Also by Greg Iles

Third Degree
True Evil
Turning Angel
Blood Memory
The Footprints of God
Sleep No More
Dead Sleep
24 Hours
The Quiet Game
Mortal Fear
Black Cross
Spandau Phoenix

THE DEVIL'S PUNCHBOWL

GREG ILES

**Doubleday Large Print
Home Library Edition**

SCRIBNER

NEW YORK   LONDON   TORONTO   SYDNEY

This Large Print Edition, prepared especially for Double-day Large Print Home Library, contains the complete, unabridged text of the original Publisher's Edition.

SCRIBNER
A Division of Simon & Schuster, Inc.
1230 Avenue of the Americas
New York, NY 10020

SCRIBNER and design are registered trademarks of The Gale Group, Inc., used under license by Simon & Schuster, Inc., the publisher of this work.

Manufactured in the United States of America

ISBN 978-1-61523-212-3

This Large Print Book carries the Seal of Approval of N.A.V.H.

For
Madeline and Mark
Who pay the highest price for
my writing life.

Thank you.

No man in the wrong can stand up against a fellow that's in the right and keeps on a comin'.

—Captain Bill McDonald, Texas Ranger

"You're an animal."

"No, worse. Human."

—Runaway Train

THE DEVIL'S
PUNCHBOWL

CHAPTER

1

Midnight in the garden of the dead.

A silver-white moon hangs high over the mirror-black river and the tired levee, shedding cold light on the Louisiana delta stretching off toward Texas. I stand among the luminous stones on the Mississippi side, shivering like the only living man for miles. At my feet lies a stark slab of granite, and under that stone lies the body of my wife. The monument at its head reads:

SARAH ELIZABETH CAGE
1963–1998

**Daughter. Wife. Mother. Teacher.
She is loved.**

I haven't sneaked into the cemetery at midnight to visit my wife's grave. I've come at the urgent request of a friend. But I didn't come here for the sake of friendship. I came out of guilt. And fear.

The man I'm waiting for is forty-five years old, yet in my mind he will always be nine. That's when our friendship peaked, during the Apollo 11 moon landing. But you don't often make friends like those you make as a boy, so the debt is a long one. My guilt is the kind you feel when someone slips away and you don't do enough to maintain the tie, all the more painful because over the years Tim Jessup managed to get himself into quite a bit of trouble, and after the first eight or nine times, I wasn't there to get him out of it.

My fear has nothing to do with Tim; he's merely a messenger, one who may bear tidings I have no wish to hear. News that confirms the rumors being murmured over golf greens at the country club, bellowed between plays beside high school gridirons, and whispered through the hunting camps like a rising breeze before a storm. When Jessup asked to meet me, I resisted. He couldn't have chosen a worse time to discover a conscience, for me or for the city. Yet in the end I agreed to hear him out. For if the rumors are true—if a uniquely disturbing evil has entered into my town—it was I who opened the door for it. I ran for mayor in a Jeffersonian fit of duty to save my hometown and, in my righteousness, was arrogant enough to believe I could deal with the devil and somehow keep our collective virtue intact. But that, I'm afraid, was wishful thinking.

For months now, a sense of failure has been accreting in my chest like fibrous tissue. I've rarely failed at anything, and I have never quit. Most Americans are raised never to give up, and in the South that credo is practically a religion. But two years ago I stood before my wife's grave with a full heart and the belief that I could by force of will resurrect the idyllic town that had borne me, by closing the racial wounds that had prevented it from becoming the shining beacon I knew it could be, and bringing back the prosperity it deserved. Halfway through my four-year term, I've learned that most people don't want change, even when it's in their best interest. We pay lip service to ideals, but we live by expediency and by tribal prejudice. Accepting this hypocrisy has nearly broken me.

Sadly, the people closest to me saw this coming long ago. My father and my lover at the time tried to save me from myself, but I would not be swayed. The heaviest burden I bear is knowing that my daughter has paid the highest price for my illusions. Two years ago, I imagined I heard my dead wife's voice urging me onward. Now all I hear is the empty rush of the wind, whispering the lesson so many have learned before me: *You can't go home again.*

My watch reads 12:30 a.m. Thirty minutes past the appointed hour, and there's still no sign of Tim Jessup among the shoulder-high stones between me and Cemetery Road. With a silent farewell to my wife, I turn and slip between the monuments, working my way back up toward Jewish Hill, our rendezvous point. My feet make no sound in the dewy, manicured grass. The names chiseled on these stones I've known all my life. They are the town's history, and mine: Friedler and Jacobs and Dreyfus up on Jewish Hill, whose stones read *Bohemia, Bavaria, Alsace;* the Knoxes and Henrys and Thornhills in the Protestant sections; and finally the Donnellys and Binellis and O'Banyons back on Catholic Hill. Most of the corpses in this place had white skin when they were alive, but as in life, the truth here is found at the margins. In the areas marked "Colored Ground" on the cemetery map lie the trusted servants and favored slaves who lived at the margins of the white world and earned a patch of hallowed earth in death. Most of these were interred without a marker. You have to go farther down the road, to the national cemetery, to find the graves of truly free black people, many of them soldiers who lie among the twenty-eight hundred unknown Union dead.

Yet this cemetery breathes an older history. Some people buried here were born in the mid-1700s, and if they were resurrected tomorrow, parts of the town would not look much different to them. Infants who died of yellow fever lie beside Spanish dons and forgotten generals, all moldering beneath crying angels and marble saints, while the gnarled oak branches spread ever wider above them, draped with cinematic beards of Spanish moss. Natchez is the oldest city on the Mississippi River, older even than New Orleans, and when you see the dark, tilted gravestones disappearing into the edges of the forest, you know it.

I last came here to view a million dollars in damage wreaked by drunk vandals on the irreplaceable wrought iron and statuary that make this cemetery unique. Now all four gates are chained shut at dusk. Tim Jessup knows that; it's one reason he chose this trysting place. When Jessup first called, I thought he was proposing the cemetery for his convenience; he works on one of the riverboat casinos at the foot of the bluff—the *Magnolia Queen,* moored almost directly below Jewish Hill—and midnight marks the end of his shift. But Tim insisted that the cemetery's isolation was a necessity, for me as much as for him. Swore, in fact, that I could trust neither my own police department nor any official of the city government. He also made me promise not to call his cell phone or his home for any reason. Part of me considers his claims ridiculous, but a warier clump of brain cells knows from experience that corruption can run deep.

I was a lawyer in another life—a prosecutor. I started out wanting to be Atticus Finch and ended up sending sixteen people to death row. Looking back, I'm not sure how that happened. One day, I simply woke up and realized that I had not been divinely ordained to punish the guilty. So I resigned my position with the Houston district attorney's office and went home to my joyous wife and daughter. Uncertain what to do with my newfound surplus of time (and facing an acute shortage of funds), I began writing about my courtroom experiences and, like a few other lawyers slipstreaming in the wake of John Grisham, found myself selling enough books to place my name on the bestseller lists. We bought a bigger house and moved Annie to an elite prep school. An unfamiliar sense of self-satisfaction began to creep into my life, a feeling that I was one of the chosen, destined for success in whatever field I chose.

I had an enviable career, a wonderful family, a few good friends, lots of faithful readers. I was young enough and arrogant enough to believe that I deserved all this, and foolish enough to think it would last.

Then my wife died.

Four months after my father diagnosed Sarah with cancer, we buried her. The shock of losing her almost broke me, and it shattered my four-year-old daughter. In desperation I fled Houston, taking Annie back to the small Mississippi town where I'd been raised, back to the loving arms of my parents. There—*here*—before I could begin working my way back to earth, I found myself drawn into a thirty-year-old murder case, one that ultimately saved my life and ended four others. That was seven years ago. Annie's eleven now, and almost the reincarnation of her mother. She's sleeping at home while a babysitter waits in my living room, and remembering this I decide that Tim Jessup gets exactly five more minutes of my time. If he can't make his own midnight meeting, he can damn well come to City Hall during business hours, like everybody else.

My heart labors from climbing the nearly

vertical face of Jewish Hill, but each breath brings the magical scent of sweet olive, still blooming in mid-October. Under the sweet olive simmers a roux of thicker smells: kudzu and damp humus and something dead in the trees—maybe a gut-shot deer that evaded its shortsighted poacher. When I reach the edge of the table of earth that is Jewish Hill, the land and sky fall away before me with breath-taking suddenness.

The drop to the river is two hundred feet here, down a kudzu-strangled bluff of windblown loess—rich soil made from rock ground fine by glaciers—the founda-tion of our city. From this height you can look west over endless flatland with almost intoxicating pride, and I think that feeling is what made so many nations try to claim this land. France, Spain, England, the Confederacy: all tried to hold this earth, and all failed as surely as the Natchez Indians before them. A sagging wire bench still stands beneath an American flag at the western rim of the hill, awaiting mourn-ers, lovers, and all the rest who come here; it looks like the best place to spend Tim's last four minutes.

As I sit, a pair of headlights moves up Cemetery Road like a ship beating against the wind, tacking back and forth across the lane that winds along the edge of the bluff. I stand, but the headlights do not slow, and soon a nondescript pickup truck rattles past the shotgun shacks across the road and vanishes around the next bend, headed toward the Devil's Punch-bowl, a deep defile out in the county where Natchez Trace outlaws once dumped the corpses of their victims.

"That's it, Timmy," I say aloud. "Time's up."

The wind off the river has finally found its way into my jacket. I'm cold, tired, and ready to go to bed. The next three days will be the busiest of my year as mayor, beginning with a news conference and a helicopter flight in the morning. But after those three days are up . . . I'm going to make some profound changes in my life.

Rising from the bench, I walk to my right, toward a gentler slope of the hill, where my old Saab waits beyond the cemetery wall. As I bend to slide down the hill, an urgent whisper breaks the silence of the night: *"Hey. Dude? Are you up here?"*

A shadow is advancing along the rim of Jewish Hill from the interior of the grave-yard. From my vantage point, I can see all four entrances to the cemetery, but I've seen no headlights and heard no engine. Yet here is Tim Jessup, materializing like one of the ghosts so many people believe haunt this ancient hill. I know it's Tim because he used to be a junkie, and he still moves like one, with a herky-jerky progress during which his head perpetu-ally jiggers around as though he's watch-ing for police while his thin legs carry him forward in the hope of finding his next fix.

Jessup claims to be clean now, thanks largely to his new wife, Julia, who was three years behind us in high school. Julia Stanton married the high school quarter-back at nineteen and took five years of punishment before forfeiting that particular game. When I heard she was marrying Jessup, I figured she wanted a perfect record of losses. But the word around town is that she's worked wonders with Tim. She got him a job and has kept him at it for over a year, dealing blackjack on the casino boats, most recently the *Magnolia Queen.*

"Penn!" Jessup finally calls out loud. "It's *me,* man. Come out!"

The gauntness of his face is unmistakable in the moonlight. Though he and I are the same age—born exactly one month apart—he looks ten years older. His skin has the leathery texture of a man who's worked too many years under the Mississippi sun. Passing him on the street under that sun, I've seen more disturbing signs. His graying mustache is streaked yellow from cigarette smoke, and his skin and eyes have the jaundiced cast of those of a man whose liver hasn't many years left in it.

What bound Jessup and me tightly as boys was that we were both doctors' sons. We each understood the weight of that special burden, the way preachers' sons know that emotional topography. Having a physician as a father brings benefits and burdens, but for eldest sons it brings a universal expectation that someday you'll follow in your father's footsteps. In the end both Tim and I failed to fulfill this, but in very different ways. Seeing him closer now, turning haplessly in the dark, it's hard to imagine that we started our lives in almost the same place. That's probably the root of my guilt: For though Tim Jessup made a lifetime of bad decisions—in full knowledge of the risks—the one that set them all in train could have been, and in fact was, made by many of us. Only luck carried the rest of us through.

With a sigh of resignation, I step from behind the gravestone and call toward the river, "Tim? Hey, Tim. It's Penn."

Jessup whips his head around, and his right hand darts toward his pocket. For a panicked second I fear he's going to pull a pistol, but then he recognizes me, and his eyes widen with relief.

"Man!" he says with a grin. "At first I thought you'd chickened out. I mean, *shit.*"

As he shakes my hand, I marvel that at forty-five Jessup still sounds like a strung-out hippie. "You're the one who's late, aren't you?"

He nods more times than necessary, a man who'll do anything to keep from being still. How does this guy deal blackjack all night?

"I couldn't rush off the boat," he explains. "I think they're watching me. I mean, they're *always* watching us. Everybody. But I think maybe they suspect something."

I want to ask whom he's talking about, but I assume he'll get to that. "I didn't see your car. Where'd you come from?"

A cagey smile splits the weathered face. "I got ways, man. You got to be careful dealing with this class of people. Predators, I kid you not. They sense a threat, they react—*bam!*" Tim claps his hands together. "Pure instinct. Like sharks in the water." He glances back toward town. "In fact, we ought to get behind some cover now." He gestures toward the three-foot-high masonry walls that enclose a nearby family plot. "Just like high school, man. Remember smoking grass behind these walls? Sitting down so the cops couldn't see the glow of the roach?"

I never got high with Tim during high school, but I see no reason to break whatever flow keeps him calm and talking. The sooner he tells me what he came to say, the sooner I can get out of here.

He vaults the wall with surprising agility, and I step over it after him, recalling with a chill the one memory of this place that I associate with Tim. Late one Halloween night a half dozen boys tossed our banana bikes over the wall and rode wildly through the narrow lanes, laughing hysterically until a pack of wild dogs chased us up into the oak trees near the third gate. Does Tim remember that?

With a last anxious look up Cemetery Road, he sits on the damp ground and leans against the mossy bricks in a corner where two walls meet. I sit against the adjacent wall, facing him at a right angle, my running shoes almost touching his weathered Sperrys. Only now do I realize that he must have changed clothes after work. The dealer's uniform he usually wears on duty has been replaced by black jeans and a gray T-shirt.

"Couldn't come out here dressed for work," he says, as though reading my mind. What he actually read, I realize, was my appraising glance. Clearly, all the drugs he's ingested over the years haven't yet ruined what always was a sharp mind.

I decide to dispense with small talk. "You said some pretty scary things on the phone. Scary enough to bring me out here at this hour."

He nods, digging in his pocket for something that turns out to be a bent cigarette. "Can't risk lighting it," he says, putting it between his lips, "but it's good to know I got it for the ride home." He grins once more before putting on a serious face. "So, what had you heard before I called?"

I don't want to repeat anything Tim hasn't already heard or seen himself. "Vague rumors. Celebrities flying in to gamble, in and out fast. Pro athletes, rappers, like that. People who wouldn't normally come here."

"You hear about the dogfighting?"

My hope that the rumors are false is sinking fast. "I've heard there's some of that going on. But it was hard to credit. I mean, I can see some rednecks down in the bottoms doing it, or out in the parishes across the river, but not high rollers and celebrities."

Tim sucks in his bottom lip. "What else?"

This time I don't answer. I've heard other rumors—that prostitution and hard drugs are flourishing around the gambling trade, for example—but these plagues have been with us always. "Look, I don't want to speculate about things I don't know to be true."

"You sound like a fucking politician, man."

I suppose that's what I've become, but I feel more like an attorney sifting the truth from an unreliable client's story. "Why don't you just tell me what you know? Then I'll tell you how that fits with what I've heard."

Looking more anxious by the second, Jessup gives in to his nicotine urge at last. He produces a Bic lighter, which he flicks into flame and touches to the end of the cigarette, drawing air through the paper tube like someone sucking on a three-foot bong. He holds in the smoke for an alarming amount of time, then speaks as he exhales. "You hear I got a kid now? A son."

"Yeah, I saw him with Julia at the Piggly Wiggly a couple of weeks ago. He's a great-looking boy."

Tim's smile lights up his face. "Just like his mom, man. She's still a beauty, isn't she?"

"She is," I concur, speaking the truth. "So . . . what are we doing here, Timmy?"

He still doesn't reply. He takes another long drag, cupping the cigarette like a joint. As I watch him, I realize that his hands are shaking, and not from the cold. His whole body has begun to shiver, and for the first time I worry that he's started using again.

"Tim?"

"It's not what you think, bro. I've just been carrying this stuff around in my head for a while, and sometimes I get the shakes."

He's crying, I realize with amazement. *He's wiping tears from his eyes.* I squeeze his knee to comfort him.

"I'm sorry," he whispers. "We're a long way from Mill Pond Road, aren't we?"

Mill Pond Road is the street I grew up on. "We sure are. Are you okay?"

He stubs out his cigarette on a gravestone and leans forward, his eyes burning with passion I thought long gone from him. "If I tell you more, there's no going back. You understand? I tell you what I know, you won't be able to sleep. I know you. You'll be like a pit bull yourself. You won't let it go."

"Isn't that why you asked me here?"

Jessup shrugs, his head and hands jittery again. "I'm just telling you, Penn. You want to walk away, do it now. Climb over since she was four years old and played the princess in her nursery-school play) Linda has searched for a real prince, for a gentle man who could lead her out of the thorny maze that's been her life ever since the other kind of man had his way with her. When she first met the man using her now, she believed that magical moment had finally come. Only a year shy of thirty and with her looks still holding despite some rough treatment), Linda had finally been placed by fate in the path of a prince. He looked like a film actor, carried himself like a soldier, and best of all actually talked like a prince in the movies her grandmother used to watch. Like Cary Grant or Laurence Olivier or . . . somebody.

But not even Cary Grant was Cary Grant. He was named Archie Leach or something, and though he was probably an okay guy, he wasn't who you thought he was, and that was the truth of life right there. Nothing was what you thought it was, because no one was who they pretended to be. Everybody wanted something, and men mostly wanted the same

that wall and slide back down to your car. That's what a smart man would do."

I settle against the cold bricks and consider what I've heard. This is one of the ways fate comes for you. It can swoop darkly from a cloudless sky like my wife's cancer; or it can lie waiting in your path, obvious to any eyes willing to see it. But sometimes it's simply a fork in the road, and rare is the day that a friend stands beside it, offering you the safer path. It's the oldest human choice: *comfortable ignorance or knowledge bought with pain?* I can almost hear Tim at his blackjack table on the *Magnolia Queen:* "Hit or stay, sir?" If only I had a real choice. But because I helped bring the *Queen* to Natchez, I don't.

"Let's hear it, Timmy. I don't have all night."

Jessup closes his eyes and crosses himself. "Praise God," he breathes. "I don't know what I would have done if you'd walked away. I'm *way* out on a limb here, man. And I'm totally alone."

I give him a forced smile. "Let's hope my added weight doesn't break it off."

He takes a long look at me, then shifts

his weight to raise one hip and slides something from his back pocket. It looks like a couple of playing cards. He holds them out, palm down, the cards mostly concealed beneath his fingers.

"Pick a card?" I ask.

"They're not cards. They're pictures. They're kind of blurry. Shot with a cell phone."

With a sigh of resignation I reach out and take them from his hand. I've viewed thousands of crime-scene photos in microscopic detail, so I don't expect to be shocked by whatever Tim Jessup has brought in his back pocket. But when he flicks his lighter into flame and holds it over the first photo, a wasplike buzzing begins in my head, and my stomach does a slow roll.

"I know," he says quietly. "Keep going. It gets worse."

CHAPTER

2

Linda Church lies beneath
who pays her wages and trie
the fear behind her eyes. As
into her, his eyes burning,
head dripping sweat, she
she's a stone figure in a
with opaque eyes that reve
Linda reads fantasy novels
off hours, and sometimes
ines she's a character in
noblewoman forced by a c
fate to do things she ne
she would. Things like tha
to heroines all the time. A

thing. If her prince had turned into a frog, she would at least have had the comfort of familiarity. But this story was different; this false prince had morphed into a serpent with needle-sharp fangs and sacs of poison loaded behind them. Linda now knew she was only one of twenty or thirty women he'd slept with on the Magnolia Queen, and was probably still screwing, no matter what he claimed. With good-paying work so hard to find, who could afford to say no to him?

"What's your problem tonight?" he grunted, still going at her without letup. "Squeeze your pissflaps, woman, and give the lad something to work with."

She hates his voice most of all, because the beautiful way he speaks in public is just another cloak he wears to hide what lies beneath his skin, and behind those measuring eyes. He really is like a character in one of her books, but not a hero. He's a shape-shifter, a demon who knows that the surest way into the souls of normal people is to appear to be exactly what they most want, to make them believe he sees them exactly as they wish to be seen. That was *how he'd snared Linda. He'd made her believe her most secret fantasies about herself, just long enough to make her willingly give herself, and then . . . the mask had come off.*

The horror of that night is graven on her soul like scar tissue. In the span of a few minutes, she saw what she'd allowed inside her, and something in her withered away forever. It happened in this very room, a cavernlike hold in the bowels of the Magnolia Queen, one of the only two rooms on the casino boat without security cameras. Linda works upstairs in the bar called The Devil's Punchbowl, but the women on the Queen call this off-limits room the real Devil's Punchbowl. For it's here that the demon inside her conducts all business that cannot stand the light of day. Here he brings card counters and other troublemakers, to strap them into the chair bolted to the floor in the middle of the room. Here he brings the women who endure what Linda suffered that night after the mask came off. . . .

After he'd gone, while she put herself together as best she could, she'd told herself she would quit the boat. But when it came to it, she hadn't had the nerve. Partly it was the money, of course, and the insurance benefits. But it was also the mind's ability to lie to itself. A familiar voice began telling her that she was mistaken, that she'd misinterpreted some of the things he'd done, that she had in fact asked for those things, if not verbally then by her actions. But each new visit brought further confirmation of her warning instincts, and the fear in her had grown. She wanted desperately to stop, to flee the Queen and the city, yet she didn't. This demon seemed to have—no, he had —some strange power over her, so much that she was afraid to mention her predicament to anyone else. In rational moments, this made her furious. Surely she had an open-and-shut case for sexual harassment. Of course, he might argue that the relationship was consensual. She's given him enthusiastic sex in several places on the boat, and except for his office and this room, every inch of the casino is covered by surveillance cameras—even the bathrooms, no matter what the law says.

She's thought about asking some

other girls to go to a lawyer with her, but that would be riskier than laying all her money down on one of the table games upstairs. Linda only knows about the other girls because she's heard a couple of the trashier ones talking about how they did a group thing with him and a big player from Hong Kong. Knowing that the man inside her now has been inside those other women makes her shudder, yet she doesn't cry out or try to throw him off. Why? A heroine in one of her novels would do just that: find a hatpin or a dagger and stab him in the back during his "moment of greatest passion." But real life isn't like that. In real life that moment comes and goes, and when he rolls off of you, you feel like your soul has been ripped out by its bloody roots, leaving only a husk of what you were before.

That was the state she'd been in when her true prince walked into her life. He wasn't riding a white charger or wearing a doublet or a wizard's robe; he was wearing a blackjack dealer's uniform, and watching her with an empathy that cut right through her hardened defenses. His eyes were the opposite of those burning above her now: soft and kind and infinitely understanding. And somehow, she'd known, he had seen her torment before speaking to her. He didn't know the nature of it; that would have killed him, literally, for he would have tried to stop what was going on, and he is no match for the shape-shifter. He's too good for the job he has—too good for her, really—*but he doesn't think so. He loves her.*

The problem is that he's married. And to a good woman. Linda despises herself for wanting the husband of another woman. But what can you do if you truly love someone? How can you banish a feeling that is stronger than the darkness that's eating you from the inside out?

"You're making a bloody bags of it," the demon growls in contempt. "Do ye want me to change at Baker Street?"

Linda shrinks in fear, moves her hips faster. She's picked up enough slang to feel nausea at the innocuous-sounding euphemism. Her extra effort seems to allay his anger; at least there's no more coded talk of turning her over.

She shuts her eyes and prays that the demon moving inside her won't discover her secret prince, or what he's doing at this very moment to put the world in balance again, like the heroes in her novels—not until it's one delicious second too late. For if the demon or his henchmen discover that, Timothy will die—horribly. Worse, they will surely make him talk before the end.

That's one of their specialties.

CHAPTER

3

"Penn?" Tim says softly, touching my knee. "Are you okay?"

I'm bent over three blurry photographs in my lap, trying to absorb what's printed on the rectangles of cheap typing paper, with only the wavering flame of a cigarette lighter to illuminate them. It takes a while to truly *see* images like these. As an assistant district attorney, I found that murder victims—no matter how brutally beaten or mutilated—did not affect me quite so deeply as images of those who had survived terrible crimes. The mind has a prewired mechanism for distancing itself from the dead, surely a survival advantage in our species. But we have no effective filter for blocking out the suffering of living humans—none besides turning away, either physically or through denial (not if we're "raised right," as Ruby Flowers, one of the women who "raised" me would have said).

The first picture shows the face of a dog that looks as though it was hit by a truck and dragged a hundred yards over broken glass. Yet despite its horrific wounds, the animal is somehow standing under its own power, and staring into the camera with its one remaining eye. Wincing with revulsion, I slide the photo to the bottom of the group and find myself looking at a blond girl—not a woman, but a *girl*—carrying a tray filled with mugs of beer. It takes a moment to register that the girl, who's no older than fifteen, wears no top. A vacant smile animates her lips, but her eyes are eerily blank, the look of a psych patient on Thorazine.

When I slide this photo aside, my breath catches in my throat. What might be the same girl (I can't be sure) lies on a wooden floor while a much older man has intercourse with her. The most disturbing thing about this photo is that it was shot from behind and between a group of men watching the act. They're only visible from knee to shoulder—three wear slacks and polo shirts, while a fourth wears a business suit—but all have beer mugs in their hands.

"Did you take these pictures?" I ask, unable to hide my disgust.

"No— *Damn!*" Tim jerks the hand holding the cigarette lighter, and the guttering light goes out. "You seen enough?"

"Too much. Who took these?"

"A guy I know. Let's leave it at that for now."

"Does he know you have them?"

"No. And he'd be in serious shit if anybody knew he'd taken them."

I lay the pictures beside Tim's leg, then close my eyes and rub my temples to try to stop an incipient headache. "Who's the girl?"

"Don't know. I really don't. They bring in different ones."

"She didn't look more than fifteen."

"If that."

"Those pictures were taken around here?"

"At a hunting camp a few miles away. They run people to the dogfights on their VIP boat. Change the venues each time."

Now that the lighter is out, my night vision is returning. Tim's haggard face is wan in the moonlight. I expel a rush of air. "God, I wish I hadn't seen those."

He doesn't respond.

"And the dog?"

"The loser of a fight. Just before his owner killed him."

"Christ. Is that the worst of it?"

Tim sighs like a man stripped of precious illusions. "Depends on your sensibilities, I guess."

"And you're saying this is being—what, promoted?—by the *Magnolia Queen*?"

Tim nods but does not speak.

"Why?"

"To pull the whales down south."

"Whales?"

"High rollers. Big-money players. Arab playboys, Asian trust-fund babies. Drug lords, pro athletes, rappers. It's a circus, man. And what brings 'em from the farthest away is the dogfighting. Blood sport." Tim shakes his head. "It's enough to make you puke."

"Is it working? To pull them in?"

"Yeah, it's working. And not just specta-tors. It's the competition. Bring your killer dog and fight against the best. We had a jet fly in from Macao last week. A Chinese billionaire's son brought his own dog in to fight. A Bully Kutta. Ever hear of those? Bastard weighed more than I do. The dog, I mean."

I try to imagine a dog that outweighs Tim Jessup. "Through the Natchez airport?"

"Hell, no. There's other strips around here that can take a private jet."

"Not many."

"The point is, this is a major operation. They'd kill me without a second's hesita-tion for talking to you. I'd be dog bait, and that's a truly terrible way to die."

Something in Tim's voice when he says "dog bait" touches a nerve in me. It's fear, I realize. He's watching me closely, trying to read my reaction.

"Why do I feel like I'm waiting for the other shoe to drop?"

Jessup hesitates like a diver just before

the plunge. Then he clucks his tongue and says, "They're ripping off the city, Penn."

This sudden shift in focus disorients me. I settle back against the bricks and watch the wings of an angel twenty yards away. The dew has started to settle; the air around me seems a fine spray that requires wearying effort to pull into my lungs—maybe thick enough for a stone angel to take flight. The low, churning rumble of a push boat on the river far below tells me that sound travels farther than I thought tonight, so I lower my voice when I ask, "*Who's* ripping off the city?"

Tim hugs himself, rocking slowly back and forth. "The people I work for. Golden Parachute Gaming, or whatever you want to call them."

"The parent company of the *Magnolia Queen* is ripping off the city? How could they do that?"

"By shorting you on the taxes, dude. How else?"

Jessup is referring to the portion of gross receipts that the casino boat pays the city for its concession. "That's impossible."

"Oh, right. What was I thinking? I just came out here for old times' sake."

"Tim, how could they short us on taxes without the state gaming commission finding out about it?"

"That's two separate questions. One, how could they underpay their taxes? Two, does the gaming commission know about it?"

His cold dissection of what would be a nightmare scenario for me and for the town is getting on my nerves. "Do you know the answers?"

"Question one is easy. Computers. Teenagers have hacked into freaking NORAD, man. Do you really think the network of a casino company can't be manipulated? Especially by the people who *own* the network?"

"And question two?"

"That's tougher. The gaming commission is a law unto itself, and I don't know enough about how it operates to know what's possible. There are three men on it. How many would have to be bent to provide cover for the operation? I don't know."

I'm still shaking my head. "The auditing

system we use was evolved over decades in Las Vegas. No one can beat it."

Jessup chuckles with raw cynicism.
"They say you can't beat a lie detector,
either. Tell you what," he says gamely, and
in his eyes I see the energy of a man who
only comes into his own during the middle
of the night. "Let's assume for a second
that the gaming commission is clean and
go back to question one. There's no way to
distort the take from discrete parts of the
casino operation, because everything's so
tightly regulated, like you said. The company's own security system makes it
impossible. Every square inch of the boat
is videotaped around the clock with PTZ
cameras and wired for sound. The cameras are robotically controlled—from
Vegas, not Natchez. A buddy let me into
the security center one night, and I saw
Pete Elliot fingering his brother's wife in
the corner of the restaurant."

"I don't need to know that crap."

"I'm just saying—"

"I get it. What's your point?"

"The *only* way for the company to rip off
the city is to understate the gross. You
guys see a big enough number, you figure

your cut and don't look any deeper. Right?"

"To an extent. The gaming commission looks deeper, though. How much money are we talking about?"

Jessup flicks his lighter and examines his burned thumb, then squints at the flame as though pondering an advanced calculus problem. "Not that much, in terms of the monthly gross of a casino boat. But that's like saying a thousand years isn't much time in geological terms. We're talking serious bread for an ordinary human being."

"Wait a minute," I say. "There's a flaw in your premise. A fatal flaw."

"What?"

"There's no upside for the casino company. However much they rip us off by, their gain is minuscule compared with the risk. They're practically minting money down there. Why risk killing the golden goose to steal a couple of extra million a year? Or even a month?"

Jessup smiles sagely. "*Now* you're thinking, dude. Doesn't make sense, does it?"

"Not to me."

"Me, neither." He lights another cigarette and sucks on it like a submerged
man breathing through a reed. "Until you
realize it's not the corporate parent doing
the ripping, but a single guy."

"One guy? *That's* impossible. Casino
companies never give an individual that
kind of power."

Tim expels a raft of smoke. "Who said
they gave it to him?"

"No way, Timmy. The casinos do
everything in their power to avoid that situation."

"Everything *in their power.* And they're
good. But they're not *God.*" He grins with
secret pleasure, as though he's smoking
pot and not tobacco. "The company
makes certain assumptions about people
and situations, and that makes them vulnerable."

I run my hand along my jaw. The fine
stubble there tells me it's getting late.
"Obviously you have a suspect. Who is it?"

Tim's smugness vanishes. "You don't
want to know that yet. Seriously. For tonight he's 'Mr. X,' okay? He Who Must
Not Be Named. What matters is that he's

been with the company long enough to put something like this together."

I know a fair amount about the Golden Parachute Gaming Corporation. But rather than scare Tim off by speculating over which executive might be the one, I'd rather take what he's willing to give me. For now. "Let me get this straight: Mr. X is also behind the dogfighting and the girls?"

"Hell, yeah. The side action's what brings the whales down here, which in turn makes the *Queen* all the more profitable, while making Mr. X some serious jack on the side."

I sigh deeply, sickened by the thought that I, who reluctantly courted Golden Parachute and helped bring the *Magnolia Queen* to town, may also have helped to infect my town with this virus. But rather than blame myself, I turn my frustration on Tim. "You picked a hell of a week to come forward. This is balloon-race weekend. We've got eighty-seven hot-air balloons coming to town, and fifteen thousand tourists. I've got a CEO expecting the royal treatment, which I'll have to give him to try to pull his new recycling plant here."

Tim nods. "Read about it in the news-paper. Sorry."

"Seriously, Tim. I don't see how you expect me to help you without knowing Mr. X's identity. I can't do anything with-out that."

Tim goes back to his submerged-man routine with the cigarette. In its intermittent glow, I watch his eyes, and what I see there frightens me. The dominant emotion is fear, but mixed with that is something that looks and feels like hatred.

"What's your idea of help?" he says softly.

"What do you mean?"

His eyes tick upward and lock onto mine. "You worked for a big-city DA. You know what I mean."

"I saw the pictures," I say gently. "I know this is bad. That's why we have to let the authorities handle it."

"*Authorities?*" He almost spits the word. "Didn't you hear what I said on the phone? You can't trust anybody around here with this."

"My own police department? Do you really believe that?"

Tim looks astounded by my ignorance.

"They're not *yours*. Those cops were on the job before you got into office, and they'll be there when you're gone. Same for the sheriff and his boys. To them, you're just a political tourist. Passing through."

His casual damnation of local law enforcement disturbs me. "I trust a lot of those men. We grew up with most of them, or their fathers."

"I'm not saying the cops are crooks. I'm saying they're *human*. They're looking out for themselves and their families, and they like to have a little fun on the side, same as the next guy. How many guys you know wouldn't look the other way to get a beer-drinking snapshot with a star NFL running back? I've been to a couple of these barn burners, okay? I know who I've seen there."

Like the full import of a cancer diagnosis, the ramifications of what Jessup is telling me are slowly sinking in. "You've personally witnessed Mr. X at these dogfights? You've seen him encouraging underage prostitution?"

Jessup snorts in contempt. "Are you serious? You want to arrest Mr. X for promoting dogfighting? On *my* word? The

bastard could get a dozen upstanding citizens to swear he was on the *Queen* any
day or night we name."

"Dogfighting is a felony in Mississippi," I
say evenly. "Just *watching* one is a
felony. The maximum sentence is ten
years. And with multiple counts? That's
hard time."

This seems to get Tim's attention. But
even as I point out the facts, I silently concede that Jessup has a point about his
being a problematic witness. "Obviously,
nailing them for defrauding the city would
be the lethal hit. Golden Parachute
would lose its gaming license, and that
would shut down five casinos in one pop.
The IRS would eat them alive. The partners would lose hundreds of millions of
dollars."

"Now you're talking," Tim says bitterly.

"So how do *you* propose we handle
this? Do you have any documentary evidence, other than the pictures I saw?"

He licks his lips like a nervous poker
player. "I'm not saying I got nothing, but I
need more. I've got a plan. I've been working on it for a month."

A sense of foreboding takes hold deep

in my chest. Everything he's told me up to now has been leading to this. "Tim, I won't help you risk your life. I do have experience with this kind of operation, and I've seen more than one informer wind up with his throat cut."

Jessup has the faraway look of a martyr walking into the flames. Without warning he seizes my wrist with a startlingly powerful grip. "This is *our* town, man. That still means something to me. I'm not going to sit still while these carpetbagger motherfuckers ruin everything our ancestors worked to build—"

"Shhh," I hiss, feeling blood coming into my cheeks. "I hear you, okay? I understand your anger. But it's not worth your life. It's not even worth taking a beating. People in this town were gambling, selling slaves, raping Indian women, and cutting each other's throats before Paul Revere sold his first silver candlestick."

Tim's eyes are glistening. "That was centuries ago. What the hell's wrong with you, Penn? We're talking about innocent lives. Underage girls and defenseless animals." He lowers his voice at last, but the urgency does not leave it. "Every week

Mr. X sends out four pickup trucks with cages in the back, a hundred miles in every direction. When those trucks come back, the cages are filled with house pets—cocker spaniels, poodles, dalmatians, cats. The trainers throw 'em into a hole with starving pit bulls to teach the dogs how to kill, or tie 'em to a jenny to make the dogs run. Then they feed them to the dogs when it's all over. Every one of those animals gets torn to shreds."

Even as the shiver goes through me, I recall that a neighbor who lives three houses down from me lost her seven-year-old cocker spaniel last month. She let the dog out to do its business, and it never came back.

"I didn't ask for this," Tim says stubbornly. "But I'm in a position to do something about it. *Me,* okay? What kind of man would I be if I just turned away and let it go on?"

His question pierces me like a blade driven deep into my conscience. "Timmy . . . shit. What would you say if I told you that the only reason I'm still mayor of this town is that I haven't figured out how to tell my father I'm quitting?"

Jessup blinks like a stunned child trying to work out something beyond its grasp. "I'd say you're bullshitting me. But . . ." A profound change comes over his features. "You're not, are you?"

I slowly shake my head.

"But why? Are you sick or something?"

He asks this because our last mayor resigned after being diagnosed with lung cancer. "Not exactly. Soul sick, maybe."

Tim looks at me in disbelief. "*Soul* sick? Are you kidding? I'm soul sick too! Man, you stood up all over this town and told people you were going to change things. You made people believe it. And now you want to quit? The Eagle Scout wants to *quit*? Why? Because it's tougher than you thought? Did somebody hurt your feelings or something?"

I start to explain, but before I can get a sentence out, Jessup cuts in, "Wait a minute. They came to you with money or something, right? No . . . they threatened you, didn't they?"

"No, no, no."

"Bullshit." Tim's eyes flash. "They got their claws into you somehow, and all you know to do is run—"

"Tim!" I grab his leg and squeeze hard enough to bruise. "Shut up and listen for a second!"

His chest is heaving from the excitement of his anger.

I lean close enough so that he can see my eyes. "Nobody from any casino has come to me with anything. Not bribes or threats. I wanted to be mayor so I could fix the school system in this town, which has been screwed since 1968. It's been our Achilles' heel for nearly forty years. But I see now that I can't fix it. I don't have the power. And my child is suffering because of it. It's that simple, Timmy. Until tonight, all this stuff you've told me was just whispers in the wind."

"And now?"

"Now I can't get those goddamn pictures out of my head."

He smiles sadly. "I told you. I warned you."

"Yeah. You did."

He rubs his face with both hands, so hard that his mustache makes scratching sounds. "So, what now? Am I on my own here or what?"

"You are unless you tell me who Mr. X is."

Jessup's eyes go blank as marbles.

"Come on. I know law enforcement people who aren't local. Serious people. Give me his name, and I'll get a real investigation started. We'll nail his hide to the barn door. I've dealt with guys like this before. You know I have. I sent them to death row."

With slow deliberation, Tim stubs his cigarette out on the mossy bricks behind him. "I know. That's why I came to you. But you have to understand what you're up against, Penn. This guy I'm talking about has got real juice. Just because someone's in Houston or Washington doesn't mean they're clean on this."

"Tim, I took on the head of the FBI. And I won."

Jessup doesn't look convinced. "That was different. A guy like that has to play by the rules. That's like Gandhi beating the British in India. Don't kid yourself. You go after Mr. X, you're swimming into the shallow end of Lake St. John, hoping to kill an alligator before one kills you."

This image hits me with primitive force. I've cruised the shallow end of the local lake from the safety of a ski boat at night, and there's no sight quite like the dozens of red eyes hovering just above water level among the twisted cypress trunks. The first thrash of an armored tail in the water triggers a blast of uniquely mammalian fear that makes you pray the boat's drain plug is screwed in tight.

"I hear you, okay? But I think you're a little spooked. The guy is human, right?"

Jessup tugs at his mustache like the strung-out junkie he used to be. "You don't know, man . . . you don't *know.* This guy is smooth as silk on the outside, but he's got *scales* on the inside. When the dogs are tearing each other to pieces, or some girl is screaming in the back of a trailer, his eyes turn from ice to fire right in front of you."

"Tim—" I lean forward and grasp his wrist. "I don't understand is what you want from me. If you won't go to the professionals, how do you propose to stop this psycho? What's your plan?"

A strange light comes into Jessup's eyes. "There's only one way to take down an operation like this, and you know it."

"How's that?"

"From the inside."

Jesus. Tim has been watching too many cop shows. "Let me get this straight. The guy you just described as Satan incarnate, you want to wear a wire on?"

Jessup barks out a derisive laugh. "Fuck no! These guys carry scanners into the john with them. "

"Then what?"

He shakes his head with childlike stubbornness. "You don't need to know. But God put me in this position for a reason."

When informants start talking about God, my alarm bells go off. "Tim—"

"Hey, I'm not asking you to believe like I do. I'm just asking you to be ready to accept what I bring you and do the right thing."

I feel obligated to try to dissuade him further, but beneath my desire to protect a childhood friend lies a professionally cynical awareness of the truth. In cases like this, often the only way to convict the people at the top is to have a witness on the inside, directly observing the criminal activity. And who else but a martyr would take that job?

"What are you planning to bring me?"

"Evidence. A stake to drive through Mr. X's heart, and a knife to cut off the company's head. Just say you're with me, Penn. Tell me you won't quit. Not until we take these bastards down."

Against all my better judgment, I reach out and squeeze Tim's proffered hand. "Okay. You just watch your back. *And* your front. Informers usually get caught because they make a stupid mistake. You've come a long way. Don't go getting hurt now."

Tim looks me full in the face, his eyes almost serene. "Hey, I have to be careful. I've got a son now, remember?" As if suddenly remembering something, he seizes my wrist with his other hand, like a pastor imploring me to accept Jesus as my savior. "If something does happen, though, don't blame yourself, okay? The way I see it, I've got no choice."

Your wife and son wouldn't see it that way, I say silently, but I nod acknowledgment.

Now we sit silently, awkwardly, like two men who've cleared the air on some uncomfortable issue and have nothing left

As the white beam leaves the Turning Angel and arcs up toward me, I jog back to the walled plot that sheltered Tim and me. My old friend has vanished as silently as he appeared. The odor of burnt paper still rides the air, and two tiny embers glow orange in the corner of the plot—all that remains of the evidence in a case I have no idea how to begin working. After all, I'm no longer a prosecutor. I'm only the mayor. And no one knows better than I how little power I truly have.

to say. Small talk is pointless, yet how else can we part? Cut our palms and take a blood oath, like Tom and Huck?

"You still dating that lady who runs the bookstore?" Tim asks with forced casualness.

"Libby?" I guess word hasn't spread to Jessup's social circle yet. "We ended it about a week ago. Why?"

"I've seen her son down on the *Queen* a few times in the past couple of weeks. Looked high as a kite to me. Must have a fake ID."

After all I've heard tonight, this news falls on me like the last brick of a backbreaking load. I've spent too much time and political capital getting my ex-girlfriend's nineteen-year-old son out of trouble with the law. He's basically a good kid, but if he's broken his promise to stay clean, the future holds serious unpleasantness for us both.

Tim looks worried. "Was I right to tell you?"

"Are you sure he was high?"

Suddenly Tim hops to his knees, tense as a startled deer, holding up his hand for silence. As he zeros his gaze somewhere past the wall between us and the river, I realize what has disturbed him: the sound of a car coming up Cemetery Road. We listen to the rising pitch of the engine, waiting for it to crest and fall . . . but it doesn't. There's a grinding squeal of brakes, then silence.

"Stopped." Tim hisses. "Right below us."

"Take it easy," I whisper, surprised by my thumping heart. "It's probably just a police cruiser checking out my car."

Tim has his feet under him now. Almost faster than I can decipher his movements, he grabs the photos from the ground, shoves them into the corner of the plot, and sets them ablaze with his lighter. "Cover the light with your body," he says.

As I move to obey, he crab-walks over two graves and lifts his eyes above the rim of the far wall. The photographs have already curled into glowing ashes.

"Can you see anything?" I ask.

"Not yet. We're too deep in."

"Let me go take a look."

"*No way.* Stay here."

Exasperated by his paranoia, I get to my feet and step over the wall. Before I've covered twenty feet I hear the tinny squawk

of a police radio. This brings me immediate relief, but Tim is probably close to bolting. With a surprising rush of anxiety, I trot to the bench beneath the flagpole and peer over the edge of Jewish Hill.

An idling squad car sits behind my Saab. There's a cop inside it, talking on his radio. He's undoubtedly running a 10-28 on my license plate. In seconds he'll know that the car in front of him belongs the mayor of the city, if he didn't already know. As I watch, the uniform gets out his car and switches on a powerful flashlight. He sweeps the beam along cemetery wall, then probes the hedge below Jewish Hill. Our officers carry Surefires, and this one is powerful enough transfix the Turning Angel in its ghostly ballet of vigilance over the dead.

Given a choice between waiting for cop to leave and walking down to him, I choose the latter. For one thing might not leave; he might call a tow instead. For another, I *am* the mayor it's nobody's business what I'm doing here in the middle of the night. I well be having a dark night of the soul visiting my wife's grave.

CHAPTER

4

Julia Jessup watches her seven-month-old son sleep in the crib her sister-in-law sent from San Diego. Julia envies her little boy, that he can sleep so soundly while his father is away. A perfect shining bubble of saliva expands from his cherub's lips as he exhales, then pops on the inspiration. Julia almost smiles, but she can't quite manage it. Somewhere between her belly and her heart a great fear is working, like a worm eating at her insides. Tim has promised that everything will be all right, that he will return safely from wherever he went, but her fear did not believe him.

Julia has come so far to reach this place, this little haven from the hardness of the world. A hundred years ago, she married her high school boyfriend, the quarterback of St. Stephen's Prep. The school's golden boy got her pregnant at nineteen, married her a week later, and gave her herpes two weeks before the baby came. Julia discovered this when the baby contracted the virus during delivery and died in agony eight days later. It was hard to hold on to her romantic illusions after that. But she'd tried.

She suffered through the barhopping with his moronic friends and the vacuous sluts they hung out with, his long absences in the woods during deer season, paintball tournaments during the workweek, sweating in a mosquito-clouded bass boat while he fished. But in the end, she'd had to face that she'd bound herself to a boy, not a man, and that any future with him meant sharing him with every trash monkey who caught his eye, and catching whatever STDs she didn't have yet.

The first years after she divorced him were leaner than she'd known life could be. Julia had come from a good family, but when the oil business crashed in the eighties, her father couldn't find another way to make a living and ended his erratic job search with a bullet in the head. After her divorce, she was pretty much on her own. She waited tables, worked a cash register, parked cars at parties, and sold makeup to women who paid more for facial creams in a week than Julia paid for a month's rent. She steered clear of men for the most part, and watched her friends who hadn't left Natchez screw up in just about every way possible where the opposite sex was concerned. When Julia needed companionship, she chose older men—married ones who had no illusions about where things were headed—and bided her time.

Then she'd met Tim Jessup, or remet him. She'd known him in school, of course, but they'd never dated, since he was three years ahead of her. Back then he'd been one of the cocky ones who thought that the good life lay waiting ahead of him like a red carpet spread by fate. But soon after high school, he'd learned different. Julia hadn't thought of Tim much after that, not until she took a job serving hors d'oeuvres on the casino boat one night. Tim had watched her from his blackjack table, then waited for her to finish her work. They went for breakfast at the Waffle House, talked about the good old days at St. Stephen's, then, surprisingly, opened up about the not-so-good days that had filled most of their lives since. By the end of that night, Julia had known Tim might be the man she'd been waiting for. There was only one catch. He had a drug problem.

She could see it in his eyes, the itchy anxiety that worsened until he made a trip to the bathroom and returned with a look of serenity. But then he'd disarmed her by admitting it, that first night too. They'd seen a lot of each other after that, and within a month Julia had made a deal with herself. If she could get Tim clean—really clean—

then she would take a chance on him. And to her surprise, she had suc- ceeded. Nothing in her life had been tougher, but she'd set her whole being on seeing him through to sobriety, and she'd done it.

The results were miraculous. Tim quit working the boat his druggie friends patronized, hired on with the new outfit, and began working every shift the Mag- nolia Queen would give him. He'd even talked his father into giving him a loan for a small house, and in his off hours began fixing it up himself, sawing and hammer- ing like a born carpenter, not a privileged surgeon's son. Julia watched HGTV every chance she got, ripped up the stained carpet of the previous owners, and refin- ished the hardwood underneath. Installed the bathroom tiles too. Her pregnancy was something they kept to themselves, a treasure they hugged together in the cocoon of their changing house, until they'd gone so far down the road to nor- malcy that people wouldn't roll their eyes when she revealed it. By the time she began to show, the change in perception had begun. Even Tim's father had warmed to her, in his own way. Some days, in the early mornings, or late at night, she would see his silver Mercedes glide past on the lane outside, and she'd know he was checking his son's progress. When the baby finally came, perfect and round and without flaw because Julia had taken acyclovir for the last month, every pill at the exact moment she was supposed to, the transformation was complete. She could hardly believe this was her life, that by sheer force of will and faith in herself and her husband she could bring goodness out of fear and regret. But she had done it.

If only Tim's evolution had stopped there. . . .

As her husband slowly regained the bearings he'd lost during his early twenties, he'd begun to experience a kind of emotional fallout. His memory, which had blocked out so much during his lost years, began to fill in the gaps, and waves of guilt and regret would assail him. Tim rediscovered God, which might have been all right had he not acted like a religious convert, more zealous than those born into the faith.

He saw choices starkly, as either right or wrong, and despite his own past he judged those who didn't measure up to his idea of ethical responsibility. It wasn't a moral prissiness—he didn't condemn people for the common human lapses—but he began to obsess about the big things in life. Politics. Organized religion. The diamond brokers in Sierra Leone, the starving children in the Sudan, the good Muslims in Iraq. The uneducated blacks right here in Mississippi.

And then it happened. Exactly what, Julia didn't know. But it was something at work. Tim had witnessed something terrible, or overheard something, and from that night forward he'd been a man possessed. With each passing week he'd grown more withdrawn, more irritable, to the point that she feared he'd begun using again. But it wasn't that. Tim had apparently discovered something that so outraged him he felt compelled to right the wrong himself. And that terrified her. Tim wasn't the kind of man to take on that kind of trouble. He was smart, and he was good-hearted, but he wasn't hard inside, the way her first husband had been. Tim had illusions about people; he wanted them to be better than they were, and you couldn't fight evil men if you thought that way. You couldn't win, anyway. Julia had lived enough life to know that.

The only thing that had given her any comfort was Tim telling her that Penn Cage would be helping him. Julia had known Penn in high school too. She'd even kissed him once, beside a car one night at a senior party that she and a friend had sneaked off to. Penn Cage wasn't like Tim. He wasn't timid or uncertain; he made decisions and stuck with them, and life had worked out for him. It wasn't as if he hadn't suffered; he'd lost his wife to cancer; but everybody paid for the things they got, some way or other. You had to pay just for being alive.

And that, Julia guessed, was what Tim was trying to do. He wanted to make up for all the years he had wasted, for all the things he could have accomplished and had not. It wasn't for her, she knew, and this both relieved and wounded her. She'd done all she could to prove to Tim that he owed her nothing—nothing except all the time he could give to her and the baby. But that wasn't enough for him. Tim's obsession was rooted in his relationship with his father. He felt he had betrayed his father as well as himself, and something was driving him to prove that he was in fact the man his father had dreamed he might one day become.

Julia hopes Tim wasn't lying about Penn, that he didn't simply tell her whatever he thought would quiet her while he went off to God-knew-where to earn the right to feel good about himself again. And so she waits, and watches her baby, and prays that someone will take the cross from her husband's back and carry it for him. For in the inmost chamber of her heart Julia is certain that if Tim goes on alone, he will die before finding the salvation he seeks.

CHAPTER

5

I should probably drive straight home from the cemetery, but as Tim predicted, I cannot free my mind from the terrible images in his photographs. Instead, I drive up Linton Avenue, turn on Madison Street, and cruise past the newspaper building, where my old lover once worked as publisher. While Caitlin Masters lived in Natchez, everything she could uncover and verify about the city was printed in the paper. Now, despite the fact that her father still owns the *Examiner,* much of the investigative fire seems to have gone out of the staff. If Caitlin were still here, I suspect, the rumors that Tim fleshed out tonight would already be halfway to the front page.

I turn on State Street and negotiate a series of right angles on the city's notorious one-way streets, checking for a tail as I make my way to City Hall. The cop at the cemetery proved easy enough to handle, but I'm not sure he bought my explanation of visiting my wife's grave. He kept glancing over my shoulder as though he expected a half-dressed woman to appear from among the gravestones beyond the cemetery wall. Of course, he might also have been searching for Tim Jessup, and that's why I'm keeping my eyes on my rearview mirror as I drive. I'd like to know just how interested the police are in my movements.

Unlike most Mississippi towns, Natchez has no central square dominated by a courthouse or a Confederate soldier on a pillar. The lifeblood of this city has always been the river, and the stately old commercial blocks platted in 1790 march away from it as though with regret, toward onetime plantations now mostly subdivided into residential neighborhoods. City

Hall faces Pearl Street and abuts the county courthouse at the rear. The courthouse is the larger of the two buildings, but people often see them as a single structure, since only a narrow alley separates them.

Parking before the cream-colored stone of City Hall, I walk beneath hundred-year-old oaks to the main entrance. The building is usually locked by 5:00 p.m., but the chandelier in the foyer blazes like the ballroom of the *Titanic,* and I use its light to find the proper key on my ring. A couple of years before I was elected mayor, the previous board of selectmen awarded me a key to the city. This token of recognition didn't mean much at the time—it was the kind of honor you might dream about as a kid watching a Disney movie—but tonight, unlocking City Hall with the actual key to the building, I feel the crushing weight of my responsibility to the people who elected me.

Upstairs, in my office, I kneel before my safe and open its combination lock. The few sensitive documents I deal with as mayor reside in this safe, among them my file on the Golden Parachute Gaming

Corporation, the Los Angeles–based company that owns the *Magnolia Queen*. Feeling strangely furtive, I slip the thick file inside my button-down shirt before I walk downstairs and lock the door. With the file still tucked against my belly, I drive the ten blocks required to reach my home on Washington Street three blocks away, my eyes alert for police cars.

When I moved back to town, I had the morbid luck to arrive shortly before the patriarch of an old Natchez family died, which resulted in their family home coming up for sale after a century of benign neglect. I bought it the same day, and I've never regretted it. An elegant, two-story Federal town house of red brick, it stands at the center of one of the most beautiful enclaves of the city. Town houses of various styles and pedigrees stand along both sides of the street like impeccably dressed ladies and gentlemen from another era, gradually giving way to the Episcopal Church, the Temple B'nai Israel, Glen Auburn—a four-story French Second Empire mansion—and Magnolia Hall, a massive Greek Revival mansion and the headquarters of one of the once-powerful local garden clubs. The town houses aren't antebellum for the most part, but rather the dwellings of the merchants, lawyers, and physicians who prospered in Natchez in the Victorian era. The entire downtown length of Washington Street is lined with fuchsia-blooming crape myrtle trees, which are tended by ladies obsessively dedicated to their survival.

As I park and exit my car, a faint but steady glow from the second floor of the house across the street catches my eye. My stomach gives a little flip and I pause, trying to recall whether I've seen that light in the past few weeks. The question has some importance, for the house still belongs to Caitlin, though she hasn't lived in it for eighteen months, preferring to spend most of her time in Charlotte, North Carolina, where her father's newspaper chain is based. But the house remains furnished, and she does not rent it out. Caitlin and I parted on good enough terms that I still possess a key, in theory so that should any kind of emergency befall the house, I could help the proper people to deal with it.

The reality is that for six of the past

seven years, Caitlin and I lived as a couple. Her owning a house across the street from mine helped maintain the fiction that we were not "living in sin," which people still say here, and only half-jokingly. Caitlin often spent the night when Annie was in the house, but Caitlin's an early riser, and she was usually at work by the time Annie got up to get ready for school. As I remember those mornings now, something catches in my chest. It's been too long since I felt that relaxed intimacy, and I know my daughter misses it.

For most of the time we were together, Caitlin and I planned to marry. We took it for granted in the beginning, when we still believed that fate had brought us together. We met during the civil rights case that seized control of my life after I returned here, and before the resulting trial ended, we'd discovered that though we were ten years apart in age and quite different on the surface, we were joined as inseparably as siblings beneath the skin. The only tension in our relationship developed later, when living and working in a small Southern town no longer felt charming to Caitlin, but rather like a prison. She was born and raised for the big canvas (her coverage of our case earned her a Pulitzer at twenty-eight), and while Natchez sometimes explodes into lethal drama, for the most part it remains a quiet river town, trapped in an eddy of time and history, changing almost imperceptibly when it changes at all.

My decision to run for mayor threw our differences into stark relief and ultimately made the relationship untenable. Caitlin came to Natchez as a flaming, Ivy League liberal with no experience of living in the South, but after five years here, she'd developed ideas more racist than those of many "good ol' boys" I'd grown up with, and she was ready to get out. Our sharpest points of contention were (a) whether the city was worth saving, and (b) if so, was I the person to save it? Caitlin claimed that people get the government they deserve, and that Natchez didn't deserve me. *She* did, in her view, and added the argument that Annie deserved a culturally richer childhood than she would have here. In short, Caitlin wanted me to leave my past behind. But true Southerners don't think that way. I was willing to risk being turned into a pillar of salt, if by so doing I could help renew the city and the land that had borne me. More than this, I believed that living closely with my parents would provide my daughter an emotional bedrock that no amount of cultural diversity would ever replace. In the end, I followed my conscience and my heritage, ensuring that my future marriage became the first casualty of my mayoral campaign. Caitlin cried—as much for Annie as for us—then wished me well and went back to North Carolina, to the New South of glass office towers, boutique restaurants, and the Research Triangle. I stayed in the land of kudzu and Doric columns and bottleneck guitars—one short ride away from James Dickey's Land of Nine-Fingered People.

There's no denying the light glowing softly through the curtain in the upper room across the way. But if Caitlin has returned to Natchez, she's most likely come back in some connection with the Balloon Festival. Still, something else might have influenced her unexpected appearance, and it's worth considering. Ten days ago I ended my relationship with Libby Jensen, after seeing her for nearly a year. Was ten days sufficient time for that news to reach North Carolina? Of course. One e-mail from a gossipy *Examiner* employee would have done it, and a text message would be even faster. If Caitlin has returned, her timing is certainly suggestive.

The casino file has grown damp under my shirt by the time I climb the porch and reach for my front door. Before my hand touches the knob, the door squeaks open, startling me, and the tenth-grade honor student who babysits Annie speaks uncertainly through the crack.

"Mr. Cage? Is everything okay?"

Because of my experiences with Mia Burke, the senior who used to sit for Annie, I no longer allow babysitters to use my first name. "Everything's fine, Carla. What about here?"

She pulls back the door, revealing her blue-and-white jumper and eyes red from sleep or studying. "Yeah. I was kind of scared, though. I heard the car stop, but then you didn't come in . . ."

I smile reassuringly and follow her inside, keeping the file pressed inside my shirt with my left hand while I dig for my wallet with my right. Having no idea how long I've been gone, I pull a couple of twenties and a ten from my billfold and give Carla permission to go with a wave.

"Annie did all her homework," she says, slinging a heavy backpack over her slight shoulder. "Paper's written."

"Did she do a good job?"

"Honestly?" Carla laughs. "That girl knows words I don't know. I'd say she's about one year behind me, gradewise."

"I feel the same way sometimes. Thanks again. What about this weekend?"

Carla's smile vanishes. "Um . . . maybe some late at night, if you need me. But I'm going to be at the balloon races most of the time. They have some decent bands this year."

"Okay. Any time you can spare, I'll pay you extra. This weekend is crazy for me."

She smiles in a way that doesn't give me much hope.

After closing the door behind Carla, I pour a tall iced tea from the pitcher in the kitchen fridge, carry it to the leather wing chair in my library, and spread the file open on the ottoman.

Golden Parachute Gaming Corporation pitched itself to the city as the Southwest Airlines of the casino industry. Capitalized by a small, feisty group of partners led by a Los Angeles entertainment lawyer, the company evolved a strategy of moving into secondary gaming markets and undercutting the competition's prices in every way possible, while simultaneously providing personable and personalized service, even to its less moneyed patrons. They run a phenomenally efficient operation, but what's opened many stubborn doors for them is their practice of forming development partnerships with the communities they move into, building parks, ball fields, community centers, and even investing in the development of industrial parks in some cities. Small town officials eat this up, and Natchez was no exception.

More than anything, though, Golden Parachute's success in penetrating our market came down to timing. They applied for their gaming license in the aftermath of Toyota's disastrous decision to build a new plant in Tupelo versus Natchez. Citizens were bitter about the lost jobs and ready to climb into bed with someone else—almost anybody else—on the rebound. Golden Parachute already had successful casinos up and running in Tunica County, near Memphis, and Vicksburg, just sixty miles north of Natchez. With that track record, they had no trouble getting local heavyweights to lobby the state gaming commission to grant a fourth license for Natchez.

Bringing another casino boat to town had not been one of my goals when I ran for mayor. (In truth, none of the floating casinos are navigable vessels; they are barges built to look like paddle wheelers from the era of Mark Twain, but at five times historical scale.) My platform was reforming education and revitalizing local industry. But after considerable persuasion by the board of selectmen, I agreed to help close the casino deal. My reasons were complex: exhaustion in wake of the Toyota failure; a savior complex running on adrenaline after the depletion of my initial inspiration; disillusionment with my colleagues in government and with many of the citizens I was supposed to be serving. I was also frustrated that the board of selectmen were often divided along racial lines: four black votes and four white, with me the deciding factor. I voted my conscience every time, but few people saw it that way, and with every vote, I lost more allies on one side or the other. The only thing the board could agree on was any proposition that could bring money or jobs to their constituencies. And so . . . Golden Parachute found a receptive audience for its sales pitch.

The problem, as it so often is with casinos, was site approval. Golden Parachute wanted to moor the *Magnolia Queen* on riverfront property donated to the city by a prominent Natchez family—the Pierces—by means of a complicated trust. One stipulation of that trust was that Pierce's Landing never be developed as a casino or shopping mall while the matriarch of the family remained alive. Inconveniently for the selectmen, Mrs. Pierce had lived to the ripe old age of ninety-eight, and she was still, as the saying goes, as sharp as a tack. That tack lay directly in the path of the inflated giant that was the Golden Parachute deal.

My first instinct was to try to persuade the company to find another property, but the company wouldn't budge. Golden Parachute wanted the Pierce land, which was not only the last suitable river property within the city limits, but also the finest, barring the Silver Street spot taken by *Lady Luck,* the first riverboat casino in the state. Predictably, Golden Parachute began making noises about scrapping its plan to come to Natchez, and just as predictably the selectmen went into panic mode. I heard whispers about the new eminent-domain law, which allowed the government to seize private land for commercial development. I viewed this as one of the most anti-American laws ever put on the books, but my fellow officials did not share my feelings. Only Selectman Paul Labry stood with me in resisting this Stalinist move. Desperate to prevent the use of this tactic, Labry and I quietly went into action.

First we met with one of the Pierce heirs, who'd graduated several years ahead of

me at St. Stephen's. He got us a copy of
the actual document governing the trust,
which few people had seen, outside the
preservationists who'd helped to write it,
and the former mayor, who'd died of lung
cancer shortly after leaving office. To my
surprise, I discovered that Mrs. Pierce possessed the authority to unilaterally revoke
the clause preventing casino development.
Disturbed by the board's increasing clamor
to seize the land in question, I requested
an audience with the grand old dame of
Pierce's Landing.

I met the distinguished lady in a conference room at Twelve Oaks Gardens, an
assisted-living facility on the outskirts of
town. As the granddaughter of an officer
who had served under General J. E. B.
Stuart at Gettysburg, Mrs. Pierce presided
over an entire wing of the facility like a
dowager empress. Her children had
offered to take her in, but they had all settled in other states, and Mrs. Pierce pre-
ferred to remain in the city she'd lived in
all her life, and to "be around people"
rather than to live in her mansion with
round-the-clock nurses (or "watchers," as

she called them, as in "They're here to watch me have my final heart attack.") Mrs. Pierce granted me the audience because my father had treated her for more than thirty years, and because, she told me, she had enjoyed several of my novels on tape. At ninety-eight, she confessed with some embarrassment, her eyes were not what they had once been.

For the best part of an hour, I made the case for allowing a casino riverboat to be moored to her ancestral land. Early in our conversation, I discovered that Mrs. Pierce was neither a religious zealot nor a hidebound moralist. She confided that her father had hated gambling in all its forms, not least because his brother had lost a fine home and several hundred acres of farmland during a drunken poker game. She also mentioned that forty years earlier she'd become aware of quite a bit of "unpleasantness" going on across the river, all related to gambling. One of her maids had actually been accosted on the road by men who'd believed she was a prostitute. After realizing the basis of her objections, I pointed out that legalized casino gambling was far different from the illicit juke-joint operations she remembered. Gambling was now a legitimate industry of strictly regulated corporations that had brought prosperity to our struggling state. In making this argument, the numbers were all on my side.

Legalized casino gambling lifted Mississippi's Tunica County—once the poorest in the United States—from wretched poverty to wealth in fifteen years. A rural county serviced by open sewer ditches in 1991, Tunica has doubled its per capita income while going from two thousand total jobs to over seventeen thousand. They've invested $40 million in school improvements, poured millions into police and fire protection, built a sports arena, doubled the size of their library, and invested over $100 million in their road system. Statewide, the verdict on gambling is beyond question. Since 1992, the casino industry has come to provide nearly 5 percent of the state's total tax revenue.

Despite Mrs. Pierce's suspicion that "vice is vice, whatever cloak it wears," I knew I was making headway when she told me that she'd always chastised her friends who had blindly resisted change and felt they had hobbled the city's efforts to keep pace with the rest of the country. I knew I was almost home when she said softly that she'd never imagined she would gaze down the hill that led to her "home place" and see a neon casino sign. I promised her that if that was her final objection, she never would. The city would submit all of Golden Parachute's signage plans to her for approval. My mouth fell open when the old belle said she wouldn't carp about the sign if the company would devote one-half of 1 percent of its revenues from the *Magnolia Queen* to helping the city's underprivileged children. (Mrs. Pierce actually said "colored," but her heart was in the right place.) In the end the company agreed to one-quarter of 1 percent, but that has amounted to $162,000 this year.

Two days after our meeting, Mrs. Pierce revoked the restrictive clause, and the Golden Parachute casino deal went forward. This made me a hero to the board of selectmen, but I felt like a heel. What I feel tonight is immeasurably worse. Mrs. Pierce died one month after revoking that

clause, and if even half of Tim's allegations are true, it's a mercy that she did.
The town at large never learned that it
was I who opened the final gate to Golden
Parachute, but that does not lessen my
guilt. Tonight I feel more like I lifted our
hoopskirt and pulled down our petticoats.

Nevertheless, dogfighting, drug use,
and prostitution went on here before the
Magnolia Queen arrived, just as they do in
every city in America. The thesis that
Golden Parachute is defrauding the city of
millions of dollars in taxes is an accusation
of a different order. This kind of crime,
while not as disturbing on the surface as the
others, is more harmful in the end, because
it impacts every man, woman, and child in
the city. If this allegation is true, then food
is being stolen from the mouths of the children Mrs. Pierce wanted to help.

Yet this is the part of Tim's tale that I find
impossible to believe. I don't know enough
about computers to judge the feasibility of
distorting the casino's gross receipts, but
even if such fraud were possible, the central question remains: *Why would Golden
Parachute risk it?* Especially now.

Forty-six days ago, Hurricane Katrina

roared over the floating gold mines that were the casinos at Biloxi and Gulfport and left behind something resembling Omaha Beach on D-day. A single storm wiped out a $100-million-a-month industry. But 150 miles to the northwest, in Natchez, the *Magnolia Queen* and her sister casinos simply battened down their hatches and rode out the winds and rain. The city sustained severe damage, and some areas were without power for more than a week, but the *Magnolia Queen* was running on her generators the day after the hurricane. And no sooner had some refugees gotten settled into the shelters at the local churches and school gymnasiums than they found time and means to get down to the river and gamble away what little money they'd brought with them (or had been given by the churches). That image brings a sick feeling to the pit of my stomach, but more than that, it tells me that the partners of Golden Parachute Gaming would have to be insane to risk their gaming license to pick up a few extra million when God is going to dump ten times that amount into their coffers over the next year.

Moreover, until tonight, the company has given me no reason to regret bringing them to town. They've paid their taxes promptly and followed through on the community investments they promised. I enjoy cordial relations with their general manager, an Englishman named Sands who works the city with the professional charm one would expect from a manager in Las Vegas, not Mississippi. The only part of Golden Parachute that's ever rubbed me the wrong way is their chief of security, a coarse Irishman named Seamus Quinn, who looks and talks like an overdressed thug from the London underworld. But Sands vouched for Quinn's credentials, and I decided my problem with the security man was more a matter of style than anything, like my problem with some cops. The bottom line is that I've watched Golden Parachute operate without incident in every market they serve. So I find myself at a loss when trying to reconcile Tim Jessup's allegations with what I know of the company.

My eyes are blurring with fatigue near the end of the file, but I blink myself awake when I find a note I wrote in the margin of one document over a year ago. In red ink, on a copy of Golden Parachute's original application for its gaming license, I see the words *Voting trust. % voting power reflect actual ownership?* Something Tim said tonight makes this note resonate within me, and suddenly my only serious suspicion about the original Golden Parachute deal returns to me.

By law, anyone who plans to own more than 5 percent of a casino in Mississippi must submit to a comprehensive investigation of his past. This is no simple background check; no aspect of the prospective owner's life is off-limits, and the subject must pay for the investigation himself. The gaming commission maintains a full staff of investigators for this purpose, and they will not hesitate to fly to the Philippines to subpoena the contents of a safe-deposit box if they deem it necessary to determine the "suitability" of an applicant. In fact, most rejections of gaming applications have been based on the "unsuitability" of investors.

During the Golden Parachute deal, I learned from talking to an old law school classmate that there is a way around this statute. Lawyers can establish a "voting trust," which may own all or part of a casino. Behind such a trust lies a group of investors with a private understanding of who owns what percent of the company, but on paper 95 percent of the voting power is held by the one partner who has nothing to fear from a background investigation. The other partners are named in the application, but since on paper they own only the remaining 5 percent between them, they are not subject to similar scrutiny. A neat system. But what happens, I asked my friend, if the squeaky-clean front partner decides to actually start using his voting power to make the decisions? My friend laughed and said that because most of the "five percent partners" tend to have names that end with vowels, this rarely happens. When it does, the front partner usually winds up inside a fifty-five-gallon drum in a convenient body of water.

Golden Parachute Gaming is owned by a voting trust called Golden Flower LLC. Flipping to the back of the application, I see that it was signed only by the front partner—the L.A. entertainment lawyer—and not the "five percenters." What stuck in my mind tonight was Tim's comment about a Chinese billionaire's son flying in from Macao to fight his dog in Mississippi. Why, I wondered, would a billionaire come so far to do something he could easily do in Macao? Was he simply seeking new competition? After all, for a man with a private jet, distance means little. But I'm almost sure I remember that two of the five percent partners in Golden Parachute were Chinese. By the time I learned this, the deal was so far along that I gave it little thought. I simply made this note in the margin and moved on, caught up in the next day's business. No one wanted to rock the boat by then, not even, apparently, the gaming commission. But tonight, I realize, I need an answer to the question I wrote in this margin so long ago.

Who really owns Golden Parachute?

With a last swallow of diluted tea, I close the file and slip it behind my collection of Patrick O'Brian novels on the third shelf. As I walk upstairs, my thoughts and

feelings about what I heard in the cemetery start to separate, like solids precipi-
tating from a solution. On one hand, I
don't doubt that Tim witnessed the horrors he described. On the other, if someone shook me awake at 4:00 a.m. and
asked whether I was sure that Jessup
hadn't started snorting coke again—or
heroin or crystal meth or whatever he was
doing before Julia Stanton got him
straightened out—I would be hard-pressed
to say I was. Most people who know us
both would assume the worst about Tim. I
don't, but it wouldn't be hard to convince
myself that he's dreamed up a conspiracy
in which he can play the hero to belatedly
make up for the real-life drama in which
he played the villain.

During his first year at Ole Miss, Tim
agreed to host two prospective freshmen
from St. Stephen's Prep, our alma mater,
during a football weekend. Like a lot of
other students, he made several high-
speed trips to the county line to procure
cold beer, which was not legally available
in Oxford, Mississippi (and still isn't). During his third beer run, Tim drove his Trans
Am eighty-eight feet off the highway and

into a pecan tree standing at the edge of a cotton field. Tim and one of the high school boys were wearing their seat belts; the third boy was not. The impact ejected him from the backseat through the front windshield and into the branches of the tree, where with any luck he died instantly. Because of the alcohol found at the scene, both sets of parents sued Jessup's father, and Tim served a year in jail for manslaughter. Pleading the case down from vehicular homicide probably cost Dr. Jessup all the goodwill he'd built up in twenty years of practicing medicine, not to mention the cash that must have changed hands under the table. But despite the light sentence, things were never really the same for Tim after that. As his life slipped further and further off track, people blamed drugs, weakness of character, even his father, but in my gut I always knew it was the wreck that had ruined him.

Now, with his new wife's help, Tim seems to have clawed his way back to a decent life. But a casino boat is probably a tough place for a guy with his past to stay clean. *Stop,* says a voice in my head. *Stop blaming the messenger. Just because you don't want to hear what he said doesn't mean it's not true. Remember the pictures.*

A mangled dog. A half-naked teenager serving beer. A middle-aged man screwing the young girl on a board floor while four other men drink and watch. I saw those three images for only seconds, but I'll never forget them. When I close my eyes and recall them in detail, I feel nauseated. And that nausea is the reason I promised Tim that I'd help him.

As I walk down the hall to check on my daughter, a different sensation chills me. Fear. Raw fear. After twelve years in the Houston DA's office, it's a familiar feeling. As I told Tim, I've run investigations using confidential informants, and more than one ended badly for the person wearing the wire. Highly trained FBI agents trip up under the pressure of living double lives, and even the best undercover agents can be burned by a random event. The reality of tonight's meeting with Tim cannot be pushed aside: by encouraging him to proceed with his plan, I could be sending an impassioned amateur to his death.

I pause beside Annie's door and peek through the crack. A pale green night-light limns her form, bunched beneath the covers. That she can sleep alone in her own room brings me an abiding sense of peace. After Sarah died, Annie not only had to sleep in my bed, but also had to be in direct physical contact with me. If her hand fell from my arm or hip, she'd jerk awake with night terrors. The peace she now enjoys is a testament to the soundness of my decision to bring her back here. Living near my father and mother brought Annie the gift once enjoyed by all societies that revered the extended family: a profound sense of security. That decision cost me my future with Caitlin, but Annie's recovery has given me the strength to deal with that loss. And yet . . . tonight a nagging voice echoes endlessly beneath my conscious thoughts: *We've stayed too long . . .*

After I undress and brush my teeth, I walk to my bedroom window and gaze across sixty feet of space to the second floor of Caitlin's house. Is she there? Did she fall asleep with the light on? Or is she down at the *Examiner* offices, badgering the editor about the layout of tomorrow's paper? This thought brings a smile, but then I realize Caitlin could just as easily be dancing at one of the bars on Main Street, or exercising her gift for irony at the expense of some pompous, nouveau-riche redneck who threw a balloon-race party. I feel a compulsion to walk down and check her garage for a rental car. Has eighteen months of separation from her turned me into a stalker? The reality is that she could pull up to her house right now with a man and disappear inside for a night of recreational sex behind that familiar curtain.

Christ. As selfish as it sounds, this image has a more violent effect on my adrenal glands than the photos I viewed in the cemetery. If I'm this jealous, can I possibly be over her? One thing is sure: I'll be damned—truly damned—if I stand here mooning at her light like a latter-day Gatsby, until the very scene I fear transpires before me. Caitlin left me because I believed the path to my future lay through the past. So what the hell is she doing back here, where the past is never past?

As I drift toward sleep, the images from

Tim's cell phone snapshots rise again, but they seem remote, like evidence dropped on my desk by cops I dealt with in Houston. Can young girls be raped and dogs be slaughtered within sight of the town I love so dearly? In the foggy frontier between sleep and wakefulness the idea seems far-fetched, yet one burden of my legal experience is the knowledge that savage crimes occur in the most benign settings, that screams go unheard, that pleas for mercy are ignored, even relished.

When thoughts like these trouble my passage into sleep, I use a trick taught me by a sixties-era rock musician I saved from going to jail in Houston. Whenever drug withdrawal sent him into paroxysms of pain and need, whenever the demons came for him, he would picture a virgin field of ice, blue-white and impossibly clean, so remote that no footprint had ever marred its surface. He would focus on that scene until he felt himself inside it, and sometimes peace would come. To my surprise, I found this sometimes works for me as well. But tonight, as I carefully construct my Zen-like sanctuary, I cannot keep the demons out. Dark shapes move beneath the ice like predators prowling a vast sea, ever alert for the shadows of prey on the white sheet above.

Tonight I'm *on* the ice, I realize, one more shadow to be hunted. A penumbra the size of a small car flashes beneath me, and I run. Though I lie supine in bed, my heart thumps in my chest, and the blood rushes through my veins. Far ahead, I see a blue mark on the ice. A hole. Beside it Tim Jessup stands shirtless and blue from the cold. As I crunch toward him, he removes his pants and looks down into the hole. I shout for him to wait, but he doesn't hear. He sits down, dangles his legs in the water, then, with a gentle shove like a boy edging himself off a roof, drops through the blue-black opening. I start to scream, but a new vision stops me. Stark against the horizon, a wolf stands watching me. His fur is bone white, and his eyes gleam with unsettling intelligence. I try to stop running, but I slide forward, hopelessly out of control. As I come to rest, the wolf begins to move, walking at first, then loping toward me with single-minded purpose. His eyes transfix me, and as I try to force my legs to backpedal, I hear Tim's hysterical voice crying, "You don't know, man! You don't *know. . . .* "

CHAPTER

6

Julia sits at her kitchen table, staring at a Ziploc sandwich bag filled with speckled pills and white powder. She found it an hour ago, when the running toilet got on her nerves badly enough to make her remove the tank cover. The baggie was sealed inside a small Tupperware container weighted with a handful of bolts. The edge of the Tupperware lid was keeping the toilet flapper from sealing. Tim had been clean for so long that the first moments after lifting the container out of the tank filled Julia with confusion. But after removing the lid, she'd felt her universe imploding as surely as if a black hole had swept into it.

She'd set the baggie on the kitchen table and simply stared at it for a while, shivering with anger and her sense of betrayal. But mostly she felt fear, because she hadn't seen any sign that Tim was using again. To stop her hands from shaking, she got out her crocheting needle and tried to crochet the way her grandmother had taught her, but her mind was unable to direct her fingers. So she waited, her gaze moving from the dope on the table to the clock on the stove, an endless motion of eyes that offered no solace.

Julia tenses now, listening for sound from the baby's room. It's 3:45 a.m., almost time for a feeding. She has preternatural hearing when it comes to her baby; Tim is constantly amazed by the things she picks up. It's like she's bound to the child by an invisible thread, a silken strand like a spider's web, and if little Timmy moves, it pulls something down in Julia's belly. She knows what that something is.

When you lose a child and God grants you another, you take no chances. She feels the same way about Tim, but on that score there isn't a lot she can do. Someone has to stay with the baby. She's been worried recently, but not about drugs—not for a long time. It infuriates her to think that she was afraid for Tim tonight. Before she found that baggie, she'd believed he was doing something about whatever he'd seen at work, and trying to protect her by not telling her details. But he'd been almost three hours late even then. She feels so stupid that she wants to tear out her hair or whip herself.

As if Penn Cage would stay out this late with Tim! Penn is home in bed with Libby Jensen, or somebody like her. Someone smart who can still laugh with innocence in her eyes, someone who has her shit together. Julia wonders briefly why Penn left Libby. Maybe Libby doesn't have her shit quite as together as she seems to. Maybe she doesn't really understand what's important in life. Or maybe Penn just grew bored with her, the way men do.

Julia hadn't thought Tim was bored with her, but there's the dope, right there on the table. What else could it mean? That he can't cope? With what? With happiness? With a loving wife and a beautiful son? This thought terrifies her. Julia once thought Tim was smarter than she, and he is, in book smartness. But what good is that when the issue is survival, as it has been for them? Julia's common sense and fortitude have gotten them through some tough times. To sit facing the prospect of reliving the hell she thought long behind them is almost more than she can bear. She has gone from fury to terror and back a thousand times. The pills make her wonder about other women. A woman might push Tim back to using, if she was an addict, a woman from the boat, maybe—

An unfamiliar scraping sound brings Julia to full alertness, the yarn stretched taut between her fingers and the hook. That noise didn't come from the baby's room—she's sure of that. It sounded like someone raising the window in the guest room at the back of the house.

She swallows hard, then goes to the

cabinet above the stove and takes down the pistol Tim stole from his father's safe back when he was using. He'd tried to give it back later, but his father told him to keep it. The gun is heavy and black, but Julia grips it firmly in her flexed fist and tiptoes to the back of the house.

Terror hits her, gluing her bare feet to the floor. She can hear shoes moving behind the door. They creak as the intruder shifts his weight. Could it be the police? No—they would crash through the door. It might be another junkie, coming to steal Tim's stash. When the window slides back down, Julia tightens her finger on the trigger and almost fires through the door.

She's on the verge of bolting for the baby's crib when she realizes that the intruder must be Tim, because there's no light on in the guest room, yet the person inside is moving with assurance. She slides back three steps and aims the pistol at the door. If it opens and anyone but Tim appears, she will fire. She hears a muttered curse, and then the door opens.

Tim jerks as though he's been hit with a cattle prod when he sees the gun pointed at his face. Then suddenly he is apologizing, begging her to forgive him. She's so angry that she wants to shoot him, but her relief is even stronger.

"Where were you?" she cries in a squelched scream. "It's four in the morning!"

"Hey, hey," he says soothingly, throwing some balled-up clothes onto the floor. "It's going to be all right now."

"Bullshit!" she hisses. "I almost shot you! You fucking liar! Liar liar LIAR!"

Tim's forehead wrinkles with puzzlement. "What are you talking about? I've been with Penn, honey. You don't want to know more than that."

Julia wipes her eyes with a quivering hand and looks at him the way she used to when she had to manage every moment of his life to keep him from sliding back into the abyss. She means to ask about the drugs, but what she says is "Just with Penn?"

Something in the quick blinking of his eyes tells her that whatever follows is going to be a lie. As she turns away, the fine cracks that have accumulated in her trust over the past weeks give way, and the true fragility of her existence is revealed. She stifles a wail, then goes to the kitchen cupboard and takes out a bottle of Isomil to heat on the stove.

She now knows that what she told herself after leaving her first husband was a lie. If a man ever cheats on me again, I'll leave him in a second. *So easy to say, but with a baby in the nursery things get a lot more complicated.*

"Julia?" Tim says awkwardly.

If he tries to approach her, she will move away to avoid smelling another woman on him. "There's something for you on the table," she says coldly.

"Huh?"

"The table!" She watches the gas flame glow at the edge of the pot.

"Oh, God," Tim breathes. "Julia—"

"Mm-hm?"

"It's not what you think."

"It's not? That's not dope on the table? That's not Vicodin and cocaine?"

"No. I mean . . . it is, yeah. You know it is."

"Let me guess. It's not yours, right? You're just holding it for somebody."

Hearing the floor creak, she holds up a hand to ward him off. He stops.

"Baby, I know what you think, but that stuff is part of what Penn and I are doing."

Even Julia is surprised by the harshness of her laughter. "Oh, right. I understand now. You and the mayor are using a bag of dope to save the city."

There's a brief silence. Then Tim says, "Actually that's about it. Penn doesn't know about that part of it, but it's the only way. That's all I can really tell you now. Anything else would be dangerous. In a few days, though, I should be able to explain it to you."

"If you're not in jail, you mean?"

Tim sighs in what sounds like exhaustion. "I just wish you'd believe me. Haven't I earned that yet?"

Julia grips the pot handle with her shaking hands. Part of her wants to throw the hot water on him, to scald him for lying to her. But part of her wants to believe. Tim sounded like he was telling the truth about the drugs, and she truly hasn't seen any signs of his being high. But he's lying about something—that she knows.

"Julia?"

"You're home now," she snaps, her eyes locked onto the milk bottle warming in the pot of water. "Whatever you're doing, get it done, so we can get back to living."

Tim keeps his distance. "Okay."

"All right," she says, cutting off further discussion. "Go get Timmy, please. You know what time it is. He's going to start crying any second."

The kitchen is so small she can feel Tim nodding in the shadows. "Okay," he mumbles in surrender.

Julia opens the bottle and touches some hot milk to the inside of her wrist. She knows what's important.

CHAPTER

7

I come awake swatting at my bedside table like a man battling a horsefly. According to the alarm clock, I got four hours of sleep. It's all I can do to walk blindly into the shower and stand under scalding spray until my synapses seem to be firing normally. After making sure Annie is awake, I dress a little sharper than usual, since I have to spend at least two hours giving Hans Necker, the visiting CEO, a tour of sites for his recycling plant. Annie gives me a thumbs-up when I walk into the kitchen, a rare seal of approval for my day's outfit. She's eating cereal and some

garlic cheese grits my mother made yesterday. I finish off the cheese grits, drink
the cup of coffee Annie has made me,
and follow her out to the car, so exhausted
that I forget to glance into Caitlin's driveway for a car.

Annie is uncharacteristically quiet during the ride to St. Stephen's, but as we
near the turn for the school, I discover
why.

"I dreamed about Caitlin last night," she
says softly.

"Did you?" I wonder whether my
daughter could have seen or heard something across the street that told her Caitlin
might be in town.

Annie nods with slow deliberation. As I
watch her from the corner of my eye, it
strikes me that the topless teenager
serving beer in Tim's photograph was
probably only four years older than my
daughter. This realization is freighted with
such horror that I have to clear my throat
and look away. Annie knows nothing of
such things yet, or at least I hope she
doesn't. Right now one of her deepest
concerns is the women in my life.

"Have you ever dreamed about Caitlin before?" I ask.

"Yes. Not for a long time, though."

"What was last night's dream about?"

Annie keeps her eyes forward. "I don't want to say."

Strange. "Why not? Was it scary?"

"Not at first. But then it was, kind of."

Recalling my own nightmare of the ice field and the wolf, I turn into the school's driveway and pull up to the door of the middle school building. "Sometimes things are less scary if you talk about them."

Annie looks at me with her mother's eyes. "I just want to think about it for a while."

Her enigmatic expression tells me she's already beyond my understanding. "You know what's best for you, I guess."

She gets out and shoulders her backpack like a younger version of her babysitter, but as she walks through the big doors, I see her mother in every sway of her body. It's moments like these—the most commonplace events—that hit me hardest, reminding me that *widower* is more than an archaic word. As my eleven-year-old disappears into the halls of the same school I attended at her age, I wish fervently that the woman who supplied the other half of Annie's DNA could have lived to see who she's becoming.

"Baby girl," I whisper to the breath-fogged window, "Mama sees you."

In this affirmation lies a hope that I've never quite been able to sustain, yet still I continue to affirm it. I don't believe Sarah sits in heaven looking benevolently down upon our daughter; but I do believe she survives within Annie—in her face, her voice, in her quick perception and even temperament. In my years with Caitlin, seeing these avatars of my wife in my daughter brought pleasure, not pain. But now, alone again, I find that each memory carries a sharp edge on its trailing side. Whatever brings you comfort can also bring you pain.

I turn onto Highway 61 and force my thoughts to the business of the city, which takes more effort than I would have believed possible two years ago.

Whoever said, "Be careful what you wish for," must have served as mayor of a small town. If there were ever a case of being punished with one's dream, being elected mayor of Natchez is it. The mayor of a city like Houston has a certain amount of insulation from his electorate, which he can justify in the name of security. But when you're mayor of a small town, every mother's son believes your time is his, no matter where you are or what you might be doing. A call from a Fortune 500 company might be followed by an irate visit from a man whose neighbor's goats keep eating his rosebushes. If you keep your sense of humor, you can tolerate these situations with equanimity, but I've been having difficulty maintaining mine for some time now.

Today it's neither goats nor roses, but a Minnesota millionaire with a bold—or possibly crazy—scheme to recycle waste from all the cities along the Mississippi River and its tributaries. Hans Necker plans to gather aluminum, plastic, and paper refuse, compress it at collection points, then float the resulting cubes downstream on barges to a recycling facility at Greenville or Natchez or Baton Rouge— wherever he ultimately decides to locate his plant. One thing is sure: Katrina just scratched New Orleans off his short list. We have three potential sites for such a facility in Natchez, all close to one another. Despite this, Necker has chartered a helicopter to view them, as well as the city and its environs. Even the thought of spending hours bobbing and pitching over the city in a chopper gives me a mild case of airsickness, but what choice do I have? Hans Necker wants a sky tour from the mayor, so a sky tour he will get.

Halfway to the airport, Paul Labry, one of the few selectman I consider a friend, texts me that Necker is running late. The CEO has already spent more time in Greenville than he'd expected to, and the selectmen are drawing all sorts of negative conclusions from this. I can't get too stirred up about it. Compared to what I'd have to deal with if Tim Jessup were to uncover proof of his allegations, losing a possible recycling plant seems like small potatoes.

With the jarring synchronicity I experience so often in life, my cell phone vibrates against my thigh. I take it out, expecting another update from Labry, but I find a text message from a number I don't know. I don't even recognize the area code. When I click READ, the words make my mouth go dry.

Xing the Rubicon. Stay close to ur fon & n range of a tower. Don't respond 2 this msg! Mrs. Haley.

"Shit," I whisper. Mrs. Haley taught Tim Jessup and me Latin in the eighth grade. *Crossing the Rubicon?* What the hell is Tim playing at? I figured he'd wait at least a few days to try whatever it is he's been planning. Doesn't he understand how important this weekend is to the city? *"Shit,"* I say again, unable to get my mind around the idea that Jessup could be committing any number of felonies at this moment, endangering both himself and the future of the casino industry in Mississippi.

"Tim, you crazy son of a bitch," I mutter, and start to reply to his message with a warning. But before I hit SEND, caution wins out over anxiety, and I shove the phone deep into my pocket.

Locking my car, I march out onto the tarmac where a few single-engine planes wait in lonely silence. There isn't much to see at the airport. Natchez hasn't had

steady commercial service since the
1970s, when the oil business was boom-
ing and the DC-3s of Southern Airways
flew in and out every day. I remember
being led aboard one of the sturdy old
planes by a pretty stewardess when my
parents took my sister and me to London
as children. I've always believed that trip
generated my sister Jenny's love of
Britain, a love that eventually pulled her
away from us for good. If I close my eyes,
I can still feel the buffeting wind from the
big propellers as they revved up to carry
us to the Pan Am 747 waiting in New
Orleans. Two slices of Americana gone
forever.

I need that prop wash this afternoon.
Last night's wind died this morning, and
the sun blazes white over the runways,
roasting me as I check the northern sky
for Hans Necker's Gulfstream IV. The lack
of wind was good for the Balloon Festival's "media flight" this morning, but it
sucks for a man wearing a long-sleeved
button-down, even Egyptian cotton. The
humidity in south Mississippi could drown
a desert dweller if he breathed too fast.

After shedding another pint of sweat, I

finally spy a silver glint in the sky far upriver. As Necker's jet descends toward me, I hear the *whup-whup-whup* of a helicopter approaching from the south. The Gulfstream circles and executes its approach from the southeast, landing as gracefully as the first duck of winter on a dawn-still pond. As the jet taxies up to the small terminal, a blue Bell helicopter descends toward the tarmac twenty yards away from me. Then the aft door of the Gulfstream opens and the steps unfold to the ground with a hydraulic hum.

Hans Necker emerges alone, a stocky, red-faced man of about sixty with a grip of iron. "Penn, Penn! Face-to-face at last," he says, walking exuberantly while we shake hands. "Sorry to be late, but we made up most of the time in flight."

I greet Necker with as much enthusiasm as I can muster while he guides me past the tail of his jet and toward the settling chopper. *Straight to business, then. Suits me. The sooner we go up, the sooner we get back.*

The moment the chopper's skids touch down, Necker yanks open the side door, pushes me into the vibrating craft, and

climbs in next to me. The pilot points at
two headsets lying on the seat. I slip one
on, then grip the handle to my left in anticipation of takeoff.

"Take her up, Major!" Necker shouts in
my crackling headset.

The chopper rises like a leaf on a gust of
wind. Then its nose dips and we start forward, rapidly gathering speed as we climb
into the blue-white sky.

"Penn," Necker says over the intercom
link, "our pilot's Danny McDavitt. Flew in
Vietnam."

"Good to meet you," I tell the back of
the graying head in front of me.

"You too," says a voice of utter calm.

I recognize McDavitt's name from an
incident about six months ago involving a
helicopter crash-landing in the river. There
was some talk about the pilot and a local
doctor's wife, but there's so much talk like
that all the time that I only pay attention if it
involves me or the city. The idea of a
crash awakens a swarm of butterflies in
my stomach, but in the sixty seconds it
takes us to sight the Mississippi River to
the west, Danny McDavitt convinces me
that he's an extension of the machine

carrying us, or that the machine is an extension of his will. Either way, I'm happy, because this chopper flight is the first I've ever endured without my stomach going south on me.

"How did the media flight go this morning?" Necker asks, his face pressed against the glass beside him.

"Great!" I reply too loudly. "Weather looks good for most of the weekend. Except maybe Sunday."

"Good, good."

"How was your visit to Greenville?"

"Fine. Got some good people up there, and they really want the plant. I still like this place, though," Necker says almost wistfully. "It's got a romance to it that the other cities don't have—apart from New Orleans, and there's no possibility of making that work now."

I figured as much, but it's a relief to hear it confirmed.

"I did an overflight three days after the levees broke," he says, looking down at a string of barges on a bend in the river below. "Hauled some relief supplies down to Biloxi. Christ, it looked like the End of Days down there. There were *still* people stranded on the interstate. I couldn't believe it."

I shake my head but make no comment. The enormity of the havoc wreaked by Katrina is beyond words. We do what we can, then start again the next day. "You want to view the industrial-park sites first? Or look at the city?"

"Let's head straight down to the old Triton Battery site. I'm pressed for time today. Okay with you, Major?"

"It's your nickel," McDavitt replies.

On any other day, Necker's haste might worry me, but today I'll take any excuse to get time alone with my thoughts. As we drone southward, following the vast river, the city unfolds beneath us like an Imax film, the classic city on a hill, one of only three on the eastern side of the Mississippi from Cairo to New Orleans. From two thousand feet, you can see the nineteenth-century scale of Natchez, the church steeples still taller than all but two commercial buildings; yet we're still low enough to take in the *Gone With the Wind* aura of the grand mansions set amid the verdant forests of the old plantations. A year ago I could rattle off our claims to fame with poetic enthusiasm: how Natchez in 1840 had more millionaires per capita than any city in America; how we survived the Civil War with our property intact, if not our pride; and how, after the white gold of cotton failed, the black gold of oil replaced it. But experience has drained my enthusiasm, and my ambivalence is difficult to mask.

Still . . . a more picturesque American town could not be found anywhere. For sheer beauty Natchez is unmatched along the length of the river; with its commanding site above the river Mississippi it surpasses even New Orleans, and one would have to travel to Charleston or Savannah to find comparable architecture. But gazing down from this helicopter, I no longer see the city I knew during the first eighteen years of my life, nor even the town I found when I returned seven years ago. Now I see Natchez through the mayor's eyes, and what I see is a town crippled by a mistake made thirty years ago, when the majority of whites pulled out of the public school system in response to forced integration. A city whose public schools are 90 percent filled with the descendants of slaves, and whose four private schools struggle to provide a superior but redundant education to mostly white students, leavened by a few lucky African-Americans (the children of affluent professionals or dedicated middle-class parents—or those kids recruited to play football) plus the majority of Asians and Indians in the county, who avoid the public school system if they can. Changing this state of affairs was my primary reason for running for mayor, for until it is changed, we're unlikely to attract any new industry larger than Hans Necker's as-yet-unborn recycling plant. But thus far I have failed in my quest—publicly and miserably.

Necker asks a lot of questions as we fly, and I answer without going into detail. Every road, field, park, school, and creek below holds indelible memories for me, but how do you explain that to a stranger? Necker seems like the kind of guy who'd like to hear that sort of thing, but the truth is, I'm simply not in the mood to sell. That's one good thing about casino companies: you don't have to sell them. They come to the table ready to deal. And like the plain girl dreading prom month, we can't afford to be too picky about whom we say yes to. We got our prison the same way. (It might look like a college athletic dorm, but the razor wire doesn't let you forget its true purpose.)

After flaring near the earth beside the river south of town, Major McDavitt sets the chopper down on the partially scorched cement where the gatehouse of the Triton Battery plant once stood. For me this is an uncomfortable visit, because I set the fire that destroyed the shuttered hulk that remains of the factory.

"You okay?" Necker asks with a smile.

"Not bad, actually. Thanks to Major McDavitt."

The pilot holds up a gloved hand in acknowledgment.

"Take a walk with us, Danny," Necker says.

McDavitt removes his headset.

"I always use military pilots," Necker explains, climbing out of the chopper. "Combat pilots when I can get them. They don't lose their cool when things go awry, which always happens, sooner or later."

I follow the CEO down to the cracked concrete, bending at the waist until I clear the spinning rotors. McDavitt gets out and walks a couple of strides to our left, like a wingman on patrol. He looks about fifty, with the close-cropped hair and symmetrical build of a Gemini-era astronaut.

"Lots of history around this town," Necker says, walking toward the burned-out battery plant. "Not all of it ancient."

I feel Major McDavitt come alert beside us.

"For example," Necker goes on, "this plant here was used by a drug dealer as a hideout until somebody in present company took care of business."

Danny McDavitt gives me a sidelong glance.

"And we're not too far," Necker continues, "from where somebody ditched a chopper under suspicious circumstances." The CEO beams with pleasure at the hitch in McDavitt's step. "I just want you boys to know I do my homework. I've checked you both out, and I figure whatever you did, you had good reasons. I check out everybody I plan to do business with, and I'd like to do some business in this town."

I stop, and they stop with me. Necker has to look up at me, since I'm three inches taller, but I'm the one at a disadvantage.

"I'm going to be straight with you, Penn," he says. "I want to bring my plant here. I want to buy that old factory there and recycle all the debris to show the town I mean business. There's one obstacle in the way, though. This has been a union town since 1945. I used to be a big supporter of unions—belonged to one myself when I worked as a meat packer. But they got out of hand, and you see the result." He waves his hand at the abandoned battery plant.

It's a little more complex than that, I think, but this doesn't seem the time to argue U.S. trade policy.

"Mississippi has a right-to-work law, and I plan to use that. But bottom line, I need to know one thing." A stubby red forefinger shoots up. "When push comes to shove on something—and it always does—am I gonna have your support? Are you going to be in office a year from now, when I need you? If I'm going to bring my plant down here, I need to know you're going to be the man in charge. I can't afford some yokel, and I can't afford the other thing."

Major McDavitt cuts his eyes at me. *The other thing?*

"Don't get the wrong idea," Necker says quickly. "I don't care what color a man is, so long as he can tell red ink from black. But race politics gets in the way of business, and with your fifty-fifty split, I can foresee some problems. I figure you're my best shot at solving those problems."

"You're saying that if I answer yes to your question, you'll bring your recycling plant here?"

"That's the deal, Mr. Mayor."

"What makes you think I won't be here in a year?"

Necker flashes a knowing smile. "For one thing, this is a detour from your main career. For another, I've heard you might not be too happy in the job."

"I won't lie to you. It's been wearing me down pretty fast. It's tough to get everybody swinging on the same gate, as they say around here."

Necker nods. "Politics in a nutshell. But

my research also says you're no quitter, and you're as good as your word."

Yesterday I might have confessed that I might not be here next October. But given my involvement with Tim, I'm not sure how to reply. "Can you give me a few days to answer you?"

"How does two weeks sound?"

"I'll take it."

Necker grins and starts to say something else, but his cell phone begins blaring what sounds like a college fight song. He holds up his hand, checks the screen, then with a grunt of apology marches away to take the call, leaving me staring out over the mile-broad Mississippi with Danny McDavitt. A mild breeze blows off the reddish brown water, and the pilot squints into it like a man measuring wind speed by watching waves.

"What do you think about Necker?" I ask, casually checking my cell phone for further messages. There are none.

"Kinda pushy," McDavitt says after a considerable silence. "But they're all like that."

"You fly a lot of CEOs?"

The pilot's lips widen slightly in what might be a smile. "Not these days. I flew charters in Nashville after I got out of the air force. Don't ask. At least this guy knows he puts his pants on same as the next guy."

I look back toward the Triton Battery plant and see Necker speaking animatedly into his phone. "You think he'll do what he says? You think he'll bring his plant here?"

McDavitt spits on the rocks at the edge of the parking lot. "Yep." Then he turns toward me, and his blue-gray eyes catch mine with surprising force. "Question is, will you be here when he needs you?"

While I ask myself the same question, Necker suddenly appears beside me. "I'm afraid we've got to head back right away. I've got to make an unexpected stop on my way to Chicago."

"Chicago?" This is the first I've heard about Chicago.

Necker leads us quickly back to the helicopter. "I thought you knew. I promised my granddaughter I'd watch her first dance recital. And now I have to make a stop in Paducah on the way."

The selectmen will panic if Necker isn't in town for the festival. "Are you coming back for the balloon race?"

The CEO grins. "Are you kidding? I can't wait to see your face when the canopy starts flapping and the lines start creaking at three thousand feet. I'll be back by dawn tomorrow." Necker turns to McDavitt. "Let's get airborne, Major. And don't waste any time getting back."

McDavitt nods and climbs into the cockpit. As I clamber in behind him, I feel my cell phone vibrate on my hip. With Necker beside me, I almost ignore the message, assuming it must be Paul Labry asking how my sales pitch is going. But then I remember Tim's text and decide to check it. This text is from the same number as before. Tilting the phone slightly away from Necker, I read, *Tonight, bro. Same place, same time. Don't respond 2 this message. No contact at all. And bring a gun, jic. Peace.*

As I reread the message, the free-floating anxiety that has haunted me since last night suddenly coalesces into a leaden feeling of dread, as close to a premonition of disaster as anything I've felt before.

"Everything copacetic?" Necker asks from what seems a great distance.

"Fine," I rasp, still staring at the message. "Just my daughter texting me from school."

I grab for my seat as the chopper bucks into the air .

"Easy, now," Necker says soothingly. "Sit back and enjoy it. Boy, what I'd give to still have my little girl at home. It goes by so damn fast, you miss most of it. It's only later that you realize it. That you were in the presence of a miracle. You know?"

I nod dully. *Bring a gun? Jic? Just in case? In case of what?* I'd give anything to take back the encouragement I gave Tim to pursue evidence against Mr. X and his employers. Yet somewhere beneath my panic surges the hope that Jessup, even after thirty years of drug abuse and aimlessness, has somehow proved able to do what he promised to do.

"Don't you miss a minute of it," Necker advises. "But, hell, what am I telling you? You had the sense to get out of the city and bring your kid to a place like this. A place where people are who they say they are, and you don't have to worry about all the sick crap that goes on out there in the world."

I flick my phone shut and force myself to nod again.

"A goddamn *sanctuary*," Necker pronounces. "That's what it is. Am I right?"

"Absolutely."

I guess I'm not above a little selling after all.

CHAPTER

8

The hours after receiving Tim's text message are an emotional seesaw for me; panic alternates with wild hope that Jessup has somehow obtained evidence of fraud and gotten safely away with it. This hope is a tacit admission that Tim's allegations are neither exaggerations nor paranoid fantasies. The maddening thing is that I'll have to wait until midnight to talk to him. I assume his choice of hour means that he intends to stay on board the *Magnolia Queen* until the end of his shift. Why doesn't he simply walk off the boat, I wonder, and race up to my office at City Hall?

My endless analysis of this question puts
me into such a state that Rose, my secretary, asks repeatedly whether I'm all right
and even convinces me to lie down for an
hour on a cot in the civil defense director's
office. Lying by the director's red phone, I
find it almost impossible not to call Tim,
but somehow I manage it. If he's willing to
risk his life, the least I can do is take his
precautions seriously.

The afternoon passes slowly, with
Rose doing her best to handle the calls
from the various committees and chari-
ties using the Balloon Festival to generate support or contributions, and Paul
Labry fielding complaints from merchants
and residents involving zoning and noise
violations. Like the other selectmen,
Labry has a full-time job, but he always
makes an extra effort to help me during
crunch times.

From the volume of calls and the traffic
outside City Hall, one thing is certain: Even
if Jessup is right and Natchez is festering
with corruption beneath its elegant facade,
the "Balloon Glow"—tonight's official opening ceremony of the Great Mississippi
River Balloon Festival—will go on.

I manage to get out of City Hall by six and collect Annie from my parents' house, where she usually spends her after-school time. I can tell she's excited as we drive toward the bluff, and she blushes as the police wave us through the big orange barricades at Fort Rosalie. Annie's at the age where anything that makes her stand out from her friends mortifies her, but I sense that she's enjoying the VIP treatment.

The sun has already set below the bluff, and the truncated roars of flaming gas jets sound from beyond the great mansion whose grounds provide the setting for the town's biggest festival. Annie gasps as we round the corner of Rosalie, and I feel my heart quicken. The term *balloon glow* perfectly describes this night ritual; from a distance the balloons glow like giant multicolored lanterns against the black backdrop of sky. But up close, among the inflated canopies swaying in the wind, the experience is much more intense. When the pilots do "burns" for the spectators, you can feel the heat from thirty feet away. Yellow and blue flares light the night like bonfires, awing children and adults alike. The tethered balloons tug against the ropes binding them to the earth, and kids who grab the edges of the baskets feel themselves lifted bodily from the ground. The ceremony is a perfect prologue for tomorrow's opening race, when the balloons will leap from the dewy morning grass and fill the skies over the city, pulling every attentive soul upward with them.

"I'm glad ya'll decided to go ahead with it," Annie says, grabbing my arm as we hurry to join the people streaming among the balloons. "This will help the refugee kids forget about the hurricane."

She tugs me toward the nearest balloon, and I use her momentary inattention to check my cell phone for further text messages. I don't know if I'm hoping Tim will cancel the meeting or move it forward. All I know for sure is that I want the truth about Golden Parachute. But there's no message.

I spend the first forty-five minutes with Annie, looking at everything she instructs me to and buttonholing pilots so she can ask them all kinds of questions about the flight parameters of hot-air balloons. I get buttonholed myself a few times, by citizens with questions or complaints about their pet interest, but Annie has become adept at extricating me from such conversations. TV crews roam the grounds of Rosalie with their cameras: one from Baton Rouge, ninety miles to the south; another from Jackson, a hundred miles to the north. I promise a producer from the Baton Rouge station that I'll give her five minutes at the gate of Rosalie, where they're interviewing pilots and Katrina refugees. I plan to take Annie with me, but two minutes after I make the promise, we walk right into Libby Jensen, and something goes tight in my chest.

"Libby! Libby!" Annie cries, running forward and giving her a hug. "Aren't the balloons *awesome*?"

"Yes, they are," Libby agrees, smiling cautiously at me above Annie's head.

Libby is a Natchez native who went to law school in Texas, married a partner at her Dallas firm, had a child by him, then divorced him after discovering that he'd kept a series of mistresses during the first decade of their marriage. She liked practicing law about as much as she liked being cheated on, so she brought her son back home and used her settlement to open a bookstore. Her charisma and sharp business sense have made the shop a success, and several author friends of mine stop to sign books there when making the literary pilgrimage from Oxford to New Orleans. After Caitlin left town, Libby and I found that our friendship quickly evolved into something that eased the loneliness we both felt, and that mutual comfort carried us through most of a year. But her son, Soren, has some serious anger issues—not to mention a drug problem—and Libby and I disagreed about how best to handle that. In the end, that disagreement drove us apart.

Tonight is the first time we've found ourselves together since ending our relationship, and I've worried it would be awkward. But Libby's soft brown eyes shine as she hugs Annie, and in them I see an acknowledgment that the sadness she feels is in part her own choice.

"Where's Soren?" Annie asks, reminding me that Tim said he'd seen Libby's son down on the *Magnolia Queen,* looking high as a kite.

Libby rolls her eyes to disguise the anxiety that's her constant companion. "Oh, running around with his friends, complaining about the bands they booked this year. Where are you guys headed?"

"Daddy has an *interview*," Annie says, obviously not enthused by the idea of standing by while I play talking head.

"Well, you can just come with me while he acts like a big shot for the cameras." Libby gives me a wink. "I just saw some of your friends diving into the Space Walk."

"Can I, Dad?"

I question Libby with a raised eyebrow, and she nods that she meant the invitation sincerely.

"Okay. I'll catch up in a half hour or so. We're not staying long, though. I have some work to do tonight, and I want to be rested for that balloon flight tomorrow."

"I'd like to see that," Libby says, chuckling like a wiseass.

"I'm making him take a barf bag," Annie tells her. "Seriously."

I wave them off and head back toward Rosalie, wondering where Tim Jessup is at this moment. Dealing blackjack on the boat docked below the cemetery? Or hiding out in some hotel room with stolen evidence, chain-smoking cigarettes while he waits for midnight to come? *There are no hotel rooms available,* I answer myself. Implicit in my worry about Tim is a fear of violence, and it strikes me that violence has always been a part of the ground beneath my feet. Fort Rosalie, the original French garrison in Natchez, was built in 1716. In 1729 the enraged Natchez Indians massacred every French soldier in the fort to punish them for ill treatment—for which French reinforcements slaughtered every native man, woman, and child they could find the following year. Rosalie went on to become General Grant's headquarters during one night of the Civil War, but by then it had presided over untold numbers of robberies, rapes, and murders in the Under-the-Hill district that lay in its shadow. *Is it possible,* I wonder, *that in some dark clearing across the river men are gathering to watch starving animals tear each other to pieces while half-naked girls serve them drinks?*

As I round the east corner of Rosalie's fence, a tungsten video light splits the dark, and several brown heads begin bobbing in its glare. If the gas jets of the balloons look like lanterns, the video light is a white-hot star illuminating a blond woman with a handheld mike standing before Rosalie's gate. She's interviewing some children who apparently fled here from the Lower Ninth Ward in New Orleans in the wake of Katrina. Two TV trucks are parked nearby, and more than a dozen journalists call questions to the kids from the shadows behind the light.

As I near the spotlight's halo, the producer I spoke to earlier waves me over and tells me what she wants: the basic Chamber of Commerce routine. When the kids finish, I take their place before the gate and squint against the glare while my pupils adapt.

On TV I tend to come across more like a district attorney than a mayor, and this has been a double-edged sword. Despite my diminished enthusiasm for the job, after two years in office I can give the city's PR line on autopilot. This year's Balloon Festival, however, has more meaning than usual. With the city's hotels and shelters filled to bursting with suffering families, many locals believed we should cancel the races out of respect for the hurricane refugees, and also to keep from straining the city's overtaxed resources. But the Balloon Festival is a twenty-year tradition, and I, along with several community leaders, championed the idea that the work required to bring off the races under extraordinary circumstances would prove a unifying force for the community. As I explain this to the brightly blank eyes of the TV reporter, she acts as though my words amaze her, but I know she's thinking about her next question, or her eye makeup, or where she can get a sugared funnel cake like the one a refugee kid is eating. I try to wrap up my pitch with some enthusiasm for the citizens who'll see the report from home.

"Critics argued that with the hotels filled, the balloon pilots would have nowhere to stay," I say, "but dozens of families have generously opened their homes so that the festival could go forward. We've had more volunteers for the support crews than we've ever had before. After feeling the outpouring of energy up on the bluff tonight, I believe events are going to bear out our optimism. The best thing you can do in the aftermath of tragedy is to focus on the present, because that way lies the future. Thank you."

I move to step out of the light, but suddenly a cool, calm female voice with no accent reaches out of the dark and stops me.

"Mr. Mayor, some refugees have claimed that they're not receiving the relief checks that the federal government promised them. Could you comment on this for our readers?"

Caitlin. She *is* here.

I shield my eyes from the glare. "What paper are you with?" I ask innocently.

"The *Natchez Examiner,*" Caitlin answers with the faintest trace of irony. "Caitlin Masters."

"Well, Ms. Masters, welcome back to Natchez. As for the relief checks, they're a federal matter and consequently not within my purview. Could someone kill that light, please?"

"What about the contention of two of your selectmen?" Caitlin continues, a fine barb of challenge in her voice. "They say there's been a great deal of fraudulent application for relief by refugees, with some people going through the check line three and four times with one Social Security number."

To my surprise, the spotlight goes dark, but I can't pick Caitlin's face from the red afterimage floating before my eyes. "As I said, those relief checks are being issued by the federal government; therefore, fraud in obtaining them falls under federal jurisdiction. I suggest you speak to the FBI or the Department of Homeland Security."

"I intend to."

"Good luck. Thank you, ladies and gentlemen. Enjoy the festival."

The knot of reporters breaks up quickly, leaving Caitlin and me with two techs packing equipment. My eyes having recovered, I see immediately that she looks as good as she ever did, unique among the women I meet in my daily life. Caitlin's bone-white skin, her waterfall of jet black hair, and her startling green eyes combine to radiate an almost disconcerting sense of self-possession. This woman is smart, you sense on meeting her, probably too smart for her own good, or anybody else's.

"You want to walk?" she asks.

"Sure."

She gives me an easy smile and starts away from Rosalie, walking across the head of Silver Street, the hill road that leads down to one of our casino boats, then toward the bluff proper. Caitlin leads me along the fence, on the asphalt path laid by the Corps of Engineers when they reinforced the bluff. Eighteen inches beyond the fence, the land drops like a cliff to the banks of the river below.

"You never were much of a walker," I comment, "unless you were headed somewhere specific."

She laughs softly. "Maybe I've changed."

I murmur in surprise.

"So . . . how's it going?" she asks, her words banal but her tone something else altogether.

When you practically live with someone for six years, you come to know their rhythms the way you know your own. Their way of talking, the way they breathe, sleep, and walk. Changes in those things communicate messages if you pay attention, but as I walk beside my old lover—old in the sense of long experience together—I find that our separation has dulled my perception of her secret language. That is if she means anything beyond her literal words. Maybe in this case a walk is just a walk.

"It's been hard," I say quietly. It's tough to admit you were wrong about something, and even harder to admit someone else was right. "Harder than I thought it would be."

"People don't like change," she says. "I see it every day, wherever I go."

"You said you've changed."

Her green eyes flicker. "I said maybe."

The small park we've entered was the main venue for festivals when I was a child, the white gazebo atop the bluff a gathering place for painters and musicians and even ham-radio operators, who came because the ground was the highest for miles around. At the gazebo steps, I let her ascend first, watching the clean line of her shoulders, the graceful curve of her back. God, I've missed her. She walks to the rail and looks out into the night sky over the river.

"It smells the same," she says.

"Good or bad?"

"Both."

Across the river, lines of headlights move east and west on the main highway crossing the hard-shell Baptist country of Louisiana. Twelve miles into that darkness, Jerry Lee Lewis and Jimmy Swaggart were raised under the flaming shadows of God and Satan, while around them sharecroppers toiled in the cotton and sang their pain to the uncaring fields.

"People think they're in the South when they're in the Carolinas," she says. "And they are, I guess. But this place is *still* the South, you know? It's unassimilated."

I murmur assent, but I still don't engage in conversation, preferring to study her from an oblique angle. This is the closest I have been to Caitlin in months. In a crowd of Mississippi women she stands out like a European tourist. In our moist, subtropical climate, the milk-fed, round-cheeked faces of the belles usually last until thirty-five, like a prolonged adolescence. This beauty seems a gift at first, but when it goes, the rearguard action begins, a protracted battle against age and gravity that leaves many with the look of wilted matrons masquerading as prom queens. Plastic surgery only makes the masks more startling in the end. Caitlin's face is all planes and angles, a face of architectural precision, almost masculine but not quite, thanks to feline eyes that shine like emeralds in the dark. Her every movement seems purposeful, and if she has nowhere to go, she stands like a soldier at rest. She never drifts. And remembering this, I realize that this walk is not just a walk.

"What brought you back here?" I ask softly.

She hugs herself against the wind shooting up the face of the bluff. "Katrina."

This answer is certainly sufficient, but it seems too easy. "You're covering the aftermath?"

"I'm taking it in. Trying to process it. I've heard a lot of disturbing things about what happened down there. The Danziger Bridge shooting, wide-open rules of engagement. The administration's response on the humanitarian side, or lack of one. Talk about too little, too late."

There's nothing original in this view. And I'm not much interested in a privileged publisher taking a luxury tour through the dark side of our national character. This reminds me of Caitlin as I first met her, a Northern dilettante who preached liberalism but who had no experience of the world outside a college classroom or a newspaper owned by one of her father's friends.

"Disturbing things happen everywhere," I say, "all the time. In Natchez, in Charlotte, wherever. You can find a window into hell a mile from wherever you are, if you really want to."

She inclines her head, almost as though in prayer.

I didn't mean to sound so cynical, but I have little patience with selective outrage. "You could just as easily be doing a story on how the white Baptist churches are sheltering black refugees, but that won't sell as many papers as a white-cops-shoot-black-civilians story, will it?"

"You always kept me honest, didn't you?"

"And you, me."

She turns from the rail, and her green eyes throw back reflections of the street-lamps behind me on Broadway. A thumping bass beat booms from the tavern across the street, then a blast of calliope music blares dissonant counterpoint from below the bluff.

"Wow," Caitlin exclaims. "The boats must really be crazy tonight."

With a start, I realize that for a few peaceful minutes I haven't thought of Tim Jessup. "I really should get back to Annie," I say, suddenly anxious about the depth of my need to be near Caitlin. "I've got a really long day tomorrow."

"No doubt. I heard you're on the morning flight," she says with a knowing smile. "Is that true?"

"No way out of it, I'm afraid. I'm schmoozing a CEO who could bring a new plant here."

"I heard. You think you may swing that, Mayor?"

"No comment."

She laughs dutifully, but her eyes are troubled. "I can't read you like I used to."

"I know how you feel." Despite my anxiety, I realize that the dread I felt earlier has been replaced by an exhilarating feeling of lightness under my sternum, as though I've ingested a few particles of cocaine along with Caitlin's words. An electric arc shoots through me as she takes my hand to lead me down the steps.

"Is Annie with your mother?" she asks. The path along the bluff is filling up with people preparing to watch the fireworks display across the river in Vidalia. "I haven't seen your parents in so long. I feel bad."

"They still talk about you. Dad especially." I don't want her to ask any more about Annie. I don't feel she has the right to, really.

"You know, Charlotte's not what I thought either," she says.

"No?"

"It's a lot smaller than I expected. Boston too. I'm starting to think that no matter where you go, it's basically a small town. The newspaper business is a small town. L.A.'s a small town. *Paris* is a small town."

"Maybe those places only look small from the window of a limo. When you have the phone number of everybody who matters."

She doesn't respond to this, but after a moment she lets my hand fall. As we near the festival gate, she stops and gazes at me without the guard of irony up. "That's the question, isn't it?"

"What?"

"Who matters?"

"Yep."

Her eyes hold mine steadily as the crowd swirls around us. "What's your answer?"

"That's easy. Annie."

"Touché. You're right, of course." She looks back toward the carnival lights beside Rosalie, brushes the black veil of hair away from her face. "This feels strange. So familiar, and yet . . . I don't know. You don't seem quite yourself." She tilts her head and tries to penetrate the time that hovers between us like an invisible shield. "Is it just me? Or is something really wrong?"

"What are you doing here, Caitlin?"

Her eyes narrow. "I told you. Working a story."

"A New Orleans story?"

She glances away for the briefest of moments. "There might be a Natchez angle."

Before I can ask about this, a male voice

cries her name twice in quick succession. "*There* you are!" says the newcomer, a handsome man of thirty-five who disengages from the chaos with some difficulty. He has a bohemian look—bohemian chic might be more accurate—and he clasps Caitlin's right hand in both of his. "I've been looking all over for you. I ended up down at the stage, talking to some gospel singers. They're fantastic!"

Caitlin casually extricates her hand and introduces me as the mayor of Natchez. The bohemian's name is Jan something.

"Jan's doing a documentary on the Danziger Bridge incident."

"Bridge *massacre*," Jan corrects, as though quoting the title of the film.

On the Danziger lift bridge in New Orleans, four white cops responding to an "officer down" call received sniper fire from a group of black men, returned fire, and killed two of them. The black group later contended that they had been unarmed. As with so much of what happened in the first days of Katrina's flood, no one has yet been able to ascertain what really transpired. "I'm sure they'll eat that up in Park

City," I say with a brittle Chamber of Commerce smile.

Jan draws back in momentary confusion, and Caitlin looks startled. I usually cover my emotions better than this, but tonight I just don't give a damn.

"You guys have fun. I need to find my daughter."

And with that I'm away from them. I couldn't have stood much more, and that knowledge frightens me. Yet as I walk through the festival gate, making for the flashing neon above the rides grouped on the bluff, it's not heartache that preoccupies me, but some of Caitlin's last words: *working a story. . . . There might be a Natchez angle.*

As improbable as it seems, I wonder if she's somehow picked up the rumors of dogfighting, prostitution, and illicit drugs surrounding the *Magnolia Queen.* A word from one of her local reporters would be enough to pique her interest, and every facet of that story would engage her. If Caitlin does have reporters working that story, she might well elide it from any conversation with me. At one time we told each other everything. But as our relationship wore on, we found that the professions of lawyer and journalist—even novelist and journalist—gave us separate agendas where privileged information was concerned, and that led to conflict.

Thirty yards ahead, I glimpse the familiar rounded line of Libby's shoulders, and a blade of guilt pierces me. Though we've officially ended our intimate relationship, it would hurt her to learn that a few moments with Caitlin affected me so deeply. As I near Libby, Annie and a friend cannonball through the exit of the Space Walk and roll squealing onto the ground beside her. Only now do I remember that I need someone to stay with Annie while I'm out on tonight's midnight rendezvous. There's little chance of getting a high school sitter this late on a balloon-race Friday; I'll have to ask my mother to spend the night at my house.

"You've been gone awhile," Libby says with a shadow of suspicion.

"They had a lot of questions about Katrina," I say in an offhand voice.

"We want to ride the Tilt-A-Whirl!" Annie and her friend scream in unison.

I'm hesitant to be alone with Libby, but she nods quickly and they set off for the Tilt-A-Whirl at a run.

"I saw an old flame of yours earlier," Libby says, her eyes boring into mine with uncomfortable intensity. "Was she there for the interview?"

"One of a dozen or so."

Libby sucks her lips between her teeth and looks pointedly off into the crowd.

"Have you seen Soren yet?" I ask.

"No. I guess Caitlin heard we broke up."

"She didn't mention it."

Libby tries to suppress a tight smile of judgment or envy. "She wouldn't."

"Did Annie see her?"

"I don't think so."

"Libby . . . we knew there were going to be some awkward times, but—"

"Don't," she says quickly. "You don't have to apologize. It's not even unexpected. I'm just surprised to see her this fast. But I guess I shouldn't be. Caitlin's been a quick study all her life."

I stifle a sigh and turn toward the Tilt-A-Whirl, where Annie and her friend spin through the air, trailing green and fuchsia light.

When I look back again, Libby is gone. Then I catch sight of her moving through the crowd toward the Tilt-A-Whirl. I follow, but time my arrival to coincide with Annie's disembarking from the ride.

"Should we look for Soren?" I ask half-heartedly.

"Sure," Annie says. "I haven't seen him yet."

Libby forces a smile and pats her in the small of the back. "Oh, he's with his older friends. You guys go have some fun. I need to get back and let the dogs out."

This patent lie brings another rush of guilt, but there's nothing to be done other than to let things take their course.

Libby bends, hugs Annie, then gives my wrist a quick squeeze and musters an almost genuine smile. With an awkward wave she turns and joins the flow of the crowd.

Annie stares solemnly after her diminishing figure, as though watching the departure of a family member she might never see again. After Libby disappears, Annie turns and looks up with wide eyes. "Daddy, I saw Caitlin here."

A strange numbness fills me, slowing my responses. "Really? Where did you see her?"

"She was talking to a man with a camera. She was far away, but I know it was her."

I'm not sure how to respond, but I don't like to lie to my daughter. "I saw her too, baby."

Annie's eyes widen still more. "Did you talk to her?"

"She interviewed me a few minutes ago, with some other reporters."

Annie nods slowly, taking this in. "I miss Libby, Dad."

"I do too."

When no explanation follows, she says, "Did ya'll break up?"

God, she's perceptive. "What makes you ask that?"

"I don't know. Did you?"

I take Annie's hand, then kneel and look into her eyes. "We did. I'm sorry I didn't talk to you about it first."

She looks back at the place where Libby vanished, but all that remains is a crowd of laughing revelers.

"She's really sad," Annie says, looking back at me with damp eyes. "I am too. I knew something was different."

"I'm sad too, baby."

"I think she's scared about Soren. Do you think so?"

"I think Soren has some problems. Lots of teenagers do. But that's for Soren and Libby to work out."

Annie wipes a tear from her eye.

"Come on," I say, leading her down the long row of brightly lit carnival booths, a sanitized version of the sleazy carnies that used to camp on the edge of town when I was a boy. The barkers shout their come-ons, but their hoarse voices scarcely penetrate the confusion surrounding my little girl. And yet, as sad as she is, I know that the grief Annie feels over the loss of Libby as a potential mother figure is tempered by hope that Caitlin has reappeared for a very different reason than covering a news story. If it weren't for my fear for Tim Jessup, I might be unable to think about anything else myself.

When the first rocket detonates over Louisiana, filling the sky over the river with sizzling arcs of blue and white light, it takes a couple of seconds for the report of the explosion to reach us. When it does, every muscle in my abdomen clenches, as though steeling against a bullet. This, I realize, is sympathetic fear. My daughter's hand is in mine, love is near, life is good. But somewhere not far away, Tim Jessup is risking all he has to right what he believes is an unendurable wrong. *Please be careful,* I intone in a private prayer. *Don't try to be a hero.* My father never spoke much about his service in Korea, but one thing he did share has been borne out by my own experience: *Heroism is sacrifice.*

Most of the heroes I've known are dead.

CHAPTER

9

It took all my willpower not to call or text Tim once my mother got Annie to bed. That was at ten thirty. The following hour passed like a car stuck in low gear, and I fought the urge to swallow a couple of shots of vodka to help me endure the wait. When it finally came time to leave, my mother saw me off without any question about my destination. She probably assumed I was seeing a woman, and I did not disabuse her of the notion. The only difficulty I had getting out was sneaking a pistol past her. In the end I opted to slip my short-barreled .357 Magnum into my briefcase and carry it right by her to the car.

Now I'm cruising down Washington Street with a half hour to kill before my meeting with Tim. I'm only a couple of miles from the cemetery—as the crow flies—so I have some time to ponder why he thinks I need a weapon when we meet.

Or so I think until my cell phone rings. The caller isn't Tim, as I expected, but Libby Jensen. She's so upset that at first I can't make out what she's saying. For a moment I labor under the mistaken impression that she's upset about our relationship, but then it registers—as it should have in the beginning—that she's calling about Soren.

"They arrested him!" she sobs. "They say he has to spend the night in jail. They think he was driving the car."

"Whoa, whoa, slow down. What happened?"

"There was a *wreck,*" Libby says, her voice still riding the rapids of hysteria. "I'm not sure what happened. Soren was in a car that hit another car. The police say he was driving, but Soren says he wasn't." Libby's voice drops to a frantic whisper. "Penn, he's so drunk I don't know whether to believe him or not. At least I hope he's drunk. They might have found some drugs. They won't tell me. I'm so scared. You know what Mackey said the last time he got in trouble."

On the occasion to which Libby is referring, Soren was busted with Lorcet Plus and Adderall. On my advice Libby hired Austin Mackey, a onetime classmate and the former district attorney, to represent him. At Mackey's suggestion—and against all my better judgment—I used my influence with the present district attorney, Shadrach Johnson, to try to ensure that Soren's case never went to trial. Mackey turned out to be right. After I promised my old political nemesis enough favors, the drug arrest was removed from Soren's record altogether. If Libby wasn't in love with me by that point in our relationship, the final transformation was completed that day. I can date my ultimate decision that things would not work out between us to that day as well.

"Have you left yet?" Libby asks, the pitch

of her voice rising. "Where are you? Are you on your way?"

"Have they booked him?" I ask, glancing at my watch. Twenty-two minutes till midnight. "Have they charged him?"

"I don't know! I can't even think. What will they do to him?"

What they probably should have done last time, I reply silently. Mackey's final advice to Libby and Soren was that the boy never get within a hundred yards of an illegal drug while he was in Adams County, because the next time he was caught, Shad Johnson would throw the book at him. That day has come, and I feel Libby grasping at me like a drowning woman. But even if I could somehow blunt Shad's vindictiveness, I can't go on enabling Soren to ruin his life, and his mother's with it.

"Libby, you've got to calm down," I say in a steady voice. "You can't help Soren if you can't hold it together."

"Tell me you're on your way," she says with single-minded urgency. "They're going to take him to the cell in a minute!"

Damn. I close my eyes briefly as my car drifts across Franklin Street and heads into the Victorian part of town. "Libby, I want you to listen to me. I will come down there and try to help, but you can't—"

She gives a plaintive moan that sounds like the preface to an emotional plea, but then without warning the sound shatters into a shrill scream of terror.

"What is it?" I yell. "What happened?"

There's a rattle that sounds like Libby's cell phone skating across a tile floor. I hear confused shouts, several slaps, then a shriek followed by a bellow of rage and anguish. The phone rattles again, and then I hear sobbing. Libby has the phone. After twenty seconds of gulping air, she begs me in a torrent of words to come to the station. I wait until she runs out of air, then ask again what happened.

"They're beating him up! They *maced* him."

I try to picture this scene, but I can't see the Natchez police beating a nineteen-year-old kid without some physical provocation. "Did Soren do something first?"

"He hit one of the cops," she whispers. "They were dragging him back to the cell, really being rough, and he lashed out at somebody. It was just a reflex! Penn, help me. Please! I'm so scared they're going to do something terrible to him, or put him back there with somebody horrible. If you ever cared for me at all, please, come now."

A minute ago, I would have said nothing could keep me from meeting Tim at the stroke of midnight, but guilt is a powerful motivator. With a silent *Goddamn it,* I wrench the wheel right on Madison Street and speed northward to the police station.

It's thirteen minutes after twelve when I finally squeal out of the police station parking lot, my hands shaking with anger and fear. Libby is shouting after me, but not as loudly as her son is screaming mindless profanity in the drunk tank. The police found half a pound of grass in the trunk of the car Soren was driving, but I'm almost positive he was high on crystal meth. Soren is essentially a gentle kid, not prone to violence, but when he drinks or ingests any drug but marijuana, his anger at his father surfaces, and he gets unpredictable.

A passenger in the car that he T-boned

had to be evacuated by helicopter from St. Catherine's Hospital to University Medical Center in Jackson. Worse than that—for Soren, at least—was the poke he took at the cop who was trying to drag him from the booking area to the cell-block. That blow placed Soren Jensen on the wrong side of a stark line for the Natchez Police Department. The cop required three stitches for the blow to his cheek, and Soren went to the cell with a faceful of pepper spray; but this is merely prologue for what will happen when Shad Johnson gets hold of the case.

All this minutiae drains quickly away as I race westward toward the cemetery. Even if a patrol car doesn't stop me for speeding, I'll be nearly half an hour late for my rendezvous with Tim.

Flying up Cemetery Road, past the pre-possessing silhouette of Weymouth Hall, I realize why Tim chose Jewish Hill for our meetings. The cemetery's front lower level, which houses the Turning Angel, is bathed in a yellow-orange glow from the sodium streetlights on Cemetery Road. But because of its height, the tabletop of Jewish Hill remains shrouded in darkness.

Is Tim still here? I see no car parked along the cemetery wall, but then I saw none last night either. I still don't know how Tim approached me from the back of the cemetery, since the only entrances I know about face Cemetery Road. But an old dopehead like Jessup probably knows a lot of things I don't about the deserted areas of the city.

An hour ago I planned to park more secretively than I did last night, but there's no time for that now. I stop at the foot of Jewish Hill, take my pistol from my brief-case, shove it into my waistband, and leave the car. A quick push takes me through the hedge behind the wall, and then I'm climbing the steep face of the hill, toward the wire bench and the flag-pole.

As feared, I find no one waiting at the top. No one was waiting for me last night either, but tonight feels different some-how. There's a different silence among the stones. The air doesn't seem quite still, as though it's recently been stirred, and the insects are silent. That could be the result of someone approaching, but my instinct says no. I feel a dreadful certainty that Tim has already been here and gone. Turning my back to the river and the moon, I walk deeper into the marble necropolis, scanning the darkness for signs of movement.

Out of the pulse beat of my blood comes a deep, subsurface rumble, almost too low for my ears to detect. It seems to vibrate up from the very ground. Thirty seconds later, I realize I'm hearing the engine of a push boat driving a great string of barges upriver, its massive cylinders propelling an unimaginable weight against the current. Turning, I see the red and green lights on the bow of the foremost barge, a third of a mile forward of the push boat's stern. The pitch of the engine changes as the boat moves northward, then out of its steady drone a higher hum rises. A blue halogen wash fills the near sky, dimming the bow light on the barge, and I realize a vehicle is passing below me on Cemetery Road. It's coming from out in the county, from the direction of the Devil's Punchbowl, heading toward town.

I'm too deep inside the cemetery to see the vehicle. On impulse, I run back along the top of Jewish Hill, but too late. All I see are vertical taillights winking through the leaves of the ancient oaks in the low-lying part of the cemetery where Sarah is buried. The taillights look as if they belong to a truck or an SUV, not Tim's Sentra.

My watch reads 12:37. The pistol feels awkward in my waistband but not completely unfamiliar. As a prosecutor of major felony cases in Houston, I was sometimes forced to carry a weapon for extended periods. Even after retiring from that position and taking up writing, certain circumstances have required me to carry a gun for protection, and on several occasions I've been forced to use it, sometimes with fatal results.

I feel an almost unbearable compulsion to call Tim's cell phone, but I resist it. Tim might simply be later than I am. Certainly, more things could have delayed him, or so I'd guess. After jogging in place for half a minute to relieve my anxiety, I sit on a low grave wall that commands a good view of Cemetery Road. With my mother watching Annie, I can afford to give Tim an hour of my time. I only wish I had a cup of coffee to keep me warm and alert. I'd like to lay my cell phone on the wall beside me, but I'm afraid its light will betray my position if anyone is watching.

My body has just begun to gear down when the Razr in my pocket vibrates, bringing me to my feet. I dig the phone from my pocket and cup it to my chest like a man trying to light a cigarette in a strong wind. I didn't expect to recognize the number, and I don't, but it has a Mississippi area code and a Natchez prefix.

"Hello?" I say in a stilted tone.

"Is this Penn Cage?" asks a voice both familiar and unfamiliar.

My heart rises into my throat, and for some reason I glance at my watch. Nine minutes have passed since I saw the taillights on Cemetery Road. "Who is this?"

"Don Logan, chief of police. Is this the mayor?"

A dozen reasons the chief might be calling me after midnight come to mind, none of them good. The most likely is something to do with Soren Jensen—the last thing I want to talk about right now.

"Yeah, Don, this is Penn. Don't tell me the kid's done something else."

There's a brief silence, then Logan speaks with the gravity I heard too often from homicide cops in Houston. "No, it's not that. I'm down by Silver Street on the bluff—well, underneath it really—forty feet underneath it. I'm in that drainage ditch that runs along the foot of the retaining wall."

"Uh-huh," I reply, my throat tightening.

"We've got a situation down here, Penn. Bad."

"Okay." I look desperately around the cemetery for a sight of Tim.

"We got what looks to me like a homicide. Or a suicide, I'm not sure which yet. Guy went over the fence and hit the cement"—Logan says "*see*-ment"—"and I was wondering if you might come down here and look at the scene."

This request is unusual, but I have a lot of experience with homicide cases. Maybe the chief wants my opinion on some evidence. "What do you think I can do for you, Don?"

"Couple of things, I figure. I don't really want to say on a cell phone. But you knew the victim."

As the chief finishes speaking, the last

threads of Tim's destiny are pulled into place. "Who is it?"

This time the silence lasts awhile. I suspect the chief wants to ask me if I already know. "Initials are T.J. That ring any bells for you?"

Logan probably mistakes the silent seconds I require to endure this blow as my trying to figure out whose initials those are. Only now do the squawks of police radios cut through the staticky silence of Logan waiting. "I'm too tired for guessing games, Don. Let me just get down there and see for myself."

"How long will it take you? We've got quite a crowd gathering here."

"Have you got Silver Street blocked off?"

"Hell, I can't block Silver Street. The casino would go crazy. I've got the runoff gutter where the victim landed blocked. But all the rubberneckers have to do is lean over the fence for front-row seats. Bowie's Tavern was busting at the seams with tourists when this happened."

"Get a goddamn tent over the body!"

"I'm working on it, but we've lent all our stuff out to the Katrina shelters."

"Well, grab something from the carnival up at Rosalie. Just take it."

"Good idea. I'd disperse this crowd, but some of them are witnesses. I have the people who were on the balcony at Bowie's—"

"Detain anybody who might have seen any part of what happened, whether it seems important to your men or not. And don't let anyone contaminate that crime scene."

"You sound awful sure it's a murder all of a sudden."

"Suicide's a crime too. Common law, anyway. Is Jewel Washington there?" Jewel is the county coroner.

"She just got here."

"Good." The potential for collateral damage suddenly strikes me. "Has anybody told— Have you informed the next of kin?"

"Not yet. I was kind of thinking you might want to do that." When I don't reply, Logan says, "You figured out those initials yet?"

"I've got a bad feeling that I might have. If I'm right, then I agree with you. I'd better do the telling."

"Works for me."

"Don't let your men mention his name on the radio."

"It may be too late for that. Plus, we got sheriff's deputies wandering around, and I've got no authority over them."

For the thousandth time I curse the territorial problems caused by overlapping jurisdictions. "It's your crime scene, Don. Don't let anybody tell you different. And get that tent up over his body. Everybody on that bluff has a cell phone, and somebody's going to recognize him."

"I doubt it. He's facedown right now, and he's busted up pretty bad."

Jesus. "I'll be there in three minutes, and I won't be driving the speed limit. Let your cruisers know."

"Hell, all my guys are down here. Floor it, brother."

CHAPTER

10

The scene atop the bluff where Silver Street joins Broadway looks like Bourbon Street during Mardi Gras. More than two hundred people are milling over the broad expanse of grass and pavement between the fence where Caitlin and I walked a few hours ago and the tavern across Broadway. The buzz of recent tragedy is in the air, and as I shoulder through the crowd, I see that about a third of the people are carrying styrofoam go-cups or beer bottles.

I spent most of the ride from the cemetery trying to decide whether to phone Julia

Jessup with news of her husband's death. No one should get that kind of blow by telephone, but it will be worse if someone else calls her first, someone reveling in the thrill of passing on the ultimate gossip. With so many people near the crime scene, there's a real danger this could happen before I can get to Julia's home, but still I wait. I need to see Tim's body before I talk to his wife. I know what kind of questions survivors ask, and the one at the top of the list is always "Did he suffer?"

Silver Street sweeps down at a precipitous arc from Broadway on the bluff to historic Natchez Under-the-Hill and the Mississippi River. I can't imagine how the horses handled it in the 1840s, when they had to haul freight up from the landing and the slave market. When I was a boy, we used to ride skateboards down this street, taking our lives in our hands every time we descended the half-mile-long hill. Then, as now, there was no stopping place on the narrow road. But tonight, about thirty yards down the hill, the police have placed an aluminum extension ladder against the guardrail to provide restricted access to the concrete drainage ditch that follows the base of the colossal retaining wall built to stabilize the bluffs. This wall runs more than a mile from end to end and is held in place by steel anchors that reach a hundred feet back into the bluff. At some places the wall towers a hundred feet from top to bottom, but here it averages about forty, as Chief Logan estimated on the phone.

Two uniformed cops stand at the head of the ladder. They're obviously expecting me, because one trots forward and escorts me to the ladder while the other marches up the hill to ward off an inquisitive drunk who has followed me. Mounting the ladder, I climb carefully down into a well of darkness, but at the bottom I see a hazy glow coming from beyond a bend in the wall. The air is thick with the scent of kudzu and backwater, but even with more light I could not see the river. A wall of treetops stands between me and the water, reminding me that I'm walking on an earthen ledge, a shallow step-down only halfway to the bottom of the bluff.

When I round the bend in the wall, two more uniforms confront me, but after shining a SureFire in my face, they wave me through. Thirty yards beyond them, a bubble of artificial light whites out the night. Men in uniforms and street clothes move deliberately through that light, and even from this distance I see the rumpled mess they are orbiting. I feel a rush of vertigo that could have been caused by the ladder climb, but I know better. A man I knew from the age of four is dead, and I am about to look into his empty eyes. I pause to gather myself, then walk forward.

As I get closer, Chief Logan notices me and breaks away from the others. Logan is thin and fit and looks more like an engineer than a cop. Tonight he's wearing street clothes and carrying a small flashlight, which he aims just in front of his feet. A wise man. I'd hate to know how many venomous snakes are within a hundred feet of me right now.

"That *was* quick." Logan gives my hand a quick but firm shake. "I didn't want to say any more on the phone, but you'd better steel yourself. It's bad."

"I've seen a lot of homicide victims," I say with more bravado than I feel. The truth is, I've seen a lot more crime-scene photos of victims than victims themselves, though I have seen my share of violent death. But when it's someone you know, it's different. Once the insulating barrier of professional detachment is breached, there's no telling what emotions will come pouring out.

"Did he have his wallet on him?" I ask, moving closer to the scene. "Is that how you knew who he was?"

"No sign of his wallet. A patrolmen recognized him. I doubted it at first, the face was so messed up by the fall, but my man seemed sure. Says he played blackjack at Jessup's table some."

I'm close enough now to see the dark blood pooled under Tim's upper body. Turning away from the carnage, I look Logan in the eyes. "What made you call me?"

The chief stares straight back at me. "Jessup had a cell phone in his back pocket. He landed on his face and hands, so the phone was still working. I took a look at the call log, and the last call he placed before he died was to your cell phone."

This revelation leaves me speechless. I haven't spoken to Tim in the past twenty-four hours. But if he called my cell phone, it should have rung. I was standing on one of the highest points in the city.

"I didn't get any call from Jessup tonight."

Logan chews on this for a few seconds. "He actually called you four times. Or tried to, anyway. Three times about twelve minutes before he died, and then once in the seconds right before he went over the fence. That's the best I can figure anyway. Did you have your cell phone on?"

"Yes."

Logan doesn't ask to see my phone. He doesn't have to. He can easily check my records, and I'm sure he will. To save him the trouble, I call up the log on my Razr. It shows no incoming calls from Jessup. I move to Logan's side so he can see this information.

"Were you in a dead spot or something?" he asks.

"No."

"Huh. I can't figure it, then. When was the last time you talked to him before today?"

"I don't remember," I say in an offhand voice. "You know how it is. I've seen him to say hello in the street, but no real conversation."

Logan nods, but his eyes are watchful.

"I'd like to look at his body now, Chief. Do you mind?" I ask permission because I must. Logan's allowing this would be purely a courtesy. To help him decide, I add, "I want to get to his house and tell his wife as quickly as possible."

"Don't you want to know how it happened?" Logan asks. "How he went over, I mean?"

I can't believe I haven't asked this yet, but then the reason comes to me: I'm a lot more concerned about what Tim might have been carrying when he went over the fence than the circumstances that caused him to do so. "I'd prefer to see his body first. Could you clear those people out of there, Chief?"

"Everybody but the coroner. She doesn't answer to me."

The truth is, the coroner is one of the few people whose presence I can tolerate in this situation. Jewel Washington is a nurse who ran for office after being laid off from one of the two hospitals in the city. An MD isn't a requirement to be a coroner in Mississippi, but Jewel is a knowledgeable and conscientious nurse, and she does a better job with the dead than was sometimes done in the past.

As I step into the pool of light, I see that Chief Logan didn't exaggerate. Tim's body sustained massive trauma as a result of the fall. The impact broke both his forearms and split his skull above the eyebrows. The one eye I can see is wide and cloudy, the eye of a dead fish on a pier. In my mind I hear my father's voice telling me about René Le Fort, the French army physician who created the system for classifying facial fractures by throwing cadavers off the roof of an army hospital. Though Tim is almost unrecognizable, it's not his shattered face that holds my attention. It's his chest and arms. His shirt is shredded and covered with blood, and his broken forearms look almost as though they were mauled by a wild animal. His chest and neck also show puncture wounds and tears. Unless he fell forty feet into a pile of nails and broken glass, I don't see how he could have got those injuries.

"I turned him over," Jewel Washington says from the darkness behind me. "Soon as I did, I wished I hadn't. You ever seen anything like that?"

The coroner's voice seems to come from far away, as though we are hikers separated in a twisted canyon. *I've seen worse than this,* I reply silently, *but not on someone I knew well.* "You mean his arms?"

"Yeah, his arms. He didn't get those wounds in no fall."

I bend over Tim, squinting down at the torn flesh. "Could animals have gotten to him before anyone else did?"

"I guess it's possible. Histamine tests will tell us that. But you ask me, that stuff happened antemortem."

"Christ," I whisper.

"Christ, indeed. This world done gone crazy, I believe."

Jewel speaks with the weary resignation of a middle-aged black woman who has sacrificed a lot to send her two sons to junior college. Because she has worked closely with my father in the past, I know I can rely on her to give me all the help in her power.

I stand and give her a hug from the side. "Did the fall kill him?"

"Can't say. Not yet, anyway. He's got some kind of wounds on his leg that smell like cooked pork to me. Got to be burns, but

I don't know how he'd get those." Jewel's bloodshot eyes hold mine. "Do you?"

I shake my head, trying to repress images of Tim being tortured for information, yet wondering what his torturers did to tear him up so badly.

"We won't know about this one until they do the autopsy up in Jackson," Jewel observes.

"Well, let's make sure they do it in a hurry." I turn back to the coroner and give her a small glimpse of my outrage. "Don't miss a lick on this one, Jewel. Push for every test you can get. Toxicology, everything."

"I plan to." She grunts noncommittally. "Let's just hope the DA is on board for it."

I expel a lungful of air at the thought of Shad Johnson being in charge of Tim's case. "I'm going to inform the victim's wife."

"Lord," Jewel says softly. "That's one visit I'm glad I don't have to make."

"If anybody asks you tonight, he died instantly. Okay?"

She nods slowly. "I can live with that until tomorrow. I hope it's the truth too."

I lean closer and look into her dark eyes, holding her gaze. "Has anybody searched the body?"

"Not since I been here. But you know they did before I got here." Shouts reverberate along the wall from atop the bluff, and I see drunken spectators peering down at Tim and us.

"We ought to charge admission," Jewel says bitterly. Seeing my quivering chin, she squeezes my arm above the elbow and says, "Tent's on the way."

Her small gesture of compassion cracks the armor plating I buckled over my emotions back at the foot of the ladder. Deep within me, a caustic soup of guilt and rage boils upward, searching for an outlet. Jewel squeezes my arm harder.

"Easy now."

"We grew up together," I whisper by way of explanation.

Jewel nods in sympathy. "I imagine this boy had a tough time growing up. I used to work with his daddy some. Never liked Dr. Jessup. Cold as an old-time scalpel."

Jewel has cut right to the heart of Tim's family. The corpse lying on the ground was alive for forty-five years, but the soul that occupied it until tonight never managed to escape boyhood.

"Stay in touch?" I ask.

Jewel gives me a sad smile of encouragement. "You know I will."

I turn and walk back to the dim perimeter of the light, where Chief Logan stands talking to a man in the shadows. As I near the pair, I realize that the newcomer is Shadrach Johnson, Natchez's district attorney, the man I defeated for mayor two years ago. The scars from our campaigns still sting, but our troubled history predates that election by five years.

"Well, look who we've got here," Shad says with mocking reverence. "You're out mighty late considering all the mayoral duties you've got this weekend."

Shad was born in Natchez but moved to Chicago while he was still a boy. He attended college there on scholarship and worked as a big-firm lawyer until he was forty, when he returned to Natchez to run for mayor. His Southern accent waxes and wanes with his moods and motives. As usual, he's dressed to the nines, wearing an expensive suit and tie on a weekend when most people are dressed like fans at a Jimmy Buffett concert.

"Why don't we skip the bullshit tonight?" I ask. "Tim Jessup was a friend."

"My condolences," Shad says without empathy. "Seems like an odd friendship to me, the mayor of the city and a no-count blackjack dealer."

I take a deep breath and focus on Logan. "Could I speak to you alone, Chief?"

Logan starts to step away, but Shad catches hold of his arm. "Not so fast, Chief. You need to finish my briefing here, and that might take a while."

"I just need a minute," I add with as much civility as I can muster.

"Well, Mr. Mayor," Shad says with relish, "you're just going to have to wait. I know you're not accustomed to waiting, but I *am* the chief law enforcement officer of Adams County."

I pointedly ignore Shad, keeping my eyes on Logan. "Did you find anything else on Jessup besides his cell phone?"

The chief shakes his head.

"If somebody stole his wallet, it seems like they'd take his phone too."

"Seems like," Logan agrees.

"Could I see his phone?"

"You know that's a police matter," Shad interjects. "You expecting them to find something special?"

The anger I felt beside Tim's body is reaching critical mass, and the DA is too convenient a target. I need to get away from him as fast as possible.

"No, but I'm going to inform the widow in a few minutes. I'd like to be able to answer her questions and pass along any personal effects. Knowing the circumstances of his death would help."

Logan's alert gaze is on me again, but he says nothing further. He glances at Shad, who gives a slight nod.

"There were twentysome-odd people up on the balcony at Bowie's," the chief says. "Plus a couple over there in the gazebo, making out. There were probably some other people on the bluff too, but we haven't got them separated from the mob yet. Thank God, the big doors of the bar were closed to enforce their cover charge. "

"What did the wits see?"

"Different things, of course. Or different versions of the same thing. After listening to everybody, the best I can figure is this. A tan or light-colored SUV, probably a Lincoln Navigator, came down Broadway from the direction of the Callon building. Nobody was paying much attention at that point. Then about a hundred feet past the gazebo, the SUV skidded to a stop. It squealed loud enough to make people turn. The guy on the gazebo saw Jessup running from Broadway toward the fence. He must have jumped out of the SUV. Then a second guy jumped out of the backseat and started to chase him. The second guy stopped in the grass. Jessup was screaming for help by then. The guy on the bandstand called 911, but we couldn't get here fast enough to do anything."

Logan pauses as if expecting me to question his department's response time, but I motion for him to continue.

"By this time people on the balcony were looking in that direction, but there are a few trees up there, so they couldn't see a lot. It looked like the guy chasing Jessup disappeared under the trees. He must have been getting closer because Jessup climbed over the fence and started running along the ledge toward Silver Street. Nobody's sure whether the second guy ran up to the fence or not. Half the witnesses figured Jessup and the other guy were just drunks horsing around."

"But the guy in the gazebo called 911."

"His wife made him do it," Logan explains. "Anyhow, for whatever reason, Jessup stopped on the ledge. He was twisting around like he was fighting an invisible man—that's what the guy in the gazebo said—and then he went over the edge. That's it. For now anyway."

I look up to the ledge forty feet above and try to imagine Tim desperate enough to make that leap voluntarily. If the man chasing him had been torturing him, Tim might have leapt from the ledge in the hope that he could clear the drainage ditch and hit the limbs of the trees beyond it. But the odds of death would still be high. The logical thing would have been to run back toward the tavern, or even down the ledge along Silver Street. Cars travel that hill at all hours, and he might have flagged someone down.

"Did anybody see the plates on the vehicle?"

Logan shakes his head. "The SUV got out of here in a hurry. Nobody's even sure it had Mississippi plates."

"Damn. What do you make of all that?" I ask, more to observe Logan's reaction than to learn anything valuable.

"Could be a lot of things. Jessup was a known drug abuser."

"He's been clean for a year."

Shad Johnson, quiet up to now, snorts in derision. "Jessup rear-ended a friend of mine a couple months back, and my friend swears he was fucked-up at the time."

Tim was high two months ago? "Did the police do a blood test?"

Shad shakes his head. "Wasn't that much damage. And Jessup wasn't worth suing. He didn't have anything but debts."

Logan winces. He doesn't like being caught between us.

"This could have resulted from any kind of dispute," the DA speculates. "Argument over a woman. Jessup's dealer taking the price of dope out of his ass. I expect we'll know by Monday or Tuesday."

"Have you done a grid search around the body?" I ask Logan.

"Best we could. We didn't find anything

within throwing distance, but there's a lot of damn kudzu and trees down there. If he threw something full force from the top of the bluff, it'll take daylight to find it." Logan stops speaking, but his engineer's eyes ask me what I think Tim might have been carrying. "If he threw something with some weight, he might have thrown it all the way to the river."

"Dope doesn't weigh that much," Shad says. "Not throwing size, anyway. You'll find his stash in the morning, if the rats and coons don't eat it first."

"What are *you* doing at this crime scene?" I ask pointedly. "You usually stay away from the dirty work."

Shad's lips broaden into a smile; he enjoys a fight. "I was at a party a few blocks away. I'm only answering you as a courtesy, of course. You're not the DA, Penn Cage. No, sir. This investigation is in my hands, and I'll decide what gets done and when."

"You're in charge, all right. Just remember that with power comes responsibility. You'll be held to the highest standard, make no mistake about that." I turn to

Logan. "Let's put a rush on that autopsy, Chief."

"There he goes again," says Shad, "giving orders like he's the district attorney."

Instead of taking the bait, I turn and stride back toward the ladder. As soon as Shad leaves my field of vision, he leaves my mind. My anger remains unquenched, perhaps even unplumbed, but its urgency recedes as I climb back up to Silver Street and make my way through the chattering crowd toward my car. Several acquaintances call out, but I brusquely wave them off. A cold heaviness is seeping outward from my heart. I'd rather clean and embalm Tim's mutilated body than tell Julia Stanton that the father of her baby is dead. But some duties cannot be shirked. If Julia asks why Tim died, I wonder if I'll have the courage to tell her the truth? That her husband almost certainly perished because I was late to our meeting.

CHAPTER

11

Tim Jessup's wife and son live in Montebello subdivision, a cluster of small clap-
board homes built in the 1940s to house
the employees of the International Paper
Company. For most of their history, these
structures sheltered generations of working white families, but in the past ten
years, quite a few have been taken over
by African-American families. Despite the
age of the houses and the inexpensive
materials with which they were built, most
are well kept up, with fresh paint and well-
tended lawns. What sticks in your mind
when you drive through during the day is

the abundance of kids, dogs, bicycles, flowers, lawn ornaments, and glitter-painted bass boats parked on the grass beside the driveways. Tim and Julia bought one of the more run-down houses when she got pregnant, then spent eight months fixing it up for the baby. Montebello is a long way down from the tony subdivision where Jessup grew up, but after he turned thirty, Tim stopped caring about things like that. His father never did. After my return to Natchez, I learned it was better not to mention Tim when I ran into Dr. Jessup. Whenever I did, all I saw in the old surgeon's eyes was shame and bitterness.

I turn off Highway 61 at the Parkway Baptist Church and take the frontage road down into Montebello. A warren of curving, tree-shaded streets divides the neighborhood into asymmetrical sections, and it's easy to get lost down here if you haven't visited in a while. After one wrong turn, I find Maplewood and swing around a broad curve through the parked cars and pickups that line both sides of the street.

In less than a minute I will shatter the

life of Julia Stanton Jessup, and I'm suddenly aware that my outrage over Tim's
death is an order of magnitude smaller
than what she will experience after the initial shock wears off. The explosion might
even be immediate. Julia is no shrinking
violet. She began life in a coddled existence, but fate soon had its way with her
family, and she did not pull through without becoming tough. I still remember kissing her once at a senior party, when she
was in the ninth grade. We've never spoken of it since, but the image of her as
she was then remains with me, a beautiful girl just coming into womanhood, and
unlike Tim she retained the glow of her
youth through the hard years. I suspect
that tonight's shock may take that from
her at last.

The instant Julia's house comes into
sight, I know something's wrong. The front
door stands wide-open, but there's no car
in the driveway and no one in sight. The
doorway appears as a rectangle of faint
yellow light coming from deep within the
house, though *deep* is not exactly accurate in terms of a house that small. I reach

under my seat for the pistol Tim told me to bring to the cemetery meeting. The cold metal is my only comfort as I leave the relative safety of my car and walk through the shallow yard toward the house. I should call Logan for police backup, but Tim's words from last night keep sounding in my head: *You can't trust anybody. Not even the police.*

The neighborhood is relatively quiet. I hear the thrum of a few air-conditioning units, still laboring hard in mid-October. A couple of TV soundtracks drift through the air, coming from the houses that have opened their windows to the damp, cooling night. I press my back to the wall outside Jessup's door, then crash through in a crouch, the way a Houston police detective taught me. The last thing I thought I'd be doing tonight was clearing a house, but at this juncture, there's no point in analyzing my instincts.

As I move from room to room, it becomes obvious that the house has been thoroughly searched. Every drawer and cabinet has been opened, the books pulled from the shelves and rifled, and the mattresses slit to pieces. Even the baby's mattress was yanked from the crib and slit open.

The house has only six rooms, all clustered around a central bathroom. I call out Julia's name, half-hoping she might be hiding somewhere. But I'll be happier if she's not. I hope she's miles away from this place, safely hidden or running for her life. For the state of this house tells me one thing: Whatever evidence of crime Tim was looking for today, he found it. And that discovery cost him his life. The only questions remaining are what did he find, and where is it now?

I lean out the back door, but all I see in the backyard is a plastic playhouse bought from Wal-Mart, looking forlorn and abandoned. I'm raising my cell phone to call Chief Logan when it buzzes in my hand. I jump as though shocked by a wall socket, and this makes me realize how tense I was while I searched the house. The number has a Natchez prefix, a cellular one.

"Penn Cage," I answer, wondering who might be calling me after 1:00 a.m.

The first sound I hear is something

"What? Why thirty minutes?"

"Because I'm going to call you back and give you some instructions. I have to make some arrangements first. Don't forget to switch off your phone. The people who—who hurt Tim—can use that phone to track you down."

"Oh, God. Oh . . . I knew it. I told him not to do anything."

"Julia! Don't say anything else. Don't trust anyone Tim didn't mention specifically. And don't come home. Don't even think about it. I'm there now, and the place has been torn to pieces." I glance at my watch as Julia whimpers incomprehensibly. "I'll call you back at one thirty-five. I'm hanging up now."

It's hard to do, but I press END and run for my car. My hand is on the doorknob when two police cars roar around the bend of Maplewood and screech to a stop behind me. A blue-white spotlight hits my face and a harsh voice speaks over the car's PA system.

"Stop right there! Put your hands up and step away from the vehicle!"

I feel no fear at this order, only anger and impatience. And curiosity. I haven't had time to call the chief and tell him that Jessup's house was broken into. It might make sense that Logan would send some-one to make sure I'd informed the widow— or even to search Jessup's house—but to see a brace of squad cars wheeling around Maplewood as though responding to a home invasion is more than a little surprising. Yet all I can think about as two cops approach is how I'm going to get Julia to safety.

"Who are you and what are you doing here?" barks the first cop.

"I'm Mayor Penn Cage. I came here to inform Julia Jessup that her husband was killed tonight. Chief Logan can confirm that, and you'd better call him right now. I don't have all night to stand out here talk-ing."

The cop on my left looks closer at me, then taps his partner on the upper arm. "It's okay. He's the mayor."

"You sure?" asks the second guy.

"What the fuck, am I *sure*? My dad went to school with the guy, dude."

On another night I would ask the young cop who his father is, but not this time. "Guys, I've got to go. Somebody took that house apart. You need to lock it down. Don't let anybody inside."

"The wife's not here?" asks the young cop.

I answer him while climbing in to my car. "Still trying to find her. I'll update the chief later."

I jerk the Saab into gear and head back to Highway 61. I can be at my house on Washington Street in less than five minutes, and I need a plan of action by the time I get there. Julia could come apart in less time than that, and a wrong move on her part could be fatal. But my options are almost nonexistent. All the resources I would normally use in this kind of situation have been placed out of bounds by Tim's warnings. Last night I wasn't sure his caution was warranted, but after seeing the condition of his body and the state of his house, I have no intention of risking the lives of his wife and son on assumptions.

I've called on other, private resources in extraordinary situations, but none are ready to hand tonight. The man I trust most to help me in a crisis is in Afghanistan, working for a security contractor based in Houston. His company may have some operators Stateside who could help protect Julia, but none would be any closer than Houston—seven hours away by car.

Most people who felt they couldn't trust local law enforcement would probably call the FBI, but that option presents problems for me. Seven years ago I forced the resignation of the Bureau's director, when I proved that he'd been involved in the cover-up of a civil rights murder in Natchez in 1968. That won me few admirers in the Bureau (open ones, anyway) and made me a liability to the field agents I'd befriended during my successful career as an assistant district attorney in Houston.

"Damn it!" I shout, pounding the wheel in frustration. *"What the fuck is going on?"*

It's like screaming inside a bell jar, but at least my outburst gives vent to the rage and frustration that have been building since I saw Tim's body. Closing my right hand into a fist, I pound the passenger seat until my wrist aches. When the national park at Melrose Plantation flashes by, I realize I'm driving eighty—forty miles an hour over the speed limit.

Settle down, I tell myself, remembering my father, who becomes calmer the more dire the medical emergency. When everything is at risk, good judgment, not haste, makes the difference between life and death. *Panic is the enemy. . . .*

My decision to run every stop sign on Washington Street is perfectly rational. They are four-way stops, and unless someone else is doing the same thing I am at exactly the same place and time, I have enough visual clearance to safely jump the intersections.

I park on the street, exit my car, and move toward the house in continuous motion, my mind in flux. Taking the porch steps at a near run, I notice that the cast-iron lamp hanging above me is out. Mom must have inadvertently switched it off. That isn't like her, but I don't have time to worry about personal inconsistencies tonight. I'm slipping my key into the lock when a man's voice speaks from the shadows to my right.

"That'll do, Mr. Cage. Stand easy where you are. No need to disturb the women."

I fight the urge to whirl toward the sound. I've tried too many cases where people were shot because they saw the face of someone who didn't want to be remembered. Yet from the voice alone, I'm almost certain that the man in the shadows is Seamus Quinn, the security chief on the *Magnolia Queen.* I've never heard an Irish accent like Quinn's outside the movies, and even then only in Irish-made films.

"What do you want me to do?" I ask.

"I want you to listen. It's all right to turn. I *want* you to see."

By now my eyes have adapted to the darkness, so when I turn, I see enough to register how wrong I was: The face staring at me out of the shadows belongs not to Seamus Quinn, but to his boss, Jonathan Sands.

Wait, I think, *the voice is all wrong.* Gone is the refined English accent of the *Magnolia Queen*'s general manager, replaced by a coarse, working-class Irish accent identical to that possessed by Quinn. Then it hits me: I'm looking at Sands, but it was Quinn who spoke. *The Irishman must be standing behind his boss, down in the flower bed.* I glance past Sands, but all I register is something low and pale in the blackness behind him, like a crouching animal.

Sands moves his hand slightly, which pulls my eyes back to him, and then I see his gun, a small but efficient-looking automatic held at waist level.

"Easy now, darlin'," he says. "I only brought this wee pipe so I don't have to lay hands on you."

With a start I realize it was Sands who spoke the first time. He's simply speaking with Seamus Quinn's voice rather than the cultured English accent he doles out for public consumption. I only know about British accents because my sister, Jenny, lives in England. She went to Britain as a visiting professor of literature at Trinity College, dated a Dubliner for several years, then married an Englishman and settled in Bath. For this reason, what would sound like a British accent to most other Southerners sounds like Belfast to me, and it tells me I know a lot less about Jonathan Sands than I thought I did. Tonight he sounds like a cross between Bono and the lead singer of the Pogues.

"You're not English," I murmur, trying to get my mind around it. "You're *Irish*."

"As Paddy's goat, Your Honor," he says, chuckling softly. "But let's keep that between us, eh?"

While Sands's eyes flicker with private mirth, the evil that Tim hinted at fills my soul like a squid's ink. I know without doubt that everything my dead friend suspected must be true.

"What do you want?"

"Your undivided attention. Do I have that, Mr. Cage?"

"Obviously."

"Before we talk, I'll ask you to hand over that weapon you've got in your pocket. Two fingers only."

Sands materialized so suddenly on my porch that I actually forgot I was carrying a gun. But his ability to spot my concealed pistol in the dark tells me that trying to use it against him would be the last thing I'd do on earth. As directed, I carefully draw the Smith & Wesson and pass it to him, butt first.

With the sure movements of a man accustomed to handling firearms, he slips the gun into his waistband at the small of his back, then gives me a courteous nod. "Fair play to you, Mr. Mayor. I'm going to pay you the compliment of speaking frankly, because this town is full of *cute hoors,* but you're not one of them. A friend of yours died tonight, and died hard. He died because he stepped over the line into other men's business. Timmy Jessup thought he was the little Dutch boy with his finger in the dike. When the flood rose and rolled over him, he sucked in his breath and kept his finger where it was. Pity, really, because he was all alone. Everyone else in this *culchie* town is swimming in the flood—sunbathing beside it, *windsurfing* on it. Because it's a flood of money, Mr. Mayor, not water. And if you try to put your finger in the hole Jessup left . . . Well. What matters now is that he's dead, and nothing can bring him back."

As the initial shock of being surprised on my own doorstep begins to fade, my outrage boils over. "You sorry son of a bitch. Are you telling me you killed—"

Sands silences me with an upraised hand. "Quiet now, mate. You're in more danger than you know."

CHAPTER

12

My mouth has gone dry. It's not the screamers who scare me; it's the men who don't let emotion get in the way of what they want. They're the ones who'll kill without hesitation. "I'm listening."

"Grand. Because this is all the talking I'm going to do. After this, I act, immediately and irrevocably. Understood?"

I nod.

Sands puts his hands behind his back and looks down like an officer contemplating a job in progress. A born soldier was my immediate impression of the man when I met him, for his bearing seems altogether military, though somewhat more fluid than that of the regular officers I've known. Sands has little skin fat; his face looks like a skull overlaid with the optimum amount of muscle, and little else. He's losing his hair in front, but his baldness gives no impression of weakness; rather, the heavy brow and blue-gray machine gunner's eyes give one the feeling that hair was simply an inconvenience better dispensed with. He stands right at six feet, but his trim waist and thickly muscled shoulders give one a much more aggressive perception of his height.

"I have a problem, Mr. Cage," he says. "I'm here because I want you to solve it for me."

"What's your problem?"

"Your friend Jessup stole something from his place of employment."

I blink slowly, a man trying to find an appropriate response.

"You don't look surprised enough to suit me, Mr. Mayor. Not nearly."

"Tim wasn't exactly a Boy Scout," I say as calmly as I can. "What did he steal? Money? Drugs?"

The Irishman gives me a tight smile. "You know better than that."

"What I know about Tim Jessup is that he was a fuckup. And I don't know what any of this has to do with me."

Sands takes a deep breath and exhales slowly. "I have a decision to make tonight, Mr. Mayor. A decision about you. And you're not helping yourself. Your family either."

At the word *family,* something squirms in my belly.

"The question," Sands enunciates softly, "is can I trust you? For example, you may already know what Jessup stole from my boat. Do you know that, Mr. Cage? Don't lie. If you lie, I'll know it."

By God, I just about believe you. "I have no idea."

The blue eyes don't waver; this man has spent a lifetime calculating odds. "Don't you now?"

I shake my head deliberately.

After what seems a full minute, Sands says, "Would you bet your daughter's life on that answer?"

An image of Seamus Quinn holding

Annie prisoner upstairs fills my mind, and terror compresses my heart. I grab for the door handle, but before I can turn it, something white explodes out of the flower bed, and iron jaws clamp around my wrist, pinning it motionless in the air. I try to jerk away, but the jaws tighten, numbing my fingers as surely as a nerve block.

A white dog more than half my size stands like an apparition between Sands and me, its eyes cold and blue above the wolfish mouth locked around my arm. Hot saliva runs down my tingling fingers, yet I can't quite accept the evidence of my eyes. No sound preceded this attack, not a growl or a bark or a word of command— only a quick swish of foliage from behind Sands.

"Easy now," he says either to me or to the dog, maybe to both of us. "Your daughter's just fine, Mr. Cage. For the moment, at least. She's sleeping soundly, with your sainted mother beside her in the scratcher. But if you step through that door before we come to an accommodation, that could change very quickly."

I try to back away from the door, but

the dog's forelegs are braced like white-painted fence posts, its jaw locked like a steel wrench. After a few moments, Sands makes a clicking sound with his tongue. The dog releases my arm, then walks to his master's side and sits at attention like an obedient soldier. I stare at the animal as I rub the circulation back into my hand. I've never seen its like before, not even a similar breed; an oversize pit bull might be its closest cousin, but this dog has a wrinkled face that throws me. White from nose to tail, he has cropped ears and a thickly muscled chest to match his master's. The animal has an unearthly silence about him, as though spectral and not a thing of blood and flesh, but I can still feel the imprints of his teeth in my muscles; I'll have blood bruises in the morning.

"You're not a stupid man," Sands says, rubbing the dog's head affectionately. "Don't start playing at it now. I make it my business to know who I'm dealing with. I know you put a lot of hard men in prison back in Texas. Rapists. Robbers. Murderers. Aryan fanatics. Got some of them executed too. I also know you've taken on men from your own side of the table. That FBI bastard, for example. I only mention this because you need to understand something. Despite your grand experience, you've never come across a man like me." A smug smile. "I'm sure you've heard that one before, eh? The innocent man on death row. The whore with a heart of gold. But every now and then you come across a bloke who knows what he's on about." Sands smiles to himself. "That would be me. And this is how you know."

He utters a low whistle, and suddenly the dog is upon me again, rearing on his hind legs and pinning me to my front door with his forepaws. His mass and strength are astounding, and the hot breath in my face triggers a primitive, almost subhuman fear. The dog still hasn't made a sound, but it's all I can do not to piss down my leg.

"Starting this minute," Sands says, looking at this watch, "you have twenty-four hours to find the property your friend stole and return it to me. Use any resource at your disposal, but don't mention me or my company to anyone. If you do, I'll know it, and a penalty will be exacted. If you talk to the police or the sheriff's department, I'll know. If you contact the FBI, I'll find out faster than you'd believe possible. If you talk to the state gaming commission, you're fucked. You call the governor, a senator, or your old friend the district attorney of Houston, I'll know that too. And if I find out you've done any of these things . . . I'll kill the little girl sleeping upstairs."

Sands moves up beside his dog and drags the cold barrel of his gun along my stubbled jaw. "And I won't use a gun. I'll use this."

A needle point of steel pierces the skin just below my navel, sending a shock of fear through my intestines.

"I'm very good with a knife," Sands says softly. "And I'd take my time about it. Understand? Now"—he presses the gun into a hollow beside my trachea, and the knifepoint digs a little deeper—"*after* your daughter's dead, you might bring me into a court and try to punish me. But you've dealt with enough victims' families to know how useless that is. If you executed me five seconds after I killed her, it wouldn't bring her back, would it?"

Out of the numbness that has enveloped me like a fog, I shake my head.

As Sands presses his right ear almost against my lips, the knifepoint vanishes; then I feel it burrowing into the skin between two ribs on my left side. "I didn't hear you, Your Honor."

"I understand."

"Course you do," Sands says almost musically. "But that quick mind of yours is already working, trying to squirm out of the trap. Hide the girl, yeah? You'd have to hide your mum and dad too. And of course your sister in Bath, and her husband, and the two brats. I have a lot of mates in England who owe me that kind of favor. Then there's yer one who owns the local bookstore, and her langer of a son. And let's not forget the lady newspaper publisher, fresh back from the big city. A mouthy cunt, I'll wager, but the prettiest piece of them all. So, let's put an end to that nonsense. Either you get me back what your friend stole, or you pay the price. There's no third choice."

My hands have begun to shake, but whether from fear or rage I don't know. "You still haven't told me what he stole."

"And I don't intend to, do I? That's your job."

"How can I find something when I don't know what it is?"

The knife pierces skin again. I tense, and Sands's eyes flash. "Give me your best guess."

"Documents?" I grunt. "Data?"

"Brilliant. It's a disc, right? A DVD. Started out as one, anyway. The data could have been copied onto something else by now. USB drive, digital tape, hard drive, even a fucking iPod. What the data is, I won't tell you, but you'll know it when you see it."

"How?"

"It's encrypted."

The knifepoint withdraws a fraction of an inch. "Are you a betting man, Mr. Cage?"

"No."

"Good. That's a sign of intelligence. I don't gamble either. Because the house always wins. People can't seem to remember that. But I'm trusting you will."

The knife again. I wince and try not to cry out.

"I know this is a lot to take in," Sands

says. "You lost a mate tonight, and that's never easy. But the truth is, you cut yourself loose from Jessup a long time ago. And rightly so. The man was a header. Christ, he got weepy whenever he talked about how you two were lads together, watching the moon shots on the telly."

The revelation that this meant so much to Tim almost brings tears to my eyes. I steel myself and keep my eyes on Sands's face to avoid looking into the dog's eyes.

"Listen to me now," he says. "Let the rupies investigate Jessup's death. Do everything you planned to do before Jessup died. Show the visiting CEO the town, give interviews, fly around in the balloons. But while you're having your *craic,* you find time to find my property. If I find it first, I'll let you know. Remember, I'll be watching. And listening." In a blur, he raises the knife and pricks the soft skin beneath my left eye. "Don't play games with me, mate. Remember the first rule: The house always wins. And I'm the house."

Sands bends and slips his pistol into an ankle holster, then takes my gun from the small of his back, removes the clip, ejects the remaining round from the chamber, and hands the pistol to me. As he slides the clip into my front pants pocket, his dog pushes off my chest, retrieves the ejected bullet from the flower bed, and drops the brass into his master's hand. Sands rubs the dog between its cropped ears, then drops the loose round into my pants pocket.

"One last thing." Sands kneels at the edge of the porch, reaches down into the shadows behind him, and brings up a black leather briefcase.

"What's that?"

"A quarter million dollars."

"Why is it here?"

"Why, it's the money you asked for." Sands gives me a theatrical hug, then says sotto voce, "For the cameras, mate." Then loudly again: "Like you said, you have the biggest job in town, and that's why we pay you the big bucks."

"You're not serious."

"Just smile and say thank you," he whispers. "So your daughter keeps breathing."

Given no choice, I accept it. "Thank

you," I mutter. What else can I do? Seamus Quinn could be upstairs with a knife, waiting for a signal from Sands.

Jonathan Sands pats my arm and walks down the steps as lightly as Fred Astaire, and again I sense the fluid efficiency of his motions. He waves airily.

"I wish you the pleasure of the evening. And I look forward to hearing from you."

Only now do I realize that his uppercrust English accent has returned. The working-class Irish has vanished like a vapor trail, like it was never there at all.

As I stare after him, he stops and calls, "Oh, if you're worried about the grieving widow, rest easy. If I wanted her out of the picture, she'd be room temperature already. The lad too."

My face must betray something, because he adds, "Sure, I heard every word you said to her tonight. I know she doesn't have my property, so ring her up and tell her to get a good night's sleep. In fact, if you find the disc before morning, I'll toss in a few quid for the widows and orphans' fund." He smiles at the thought, then gives me a parting shot in his native accent. "Have a grand night altogether, now."

With that, Jonathan Sands strolls off down Washington Street, the massive dog walking at his heel like a royal escort. When Sands pauses to study the smooth trunks of the crape myrtles in the pink glow of the streetlamps, the dog stops and sits beside him. As I watch, a long, black car glides soundlessly up to him, gathers up him and his dog, and rolls quickly out of sight, making for the river.

As I stare at the blackness where the taillights faded, I realize that I'm shaking uncontrollably. I can hardly grip my key to get it out of the lock.

I'm no stranger to threats. I've confronted dangerous men in my life, some of them psychopaths. A few vowed to avenge themselves upon me for criminal convictions or for the executions of relatives. I once shot a man dead to prevent him from killing my daughter in retribution. But never have I experienced the paralyzing terror I felt while listening to the clear and passionless voice of Jonathan Sands.

God, what Tim must have suffered before he died.

With shaking hands I take out my cell phone and call Julia Jessup. I'm three minutes late, but she answers, sounding like she's close to hyperventilating. I don't know what Sands's promise to leave Tim's widow alone is worth, but I must protect my own family now. After instructing Julia to seek refuge with Tim's parents, I carry Sands's briefcase inside, lock the door behind me, and race up the stairs to Annie's door. In the night light's glow, I see her tucked into the bow of my mother's larger form beneath the covers. Relief washes over me, but fear quickly burns through it. As I watch my sleeping daughter, a disturbing certainty rises from the chaos in my mind. Tim was right about "Mr. X." Jonathan Sands is not like anyone I've ever faced before. I've dealt with the man for nearly a year and not once suspected his true nature. But there's no time for self-recrimination now. Or for doubt. Sands may have convinced himself that I'll be like the others he's bought off or threatened into cooperating with him, but in twenty-four hours he'll know different. Before I can act, though, I must get my daughter to safety.

Hurrying down the stairs, I lock Sands's briefcase—which is indeed full of cash—in the safe in my study, mentally ticking off the obvious obstacles: *The house will be watched. My phones will be tapped—cellular and landlines. The house may be bugged or even covered by video cameras, considering that Sands was waiting for me when I got home. He could be checking my e-mail, text messages, and any other form of digital communication. So . . . what options remain?*

For some people, mortal danger brings paralyzing confusion. For me—after the first minute of panic—it brings clarity. So it's with utter certainty that I pick up my kitchen telephone and dial my father's home number. The phone rings three times, and then a mildly groggy baritone voice answers, "Dr. Cage."

Even before I speak, something in me arcs out over the wires, instinctively reaching for the protection of blood kin. "Dad, it's Penn."

From three miles away, I feel him come alert in the dark. "What's the matter? Is Annie all right? Is it Peggy?"

I let some anxiety bleed into my voice. "Annie and Mom are fine, but something's wrong with me. My heart's racing. I think I'm having a panic attack."

"Tachycardia? Is it a stress reaction?"

"No, it just started a couple of minutes ago. I'm a little short of breath, and my pulse is about a hundred and ten. I feel like I may throw up. I guess maybe I'm worried about taking that balloon ride in the morning."

There's a brief silence. "We'd better go down to my office and get an EKG on you."

"No, no, I think it's just anxiety. I had to fly in a goddamn helicopter today. I think I just need some Valium or something."

"A helicopter? Hmm. Maybe you're right. Do you have any Ativan there?"

"No. Do you think you could bring me something? I'd come there, but I don't want to drive while this is going on."

I hear him grunt as he heaves himself out of bed. "I'll pull on some clothes and get my bag. I want to listen to your chest."

I press my palm so hard against my fore-head that my arm shakes. "Thanks, Dad. I

appreciate it. The front door is unlocked.
Just walk in. I'll be in my bathroom."

"Okay."

I should hang up, but I can't help adding,
"Try to hurry, okay?"

"I'm on my way."

CHAPTER

13

Linda Church hugs the toilet in the ladies' room of The Devil's Punchbowl Bar and Grille, shuddering as she retches into the bowl. She's supposed to be seating patrons, but she can no longer carry out the basic functions of employment. Two minutes ago she received a text message from Tim, but the message made no sense. She wipes her mouth with toilet tissue, then flips open her phone and reads the letters again, being careful to hide it from the hidden camera above.

Thiefwww kllmmommy. Sqrttoo.

The message came from a number she doesn't recognize, not even the area code, but this is the strongest proof that Tim sent it. He's told her that one of his security tactics is to use the phones of strangers when their attention is elsewhere. He's even stolen cell phones for this purpose. But this message has taken her to the edge of panic. Kllmmommy? Sqrttoo? It almost sounds like an order to kill Julia and the baby.

"No," she whispers, as the possibility that this message might have been meant for someone else sinks into her bones. "Not possible. He loves that baby. He loves Julia."

Linda hears footsteps enter the restroom. She grabs the handle and flushes for cover, and cold spray hits her face.

"Linda?" asks a worried voice. "It's Ashley. Are you okay? Janice said you really look like shit."

"I'm okay, Ash. Stomach flu, I think. I'll be right out."

"Yuck. I'll tell Janice."

"Thanks."

Linda frantically plays back the

sequence of events that brought her here. Four hours ago, Tim walked past the door of The Devil's Punchbowl whistling "Walking on the Moon," by the Police. The song was a coded signal, arranged last night after Tim met with Penn Cage. If Tim had whistled "Every Breath You Take," it would have meant, "Get out now. Don't wait for anything." "Walking on the Moon" meant Linda should work until the end of her shift, then throw her cell phone in the river, get into her car, and drive three hours to New Orleans, to her aunt's house. Tim would call her in transit using a pay-as-you-go cell phone he'd bought at Wal-Mart, and she would answer with the same type of phone. Hers was in her car now, under the front seat.

"Walking on the Moon" was supposed to signal that everything was going according to plan, but the moment Linda recognized the tune, her insides had started to roil with apprehension. She'd forced herself to keep doing her job, even though she had to remain on the boat an hour after Tim's shift ended. She'd almost snapped at midnight and simply run down the exit ramp as he left the boat, but that would have busted them for sure.

"I shouldn't even be here," she says almost silently, ever conscious of the hidden microphones. *The Devil's Punchbowl usually closes at 11:00 p.m., but Sands has ordered all the food service to run on extended hours during the Balloon Festival.*

The door bangs open again, and Ashley calls, "Darnell just came by and asked why you weren't on duty. She's on the warpath. You'd better get back out there if you can walk."

Sue Darnell was the personnel manager, a cast-iron bitch from Dallas. "Almost done. I'm just fixing my face."

"Down there? I'm looking at your heels, girl."

"I'm coming, Ash! I got vomit on my blouse."

"It's your funeral, honey."

Don't even think that, Linda says silently. With a handful of tissue she wipes clammy sweat from her face and forehead, then gets to her feet and checks her uniform for any signs of vomit. She was lucky.

The ladies' room opens into Slot Group Seven, a jangling circus of noise filled with smoke and drunk gamblers. The extraction fans don't work for shit up here. Linda smooths her skirt against her thighs and tries to walk with something like grace as she moves through the suckers and back toward the Punchbowl.

She's thirty feet away when she realizes something is wrong. Ashley and Janice are standing by the cash registers, talking to each other without any regard for three patrons waiting to be seated. Ashley's mouth forms a perfect O, then Janice nods and begins chattering. When Ashley catches sight of Linda, she motions her over with a quick wave.

"What is it?" Linda asks, fighting the urge to bolt for the main-deck gangplank.

"Janice just got a text from her ex-husband. He's up at Bowie's. He said some guy fell off the bluff up by Silver Street. He was goofing on the other side of the fence or something, and he fell.

He's dead. *Some people are saying he jumped."*

Linda blinks, trying to absorb this, but a low ringing has begun in her ears.

"Drunk, probably," Janice *says. "Jimmy's drunk, anyway. You couldn't get me on the other side of that fence even if I was toasted. There's only about a foot of concrete, and then* nothing."

"A whole lot of nothing," Ashley agrees. "I wonder who it was."

"A tourist, I bet," says Janice. "Somebody here for the race. Wait." Janice takes a cell phone from her pocket and checks a message. "Now Jimmy says somebody threw the guy off the bluff. Jesus."

Linda is looking at Janice, but what she sees is Tim flying through the air, head over heels, spinning through the dark—

"Linda?" says Ashley, her voice tinged with real concern. "Are you going to puke again?"

Janice grabs the trash can from behind the register, but Linda ignores it and walks back toward the ladies' room. The girls say something behind

her, but she doesn't catch the meaning. She passes the door of the restroom and walks to the thick glass door that leads to the observation deck. The October wind hits her face-on, and she's glad for the chill. Looking upriver, she sees the lights of the houses on Clifton Avenue, then Weymouth Hall. Somewhere up there, Tim is supposed to be meeting Penn Cage tonight. She doesn't let her mind go any further than that. Tim is there, she says silently. Right now, he's handing over whatever he got tonight. With this article of faith set in her heart, she slips her personal cell phone from her pocket and flicks it through the rail, toward the river three decks below. She doesn't hear the splash, but she sees a spurt of silver rise in the moonlight as the phone goes under. She knows her body was between her hand and the surveillance camera when she threw the phone, because she's rehearsed this move a dozen times in her mind, just as Tim instructed.

"Keep moving," she mouths to herself, walking to the companionway used by the service staff to get to the main deck. "Don't stop long enough to let fear paralyze you."

She's quoting Tim now, like a heroine echoing her mentor in her mind. She slips through the gift shop, then past the foot of the escalators. This is the hardest part of her journey. Every atom of instinct is screaming for her to march down the big aisle between the slots, through the main entrance, and right across the broad exit ramp—but she can't.

She doesn't have her car keys.

For one wild moment she considers leaving anyway, breaking into a sprint and racing out to freedom. But if she did that, she'd be cutting herself off from Tim. The TracFone from Wal-Mart is under her car seat, and that's her only sure link to him now. To reach it, she has to have her keys.

Why didn't you tell me to keep my ignition key in my pocket? *she asks Tim silently.* Why didn't I think of it? *For the first time a blade of raw terror slices through her, cold and true. If Tim didn't think of this contingency, what else did he forget?*

Linda grits her teeth and forces herself to breeze past the center aisle without looking at the exit. Point of no return, *she thinks, spying the service door that leads belowdecks to the restricted area of the boat. Operations, Security, the physical plant of the barge.*

She has to show her badge to the security officer at the top of the stairs. He gives it a bored look, then lets her walk down the steps. She can feel his eyes on her backside as she reaches the lower deck.

The smell changes in the lower holds. It's like entering the service elevator in a hotel by mistake. The illusion of cleanliness and luxury falls away, leaving the sticky floor of reality. The air down here reeks of bad cafeteria food and other things she can't quite recognize. Employee resentment . . . paranoia. Linda quails at the idea of going near the security control area, but she has no choice. The lockers and changing room are aft of the security suite.

Because everyone is still on shift, she's alone on the lower deck. If the security guys poke their heads out, she'll tell them she's puking nonstop and has to get to the emergency room.

A long corridor runs past the door of the security suite, then the off-limits room they call the Devil's Punchbowl. She makes the length of the passageway on a single held-in breath. Halfway home now. Through the hatch that leads to the changing rooms, past the clock where she punches in, around the corner . . . and there. *The employee lockers.*

Linda licks her lips, takes a breath, then dials the combination on her locker. The lock clicks. In her mind she sees the yellow Dooney & Bourke purse she bought at Dillard's in New Orleans, a birthday splurge. And inside the purse, her car keys.

She opens the door and reaches into the locker, but her purse is gone. Withdrawing her hand, she leans back so that more light can get into the space. It's a mistake, she thinks, feeling the way she does when she somehow loses the milk carton in the refrigerator.

Lying where she left her purse is the black TracFone Tim bought her at Wal-Mart—the phone she last saw before shoving it under the front seat of her Corolla.

"You fucking slag," growls a male voice filled with rage. Seamus Quinn. *"Do you have any idea what you're in for?"*

Linda closes her eyes and grips the cold metal edge of the locker door. Without it, she would have fainted to the deck.

Quinn starts to speak again, but the air in the room changes suddenly, and his words become a mute exhalation. Linda hears rapid, shallow breathing that sets her nerves thrumming.

"Close the locker, Linda," says Jonathan Sands. "We're a bit pressed for time."

Tim is dead, *says a voice inside her, the voice that has known it all along. Hot tears slide down her cheeks as she closes the locker door.*

"That's it, darlin'," says Sands. "Now turn around."

Linda wipes her face on her sleeve

and turns slowly. Quinn is leaning against the wall behind her, his shoulder wedged against a flyer that reads NEED HELP MANAGING YOUR 401(K)? Sands stands in the corridor that leads past the security suite, arms folded across his chest, dressed as perfectly as if he were attending a wedding or a funeral in fifteen minutes. His hyperobservant eyes glide over her face and clothing, missing nothing. Beside him sits the huge white dog that sometimes accompanies him on the boat. Sands told her the dog was bred in Pakistan, for fighting and for war. She has never heard the dog make a sound.

Poor Tim, *she thinks in a rush of despair that almost drops her to the floor.*

"Can't trust a fucking cunt," Quinn mutters. "All the same."

Linda's heart flutters like a panicked bird trying to beat its way up through her throat. Move, *she tells herself.* Run—

"Don't be a fool," Sands says. "There's nowhere to go."

The wild urge to flight twists inside her.

"Come to me," Sands says, beckoning her toward the hallway. "We need to ask you some questions about Timothy."

The last ember of hope dies in her soul.

They know.

CHAPTER

14

The second my father walks into my bathroom with his black bag, I put my finger to my lips and shove a piece of paper into his hands. On it are printed the words:

I'm not sick. Annie is in danger. We all are. House may be bugged. Act like I'm having a panic attack. Follow my lead. We're going to type messages on the computer on the counter. I'll turn on the bath taps to cover the noise of the keyboard.

Dad looks up after reading for only two seconds, but I shake my head and point at the paper, and he goes back to reading. My father is seventy-three years old, and he's practiced medicine in Natchez for more than forty of those years. He's the same height I am—an inch over six feet—but the arthritis that's slowly curling his hands into claws has bowed his spine so that I am taller now. His hair and beard have gone white, his skin is cracked and spotted from psoriasis, and he has to take insulin shots every day, yet the primary impression he radiates is one of strength. Thirty years past triple-bypass surgery, he's sicker than most of his patients, but they think of him as I do: an oak tree twisted by age and battered by storms, but still indomitable at the core. He licks his lips, looks up slowly from the paper, and says, "Is your heart still racing?"

"I think it's worse. And the nausea's worse. I vomited twice after I called you."

"Wonderful." Dad glances toward the bathroom counter. Between the two sinks are the articles I assembled while I waited for him: my keys; a black Nike warm-up suit and running shoes; Annie's MacBook computer, booted up with Microsoft Word on the screen; a Springfield XD nine-millimeter pistol, and a short-barreled

.357 Magnum. "I brought you some Ati-van," he says, "but I want to listen to your chest first."

"Do you mind if I get in the bathtub? I want to clean myself up."

"That's fine. Just get your shirt off."

I nod and turn on the cold-water tap, then strip off my clothes and pull on the warm-up suit. Dad moves in front of the computer as I pull on the top and pecks out the words *What the hell is going on?*

He steps aside for me to type my response, and we begin a sort of waltz in place, during which I explain our dilemma. He always typed much slower than I, but it's worse now because of his hands; it hurts to watch him struggle to strike the keys.

Tim Jessup was murdered tonight. It has to do with his work at one of the casinos. The man behind his death just threatened to kill Annie. The motive is too complex to explain like this. They threatened Mom's life, and yours too. Even Jenny, and she's on the other side of the Atlantic.

Who are these people?

People I misread very badly.

They really killed Jack Jessup's boy?

I left his body under the bluff an hour ago. I think they tortured him.

Christ. Do the police know?

Yes, but I'm not sure I can trust them. One word in the wrong ear, and these people take or kill Annie. They have a lot to lose.

What about FBI?

First priority is getting Annie and Mom to safety. We've learned that the hard way, haven't we?

Dad nods slowly, and I know his memories mirror my own: I see the house that he and my mother lived in for thirty years going up in flames, and the maid who raised me and my sister in agony on a table in the emergency room.

"Take a deep breath," Dad says in his medical voice, as though he's listening to my heart with his stethoscope. "Again . . . okay . . . again."

There's only one real option, I type. *I'm going to call Daniel Kelly's firm in Houston. Blackhawk. With any luck they'll be able to send a team our way almost immediately. They'll take Mom and Annie somewhere safe—to an actual safe house, just like the movies.*

Dad's face goes through subtle changes of expression as he absorbs all this, but in a short while he nods and types again.

All right. What about Kelly himself? He's in Afghanistan.

Where do the girls go? Houston?

I'm not sure. But wherever it is, you should go with them.

His contemptuous expression tells me his answer to this, but he types:

Kelly's people will take better care of them than I could, and I have three patients dying right now. One in hospice and two in the hospital. I'm not going anywhere. You haven't called Kelly's people yet?

I have to leave the house for that. Was waiting for you.

Where are you going?

Not far. I should be back within 15 minutes, but don't panic unless I'm gone an hour.

He digests this, then types:

What if somebody tries to break in

while you're gone? Is that what the guns are for?

I pick up the big revolver and slip it into his arthritic hands.

Can you still fire a pistol?

He eyes his crooked fingers doubtfully.

If they bust in here, I guess we'll see. It can't be any harder than giving a goddamn prostate exam. You don't have a shotgun, do you?

Sorry. Wish I did.

He shrugs philosophically.

If someone does come, shoot before you talk. I'll come running, and I should get here fast enough to be of help.

Dad sucks his teeth for a few seconds, and I know he's thinking of options. With a grunt he bends and types: *There are a couple of guys I could call to help out. Old patients. Ex-cops.*

Not this time. The bad guys might believe I panicked and called you for some Ativan, but if anybody else shows up, we're asking for trouble. We have to do this the old-fashioned way.

Dad shakes his head and types: *Like Matt Dillon and Festus spending the night at the Dodge City jail, by God.*

That's about the size of it. I figure you're more Doc Adams than Festus.

I'm older than Milburn Stone ever got on that show, I'm afraid.

I smile, then type: *I still trust you with Annie's life.*

Something hard and implacable comes into my father's eyes as he reads the words, and I know that the first person who tries to break into my house will take a lethal bullet from a man who knows exactly where to aim.

I'm going now, I type. *Hope for 10 minutes, but give me an hour.*

"You're heartbeat's slowing a little," Dad says. "How do you feel?"

"Better. I think I just want to sit here in the tub awhile."

He nods understanding. "I'll just go watch some TV in the den. If the nausea doesn't ease up, give a yell, and I'll give you a shot of Vistaril."

"Thanks, Dad. Jesus, this really scared me."

"Don't thank me. You're not out of the woods yet."

I start to walk past him, but he grips my arm with startling force, pulls me back to the MacBook, and types: *What if you don't come back?*

He's right to ask. If I leave this house, no matter how stealthy I try to be, I might be signing my death warrant.

If I don't come back, I'm dead or taken. Call 911 and start screaming there's a home invasion in progress. Then call every cop you ever treated and put a ring of steel around this house. I start to leave, but then I add, *And raise Annie like you know I would. Like you raised me.*

He stares at the screen for a long time, and I see his jaw muscles flexing. Then he shakes his head and types: *Go fetch the cavalry, Matthew. I'll hold the fort.*

I use the rear basement window to leave my house. The lower halves of those windows sit in a narrow concrete moat that surrounds the house, and I am thankful for it tonight. I see no one as I sneak out of my backyard, but as I prepare to slip across Washington Street two blocks from my house, a cigarette flares at the corner of my block, illuminating the pale moon of a beardless face. Knowing the watcher will be night-blind for a few moments, I dart across the road and into the foliage of a neighbor's yard.

My destination is Caitlin's guesthouse, a renovated servants' quarters that can be opened with the same key that opens her front door. I move carefully between my neighbors' homes, using my knowledge of pets and gardens to steer clear of problems. When I reach Caitlin's backyard, I experience a moment of panic, thinking she returned while I was making my way here, but what I thought was her car is simply three garbage cans lined up for collection.

A rush of mildewed air hits me when I open the guesthouse door. Leaving the lights off, I move carefully across the dark den, toward the glowing red light in the kitchenette. With all hope suspended, I lift the cordless phone and press the ON button. A steady dial tone comes to me like a lifeline thrown into a black ocean.

Taking my cell phone from my pocket, I check its memory for the number of Kelly's employer in Houston, then enter it into the cordless landline. The phone rings twice, then a cool female voice answers, "Blackhawk Risk Management."

She's wide-awake at two thirty in the morning, and this gives me some confidence.

"This is Penn Cage calling. I was given this number by Daniel Kelly. He's a personal friend."

"Yes, thank you. Did Mr. Kelly give you a code word?"

I close my eyes in silent thanks to Kelly. "It's been some time, but he once told me to say *Spartacus* if I had an emergency and couldn't reach him."

"Thank you, transferring you now. Please remain on the line."

There's no hold music, only a hiss cut short by a squawk. A male voice says, "Call me Bill, Mr. Cage. Dan Kelly is on assignment at this time. What is the nature of your emergency?"

"It's life or death. I wouldn't call otherwise."

Bill seems unfazed by this; he continues speaking with the practiced calm of a fighter pilot. "Are you in danger now?"

"Yes, but I can talk."

"How can we help?"

"I'm in Natchez , Mississippi. Five fifty Washington Street, a residence. My family has been threatened by men who committed murder tonight. I'm not sure I can trust the police. I need someone to take my mother and daughter to a safe location. Can you do that?"

The pause is brief. "We can do that. We have some operators arriving for Stateside rotation, and we can send a team. What's the time frame?"

"How soon can they be here?"

"Seven hours by road. Our company planes are committed at this time. If danger is imminent, I can charter a jet, but cost may become a factor to you at that point."

I think quickly. If Jonathan Sands has somehow overheard this call, he can retaliate even before a jet gets here. Annie's safety lies in my getting back to my house unseen and playing out my bluff. "Cost is no object, but seven hours will work fine."

"You'll have a team at your front door in seven hours or less. Have the packages ready."

"I will."

"Should we expect opposition?"

"I think the opposition will be too surprised to act quickly. But your men should be ready just in case."

"Understood. Mr. Cage, while we were talking, I messaged Dan Kelly via secure digital link. His reply says that if you can remain at your present number, he will call you within thirty minutes."

I stand and pace the floor of the guest-house in the dark. "I can do that. But under no circumstances should Kelly try to call my cell phone or home phones. Those are compromised. It's this line or nothing."

"Understood. We'll see you in seven hours. Six, if we can manage it. Stay well."

I feel a rush of relief so powerful that my face goes hot. "Thank you."

Waiting in the dark with my hand on the phone, I sense the fragility of those who matter most to me, as though they're barely clinging to the planet as it spins through its orbit: my mother and daughter sleeping across the street with only my aging father to protect them; my sister in England, going through her day without even a hint that she could be in danger; Julia Jessup hiding in or near the city, or running for her life with a fatherless child to protect. Swirling around them are people whose paths I can neither control nor predict: the men watching my house, who may realize I'm gone and call their master; Caitlin, who might return at any moment and discover me; Sands himself, who might decide he can't trust me after all and consign me and mine to Tim Jessup's fate.

The half hour I must wait for Kelly's call is measured in clenching heartbeats, rapid-fire eyeblinks, startle reflexes, sudden bowel constrictions, and drops of sweat. When I don't see the ghostly white dog peering at me through the guesthouse window, I see images of my friend's brutalized body, or his wife and young son hiding in terror and grief. Strangest of all is my memory of last night's dream of Tim on the ice sheet, and the white wolf watching me. How did I dream of an animal I'd never seen before? Or *have* I seen that white dog around town somewhere, perhaps even with Sands, and stored the memory in some reptilian neurons, where they waited to be triggered by Tim's twisted tale?

When the phone rings, I jerk it to my ear so fast the chirp fades almost before it's begun.

"Hello? Hello!"

There's only silence at first. Then Kelly's voice comes into the receiver as though it's being transmitted from a distant spacecraft. "What's happening, man? Somebody threatened Annie?"

"Jesus, Kelly, it's great to hear your voice. We're in trouble here. They threatened Annie, my parents, my sister, everybody. They already killed a friend of mine tonight. A guy I went to school with."

"Slow down. Are you safe where you are?"

"Yeah, but I don't have much time. Are you still in Afghanistan?"

"Yeah. The mountains. Look, talk to me. Who's your problem?"

"The main guy is Irish. He runs one of the casinos here. He pretends to be English, but that's just a front. He goes by the name of Jonathan Sands. I have no idea who he really is. Paramilitary type, but hiding it in a suit."

"I don't like the sound of that," Kelly says reflectively. "Ex-IRA, maybe?"

"He definitely knows how to handle weapons."

"What the hell have you got into?"

"I'm not sure. But I didn't take it seriously enough at first, and a friend died because of it. According to him, I can't use conventional law enforcement. Sands has got a lot of people on his payroll."

There's a long silence. Then Kelly says, "It could take forty-eight hours."

"What could?"

"Me getting there. The company will get Annie and your mother sorted out, but it could take me two days to get back to the States."

"Dan . . . are you sure?"

"Hey, it's only money."

"You know I'll—"

"Shut the fuck up, okay? Before you embarrass both of us. And try to keep breathing for the next forty-eight hours."

"I'll do my best. Look, you can't call me, okay?"

"Understood. The Blackhawk team is going to bring you a secure telephone. A satellite phone. You'll have to decide when it's safe to use it. Update the company when you can. Just keep using *Spar-*

tacus as your code. They're also going to bring a gear bag. That's for me. I'll have them stash it somewhere in town, and you can pick it up if you're not being tailed."

"Okay. Daniel—"

"Hold up. If you get in a really tight spot after the team leaves and before I get there, there's couple of guys in your area I trust. They're from Athens Point, down the river."

"Who are they?"

"One's a young guy, ex-marine. Carl Sims. Met him at the range there. He's a black guy, a sniper. I don't care what you're mixed up in, use my name, you can trust him."

"Okay. Who else?"

"There's a guy used to fly for the sheriff down there at Athens Point. Ex–air force. Name's McDavitt. He's the real deal. If you need to get somewhere fast, or get away fast, he's your man."

A jolt of synchronicity makes my scalp tingle. "I met McDavitt *today.* No shit. Some corporate big shot hired him to fly us around the city."

Kelly laughs softly. "You see? Things

don't look as bad as you thought. Now, you get back to Annie. We'll take care of things on our end. See you in a couple of days. I'm out."

I wait until I hear the click, then slowly hang up.

The circuitous trek back to my house doesn't seem to take nearly as long this time; I feel Daniel Kelly sitting on my shoulder like one of Odin's crows. The watcher on the corner is still in place, but I move across Washington as though cloaked in darkness. Just as I slip through the hedges into my backyard, I see a man walking across the parking lot of the bank behind my house. I silently double my pace, drop into the moat beside the basement window, and slide into the relative safety of my home.

My father is standing watch at the top of the stairs. He looks old in the shaft of light falling from my bedroom door, like a monk meditating over a gun he found by chance.

"Don't shoot," I hiss from the bottom of the staircase.

"Son of a bitch," Dad whispers with relief. "I was about a minute from calling 911."

"I'm feeling a little better now," I say loudly, hurrying up the stairs.

"I think that was worse than Korea," Dad whispers, standing slowly and rubbing his lower back. "Except for the frostbite. I took two nitro pills while you were gone. Let's get to that damned computer so we can talk."

He follows me into my bathroom, and I bend quickly over Annie's MacBook.

Kelly called me himself from Afghanistan. I had to wait a half hour, but it was worth it. Blackhawk dispatched a team as soon as I told them we were in danger. They'll probably come in an armored SUV. I imagine they've already left Houston. They'll be here in less than seven hours.

Dad nods thankfully, then pecks out two words: *And Kelly?*

Kelly's coming himself. 48 hours minimum before he gets here though.

Good. So. What do we do now?

Wait for the cavalry. We should probably stop using the computer. There are lasers that can read keystrokes by the vibrations of window glass. This is sci-fi stuff we're up against.

As Dad shakes his head slowly, I type:
*We'd better stay upstairs. We can pull
shifts. One of us by Annie's bedroom door
while the other catches a catnap in my
bed.*

**You think I can sleep a wink after
what you told me tonight? Drag a
couch out here and we'll play cards
until dawn.**

Cards? You don't play cards!

A smile that's almost a grimace makes
my father's eyes squint.

**Haven't since Korea. Bores the hell
out of me.**

But tonight?

**The enemy's out there. Tonight we
play cards.**

CHAPTER

15

Linda doesn't know whether she's paralyzed by fear or whether she's entered a place beyond fear. Her mind has given way to grief or shock, or some mixture of both. They have taken her deep within the bowels of the barge that supports the faux riverboat above her head, to the long hold with black foam on its walls, like the foam in a recording studio. It's dim, but it doesn't stink of mildew as some areas of the lower deck do. This hold smells like a new car. It's here that Sands brings Linda and his other mistresses when he wants sex during business hours. A sofa bed in the corner faces two large LCD screens that display an ever-changing feed from the security cameras upstairs. On those screens Sands can monitor all areas of the casino, even during sex. This room has other uses too. Here they bring the troublemakers and scam artists who aren't lucky enough to be handed over to the police. For these occasions, a single chair stands in the center of the hold, and beside it a shiny cart like a printer trolley. But the square device on the cart is not a printer. It's smaller, with thin wires coming off it, like the EKG machine at a doctor's office. It's that machine that makes the staff refer to this hold as the real "Devil's Punchbowl."

As Quinn leads her by her elbow to the chair, Sands following behind—she can feel his presence—Linda sees something against the far wall of the room. It's a person, a small man with dark skin and short black hair. She cannot see his face. He's lying on his side, facing away from her. He's wearing a T-shirt that says THEY MIGHT BE GIANTS across the shoulders, but his legs are bare. His naked thighs and buttocks look strangely vulnerable, like a boy's behind, and something dark is smeared across one calf.

"Sit," Quinn says.

As Linda turns to obey, she sees that the chair is bolted to the floor. This registers like something on a movie screen, not reality; she cannot suspend her disbelief. Before that occurs, before reality breaks through, Quinn has folded thick leather straps over her wrists and ankles and fastened them tight. Quinn's usual curses and grunts are strangely absent. He's acting like a pious man in church; he has entered what he feels to be a sacred place. She feels a thick, padded strap tighten around her abdomen, hears the soft rip as Quinn hitches, then rehitches the Velcro that holds it fast.

"Don't do this," she whispers.

"Don't make us," Sands answers, then steps into her field of vision.

The look in his eyes is terrible to behold. Yet he speaks softly, like a man talking to a child. Behind him the white dog stands alert, awaiting a command. He looks something like a giant pit bull, but his face is wrinkled, and his eyes project a sentience that makes her shiver.

"I need to know some things, girl. And I don't have a lot of time."

She nods quickly, submissively. "Can I ask a question first?"

"One."

"Is Tim dead?"

Sands inclines his head slowly.

She doesn't want to let them see how this hits her, but she shuts her eyes before she's even aware of it, shuts them the way a little girl does hearing her father has been killed in a car wreck, as hers was when she was nine.

"How did he die?"

"That's two questions. We've no time for tears, Linda. Timothy tried to bite the hand that fed him. He stole something from me, and we have to get it back. Answer up the first time. Don't make me ask twice."

"I don't think I know anything. But I'll tell you what I do."

"Fucking right you will," Quinn mutters from behind her.

Sands raises a hand to silence him. She has never seen Sands this way. He is more focused now than he is during sex. The pupils of his eyes gleam like scorched motor oil. When he looks at her, she feels her will sapped away, like a bird being hypnotized by a snake.

"What did Timothy tell you he was going to do tonight?"

"He told me he was going to stop you. That's all I know. I don't know what he was after, exactly. I tried to talk him out of it. I knew he'd never get away with it."

"Fucking right," grunts Quinn again.

"What did he want to stop me from doing?"

"The dogs," she says, trying to think. "He had a thing about dogs. He went to a dogfight on the river. Remember? You must have said he could go. It upset him. Something happened to him there. The dogs . . . and the girls. He couldn't deal with it."

"The girls?" says Sands.

Quinn laughs. "He was bending you over the aft-deck head while his wife nursed a kid at home. What did he care about some runaway whores?"

Linda shrugs. "He did. He was like that. I don't know."

"There's more," Sands says. "A lot more. Give us the rest."

"There isn't any more. He wasn't complicated."

"He had a plan. You had the Trac-Fone hidden in your car."

"That was just so that he could find me afterward."

"You were running away together?"

"Not like that. We had to leave for a while, he said, until it was safe. He wasn't leaving his wife and son, though."

"How long was it going to be before it was safe?"

She shrugs. "I don't know. A few days. A week. He never really said. I don't think he knew."

Sands's eyes bore into hers like the

light the ophthalmologist shines into your eye to see the very back of it, where the blood vessels and the nerve go in. Sands knows she's concealing something. If Tim could see her now, he would want her to save herself, to spare herself pain. But he wouldn't want her to sell out Penn Cage. Penn has a child, and that child needs him.

"Where's your cell phone?" Sands asks. "Your personal phone."

"I lost it." She knows this is stupid even before she finishes speaking.

Quinn makes a mocking sound, but Sands only sighs. "I've known you for seven months and I've never once seen you without your phone. I've read your text messages to Timothy. Everything from 'I love you, my darling' to 'I want you to come in my mouth tonight.' If he'd known the things you did for me . . . the boy would've gone mad."

Hot tears streak her face. Sands is right: Tim never got pleasure from degrading her; but Sands lived for it. Worse, he knew that some sick part of her derived pleasure from it as well.

Once you'd been wired that way, there was no way to short-circuit those urges and reactions. A harsh voice and a slap made her wet, like Pavlov's dogs hearing the dinner bell. All you could do was struggle against it, try to drive it out with something else.

"How long has Timothy been talking to Penn Cage?"

Linda blinks but says nothing. Hope has flickered in her breast with religious power. Tim was supposed to meet Penn tonight. Either Tim missed that meeting or he delivered his evidence to Penn. Either way, she has reason to hope. If Tim missed the meeting, Penn will surely turn the town upside down to find him, starting with the Magnolia Queen. *And if Tim did manage to get him the evidence, Penn, being the mayor, must certainly know by now that his friend is dead. Either way, his first instinct will be to have Sands arrested. That's why Sands feels pressed for time. The mayor could be on his way down to the boat with a squad of police at this moment.*

You have to stay on the boat, *says a voice. Tim's voice.* If they take you off this boat, you're dead. Or lost, because no one will know where to look for you. But as long as you're here, you can be found. Whatever they do, you have to take it—

A stalling strategy occurs to Linda, one learned so long ago that it feels inborn. I'll give them things in stages, *she thinks.* Lie first, then give up something true. Something to keep them trying. When they feel I'm cooperating, resist again, then give up the next bit. *It was like negotiating with a boy in the backseat in junior high. Let him slide his hand under your shirt, but not your bra. Kiss awhile, then push his hand out and kiss some more. When he's finally, really angry, let him push up the bra and feel them for real. Then the game begins again with the belt and the snap to your jeans.*

Only this was no backseat. And these weren't junior high boys. Every minute of delay would be bought with pain.

You have to take it, *Tim's voice says from within her.* Whatever it is—

Sands reaches out and lays a hand on the gleaming metal printer cart. A black rag lies on it. Sands lifts the rag like a

*magician beginning a trick, and her eyes
track to what's beneath it. The wires end
not in EKG leads, but in shiny metal clips.
Alligator clips, she remembers from a lab
in high school. One of the wires is connected to a metal bolt about five inches
long. Dried blood coats it.*

When Linda recognizes the blood,
her mind jumps to the man on the floor
with no pants, and the idea she had
before—that she was in some place
beyond fear—vanishes like water
thrown onto a hot skillet. She's only
crossed the threshold of fear. When
she first entered this room, her grief
over Tim had smothered everything,
even her will to live. Now she wants
only to keep breathing, to avoid pain.

Sands moves closer, leans down,
pushes a strand of hair from her eye.
With an intimate caress he wipes a tear
from her cheek, then raises his finger
to his mouth and licks it.

"Linda, girl," he says softly, "there
are things far worse than death in this
world. I've seen people beg to be where
Tim is now. There are . . . appetites.
Appetites that fall outside the pale.

Quinn is a man of such appetites. I, on the other hand, prefer the shortest path from A to B."

This statement confounds her.

"In business," he clarifies, seeing her reaction. "This machine generates electric current, in varying intensity. The clips attach to things that protrude, and the bolt is for . . . insertion."

Linda's stomach heaves.

"Get the bucket," Sands says.

Quinn moves behind her; a door opens and closes. Then Quinn returns and places a bucket stinking of vomit on the floor. The stench is so primal that it cuts through every last illusion.

They're not going to stop until they know everything, *she realizes.* Maybe not even then. Because he'll have to be sure. *Linda has never known such despair. She can protect no one. They'll find out about Penn Cage, where Julia is hiding—*

The generator hums ominously when Sands switches it on, like the motor in a dentist's office revving up to drive a drill. At the sound, the dog tenses with arousal. Despite its remarkable discipline, it cannot remain still.

"Where's your cell phone?" Sands asks.

"I threw it overboard."

"Why?"

"Tim told me to. He said you could track us with it."

Sands shoots Quinn a brief glance. "What else? What was on the phone? I can get your records."

"I got a text message I didn't understand."

"From who? Timothy?"

She nods quickly. "I think he used a stranger's phone. He thought that was safer."

"What did it say? Word for word."

"It wasn't words. Not really. It didn't make sense."

Sands picks up the bloody bolt on its wire. "It's very important that you remember, Linda."

"It was just letters that only half made sense. I thought he meant to send it to someone else."

"What were they?"

"*The first word was* Thief *with a capital* T." *Then* www, *like for 'World Wide Web.'*"

Quinn takes a small pad from his pocket and begins writing on it.

"What else?" Sands asked.

" 'Kill mommy,' that was next."

"Kill mommy?"

"I know, it makes no sense."

"Was there more?"

"The last said, 'Squirt too,' or something like that."

Sands's eyes narrow in confusion. "Are you lying to me, Linda?"

"No."

Sands sighs and nods to Quinn. Quinn steps forward and rips the blouse from her chest, his eyes flashing.

She struggles not to void on the chair. "What do you want to know?"

"Was that a code for something else? Who would Timmy be sending that to?"

"I don't know! I swear to God!"

"Wire her up," Quinn says. "Give her a jolt."

"I might, just," said Sands, "depending on how she answers the next question."

Sands nods toward the corner. "Turn the boy over. Show her his face."

Linda's gaze follows Quinn as he walks to the wall. He bends and pulls the bare-bottomed man over on his back. She's afraid the face will be butchered, but it's not. She recognizes a young Asian man she has seen a few times on the boat. Ben Li. She only knows who he is because of Tim. Li works in the security area, running the computer accounting system. On paper he's listed as a gaming consultant, but his real job is working some sort of illegal magic on the computers that track the profits. Tim only found this out because Ben is lonely, and he uses drugs to dull the ache. Unlike the other employees, Li isn't given monthly drug tests. In the past few weeks, Tim has become Ben's supplier. That somehow played into Tim's plan. Linda only learned this last week, and she wasn't sure she wanted to know, but it seemed important to Tim to tell her. It was as though by telling her this—information that could get him killed—Tim was proving how much he loved her, trusted her.

"Do you know who that is?" Sands asks.

"Ben Li."

"Jaysus," whispers Quinn. "Fucking Jessup."

"Do you know what he does?"

"Something with computers, that's all I know. I only found that out a couple of days ago."

Quinn savagely kicks the body on the floor. Ben Li doesn't flinch.

"Is he dead?" Linda asks.

"Not yet," Sands replies. "Soon."

Gooseflesh rises on the back of her neck. She tries to shift, but the straps hold her fast to the chair.

"Will you move that bucket?" she asks. "It's making me sick."

"Tell me about Penn Cage."

"What about him?"

"We don't have time for this," Quinn snaps. "Juice the cunt and get it over with. Give me five minutes with the lying sleeveen."

"Please," she whimpers, searching for something human in the depths of Sands's eyes. "Please. I'll tell you whatever you want to know. Tim is dead. What's the point in hiding anything?"

Sands's eyes offer her nothing. "Penn Cage."

"Tim went to school with him. He worshipped the guy. He called him the Eagle Scout. He said Penn was the only man he knew he could trust to do the right thing."

"And what did he mean by 'the right thing'?"

"Arrest you, I guess. Tim was going to steal something that could stop what's been going on. He wouldn't tell me what, and I didn't want to know. I tried to talk him out of it, I swear. He was like a little boy. He had no idea what he was up against."

"Too fucking right," says Quinn.

"Look, I don't care what you're doing. You know that. I worked one of those fights, for God's sake. Remember? That's where you first really noticed me. But I didn't tell a soul what happened there. I never have!"

Sands gives her a chiding smile. "You told Timothy."

She closes her eyes in surrender.

"How many times did he talk to the mayor?"

"Just once that I know of. Last night."

"And he was going to meet him to-night?"

"Yes."

Sands reaches out with the bloody bolt and touches its tip to the hollow of her neck. The cold metal alone seems to shock her. "One more question," he says, dragging the bolt down and across her chest, stopping at her left nipple. "The most important one."

"What?"

"Did Tim say anything about making copies of what he stole?"

"No."

Sands circles her aureole with the head of the bolt. "Not so fast. Think about it, Linda. Tim was smarter than I gave him credit for. And a smart man would know that he might not make it off the boat with a disc. Did he mention hiding a copy anywhere?"

"No. He didn't tell me anything about a disc. He didn't want to put me in danger."

Sands smiles. "But he did, didn't he?"

Dropping the bolt on the cart, Sands picks up one of the alligator clips. "Hold her head," he says mildly.

Quinn moves behind the chair and locks his forearm around her neck, cutting off all air.

Sands forces open the clip, then attaches it to her upper lip, just beneath her nose. Quinn gives her neck a hard squeeze, then releases her head. Sands steps back and rubs his stubbled chin, regarding her without emotion.

"Did he ever sneak a notebook computer on board?"

"Not that I know of."

"He never talked about trying to transmit what he stole while he was on the boat?"

"No. He didn't tell me anything like that."

Sands lets his hand fall on a black dial atop the generator.

"Don't," she pleads softly. "I've told you everything. If I ever meant anything to you, don't do this."

"Your word's not enough. I have

to know if you're holding back. Last chance to come clean."

She shakes her head. "Didn't I always do what you wanted? Did I ever say no?"

"No, you didn't. But you lied, Linda. It's not that you fucked him, you understand? You're as human as the next woman. But you tried to help him take me down."

Her brain is transmitting a speech signal when the current hits her, scrambling every impulse in her body. She flails her head, trying to escape the blowtorch burning her lip, but it follows wherever she goes. The pain arcs up her nose to a point between her eyes, which feel as if they'll explode if the electricity doesn't stop.

Then it stops.

"Pissed herself," Quinn observes. "Should have made her go before-hand."

Linda is sobbing in the chair, with relief that the pain has ended, with ter-ror of the agony to come. The white dog shivers from the effort of remain-ing still.

"Tell me the rest," Sands says patiently. "You don't want any more of that, do you?"

She shakes her head hopelessly.

"Quinn will put that clip anywhere I tell him, and he'll run the generator all night long. He'd like nothing better."

"Nothing," Quinn says simply. "I think she wants the bolt, mate."

A sharp ringing startles them all. It's a telephone, Linda realizes, not a cellular, but a hard line. It must be lying on the floor in the corner. Quinn curses and walks to the corner, then crouches to answer the phone. After speaking softly, he hangs up and says, "They want you up in the cashier's cage."

Sands sniffs, then shoots his cuffs and pats the dog's head. "Take the clip off."

Quinn blinks in confusion. "What?"

"Get it off."

While Quinn reluctantly obeys, Sands reaches under the top shelf of the cart and brings out a paper cup.

"Drink this," he says, offering it to Linda.

"What is it?"

"Just drink it and be thankful."

"Will it kill me?"

"No. It will make you sleep."

She sniffs the cup. The clear fluid inside smells like Sprite. "Will it hurt?"

"No. It's a drug called Versed. It's like Valium. It's what they give children before they sew them up in the casualty ward."

"Casualty ward?"

"Emergency room."

A faint memory of a kind doctor stitching her knee long ago brings fresh tears to Linda's eyes. For some reason, she is suddenly sure the doctor was Penn Cage's father, Tom Cage. With a silent prayer that Penn and his daughter will be all right, she nods to Sands and opens her mouth. The fluid tastes just the way it smells. Sprite, gone half-flat. She coughs as she swallows, but it all goes down. She half believes the drink will kill her, but she's past caring. She cannot endure the clips or the bolt.

Sands walks forward and gives her a strange smile. "You gave a good ride, I'll say that. One of the best.

Quinn's been itching to have a go at you from the beginning. Now he'll get his chance, I guess."

She shakes her head slowly. "Don't leave me with him. Please. Give me enough of that stuff to finish it. Please."

Quinn's eyes flash behind Sands. "Now where's the fun in that?

Linda feels herself fading already. The hum of the generator is the brightest thing in the room.

"Where are you taking them?" Sands asks. "The farm or the island?"

"The farm. I'd just as soon stay out there tonight, if you're okay with it?"

Sands's voice is tight. "I don't care what you do with her, if that's what you're asking."

That's it, right there, *Linda thinks. No one had ever really cared what anyone did with her. No one but Tim.*

"Cunts like this run off all the time," Quinn says. "With Jessup dead, no one would even ask what happened to her, if it weren't for the pictures."

"The pictures sell the story," Sands says. "Just make sure no one finds her."

Quinn laughs, dark and low. "Don't worry. The lads are starving."

A black curtain falls over the world.

Linda awakens to a cold wind on her face, a sky filled with stars. A silver moon shines down like a pitiless eye, made hazy by fog. She hears a motor, feels herself pitching like someone trying to lie on a trampoline while someone else jumps on it. She tries to brace herself, but her hands are bound with rope. Worse, they're numb. On the next bounce, she rolls over and retches on hard, white plastic.

Boat, *she realizes.* I'm in a boat. A *real* boat.

She looks up from the white deck. Seamus Quinn sits behind a steering wheel, the wind blowing his curly black hair wildly behind him. He grins down at her, his eyes flickering like silver points of light.

"Wakey wakey," he says, mocking an Australian accent. "You've got company now, Benny lad."

Linda turns her neck and looks behind her. Ben Li lies hog-tied on the deck behind her, a strip of duct tape over his mouth. His eyes bulge, and in them she reads a desperate plea for help. As if she could do anything. After the first few moments, he stops straining against his bonds and falls back against the deck. Ben Li graduated from a college called Cal Tech, she remembers. His parents are Chinese immigrants. Tim said Cal Tech was better than any school in the South, when it came to computers. Linda wonders if Ben Li ever imagined he would end up hog-tied in a boat in the Mississippi River.

"Where are we going?" she asks.

Quinn laughs. "You know where. To have some fun."

"Fun for who?"

He laughs harder, then jerks the speedboat's wheel as though to avoid an obstacle in the water. "Me first. Then the dogs."

Linda swallows, trying to block her memory of the one night she worked a dogfight for the company. It was like stripping in Vegas after a fight. All the girls hated it. Boxing earned millions because men were drawn to violence like a drug. But dogfights took it to another level entirely. . . .

It was as if ten thousand years of civilization had been stripped away in an hour. Every guy in the place wanted to fuck or fight, and half didn't care which. If they got you in the VIP room, they wouldn't take no for an answer, and if they fought, it hardly mattered who won or lost. They just craved the release.

Fighting was the only way some men could have sex with other men. Men like Quinn. Fighting or sharing a woman. That was what they really wanted, and what she'd narrowly escaped the night of the dogfight. She'd only needed one night to know she'd never go back. How many times had the drunks started chanting, "Train! Train! Train!"? She'd finally persuaded Sands to take her to a separate building, and she'd had to service him to get him to do that. But at least she'd escaped what the other girls got. Some had apparently done that kind of thing before, but others hadn't. Some had been more afraid than she was—

"I've been watching you for a long time," Quinn says. "Strutting up and down like the queen. You've been off-limits long enough. Tonight I'm going to find out what's kept the boss interested for so long."

Linda shivers and watches the moon grow fainter as the fog on the river thickens. She wishes she knew enough about the stars to know whether she's moving upstream or down. But even if she did, the heavy mist is quickly whiting out everything around the boat.

"I think you got to him," Quinn says. "Anybody else, he'd have had that bolt up their arse and the juice full on."

She shakes her head. "No. It's not in him."

Quinn laughs. "Don't be too sure. If Jessup hadn't got away, he'd have suffered like a saint."

Linda looks at Quinn in alarm. "Got away? I thought Tim was dead."

"That's what I mean. Falling off that bluff was the best break that header ever caught. If he'd lived, Sands would have made the crucifixion look like a mild digging. You cross the boss, you get special treatment. Like Benny back there."

Quinn wants me to talk, *she realizes.* He wants a relationship.

"You ever see anything eaten alive?" he asks, turning the boat slightly to starboard.

Linda doesn't answer, but one of her cats used to catch chipmunks and torture them for hours before she killed them. Let the pitiful creature run a few feet, feel a taste of freedom, then pounce and rip its belly open with a claw—

"Nothing like it in the world," Quinn says, marveling at his insight. "That's why the Romans loved the games. That's life, right in front of you. Kill or be killed. Eat or be eaten. You're a predator or you're prey. And deep down, everybody knows which they are, right from the beginning."

A huge beam sweeps over the boat, stops, comes back, then arcs away. Linda has an impression of treetops shot with a flashbulb to her right.

"Just like that stupid bastard," Quinn says, nodding at Ben Li. "Too clever for his own good. He makes more money in a day than his parents earned in ten years, but it wasn't enough. Had to fuck it up. Look at him. A genius, they say. By noon tomorrow, a pit bull will be shitting out his brains. Next morning, his bones will be gnawed to powder."

Linda's stomach rolls. The night of the dogfight, she'd kept away from the pit as much as possible. The noise alone had sickened her, and the brief glimpses she'd been unable to avoid were burned into her memory. Two blood-soaked, muscle-bound animals locked in nearly motionless combat for an hour, one's massive jaws buried in the chest of the other, each struggling for advantage while two dozen screaming men goaded them to kill.

"And me?" she forces herself to ask.

Quinn purses his lips like a man figuring a price on something. "The day after, maybe. Depends on how interesting you make things. If you didn't know so fucking much, I'd keep you around for the weekend. Rent you out. Lots of big boys coming in for the next couple of weeks. They like their business mixed with pleasure."

The boat leaps free of the water, then smashes back down. Soon it's bouncing like a tractor over farm rows. It's a wake, *Linda realizes.* Now the spotlight makes sense. We must be overtaking a tugboat pushing barges.

"I have to go the bathroom," she says. "Bad."

"Go in your pants. You already did it once."

"*No, I mean* really *go. I can't hold it. I'm sick. You don't want it in the boat.*"

"Christ on a crutch. There's an ice chest under the seat behind Benny. Go in that."

Linda works herself up onto her elbows, which is more difficult than she thought with her hands bound, then crawls back to the stern, where Ben Li looks desperately at her through bloodshot eyes. Putting her mouth beside his ear, she says, "I wish I could help you. I'm sorry."

She smells fear coming off him like body odor. She remembers her thought back on the Queen, *that she'd entered a state beyond fear. Then later, in the chair, she'd realized that only the dead are beyond fear. But now, struggling to her feet, using Ben Li as a prop for her bound hands, she isn't so sure.*

For a moment the fog breaks, and she can see the shore, lone treetops whipping past fifty yards to her right. To her left she sees only mist. A hundred yards in front of them, a tugboat churns the river into a maelstrom. Quinn is running fast enough to pull a half dozen water-skiers.

"Can you slow down a little?" she calls.

"Just do your business! Christ."

Bending carefully at the waist, Linda pulls the edge of the rear seat up with her bound hands. She marvels at the bright white lid of the Igloo. The logo brings tears to her eyes. She remembers picnics and parties from years long past, reaching down with a sweating arm and pulling a wine cooler from the ice—

"I thought you had to go," Quinn shouts, looking back at her with annoyance. "Take your bloody pants down. Give us a preview, eh?"

Linda glances down at Ben Li. Before, his eyes had been pleading, but now they watch her with a strange fascination, waiting to see if she'll take down her pants. It is all about power, she knows. Ben Li heard Quinn talking about him and the dogs. He knows he'll be the first to die, and all he can do is lie there watching, waiting, probably praying for some kind of miracle, or even just a diversion before death.

Around the boat the fog has thickened again, turning the night a deeper shade of black.

Linda straightens up. From deep within her, so deep that she's forgotten it was there, something begins to rise. The density of it fills her as it expands. It's love, she realizes. Or whatever you call the thing that huddles in the last dark closet you've locked against the world, waiting to find something like itself. Linda has never known why she let herself go so far with Tim. She knew all along that he wouldn't leave his family. She wouldn't have asked him to, though she wanted it desperately. But now—standing almost in the river Tim died within sight of—she knows.

She wanted a child.

Over thirty and she'd never even been pregnant. But she was still young enough. And Tim wouldn't have had to leave Julia to give her that. Tim was the closest thing Linda had ever had to a child of her own, a big little boy who wanted the world to be better than it was. Now he was gone, and with him her hope of a child.

"He loved me," she says aloud, once, for all the times she'd yearned to say it to the people around her.

This knowledge surges in her breast, filling her so profoundly that a faint radiance shimmers from her skin. She feels like the Madonna in the old Italian painting printed in her grandmother's Bible. All of this she gives to Ben Li in a single downward glance, one long look that holds a woman's infinite mercy.

"Do you have to go or not, you crazy cunt?"

Seamus Quinn's angry voice pierces night and fog, but not the light that shines from Linda Church.

"Yes," she says. "I have to go."

With the grace of a bird taking flight, she steps onto the lid of the Igloo and leaps into the river.

CHAPTER

16

If physicists want to develop a time machine, they should explore fear. Fear dilates and compresses time without limit. For desperate people awaiting rescue, every instant stretches into unendurable agony; for those awaiting death by cancer, the earth spins relentlessly, shortening the days until they pass like fanned pages in a book. Trapped in our bodies, perception is all, and the engine of perception is hunger for life.

Before tonight, I could not have imagined playing a six-hour card game with my father. Yet here we sit, betting matchsticks without expression, occasionally searching each others' eyes or looking with disbelief at the guns lying between us on the sofa. I'm not much of a card-player, so it's been a one-sided contest. We've spoken enough to persuade who-ever might be listening that we're passing a long night while Dad waits to see that my heart is all right, and typed enough that Dad is fully caught up on the circum-stances surrounding Tim's murder. I'm fairly confident that there's no video sur-veillance of my upper hallway—ditto any keystroke-sensing technology around the house—for our desultory computer con-versations would surely have earned us a call from Jonathan Sands by now.

"Ante," Dad says.

"Sorry." I push a red-tipped matchstick across the tatted surface of the sofa cush-ion.

"You keep playing like this, I'm going to own this house before the sun comes up."

"Sorry I'm distracted. I keep thinking I feel my heart starting up again."

"Let me worry about that. You play poker."

We have not been without interruptions.

Libby Jensen called twice, nearly cata-
tonic with panic about what might happen
to her son in jail. I did what I could to reassure her, but in truth the time has come
for Soren to pay a price for his misbehav-
ior. Looking at life through cell bars for a
few weeks will probably do more than any
treatment center to convince him that he's
had all the drugs he needs for a while.
During her second call, Libby asked if
she could come over, but I shot that idea
down immediately, in a voice that brooked
no appeal.

Two minutes after we hung up, I heard
an engine stop in the street before my
house. Thinking Libby had come anyway,
I got up and walked to the front window. A
Chevy Malibu with rental tags was parked
in front of Caitlin's house. The passenger
door popped open, and Caitlin got out
laughing. She said something to someone
in the car, then ran up to her front door
and waved back at the car. The bohemian
filmmaker I'd met earlier got out and
walked lazily—perhaps drunkenly—up to
the porch and followed her inside. I heard
their laughter even through my closed
window. Pathetically, I hoped the car was

still running, but it didn't seem to be. I stood looking down at the car until I sensed my father standing at my shoulder.

"What is it?" he whispered.

"Caitlin."

"Huh."

"She already went in." I gave it a moment. "Not alone."

Dad thought about this, then sighed, squeezed my arm, and walked back to the couch. I should have followed, but I stood there stubbornly, stupidly, waiting for the light in her bedroom to click on and destroy whatever hope remained that she had somehow returned to town for me, and not for a quick party with her new playmate.

My breath fogged the glass, faded, fogged it again. A dozen times? A hundred? Then I heard a bang, and Caitlin ran back out of the house. She was still laughing, and the filmmaker seemed to be chasing her. She carried a wine bottle in one hand, and she held it up as though she meant to brain him with it. This time she jumped into the driver's seat, and the man—Jan, I remember now—barely got himself folded into the passenger side

before she sped up Washington Street
toward the bluff and the river, never once
looking at my house.

I walked back to the sofa, trying to dis-
sociate myself from the anger rising in
me. In the wake of Tim's murder, Caitlin's
laughter seemed obscene. Surely, I
thought, she must know about his death
by now. Tim wasn't a close friend of hers,
but she'd known him, and she knew we'd
been close friends as boys. But all she
seemed to be thinking about was getting
drunk and finding a good time.

Two hours after the wine-scavenging
trip, her car drew me to the window again.
This time the Malibu pulled into Caitlin's
driveway. She emerged unsteadily but
alone and walked to the side door. For a
brief moment she glanced across the
street, up toward my window, but by then
I was far enough behind the curtain that
she couldn't see me. She turned away
and vanished into the house.

"I want to look up something on Med-
line," Dad says. "I might want to prescribe
you something." With a groan he picks
the MacBook off the floor, pecks out a

long message, then pushes it over the matchsticks to me.

I've been thinking about Tim's story. This isn't the first time we've had that kind of thing around here. And I'm not talking about the flatboat days, either. I mean the 1960s and 70s. Just down the river on the Louisiana side, at Morville Plantation. They had a big gambling operation and some white slavery too. Literally. They had taken girls from God-knows-where and were holding them against their will, using them as whores. The sheriff ran the whole parish and took a cut of all the action. I've heard horror stories from patients, and I had a couple of brushes with the place myself. My point is, the situation was the same as now, in that the people who were supposed to stop those problems were making money off them instead.

I read his message carefully, then type *I've been thinking too. Corruption doesn't have to be widespread to serve its purpose. All it takes is one well-placed cop, one sheriff's deputy, one FBI agent, one*

selectman, or one assistant in the gover-
nor's office etc. to keep Sands informed.
The spider pays off a dozen of the right
people, and he has his web. And God
knows the casinos have the money to
buy anybody.

Dad motions for me to give him back
the computer. *You need somebody from*
the outside, Son. Way outside. Somebody
with experience handling this kind of
thing. I've been thinking all night, and I
keep on coming back to Walt Garrity.

The name brings me up short, but two
seconds after I read it, I sense that Dad's
onto something. Walt Garrity is a retired
Texas Ranger I met while serving as an
assistant DA in Houston. He was the chief
investigator on a capital murder case I
was working, and when he heard I was
from Mississippi, he asked if I knew an old
Korean War medic by the name of Tom
Cage. That brought about the reunion of
two soldiers who'd served in the same
army unit in Korea decades earlier and
also started a new friendship for me, one
that lasted through several cases. I haven't
talked to Garrity in a couple of years
(since I last pumped him for information

while researching a novel set in Texas), but my memory of him is undimmed. He's a cagey old fox who seems reticent until you get him talking; then you realize he has a dry sense of humor and long experience dealing with human frailty in all its forms. Walt Garrity is the kind of lawman who'll try almost anything before resorting to gunplay but, once pushed to that extreme, is as dangerous as any man on the right side of the law can be.

Dad takes back the computer and types, *Walt helped take on the big gambling operation in Galveston in the fifties and sixties, when he first became a Ranger. I know that sounds like a long time ago, but vice doesn't change much.*

This reminds me of Mrs. Pierce's warning—"Vice is vice, whatever cloak it wears"—but I'm not sure that's true, given the technology of the digital age. Still, I can't deny that the thought of Walt Garrity gives me some comfort. Walt may be over seventy and officially retired, but I've heard he still takes on occasional undercover jobs for the Harris County DA's office.

You might have something there, I

type. *But I can't risk calling Walt until I have a secure line of communication.*

You leave Walt to me, Dad types. *I'll set it up. And don't warn me to be careful, goddamn it. I know how to sneak around.*

As if summoned by my dad's assertion about sneaking around, my mother's voice floats down the hall. "What are you doing here, Tom?" she asks in the stage whisper common to grandmothers who don't want to wake sleeping children.

Dad and I look up simultaneously, startled by the image of Mom gliding up the hallway in her housecoat, her eyes fully alert. The Deep South still boasts a few women like Peggy Cage, "society" ladies in their seventies who spent their childhoods on subsistence farms during the Great Depression, and who, by virtue of backbreaking work and sacrifice, managed to attend college, marry a man with an ironclad work ethic, and rise to a level their parents never dreamed of. My mother may look at home in a Laura Ashley dress and know which fork to use, but she picked cotton all the way through college. If World War Three broke out tomorrow, she could plant a truck garden and start raising hogs the next day. As I heard her tell one of my biology teachers at school, "Once you twist the head off a chicken, you never really forget how to do it."

"Penn had a little panic attack," Dad says, motioning her over to the computer.

My mother freezes where she is, her eyes moving from my father's face to mine, then to the computer. She moves forward and kneels before the sofa.

Dad types, *We have a problem and we can't discuss it out loud. You and Annie are in danger. Your lives have been threatened. We have people coming from Houston to take you to a safe place.*

I watch my mother process this information. She looks shocked, then angry. Then she types, *How serious are these threats?*

Dad responds, *Jack Jessup's boy has already been murdered.*

Mom closes her eyes and sighs deeply. *When are they getting here?*

An hour or less.

What about school?

I shake my head and type, *Think Ray Presley times ten,* referring to a man my mother thought of as evil incarnate. *If you want to take Annie's textbooks along and work with her, that's great, but safety is the priority. We've learned that the hard way.*

Mom nods with resignation. *I'll get Annie's things ready,* she types, *but if we can't discuss this, I don't want to wake her until the last minute. I'll tell her it's a surprise vacation just for us.*

I nod agreement and start to type a reply, but as my fingers touch the keyboard, I hear the sound of the downstairs television rise. Dad and I left it on to distract any listeners, but I'm positive the audio track has suddenly doubled in volume. My father lost most of his high-frequency hearing long ago, but even he notices the amplitude change. He's already holding the .357 snubnose in his hand.

I lean down to Mom's ear and whisper, "Get back to Annie's room. If you hear a shot, call 911."

She looks longingly at the pistol on the sofa, but I motion for her to move to the bedroom. Dad is already moving toward the head of the stairs, but I catch up to him and pull him back.

"I'm going down first," I whisper. "You back me up. If there's more than one target, I'll hit the deck and fire low, you shoot high."

"Could it be Kelly's friends?"

I glance at my watch. "Not unless they drove eighty-five all the way."

Dad nods and moves aside so that I can reach the stairs. I slip off my shoes, then step on the top tread and move quickly downward, staying close to the wall to minimize the creaks.

Halfway down, I see a well-dressed man standing in my front hall holding a sign in his hands like a limo driver in an airport. My finger tightens on the trigger, but the word BLACKHAWK printed in red at the top of the sign stops me.

I hold up my hand to stop Dad, then read the words below the company name: YOU'RE SAFE NOW. WALK FORWARD. With relief surging through me, I look back upstairs and give Dad the OK sign. After he lowers his gun, I move up and whisper, "The cavalry's here. Get Mom and Annie ready."

He turns without a word and moves up the stairs with what for him is dispatch.

When I reach the ground floor, the Blackhawk operator sets the poster aside and gives my hand a businesslike shake. He's wearing a black sport coat with a gray polo shirt beneath it, and he obviously chose his position because it's not visible from the street. Like Daniel Kelly, he looks about thirty-five, but his hair is cut military-style, where Kelly has the blond locks of a tennis pro. Before I can speak, the operator passes me a handwritten note and a typed sheet of paper. The note reads, *I'm Jim Samuels. There were two men watching your house. They're alive but neutralized. We took their guns and cell phones. We need to get the packages moving in under ten minutes. Are they ready?*

I nod, then hold up my hand and splay my fingers to indicate five minutes. Leaning up to his ear, I whisper, "How did you guys get here so fast?"

Samuels smiles briefly, then whispers, "Dan Kelly called me and told me to gun it all the way."

While I say a silent thank-you to Kelly, Samuels points to the typed sheet in my hand. It reads, *Daniel Kelly should arrive*

Natchez in approximately 40 hours. We've rented room 235 at the Days Inn. Kelly's gear bag is waiting for him there. There's a satellite phone in your kitchen pantry, detailed instructions with it. There's a number programmed into the phone that you can call for updates on your mother and daughter. We'll be encrypted on our end, but be careful where you use the phone. Kelly told us to make absolutely sure that you don't want to come with us and wait until he gets here before you proceed with anything.

I look up and shake my head, and the Blackhawk man acknowledges with a sober nod. Leaning forward again, I whisper, "Do you feel confident about getting out of town safely?"

Samuels gives me a thumbs-up with such assurance that I suddenly wish I were going with them. Then he leans in close and says, "We were gentle with your watchers, to minimize reprisals against you. You'll have to decide how best to handle the situation. We left them behind the house."

It takes a moment to absorb that. "May I have their cell phones?"

Samuels digs in his pocket and brings out two identical BlackBerrys. I lay them on the side table. "Thanks."

"We can get you the phone records on those numbers, if you like."

"I'd appreciate it. What about their guns?"

He shrugs. "It's your call. They're going to be pretty angry at whoever they see next."

"I'm better off giving the guns back, I think."

Samuels goes to my kitchen and returns with two Glock automatics. For a puzzled moment, I watch him crouch quickly and slip the guns into the side table's bottom drawer. Then I realize my mother is escorting Annie down the stairs.

Annie's wearing the clothes she had laid out to wear to the balloon race, and she's carrying the "grandma's house" suitcase that she packs for weekends with my parents. My mother has put on slacks and a light sweater, and her gray hair is pinned up in a bun.

I'm not quite sure how to handle this situation, but Samuels walks right up to my mom and introduces himself calmly and quietly. It's easy to believe these guys spend their days guarding traveling CEOs and foreign heads of state. After a few seconds, Samuels breaks away from Mom and speaks quietly beside my ear.

"In sixty seconds, our escape vehicle will pull onto the sidewalk in front of your door. My partner's in your kitchen now, covering our flank. We'll take your mother and daughter out in a quick rush, then my partner will return for the bags. If we have any problems, we'll leave the bags and buy whatever they need at the destination. Understood?"

"Yes."

Dad steps up beside me, but before he can speak, Samuels gives us both a look of surprising empathy. "You've only got twenty seconds to say good-bye," he says. "Don't show any fear. They're going to be as safe as the crown jewels. Give them a smile to remember until they see you again."

Dad moves quickly to Mom and Annie, but my mother steps past him and looks at me with utter clarity. "I know whatever you're doing must seem important, but please remember this. You are the only parent that little girl has left. She's the most important thing in this family. Tom and I are old now. She needs you. Nothing matters more than Annie, Penn. *Nothing.* Not honor or justice or anything you learned in school. Your flesh and blood." Mom reaches up and touches my cheek. "I'm only saying what Sarah would if she were alive. Sometimes men forget what's important. Don't."

"I won't," I promise, knowing that despite my best intentions, I have done so before. But that's why I'm acting decisively now.

"Time," says Samuels.

"Daddy?"

I step past Mom and sweep Annie up into my arms. At eleven, she's no longer a little girl, but I could still carry her five miles if I had to. Her eyes are crusted with sleep, but even now they project the perception I know so well.

"Where are we going?" she asks.

"It's a surprise. I'm coming to see you soon, though. Will you take care of Gram?"

Annie smiles. "You know I will. I sure hate to miss the races. I wanted to fly in a balloon."

"When you get back, I'll get Mr. Steve

to take us up. As many times as you want. Okay?"

She nods, but balloon races aren't what's on her mind. She pushes her mouth close to my ear and says, "Will you tell Caitlin I've been missing her?"

I close my eyes and force down the emotion welling up from within.

"Mr. Cage, our ride's coming up the block. We've got to move."

I hug Annie tight and murmur, "I'll tell her," in her ear. Then I hand her to Jim Samuels, who carries her to the front door while Annie stares back at me over his shoulder.

Another hard shoulder brushes past me, and Samuels's partner joins him at the door. He's wearing an earpiece, and he seems to be receiving updates from it. He and Samuels communicate with hand motions; then Samuels tells my mother something, and she nods. He looks back at me, raises his hand to indicate five seconds, and ticks his fingers down one by one.

My heart tries to race ahead of itself, then the door is open and the Blackhawk men are rushing Mom and Annie across the open space like the royal family through a tunnel of paparazzi. I glimpse a big black Suburban before the door slams, then the growl of a modified V-8 roars loudly enough to shake my front wall and wake everyone on the street. With a screech of rubber the Suburban blasts up Washington Street like an Abrams tank heading off to war.

"Good God," Dad says, still staring at the front door. "What now?"

"You go to work."

"What are you going to do?"

I take the confiscated guns from the side table and shove them into my waistband. "Return some personal effects."

"Who do those belong to?"

"The men who were watching the house. The Blackhawk guys took them."

"Jesus. Don't you want me to come with you?"

"Nope. I'm just going to give them a friendly message for their boss."

Dad studies me for some time, then takes his keys from the tabletop. "I have my cell phone. Call me if you need me."

I give him a smile of gratitude. "I did."

He smiles back. "I guess you did. Okay. I'll take care of that other thing."

I'm puzzled for a moment, but by the time Dad says, "The medicine for your heart," I've remembered: *Walt Garrity.*

With three guns in my waistband, I grab a paring knife from the kitchen, then walk out my back door, wondering what I'll find.

The previous owners installed a stone fountain on my back patio, and this morning two men wearing dark windbreakers are sitting on the bricks, leaning back against the fountain's basin. Their hands and feet are bound with plastic restraints, and their mouths are covered with black tape. When they see me, their eyes bulge with anger, but fear as well.

I walk slowly toward them, making sure they see the guns in my belt. Both men have the thin legs and overdeveloped upper physiques of bodybuilders. The right breasts of their windbreakers read MAGNO-LIA QUEEN. Above the letters is an embroidered paddle wheeler; above this a pair of dice. I squat before the men and smile.

"Surprised to see me?"

The guy on the left nods meaningfully,

silently promising revenge. He has hair like black steel wool, and his sweat smells of alcohol.

"Here's the deal," I tell him. "Option one, I give you back your guns and phones, and you take a message to your boss for me. Option two, I call Sands and have him drive down here and see you like this. Now, I'm going to take the tape off your partner here, and he can make the choice."

I reach out and rip off the tape with one fast jerk. The second man gasps in pain.

"Best way, really," I tell him. "I've experienced it myself."

"You are *soooo* fucked," he says. "I wouldn't trade places with you for a million bucks."

I smile and start to reapply the duct tape. "I guess that's option two."

"Wait!" he says, all bravado gone. "No matter what message you give us, he'll send us back to bring you to him. You might as well come with us now."

My watch reads 6:51 a.m. I'm scheduled to fly in the first race at 7:15, but I have no desire to do so. Hans Necker will be disappointed if I don't show, and the selectmen will go batshit, but maybe that's a good thing. At least I can promise Sands that if he kills me this morning, half the town will be searching for me in less than an hour.

With two quick jerks of the knife, I free both men's legs. They hold out their bound hands, but I shake my head, wondering if either of these men was present when Tim was tortured.

"I don't think so, guys. Let's go see the boss man."

CHAPTER

17

Julia Jessup awakens to the crying of her son. She blinks crusty eyes, rolls onto her husband's thigh. Groaning in exhaustion, she reaches down to shove Tim's leg, to tell him to go get the bottle—

—and freezes where she lies. Her hand is not on Tim's leg. It's on the baby's belly.

For a few blessed moments she'd forgotten. Now, in the span of a closing synapse, the infinite weight of death and grief returns, pressing her into the mattress.

He left you, *says her father, dead almost twenty-five years now.*

Alone, *says her mother, who followed him not long afterward.* Who'll help you now? Who cares whether you live or die?

Julia rolls all the way over and sees faint light showing through the curtain. This is Daisy's house. It was the only place she could think to run, the last place anyone would look. Daisy took care of Julia when she was a baby, before her father lost it, when they still had money to pay for a maid. Daisy's house is old, not even a house really. A shotgun shack, like the ones in New Orleans. The floor is rotted through in places, and when the wind blows hard, the holes whistle and the bedclothes sway.

The baby's cry grows louder, more insistent. Tim junior is hungry. He doesn't care that his father is gone. He knows only the ache in his belly. But Julia knows. Her father killed himself when she was eighteen, and she's missed him every day since. So many times she's needed him, or someone. God, how different everything would

have been had he lived. And how different will life be for her baby? His childhood will be a struggle against want,
his mother always away, struggling in
vain to keep ahead of the bills. This
dark foreknowledge is like a festering
mass in her stomach. Tim left nothing
behind him but a mortgage. It wasn't
his fault, really. He had nothing to
leave—

"Now, now, I hear that baby cryin',"
sings a chiding voice. "He just a
bawlin', and you lyin' in bed like Miss
Astor."

Daisy is close to eighty now, but she
still gets around like a woman of sixty-
five, despite her arthritis. Her flower-
print dress crinkles as she sits on the
bed and gives the baby a bottle to
suck. Tim junior's eyes go wide and
blue as urgency changes into bliss,
and he grips the bottle with one strong
hand. Daisy tries to take the other in
hers, but the child will not be led.

"I used to look at you like that,"
Daisy says wistfully.

"I know," Julia whispers. "I wish I
was back there again."

Daisy shakes her head, her eyes on the baby. "Everybody wish that sometime. But there ain't no going back."

Julia closes her eyes. The smell of her own breath sickens her. She ran out of the house without even a toothbrush.

"You hungry yet?" Daisy asks.

"No."

"You gotta eat sometime. Can't take care of no baby without getting something down yourself."

There's a sound of horsehair rope being stretched, and Julia knows that's Daisy turning her head. She looks up into the yellowed eyes and says, "Thanks for letting me stay here. I didn't have anywhere else to go."

Daisy smiles. "Well, I think you gon' be here a while yet."

Julia goes still. "Why is that?"

"Well, there was something in the newspaper this morning. I hate to say nothing about it, but I guess there's no point hiding it."

"What was it? Something about Tim?"

Daisy's crinkled lips curl around her

dentures like dark papier-mâché. Julia's glad Daisy put her teeth in. Last night, the old woman looked one step away from the grave. "I can't read too good no more," she says, "but it didn't sound good."

"Where is it?" Julia asks, sitting up in alarm. "What did they say?"

"On the kitchen table."

Julia bounds out of bed and runs for the kitchen.

CHAPTER

18

The guard at the gatehouse of Jonathan Sands's home stands gaping at the two bound men in the backseat of my Saab.

"I said I want to see Mr. Sands."

"Does he know you're coming?"

"No. I have a trespassing problem I'd like to discuss with him."

"Just a minute." The guard vanishes into his hut. Like the men in the backseat, he is American, not Irish, but the brief look he gave my passengers told them all they need to know about the trouble coming their way.

"Are you armed?" the guard asks, reappearing at my window.

I point down at my waistband, where the butts of three handguns jut from my waistband.

"You need to leave those with me."

"I go in like this, or I drive away now."

The guard vanishes again. I check my watch. The first balloons should be taking off any minute. Judging from the treetops, the wind looks to be gusting seven to ten miles per hour, which is enough to stop many pilots from launching. During the drive over from Washington Street, I received a text from Paul Labry, informing me that the balloons would be taking off from a vacant lot just off Highway 61 South. The destination of this morning's "race" is predetermined, but the launch point varies according to the direction of the wind, with various pilots making complex calculations and jockeying for takeoff positions in spaces just big enough to accommodate a launch without hitting power lines or other lethal obstacles. I texted Paul that a family emergency would prevent me making the launch in time and that he should fly in my place. Labry has already sent four anxious text messages in reply, asking what the problem is. I've responded by begging him to trust me and to try to keep Hans Necker from getting too upset.

I'm receiving yet another message from Labry when a black Jeep thunders up behind my Saab and skids to a stop. In my side mirror, I see Seamus Quinn jump out and march toward my car. The Irishman must have driven all the way over from the *Magnolia Queen.* I roll down my window, allowing an endless stream of curses into the car.

"What the fuck do you want, just?" he growls. Quinn is a darkly handsome man with bad teeth and eyes that glint like polished metal.

"I want to talk to your boss. It won't take long."

Quinn plants both hands on the side of my car and glares into the backseat. "You fuckers banjaxed it, did you?"

In my rearview mirror the two bruisers hunch in the backseat like toddlers dreading a spanking. Quinn stares in amazement as I take two Glocks from my waistband and hand them to him butt-first.

"I'm already late for something, and if I don't show, people are going to come looking."

The glinting eyes narrow, but Quinn finally waves me forward with a guarded smile. "I'll follow you in, your lordship."

As he walks away, the gate rattles open on its electric chain, and I drive through under the watchful eye of a video camera mounted on a pole to my right. Is Sands watching from his bedroom? I wonder as my car tops a low rise, and I see the casino manager's house for the first time. In a city famed for Greek Revival, Spanish, and Italianate mansions dating to before the Civil War, Sands has chosen the closest thing to a Miami drug lord's palace as his residence. The linked boxes of white stucco may overlook the river, but they look like alien spacecraft that landed in the antebellum South by mistake, crushing an acre of pink azaleas when they set down.

"Why does Sands live here?" I ask the guys in the backseat.

"Why not?" one says sullenly.

"There's concrete and steel under that stucco," says the other. "He won't sleep in a house that won't stop a bullet. I think it's an Irish thing."

"Must be."

"You are *sooo* fucked," the second guy says for the tenth time. "I can't believe you're driving into this place. If I had the keys, I'd be halfway to Mexico by now."

"I'm not the one who banjaxed it" is my reply. "Whatever that means."

Sands's driveway is a long ellipse, and the river shows to great advantage, for the bluff is lower here than in town and steps down gently to the water. As I brake to a stop behind an Aston Martin Vanquish—an automobile beyond the reach of any honest casino manager—it occurs to me that the best way to go after these guys might be to put the IRS on their tails.

Quinn skids to a stop behind me, jumps out, and opens my door. "Here we are, guv'nor," he says, his voice dripping mockery. "Let's go see the man."

"If you're waitin' on me, you're walkin' backwards."

Quinn's eyes become slits. "Eh?"

"Never mind."

The Irishman opens the back door and motions for his two thugs to get out. After some effort one of the guys manages to work his way out of the small backseat with his bound hands. Quinn regards him silently for about ten seconds. Then he takes something out of his pocket and fits it over his right hand. I catch the gleam of brass just as Quinn swings, a powerful uppercut delivered with such speed that it would have taken a stop-action camera to capture it. The snap of bone shatters whatever illusions of security I might have had.

"That's battery," I say stupidly.

Quinn gives me a grin that's close to a leer. "You're seeing things, Mr. Mayor. He fell down." He extends a hand toward the mansion. "After you."

Jonathan Sands awaits me at his kitchen table in a white terry-cloth robe, a steaming cup of coffee and the *Natchez Examiner* laid out before him. The kitchen looks like an operating theater: The cabinets are white, the appliances steel, the countertops architectural concrete. The only raw touch in the room is the owner's unshaven face. Sands's sniper's eyes rake left and right as he scans the *Examiner,* but he says nothing.

Before entering the front door of the house, I was hand-searched, scanned by two electronic wands, and had my gun and personal cell phone taken away, along with the BlackBerrys belonging to the unfortunate men sent to watch me.

"I'm told you have a message for me," Sands says in his artificial accent, not lifting his eyes from the newspaper.

Why, I wonder, *does he preserve the illusion of Englishness here?* "That's right. I sent my mother and daughter away this morning. I wanted you to know that."

Sands sniffs, sips from the steaming cup, then looks up, his eyes devoid of everything but irritation. "That wasn't part of our agreement."

We have no agreement, I think. "I realize that. But you need to understand something about me. I've come close to losing my daughter before, and I can't function if I have to worry about her safety. So I took her off the board. I'm still clear about what you want. I don't care about the money you left with me, so you might as well take it back. But I will try to locate what Tim stole from you, and I will give it back to you if I find it."

After a long silence Sands says, "I find that difficult to believe, Mr. Cage."

"Which part?"

"That you'll return my property to me."

"You shouldn't. I might look to you like some Dudley Do-Right with a savior complex—and maybe I used to be that way, a bit—but I'm cured of that. When I first took this job, I was full of fire. My priority was to fix the school system, because all progress flows from that. It took about a year to realize that was never going to happen. I wanted to bring industrial jobs back to this town, and I lost my best chance of that when Toyota pulled out. I got your boat instead. The truth is, I've been thinking about stepping down for some time. My priority is my little girl, not this town. So, if you want to rake a little extra money out of the local yokels' pockets, it's fine by me. I'm ready to get out, and I mean *out.*"

A lopsided smile has lightened Sands's face. His teeth are perfectly straight and startlingly white; much too perfect for a working-class Irishman. *He wears dentures,* I realize.

Before he can reply, a door to my left opens, and I go rigid, half-expecting the eerie white dog to enter the kitchen. Instead, a brown-skinned Asian woman of startling beauty glides into the room with grace so effortless the most cultured belle would be hard put to match it. Scarcely five feet tall, she radiates a self-possession that seems to affect Sands as profoundly as it does me. When she takes the chair nearest me and gazes up at me, her eyes take my breath away. They are aquamarine, but they shine from the perfect archetype of a Chinese face. I'm put in mind of some English smuggler who spread his seed during the Opium Wars or the Boxer Rebellion and left half-caste beauties like this one behind to suffer the fate of mixed-blood children.

"We have not yet been introduced," she says, and in those six words I hear the pure source of the English accent Sands mimics so well. The woman looks no more than twenty, but she must be older.

"I'm Penn Cage."

She grants me the slightest of smiles.

"I've seen your photograph in the newspaper. I am Jiao. I did not mean to interrupt. Please continue."

Jiao's unexpected appearance has jarred my sense of purpose. "I've already said what I came to say," I say awkwardly. "My only concern is the safety of my family."

Sands's lopsided grin has returned. "And your friend? Jessup? What about him?"

"Whatever Tim did to you, he was on his own. I'm sorry he's dead, but I warned him not to do anything stupid. When you stick your nose in other people's business, you get hurt sometimes."

"Just so," Jiao says gravely. "In business and politics, casualties are a fact of life."

I incline my head toward her.

"It's rare for an American to understand this," she says.

"Oh, we understand it. We just don't like to admit it in public."

Sands laughs softly, but only the memory of a smile is on his lips. With almost affected care, he takes a cigarette and a gold lighter from the deep pocket of his robe, touches a hissing jet of butane to the tobacco, and draws deeply. An acrid scent fills the room.

"Mr. Mayor," he says, exhaling purplish blue smoke. "Did you know that when you line people up in front of a pit to shoot them, ninety-nine out of a hundred kneel meekly and wait for the bullet?"

Jiao's eyes remain on me; Sands's bizarre question seems not to have shocked her, or even registered at all.

Sands exhales the rest of the smoke, then leans his chair back on two legs, which creak under his weight. "Down the line walks the executioner. The shots grow louder, the bodies fall, but still the prisoners wait their turn. It's beyond me, really, but that's human nature. Once in a while, though, you get a man—or a woman—who won't wait. Sometimes they run, or leap into the pit after someone they knew. But rarest of all is the man who turns and fights. He hasn't a gun or a knife or even a club, but when he hears those shots getting closer, something in him knots tight and says, 'By God, I'll not go down like that,' and he turns with his teeth bared and his nails raking and goes for the man come to kill him." Sands grins. "I've cheered those bastards every time."

Jiao watches me with grave attention.

"Is there a point to this story?" I ask.

Smoke drifts up from the tip of Sands's cigarette, and his eyes smolder with apparent fascination. "You know there is, mate. That's *you.* You're the one in a hundred. Jessup was a fool, but you're a bloody scrapper."

Holding Annie's face in my mind's eye, I stare back with impassive eyes, as though Sands has shot far wide of the mark. "I used to be that guy," I say with seeming reluctance. "And in the right circumstances—given something worth fighting for, like my family—I still would be. But this is about money. I have all the money I need. If I lose it, I can earn more. I already lost my wife to cancer, okay? I can't replace my little girl."

Sands's eyes narrow, but he says nothing. Jiao turns to him as though for help in understanding some obscure mammal, but Sands suddenly slaps his knee and laughs out loud. Behind me, Quinn permits himself a chuckle. Still laughing,

Sands points at me as if to say, *Listen to this guy. Isn't he something?*

"Why don't you let me in on the joke?"

Sands is belly-laughing now, even though his laughter seems to annoy Jiao.

"I too am confused," she says finally.

Sands wipes his eyes on the sleeve of his robe, then sets down the front legs of the chair, leans forward, and points a thick forefinger at me. "You can't fool me, Cage. Go on! You've made a career out of sticking your nose into other people's business. You're coming after me. Of course you are. I should have seen it last night. You never even had a choice. It's your nature."

"Is this true?" Jiao asks, her translucent eyes on me.

"Course it is," says Sands. "That's why he sent his kid out of town. And his sainted mother."

"I told you why I did that."

"Bollocks! Whoever picked up your kid blew through this town like the fuckin' Secret Service. They iced Quinn's men like they were corner boys. If you wanted out of this town, you'd be *gone.* But you're still here, aren't you?"

I shrug. "This is the biggest weekend of the year for the city. I have obligations."

Sands pulls a mocking face. "I thought you didn't care about the job."

"I'm still a man of my word."

"My point exactly. You must have taken an oath when they swore you in. I'll have to get a copy of that." Sands's levity disappears like bubbles in a tube of blood. "Who got your women out of town, Mr. Mayor? The FBI?"

I shake my head. "No. Those men work for a private security company I've dealt with in the past. They have no government or law enforcement connection whatever. They'll guard anybody for the right price. Even you."

Jiao rises silently and takes two steps toward me. A scent like warm caramel reaches my nostrils. "Please do not involve yourself in our business. I can see that you care about your family. It would be unfortunate for everyone if you allowed your priorities to become confused."

"I haven't," I tell her, trying to blot out the memory of Tim's mutilated corpse. "I promise you that."

"We very much want our property back."
Yeah, I got that.

With her feline gaze still on my face, Jiao reaches out and takes hold of my hand. Then she looks down, turns my palm up, and traces out the lines that curve across my skin. Her exotic face becomes somber, as though a cloud has passed over a terra-cotta figure. She looks over her shoulder at Sands, then back at me. I try to penetrate the blue-green portals of her eyes, but I can't. At last she drops my hand, murmurs something softly in a foreign language, then leaves by the same door she entered through.

"What was that about?" I ask.

Sands raises his eyebrows. "Who knows? I'm guessing she saw something linking the two of us. Or thinks she did, anyway."

"What did she say?"

"I have no idea. Nor do I give a fuck." With his flint-hard eyes on me, the Irishman stubs out his cigarette, then lights another, drawing deeply. When he leans forward and speaks, exhaling smoke with every word, I'm reminded of how Tim characterized him in the cemetery. "Listen to me, mate. I've done things for kicks you wouldn't do to save your own life. I've lived in places where nightmares are scenery, killed too many people to remember. Man, woman, child—it makes no difference. After you've gone where I have, you understand: There are no civilians. Not on this stinking planet. Now, I gave you the rules last night. You cross me, I act—immediately and irrevocably."

"I haven't crossed you. I've only done what any father would do."

"Father," Sands echoes thoughtfully. "I suppose *your* father could serve as de facto hostage for now. While we see where you really stand."

"I can live with that," I say with apparent resignation, even as my heart begins to race. "You don't mean as a prisoner?"

Quinn laughs behind me.

"No need for that," says Sands. "We know where to find him."

"All right. Look—"

"Tell him about the USB drive," Sands says.

"Jessup made a copy of the DVD he

stole," Quinn says. "Part of it, anyway. He made it while he was still on the boat. We need you to find that too."

"Why didn't you tell me that last night?"

"We didn't know last night, did we?" Quinn says angrily. "We've been going over the computer logs, and we just found it. He copied nearly two gigabytes of data from the DVD drive to something attached to a USB port. It was probably a thumb drive, but we don't know. You just keep your fucking eyes peeled."

Real exasperation enters my voice. "How am I supposed to find this stuff? I don't even know what I'm looking for. How do you know he didn't e-mail a copy of the data to a dozen people?"

Sands shakes his head slowly. "He couldn't access the Internet from where he was. It would have set off an alarm."

"Plus there's no record of that in the logs," Quinn says.

"He could have done it from his car, couldn't he? From a notebook computer."

"If he had done, he would have e-mailed it to *you.* Do you have my property, Mr. Mayor?"

"No!"

"Then stop worrying about things we're not worried about."

"Okay. Fine. If that's all, I have somewhere to be."

Sands looks at his watch. "The first race? You've already missed it."

"I should still make an appearance."

The Irishman makes a clucking sound with his tongue. "What you *should* do is start looking for my property. While everyone else is busy. I'd start in the city cemetery."

So Tim did make it that far last night. "Maybe I will."

Sands picks up the newspaper from the kitchen table. "Yer one from the *Examiner* wrote a story about Jessup's death. They must have held the presses for that one."

I have no idea what he's talking about. My *Examiner* is still lying beside my front porch where the paperboy threw it this morning.

"See that she sticks to the script, right? And not too loud with it. Wouldn't want anything to happen to her. You might want to go back to banging her one day. If she'll have you."

As I bite off a stinging reply, Sands cuts his eyes at Quinn. "Take him back to Bedford Falls, Seamus."

Without another look at me, Sands exits through the same door Jiao used, his muscular calves rippling beneath the hem of the robe.

Quinn grins but says nothing while I follow him down the long, tiled hall to a stone portico, then out to my Saab.

The two goons I brought back are nowhere to be seen. Quinn reaches into his pocket and fishes out my cell phone, then takes my gun from the small of his back and passes it to me.

"Don't do anything like this again, Your Honor. That was local boys watching you last night. Next time it'll be my men."

"Who was that girl back there? Miss Teen China?"

A gleam of malice lights Quinn's dark eyes. "Maybe one day you'll find out."

Ignoring his implied threat, I reach for my door handle.

"Keep your cell phone switched on," Quinn says. "I like to know where my friends are."

With my gun hanging loose in my hand,

I look off toward the river, then turn back to Quinn, my eyes stripped of all affect. "You stay away from my family."

The Irishman's eyes flash with challenge. "Or what?"

"This isn't Northern Ireland. It's Mississippi. We know how to play rough here too."

"I'll remember," Quinn says, his voice filled with good humor. "Looking forward to it."

He turns and walks back toward the house.

I climb into the Saab, then check my cell phone. Quinn turned it off while I was inside. Switching it on, I drive toward the gatehouse. As soon as the phone locates a tower, it begins ringing, and also signaling missed calls. The LCD screen reads, *Caller: Hans Necker.* The Minnesotan is probably calling me from three thousand feet above the river, but as I glance back toward Louisiana, I see only a solitary balloon in the sky, scudding southward like a fast-moving cloud.

"Hello?"

"Penn! Hans Necker! Is your family all right?"

"Ah . . . yeah. I'm really sorry I had to miss the race. Everything's fine now."

"Good! Because we got delayed by wind. A couple of cowboys took off, but they were going the wrong way sixty seconds out. How far are you from the football field behind the prep school south of town?"

"St. Stephen's?"

Necker speaks away from the phone, then says, "Yeah, yeah, Buck Stadium, they call it. Big hole in the ground."

"Um . . . five minutes?"

"Perfect! Get down here. We're waiting for you. But don't mess around. We'll be one of the last to launch as it is."

As I near the gatehouse, I slow the car and look back at the stucco boxes on the bluff. When the Natchez Indians looked at the dwellings of the French interlopers who'd appeared on their land in the early 1700s, they probably asked the same questions I'm asking now: *Who are these madmen and what do they want? Do they even know themselves?* The gate guard looks puzzled by my apparent reluctance to leave. I've missed something here. Slowly I pan my gaze across the still-green landscape, past the alien mansion, to the rim of the bluff.

There.

In the shade of a scarlet oak, silhouetted against the blue-white sky, sits the white dog that pinned me to my front door while Sands prodded me with his knife. The animal is too far away for me to see its eyes, but he's not looking out over the river, as I'd first thought. He's looking at me. He seems a sculpture of alertness, his big head held high, his cropped ears erect.

As I stare, the dog raises his hindquarters until his huge body is aimed at me like a torpedo. Nearly two hundred yards separate us, but that dog could cover the distance in twenty seconds. Emboldened by the car around me, I raise my hand as though in greeting, then, irrationally, give the dog the finger. He instantly lowers his head and begins to trot toward me. After one last look, I drive through the gate.

A hundred yards down the road, a rolled newspaper lies at the foot of an asphalt driveway. I stop my car, get out, and take the rubber band off the paper. The front page carries the usual fluff about the Balloon Festival, but below the fold, I see a small story with the headline DEATH MARS POST RACE CELEBRATIONS. The byline reads *Caitlin Masters.* A quick scan of the story reveals a surprising number of facts, or perhaps not so surprising, considering the network of sources, including cops, that Caitlin developed while she lived here. But in the sixth paragraph I discover something I knew nothing about.

"Sources close to the investigation say that over a pound of crystal methamphetamine was discovered at the victim's residence by officers sent there to inform the widow of her husband's death. The widow had vanished, and the house was open. As of this writing, she remains missing. Anyone with knowledge of the whereabouts of Julia Stanton Jessup is urged to contact police immediately."

Caitlin quotes the lead detective: "With this amount of drugs involved, we're almost certainly looking at a drug murder. We need to find this woman and her child before anybody else does."

Consumed by rage, I calmly roll the newspaper back into a tight cylinder and fit the rubber band around it. A pound of crystal meth? I searched Tim's house myself, and I didn't find any drugs. And I beat the police there. If the two cops who drove up on me "found" the meth, either they planted it or they found drugs carefully planted by whoever tore up the house before I got there.

"Hey!" shouts a man in a bathrobe, from far up the driveway. "You work for the *Examiner*?"

"No, sorry," I call, tossing the paper up the driveway.

"Well, who the hell are you?"

"Nobody," I tell him, getting back into my car.

"Hey, you're the mayor, aren't you?" he shouts.

"I'm supposed to be," I mutter, leaving a foot of stinking rubber on the pavement as I fishtail onto the road.

CHAPTER

19

Two dozen balloons pass over my car in a stately if hurried procession as I drive from Sands's house to St. Stephen's Preparatory School, this morning's new launch site. As I turn into the school's driveway—painted with royal blue deer tracks the size of a brontosaur's footprints—a huge yellow sphere rises swiftly from behind the building and sails over my head breathing fire from its gas jets.

Pulling around the elementary building, I turn onto the access road of Buck Stadium, a massive oval hole in the ground lined with modern bleachers. The stadium makes an ideal launch site, not only because it's shielded from the wind, but also because its light poles are fed by underground electrical cables, which removes one of the primary risks for balloon flight.

More than a dozen pickup trucks are parked on the football field, but only two deflated balloons lie stretched on the grass like empty tube socks. The Athens Point sheriff's department helicopter is parked on the fifty-yard line, its rotors slowly turning. Beyond the chopper, several crew members hold open the mouth of a partly inflated balloon while a large fan blasts cool air into it. They'll continue until the balloon is round enough to light the burners without risk to the canopy. At the far end of the field, behind the goalposts, a single red balloon sways above the field, a half dozen people clinging to its basket, their weight just sufficient to hold it to the earth. This is the balloon Paul Labry told me to find.

Descending the hill to the floor of the stadium, I drive along the asphalt track that surrounds the gridiron. Labry's gold Avalon is parked behind a brightly painted trailer, but it's the car parked next to Paul's that brings heat to my face. Caitlin's rented Malibu. Sure enough, I see her black hair and aquiline form silhouetted against the white T-shirt of one of the big-bellied men holding down the basket of the red balloon. She appears to be badgering Labry about something. When Paul catches sight of me, he abandons the basket and starts jogging in my direction. The balloon lifts from the earth, leaving Caitlin no choice but to take Labry's place. Sighting me, Hans Necker yells and waves from inside the basket. I wave back, then focus on Paul.

"Christ, man, you gotta hurry," he says. "Necker's about to lose it."

"What's Caitlin doing here?"

"Asking about Tim's death. She's worried she got the story wrong, and she also seems to think you're mixed up in it some way."

Caitlin leaves the balloon and starts trotting toward us. She's wearing dark jeans and a light sweater. I wave her off and step closer to Labry. "I need you to do me a favor, Paul."

"What?"

"I need the names of all the partners in Golden Parachute. I checked the paperwork I have, and I don't have the names of the five percenters. The Golden Flower LLC guys. Didn't you have copies of most everything?"

Labry looks nonplussed. "Yeah, I've still got it in my garage. What's going on? Why do you need that all of a sudden?"

Caitlin has halved the distance to us. I step to my right and shout, "Give us a minute! Please."

She stops, but it won't be for long.

"Listen, Paul, if you don't have the names at your house, forget about it. Don't ask anybody else for this information. Don't try to look anything up downtown, and don't mention it to me on the phone. Just get the names if you have them at home and tell me the next time you see me in person. Okay?"

"Sure, sure. But what's it for? What's going on?"

I look hard into his eyes. "You don't want to know. The last person who asked that question was Tim Jessup."

Paul's eyes cloud with concern, then Caitlin is upon us. Thankfully, Hans Necker is screaming like a madman from the basket. Without Paul's and Caitlin's weight, the balloon is making three-foot leaps off the ground in the gusting wind.

"I have to go," I tell her, walking quickly toward the basket.

"What were you and Paul talking about?"

"City business."

"Really? It looked personal."

"How would you know anymore?" I stop ten feet from the basket. "I need to get on board."

"Why are you so angry?"

"Because I don't know what you're doing. You show up without warning, get drunk with your boyfriend, but somehow stay up late enough to write a story slandering a dead friend of mine, just in time to screw up the image of the town's most important festival."

Necker does a quick burn, and the heat of the flames reaches out to us like a living thing. I move toward the balloon, but Caitlin grabs my arm and pulls me to a stop. "Wait! What exactly are you angry about? A man was killed last night, and I wrote the facts as I knew them. Are you seriously pissed because I didn't follow

Natchez tradition and soft-pedal the story until after the festival?"

"I don't have time to discuss it." I start forward again. "Hey, Hans, sorry I'm late."

Caitlin obviously isn't worried about appearances. She catches my wrist and spins me around. "Or is it the getting drunk with my boyfriend part?"

"Come on, Penn!" Necker shouts. "The wind could kick up any second."

On any other day I would have hesitated before climbing into this basket, but today I'm grateful for an excuse to escape Caitlin's reproving eyes.

"I never said he was my boyfriend," she says close to my ear. "Not that it's any of your business."

As I turn away and climb into the basket, a strong hand grips my upper arm from behind. I turn, expecting Hans Necker's red visage, but instead I find the aging astronaut's face of chopper pilot Danny McDavitt.

"Morning, Major," I say.

As Hans Necker fires the gas burner with a roar, McDavitt leans toward me. "I hear we've got a mutual friend. You need something, let me know. I stuck my cell number in your back pocket."

I nod and offer silent thanks to Daniel Kelly.

The balloon tugs at the basket like an eager horse. Caitlin has walked a few feet away, but suddenly she runs forward and leans between two men sitting on the lip of the basket. "I want to talk as soon as you get down."

"I won't have time. Not today."

"Crew!" Necker shouts. "Let go of the basket on my count. Three, two, one, *now.*"

The crew members slide off the basket almost as one, and the balloon rises like a dandelion on the wind. Thirty feet off the ground, the butterflies take flight in my stomach. My existence is now dependent on the integrity of a few dozen yards of nylon, a wicker basket, some Kevlar cables, and rope. Caitlin's angry face dwindles rapidly. As soon as we clear the stadium bowl, higher winds catch us and hurl us westward like an invisible hand. We're moving as fast as some cars on the road below. They've slowed to watch the balloon, which must from the ground look graceful in its flight. But from inside the basket, it isn't a slow waltz of balloons and clouds; it's like scudding before the wind in a sailboat.

My cell phone vibrates in my pocket. When I check it, I find a text message from Caitlin. *Something's wrong. What is it? You're not yourself.* I shove the phone back into my pocket and look westward, toward the river.

"Only about half the pilots are flying this race," Necker says. "The winds were running eight to ten miles per hour earlier, and that scares off a lot of people. Means the winds aloft will be running pretty fast." He grins. "As you can tell."

I force a smile and try to look excited, but for me this flight is a necessary evil, a roller-coaster ride on behalf of the city. My strategy is the same I use with Annie in amusement parks: get aboard, tighten my sphincter for the duration, then climb out dazed and kiss the blessed earth. The flaw in that comparison is that few people die on roller coasters, while a significant number die in ballooning accidents, often when the lighter-than-air craft strike power lines. I've seen video of these slow-motion tragedies, and the memory has never left me. The canopy always floats into a high-tension wire with the inevitability of a nightmare. People on the ground become anxious, gasp in disbelief. Then comes the strike, a blue-white flash, and for a moment, nothing. Then the fuel tanks explode. The basket erupts into flame as if struck by an RPG, and the heat carries the balloon higher, making it impossible for the passengers to reach the ground alive. Some leap from the basket, others cling fiercely as the canopy collapses and the flaming contraption streaks earthward like a broken toy. When I've asked about these accidents, I always get the same answer: pilot error. I'm sure that's true in most cases, but the knowledge does nothing to ease my anxiety today.

My cell phone vibrates again. It's another text from Caitlin. *What did I get wrong about the story? P.S. Why isn't Annie flying with you?* Groaning aloud, I switch off the phone.

"Woman problems?" Necker asks with a wink.

"You could say that."

He chuckles. "That was a pretty girl back at the launch site. And she was giving your friend Labry unshirted hell. I imagine she's a lot to handle."

I actually find myself laughing. "You're a good judge of character, Hans."

I shudder as the canopy makes a ripping sound, but Necker only smiles and squeezes my arm with reassurance. "That's normal. These things seem like they're coming apart in a high wind, but that's because the rigging's so flexible. Can you imagine what an old clipper ship must have sounded like tearing across the Atlantic?"

As we rush along above Highway 61, rising through five hundred feet, I silently repeat my day's mantra: *Accidents are rare, accidents are rare. . . .*

I hope we stay low today. Last year a different pilot and I got caught in an updraft and "stuck" a mile above Louisiana. Rather than having the romantic ride most people experience, I was stranded in the clouds, with a view much like the one you get from a jetliner: geometric farms and highways, cars the size of ants. But today is different. The landmarks of the city are spread below me with the stunning clarity of an October morning. To my right lies the Grand Village of the Natchez Indians, a carpet of green meadows and ceremonial mounds beside St. Catherine's Creek. I scarcely have time to orient myself to the mounds before we race onward toward the river.

"Glad you made it," Necker says, slapping me gently on the back. "We're looking good. It's actually lucky you were late."

"Glad to help. It really couldn't be avoided."

The CEO nods but doesn't question me. "They've shortened the race to the first target only. Nobody's going to be able to maneuver well in this wind."

I try to conceal my relief that this will be a short flight. Some balloon races are long and complex, like magisterial wedding processions. Others are brief and chaotic, like car chases through a mountain village, with pilots trying to divine invisible crosscurrents of wind like oracles opening themselves to revelation. Today's event is the latter type, but there's a certain majesty to the seemingly endless train of balloons stretching from the Louisiana

Delta ahead of us back to Buck Stadium, which is now merely a fold in the green horizon. Two helicopters fly along the course like cowboys tending a wayward herd, but they have no control over their charges. The balloons go where the wind blows.

Necker has read the winds well. Where Highway 61 veers north toward Vicksburg and the Delta, we continue westward toward Louisiana. Far to my right I see the abandoned Johns Manville plant, to my left, the shuttered International Paper mill, and the scorched scar that is all that remains of the Triton Battery Company. All those plants came between 1939 and 1946, and the last shut its doors only a few months ago. So much for Natchez's smokestack industries. But the beauty of the city remains undiminished. From this altitude it's plain that the modern town grew over dozens of old plantations, and there's far more forest than open ground. It makes me long for the days before the lumber industry came, when—the saying goes—a squirrel could run from Mississippi to North Carolina without once setting foot on the ground.

As downtown Natchez drifts past like a ghost from the nineteenth century, I hear bass and drums pounding from the festival field beside Rosalie. A moment later I sight the crowd swelling and moving like a swarm of ants before the stage. Then we're over the river, its broad, reddish-brown current dotted with small pleasure craft, the levee on the far side lined with the cars of people watching the balloons pass.

Far ahead, near the horizon, I can see our destination: Lake Concordia, an oxbow lake created by a bend in the river that was cut off long ago. Sometimes Annie and I go water-skiing there with friends who have boats, such as Paul Labry and his family. Thinking of Labry brings a knot of anxiety to my throat. In the rush of boarding the balloon, I asked him to get me the names of the Chinese casino partners for me. So easy to do. But have I needlessly—and selfishly—put him at risk? Probably not, if he follows my orders exactly. But will he, not really knowing what's at stake?

Labry and I are only a year apart in age, but we went to different schools, and

that can be an obstacle to close friendship in Natchez. After forced integration
in 1968, the number of private schools
doubled from two to four. Labry and I
attended the two original ones: Immacu-
late Heart and St. Stephen's. The new
schools were "Christian academies" that
stressed conservative ideology and ath-
letics over academics. There wasn't much
mixing between the four institutions, and I
probably spent more time with the public
school kids than with the "Christians" or
the Catholics, who stuck together like
an extended family. But in the eleventh
grade, Paul Labry and I were sent as del-
egates to the American Legion Boys State
in Jackson. I knew Labry only slightly when
I arrived, but after spending a week with
him among strangers, I knew I'd made a
friend I should have gotten to know long
before.

Labry went to college at Mississippi
State and returned home afterward; he
was already working in his father's office-
supply business while I was earning my
law degree at Rice. When I returned to
Natchez for good, I discovered that Labry
was one of the few boys from the top

quarter of his class who hadn't immi-
grated to another part of the country to
earn his living. As mayor, whenever I
looked at the Board of Selectmen with
frustration, Labry's constant presence
and dogged, conscientious work gave me
hope for change. I think he originally har-
bored dreams of running for mayor, but
after I confided to him that I intended to
run, he told me that I should go for it, and
that I could count on his full support. He
has been true to his word, and I should
not repay a loyal friend and family man
by dragging him into the mess that has
already claimed Tim Jessup's life.

"Look at that!" cries Necker, pointing
down to a vast, swampy island enclosed
by an old bend in the river. "That's Giles
Island right there. We're setting up to win
this thing, Penn, I can feel it."

"I never had a doubt," I tell him, which
is true. Necker probably studied maps of
this area nonstop during his flight back
from Chicago.

As we start to cross the island, a loud
crack unlike anything I've yet heard snaps
me to full alertness. What frightens me
most is Necker. He's gone from a relaxed

posture to total rigidity in less than a second.

"What was that?" I ask.

Necker doesn't answer. He has leaned back to look up through the throat of the balloon, and he doesn't look happy.

"Was that a shot?" I ask, almost afraid to voice what my instinct tells me is true.

"Yes and no," Necker answers, still staring up into the canopy. "Somebody just put some lead through the canopy, but that sound we heard wasn't the gun. It was the bullet itself."

"Jesus." The balloons to the west of us seem much farther away than they did ten seconds ago. "What's the difference?"

Necker is working fast, checking the digital equipment that rests in a pouch on the inside lip of the basket. He's as grim as a fireman about to rush into a burning building. "It takes a high-powered rifle to make the sound we just heard. That bullet was supersonic."

My fear is scaling up into panic. I want to suppress it, but some reactions are simply beyond control. "What does that mean for us?"

"A stray shotgun pellet is one thing. But

you don't hit a balloon this big with a high-powered rifle unless you're aiming at it."

Before the wind carries Necker final word away, another *crack* makes me grab the edge of the basket in terror. This time I hear the bullet rip the nylon above our heads. Necker grabs the wooden handle of a rope that stretches all the way to the top of the balloon. It's fastened inside a carabiner, which Necker carefully opens while gripping the handle tight in his hand. He looks like a man about to pull the rip cord on a parachute.

"What are you doing?" I ask, trying to keep my voice steady.

His eyes meet mine with an intensity that shakes me to the core. "We've got to get down. Somebody's trying to kill us."

I want to help, but my mind is blank. Before I can say anything more, Necker pulls on the rope, and our balloon begins dropping like an elevator in a Tokyo office building. My stomach flies into my throat, and my feet tingle the way they do when I stand on a cliff edge.

"Will the canopy hold together?" I ask above the rush of the wind.

Necker nods with confidence. "We can

take quite a few holes and maintain buoyancy. But if they hit a cable or cause a big rip, we'll be in trouble."

"What if they hit the fuel tanks?"

Necker gives me a grin of utter fatalism. "If they hit a tank, we're dead."

The sound of the wind is twofold now, the air blowing past us horizontally, and that rushing upward as we plummet toward the earth.

"Can we dump the tanks over the side?"

Necker is watching the top of the balloon through its mouth. "That would take four or five minutes in my balloon, and this isn't my balloon. I'll have us on the ground in fifty seconds."

He pulls harder on the rope, and we drop still faster. I cannot bear to look outside the basket. "What are you doing?" I ask.

"Venting hot air from the top of the balloon. It's the only way to get down fast."

"How fast are we going?"

"A thousand feet a minute."

"How fast is that?"

Necker purses his lips, figuring on the fly. "A forty-yard dash straight into the ground. It probably won't kill you, but it'll hurt like hell."

Shit. . . .

He squeezes my upper arm and winks. "We'll be all right. I'll do a burn right before we hit. Try to cushion it a little."

My heart is pounding so hard that my chest hurts. "I feel like we just jumped out of a plane!"

Necker actually laughs. "A skydiver falls ten times this fast. Just keep scanning the ground. Watch for a muzzle flash. Somebody's going to jail for this."

Steeling myself, I pan my eyes over the swampy ground bounded by the snaky bend of the old river course. There's a thousand acres of trees down there that a sniper could hide behind. There's no way we're going to find him without hearing his gun go off.

The ground seems to swoop up toward us with surreal speed. I'm trying to force my gaze away from it when Necker takes out his cell phone and speed-dials a number. "Major McDavitt? We're taking ground fire. . . . That's right, rifle fire, I'd say. Could be hunters, but I don't think so. I'm hitting the deck right where we are, maximum safe descent." Necker gives me a quick glance. "Maybe faster."

A mile to the west, the Athens Point sheriff's department chopper banks toward us and accelerates. Just as my heart lifts, another bullet punches though the canopy with the sound of a bullwhip finding flesh.

"God*damn* it!" Necker bellows, pointing toward the levee road. "I think that came from the south," he shouts into the phone. "Skim the levee road on your way here and see if you see anything. Try to get a license plate."

The helicopter makes no move toward the levee, but makes for us at what must be maximum speed. Major McDavitt has decided that survival means more than punishment.

Necker's jaw is set tight, but I see a wry smile on his lips. "So that's how it is," he says into the phone. "Medevac time. Well, you'd better call ahead to the hospital. I'm AB positive. Penn, do you know your blood type?"

"O negative."

Beneath us I see an orange tractor and a propane tank beside what looks like a bunkhouse. A billy goat stands munching something beside a barbed-wire fence—

"Stop looking at the ground," Necker

advises. "You're turning green. Watch the horizon. I'll tell you when to brace. Fifteen seconds. If we overshoot and land in the water, stay with the basket. It'll float. Unless you want to try to swim right to shore."

"Shouldn't we try for the water?"

"We might not be able to swim after impact."

Good Lord. The gas jet roars above our heads, heat blasts my scalp, and the basket presses up against my feet like an express elevator slowing for the ground floor. "That old river's full of alligators anyway!" I shout.

Necker tries to laugh, but what comes out is a strangled bark. He grabs the valve of the propane tank and shuts off the fuel line. "Five seconds! Brace! Bend your knees!"

I bend my knees and grab the upper frame of the basket, bracing against our lateral motion, which is westward toward the water. We're moving a lot faster across the ground than I'd realized, but that may actually help us.

The impact is like falling from a galloping horse. My knees collapse and my pelvis slams the side of the basket, jolting me from ankles to crown, and then we're sliding over the marshy ground as the wind drags us relentlessly toward the water. Necker hauls mightily on a rope, and suddenly the canopy collapses and we shudder to a stop.

The sudden silence is unnerving, but in seconds I hear the steady beating of McDavitt's helicopter descending beside us.

Hans Necker drops to the floor of the basket like a man who died on his feet. It's only now that I remember the gunfire that caused this crash landing.

"Are you hit?" I ask.

Necker shakes his head. "Ankle's broken. One for sure, maybe both. Can you help me up?"

"Hell, yes. Let's get out of this thing."

McDavitt is already out of the chopper and running toward us. "Anybody hit?" he calls.

"No," I shout back. "We need help though!"

When McDavitt reaches the basket, he helps me lift Necker over the side. The

CEO grips the frame for a moment and smiles. "This old girl got us down alive."

"You got us down, buddy. We need to get to St. Catherine's Hospital, Major. Ready?"

McDavitt nods as we cradle Necker between us in a sitting position.

"Let's do it."

I thought the balloon was moving fast when we crossed the river, but Major McDavitt storms back toward Natchez at 120 knots, aiming for the helipad atop St. Catherine's Hospital. The town's top orthopedist is waiting for Necker in the emergency room, and the Adams County sheriff's department chopper is flying in tandem, following us in. Paul Labry is on his way to the hospital, preparing to deal with what can only be a media crisis for the Balloon Festival.

"How you doing?" I ask Necker, who's sitting with his back to the wall of the helicopter's cabin, his left calf propped on my knee to keep his foot elevated.

"Hurts like a son of a bitch," he says. "But it could have been a lot worse. You did good, keeping it together. A lot of people would have panicked."

"Oh, I panicked."

Necker laughs, then winces. "Damn, I'd like some morphine."

"Two minutes."

Necker nods. "Let's talk fast then."

"What do you mean?"

"I don't believe in luck, good or bad. We weren't the first balloon in line, or the last. But we were shot at and hit three times with a high-powered rifle. Anybody who could hit us three times could have killed us if he wanted to. All he had to do was shoot the basket. He'd have hit us or the fuel tanks, or both."

I look back noncommittally. "So . . . ?"

"So either we stumbled on a psycho hunter having a really bad day, or somebody was trying to send one of us a message. I don't have any enemies here yet, so far as I know. What about you?"

I stare back at the CEO but do not speak. Necker didn't get where he is by being dumb.

He changes tack. "A lot of people are about to ask us what happened back there. What are we going to say?"

I'm not sure what to say, to Necker or the public. I can't quite believe that Sands or Quinn would pull a stunt like that. Especially after I reaffirmed that I intended to do what they've asked of me. But who else could it have been?

"Are we off-the-record?"

Necker points at a headset on the floor to indicate that Major McDavitt cannot hear us. "Unless I'm dictating a press release, I'm always off-the-record."

I take a deep breath and look out at the spire of St. Mary's, growing larger in the chopper's windshield. "I don't think you're going to find out who fired those shots, Hans. But I may know already. Who ordered it, anyway."

"I'm listening."

"That was a message telling me to keep my nose out of something. Or my mouth shut. I'm not sure which yet. It had nothing to do with you or the race. I can't give you details. I wish I could, but I can't. It's just not an option."

"You don't think any other pilots are in danger?"

"No. Not unless we get some nutty copycat or something."

Necker's appraisal of me is cold and swift. "This isn't something personal, is it? Like diddling somebody else's wife?"

"Hell, no. It's criminal activity. That's all I can say. If you could help me, I'd tell you more, but you can't. Not with this."

"I know a lot of people, Penn."

"So do I. This isn't that kind of problem. Money and connections won't help. In fact, money is the problem."

"This is why you were late this morning, isn't it?"

I nod.

"Your family's okay?"

"They are now. They weren't this morning."

Necker winces again, then nods slowly. "I see. Okay. Tell me what I can do to help you. There has to be something."

I think for a moment. "Honestly?"

"Yessir."

"I need this helicopter for the rest of the weekend, and I need Major McDavitt flying it. From now till Sunday night."

Necker shifts his leg, grimaces in pain. "You've got it."

"I'll pay for his time, of course. I—"

"It's already paid for. What else?"

"I think that's all you can do for now. Other than that, I'd just ask that you not let this thing affect your view of the town, if that's possible."

Necker smiles. "Hell, I've run into strong-arm stuff in Minneapolis. You get that everywhere. I only wish you'd let me help you. I take it personally when some-body shoots at me. I'd like a few words with the son of a bitch myself."

"If I have my way, you'll get your chance."

Necker glances out the window at the hospital as we descend. "I won't keep you, then. I'm going to be on crutches for a while anyway. Go do what you have to do. Anybody asks, I'll say I think that shooting was some kids that got out of hand."

"I appreciate it, Hans."

"Would it help you to know where those shots came from?"

"It might."

"I'll get somebody to truck that balloon over here, and I'll have a look at it. I know our altitude when we were shot. If the shots were through and through, I can fig-ure the angle and probably where the shooter was standing. Approximately, anyway."

The chopper touches down on the roof like a butterfly alighting on a leaf. Necker smiles. "A lot better than our last one, eh?"

Paramedics yank open the side door and motion for me to exit the cabin. As I leave, Necker grabs my arm and says, "I'll tell Danny to be on call for you."

"Thanks."

Paul Labry is waiting for me on the helipad. I've never seen him this upset before. "What the hell happened up there, Penn?"

"I told you on the phone. Somebody took a couple of shots at us. Necker had to set down hard."

"Are you okay?"

"I'm fine. How many people know what happened?"

"Are you kidding? With cell phones? I'll bet most of the pilots know by now, and the town won't be far behind."

"Caitlin?"

"I don't know. How do you want to handle this? Some people are already saying we should cancel the rest of the flights. Today's *and* tomorrow's."

"Pilots?"

"No. Couple of county supervisors."

"I'm not surprised, but I'm not sure we should cancel. I think this was probably an isolated event. Necker agrees. The pilots are going to want input on the decision. We need to call a meeting—a closed meeting—pilots and the committee only. Let's give them long enough to get down and packed up." I look at my watch and give Paul a time.

He nods. "Where? The Ramada convention room?"

"That's fine. I need you to handle the press on this, Paul. I'll be at the meeting, but you're the point man for now."

"What? I don't know anything!"

"Necker can give you the details."

Labry looks more upset than when I first got out of the chopper. "Where are you going to be?"

"You can reach me on my cell."

Labry groans as he follows me to the hospital's roof door.

"Go on ahead," I tell him. "I have to make a call."

"Don't you need a ride back to your car?"

"My dad's giving me a ride. He's working downstairs. You go ahead."

Labry starts through the door, then stops and looks back at me. "Hey, I almost forgot. I got those names you wanted."

I pause, momentarily confused. "Names?"

"The Golden Parachute partners. That's where I was when you called. My garage. I didn't want to say anything on the cell, you were so cloak-and-dagger about it. I had to write the names down so I wouldn't forget. There are six partners sharing the five percent stake."

"Are two of them Chinese?"

Labry nods, then produces a scrap of paper that looks like part of a grocery bag. I shove it deep in the same pocket that holds Danny McDavitt's number. "Go on, Paul. You're going to have a lot to deal with. Talk to Necker first."

As Labry shakes his head and walks into the hospital, I speed-dial 1. Seamus Quinn answers the phone with a note of amusement in his voice.

"Seems like we spoke only this morning," he says, chuckling.

"What the fuck are you trying to do?" I shout.

"What would you be talking about?"

"You just tried to kill me!"

"How could I do that? I'm having a pint on the *Queen* as we speak." Quinn obviously assumes I'm taping the call.

"Look, I don't get it. I told you, I'm going to do what you want. I'm going to find your disc. But I can't do it if I'm dead."

"No idea what you're talking about," Quinn says airily. "Unless it's that balloon crash I just heard about."

"What else?"

"Well, you must be exaggerating. If somebody really wanted to kill you, they'd have blown your fuel tank."

"If you were trying to send me a message, I don't understand it."

"No message. But now that I have you on the phone, I do recall someone saying you had other things to do this morning than go riding in a balloon."

So that was the message.

Quinn continues, "I also recall telling you to leave your cell phone switched on."

"A reporter's been bugging me. I had to shut it off."

"Not my problem. I like to know where my mates are, remember. Gives me a sense of security."

I can't even think of a response.

"Got to run now, mate. Business is picking up, now the balloons have landed. You call back soon. I like to hear good news."

When the connection goes dead, something lets go in me, and I wobble on my feet. Delayed shock, probably. I grab the doorknob to steady myself, then back up and sit down on an air-conditioning unit. Hugging myself to stop the shakes, I wonder how I'm going to get downstairs to meet my father.

My cell phone is ringing in my pocket. I'm already wishing I hadn't switched it back on. This time it's not Caitlin or Labry.

"Penn, it's Chief Logan. I heard you had some trouble."

"A little bit."

"Nobody hurt too bad, I understand. Lucky break."

"Yeah."

"I was wondering if you could swing by headquarters for a minute."

"What for? Is it about the shooting?"

"No. I've had your girlfriend here threatening me with lawsuits till Judgment Day if I don't let her kid out of jail."

"Chief, I can't deal with Libby Jensen's problems right now."

Logan voice changes suddenly; all the official tone goes out of it. "We need to talk, Penn. And not on a cell phone. I'm at headquarters for another half hour. Find a way."

I sigh in resignation. "Okay. I'm on my way."

I'm only six feet from the roof door, but I feel it's a mile away. The thought of making my way to the ground floor of the hospital seems beyond me. I don't know if it's sleep deprivation or the crash. I am gathering my last reserves of energy to stand when I look to my left.

Facing me like a giant blue dragonfly is the Athens Point helicopter, its rotors turning as though they could go on for eternity. Danny McDavitt sits at the controls like a waiting chauffeur, his eyes on me.

There is my ride.

CHAPTER

20

Police headquarters is on the north side of town, far from the most recent residential and commercial development, closer to the predominantly black part of town. The low-slung, one-story structure looks like a cross between a 1970s office suite and a federal prison minus the barbed wire. Wedged between a Pizza Hut and the Entergy building, it's surrounded by car dealerships, auto parts shops, cheap motels, and a cash-for-your-car-title place. Across the street, amid this haphazard sprawl, stands Devereaux, one of the most beautiful Greek Revival mansions in the

South, now dwarfed by the massive Baptist church that has become its neighbor, the only new construction on this side of town.

Inside the glass-walled entry area of the station, I announce myself to the officer behind her bulletproof glass window. After a show of finishing some paperwork, she buzzes me through the door and points to the chief's door.

Don Logan and I have been through more than one scrape together. A year and a half ago, we were both shot at by gang members in the lobby of the city's finest hotel. As I told Tim the night before he died, I find it almost impossible to believe that Logan could be on the pad, no matter what the temptation. On the other hand, the chief might have guilty knowledge about one or more cops under his command. Situations like that have put honorable men in difficult positions before, so I must tread carefully with Logan, honest though he may be.

The chief is waiting behind a desk that's the picture of order, a compulsive engineer's desk. He wears a starched blue uniform and a silver badge, but in his wire-rimmed glasses he still looks like a high school science teacher.

"What's going on, Don?" I ask, hoping to get past titles immediately. "You sounded pretty upset on the phone."

"I'm not sure where to start."

"What's the status on Soren Jensen?" This question gives me time to read the chief's mood. What I'm picking up is serious tension.

"Jensen's being charged with possession with intent to distribute."

Seeing the shock on my face, Logan hurries on, "It's not my call, Penn. The DA's filing those charges. Shad even came down here this morning to make sure I understood his position. I don't know what you did to step on his toes, but he's out for this kid's blood."

"I hear you. What about the MVA?"

"The kid's being charged with DWI as well. He was drunk on the Breathalyzer, but I think he was full of meth too. His mother told him not to take a blood test, but Shad's going to get a court order."

I absorb this in silence. Libby is probably close to a nervous breakdown by now.

"I know he's basically a good kid," Logan says. "But he hit a cop. You know he wouldn't have done that unless he was high."

"Probably not. He needs help, though, not time in the pen."

"So do all the poor black kids who come through here, and a lot of them don't get it. So it's easy for Shad to throw the book at Jensen and look like he's being impartial. But let's move on. We've got more serious problems to deal with."

"Like?"

"Tim Jessup."

Here we go. "Are you treating his death as a homicide?"

Logan lifts a stainless steel pen from a holder and glances away, temporizing. "The autopsy results aren't back. Let's move to some specifics before we start drawing conclusions."

"I saw the story in this morning's paper. Who found the dope in Jessup's house?"

"The two patrolmen who saw you leaving there called in a K9 unit. Dog found it behind some Sheetrock in the closet. Typical hidey-hole."

"Don, somebody tore the place apart before I got there. They would have found the drugs and taken them."

Logan shrugs as if he can do nothing about the facts.

"How did Caitlin Masters find out about the meth so fast?"

"Come on," he says. "You know that woman better than anybody. She's got sources all over town, from the courthouse to Lawyers' Row to this department."

I concede this with a nod. "What concerns me is that to the best of my knowledge, Tim Jessup has been clean for a year."

"There's no way to know that."

"Julia Stanton turned that boy around. I tend to be cynical where drugs are concerned, but I don't think Julia would have stayed with him if he was using again."

Logan taps the pen on his desk, looks toward his partially open window blinds. Then he reaches into his drawer and pulls out a manila envelope. From it he takes four photographs and lays them out for me to examine. They're printed on ink-jet photo paper, and all four show a nude or partly nude woman with a stunning body posed in various erotic positions. Unlike the teenage girl in the cell phone shots Tim showed me, this woman is in her midthirties and looks confident of her sexuality.

"What am I supposed to get from these?"

"We found these in Jessup's house. Something tells me Julia didn't know about this either."

I am at a loss for words.

"Nobody leaked these to Ms. Masters, by the way," he adds.

Thank God for small favors. "Were these stashed with the dope?"

"No." Logan can't suppress a small smirk. "Folded inside *The Seven Habits of Highly Effective People.*"

"Have you ID'd the woman? She looks vaguely familiar."

"Linda Church. Hostess at the Devil's Punchbowl, one of the bars on the *Magnolia Queen.* Born right here in Natchez."

I raise my eyebrows. "Who ID'd her?"

"One of the patrolmen recognized her. I did too, when I saw the pictures. She grew up out in Morgantown, like me. She wasn't that far behind me in school. I'm eight years younger than you, remember, even if I'm losing my hair faster."

I smile and nod.

"You never saw Linda on the boat?" he asks.

"I don't gamble."

"Me either. But I go down there and eat with the wife sometimes. Food's good, and not too expensive."

"What do you know about her?"

"She stripped in Vegas. A lot of people don't know that. She went to a juco in Oklahoma, married a guy there. That lasted about ten years. No kids. He left her. She got short of money, started stripping in Oklahoma City, then moved on to Vegas. Not sure why she left, but she came back here and started working the boats. I do remember her from school, though. They called her Butterface."

"Butterface?"

"You know, everything about her was hot but her face."

I lean forward and examine the pictures more closely. Aside from her high, full breasts and tight bottom, Linda Church has large eyes and good bone structure.

"She looks pretty enough in these pictures."

"Yeah. It was acne. She had it bad in high school. She's scarred more than these pictures show. But Linda's like a lot of country girls, a ten-plus when you see them from behind, a five from the front."

"So based on these pictures, you think Tim was having an affair with her."

"Sure looks that way."

"Jessup's not in any of the pictures."

"Would you be, if you were going to keep these around your house?"

"I wouldn't keep them around my house. And neither would Tim. Julia would castrate him if she found them."

"No offense, but Jessup has a history of self-destructive behavior."

"Have you questioned this woman yet?"

Logan sighs heavily. "We can't find her."

The moment he says this, I suspect that Linda Church may never be found alive. "Was she supposed to report for work today?"

"Not for another hour yet. We already questioned her coworkers, though. One said she's positive Jessup and Linda were hooking up on the sly. They kept it secret because of workplace rules."

If Tim was having an affair with her—or if she was helping him with his plan to steal evidence—why didn't he tell me about her? As soon as I ask myself, I know the answer: Tim didn't want me to judge him for cheating on Julia, if in fact he was doing so.

"Jessup never told you about this girl?" Logan asks.

"Me? We weren't that close, Don. Not since we were nine years old."

"Right. But you're positive he wasn't doing drugs."

Frustrated by the need to conceal my relationship with Tim, I say, "I'm just telling you what I think."

"Well, here's what *I* think. To an objective investigator, it looks like an old dope-head slid back to his old ways. He was banging a waitress at work and selling meth to keep up his two women."

"That's what it's supposed to look like. Did you find any meth precursors in Jessup's house? Any cooking equipment?"

Logan shakes his head.

"It's bullshit, Don. Staged. Every bit of it."

Logan leans back in his chair and cradles his hands behind his head, his eyes regarding me coolly. "Were you and Jessup working on something together?"

I thought I was ready for this kind of question, but the directness of it takes me by surprise. "I'm the mayor. He was a blackjack dealer. What could we be working on?"

Logan's eyes remain steady. "You're also a novelist. And a lawyer. A former prosecutor."

"And?"

"And a couple of nights ago, one of my patrolmen saw your car out at the cemetery. After midnight. That's not far from where Jessup worked. And his shift ended at twelve a.m. this week."

I shrug as casually as I can. "I was feeling down, Don. I went out to visit my wife's grave. I do that sometimes."

Logan looks as if he's trying to give me the benefit of the doubt—and failing. "That's what my man said you said. I can respect that. But if anything else happened while you were out there, I'd sure like to know about it."

I shake my head slowly. "Nothing. Me and the ghosts, that's it."

Logan watches me awhile longer, then says, "There's a couple of other things you should know. One, Jessup's wife is missing."

"Meaning what? Someone filed a missing persons' report? Or you just can't find her?"

"We can't find her or her son."

I shrug again. "I don't know where she is, if that's what you're asking. Do you have Tim's car?"

"That's the other thing. It's missing too. Thing is, I've got Linda Church's cell phone records, and she received a pretty disturbing text message last night shortly before midnight."

"What did it say?"

Logan reaches back into the manila envelope, takes out a small piece of paper, and slides it across his desk. Written on it in pencil are the letters: *Thief-www kllmmommy. Sqrttoo.*

"What do you make of this?" Logan asks.

"Tim sent this?"

"It was sent from the cell phone of a man whose phone was stolen while he was on the *Magnolia Queen* last night. I think Jessup's been doing a lot of that lately."

Logan's inquisitive eyes probe mine, but I say nothing. At length he says, "In my experience, strippers have been exposed to pretty much everything. Getting mixed up in a murder for hire wouldn't be that big a step for some of them. An objective investigator might look at that text message and see an order to kill Jessup's wife and child."

I can't believe the chief is serious. "Tim was planning to murder his wife? The woman who saved his life? That's ridiculous. You know it is."

"Brother, two years ago I'd have said it was ridiculous if you told me Dr. Drew Elliot was porking a high school girl. If this job has taught me anything, it's that you have no idea what people are capable of, not even the people you think you know best."

"Fair enough. But I'm telling you, Julia Stanton was Tim Jessup's salvation."

Logan taps one of the photos on his

desk, his finger coming to rest on Linda Church's shapely derriere. "Maybe Tim thought *this* was his salvation."

"That's sure what somebody wants you to think. You and everybody else in town."

"You really believe he's being framed? After his death? Who has a motive to frame Tim Jessup?"

"Cui bono, my friend."

"What?"

"Who benefits?"

"From his death?"

"Yes. And from smearing what remained of his good name. It's pretty clear that someone wants Tim's death to look like a run-of-the-mill drug murder. Guaranteed to go in the 'unsolved' file."

Logan looks uncomfortable.

"Which is exactly how Shad Johnson seemed to be reading it last night at the crime scene," I remind him. "Before any such evidence had been discovered. By the way, when Shad was here to make sure you threw the book at Soren Jensen, did he give you any sense of urgency about solving Jessup's murder?"

The chief can't meet my eyes now. "Not exactly."

"Uh-huh. I'd say the situation's pretty self-explanatory, Don."

Logan gets up from his desk and walks to the window, toys with the blinds. "Let me ask you a question. You know a lot about this town. You were raised here, you've written about it."

"What do you want to know?"

He turns and looks me squarely in the eyes. "Who actually runs this place?"

This is a question I've asked myself since I was a boy.

"You're the mayor. Do you run it?"

"Far from it. In fact, our kind of city government is literally defined as the 'weak mayor' form of government."

Logan gives me a guarded look. "You've got the power to fire me."

"I'd happily trade that for the power to fire the district attorney."

The chief grunts as if he agrees. "My folks always told me Natchez was run by the garden clubs. Maybe that was true once, but that idea's a laugh and a half now."

"They never really did, Don. This town was always run by a few big men behind the scenes. Men like Leo Marston. Judges, bankers, lawyers, oilmen. But things have changed. The big money's mostly gone or spread among the heirs. There's not that much power here anymore. It's a free-for-all. White or black, everybody's chasing whatever money they can find. We're just like the rest of the country that way."

Logan nods dejectedly, but something else seems to be eating at him. "I tell you, I'm starting to feel like the marshal in a company town. Mining town, lumber town, whatever."

"Gambling town?" I suggest quietly.

A quick, worried glance. "You said that, not me. Look, gambling is gambling, and everybody knows what comes with it. But it's legal now, and given that, I have to say the casinos have been good partners."

"You sound like a lot of people when they talk about casinos."

"How's that?"

"Careful."

"Well. It's like being police chief in a town by an army base. If you're not pro-army, you're in the wrong job. The way I see it, my job is to collect evidence and make arrests. I can only go by the evidence I find."

"Chief, your job is to uncover the truth."

Logan looks at me with a dogged defiance in his eyes. "No, sir. That's a jury's job. And a judge's. Lawyer's, maybe. And it don't make a bit of difference how much detective work I do if the DA doesn't want to prosecute something."

Now I stand. "If you find solid evidence, Shad will have no choice."

"You really believe that? You were an assistant DA yourself. You know how political that stuff gets."

"Murder is murder, Don."

The chief makes a clicking sound with his tongue. "Well, I'll sure be interested to see the results of Jessup's autopsy."

"When will you get those? Next week?"

"Actually, Jewel Washington put a rush on it. She's pretty tight with the people at the crime lab in Jackson. I think the pathologist may be cutting Jessup late today."

A fillip of excitement shoots through me. "Does Shad know that?"

Logan shakes his head. "I wouldn't want to be Jewel when he finds out either."

"If he tries to retaliate against Jewel for doing her job the way it ought be done, Shad'll find out just how much power I *have.*"

"Penn, look—"

"No, this is bullshit. You tell me one thing. If the autopsy comes in conclusively as homicide, are you going to press the investigation or not?"

Logan straightens up with impressive dignity. "If it comes back homicide, I'll be investigating a homicide. I'll do it by the book, and I won't miss a lick. But, brother, in the end, being chief of police is a lot like being mayor. Unless you're backed up by the people above and below you, it's just a nice-sounding title."

As Logan grimaces under the burdens of his office, something disturbing strikes me. "Don, we've been talking quite a while, and you haven't asked me anything about my balloon getting shot down."

He takes a deep breath, then answers with carefully chosen words. "First off, I can see you weren't hurt bad. Second, it happened over Louisiana. Not my jurisdiction. Mine ends at the river."

I sense barely contained anger behind his eyes, but he will not voice it.

"One thing has troubled me since last night," I tell him. "You said Tim tried to call me several times before his death. I was in one of the highest parts of the city, but I never got those calls. No texts either. How could that be?"

Logan folds his arms and looks at the institutional green carpet.

"May I see Tim's phone?"

The chief shakes his head. "I can't do that."

"Why not?"

"Ask the district attorney, not me."

"Do you *have* the phone? Is it in the evidence room?"

Logan keeps his gaze on the carpet. "You're outside the bounds of what I can answer."

"Jesus, man, what *can* you tell me?"

Logan chews on his bottom lip for a while. Then he glances at his door and walks to within a foot of me. "Last night, there were two localized interruptions of cellular service. In two different places, and at two different times."

I ponder this for a minute. "Let me guess. The first was around midnight, near the cemetery."

Logan nods almost imperceptibly.

"And the second was right around the time Tim died. When he jumped out of the SUV and was trying to get away from whoever was inside."

"You get the prize."

"How widespread was the interruption?"

"From the complaints, the best I can figure was about half a square mile near the cemetery. Up on the bluff it was more widespread, but it had a shorter duration. Generated a lot more complaints, though, with all the people partying up there."

"Were all carriers interrupted, or just one?"

"All."

"Shit. Somebody was jamming the radio spectrum."

Logan licks his lips but says nothing.

"That's serious business. Have you talked to the cellular providers?"

"No way. I figured this out from the complaints of witnesses. And a couple of my black officers live out by the cemetery."

"You know what happened. Whoever killed Tim jammed the cell signals around the cemetery while they were chasing him out there. They stopped it after they had him in the SUV, when they were torturing him. Then they started jamming the lines again when he broke loose and ran for the fence."

Logan sniffs and looks back toward his door. "Are you prepared to tell me who 'they' are?"

Is he asking me this honestly? I wonder. *Or is he testing me? And if he's testing me, is it for himself or for Jonathan Sands?*

"Do I need to tell you?"

The chief walks back behind his desk. "Six months ago I got an offer to be chief of police in a little town on the Florida coast. Ever since I saw Jessup lying in that ditch, I've been wishing I hadn't said no."

I walk forward and lay a hand on his shoulder. "It's a sad day when two Mississippi boys can't trust each other any more than this."

"Yes, sir, it is. Things have slid a long way out of whack."

"Maybe we need to try to do something about it."

Logan's eyes open a little wider. "Maybe. Let's see what that autopsy says. You stay in touch, Penn."

I turn to go, but the chief's voice stops me at the door.

"How's that little girl of yours doing?"

"She's fine," I reply, my eyes hard and flat. "It was good to see you, Don. Take care of yourself."

CHAPTER

21

I'm standing before the grave of Florence Irene Ford, who died in 1871 at age ten. Because the child was afraid of storms, Irene's mother had a glass window installed in the casket, so that during inclement weather she could descend the little stairway behind the gravestone and reassure her child. This tale always fascinated Tim Jessup, so I thought Florence's stairway might make a good hiding place for the stolen disc. But a locked metal trapdoor protects the stairway now, the price of protecting the cemetery from vandals.

For ninety minutes I've crisscrossed the cemetery in search of Jonathan Sands's missing disc, following a map that only I could have drawn. Sketched hastily in my Moleskine notebook, it shows the locations of graves of people that Tim and I both knew. If Tim were running for his life and meant to hide evidence with the intent of retrieving it later—or in the worst case for me to retrieve it—I figured he would choose a spot I might think of on my own. A grave we both knew seemed the likeliest place. Had I chosen to include deceased people from my parents' generation, it would have been a long list indeed, but knowing that time was short, I included only ours, with two exceptions. Still, I could easily think of nine, and they were spread throughout the vast cemetery.

There was Mallory Candler, our Miss Mississippi, who was murdered in New Orleans. Tim's in-laws are also buried here: Julia's father, a suicide at forty-nine, and her mother, dead from a stroke two years later. Two St. Stephen's schoolmates who died in accidents also made the list: a boy shot by his brother while hunting, and a girl who broke her neck diving into a pond when she was twelve. Kate Townsend, a St. Stephen's student who was murdered a year and a half ago, also went on my map, but I found no sign of anything hidden near her—or any other person's—tomb.

My next step was to include the famous monuments of the cemetery, figuring that in the dark Tim might not have had time to search out the stones of the recently deceased. This trek took longer, for the older sections have no modern grid layout or uniform tombstones. Sweating from the midday heat, I crawled through a world of fantastical sculptures, mausoleums fenced with heavy wrought iron, cracked marble and masonry filled with crannies ideally suited to hide contraband. I probed like an archaeologist beside the graves of the principals in the Goat Castle murder case; of Rosalie Beekman, the only casualty of the Civil War at Natchez; of Louise the Unfortunate, an unknown woman from the North who died in a Natchez brothel; and of Bud Scott, the famed black bandleader many believe to be the father of Louis Armstrong, who spent several summers in Natchez as a boy. Yet none of these mossy monuments concealed the treasure I sought.

While concealed in the shadows between two mausoleums, I used the Blackhawk satellite phone to check on Annie and my mother. They had already reached Houston, and were nearly to the safe house that awaited them. I gave the Blackhawk dispatcher the names of the five percent investors in Golden Parachute and asked if the company could check out the two Chinese investors for me. After promising this would be done, the dispatcher informed me that Daniel Kelly could arrive in Natchez in twelve to fifteen hours, depending on certain variables. This was faster than I'd hoped, and welcome news. During bad times, Kelly makes good things happen, and when he can't manage that, he at least deters those who would like to make things worse.

Knowing that the missing disc is all that might bring my family safety from Sands— or give me the weapon I need to destroy him—I prepare to continue my search, but the sheer size of the task is overwhelming. I see why Quinn was so anxious for me to take it on. It would take strangers weeks to search this graveyard.

When my cell phone rings, I half expect to hear Seamus Quinn's voice, but the caller is Paul Labry.

"Penn, you need to get over here," he says.

"Where? The Ramada?"

"No, we moved the pilots' meeting to the Visitors' Center. We needed the space. All the pilots know about the shooting, and they all want a say in what happens next."

"Well, that's the city's decision. The pilots can stay or leave as they will."

"Most of them want to hear what happened from the horse's mouth before they decide. I really need you to get over here. The meeting is controlled chaos right now. Another fifteen minutes, and it could be a riot."

"I'm on my way."

The Natchez Visitor and Reception Center looks like the student union building of a junior college. Cut into a slope in the shadow of a Hampton Inn and a casino hotel, it's almost invisible as you cross the bridge from Louisiana to Mississippi.

When large events are held here, access is virtually impossible. Nearly a hundred pickups with balloon trailers have wedged themselves into the parking lot. There would be enough room were it not for the regiment of cars that have filled every remaining space in the lot and even the grassy shoulders. The license plates tell me these are local people drawn to the scene by the rumor of this morning's shooting. Making my way up the sloping asphalt, I realize it could take me a half hour to get through the milling crowd of locals. As I near its periphery, though, Paul Labry texts me to walk around to a service door behind the center, where he will be waiting.

True to his word, Labry admits me to the building and rushes me down a bland corridor to the main meeting area, which looks like a breakout meeting room in a convention hotel. A hundred men and half as many women sit in folding chairs before a lectern on a small riser. Eddie Jarvis, one of the city selectmen, is speaking to them, and everyone seems amazingly calm. Labry is talking in my ear, but it takes me a few moments to register the import of his words.

"Hans Necker just saved our ass. He called some key pilots as soon as he got out of surgery and told them he thought the shooting was a freak accident, some kids out hunting who got out of hand. About half the pilots wanted to keep flying anyway. The weather hasn't been this good in years, and there's always the prize money."

"What's the festival committee say?"

"What do you think? Balloons in the air means money, especially tomorrow. Sunday without balloons is always a dud, financially speaking."

"Do I need to talk at all?"

"Just a quick word of thanks. Show them you're all right. Reassure them."

Many in the crowd have noticed me, and they're watching me now, not Eddie Jarvis. Jarvis waves me forward, and I take the lectern.

"Ladies and gentlemen, I want to thank you for getting here on short notice. What happened to Hans Necker and me today has rattled everyone, I'm sure. But I want you to know that I agree with Hans. I feel sure this was an isolated occurrence. I think everyone should make his or her own choice about whether to continue flying, but we intend to go on with the festival. Law enforcement will have a strong presence along the course this afternoon and tomorrow."

"Will you be flying this afternoon?" someone calls, and there's some muted laughter.

"I will. But I'll be aboard a sheriff's department helicopter, helping to scout the course. I don't want to put any of you good people at risk by asking you to fly me. It could be that today's gunman was a disgruntled constituent of mine."

There's more laughter this time. Balloon pilots are an intrepid bunch, but not all of them seem reassured.

"I was in the balloon behind you guys," says a mustached man in the fourth row. "I heard the bullets flying, but no gunshot. Do the police think the shooter used a silenced rifle?"

There's some murmuring at this.

"I was in the service," the man explains. "That's what it sounded like to me."

"The police and the sheriff's department are looking into all the available evidence. If we learn anything that bears on the safety of future flights, you'll all be informed immediately. I'm going to arrange the helicopter flyovers now. Thank you again for all you've done to help make the festival a success. Mr. Jarvis?"

I wave and leave the lectern, joining Labry by the door.

"That was just right," he says. "Best you could hope for."

"How many do you think will keep flying?"

"Half. And half is plenty. If half of them fly, and this weather holds, the festival could still break a record."

"I need a phone, Paul. Not your cell either. A hard line."

He gives me a strange look. "What's with all the cloak-and-dagger this weekend?"

"Nothing. I just don't want anybody hearing our security arrangements."

Labry steers me toward a door, then pushes it open and speaks to a middle-aged woman sitting at a desk inside. "Could we borrow your office, Margaret? City business."

"Of course," she says, picking up her purse and coming around the desk. "Glad to see you're all right, Mr. Mayor."

"Thank you."

I motion for Labry to follow her out, then take Danny McDavitt's cell number from my pocket. He answers immediately.

"Do you know who this is?" I ask.

"I do."

"Where are you, Major?"

"Adams County Airport. Topping up the tank."

"Can you pick me up somewhere close to town?"

"No problem. Where?"

I think quickly. "There's a big field right in the middle of town, on the north side. It's right behind the Children's Home on Union Street. Not a lot of people know about it. I'll be waiting there. If you touch down just long enough for me to jump on, nobody watching from a distance will even know you landed."

"Got it. I'll see you in fifteen minutes."

When I leave the office, Labry is there to escort me back to my car.

"Keep your head down as we pass the crowd," he says. "Caitlin nearly beat down the door to get access to that meeting. She's liable to have an ACLU lawyer out there."

We exit the building at the rear, beneath the whipping flags of England, France, Spain, the Confederacy, the United States, and of course Mississippi, which still sports the Confederate battle standard in its top left corner.

Making a wide circle around the crowd outside, we move down a row of cars toward my Saab. We're thirty feet away when Caitlin steps from behind a balloon trailer with a cell phone held to her ear.

"Well, here you are at last," she says. "Paul, I need a minute with the mayor."

Labry looks at me. I sigh in exasperation, then wave him off. He moves back toward the Visitors' Center at a vigorous march.

Caitlin pockets her cell phone and walks toward me, her green eyes intent, probing mine with the power of the quick mind behind them.

"One minute," I tell her.

"I just heard the flights are going to continue."

"Yes."

"There's no way you would have supported that unless you knew that the shooting today was directed at you alone."

"What do you want, Caitlin?"

I try to keep the frustration out of my voice, but my resentment at her decision to leave Natchez has not left me. She looks hurt, but also resolved to press forward.

"I just saw some pictures that were found at Tim Jessup's house. Nude pictures. Of a woman who worked on the *Magnolia Queen*."

"Some cop is going to lose his job this week."

"Listen to me, Penn, please. I think someone is trying to play me. I'm not even having to fight to get this stuff out of them. They're using me to put out a story, I can feel it."

I don't respond.

"Won't you tell me what's happening? Let me help you."

"Don't you mean help yourself? You're in the hunt for another Pulitzer, aren't you?"

Her eyes flash. "I'm hunting for the truth. As always."

"I can't help you."

"So where does that leave us?"

"What else do you have?"

She takes a deep breath, looks off toward the crowd, which is dispersing into the cars now. "Not much. But that's going to change. You know it will."

Conscious of my rendezvous with McDavitt, I make a fast decision. "Caitlin, let's pretend no time has passed since we were together. None. No hurt feelings, nothing. I'm telling you that if you pursue this thing, your life is in danger. More than when we worked the Del Payton case, even. You won't be helping Tim or what he was trying to do. You won't be serving the public interest. And you'll be putting me and my family at risk, as well as yourself. In a few days, I may be able to tell you more, but for now, that's it."

She looks back in disbelief. "So, I'm just supposed to walk away?"

"Weren't you planning to anyway? I thought you were on your way to New Orleans with your friend?"

"He's already gone."

"Why aren't you?"

She starts to answer, then bites her

bottom lip and shakes her head. "I don't know. I really don't. Thanks for the minute. It was a real education."

She turns and follows Labry's path up toward the Visitors' Center, her jet hair blowing in the breeze from the river.

Eight hundred feet over the Mississippi River, my stomach starts to go on me. The balloon crash was too recent; I have to belt myself tightly into the chopper just to keep my nerves together. Danny McDavitt is sitting in front of me, in the left seat of the Athens Point sheriff's department helicopter. Folded into the right-hand seat is a tall, lean black man in his twenties named Carl Sims. Carl is the former marine sniper that Daniel Kelly told me about on the phone. He works as a deputy for the Athens Point sheriff's department, but today, like most people who live within fifty miles of town, he was attending the Balloon Festival. His black jeans and blue hoodie contrast with McDavitt's faded khakis and polo shirt. Though Sims and McDavitt are thirty years apart in age, they seem to know each other well. They communicate in brief phrases or dry jokes, and even their silences seem charged with exchanges of information.

Ostensibly, we're flying the course of the afternoon balloon race, watching the ground for signs of snipers. In fact, we're searching for Tim Jessup's car. When a child is kidnapped, the Investigative Support Unit of the FBI recommends getting a helicopter airborne as fast as possible, equipped with a vehicle description. Choppers are remarkably effective at locating cars on the run, and I don't see why they should be any less effective at locating cars that have been abandoned. If Tim's car has purposely been hidden, of course, our search is probably pointless. But since I have access to the chopper, searching for the missing car seems a better use of my time than riding shotgun for a bunch of balloons that won't be fired on unless I'm flying in one of them.

Once again, because of prevailing winds, the race course crosses the river from Mississippi to Louisiana. More than half of the pilots have decided to stay for the remainder of the festival, and half of these have already crossed the river and are sailing southwest under a glorious blue sky. The remaining balloons are stretched out to our left at various altitudes, from the twin bridges back to the launch site at the Natchez Airport. The wind has settled down since this morning, and from this distance the balloons look painted on the sky.

To the west, the Adams County sheriff's helicopter is running along the levee on Deer Park Road like a gunship preparing to lay down suppressing fire on enemy troops.

"I think they've got the primary mission under control," McDavitt says over the interphone. "What say we get to work?"

"I still don't know exactly what we're doing," Carl Sims confesses, looking back from the front seat. "I'm happy to help, but a little detail would be appreciated."

I don't see any reason to burden McDavitt or Sims with more knowledge than they need. "Guys, let me put this as simply as I can. Last night, a friend of mine was murdered. Who did it isn't important at the moment. But they've threatened my family. Right now we're looking for my friend's car. It's a blue Nissan Sentra, five or six years old. I'm not sure what it can tell me, but there might be evidence inside that could nail the people who killed him. Is that enough for you?"

"Where are we looking?" McDavitt asks.

"I think they caught him somewhere out past the city cemetery, on Cemetery Road or one of the dirt roads that turns off it."

The major executes a pedal turn and heads toward Weymouth Hall, a mansion atop the bluff not far from Jewish Hill. As we approach the widow's walk atop the house, he turns north and starts following Cemetery Road at about four hundred feet. The cars parked at the houses and shacks below are easily identifiable, and this gives me some hope.

"Got a license plate number?" Carl asks.

"No."

"I can get that for you. One call to the dispatcher in Athens Point."

"Can't risk it. This has to be totally under the radar."

After a brief glance at McDavitt, Carl says, "Right. Blue Nissan Sentra."

The Athens Point helicopter is brand-new, and far more advanced than the

Adams County chopper, having been pur-
chased after the crash Hans Necker mentioned during our stop at the old Triton
Battery plant. It's a Bell JetRanger, with a
lot of bells and whistles I don't understand,
but one that I do is FLIR, or Forward Looking Infrared Radar. This formerly military
surveillance system is based around a
pod mounted beneath the chopper's nose,
which contains an array of sensors that
detect both infrared and visible light. Its
readings are processed by a computer,
then displayed on a screen mounted on
the instrument panel in front of Major
McDavitt. Modern FLIR units are so sensitive to heat that they can "see" the transient "handprint"—actually a heatprint—of
a fugitive who has momentarily touched a
car as he flees from police in total blackness. In daylight, FLIR signals can be
blended with the signals from visible light
cameras to create a sort of God's-eye view
of the terrain below. The Athens Point unit
was donated by a lumber millionaire and
avid hunter who occasionally uses it to
monitor the white-tailed deer population
on the thousands of acres he owns.

McDavitt seems to be flying with one

eye on the ground and the other on the FLIR screen. When I ask about this, he explains that he flew Pave Low helicopters in Afghanistan, one of the most advanced choppers in the world, and that he became accustomed to using instruments as his primary interface with the world. Carl Sims searches the old-fashioned way, as befits a former sniper. His forehead is pressed to the curved windshield beside him, and he takes occasional breaks to survey the ground through the "chin bubble" below his feet.

Our main problem is not that Cemetery Road runs through a vast forest, but that this forest is laced with dozens of dirt roads, most cut long ago by loggers or oil drillers, and few are well maintained. If Tim was fleeing from pursuers in his car, he could have turned down any of these roads, hoping to find a wooded sanctuary.

"How far off the road do you want me to look?" McDavitt asks, obviously sharing my concern.

"Half a mile, I guess. Much more than that, and we won't be able to see anything anyway."

"Half a mile, it is."

The pilot begins banking from side to side, and as the chopper dips and rolls, my stomach begins to churn. Following advice I've heard about seasickness, I fix my gaze on the horizon line across the river. Carl and Danny make occasional comments about the landscape below, and several times the pilot drops to tree-top level to examine a car more closely. Sims even spots a Sentra, but when we descend to check it, we find that its paint is actually green.

A couple of minutes after this disap-pointing reconnaissance, McDavitt says, "Son of a bitch," and brings the ship into a hover over a high bluff not far from the river. He points to the FLIR screen. "Look at that, Carl."

"I'm seeing it."

"What is it?" I ask, leaning forward into the cockpit.

"A car," the pilot answers. "And it's hot."

On the screen I see a tiny black rectan-gle partially obscured by masses of gray that must represent the foliage. "How hot?"

"It was probably still on fire this morn-ing."

"Vehicles can burn for a long time," Sims explains. "Upholstery and stuff. I saw it in Iraq."

"It looks . . . I don't know, sort of far away. A lot lower than the trees."

"It's in a hole," says McDavitt.

"How deep?"

"I can't tell. I tried putting the laser on it, but there's too much vegetation to get an accurate reading. Just guessing, I'd say three hundred feet below those treetops."

I lean into the window and gaze out over the Mississippi River. After orienting myself to the angle of the bend, and the lake not far beyond the river, a sense of certainty much like triumph settles in me.

"I know where we are."

"Where?" Carl asks.

"The Devil's Punchbowl."

The sniper whips his head around and stares at me. "No shit?"

"No shit."

"How do you know?" asks McDavitt.

"I spent the night down there once. A long time ago."

"Bullshit," says Sims.

"Seriously. I was seventeen. It was a

Boy Scout thing. Merit Badge. Camping out overnight by yourself. Being a typical teenager, I chose the scariest place I could think of."

"I never knew anybody who's actually been down there," Sims says. "I always heard outlaws dumped the bodies of their victims there back in the old days. Heads separated from the bodies, and all."

McDavitt points at the FLIR screen. "I think somebody else heard the same stories. Got inspired, maybe."

"Maybe so," I agree, trying to let the truth of what happened last night find its way to my consciousness.

"What did you see down there?" Carl asks me. "Find any skeletons?"

"No. Wildlife, mostly. Lots of deer, foxes. I saw some black-bear tracks. I almost stepped on a six-foot rattlesnake."

"How deep is it? For real?"

"I didn't have any way to measure it. But it got dark down there in the afternoon. And I almost drowned that night. It started raining, and before I knew it, I was in the middle of a flash flood."

McDavitt chuckles softly. "I always

heard that Jean Laffite might have hid his treasure down there. You didn't find any pieces of eight, did you?"

"Not for lack of trying. I took a metal detector with me. And I did find a treasure, of a kind. But not pirate gold."

"What did you find?" Sims asks, his eyes bright.

For a few moments I resist answering. This memory I've always kept to myself. "A cougar. I saw a cougar down there. They're supposed to be extinct in these parts, but I know what I saw. He was on a limb looking down at a game path. There were deer tracks all through there. He was waiting for supper to walk by."

"What happened?"

"He looked at me, I looked at him, and then he was gone. Never made a sound. I didn't sleep a wink. All night I expected him to pounce on me out of nowhere. But he never did."

"He didn't like the smell of you," Carl says.

"Can't say I blame him," McDavitt says in a deadpan voice. "I'd have to be awful hungry to choose you over venison. But let's not get sidetracked. Anybody watching this ship is going to see us hanging over this hole like a buzzard circling a carcass. What's the plan?"

"That's got be Tim's car," I aver. "The question is, did he run it down there himself, or did the bad guys dump it there?"

"Why would he do it himself?" Carl asks.

"If they were chasing him, he might do it to make them think he'd crashed and died."

McDavitt nods thoughtfully. "If he did that, then the bad guys might not have searched it yet."

"If they know it's there, they've searched it. And they probably do know," I say, recalling Sands's certainty that Tim did not e-mail the stolen data to anyone. "But we can't be sure." I could call Seamus Quinn and save myself a lot of trouble, but if Quinn doesn't know about the car . . . "I need to get down there, guys."

"How you going to do that?" McDavitt asks. "My hoist won't even get you halfway."

"Same way I did when I was seventeen, I guess."

"How long did that take you?"

"Most of a day."

An intermittent beep sounds in the muffled hum of the JetRanger's cabin.

"What's that?" McDavitt scans his instrument panel. "That's not coming from the chopper."

I pull off one earpiece of my headset. "Sorry. It's a satellite phone." I lift the phone from the floor, click the SEND button, and put the receiver to my ear. "Hello?"

"Penn, it's Dad."

"What's going on? Is something wrong?"

"No, but I think you ought to come by my office."

"Right now?"

"Right now. There's somebody here to see you."

"Can you say who it is?"

"I'd rather not."

I feel momentary panic. "Are you all right?"

"I'm fine, don't worry."

"Did you call from your office line?"

"Hell no. I borrowed Chris Shepard's cell phone."

"Okay." Chris Shepard is one of my father's younger partners.

"Just get over here now, if you can."

"I'm kind of in the middle of something important."

There's a brief silence. Then my father says, "Well, let's see how important. I've got Jewel Washington sitting here with the results of Tim Jessup's autopsy, which she's under instructions not to share with anybody. Is that important enough?"

Shit. "Don't let her leave. I'll be there in fifteen minutes."

"That's what I figured."

I hang up and look down at the forest below, then at the men in the front of the chopper. "I need to get back to my car."

McDavitt nods. Carl keeps looking at me, then expels a lungful of air. "If you really think what you're looking for could be down there, I can check it out for you."

A rush of gratitude flows through me. "Are you sure? That's a deep hole."

Sims laughs. "Yeah, well. I've heard about that place all my life. Might as well see for myself what's at the bottom."

"What exactly is he looking for?" McDavitt asks.

"A DVD, probably. Any form of digital media."

"Any digital media in that car has been burned to a crisp," the pilot points out.

"Could have been thrown clear," Carl says. "If it was in a bag or a case, say."

"You *want* to go down there," McDavitt says, shaking his head. "Can you tell this guy was a marine or what?"

"You could be right about the fire," I concede. "But if we don't look down there, we'll never know for sure."

Carl speaks with his face pressed to the window. "If you got in and out when you were a Boy Scout, I can sure as hell do it. Can't be any worse than Iraq, right?"

"I don't think they have rattlesnakes or bears in Iraq."

"Or cougars," McDavitt adds with sarcasm.

Carl nods thoughtfully. "You got a point there. But I've got good boots. And if I have to shoot, I hit what I aim at."

"The trick," says McDavitt, "is seeing the threat in *time* to shoot."

The sniper smiles. "I'll keep my eyes open."

"Okay," says McDavitt. "Where's this traveling circus headed next?"

"My car," I tell him.

"Then mine," Sims says. "ASAP. I don't want to be at the bottom of that hole when night falls."

McDavitt swings the chopper out over the river and roars back toward town.

CHAPTER

22

My father's medical office looks like something that belongs in the Smithsonian Institution, the refuge of a doctor who loves history and the art of medicine, and who exhibits his disdain for modern gadgetry by banishing his notebook computer to the nurses' station outside his inner sanctum. The office is almost a museum itself, housing a gargantuan collection of medical books, Civil War memoirs, English novels, ship models, antique surgical instruments, and meticulously hand-painted lead soldiers from the Napoleonic Wars, each one accurate to the last detail. Every inch of fabric and leather in the room exudes the smell of cigars, which announces to patients old and new my father's long-held medical philosophy: *Do as I say, not as I do.*

I find Dad sitting behind his desk, his feet resting on a stool, while Jewel Washington laughs at something he said before I entered. I could swear I see a trace of embarrassment in Jewel's dark cheeks. It's hard to imagine what would make a nurse who's made it past fifty blush, but if anybody knows what that would be, it's Tom Cage. Jewel stands to greet me, and we hug briefly.

"Sit by me on the couch," she says. "I didn't bring any paperwork, for obvious reasons. I ain't supposed to show you the autopsy, so how about I just summarize it verbally?"

"Did Shad Johnson tell you not to show it to me?"

Jewel's eyes glint with submerged meaning. "Let's say the district attorney advised the county coroner that a homicide investigation is no business of the mayor's."

"Duly noted. What did the autopsy show?"

"Your friend was shot."

A chill races along my arms. I expected anything but this. "Shot?"

"Pathologist in Jackson dug a .22 Magnum slug out of his heart."

"Why didn't we see the entry wound? Was it masked by one of those dog bites?"

"You got it. Dog mauled that boy something terrible."

"Are you sure it was a dog?"

"I got out the textbooks and took measurements. That man was tore up by a canine—a big one—and the wounds definitely occurred prior to death."

Dad shakes his head in disgust.

Jewel says, "You combine that with the burns, and—"

"Just a minute. What caused the burns?"

"Some were from an electric cigarette lighter, like in a car. Others from an actual cigarette, which gets hotter than a car lighter. A lit cigarette burns at over a thousand degrees Fahrenheit. Draw on it, it heats up to nearly thirteen hundred degrees. That's a world of pain right there."

"Sons of bitches," Dad mutters.

"Add up those two things, you get one answer. Somebody tortured that man. Why? For kicks? For revenge? Something he knew? I'm guessing you'd know more about the motive than I would."

"I don't know anything at this point, Jewel."

She gives me a long look. "You sound more like Shad Johnson than Penn Cage."

"Let's get back to Shad in a minute. What else did the postmortem show?"

"They only have the initial toxicology panel back, but there were definitely drugs in the victim's blood."

Damn it. "What kind of drugs?"

"Opiates, some crystal meth."

I shake my head, unwilling to accept that Tim had gotten high before carrying out his secret mission.

"Funny thing, though," Jewel says. "There was some bruising at the injection site. Antecubital vein, which is unusual. Most addicts try to hide needle marks. This guy wasn't a habitual user, at least not that way. His veins were in decent shape, except for some old scarring between his toes and on his penis."

"What killed him, Jewel? The fall or the bullet?"

"The fall, but only because it happened so soon after he was shot. Bullet wound would've killed him in a minute or two."

"Did anybody hear shots on the bluff prior to Tim's fall? I don't remember Chief Logan saying anything about that."

"Not as far as I know."

"And you said the wound would have killed him in a couple of minutes."

"Yes."

"If he'd been shot in the SUV, could he have made the run to the fence, and then run along it like he did?"

Jewel is considering this when Dad says, "It's possible. I've seen men hit several times with higher-caliber bullets continue fighting for over a minute."

Jewel and I look at my father in silence, knowing that this kind of knowledge was not absorbed in medical school, but in Korea.

"In that situation," Dad goes on, "being tortured, his adrenaline would have been off the charts. And he obviously summoned the strength to break away from his captors."

"Okay, maybe that explains it. But if he was shot at the fence, then someone used a silenced weapon."

"Like with the balloon," Dad says. "I see."

Jewel looks between us but says nothing. Like a lot of people in town, she has heard about the crash landing, and the rest is simple enough to piece together.

"Any other significant findings?" I ask.

Her eyes fix on me. "You could say that."

"Well?"

"Penn Cage, I didn't carry my tired old butt out here to be doing all the givin' without gettin' nothing in return. You tell me what's going on. Who killed that man like that? And why?"

I look to my father for support, but he only shrugs. "Jewel," I say, "I want you to listen to me. Listen like I'm telling you about one of your children. You don't want to know any more about this case than you already do. You could end up on the same table Tim was cut on. Tell me you understand what I'm saying. I don't want to add your safety to my list of worries."

The coroner shakes her head, but I can't tell if she's offended or not. "What are you telling me? Stop working this death?"

"No. Just don't do anything out of your normal investigative routine. Follow the book, and nothing more. And by that standard, I think you're finished."

Now she looks offended. "If I'd followed the book, you wouldn't know what you know now."

"I realize that. And I appreciate it. But the risk is mine to take, not yours."

"Why's that?"

"Because I owe somebody."

A small, strange smile shows on Jewel's face. "Now you sound like your daddy. Okay, then. You're telling me I'm at risk just by coming here, right?"

"You could be. If they're watching Dad. You need to come up with a plausible reason for your visit."

"Prescription," Dad says. "Is your mother still having problems with peripheral neuropathy?"

Jewel smiles broadly now. "Do you ever forget anything about a patient?"

"Hell, yes. More every day."

"I don't believe it."

I touch the coroner's wrist. "You said there was something else."

"Pathologist found something in your friend's rectum."

"What? Drugs?"

"No. The cap from a thumb drive."

My heart thumps against my sternum.

"A thumb what?" Dad asks.

"A flash-memory device," Jewel explains. "USB type. Made by Sony. It's about two inches long and a third of an inch wide."

"Only the cap?" I ask, certain that I'm a lot closer to at least the copy of the data on the DVD Tim stole from the *Magnolia Queen.* "Not the actual device?"

"Right. Weird, huh?"

"Maybe not."

Jewel ponders my face. "He stuck the drive up there to hide it from whoever killed him, didn't he?"

To smuggle it off the boat, I think. "Probably."

"This guy worked on the *Magnolia Queen,* right?"

"Jewel—"

"So was he smuggling information off the boat."

"Please stop, right there. I'm not kidding."

She frowns and waves me away as she might a pestering child. "I ain't tellin' nobody nothin' 'bout this. I just want to know for my own self. So when I sit up at night thinking about it, like I always do, I'll eventually be able to get me some sleep instead of puzzling about it till the sun comes up."

"You're on the right track, that's all I can tell you."

"Okay. So the question is, who has the USB drive now?"

I nod.

"Well, your friend left work just before midnight, and he died around twelve thirty-five. So whoever tortured him didn't have him long, not even if they had him that whole time, which they probably didn't. Jessup had lots of welts and abrasions on his legs and arms, like he'd been running through the woods."

"Really?"

"Mm-hm. So let's say they had ten

minutes to torture him in the backseat of that SUV. I doubt they had time to do a cavity search."

"Don't be too sure. Some professionals do that kind of thing automatically."

Jewel's brow furrows. "What kind of professionals? You talkin' 'bout cops?"

"Not exactly. Military types. Ex-military. Paramilitary, maybe."

"What exactly does *para*military mean?"

"*Sort of* military," Dad explains. "Like *para*medic. Not quite a doctor."

"They didn't expect Tim to get out of that vehicle," I reason aloud. "They injected him with drugs, started torturing him, but somehow he got out while they were driving down Broadway. So unless they cavity-searched him, or he gave up the USB drive's location right away, he got out of that vehicle with it. Who had access to the body, postmortem?"

"The cops at the scene," Jewel says.

"You think they'd pull his pants down and cavity-search him with spectators hanging over the fence like they were?"

"They could have," Dad says. "They could have leaned a bunch of guys over him to shield it, the way NFL teams do when they want to hide an on-field injection from the camera."

"No. That would take too many dirty cops. Let's assume the drive was still in situ when Jewel got the body. Who had access after that?"

Jewel's still looking at the ceiling, nodding slowly. "It was so late that I put him in the morgue at St. Catherine's rather than drive him to Jackson. University said they'd rush the autopsy for me, but it wouldn't speed it up any for me to drive him up in the middle of the night. And I'd been all day under that hot sun—"

"The morgue is locked, right?"

"Most of the time. And the drawers are locked. But it ain't like I got the only key. They gave me my key to the drawers when I got the job. I probably should have put new locks on them, but the administrator might not appreciate that, seeing how I don't own the hospital. So, I guess anybody with a key to the drawers could get to the body. The local pathologist for sure. Maybe some med techs or even nurses. Hell, maintenance might have a key, for all I know."

"We need to find out."

Jewel snorts. "The way things are at that hospital right now, you could ask questions for a month and never find out everybody who's got a key. That's like asking who's got a key to a church or a school. And if I start asking, everybody's gonna know it. That how you want to play this?"

"No. Forget that. But as far as you know, no cops have reported a USB drive being found?"

"Nope. They don't even know about the cap, or I'd have already heard a dozen jokes about somebody 'putting a cap in his ass.'"

"I think we need to get Jewel moving," Dad says.

"One last thing," I say. "Shad Johnson."

Jewel's brown eyes filled with an emotion I can't read. "Pardon my French, Penn, but that man's sure got a hard-on for you. I reckon ever since you beat him out for mayor, he's been out to get you."

"It goes back farther than that. It was the Del Payton case."

"*Mm-hm,*" Jewel responds with a unique emphasis that I've only heard from black women. "That's why he lost for mayor. Betrayed his own people. And we knew it. We're finally past the time where black folks always gonna vote for you just 'cause you black."

"Shad explicitly warned you not to share any information with me?"

"Yes, indeed."

"Did he give you a reason?"

"He said the victim was a friend of yours, and you might be involved in the case somehow. Giving you any kind of information would be improper, maybe even illegal."

"Were those his exact words?"

"He said something about a 'firing offense.'"

"Yet here she is," Dad says. "Good people."

"I do appreciate it, Jewel," I tell her. "More than you know. But from now on, you need to lie low. There's nothing more you can do."

She pulls a wry face. "I ain't so sure about that. But you won't hear from me unless I've got something you really need."

"How will you know that, if you don't know what I'm trying to do?"

"Boy, I know what you trying to do. You trying to prove your friend was a good man and nail whoever killed him. And that's something I can get behind. Shad Johnson can kiss my big ass if he thinks he scares me. I could break that man over my knee."

"It's not Shad you have to worry about."

Jewel nods slowly. "I hear you. But I know how to walk soft when I need to. Now, let me get out of here. I'm dying for a cigarette. I hate to admit it, but it's the Lord's truth."

I'm rising to shake her hand when my cell phone rings.

"Go on and get that," she says. "You gonna give me that 'scrip for my mama, Doc?"

I move into the hall. "Hello?"

"Penn, this is Julia Jessup."

"Julia! Are you all right?"

"*No.* I just got off the phone with that girl you used to date, or live with, or whatever."

"Who? Libby Jensen?"

"No! The one that wrote those lies in the paper this morning!"

"Caitlin Masters? Wait a minute. How did you talk to Caitlin? Did she call your cell phone? You're not supposed to have that switched on."

"I called *her*. I'm not going to have half this town believing Tim was dealing drugs. There wasn't any damn meth in our house."

"I know that, Julia." *Jesus.* "And I know you're upset. We need to talk about this face-to-face."

"What you *need* to do is call that bitch and tell her what you just told me. Tell her to write a retraction in tomorrow's newspaper."

"Julia, listen, please. The last thing you want right now is Caitlin Masters poking around this story. All that matters is you and your son staying safe. That's all Tim would want."

I hear a child crying, then what sounds like a hand patting flesh. "You don't know what Tim wanted," she says. "It doesn't sound like you do, anyway. He wanted to make those bastards he worked for quit whatever they're doing. I tried to talk him out of it, but he wouldn't listen. He said you were helping him, and now he's dead. And I don't see you defending him. Maybe if Caitlin Masters put all this on the front page, something would get done. I'll bet she'd do it too. She already asked me for an interview."

Beads of sweat have sprung up on my face. How can a woman who just lost her husband not see that what she's proposing could cost her and her son their lives? Just saying it on the telephone has put her at risk, and Caitlin too.

"Julia, Tim came to me for a reason. He trusted me because I've dealt with this kind of thing before, and because he knew I would do the right thing. But the right thing is rarely what your emotions tell you to do when you're upset. I know you can't see that right now, but you have to try. Julia . . . ? Are you still there?"

"I'm here."

"Please forget about talking to Caitlin. Nothing good will come of that, and it could cost you everything. *Everything.* Do you understand? Julia? Do I have to spell this out for you?"

Her only reply is a strangled growl, a mixture of rage and frustration that rises to a crescendo, then abruptly ceases.

"Julia, as long as you stay where you

are and keep quiet, you'll be safe. You can call me tonight, and we'll work out a way to see each other. All right?"

"Christ," she says in disgust. "I'm hanging up."

The phone goes dead.

I walk to the open door of my father's office. Dad is bending over his desk to sign a prescription, while Jewel studies a photograph of our family when I was eleven and my sister seventeen.

"Ya'll ever see Jenny anymore?" she asks.

"Not very often," Dad confesses.

"She looks just like Mrs. Peggy, almost exactly."

"I'm sorry, I've got to run," I tell them.

"Where are you going?" Dad asks.

"I have to find Caitlin. Thanks for everything, Jewel. No more warnings from me."

The coroner smiles. "Boy, I didn't make it this far not knowing how to take care of myself. Get out of here."

With a quick wave, I turn and run for my car.

CHAPTER

23

Tim Jessup's father is the last man I expected to hear from today, but four blocks from Caitlin's house, I answered my cell phone and heard the old surgeon's voice in my ear. Jack Jessup is the opposite of my father: arrogant, greedy, brusque with patients. Golf, money, and the respect of society are his primary obsessions, at least the ones I know about. Seen through his father's eyes, Tim must have seemed a complete failure from the time he entered high school.

Dr. Jessup gave me no specifics, but asked if I could stop by the Catholic rectory in the next half hour. I assumed that he intended to ask me to read or say something at Tim's wake. I wanted to see Caitlin as soon as possible—she had agreed via text message to meet me at her house—but since the cathedral and rectory are only a few blocks away from our houses, I agreed to meet the surgeon.

It's close to dark when I pull up to the imposing mass of St. Mary's Minor Basilica, a monument to the Irish immigrants who came to Natchez in the nineteenth century. The Irish dominated the Catholic faith here, leavened by a few Italian families who escaped indentured servitude upriver in Louisiana. Of course, Natchez has black Catholics as well, and they worship at the historic Holy Family Church on St. Catherine Street, but their journey, like so many in Natchez, was a parallel one. The dual cultures, shadows of each other, stretch out toward infinity, a single breath apart, but never quite meeting.

The rectory is a modest building, built of the same brick as the cathedral. A long, gray Mercedes is parked in front of it, and behind this an older Lincoln Continental. As I approach the door, a woman bursts through and rushes past me. She looks familiar, but all I really register is a graying bouffant and pancake makeup concealing a face twisted into a grimace of rage and anguish. She disappears into the Lincoln, then races down the street with a squeal of rubber.

What's going on here? I wonder.

Father Mullen is a new priest, and young. I've only met him on a couple of occasions, at civic functions. A well-educated Midwesterner, he seems somewhat bemused by the Southernness of his new flock. I wonder how he sees Jack Jessup, a clotheshorse who used to charge $1,000 to remove a mole my father would have cut off for $75.

I find Dr. Jessup and Father Mullen in the priest's office, the surgeon's expensive chalk-stripe suit a marked contrast to Mullen's black robe. I can tell by Jessup's posture that he's disturbed about something. He's leaning over the priest's desk like a naval officer at the rail of a ship about to go into battle.

Judiciously clearing my throat, I say, "Excuse me?"

The surgeon turns sharply, but his face

softens when he recognizes me. He motions me forward, and I shake his hand.

Behind him, Father Mullen looks as though he would rather be mortifying his flesh in a monastery than dealing with Dr. Jessup in his present state. The surgeon has intimidated more formidable men than priests.

"What can I do for you, Dr. Jessup?" I ask.

The surgeon's mouth works behind his closed lips for a few moments, as though he's being forced to chew and swallow a day-old lemon wedge. When Dr. Jessup finally speaks, I realize his voice is choked with indignation.

"Did you see who just left?"

"She looked familiar, but she passed me so fast, I didn't recognize her."

"Charlotte McQueen."

I blink in surprise, but it takes less time than a blink for me to decode the subtext of this situation. Charlotte McQueen is the mother of the boy who died when Tim ran his car off the road in college during his beer run to the county line. In fact, she's the one who pushed the DA into making Tim do jail time. Mrs. McQueen is an

influential member of the Catholic church,
and I doubt she came to express her condolences.

"I see," I temporize. "Well, how exactly
can I help, Doctor?"

Dr. Jessup jerks his head toward Father
Mullen. "I'll let *him* explain it to you."

The priest tries a conciliatory smile as
he stands and walks around his desk, taking care to make a wide arc around Dr.
Jessup. I can only imagine what must
have transpired before I entered the rectory. "Mr. Mayor," he begins in a soft voice,
but then he stops and looks closely at me.
"Are you all right, Mr. Cage?"

"What do you mean?"

"Your eyes are very red."

"I haven't gotten much sleep this weekend. Please go on."

"I'm not sure we should even be having
this conversation, but Dr. Jessup feels
that your input might help shed some light
on the situation."

"What exactly is the situation?"

"Well, as you may know, Timothy Jessup was—"

"Just tell him what the woman said," Dr.
Jessup snaps. "Tell him what she wants."

Father Mullen gives the surgeon a pained look. "Dr. Jessup, I really don't think you need worry about Mrs. McQueen's request. What she asked—"

"Demanded."

"Yes . . . yes, I suppose she did. Nevertheless, it's really very rare nowadays. Only in the most extreme cases does—"

"Stop all the mushmouth! Just tell him."

Father Mullen turns to me. "Well, as you probably know, Mrs. McQueen's son Patrick died twenty-seven years ago on a highway near Oxford, Mississippi."

"Yes, I know. Tim Jessup served time for manslaughter as a result. How does that bear on the present?"

"The vindictive old bitch doesn't want Tim to have a Church funeral," Dr. Jessup says in a choked voice.

Blood rises into my cheeks. "Is that true?"

Father Mullen diplomatically retreats a step. "Not exactly. But in broad terms, yes. I don't believe Mrs. McQueen has ever gotten over the death of her son."

"Of course not. No one does. But I fail to see how that would have any bearing on Tim's funeral."

"Well," Father Mullen says in the tone of a man being forced to point out the most inconvenient of truths, "according to canon law, certain persons may be prohibited from having Catholic funerals. If the person is known to be an apostate or a heretic, or is such a publicly manifest sinner that having a Church funeral would cause a scandal among the congregation, the mass may be—and occasionally is—withheld."

Dr. Jessup is shaking his head in disgust. "I can't believe my ears. I've been coming here for thirty-seven years, and—"

"Just a moment, Dr. Jessup," I say. "Father, are you seriously considering Mrs. McQueen's request?"

"Well, not in the way you might think. But given the situation, I don't feel I can simply reject it out of hand. The problem is that the congregation has become aware that a large quantity of drugs was found in Tim's home on the night he died."

"The night he was *murdered*," Dr. Jessup corrects. "Isn't that right, Penn? Wasn't my son murdered?"

"He was."

Father Mullen nods awkwardly, as

though this information hardly advances Tim's cause. "It seems that some embarrassing pictures have surfaced as well— pictures of a young lady not Mr. Jessup's wife. They were also found in his home."

Dr. Jessup snorts. "You want to start going through the closets and computers and cell phones of everyone in this congregation and see how many pictures like that you find?"

Father Mullen blanches at the prospect. "From an ecclesiastical point of view, the issues are several, and I suspect Mrs. McQueen researched them thoroughly before she came to me. Canons 1184 and 1185, to be precise. First, Tim hadn't been a practicing Catholic for many years. Second, he never had his child baptized into the faith nor showed any intent to do so. Third, he's known to have made statements to members of the congregation that he stopped believing in God decades ago. With all respect, Dr. Jessup, Tim appears to have led a life of dissolution from the time of the drinking incident in which Patrick McQueen died up to the night of his own death, when police say he was selling drugs for a living. But most important, if Tim was indeed murdered, it's unlikely he got a chance to repent these actions. Any or all of these issues could technically make Tim ineligible to receive the liturgy at his funeral."

Behind all the Churchspeak, I sense a man being tested in a way he never foresaw until tonight. "What do *you* think, Father?"

"The padre thinks it's time to punt," Dr. Jessup says bitterly. "He wants to call the bishop."

"Dr. Jessup," Father Mullen says in the soothing voice he must use at hospital bedsides, "almost no one is denied a funeral, or at least a Catholic burial, nowadays. With our modern understanding of psychology, the Church frequently gives even those who take their own lives a mass and burial. I think that in this case, it's simply a matter of showing Mrs. McQueen that I've taken her request seriously by passing it on to the bishop, who I am sure will make the appropriate decision."

"Translation," says Dr. Jessup, "they don't want to upset any big contributors. Or the women who keep the Church going.

I guess I didn't put enough of the Almighty Dollar in the plate over the years."

"Doctor," the priest says with an edge of indignation, "I don't think that's fair."

"I thought you asked me here to talk about Tim's wake," I say, still not quite believing the situation.

Dr. Jessup brings a quivering fist to his mouth, and I realize I'm seeing something I've never witnessed before. Jack Jessup, a surgeon who, for as long as I can remember, appeared to be as stony and remote as a Victorian banker, is crying.

Father Mullen starts toward him as though to commiserate, but I warn the priest off with a glance. When a man like Jack Jessup breaks down, he's capable of anything.

"Mr. Mayor," Father Mullen says softly, "Dr. Jessup felt that before I called the bishop, you might be able to give me some details unknown to the public—things that might mitigate the present appearance of things."

Despite my desire to help, I'm hesitant to reveal anything about what Tim was doing. It's not that I don't trust the priest. My fear is that Dr. Jessup, in his desire to amend people's opinions of Tim, might reveal more than he should. In truth I never liked the surgeon, but he's suffering terribly now, and if I can ameliorate that, I should. The risk of Tim not getting a Catholic funeral must be remote, but one never knows what bureaucrats will do to keep from offending those who subsidize their existence.

"Gentlemen," I say reluctantly, "I want both of you to give me your word that what I'm about to say doesn't go beyond these four walls."

Dr. Jessup's eyes narrow. "I'll never repeat anything you say here. As God is my witness."

Father Mullen frowns at the doctor, but it's hard to chide a man who has just lost his son. "You have my word, of course," says the priest.

"I want the seal of the confessional."

Mullen looks offended. "I'm not sure what you mean by that. You're not Catholic, are you?"

"You know exactly what I mean, Father. I'm sorry to insist, but I've known priests and pastors who betrayed confidences, both in private conversation and in court."

Father Mullen shakes his head with a weary sigh. "The seal of the confessional. What we say here goes no further."

Dr. Jessup is watching me like the parents of defendants I prosecuted for rape or murder watched the faces of their sons' accusers; he's waiting for some hint that his child wasn't the terrible man people believe he was—some scrap of hope to cling to as time wears him down and leaves nothing but memory.

"Father Mullen," I say softly, "I'm ashamed to admit this, but I was Tim's childhood friend, yet for the past few years I shared the low opinion people have of him. If we're all honest here, I think even Dr. Jessup shared that opinion."

A strangled croak comes from my right, but I cannot bear to look.

"In the next few days, people are going to say a lot of things about Tim. The newspaper may say he was using drugs the night he died. The police or the district attorney might even say Tim was planning to commit terrible crimes. I'm telling you now that those charges will be lies."

Dr. Jessup's shoes creak as he steps

forward and leans closer. "What do you mean? Tell us."

I keep my eyes on those of the priest, which are blue and clear and bright with skepticism. "Tim Jessup was a hero," I tell him quietly. "I don't say that lightly. Tim died trying to save innocent people from suffering, and to protect this town from evil. That may sound archaic, Father, but I've dealt with evil firsthand. I know what I'm talking about. Tim suffered terrible torment before he died. The tragedy is that his death was unnecessary. Had the rest of us been doing the work we pay lip service to doing, Tim would still be with us. I know Mrs. McQueen has suffered over her son, but Tim paid for that a long time ago. What matters most is this: Even if the truth of what Tim was trying to do never comes out, every citizen of this town is in his debt. Of that you can be sure."

Dr. Jessup clutches my upper arm like a drowning man clutches a life preserver.

Father Mullen's eyes are wide, his mouth half open. "Well . . . I think I expected a plea for the sake of the man's wife. Can you give me any details?"

"I'm afraid not. There are lives at stake."

The surgeon's hand is shivering on my arm. "Please, Penn. Anything."

I shake my head. "Father, Jacqueline Kennedy once said that the Catholic Church is at its best when dealing with death. To me, this is one of those opportunities to live up to the promise of your creed. I personally don't know what Tim believed about God, but I do know he believed *in* God. He made religious references to me the night before he died, and I know he believed he was doing God's work when he was killed. Now, you can call the bishop if you like. But I think it's best if Dr. Jessup and I just leave you alone with your conscience."

Before the priest can respond, I turn and pull the old surgeon with me to the door. Dr. Jessup is wheezing like an asthmatic, but this sound isn't respiratory distress; it's the throttled crying of a man who sealed himself off from emotion for most of his life and now finds himself unable to contain the hurt and stunted love within him.

"Can you get home all right?" I ask.

Dr. Jessup won't let me off so easy.

When we reach the steps, he seizes my arm and turns me until I'm looking into his watery gray eyes, eyes that for forty years seemed to look down from an Olympian height to the mortals who came to him to cut out their tumors and inflamed gall-bladders, and that now hold only pain and pleading. How the mighty are fallen.

"Was that true? What you said about Tim? That he was trying to do something good?"

"Yes. But don't ask me what it was. And please don't tell your wife yet. I'll tell you the rest of it someday, Doctor. When it's safe. But that's the best I can do tonight."

Dr. Jessup shakes his head slowly. "You said he—he suffered."

I look down the street, toward the corner of Washington Street. "You're going to see that for yourself when Tim's body comes back from Jackson. You're a doctor, so you'll know what you're looking at. I wanted you to be prepared. Don't let your wife see him."

"Who killed my boy?" Dr. Jessup asks in a cracked whisper. "You tell me. Tell me!"

"I can't."

"But you know, don't you?"

"No, sir. And I'm afraid the police aren't even calling it murder yet. Not officially. The next few days are going to be hard on you and Mrs. Jessup. I hope you can take some comfort in what I told Father Mullen. I don't think you'll have any more trouble about the funeral. Mullen's just young, and I'm sure Mrs. McQueen was pretty formidable. She feels about Patrick the way you do about Tim."

Dr. Jessup nods. "I know that. I see it now."

I try to turn and walk to my car, but he clings to me, his hand like a claw on my wrist. "What are *you* doing? I know you're your father's son. Are you trying to finish what Tim started?"

A car with blue headlights approaches on the street. After it hisses past, I say, "All I can tell you is this: If I have anything to do with it, Tim will not have died in vain. Now, I need to go."

"One last thing," Dr. Jessup says. "I know your father never thought much of me. All my life I chased after things that don't mean a damned thing. My son needed me, and all I could do was hate him for not being what I wanted. Well, this is my punishment, I guess." Dr. Jessup's gaze slides off my face and climbs the buttresses and spires of the cathedral. "Your father was the best of us. Our crop, I mean." The wet eyes come back to me. "And Tim thought the world of you. I wish you would say something at his wake, if you will. Even if you can't say what you told us in there."

"Of course I will."

Just as I think I'm free, the gray eyes peer into mine with a darkness like blood behind them. "If you find out who killed my boy, Penn, you pick up the telephone. You hear me? Tell me where to find him, that's all. I don't care if I spend the rest of my life behind bars and eternity in flames."

Dr. Jessup's clenched hand finally loosens as the force of his passion drains from him. For a moment I fear he's going to collapse on the steps, but then he pulls his coat around him and gets himself under control. I saw this too many times when I was a prosecutor, most often in victims' families: fathers and brothers who would readily kill to avenge those they should have loved far better when the person was alive.

"Tim will get justice. The best thing you can do for him now is take care of your grandson. Your wife and your daughter-in-law too. They need you."

With a last grimace of confusion, he shuffles past me toward the big Mercedes by the curb. As he wrestles with his key, I trot to my car on unsteady legs, hoping that Caitlin has waited for me.

Caitlin is watching from one of her front windows as I pull up. She opens the front door with only her face showing, as though she's just gotten out of the shower, then motions for me to come in, but I wave her out to the car. She extends a bare foot and calf, points to the foot, then disappears inside. I get out and walk halfway to her door. A moment later she comes out wearing shorts, sandals, and a white linen top, a puzzled look on her face.

"To what do I owe this honor?"

"We need to talk," I whisper, "and it can't be in our houses or cars. Is there a car at the newspaper office we can use?"

She's looking at me strangely, but she answers quietly. "Yes. Are you going to drive us over there?"

When I nod, she walks back and locks her door, then comes out to my car.

Caitlin never needs to be told anything twice, unless it's to keep her nose out of something. She doesn't speak as we drive across town; she's content to study me from the passenger seat. I look toward her a few times, but it's difficult to do that without making eye contact, and there's too much unsaid between us to endure that for long. It's easier to study her legs, which are long and toned and surprisingly tawny, given her pale skin. She must have spent some time in the lower latitudes recently.

"Antigua," she says, reading my mind.

"Alone?"

"No." After letting me suffer for a few moments, she says, "A corporate retreat."

"I've never really understood what happens at those."

"Depends on the company. Some put you through a week of New Age sermons on the gospel of wealth. Others encourage you to kill large mammals and screw beautiful ethnic prostitutes."

After the awful tension at the rectory, this makes me laugh. "I spent a lot of my career dealing with men who'd rather screw large mammals and kill beautiful ethnic prostitutes."

This brings a real laugh from Caitlin. In the closed car the sound rings bright and true. "Or writing about them," she says.

I nod but don't continue our old conversational rhythm, and the sparkle dies in her eyes. As I start to pull into the newspaper parking lot, she points to the side of the building, which I assume means I should park behind it. When I get to the back, I see six cars parked in a row beside a glass door.

As soon as we're inside, she says, "Are you sure you don't just want to talk here?"

"Can you get us total privacy? I don't want everyone in the building knowing I'm here."

"If you don't mind sitting on the floor of a supply room."

"Fine. Perfect."

A little way up the hall, she leads me

into a room lined with metal shelves and boxes, then locks the door behind us. After a quick survey of the shelves, she pulls down two boxes of legal-size copy paper and makes a seat. I pull down two more, and soon we're facing each other, separated by three feet of harshly lit space.

"You look bad," she says bluntly. "How long has it been since you slept?"

"That doesn't matter right now."

She considers this for a few seconds. "You know, you acted like a total shit to me today."

"You asked for it. You acted like you expected me to take you into my confidence as though we're still together. We're not together."

She looks away. "I just wanted you to have a civil conversation with me."

"No. You wanted a story. The inside story. And I couldn't give you that. No one would have benefited from that."

"Is that for you to decide?"

"In this case it is."

"You spoke in the past tense. Why are you here now?"

"Because you're in danger. The deeper

you look into Tim Jessup's death, the more likely it is you'll be hurt."

I see disbelief in her eyes, but not because she doubts the danger. "You know I've worked stories like that before."

"This is different. I've worked dangerous cases. But these people will kill without hesitation."

"What people?"

"We may get to that. But you need to know that you can't trust your phones—not your cell or the landlines at home. I'm not sure about the newspaper phones."

Now she doubts me. "Who are you talking about? Who can tap landlines? Bad cops? The FBI again? Who?"

"It's complicated. You also have to realize that people like Julia Jessup tell other people you've questioned them. They say that on open phone lines. And the wrong thing in the wrong ear will get you dead."

"Where's Annie?" Caitlin asks, ignoring my warnings.

I shake my head.

"Is she even in town? Your house never looked so empty." Caitlin thinks for a moment. "You sent her away, didn't you? Penn, what's going on?"

"Just wait a second. Do you remember the agreement we used to have about cases like this?"

"Of course."

"What was it?"

She rolls her eyes. "We tell each other all we can, but we don't use anything the other says has to stay secret."

Right, so far. "And . . . ?"

She sighs in exasperation. "I don't publish anything until you clear it. And you don't put anything in your novels that I want to save for myself."

"Okay. Can we go forward with that understanding?"

She purses her lips as though trying to judge whether I might be trapping her in some way, but at length she relents. "All right. Deal."

"I need your help, Caitlin. That must be obvious, since I wouldn't be here otherwise."

This seems to wound her. "What kind of help? I'm here, okay?"

"For how long?"

"You mean how long will I be in

Natchez? You know me. That's open-ended. What exactly do you need? You don't want to manipulate the newspaper, do you?"

"No. I need physical cover."

"Translate that."

"I need a girlfriend."

"A *girlfriend*?" Wry amusement touches her mouth. "Didn't you just get rid of one?"

"I'm not kidding. The people I'm dealing with have very sophisticated surveillance equipment and enough time to watch me around the clock, if they want to. I need an excuse to disappear sometimes. Like into your house. Or to go on a drive. They already know who you are, and they know we have a past. It's a credible cover."

"I see. And what do I get out of this arrangement? Are you proposing a friends-with-benefits kind of deal?"

The look in my eyes must be all the answer she needs, because she immediately holds up both hands in apology.

"What did you always get out of this arrangement?" I ask.

"Stories."

"*Big* stories."

"Okay, okay. I'm in. I just wanted to be

sure. So what's the story? Crystal meth in the Deep South? I really hope not."

"What do you know about dogfighting?"

"*Dog*fighting?"

"Yes."

Her face goes blank. "Nothing. Less than nothing."

"Time to learn."

CHAPTER

24

Captain Walt Garrity crosses the Mississippi River Bridge at Vidalia, Louisiana, one callused hand on the wheel of his 2004 Anniversary Edition Roadtrek RV and the other wrapped around a thermos of hot coffee. He saw the lights of Natchez long ago, twinkling high on the bluff that towers over the flatland of Louisiana. The last time he crossed the Mississippi here there'd been only one bridge, the one built right before World War Two. He'd been on Ranger business then, coming to pick up a fugitive on a murder warrant. The guy had gotten drunk, cut somebody in Under-the-Hill, and wound up in the Natchez clink. The local cops had treated Walt well, a little hero worship for a Texas Ranger was common in cops who'd been raised on Saturday-matinee westerns as boys. Walt knew better than to expect deference now. These days he rarely mentioned he'd been a Ranger, since some people (mostly Mexicans) tended to make assumptions based on the checkered history of the troop.

He's been driving for nine straight hours, not counting a stop for gas. Even with the built-in head in the Roadtrek, his first instinct when he feels the need for a bathroom is to piss in a Coke bottle, something he became adept at while racing across long stretches of Texas in the late fifties. It helps to have a long Johnson—or so say the fellows who claim to have one; Walt has to make do with what God gave him, which has always proved sufficient. Not that it matters much lately. At seventy, his pride has gone soft on him. He's heard a lot about the blue pills, but you can't take them if you're on heart medicine, and Walt has been taking nitrates since his bypass a decade ago. Carmelita, the Mexican woman who lives with him, has stayed on in spite of this, despite being ten years his junior. "Tirar isn't everything," she always says. Then she winks and adds, "And there's more than one way to skin a cat."

At the midpoint of the bridge, it strikes Walt that the last time he crossed here his wife was the woman waiting back in Nacogdoches. Frances would have been about thirty then, shining with the glow of her second pregnancy. But even that glow faded whenever Walt chugged down the long driveway and off to work. Frances was a worrier; his fellow Rangers always said that if worry and prayer could keep you alive, Walt didn't have a thing to worry about when the bullets started flying. Naturally, it was Frances that fate had taken too soon. Walt shoves down the memories and thinks again of Carmelita. She never worries when he leaves, though she knows some of his recent jobs have gotten hairy. Crime has changed in the past twenty-five years, even in Texas. Whatever code that once kept some sort of restraint operating among the criminal class vanished with the appearance of crack cocaine. Even so, says Carmelita, life is too short to spend it worrying, especially about old dogs like Walt, who always seem to find their way home in one piece.

Walt takes his gaze off the city's cathedral steeple and looks down to the foot of the bluff, where the riverboat casinos hug the shore like remora fastened to a shark's side. Two boats north of the bridge, two to the south. Walt chuckles to himself. Mark Twain would roll over in his grave. These "boats" may have been floated down the river to reach their present locations, but they were never meant to go anywhere under their own power; they don't even have engines. They're floating entertainment complexes, like something from Walt Disney World. They exist for one reason: to drain money from as wide an area as possible and funnel it to the owners of the casinos, few of whom would deign to cross the borders of a state like Mississippi.

Walt has never been a gambler by constitution. He played some poker in Korea to keep his mind off the cold, and he won enough spending money to visit the clean whores in town rather than the girls hiding in the hills by the camp, all of whom carried exotic strains of VD. He'd also done some gambling in his various undercover roles, both as a Ranger and as a special investigator for the Harris County district attorney—Penn Cage's old boss. Winning at poker was a matter of judging men quickly and accurately, and that wasn't much different from Rangering. Walt had found that his emotional detachment from games of chance gave him a significant edge over men who had the itch in their blood.

As the Roadtrek rocks and bounces down off the bridge, he swings left on Canal Street and heads into downtown Natchez. He hasn't seen Tom Cage in close to ten years, but when you've served with a man in combat, the passage of time means nothing. You're brothers until death—and beyond, if there is such a thing. From what Tom said, they need to work fast, and that means Walt establishing a cover as quickly as possible. He's traveling under one of his favorite legends—J. B. Gilchrist, a Dallas oilman—and with a little help from the Cages, he'll embed himself in the fabric of the town, then draw the target to him as surely as honey draws a bear.

It helps that Natchez is an oil town. There isn't much business left here— mostly workovers being done by men trying to suck the last few barrels from wells drilled in the 1950s and capped in the 1980s—but some big fields were discovered in the old days, and the town enjoyed remarkable prosperity. Quite a few Texas outfits still have interests in the area, and with Tom arranging for a geologist friend to let it out that J. B. Gilchrist has an override on a well being drilled next week, the town's history will firm up his cover just fine.

Walt turns on Main Street and parks outside the lobby of the Eola Hotel. As he dismounts from the big van, he sees several trailers parked crosswise in the crowded lot, most with colorful balloons painted on their sides. At the back of the lot, a couple of crews seem to be packing suitcases into their trucks rather than unpacking, as Walt would have expected. He brought the Roadtrek because Tom had told him he wouldn't be able to rent a hotel room during the festival weekend, but Walt senses that the introductory scene he'd planned to play in the lobby might just pay off with a room.

The Eola is a classy hotel from a bygone era, a grand old dame that makes even Walt feel young again. He walks up to the brass cage of the desk and nods to the harried-looking desk clerk whose name tag reads BRAD.

"Can I help you?" asks the young man, not meeting Walt's eye.

"J. B Gilchrist, checking in."

"Yes, sir. Do you have a reservation?"

"*Course I do. Check your screen there. It's G-I-L, then the name of our Lord. You follow?*"

Brad looks perplexed. "Sir, ah . . . I'm checking under G, but I don't show a Gilchrist. Could the reservation be under another name?"

"How could it be under another name?" Walt asks, upping his volume enough to turn a few heads. "I only got one name, son. Big Jim Gilchrist. And I'm tired from a damn long drive. Now, I was happy when I walked in. Why don't you get me fixed up so I can stay happy?"

"Sir, I'm afraid this is one of the most crowded weekends of the year, and—"

Walt cuts the boy off with a withering glare. "Listen, son, let's skip the formalities and get your supervisor in on this, so we can have an executive decision. Hotels always keep a couple rooms on standby for when they make mistakes, like you're making now. You just tell your boss to release one of 'em, and everything will be fine."

"Mr. Gilchrist, I don't think you understand the—"

"Supervisor," Walt cuts in. "Boss man,

jefe—are you reading me? Call whoever you got to call to make this right."

Walt turns away from the desk and walks toward a long, black grand piano that looks like an idling limousine awaiting a driver. He begins hammering out "Chopsticks," drawing curious and annoyed glances from the guests in the lobby.

"Mr. Gilchrist?" Brad calls. "Sir?"

Walt doesn't stop banging the keys, but he cuts his eyes toward the desk. "I'll bet you've got some good news for me."

"Well, actually, it turns out that we do have an unexpected checkout. If you don't mind a room that hasn't been made up yet?"

Walt laughs good-naturedly. "Son, before I struck it big, I stayed in places a cockroach would have run from. You just print me out a key. I'm ready to get down to one of them boats and lose some money."

"Yes, sir. Right away."

Walt looks around and sighs expansively. "Seems like a lot going on for this town. This ain't Pilgrimage month, is it?"

"No, sir. It's the Balloon Festival. The only reason this room is free is because we had a problem this morning with the flight."

Walt's inner sentry goes on alert. "What kind of problem?

"Well, someone took a shot at one of the balloons."

"I'll be dogged. Kill anybody?"

"No, sir. But they did have to crash-land the balloon. And the mayor was in it."

"The mayor?" Walt barks a laugh as he thinks this through. If Penn had been badly hurt, Tom would have called despite instructions not to save in dire emergency. "No kidding? He make it?"

"He's fine. They just had a hard landing."

"He must have pissed somebody off, huh? Wrote the wrong ordinance or something. I've known a couple mayors I wouldn't have minded shooting."

"They think it was squirrel hunters."

"I'll be dogged," Walt says again. "Balloons flying tomorrow?"

"Yes, sir, Sunday too. But everybody's nervous, and some of the pilots have left town. It's a pilot's room you're taking tonight."

"Sounds like I owe the lone gunman a favor. Otherwise I wouldn't have a room in this fine establishment."

The clerk slides a form toward him. "If you'll just initial here, and here, and sign at the bottom. Please note the fine for smoking in the room."

"Hell, I'll just pay you now."

Brad frowns. "It's two hundred and fifty dollars, Mr. Gilchrist."

Walt laughs like a man for whom $250 is a minute's pay, then signs his name with a flourish. "Just pulling your chain, Brad."

As the clerk tries to pull back the form, Walt leans in close. "Say, what's the action like around here?"

Brad looks confused. "The casinos are all beneath the bluff. Our concierge can help you with anything else, but he's busy right now."

Walt slides a $100 bill across the desk. "I'm talking about girls, Brad. I know where the gambling is, but that's only half the party. I've been hankering for a colored girl, to tell you the truth. Been a while, you know? This seems like the right town for that. They got girls on the boats or what?"

Obviously offended, the clerk lets his voice take on a haughty tone. "I'm sure I don't know, sir."

"What about cockfighting? I know you got some of that around here. That's the kind of action I'm talking about. Blood sport."

Brad straightens up and squares his shoulders. "Sir, if you don't mind, there are people waiting."

Walt snatches back the bill. "You're in the wrong job, sonny. You say the concierge is busy? You got an elevator man? Somebody around a hotel has to know what's what."

The clerk's cheeks are red. "Will you be needing help with your luggage?"

"I need a bellboy who can earn that C-note with some useful information, that's what I need."

"Perhaps someone can help you on one of the boats."

Walt walks away muttering loudly, "I

never heard of a deskman in an oil town who don't know nothin' 'bout the local trim." He turns and shouts, "Send a bottle of Maker's Mark up to my room from the bar. You know what that is, don't you?"

"A full bottle?"

"Jesus, Brad, where'd they find you? I want whiskey, and if you've got a pretty maid who can bring it up, send her up with it."

There was a time when the way he'd behaved in the last five minutes wouldn't have shocked any hotel man in the South, and not many around the country. I guess times do change, Walt thinks. But not that much. The clerk would gripe to somebody about the old asshole he'd had to deal with, then repeat what Walt had asked for, and soon enough, like ripples in the proverbial pond, word would reach the proper ear. It was simply a matter of waiting.

Any fisherman could tell you that.

CHAPTER

25

"Do you have any food in your backpack?" Caitlin asks. "I think better when I'm eating."

"No food, sorry."

She's pacing the supply room of the *Natchez Examiner,* studying my handwritten transcription of the text message Chief Logan showed me, the one Tim sent to Linda Church shortly before he died. I've told Caitlin all I know of the case so far, but true to character, she has set aside the larger questions to focus on an immediate challenge. She's something of a savant with puzzles, and nothing if not obsessive in all pursuits.

"I don't think this is a password," she murmurs to herself. "It's too long, plus it's counterintuitive. Have you gone to this URL, www.thief.com?"

"Yes. I don't see how the site could be related to any of this. And there's no dot-com in the text message. We're just assuming that one follows."

"Right, right. What *is* in the backpack?"

"A gun and a satellite phone."

She looks up, checking to see if I'm joking. When she sees I'm not, her gaze drops back to the message. "I suppose there could be more to the Web address, and Tim knew Linda would know what the rest of it was. But if that's the case, we're not going to find that without Linda. Not easily, anyway."

"Obviously it could be a code of some kind, but it's not simple enough for me to break it."

"Maybe," Caitlin concedes. "But the words that follow don't appear to be random. 'Kill mommy. Squirt too.' But they don't actually say that, do they? Are these letters exactly what you saw in the police station?"

"I think so, yes."

"And you don't believe Tim would have tried to get rid of his wife and kid to run off with this Linda woman?"

"No way in hell. He lived for that kid. I'll be surprised if it turns out he was even having an affair with Linda."

"I won't."

Caitlin makes another tight circuit of the room, then stops with her forefinger on the paper. "You know what?" she says, her voice suddenly bright with excitement.

"What?"

"I think this message is just what it looks like!"

"Which is what?"

"A text message."

"What do you mean?"

"Just a second." She rummages through her purse, then pulls out a small flat pen and a business card. Setting them aside, she taps at the keys of her cell phone for half a minute. Then, after scrawling on the back of the card for a few seconds, she drops the pen back in her purse and shoves the card at me with a look of triumph. "There you go. There's your message."

I look down and read aloud what she's written: "*They know. Run.* Is that it?"

"That's it."

"So he was warning her to get off the boat?"

"Yep."

"How did you get that?"

"The cell phone Tim used to send this message was in predictive text mode. Either he didn't know that or he forgot, and he typed the message without looking at the screen. Otherwise he would have seen what was happening to his intended message. Was this sent from his personal phone?"

"I don't . . . yes. This actually makes sense. He was being chased in his car. He couldn't take time to try to use his extra phones, or even to look down at his own phone."

"A lot of girls I know can do that," Caitlin muses. "Not so many guys."

"Tim probably could."

"But he didn't warn her in time. Did he?"

"I don't think so. I think Linda Church is dead. Or worse."

"What's worse?" I actually see the memory of my describing Tim's tortured body come back to Caitlin. "Oh. Never mind."

I turn over the card she gave me. *Zeitgeist Films HD.* "Ah. Your friend." She gives me a look like *Give me a break,* but I don't. "What's the deal with that guy? What did you tell him?"

"He had interviews to do in New Orleans. I didn't."

"Does he expect you down there?"

"Not so much. Look, he was starting to get on my nerves, if you want to know the truth."

"And this little adventure gives you a good excuse to blow him off."

"You don't want me to blow him off?"

"I just need to know I can count on you being here for three or four days. Without interference."

"The answer is yes. And don't forget, I'm already paying my way. I just broke your code for you."

"Thank you."

"Should we tell anyone else?"

"No."

"Then can we get out of here and get some food?"

"Not if you want to keep talking about the case."

She gives me a crafty smile, says, "Give me forty seconds," then leaves the supply room. She returns in less time than that, a set of keys with a Chrysler ring in her hand.

"This van is a mess, but there's no way it's bugged. No one would even get into it without a hazmat suit. Come on. We can talk in there."

Walking out to the van, I scan the parking lot and the street. I don't see anyone watching, but that doesn't mean anything.

As predicted, the van is a wreck, but I do feel more secure in it. The best way to beat surveillance—or even terrorists—is to abandon all patterns, to make random decisions. This is a good one.

Caitlin drives us over to Franklin Street, where a recent arrival has opened a Greek fast-food joint in an old fried-chicken restaurant. He still serves fried chicken and catfish, but now the black section of town—where this restaurant is—is getting a taste of pita and souvlaki. So far, the place is still open, and it has a drive-through window.

"So what about your high school girl?" Caitlin asks, after ordering gyro plates to go for both of us. "You two still talk?"

"Give me a break. You know nothing happened."

Her eyebrows arch for a split second. "So you say. Still at Harvard?"

"Yes."

"I thought she might flunk out, pining away for you and all."

I shake my head and look away, pressing back thoughts of Mia Burke and what she might be doing tonight. She has e-mailed me several times, and I have responded twice. But I have kept her at a remove.

"So, what are you *doing* about Tim's death?" Caitlin asks. "I still haven't heard a plan of action."

"Daniel Kelly's on his way here from Afghanistan. He should be here early tomorrow morning. Like six a.m."

"That's a good first step. Rambo with a blond ponytail."

"Sometimes that's what you need."

"Oh, I know. I was kidding. What about the local cops? You don't think you can trust Chief Logan?"

"I think it's more a matter of him not knowing who he can trust."

"Will he work Tim's murder, at least?"

"I don't think it matters much, unless he finds a smoking gun. Which he won't. Even if he did, Shad Johnson could still make it difficult to prosecute the people involved."

"And of course the FBI hates your guts."

"There are still a couple of people there I think I could talk to. I've thought about calling Peter Lutjens, just to have him troll through the computers for what can turn up on Jonathan Sands." Lutjens is an agent who works in the Puzzle Palace—FBI headquarters—and has access to almost everything in their digital data banks.

"You nearly got him fired last time," Caitlin reminds me.

"Not 'nearly.' He was fired."

"They reinstated him."

"The point is, Peter might be able to help, but I'm reluctant to put him in the same position again. I also worry that any query on Sands might trigger some kind of automatic response."

"Okay, there's my problem with this.

How could a guy working in a casino in Natchez, Mississippi, be that important?"

"If we knew that, our problems would be over."

The window attendant hands Caitlin a white bag, and she pays with a credit card. As we pull away, she plucks a triangle of pita bread from the bag and eats it in a bite. "Food of the gods," she says. "What about the Chinese angle? In the post-9/11 world, surely foreign investors in American casinos must be investigated by the CIA, even if the gaming commission gives them a pass because they have a nominally small share."

"I agree. That part doesn't make sense. If one of these Chinese investors has a criminal record, or is dirty in some way, I don't see the government allowing him to purchase part of a casino company."

"And you never thought Tim's theory of Sands ripping off the town by shorting taxes made sense. So what is he really up to?"

"When I was in Houston, I heard about some cases where casinos had been used for money laundering. An Indian casino in particular, I remember, with links to organized crime on the East Coast. But if that's what they're up to, why risk the operation with side action like dogfighting and prostitution? I mean, maybe a guy like Sands would risk it, but not some Chinese billionaire. At least I don't think he would."

"Superrich freaks exist," Caitlin says. She laughs, then digs out a strip of meat to eat with another piece of pita. "In fact, they're probably the rule, not the exception. Plenty of rich Japanese freaks, when it comes to sex and violence. China, I don't know. I've been there twice, but only as a tourist."

"You mean you didn't sleep with any natives?"

"No, I still like older white guys, for some unfathomable reason. What do you expect out of Kelly?"

"Security, for one thing."

She looks up with utter seriousness in her eyes. *Annie?* she mouths.

"Safe. That's all that matters. But Kelly won't show up empty-handed. He'll have whatever Blackhawk finds on Sands, Quinn, and Golden Parachute. Those guys don't miss much."

Caitlin gives a skeptical little *hmph.*

"What's that for?"

"They do a lot of work in Iraq, right? That hasn't turned out so well, in case you haven't noticed."

"Yeah, well, Kelly's on the first team. And he'll push to get a thorough job on this."

"I agree. Besides, I miss having a guy around who can handle a mob attack or home invasion, if I get into that kind of situation."

I know she's keeping up this patter to try to keep me from sinking into depression, but just bringing her up to speed has exhausted me. Two bites of food is like taking a shot of Demerol.

"I wasn't kidding when I said you look terrible," Caitlin says. "What were you going to do next? Like right this minute?"

"Tonight I'm going to fly the river with Danny McDavitt and try to see where the VIP boat goes."

"The VIP boat?"

"The excursion boat owned by Golden Parachute. I forgot to tell you, Tim said they usually take the excursion boat to these dogfights."

"When was the last time you slept?"

"I got a few hours last night."

"Bullshit. Your eyes look like they're bleeding."

I flip down the visor and look in the vanity mirror. She's not exaggerating by much. If I don't recharge my batteries soon, I'm going to be no use to anybody. "Actually . . . I guess the last time I slept was in my office yesterday. Couple of hours on a cot. And I only got four hours the night before that."

"What were you going to do if you found the VIP boat?"

"Nothing. Stand off and find out where it anchors. Then go home and wait for Kelly."

"I think your pilot could handle that job on his own. Don't you?"

"Yeah, I think he could. But—"

"You're in no condition to make decisions. You've done well up to now, but you need sleep. You're coming back to my house and crashing until an hour before Kelly arrives. Tell McDavitt to call me if there's a problem. I'll man the satellite phone, whatever."

"That's a tempting offer."

"It's not an offer. It's an order."

"Okay. Let me speak to Danny. I need to check on something anyway."

As Caitlin drives along Homochitto Street, I roll down the window and call Danny McDavitt on the satellite phone. His usually laconic voice sounds worried from the first syllable.

"Carl's not back yet," he says.

"From the Devil's Punchbowl?"

"Right."

"How long has he been gone?"

"I don't know exactly what time he went in, but he's almost three hours past due now."

"You think he got stuck down there in the dark?"

"He may have. He'd probably spend the night down there rather than try to climb out in the dark."

"I hope that's it."

"How are you doing?" McDavitt asks.

"I'm pretty whipped. Haven't slept for two days. Do you think you could make tonight's flight without me?"

"Just do what we talked about earlier?"

"Yeah. And stay far enough away so that they don't hear the chopper."

"I might have to make one pass at an audible level to get a good fix. FLIR has its limitations, especially when you can't afford the top of the line."

"Just be careful."

"Always. Hey, I heard from Hans Necker. He examined the wrecked balloon, and he's pretty sure the shots came from the levee road. So most likely they were fired from a parked vehicle, or from the trees near one. And definitely from a silenced rifle."

"Okay. Tell him thanks if you talk to him again, but we already know who ordered those shots fired. I was just hoping they'd been fired from private property, and we could get the name of the landowner. How are Necker's legs?"

"One bad sprain, one fracture. He's a tough bird though. I also heard from our blond friend. He's landing in Baton Rouge about three this morning. I'm going to fly down and get him, if you'll pay for the fuel."

"Absolutely."

"We can be at the rendezvous by four thirty a.m., if you want to wake up that early."

When Danny dropped me off at my car, we decided that as soon as Kelly arrived, we'd meet on a piece of private property owned by one of my father's two partners. "That's great. The sooner the better."

"Do you want a report before then?"

"Only if Carl turns up."

"Right. I'm out."

"Thanks, Danny."

"Everything okay?" Caitlin asks.

"I don't know. The guy who's checking out Tim's car hasn't come out of the Devil's Punchbowl."

"You think he's in trouble?"

"I just hope he's not down with a snakebite or something."

"You said he was a marine, right? He'll be okay."

"I guess. That food is really hitting me now. Jesus. I can hardly keep my eyes open."

"Close them. I'll wake you when we get to my house."

"If my cell rings, ignore it. If the satellite phone rings, answer it. But be very careful what you say, once we're in your house."

She reaches out and brushes my hair

away from my eyes. "Just let go, okay? We'll be home soon. You did the right thing telling me."

"Did I?" I ask, but my mind is already sliding into blankness.

"Penn, wake up."

"What?" I jerk to a half-alert state of panic. We're still in the car, parked against a vanilla brick wall. "What's happening?"

"Chief Logan just called."

"What time is it?"

"You were only asleep for a couple of minutes. We were almost home and your phone rang."

More panic. "The satellite phone?"

"No, no, your regular cell. I wouldn't have answered, but I recognized his number."

"You what?"

"I don't forget numbers, you know that."

I look out the window and see the Entergy building. "We're at the police station?"

"Logan said he needs to talk to you face-to-face."

"What else did he say? Sands's people can listen to my regular cell."

"He said the problem was Soren Jensen and Shad Johnson. I think you're okay. Apparently the boy hasn't been arraigned yet, and your old girlfriend has been raising hell. That's good cover, right?"

"Best we're going to get. Is Libby here now?"

"No. Wasn't she a lawyer before she ran that bookstore?"

"A corporate lawyer. And she's not licensed to practice in Mississippi. Look, do you mind waiting in the car?"

Caitlin gives me a disappointed look. "You don't trust me?"

"It's not that. Logan's not going to speak freely in front of you."

"Okay."

"Do you think anybody followed us here?"

"I don't think so. But what do I know? I haven't been stalked since college."

"Even so, we can't use this car anymore. If Sands's people heard that call, they'll cruise by just to see what vehicle I'm in."

"I can get more cars," Caitlin says. "Get going. You know I hate waiting."

* * *

Chief Logan looks five years older than he did yesterday.

"What's up, Don?"

"I've got the autopsy report."

"Looks like you don't like what's in it. How long have you had it?"

"A few hours."

"What does it say?"

His eyes meet mine. "I have a feeling you already know."

"I knew last night what it was going to say. Murder. You knew it too."

"Yeah. I guess I was hoping this really was a drug murder. Or just a straight killing. Over a debt, a woman . . . something."

"There's nothing straight about this, Don. What did Shad say about the autopsy?"

"Our illustrious district attorney claims this *is* a drug murder. Drugs and adultery."

"So why did they torture him?"

"That's easy to explain, if you're trying."

"What about Linda Church? Any word on her?"

"Nothing. It's like she fell off the face of the earth."

"I think she has. She knew way too much to keep breathing."

Logan sighs heavily.

"What are you going to do now, Chief?"

"Same thing I always do. Work the case."

"How?"

"That's what I've been down here thinking about. What would you do, if you were in my place?"

"I'd get a warrant for the security tapes on the *Magnolia Queen* for the twelve hours prior to Tim's death."

Logan's mouth falls open. "You're kidding, right? What would they show?"

"I don't know. But the company's reaction to the search would tell you a lot. What about the SUV Tim jumped out of before he was killed?"

"Three local casinos own similar vehicles. Golden Parachute alone owns eight of them. But I don't have a plate, so what can I do?"

"Make them account for every one of them. Look for time sheets. Try to spot the vehicles on surveillance cameras."

Logan leans back in his chair. "Jessup did something on that boat, didn't he? That's why he's dead."

"I have no idea, Chief."

"Sure you don't."

For a moment I consider telling Logan that I know where Tim's car is, but that's a risk I'm not prepared to take until I know Carl Sims is alive and well. "I'd also check every business and home on Broadway for security cameras. Maybe somebody has a tape of the minutes before Tim went over the fence and doesn't even know it yet."

"I've checked. No luck. In Natchez, you generally only find cameras at gas stations, convenience stores, and banks. Liquor stores, of course."

"And casinos," I add.

"I hear you. But what judge is going to give me a search warrant for those tapes?"

"Judge? I thought you had a stack of presigned warrants over here that you just fill out when you need one."

Logan shakes his head. "Once upon a time, maybe. But those days are gone. I can pick up the phone and get a search warrant for almost anywhere in the city, probable cause or not. But the security tapes of a casino boat? No judge wants to get into a pissing match with those people and their lawyers."

"An honest judge has nothing to worry about. You'll get the warrant if you ask for it. Try Eunice Franklin."

Logan gives me a weary sigh. "I'll think about it, okay?"

"Don't think too long. Tapes can be erased. Actually it's probably hard drives, not tapes. I'd get on top of this fast."

"In an ideal world."

"The world is what we make it," I say softly.

Logan steeples his fingers and regards me with a cold eye. "You know, when you won for mayor, I was looking for some big changes. And I think you were ready to make them. So why haven't things changed much?"

"I take your point. I realize you don't have a lot of power, Don. But you do have some. And no one can fault you for working a homicide case hard. Certainly not the average citizen. If you say you need those tapes, I'll back you up, and so will the people of the town."

"The people of the town won't be sued for harassment by a battery of attorneys."

"Who do you think pays if you lose a suit? Ultimately, it's the town."

"Okay, okay. But let me turn this around. What are *you* doing about Jessup's death?"

"Nothing," I say flatly.

Logan seems surprised, but after a few moments he seems to reconcile himself with the fact that I can't or won't say more. "Penn, what did Jessup steal? What's on that USB drive he hid up his ass? If I knew that . . ."

I turn up my palms and give him a helpless shrug. Unless he's a very good actor, Don Logan is an honest man. That he's in the dark about the missing data tells me that. But his power to help me with my problem is limited. "Are your men as ignorant of that as you are?"

His eyes never leave mine. "I wish I knew."

"Have you been threatened, Don?"

"Not in so many words. But it's no secret that nobody wants a cash cow to stop making milk." Logan gets up and gets himself a cup of coffee from a small carafe on a table to his left. "I thought I was being put through the ringer, but you look pretty rough, brother."

"I feel worse than I look."

"You'd better get some sleep."

"I'm about to. Maybe things will be better when I wake up, huh?"

Logan sips his coffee. "I wouldn't count on it. If this were a hurricane, I'd say it hadn't even made landfall. Yet."

I get to my feet and walk slowly toward his door. "I hope you're wrong."

"Any last advice?" Logan asks.

"Think hard about who you assign to this case."

"Who would you suggest?"

"Family men with no history of financial problems or substance abuse. And none with expensive habits."

He studies me in silence for a while. "What if they actually turn up some evidence?"

"I'd keep it to myself until I talked to the mayor."

Logan clucks his tongue. "What about the district attorney?"

"Obviously the DA has to be informed. At some point."

"That sounds like a dangerous game."

"It has been from the start. We just didn't know we were playing it."

* * *

When I step outside, Caitlin actually gets out and opens my door for me. "A new black Cadillac Escalade parked in the lot three minutes after you went inside."

"Where is it now?"

"The second you appeared in the entryway, it took off, headed downtown."

"It didn't pick up anybody or drop someone off?"

"No. And it had tinted windows. I couldn't see anything."

Only after I'm in and seated do I notice my open backpack on the floor at my feet. My pistol is lying on the dashboard.

"Good girl."

"Maybe it was nothing," she says.

"Don't think that for a second. You're in the middle of this now. You've been in it ever since you wrote the story on Tim's death."

"Should I drive back to the office and get my car?"

"No. This van's blown now. Let's take the shortest path to your house. I need a bed."

She pulls out of the lot and turns right,

heading toward town through widely spaced pools of sodium-pink light. "What did Logan want?"

"He knows Tim was murdered. He knows it has something to do with the *Magnolia Queen.* Beyond that . . . I don't know."

"Do you trust him?"

"I think he's clean on this. But he knows something's wrong, and that it runs deep in the town."

"Can he help?"

"Not much, if at all."

The smell of the leftover Greek food combined with the mess already in the van makes my stomach roll.

"What is it?" Caitlin asks anxiously.

"Just queasy. Exhaustion."

I feel her hand close on my left knee. "Three minutes, you'll be in my bed."

A strange laugh comes from my lips, but it sounds like someone else's voice. "I thought that would take a lot more work than this."

"Oh, I'm not worried. I don't think you could do anything about it even if you wanted to. Certainly not up to my stan-dard, anyway."

I want to offer a riposte, but my synapses don't seem to be firing properly. My eyelids are closing when my cell phone rings. I start to ignore it, but then I see that the caller is Seamus Quinn.

"Our friends from the Emerald Isle," I mutter. "Hello?"

"What the fuck are you doing?" Quinn asks with his usual diplomacy.

"Making sure the police don't turn my ex-girlfriend's son into hamburger."

There's a short pause. "Where are you now?"

"With my old girlfriend."

"What girlfriend? The bookstore woman?"

"No, my *old* old girlfriend. The mouthy cunt, as your boss called her."

Caitlin shoots me a sidelong look.

"What kind of game are you playin', counselor?"

"No game. You told me to do what I would normally do. The chief called me about Soren Jensen, I went to deal with it. I'm still looking for your property."

"And you haven't found it?"

"I covered the whole cemetery today, but I couldn't find anything."

"Keep lookin'.'"

On a hunch, I decide to take a gamble. "I did find Tim Jessup's car."

"Did you, now? Where was that?"

"Bottom of the Devil's Punchbowl."

"Ah. Well. That doesn't interest me."

So they already knew about the car. They may even have burned it and run it into the Punchbowl. But from Quinn's tone, I don't think he has Carl Sims on his radar. "Does your company own a black Escalade?"

"Don't know what you're blathering on about," Quinn says. "But stick her once for me tonight, eh? She's a hot piece."

Caitlin obviously heard this last remark. She's acting like she can't believe the guy would say that, but she knows better, and she leans close to hear the rest of the conversation.

"I'll keep that in mind. I'm sleeping at her place. Tell your goons to keep their distance."

"High and mighty," Quinn says. "Know her type well. They want it nasty. She looks a bit young for you. Give me a ring if you run out of steam."

Quinn is laughing as I click END.

"Was that Sands?" Caitlin asks.

"No, his security chief. He's a thug. A monster, probably. Sands talks like the Duke of York. At least until he takes off the mask. Then he sounds like what you just heard."

"Charming."

"Don't try to find out for yourself." I slide lower in my seat, trying to find a comfortable position. "These guys are predators, you can't forget that. Tim told me that the first night, and I didn't let it sink in. Don't make the same mistake."

Caitlin nods thoughtfully in the dark, but her eyes are bright. As it does most people, evil fascinates her. Like me, Caitlin has probed the dark side of human nature through her work. But unlike me, she has not become exhausted by the effort. As I descend into sleep, I recall a line of Wilde's that she once quoted to me: *The burnt child loves the fire.*

CHAPTER

26

It doesn't take long for a hooker to latch onto Walt. He's playing the craps table in high style, like an oilman with money to burn, and nothing draws girls like burning money. This one's young, and that fits his role: sugar daddy on the prowl. She's a bottle blonde with skinny legs, a hard face, and hard little tits, but she's not more than thirty, so she'll do. Walt likes dark-haired women, but he's somebody else tonight—J. B. Gilchrist from Dallas, Texas—and picking a wrong woman makes it easier to remember that.

Walt's working the Zephyr, not the Mag-nolia Queen. In a market this small, word of a big player will spread plenty fast. His goal is to lose enough of Penn's money that by tomorrow night, every pit boss and dealer in town will know his name.

The crowd on the Zephyr is mostly black, which he'd expected when a guy on the shuttle bus joked about him going to the African Queen. The majority of this clientele clearly doesn't have money to lose, but here they are, dropping their dol-lars into the slots and looking longingly at the table games. He feels guilty sliding the brightly colored chips across the felt under their watchful eyes, but he's got a job to do, and there's no point worrying about something he can't change.

It takes about fifteen minutes—and a good deal more of Penn's cash—before the table hits a hot streak. Walt's not the roller when it happens, but that hardly matters: Craps is the most social of casino games, with the play-ers rooting for each other, united against the house. By laying down hun-dreds per bet, Walt's become the de facto "table captain," and all eyes are on him. If he wins, everybody wins, at least in spirit.

By the time the roller has hit his fifth point, Walt's up by thousands, and the hooker's snuggling closer on his arm. His fellow players' eyes go from Walt, as he makes his bet, to the tumbling dice, then back to Walt, who's increased his line bets to a thousand dollars.

A couple of men in Western-style suede sport coats have joined the swelling crowd waiting for an opening at the table. Well-heeled rednecks by the look of them—one older with gray whiskers, the other a Tim McGraw look-alike in his midthirties—father and son, maybe. If they stick around, Walt might ask them about finding some action. They'll ogle the blonde and say, "It looks like you already found some, part-ner," but he'll shake his head and draw them in close and ask about some real sport. They might act confused, play it carefully, but the young guy's wearing an Angola Prison Rodeo belt buckle, so he can't be from too far away. Walt suspects that he, at least, knows the score.

"Five, five," the stickman calls out.

"No-field five." He pushes the dice to the red-hot roller. "High, low, yo, anyone?"

The stickman's pushing for prop bets, bad-odds wagers that only amateurs make.

"Thousand on the yo." The crowd hushes, watching as Walt tosses out two purple chips. "One for me and one for the boys."

"Thank you very much for the action, sir," says the stickman loudly, placing the chips in the middle of the table, one representing Walt's bet, the other $1,000 bet for the stickman, the pit boss, and the two dealers running the table. Now Walt has the employees' attention as well. If his bet hits, the dealers will win a tip that comes only a handful of times in a career.

"Whew," breathes the girl on his arm. "That's a lot."

Walt grins like he's lapping it up. "That's the secret of this game, hon. Soon as you get a good run going, you ride it. Ride her till she bucks ya and go home happy." He leans down to her ear and adds, "And ride some more."

"You go, Dad," says the rodeo fan. "Show 'em how it's done!"

Walt gives the kid a hard look, then softens it into a smile, hugging the girl to his side. "This'un here's the only one who gets to call me daddy."

There's general laughter from the crowd, and the roller tosses the dice.

The crowd whoops as the dice come up eleven.

"Yo eleven," says the stickman, barely controlling the excitement in his voice. "Pay the line, and pay the gentleman. Thank you again, sir."

Walt gives a casual nod as the dealers collect a total of $16,000 in tip money to divide as they see fit.

He lays down the same bet again, to sincere thank-yous from the crew. Predictably, it misses. And just as predictably, the roller's hot run ends a few throws later. Gradually, the dice make their way around the table. When they reach Walt, he gestures graciously to the hooker that she should take his roll. She squeals and squeezes his arm, then takes a gulp from her rum and coke. He drops the dice into her moist palm, tells her to blow on them before she rolls. Her eyes light up like a penny slot machine. She blows on the dice, then flings them down the table like a kid skipping rocks on a pond.

"Seven," says the stickman. "Winner, seven. Pay the line, take the don't."

The crowd roars as usual, and Walt uses its attention like a spotlight. "Let's do another bet for the boys," he says generously. "You can win it for them, right, honey?"

The hooker giggles wildly as the stickman places another thousand-dollar "yo" bet for himself and his coworkers.

The hooker rolls the dice, establishing a point of four, but losing the prop bet. The crowd sighs.

"Sorry, boys," Walt says. "Let's hit that point. What do you say, Fancy?"

"It's Nancy," the girl says with an exaggerated pout.

Walt grins for the crowd. "I knew a Fancy in New Orleans once. Or was it Dallas? Hell, I can't remember. But I sure remember her. How 'bout you be Fancy just for tonight?"

The hooker looks uncertainly around at the attentive eyes, then down at Walt's long rack of high-value chips. Her eyes flash, and she pumps her fist like a high school cheerleader at a pep rally.

"Fancy Nancy!" she cries. "Gimme those damn dice!"

The crowd chatters while Walt places the maximum odds bet on his four, then falls silent, waiting for the throw.

"Roll 'em, Fancy," Walt says. "Put the magic on 'em, baby. Give us a four. Make those old bones pay, I know you know how to do that."

The crowd laughs again, but the girl's past caring now. Walt feels like a son of a bitch, but it takes a son of a bitch to get his rocks off watching two dogs tear each other to pieces to please men who don't care if they live or die, except as extensions of their own pride.

Nancy blows on the dice again, then gives them a backhand throw, but the pit boss's eyes are on Walt now. Just like the PTZ cameras in the hanging domes on the ceiling. The guys in the security room were probably bored shitless when he started his run, but now they're watching with the same hunger as the people leaning against the table, wishing somebody would beat the house and walk away flush.

Suckers every one, *Walt thinks.* How empty does your life have to be to spend your nights in this place?

The dice come up three and one—the needed four. Nancy shrieks, and the crowd surges against Walt like a tide. It's so easy to win when you don't care one way or the other.

Walt ups his line bet, and Nancy rolls, establishing a point of four again. Walt takes the maximum odds, then places two thousand-dollar bets on "hard four"—one for him, and one for the dealers. Another crazy bet, way past the edge of probability. But a thrumming on that old taut wire stretched from his balls to his throat tells him that tonight is his night.

"Get ready, boys!" he says, feeling like Joe Namath before Super Bowl III. "You're going home with folding money tonight!"

Nancy skips the dice across the table with evanescent excitement, and they rebound half the table's length, wobbling over to a two and a two.

The dealers blink in astonishment as the crowd goes wild around them.

"Four the hard way," the stickman says with unaccustomed awe. "Hard four. Pay the man."

"And don't forget to pay yourselves, son," Walt says with grandiose intimacy, having won both men another two grand each to take home. "You're gonna remember J. B. Gilchrist, aren't you?"

The stickman smiles with genuine gratitude. "Yes, sir."

"Color me up," Walt tells the dealers, and the crowd falls silent. The dealers change his winnings into high-denomination chips that he can carry easily to the cashier.

Walt pockets the chips, then grabs the hooker and dips her low, like Fred and Ginger. Nancy squeals, but the crowd claps and cheers as Walt brings her back up, red-faced from the effort. "Time to move on, hon!" he bellows. "I like action, and the action's always moving. Anybody knows where to find it, you come talk to me. I'm always looking!"

The crowd parts as though for a prophet, and Walt leads his hooker across the casino floor like a king escorting a royal consort. He hasn't felt this good about a job in a long time. He'd never gamble with his own money, but he does believe in luck. Any man who's been in combat has seen luck in all its infinite variations, and Walt has been putting his life on the line for fifty years since he got back from Korea. He's the last of the Rangers from his old company still doing law enforcement work, and while he knows that judgment and experience have helped get him this far, without luck he would have died long ago. Driving out from the ranch, he'd wondered if he might be pushing a little too hard this time, tempting the lady to turn against him. But tonight he feels the fullness of his abilities in all their old potency. He's got his mojo working, as an old Houston cop used to tell him.

"I'm waiting for you," he says softly, thinking of the man who threatened Tom Cage's granddaughter. "Come on and take a nibble, sonny. I'll set the hook so hard it'll break your goddamn jaw."

In the parking lot on the bluff, Walt tips the driver of the shuttle bus, then steps off and joins Nancy on the pavement of the parking lot.

"Where's your car?" the hooker asks, looking up the line of modest cars in the lot. "I'll bet you drive a big old Cadillac or something, don't you? Old school, right?"

"Hell no," says Walt, pointing to the big Roadtrek van. "That's me right there."

The girl's mouth falls open. "Where? That?"

"That's me." Walt clicks open the locks from his key ring. "Wait till you see her."

The girl looks wary, but she follows him into the van, which is finished as finely as a boat cabin. "Ain't no regular RV, is it?" she marvels, turning in the small space. "You got a stove and a microwave and a flat panel and a refrigerator and a—"

"Shower," he finishes.

"Man! What did this thing set you back?"

" 'Bout a hundred," Walt says.

Nancy shakes her head and eyes the sofa in back doubtfully. "You're not sleeping in this thing, are you? I mean, you got a hotel room, right?"

"Sure. I'm at the Eola."

She smiles and nods knowingly. "Well, hell. Let's get this thing going and get up there. We'll open up the minibar and have us a party, Daddy."

Walt opens a cabinet over the sink and pours himself a shot of Maker's Mark. Then he sits at the table in back and drinks it, feeling the burn in his gullet.

Nancy looks puzzled. "You got any rum, by any chance?"

"Rum is for pirates and high school girls. You're out of high school, aren't you?"

She giggles. "Maybe I am and maybe I ain't. Do you want me to be?"

"What I want is for you to pour yourself a little whiskey and sit here by me."

Nancy pours a glass of whiskey and sets it on the table, then sits beside Walt and nuzzles her face into his neck. For an instant he feels a shiver of desire, but then her hand creeps across his thigh and down between his legs, rubbing insistently.

"Don't you want to get on over to that hotel?" she coos. "We wanna be where we can spread out. Don't we?"

Walt doesn't want to take the girl back to the hotel. He wants to go back to his room alone and call Carmelita. He can't do that, of course, not without breaking cover. He never had any intention of screwing Nancy. He figured he'd get her to do a little striptease, overtip her, then pretend to pass out and hope she didn't try to rob him. If she did, he'd "wake up" and ease her out gently. But now that they're alone, he knows he doesn't have the stomach for even that. Seeing those little tits drop out of that dress wouldn't do anything but make him think about the kids she has waiting at home, and the idea of her working with mechanical urgency to make him climax nauseates him.

What he really feels like doing is talking to her. Asking the same stupid question he asked the whores back in Korea—"How did you wind up doing this?"—which was all the more pointless back then because almost no one could answer even the simplest queries in English. Only in Japan had he received a real answer, on his extended R&R, and that had almost changed the course of his life.

"Don't you want it, Daddy?" Nancy murmurs, rubbing clumsily at his trousers. "Huh?"

He drinks off her shot, then says, "Listen, Nancy," and gently moves her hand out of his crotch. "You brought me some good luck in there, and I sure appreciate it. But I think I'm gonna call it a night."

The girl's face falls. "What's the matter, J.B.? You don't like me?"

"Oh, I like you. A lot. But I'm gettin' on up there in age, in case you haven't noticed."

Nancy gives him a conspiratorial laugh.

"Hell, I got kids older than you. I like having a girl on my arm, putting on the dog a little. But the truth is, honey, old J.B. can't really get it up no more."

Her brow furrows as though she's trying to understand an algebra problem. "What about Viagra?"

Walt chuckles as though with embarrassment. "I've got a bad ticker, hon. Can't take that stuff."

Nancy looks almost frantic. "Well, there's other things I can do. I mean, you got me out here and all. And I got to make a living, you know?"

"Oh, I know that, sweetheart. Don't you worry 'bout that." He digs out his roll and peels off five $100 bills. Nancy almost licks her lips at the sight of them, but she waits until he passes them to her. "Does that cover your time?"

The glow in her eyes tells him she hasn't seen that kind of money in a long time, if ever. "What about my tip?"

Walt hesitates, then winks like a man who knows he's being taken advantage of and peels off another hundred, which he folds into the damp little palm.

"How long you gonna be in town, J.B.?" Nancy asks, obviously thinking about her future prospects. "I can put on the dog all you want, darling."

"I'll be around all week. Got a piece of some Wilcox wells down here. You'll see me around the boats. If I'm with somebody else, you just give me the high sign, and I'll come get you if I can. If not, I'll catch you the next night. Okay?"

She nods soberly. "I got you."

Walt smiles with genuine gratitude. "Can you get home all right?"

"Yeah, my car's in the lot here."

"Where?"

"Other side."

Walt gets up and cranks the Roadtrek, then follows Nancy's pointing finger to the other side of the vast lot, where he stops beside her wreck of a car.

"It's a junker," she admits, "but it runs good. My ex is a mechanic."

Walt feels like giving her the rest of the roll, but that would be pushing it.

Nancy raises her slim frame from the seat, leans down, and kisses him on the top of the head, then walks to the door in the side of the Roadtrek. As he looks back to watch her go, she pauses and lifts her tight skirt over her hips. A thin band of black elastic encircles her surprisingly feminine hips, and the thong disappears between the firm cheeks of her rump. She bends and touches her toes without effort, then stands and turns to face him, drawing the thong away from her pubis. The hair there is trimmed flat, a dark shadow over taut skin and protuberant lips. This time something stirs in him, something beyond thought or reason, the old Adam in him coming back to life.

"Do you miss it, J.B.?" she asks softly. "Don't you just want to put your finger in it sometimes?"

Walt tries to laugh this off, but something sticks in his throat.

"Everybody wants to," she says. "You don't never get too old for that."

Walt looks into her eyes, then back at the triangular shadow.

"I'll be around," she says, letting the thong pop back into place. "You let me know."

She pulls down the clingy skirt, opens the door, and steps out of the van.

Walt drives away without looking back. Her groping touch had repelled him, but that last, unexpected display, her frank lack of embarrassment, arced across the space between them and struck something vital. It's enough to make him want to stop the van and pour another drink. A girl he wouldn't have looked at twice ten years ago has pierced his armor with a simple tease. The confidence he felt on the boat has been shaken. As he climbs the long road that leads up the bluff, he wonders, Am I getting too old for this game?

CHAPTER

27

After two nights without sleep, seven hours' rest is not enough, but ten minutes in a steaming shower at least make me feel human again. Caitlin woke me from a dead sleep at 3:45 a.m. and led me to her bathroom. Now, as I'm toweling off, she comes in and sets a cup of coffee beside the lavatory. I wrap the towel around my waist, and she perches on the edge of the commode. She's still wearing the clothes she had on at the police station.

"Have you slept?" I ask her, taking a hand towel off the rack to dry my hair.

"I've been reading about dogfighting."

"And?"

"My mind is blown. I'm serious. This is a worldwide sport—if you can call it that—and it goes back centuries. It's been outlawed almost everywhere except Japan, but it's still thriving all over the world. Did you even Google this?"

"I haven't had time."

Caitlin shakes her head as though I'm hopeless. "I pictured, you know, a mob of hicks with twenty-dollar bills in their hands gathered around a couple of bulldogs. But this is a big-money business. There's a whole American subculture out there. Two subcultures really: the old-timer rednecks—who specialize in breeding 'game' dogs and pass down all the knowledge about fighting bloodlines from the 1800s; then there's the urban culture—the street fighters, they call them. Hip-hop generation and all that. It's a macho thing. They fight their dogs in open streets, basements, fenced yards. But as different as the two subcultures are, they have a lot in common. They're highly organized, they train the dogs the same way, and they expose their kids to it very young to desensitize them . . . It's *sick*."

"'Game dogs,' you said. Is that what they call fighting dogs?"

"No, no. 'Gameness' is a quality that a dog has or doesn't have. If a dog is 'game,' that means he's willing to fight to the point of death, no matter how badly injured he is. Truly game dogs will keep fighting with two broken forelegs."

"Jesus."

Caitlin stands, outrage animating her. "Apparently pit bull terriers are among the most loyal dogs in the world, and it's that loyalty that these assholes twist to create animals that will sacrifice their lives to please their masters. You should see some pictures. When they're not fighting, these dogs live on heavy three-foot chains or on the breeding stand. That's it. And they don't live long. You know what happens to dogs that aren't considered game?"

"I can guess."

She nods. "They kill them. Kill them or use them for practice. 'Practice' means letting other dogs tear them to pieces, to give them a taste for blood. If it's the first option, they shoot them, hang them, bash in their skulls with bats, electrocute them, run them over with trucks. Sometimes they just let them starve."

"It's hard to grasp," I say, knowing this is hardly adequate. "I need my clothes."

"They're in the dryer. I'll get them. Though I kind of like seeing you this way. It's been a while."

This is what you get with a journalist like Caitlin. She can talk about horrific details in the same sentence with her desire for food or sex. I guess it's like doctors talking about suppurating infections while they eat. After a while, they just don't think about it.

"Yes, it has," I agree.

She looks at me for a few moments more, then leaves the bathroom.

The hook has been set. She will not let go of this story until she finds everything there is to know. This probably puts her in more danger than she was in before, but at least now she knows what she's dealing with, and I will be close enough to protect her.

After I dress, we take my backpack and slip out a side window, then through a neighbor's yard to a street two blocks away. There a female reporter named

Kara picks us up in her Volkswagen. She drives us to her apartment on Orleans Street, tells Caitlin to be careful, and disappears. Then Caitlin takes the wheel and follows the directions I've given her.

Our destination is a hundred acres of gated land called Hedges Plantation. Just off Highway 61 South, it's owned by Drew Elliott, my father's first junior partner, and a friend of mine since grade school. Dad is supposed to have got the key so that he can let us onto the property at 4:30 a.m. Danny McDavitt and Kelly are flying in from Baton Rouge, and McDavitt can probably set the chopper down there without anyone being the wiser. Though Hedges is surrounded by the newest residential developments on the south side of town, it's mostly wooded, and protected from casual observation on every side. Drew originally planned to build a home here, but now I hear he plans to build a high-end subdivision. Modern medicine in a nutshell. There are a couple of aluminum buildings on the property, and it's one of these that I've chosen for our rendezvous.

"Is that the one?" Caitlin asks, pointing

to a narrow gravel road just past the entrance to an antebellum home on the right.

"No, the next one."

"I see it. Okay." She slows the car, and the wheels crunch on gravel. "The thing about dogfighting," she says—it's standard procedure for Caitlin to return without warning to a previous discussion—"is that when the police do bust fights, which is rarely, they always turn up evidence of other crimes. Drugs, weapons, prostitution. The gambling goes without saying."

"Kill your lights."

"What?"

"There's enough moonlight to get us down this road."

She switches off the lights but keeps talking. "I don't mean random stuff either. The same criminals who run drugs and guns and girls love fighting dogs. It's like the ultimate expression of the male lust for power and violence."

"Your Radcliffe education is showing."

"Well, it's true."

"I know. That's why I called Kelly."

She gives me a tight smile. "Yeah, I get it now."

As we roll up to a metal gate, a tall, white-haired man steps from behind some cedar trees to our right. My father. Caitlin smiles and starts to roll down her window, but Dad pulls open the gate and motions for us to drive quickly through. After we do, he locks the gate behind us and comes to the passenger door of the Volkswagen. I get out and squeeze into the back, leaving the front seat for him.

"Well, Kate," he says, his eyes glinting as he looks at Caitlin. "It's sure been dull without you around."

"No more boredom," she says with a smile. "I guarantee that, at the very least. Have you heard from Peggy and Annie?"

Dad shakes his head. "We're talking as little as possible. And only on the satellite phone."

"I have it with me," I say. "We can get an update after this meeting."

"Good. I have a surprise for you, Son."

"What's that?"

"Walt's here."

"Garrity?"

"Right."

"What do you mean 'here?' In Natchez? Or *here* here?"

"He's in the shed now, talking to Kelly."

For the first time, I feel a rush of real optimism.

"The sly son of a bitch just appeared in my house," Dad says. "Almost gave me a coronary. I have James Ervin watching me, and he had no idea Walt was even there."

James Ervin is a black cop my dad used to treat. "That's not encouraging."

"Walt's pretty slick," Dad says.

"Who's Walt Garrity?" Caitlin asks.

"A Texas Ranger," Dad explains. "Met him in Korea, when we were still boys. He's semiretired, but I guess once you learn to sneak past Indians and Mexicans, retired city cops aren't much of a challenge. This will be the only night we see him. He wants to work totally apart from everyone else."

As well as I got to know Walt in Houston, there are many things I don't know about him. For example, I know that my father saved Walt's life during the Korean War, and that Walt later returned the favor, but I don't know the circumstances of either episode. Both men belong to a generation that doesn't talk about certain things without a compelling reason.

"I'm sure Walt knows best," I say. "We'll talk about your security later."

Dad ignores this and motions for Caitlin to continue up the road. She gives his hand a squeeze, then begins driving us deeper into the forest.

We're meeting in a sixty-by-forty-foot shed of galvanized aluminum, the kind you see along highways all over the South. My father leads Caitlin and me past a ski boat on a trailer, a 1970s-vintage Corvette with a hole in its fiberglass, an orange Kubota tractor, a zero-turn lawn mower, and various other power machinery used for grounds maintenance. Near the far end of the building, sitting in folding lawn chairs beneath two camouflage-painted deer stands, are Danny McDavitt, Carl Sims, Walt Garrity, and Daniel Kelly. At first glance, they look incongruous, like an illustration of different American types: an astronaut, an NFL cornerback, a cowboy, and a surfer with a blond ponytail. I'm surprised to see Carl Sims here, but before I can ask about his descent into the Devil's Punchbowl, Walt Garrity drawls, "Look what the cat drug in."

Rising from his lawn chair, Walt catches sight of Caitlin and quickly doffs his Stetson. "Ma'am. I didn't realize we'd be having female company."

Kelly rises to give Caitlin a hug. They met seven years ago, when we were drawn together by the Delano Payton case. "What do we have here, Penn?" Kelly asks. "The Seven Samurai?"

Carl Sims smiles from his chair. "Kind of looks like it, if you count the lady."

"Oh, she pulls her weight," Kelly says.

Gratitude shines in Caitlin's eyes as she shakes hands with Carl and Danny.

"Maybe you're right," I say. "Leaderless soldiers gathered to save a village."

"Well, I'm impressed," Caitlin says. "An air force pilot, a marine sniper, a Texas Ranger, a Delta Force commando, and a doctor."

"You left out lawyer and reporter," McDavitt points out.

"Superfluous on any important mission, I'm sure," she quips, getting a chuckle all around and putting everyone at ease.

"Not these days," Kelly says. "Even the army needs a legal department and a propaganda machine."

He unfolds three more chairs, and we sit in a tight circle, surrounded by chain saws and Weed Eaters and the oily smell of two-stroke engines. I look across the circle to Carl.

"So, you made it out of the Punchbowl?"

The sniper grins and shakes his head like a man who's spent a week crossing a desert. "Took a while, but I finally did."

Danny McDavitt says, "I would have called and told you, but I figured you needed the sleep."

"Thank you," says Caitlin. "He did."

"Did you find anything down there?" I ask.

"Not a damn thing. Not in the car or around it. I grid-searched on my hands and knees. If there was anything down there, somebody else already got it."

"Do you think the car burned when it crashed, or somebody torched it and dumped it there?"

"Somebody torched it, but I don't think they did it until yesterday. I think somebody else made the same climb I did, either to find something or to be sure they destroyed something."

As I recall the USB drive Tim concealed in his own body, Dad says, "So, where do we start? Is everybody on the same page, or whatever they say these days?"

Walt leans back and speaks from beneath the brim of his hat. His voice has been roughened by years of cigarette smoke, and the clear eyes in the weathered face give him a natural authority that the others seem ready to defer to, at least for now.

"Mr. Kelly was just telling me some things his company has learned in the past few hours. Reckon he ought to start us off."

"Everybody good with that?" Kelly asks.

The group nods as one.

"As most of you know, I work for Blackhawk Risk Management. We have a research department, and they've been checking out Jonathan Sands. In some ways, our research people aren't much different from those at any other corporation. They use Google, Nexis, et cetera. But Blackhawk also employs former counterterror operators from the U.S., Britain, Israel, Germany, South Africa—basically every major military power. We also employ former government lawyers and retired line officers. So our informal network of sources is pretty good. The initial bio I got back is detailed, but it only goes back to February 1989, when Sands left the UK. Northern Ireland, to be exact. This was just after some of the worst fighting in the so-called Troubles over there. The Brits are stonewalling on exactly what Sands did before '89, so we'll have to be content with what we have for now."

"Why would they hold back?" I ask.

Kelly shrugs. "We don't know that yet. But he has an amazing story, and I've heard a few. When Sands left Northern Ireland—one step ahead of somebody, is my guess—he worked as a mercenary for almost a decade, then settled in Macao. He started in the security department of a casino owned by Edward Po. Po is a legend, a whole separate story, so let's forget him for now. Suffice to say he's a sixty-eight-year-old Chinese billionaire, utterly ruthless and notoriously kinky. The important thing is that Sands arrived just before Macao was returned to Chinese sovereignty. It was about to expand from a serious-gamblers-only city to a Vegas-style destination, and Sands proved a valuable asset to Po. He was white, he could pass for English, and he had the kind of skill set that rough boys develop in Northern Ireland, plus what he'd learned in the interim. That doesn't explain his meteoric rise within Po's organization, though. He was promoted very quickly, and within three years he was often seen with Po at various public functions in China. And not as a security officer, but a corporate officer. Sands even seemed to overtake Po's son, whose name is Chao."

"What explains that?" asks my father.

"Dogfighting," says Kelly. "That's what I think. It's Po's passion. He's a famous breeder of Japanese Tosas, and he definitely fights them on a circuit."

"You think Sands picked up the taste for it there?" Carl asks.

Kelly shakes his head. "My gut tells me Sands grew up around it. Specialized knowledge about the sport would have got him noticed by Po."

Caitlin says, "I found a lot online about dogfighting in England and Ireland, going back centuries."

Kelly nods sagely. "Let's rewind a few

years. Before Sands arrived on the scene, Edward Po had a younger brother named Yang, who died of cancer. Yang Po was a Christian, a Baptist converted by Scottish missionaries, and he ultimately married one of their daughters. Yang had a daughter named Jiao—half-caste, white blood. Very hot—in pictures, anyway."

"I met her," I say. "She's striking, all right."

Caitlin cuts her eyes at me. "Is she part of whatever's going on here?"

"I think so, yeah. That's the vibe I got."

"That's interesting," says Kelly. "Because Yang Po had no involvement in his brother's casinos or any other criminal activity. He was a professor—a *law* professor, if you can believe that. Edward, on the other hand, was neck-deep in every racket you can run in China, and that's saying a lot. He's since exported a lot of his operations to the U.S. and Europe, as well. What's important for us is that Edward Po promised his dying brother that he'd not only take care of Jiao, but shield her from the sinful lifestyle. And he tried. He sent her to Cambridge, in fact. But when Jiao returned to Macao, she naturally fell for

Sands, the Irish bad boy, much as her uncle seems to have done. Po hoped she'd grow out of it, but when she didn't, he told Sands to get out of town or else."

"Or else what?" asks Caitlin.

"If Sands left China without Jiao, he'd get a nice severance package and the highest recommendation. If he stuck around or tried to take Jiao with him, they'd sever his genitals from his body, then his head from his neck."

Caitlin's eyebrows arch with interest, if not surprise. "So what did he do? Jiao's here now. Did Sands risk the reprisal and take her with him?"

"He's not the type to cave to threats," I say.

"Depends on who's doing the threatening," says Kelly. "The IRA thinks they know something about torture? Trust me, you have to go to Asia to learn about pain. Sands had seen Po's organization from the inside, and he knew what would happen. He did exactly what the boss wanted. He left the girl *and* China. Anyone want to guess where he went?"

"Land of opportunity?" prompts Danny McDavitt.

"You got it. Las Vegas, to be exact. With Po's recommendation, Sands got a top security job with the Palm Hotel group. Turned out his ambition was to own a casino himself. I think that's what Sands was doing with the niece in Macao, trying to marry into the business. Fast-forward a few months, and enter Craig Weldon, a Los Angeles entertainment lawyer who liked to hang out at the Vegas Palm. Weldon owns a sports management agency, and he had the same dream as Sands, to own a casino. The difference was, Weldon had the money to build one. That's how Golden Parachute was born. They made a simple plan to go into secondary markets—like Mississippi—and beat out the competition. They wanted to clean up out in the sticks, then return to Vegas as conquering heroes ten years later. Not a bad plan. But while they were putting all this together, Jiao showed up in Vegas. Couldn't stay away. True love, and all that. Now, did Sands try to send her back to China? Did he ask her to stay? We don't know. All we do know is that Po didn't send an unlicensed surgical team to castrate Sands. He let the Golden Parachute get completely unfurled, ready to catch wind, and then . . ."

"What?" asks Caitlin.

"He stole it," says Walt. "Right?"

Kelly smiles. "Lock, stock, and barrel. This is speculation, but probably very close to what happened. Right before Sands and Weldon applied for their license, Po showed up and said, 'Hello, Jonathan, my faithful servant. I appreciate all the legwork, but Golden Parachute Gaming is about to become a subsidiary of Po Enterprises, Ltd. Unofficially, of course.' And what could Sands do but grin and bear it? He knew he wouldn't live five minutes if Po decided otherwise. So, Po's name went into the five-percent silent-partner pool as a token investor, but in reality, the bulk of the money that funded Golden Parachute was his. Craig Weldon became a figurehead, either bought off with massive payoffs or scared into silence. Chinese gangsters are pros at both. California still has Triad-affiliated youth gangs who can enforce whatever the higher-ups want. Forget Sands and Quinn—Craig Weldon owns a lot of L.A. real estate, and an L.A. youth gang could permanently fuck up his portfolio with one weekend's arson and vandalism."

I wait for Kelly to go on, but he seems to have come to the end of his story. "So Golden Parachute is actually owned by a Chinese billionaire?"

"That's what my employers think."

"Does the U.S. government know that?"

"That I don't know."

After digesting this, I say, "What do you think Sands's real position is with the company? Does he even have an equity stake?"

Kelly shrugs. "Whatever his title is, he might as well be chief cook and bottle-washer. He's under Po's thumb. It's like he never even left Macao."

"Except he has the girl," Caitlin points out. "Jiao."

"How happy did he look to you?" Kelly asks me.

"Not very. Which brings us to the question I've been asking since Tim Jessup first came to me. What the hell is Sands really doing here? And is he doing it on his own, or for Edward Po?"

"Your father told me about Jessup's theory," Kelly says. "Sands *could* be stealing from the city to try to make his own pile. Get a stake and haul ass, with or without the girl. But is he that stupid? The world's not big enough to hide from Edward Po. If that's Sands's plan, he's a moron."

"He's no moron. The opposite, in fact."

Kelly stands and begins doing dips between two crossbars on the poles supporting the deer stand. His triceps flex like those of an Olympic gymnast. "So," he says, "whatever game Sands is playing with his accounting, he's doing it on orders from Po. Or at the very least, with Po's blessing."

"That brings us back to my original question. Why risk a gaming license worth hundreds of millions of dollars to steal a few hundred thousand, or even a few million, from a small town in Mississippi? Edward Po can't be that stupid."

"He's not," Walt Garrity says in the tone of someone who knows.

"Are you familiar with Po?" Kelly asks.

"Not by name," says the old Ranger. "But from what you've said so far, I think I've got the picture. Po's Chinese organized crime, right?"

"Right."

"If he has U.S. operations, they'll involve human-smuggling, prostitution, possibly drugs, and definitely money laundering."

"Right again," says Kelly, looking slightly surprised.

"I wondered about money laundering," I think aloud.

"Casinos are tailor-made for it," Walt explains. "Casinos are just banks, really, without all the pesky regulations. Wherever you have casinos, you have large-scale money laundering. The feds have passed a lot of regulations, but there's so much money to be made, crooks can bribe casino employees to ignore them."

Caitlin says, "Would the profit be enough to tempt someone as wealthy as Po?"

"It's not a matter of profit," Walt says. "Not the way you think of it. The biggest problem any criminal has is what to *do* with his profits. Take drug dealers. Cash money weighs more than the product they sell. Cash is one big pain in the ass. A guy like Edward Po needs hundreds of legitimate businesses to lay off all the cash he takes in. Maybe thousands, if he's that big in China. Import-export firms, currency exchanges, car dealerships, you name it. But casinos make the best laundries. Casinos and online gaming sites, based offshore."

Kelly, Carl, and Danny are looking at Walt with new respect. Apparently, they took the older man for what he appeared to be, a tired cowboy who might know his way around a horse and saddle, but not a computer.

"So Tim might have been right about Sands manipulating the casino's gross," I reason. "But if I understand you correctly, they could be *exaggerating* the earnings of the casino rather than underreporting."

"They might run some dirty money through that way," Walt says, "but they'd be paying county, state, and federal taxes on it, and that gets costly. The bulk of the operation would be handled by wiring large sums into the casino's bank for gamblers who show up a day or a week later, then gamble for twenty minutes, and cash out their accounts in money that's now legally clean. The casino makes false reports to the government to understate or misrepresent the wire transactions, and that's it. It's a dream setup. How many casinos does Golden Parachute own?"

"Five in Mississippi alone."

Walt chuckles softly, then begins to laugh outright.

"What is it?" asks my father, who seems to recognize Walt's tone.

"Those casinos ain't casinos at all," says the Ranger, his face reddening. "They're goddamn Chinese laundries."

Kelly's nodding thoughtfully. "That's got to be it."

"If you're right," I say, "then why would Sands risk such a sweet deal to do things like fight dogs and run whores?"

Caitlin leans forward and speaks with cutting clarity. "The same reason a dog licks his balls."

There's an awkward silence, then the men burst out laughing.

"Because he can," Carl says.

"It may be just that simple," Kelly reflects. "Men follow their compulsions wherever they are. I see it all the time overseas."

My father clears his throat and says, "This Freudian analysis is all fine and good, but what are we going to *do*? My wife and granddaughter are sitting in Houston with strangers because of these bastards. I want to know how to resolve this situation—fast."

Everyone's looking at Kelly. He stands motionless for a time, his eyes focused on the floor at the center of our circle with Zen-like calm. He's thirty-nine years old, with not a spare ounce of fat on him. When he moves, his body ripples with corded muscle, yet his blue eyes seem mild, even amused most of the time. He may work for a security company, but when I see him like this, all I can think is *Delta Force.*

"I'm tempted to pay Sands a personal visit," he muses, still looking at the floor. "Before we do anything else."

"For what?" I ask.

"To lay out some ground rules. He already threatened your family. He could strike at any time. He needs to know that any move against you will result in him being wiped from the board."

I hear a couple of audible swallows.

"I can see that," Walt says pragmatically. "The problem with going that way is you're unzipping your fly the minute you talk to him. If Sands sees what he's up against, he could pull in his horns and shut down for a while. That's the opposite of what we want. Right?"

Kelly considers this argument, then nods with certainty. "That's why we're going to end this thing tonight. Sands and Quinn are our immediate problem. We need to get them by the balls as fast as we can. Then the inevitable will happen."

"What's that?" Caitlin asks.

"Their hearts and minds will follow," says McDavitt.

Kelly looks at me. "You said dogfighting's a felony, right?"

"Right. Even attending one is a felony. And the sentences can be pretty stiff."

"Then tonight we're going to run a quiet little op. A photographic expedition. We'll shoot pictures of Sands, Quinn, and any local dignitaries who might be in attendance, plus the whores and anything else worth shooting. At that point, you'll have evidence that could put Sands in jail for serious time. Your DA will have no choice but to cooperate. I've seen dogfighting in Kabul. It's brutal stuff. If Caitlin publishes one photo spread on the *Examiner*'s Web site, the PETA people will be calling for the partners of Golden Parachute to be crucified on the Washington Mall."

Walt nods. "I've been trying to find out where they fight. Nothing yet, but I'm on it."

"What do we use for equipment?" I ask.

"I've got night-vision optics in my gear bag," Kelly says. "Scope, camera, range finder. Carl's probably got some stuff too."

The sniper nods. "We got a new scope at the sheriff's department. I can have it up from Athens Point by tonight."

"How do we get close to one of these fights without being detected?" I ask.

Kelly smiles cagily. "Most of them happen by the river, right?"

"That's what Jessup told me."

"Then we do a Huck Finn."

"A raft?"

"Not exactly. Didn't you tell me you've done some kayaking with the guy who organizes that annual race here? The Fat something or other?"

"The Phat Water Kayak Challenge."

"Right." Kelly tries to puzzle this out. "Is he a rapper or something?"

"No, he's an ex-marine, force recon. He's about fifty."

"Will he lend you a boat?"

"Sure. He'd be happy to guide us to wherever we're going."

"That's it, then. Danny will fly air support. He'll be my eye in the sky, with Carl riding shotgun with his sniper rifle. Wherever the VIP boat docks, I'll slip into shore a hundred yards away, find the action, photograph it, then get out before they even know I'm there."

"Sounds like a plan," says McDavitt. "I'll bet they go the same place they docked last night."

"Where was that?" asks Caitlin.

"A spot down the river. Louisiana side. Looked like an old farm, maybe a deer camp now. I was pretty high up, but I saw what could have been a small crowd of men under some trees."

"Wait a second," I cut in. "Those kayaks are nineteen feet long, but they only seat one paddler. We—"

"I know they only seat one," Kelly says, looking hard at me. "It's not *we* on this trip, buddy. It's me."

I feel blood heating my face. "You're not going without me."

"I'll move a lot faster without you, Penn."

"You're missing the point. I need to be

there so that I can corroborate the evidence later. We don't know what kind of legal proceedings might come out of this. You're going to go back to Afghanistan, or Iraq, or Africa, wherever. I need to be able to say I was there, that I saw you take these pictures and the action they document."

Kelly takes a deep breath and looks at my father, but Dad says nothing.

"You're forgetting something, buddy," Kelly says. "Something I heard your mother told you not to forget."

"What?" I ask, but it's coming back to me now. The morning we evacuated them with Kelly's people.

"Annie," Caitlin reminds me. "This is no Outward Bound course. There's real risk here."

"Believe it," Walt says. "Dogfighters are like drug growers, obsessed with security. They're well-armed, high-tech, and highly mobile. You should expect guards—human and canine. You might run into booby traps, laser fences, God knows what."

Kelly nods as though this is all part of a night's work. "I've been fighting Taliban insurgents for the past year, Mr. Garrity. I can handle this."

"Oh, I'm sure you can. I'm just making the point for Penn." Walt gives me a piercing look. "Your old-time American dogfighting fraternity is a tough bunch of boys. And from what you say about these Irish bastards, they could be worse. If they figure out Kelly's close, there's gonna be gunplay, no doubt about it."

I look around the ring of faces, sensing that everyone agrees with Kelly and Caitlin. "I'm not forgetting Annie," I tell them. "But I'm not forgetting Tim Jessup either. This isn't up for debate. If we can take Tim's killers down tonight, I'm going to be there."

Caitlin uses her eyes to plead silently with me, but the men are watching my father. Dad rubs his chin for a while, then says, "Peggy was right about Annie needing you. She was right that we're getting old. But she *isn't* right that nothing's more important than your children. Sometimes you have to take a stand. I'm not saying this is that time. But Tim was your friend, and I understand if you feel you have to go."

"I'm getting two boats," I tell them. "End of discussion."

Kelly nods once in surrender. "Okay. We'll put in upstream and take our directions from Danny in the chopper."

"What about comm?" McDavitt asks.

Kelly reaches into his back pocket and takes out a small, black box like a cell phone, with a short, fat antenna. "These walkie-talkies are encrypted and guaranteed across ten miles. We call them Star Treks, like the 'communicators' on the old TV show. I brought four with me. For God's sake, nobody lose one. They're army-issue, Special Forces only, and it's my ass if I go back to Afghanistan short."

"What kind of weapons are you taking?" Carl asks.

Kelly looks as if this is the least of his concerns. "I'll decide that later. I'd like to avoid violence, if possible. But if they start the party, I'll be happy to bust their piñata." Kelly gives Carl a frank look. "You down with that?"

The sniper turns the question over in his mind. "Somebody shoots at me, I gotta shoot back, don't I?"

"What if they shoot at *me*?" I ask.

Carl grins. "Just think about that insurance commercial, the one with the red umbrella. I got you covered."

"How big is your umbrella?"

"In daylight, over a thousand yards. Nighttime's a little different. But I won't be far away. You just focus on staying quiet while Kelly does his job. Danny and I will take care of the rest."

"All this testosterone is certainly reassuring," Caitlin says, "but what if you don't *find* a dogfight?"

Kelly shrugs. "We pull back, regroup, and wait for more intel. From what we know about Sands, I don't think he's worried about being caught by the locals."

"They'll be fighting tonight," Walt says with confidence. "Go outside and smell the air. *Feel* it. It's football weather. The blood is up. Animals are getting itchy, starting to move. Bucks are fighting in the woods. Fighting and fucking's what it's all about this time of year."

I think Caitlin is actually blushing.

"What about you, Mr. Garrity?" Kelly asks. "I know you didn't come all this way to twiddle your thumbs."

"That's a fact," Walt says. "I came because my old comrade-in-arms was in trouble." He nods at my father. "And I do have a plan. But I tend to play a long game. I like to move slow and careful and let my prey come to me."

Carl is listening closely. Undoubtedly, a sniper can relate to this philosophy.

In a good-natured voice, Walt says, "I'm sure that after tonight, I'll be redundant personnel. But no matter what happens, this is the last time you folks will see me. I'm like an actor playing a part. Once I get into the role, I don't break character. I almost didn't come tonight, but I wanted to see what this mess was really about. I'm glad I did."

"Is there anything we can do to help you?" Kelly asks.

"I have only one request, and it's for you."

"What's that?"

"I rather you not tell your employers about my involvement."

"No problem."

"Why not?" asks Caitlin. "You don't trust Blackhawk?"

Walt spits on the concrete floor and

looks off into the shadows. "Blackhawk is a Texas outfit, and they have some good men over there. But after 9/11 they ramped up pretty quick—sort of like deputizing a bunch of laymen for a posse. It's tough to know who you're getting when you hire that fast."

"I wouldn't argue with you," says Kelly. "Don't lose a second's sleep over it."

"I appreciate it."

Walt stands and stretches, and within twenty seconds everyone else has followed suit. As he lowers his arms, I see a leather string around his neck that triggers a powerful memory.

"You still carry that derringer with you?"

Walt smiles, then pops open the top mother-of-pearl snap on his Western shirt and lifts what looks like a child's toy from where it lies against his chest. Kelly and Carl lean forward. The derringer is smaller than a woman's hand, with burled-wood grips and metal dulled by years of sweat.

"Two shots?" Carl asks.

Walt smiles. "That's one more than you generally get, ain't it?"

"But I'm firing a .308 round."

Walt pulls a pin from the gun and

removes its cylinder, exposing the brass tails of five bullets. "Two's generally enough in the kind of situation where you use this thing, but you never know."

Carl puts his hand out and touches the gun like a talisman, but Kelly says, "I thought Texas Rangers carried Colt .45s."

Walt chuckles. "Pretty hard to hide my old Colt. I've been patted down many a time without anybody finding this little lady. She's loaded with .22 long-rifle rounds. They do the job just fine."

While Carl studies the gun, Kelly looks at me. "What's your day look like?"

"I'm scheduled to present a citizenship award on the bluff at the Ramada Inn at two p.m. There's always a big crowd there on Sunday, watching the balloons. Barbecue, lots of city employees, kids."

"It's public knowledge that you're doing this?"

"Sure. Printed in the paper. Why?"

"I may stop by to get a look at whoever's covering you."

"You going to give me one of those Star Treks?"

Kelly laughs and passes me the one from his pocket. As I take it, he turns to

Walt and says, "How about you, Mr. Garrity? You want one?"

The old ranger smiles. "Where I'm going, they'd just take it off me. A gun they might not mind, but radios are a big no-no."

"Just making sure."

"Thanks, but I work alone. Kind of a habit."

Kelly laughs suddenly, as though at Walt's expense.

"What is it?" Garrity asks, a little edge in his voice.

"I've been trying to remember something all night. Something my uncle used to say."

"What's that?"

"'One riot, one Ranger.' That's the motto, isn't it?"

Walt sighs like a man who's heard this line a thousand times too many. "That's the myth, not the reality."

Kelly says, "I understand," and offers his hand.

Garrity takes it and shakes firmly. "Good luck to you, soldier. And keep your eyes peeled for dogs."

"I'll hear the dogs," Kelly assures him.

"No, you won't. Dogfighters are like the dopers now. Once upon a time, they used guard dogs to warn you away and alert them to run. Now they sever the vocal cords so there's no bark to warn you."

A chill races across my skin.

"My God," says my father.

"They're on your throat before you even know they're there," Walt says. "A lot of cops have been hurt like that this past year. Some killed."

"Thanks," Kelly says. "I've heard of that before, but I've never seen a dog it's been done to."

"I have," I say softly. "Jonathan Sands has one."

Everyone turns to me.

"It's white, and it's *big.* I think the breed is called a Bully Kutta."

I've rarely seen astonishment on Kelly's face, but I see it now. "That's a Pakistani breed," he says. "A war dog. It's related to the Bully Ker. I've seen those fight in Kabul. The tribesmen fight them against *bears.* Two dogs against a bear, and the dogs always win."

"Who the hell are these people?" Dad asks.

Kelly pats my father on the shoulder. "I don't think we'll know that until we find out how Jonathan Sands spent the first part of his life."

"Are we going to find out?"

Kelly nods. "The British government can stonewall Blackhawk all they want, but I've got personal friends in the SAS, vets who served in Northern Ireland. We'll have the story before long."

"By tonight?" Caitlin asks.

"Maybe. In any case, I think we should get out of here. It's going to be a long day, and an even longer night. Everybody know what their job is?"

After everyone nods, Kelly reaches into his gear bag and brings out two more walkie-talkies. One he gives to Danny McDavitt, the other to my father. Then he looks at Caitlin and me.

"You two are together for the duration, right?"

She nods, and I see color in her cheeks.

"Glad to see it," Kelly says with a smile.

"I am too," says my father. "Too bad it takes a goddamn crisis to bring them together."

"Dr. Cage," Kelly says, "I'd appreciate it

if you'd scope out some safe houses for us, on both sides of the river. Think you can do that?"

"This time of year, I'm sure I can. Both of my partners' lake houses are empty."

"Hey," I say, pointing at Kelly. "Caitlin and I are together until tonight. Then I'm with *you*."

CHAPTER

28

If it were any other year, this would be my favorite day of the Balloon Festival: the "barge drop" event as seen from the Ramada Inn above the Mississippi River Bridge. The flashy trappings of the festival stand a mile away at Fort Rosalie. Here there is no grand stage, no headline act or spotlights, no carnival rides. But the Natchez Ramada Inn, a monument to bourgeois America, commands one of the most breathtaking views of the Mississippi River on the continent. Soon it will be leveled to make way for yet another casino hotel, but for locals it remains the beating heart of the Balloon Festival. A strong pilot presence gives it the buzz of a military command center from Friday until Sunday evening. You can smell the pork ribs being barbecued by the swimming pool even before you get out of your car. Every room with a river view has been rented for a year in advance, many by local organizations who use the event as an excuse for three days of uninterrupted partying.

The object of the "barge drop" is for a balloon crew to drop a beanbag onto a white cross marked on the deck of a barge holding position in the Mississippi River. Many end up landing—sometimes crash-landing—on the grounds of the hotel itself, or in the neutral ground at the foot of the massive hill the hotel stands on. But the true center of the festivities is the long hill that falls precipitously from the hotel pool toward Highway 84 and the river. Here hundreds of families gather on blankets and lawn chairs to watch their children slide hell-for-leather down the slope on flattened cardboard boxes, toward a concrete drainage ditch. Each sally is potentially life-threatening, and beyond the concrete lies a much longer slope covered with a thick mat of kudzu. I've seen fathers in their forties make twenty or thirty trips up that hill dragging a scarred Maytag box behind them, with a toddler or two still clinging to it like princes on a magic carpet. It's a miracle the hotel's owners allow this ritual in our hyperlitigious age. That a dozen lawsuits don't arise from this activity every year says more about the crowd than anything else. They're the kind of parents who, if their son broke his arm, would tell him it was his own damn fault for not stopping short of the concrete and to suck it up until they could get Dr. Cage away from his bourbon long enough to splint the bone.

I spent my first thirty minutes anxiously searching the crowd for Daniel Kelly or signs of people following me. Several times I felt someone *was* watching me, but whenever I turned, I saw nothing suspicious. Ten minutes ago, I presented the citizenship award to Paul Labry, who had no idea he had been voted the honor. I actually saw tears in Labry's eyes as he accepted the brass plaque, but my mind was only half on the presentation, because five minutes before my speech, my father had called on Kelly's Star Trek and told me that Jewel Washington, the coroner, was at the Ramada and had something important to give me. I spotted Jewel right after the speech, serving barbecue under a tent, but she gave no sign of recognizing me, so I decided to stick around until she felt an approach was safe.

Caitlin is roaming the crowd, just in case Jewel sees her as an obstacle to our communication. She has my backpack slung over her shoulder, and in it the satellite phone and my gun. We've done a good job playing the role of reconciled lovers; I only hope Libby Jensen's not here today. Normally, Libby would be able to handle the situation, but with her son in jail, she might make a scene.

"Mr. Mayor?" someone says nervously from behind me.

Turning, I look into the cornflower blue eyes of a girl of about twenty. She's mousy-haired and round-faced but pretty in her way, a hillbilly girl who will soon lose her looks along with the blush of youth. She's either tall or wearing very high heels, because I'm looking almost straight into her eyes. My first coherent thought is that someone should teach her how to apply eye makeup, because she could take off half of what she's wearing and look twice as good.

"Hello," I say. "Are you enjoying the festival?"

The girl smiles, but her eyes are filled with confusion, or even fear. Something about her seems familiar. Before I can figure out what, she shoves something into my front pants pocket. The contact startles me, but the crowd around us is intent on two balloons that are flying too close together as they sweep in off the river.

"Don't read that until you're by yourself," the girl says. "It's superimportant."

"Are you—"

"I gotta go," she says, then turns and moves into the crowd. I see her leather jacket for a couple of seconds, then only a blur of bodies.

"Who was that?" Caitlin asks, suddenly appearing at my side. She's staring after the girl, but I can no longer distinguish her from the other people swirling between us and the hotel swimming pool.

"I don't know."

"What was she saying?"

"She stuffed something into my pocket. I think it's a note. She said to read it in private. Jewel must have sent her over. Somebody must be watching Jewel."

"Or you."

"Yeah."

Caitlin takes my hand. "Let's get out of here."

I look around the grounds of the hotel. Unless you have a room, there's no privacy to be had. "We shouldn't leave until we're sure I have whatever Jewel needs to give me."

"Have some barbecue, Mr. Mayor!"

Jewel Washington's sweating brown face appears before me so suddenly that I can't quite tell where she came from. She shoves a Chinet plate piled high with tangy-smelling pork into my hands. Before letting go of it, she pinches the back of my hand, then adjusts the plate so that I feel something hard taped to the bottom it. It's small and rectangular and feels plastic.

"The pork was going fast," she says loudly. "Paul Labry told me to bring you a plate before we got down to the bone."

Jewel interposes herself between me and Caitlin, then starts talking to Caitlin in a "girl talk" tone—probably to give me time to remove whatever it is she's trying to pass me.

"Caitlin's cool, Jewel," I say softly. "What's under the plate?"

Without breaking the rhythm of her conversation, the coroner laughs loudly and squeezes Caitlin's arm, then pulls the two of us together and leans in as though dispensing romantic advice. "A tape of a voice memo Tim Jessup recorded on his cell phone right before he died. Shad has the phone. He has your cell records too. This case is getting crazy, Penn. You need to watch yourself."

"You're crazy, girl!" Caitlin says, playfully shoving Jewel's shoulder. "But if this keeps up, I might consider moving back here."

"You come on back!" cries Jewel. "We need you back here gettin' on people's case." She backs away from us. "You two be talkin' again, so you can share that plate!"

Jewel waves broadly, then makes her way back toward the barbecue tent. Two sheriff's deputies standing in line watch as she approaches, and they don't take their eyes off her as she moves behind the serving table.

Caitlin grabs my arm and pulls me around some shrubs beside the pool. "I don't know what's going on, but let's get the hell out of here and see what we've got."

Balancing the plate on my right hand, I put my left arm around Caitlin and walk toward the breezeway that leads to the hotel parking lot. Nearly everyone we pass speaks to me, and several call Caitlin by name. A local Realtor tries to stop me and talk about a zoning variance, but I plead official business and push on. The moment we get twenty yards of space around us, Caitlin says, "Is the tape in the freaking barbecue or what?"

"It's taped to the bottom of the plate."

"What kind of tape is it?"

"A minicassette, I think."

"Old school. I have that kind of recorder at the office."

"Kmart's only a minute away."

"Okay." As we make our way through the crowded lot, Caitlin says, "If the tape is what Jewel had for you, then who's the note in your pocket from?"

"Probably some nut job, if not the girl herself. There's the car. Come on."

Caitlin unlocks the car we drove here, a Corolla owned by the newspaper. Before we get in, I realize that if someone did follow us here, they could have planted a listening device in the car while we were gone. I feel like hammering my fist against the roof in frustration, but instead I take Caitlin by the upper arms, lean into her neck, and kiss her below the ear.

"Don't say anything about this stuff in the car," I whisper, surprised by the force of my reaction to her scent. "We can read the note on the way to Kmart, but don't talk about it. We'll talk in the store."

She nods and gets behind the wheel.

Before I get in, I crouch between the cars, take out the Star Trek, and call Kelly. When he acknowledges, I ask, "Are you at the hotel?"

"Yeah."

"We're driving to the Kmart, just up the highway. I want you to cover us."

"No problem. Everything okay?"

"I may have good news. Stay close to us."

"Don't worry."

As soon as I'm inside the car, I pull the tape from the bottom of the plate and confirm that it's a standard minicassette. Slipping it deep into my left front pocket, I dig out what the girl shoved down my right pocket. It's blue-ruled newsprint from the kind of tablets first-graders use when they're learning to write block print. It's been folded and refolded many times, like a love note someone passes you in junior high.

"Let's get some food for this afternoon," I say casually. "For postcoital munchies."

Caitlin laughs convincingly. "What do you want?"

"Chips and dip, drinks and stuff. You don't have anything at your house."

"What do you expect after a year and a half?"

She backs out of the parking space and carefully negotiates the packed vehicles. Soon we're coasting down the long, curving hill that leads to the highway below the bridge. Across that highway is the Visitors'

Center, where only yesterday I blew Caitlin
off in the parking lot. That feels like three
days ago. She drops a hand from the
wheel and makes a fast "hurry up" motion.

After I get the note unfolded, I see a
woman's printed script, the fancy, tightly
written kind some girls use when they
write poems or diary entries. It begins like
a thousand other letters and e-mails I've
received in the past two years—"Dear
Mayor Cage"—but when I read the first
line after the salutation, my heart starts
pumping at twice its normal rate.

> My name is Linda Church. I am hiding
> out and can't speak to you in person.
> <u>Please</u> don't try to find me. Tim is dead,
> as you probably know, and they were
> going to kill me too, but I escaped with
> my life. Just barely, though. I am hurt,
> but some good people are helping me.
> I'm writing to you because on the night
> Tim was murdered, I learned some
> things that I think he would have wanted
> you to know. Honestly, though, I'm afraid
> even to tell you these things. But <u>TIM
> TRUSTED YOU,</u> so I am taking this risk.
> I pray that you did not betray Tim and

cost him his life. I loved him and still do, and there must be some good men left in this world.

Caitlin is poking my leg; she wants to know what's in the note. To put her off, I place my thumbnail under the first line and hold the note where she can read it. The shock on her face tells me I'll have to read it where she can see it too, even at the risk of an accident.

A young man named Ben Li is probably dead by now. He worked on the boat sometimes, but we hardly ever saw him. Tim told me his job was computers. I doubt you will find his body, as I'm pretty sure they have fed him to the dogs. This dogfighting that upset Tim so much is still going on. I don't know what all Tim was trying to get from the company, and I don't know if he got whatever it was to you. I can only hope that he did, that he didn't die for nothing. You should know that Mr. Sands and Mr. Quinn are <u>MONSTERS.</u> They are not just cruel, or sick men. I knew men like that in Las Vegas, and everywhere else I've lived too. But Sands and Quinn are demons who live on other people's pain. I have prayed on this and know it to be true. I have sinned by lying with Sands, but I was in fear for my life, and I believe now to some extent that it was rape. Sands has sex with lots of girls who work on the boat, not always by their choice. He is not who or what he pretends to be. He is a demon wearing a human skin. Quinn is not a demon but he is an animal. No, worse. Animals would never do the awful things he has done. But I'm losing my track. What's important is the facts, and it's hard to keep facts in my head right now. I think my leg is infected and maybe broken too. But I can't risk going to a doctor. I feel so guilty about Julia and the baby. I hope they are going to be all right. If I get out of this alive and I ever manage to make any money, I am going to send some to Julia (Anonymous) to make up for whatever pain and worry I have caused her.

You need to know that Quinn bragged to me that "big things" were coming up soon or about to happen. "Big people" coming into town for something, I don't know what. But I worked one of those dogfights, and it is probably something like that, even though they are horrible things. The animals die and the men have orgies on the girls and stuff like that. If you could just bust one of those fights, you would find enough drugs to put them all in jail until Judgment Day. I hope I have not made a mistake in writing to you, Mr. Cage. I am trusting Tim's instinct, but I'm afraid that was not very good in life. If it was, he might still be with us and not in Heaven.

The people who are hiding me are going to get me away to somewhere safe. May the Lord bless you and keep you safe if you are doing His work.

Yours in Christ, Linda Mae Church.

The sound of Caitlin's opening her door brings me out of my trance. With one inquisitive look she asks if I still want to go into Kmart. I nod; then refold the note and put it back in my pocket. Motioning for her to hand me her purse, I take the satphone from my backpack and stuff it into her bag, then shove my pistol into my pocket.

"Let's go."

When we're ten yards from the car,

Caitlin says, "You still think Tim didn't have an affair with her?"

"Wait till we're inside the store to talk. I'll get the chips and dip and see if we're being tailed. You get the recorder, some triple-A batteries, two pairs of cheap headphones, and a miniplug splitter. You know why?"

"Because those cheap recorders only put out a mono signal."

It's good to be back with somebody who needs no spoon-feeding.

Inside the Kmart, I walk to the snacks section and grab some Doritos, then watch the store entrance. A few people come in and out, but most are black, and none look remotely like Quinn's goons. The white people are Pentecostals or older folks wearing gardening clothes. Less than five minutes pass before Caitlin appears at the head of my aisle with a stapled bag held low beside her. I walk past her and whisper, "Men's clothing department."

Grabbing two pairs of pants off a rack, I ask an older woman staffing the ladies' department to open a fitting room. She recognizes me as the mayor, makes a show of offering all the help she can, then leaves me with the room. A second later, Caitlin slips into my dressing room and opens the bag. It takes all my strength to get the plastic packaging off the tape recorder, but Caitlin's deft fingers make short work of inserting the batteries and setting up the headphones and splitter. When this is done, I take the cassette from my pocket, insert it into the recorder, and hit PLAY.

A hiss fills my left ear. Caitlin's head is tilted, tensely poised, her eyes wide and bright as though reflecting every bit of light in the cubicle. She's hearing the same thing I am, a low-quality copy of a low-resolution voice memo made on a cell phone and played back through the cheapest equipment available. Yet when I hear Tim's voice, it pierces me to the quick. He's breathless, as though he's sprinted most of a mile, but the whine of an overrevved engine in the background tells me he's in a car.

"Penn, where are you, man? I waited as long as I could, but they're onto me. I had to run. I tried to call you, but both my phones say 'No service.' They're jamming the signal like they do on the

boat sometimes. They blocked Cemetery Road, so I'm headed out into the county . . . almost to the Devil's Punchbowl now. I'm going to have to shut off this phone, because they may be tracking me with it. I can't say much, because they might get the phone. I'm doing eighty on gravel, man!"

Caitlin's eyes go wide as the creak of a car seat conjures an image of Tim craning his neck around as he races down Cemetery Road.

"They're still back there. I found what we needed, okay? It's a DVD disc. I got it through the guy who shot the cell phone pictures I showed you. He's a computer genius named Ben Li. I got him so stoned he didn't know up from down, then sedated him. He must have woken up early. He probably panicked and called them, he's that dumb. Anyway, here's how to find the disc in case anything happens to me. Ready? 'Dog pack. The Great Escape.' Okay? You'll figure it out, but I hope to God you don't have to. If I don't make it, then look where the sun don't shine, as Coach used to say. I'll be all right, though. These bastards don't

know Adams County like I do. I'm going to—wait, wait, shit, I forgot—"

It sounds like Tim dropped the phone. He yells, *"Fuck!"* and groans as if he's bending double, then his voice is close again. *"Ben said something while he was stoned. See, I always thought he had more pictures than what he showed me. Insurance, you know? To protect himself. He said I should ask his birds about the pictures. He had two cockatoos, but all I ever heard them say was stupid lines from movies. I searched their cages and couldn't find anything. Shit, they're gaining . . . I've got to shut down. No airplane mode on this bitch. I love you, man, but you picked a hell of a time to be late. Bye for now—"*

The electric silence in the headphone is cut off by a blank hiss.

My hands are shaking, my heart pounding as though the chase just happened, as though I were in the car with Tim rather than listening to a dead man talk two days after he was murdered. The realization that Tim probably died because I was thirty minutes late makes me dizzy with nausea. My ears roar as an infinite string of what-ifs blasts through my mind like a line of runaway subway cars.

"I can't believe I wrote that first story," Caitlin says in a dazed voice. "I wrote just what his killers wanted me to, didn't I?"

She doesn't cry often, but there are tears in the corners of her eyes. Behind the tears seethes anger—and wounded vanity. No one likes to be played for a fool, but some people, usually the vainest among us, truly cannot handle it.

Despite wrestling with my own guilt, I nod.

"I'm going to bury Golden Parachute," Caitlin vows. "*Bury* them." Then her eyes snap to mine. "What do the clues mean? Do you know where the disc is?"

In the maelstrom of guilt swirling inside me, childhood memories spin and flicker like buoys glimpsed through heavy rain. "Not yet. I'm thinking."

"They could be passwords."

"To what? Tim found a physical object and hid it somewhere."

"Right, right."

"*The Great Escape* is a movie. Tim and I were kids when it came out."

"Did you watch it with him?"

"I don't think so." I think frantically, trying to grasp images that float away like leaves in a swirling current. "The part about the birds was separate from that, right? From 'dog pack' and *The Great Escape*?"

"Yes."

"Because he said that guy's birds could say movie lines."

"Yes, but that first part wasn't connected to the birds. The first clues were for you alone."

I'm trying to make the missing connections, but Caitlin's urgency feels like an overcurrent shorting out my neural processes. "Just don't say anything for a minute. I'm thinking."

She nods, but I know silence requires extreme effort from her. She's a puzzle-solver by nature, and not having the tools to solve this one must drive her mad.

"Could 'dog pack' have something to do with the dogfighting?" she asks.

"Caitlin!"

"Sorry—I'm sorry."

I try fast-forwarding through my childhood friendship with Tim Jessup, but the memories are blurry, like stock images, shot poorly and faded with age. Many

involve bike riding or playing steal the flag,
but nothing related to dog packs comes—

"Oh my God," I groan, first amazed,
then appalled as the significance of the
second clue drops into place.

She grabs my arm. "What is it?"

"I can't believe I was that stupid."

"What? Do you know what it means?"

"Yes." I reach for the doorknob. "Come
on!"

"Where?"

"The cemetery! It's been there all along!"

"I thought you already searched the
cemetery."

"I did. But it's huge. Now I know where
to look."

Something vibrates in my pocket. At first
I think it's my cell phone, but then I realize
it's Kelly's Star Trek. "Peek outside," I tell
Caitlin, suddenly nervous. "Hurry."

She opens the door and freezes.

"What is it?" I ask, trying to pull the gun
from my pocket.

"I'm helping him get the things fitted,"
Caitlin says awkwardly.

"It's *Sunday*," a woman says with disgust. "There's kids out here. Why don't
you just get a *room*?"

Caitlin closes the door. I click the TALK button on the Star Trek and say, "It's me."

"We've got a problem," Kelly says in my ear.

"Short of a death, it doesn't matter. I think we're at the endgame."

"Tell me."

"Not over the air. Not even on these things."

"You found what we're looking for?"

"I know where it is. Can you cover us to the cemetery?"

"Screw that. You're in the store now?"

"Yeah."

"You have the satphone with you?"

"In Caitlin's purse."

"Walk straight back to the staff area like you own the place, then leave by their private exit door. Use a fire door if you have to. I'll be waiting out back. If anybody tries to stop you, tell them you're the fucking mayor. If that doesn't work, pull your gun. Just get to my car. The game has changed."

When Kelly's voice gets tense, I know we're in trouble.

"We're on our way."

CHAPTER

29

Linda Church sits on a folding chair in the corner of a small kitchen and studies her left knee, which is swollen and blue at the front, and purple in back. The joint doesn't hurt too bad, but she knows some gristle in it is torn because her skin is stretched tight as a drumhead and the bones slip when she walks. The lower part of her right leg looks worse. There's a tear in the bruise, and the skin around it feels like it just came out of a microwave oven.

She remembers leaping from Quinn's boat but has no memory of hitting the water—only a white flash coming out of darkness. She awakened in terror that she was drowning, but the sound of a motor in the dark told her she couldn't afford to splash. Quinn was trolling slowly back the way he'd come, searching for her with a spotlight that lit the fog yellow. She felt sure he would find her since she could hardly swim with the leg, but as the boat drew near, and she prepared to slide under the water, she'd heard something strike the hull—not hard—more like the sound of kicking shoes.

Then she remembered Ben Li.

The spotlight arced up into the sky, and some sort of commotion broke out on the boat. She heard more hollow impacts, then two shots cracked over the water. The echoes seemed to go on forever, and before they died, the big motor revved up and the boat turned south again.

Then God had saved her. She'd had no idea whether she was near the bank or in the center channel of the Mississippi, about to be run down by a barge weighing thousands of tons. But as she floated downstream, thankful for every ounce of body fat she'd cursed until then, she felt her good leg scrape sand. The river was lifting her onto a gently shoaling sandbar as surely as if God himself were holding her in his hand. When she came to rest, her eyes filled with black sky, she felt like Moses in the bulrushes.

Unlike Moses, however, no one found her lying by the river. How long she lay there, she had no idea. But sometime before dawn, she got to her feet and started limping toward the levee. Soon the sand had dirt mixed in it, then she was dragging herself over rich soil, the farmland her grandfather used to hold to his nose and smell as if it were pipe tobacco. She'd wanted to scream as she climbed the levee, but she didn't dare do more than grunt. On top of the levee was a gravel road, and she guessed it ran all the way from New Orleans to Missouri, if not to Minneapolis. The levee made her think of her grandfather too; he'd told her how during the flood of '27 they'd put the nigras and the cows onto it to save them from the rising water, and kept them there for weeks and weeks.

She knew she couldn't walk on the levee, as bad as she wanted to. There'd be trucks coming down it before dawn, and if Quinn sent even one man along the road to look for her body on the bank, he'd pin her in his headlights like a doomed deer. She couldn't move well enough to be sure of getting away in time. So she'd slid down the far side of the levee, down to the scrub trees by the borrow pits, from which they'd taken the dirt to build the levees. She limped along the pits until the sun came up, her eyes always on the ground, looking for snakes. She remembered a teenage boyfriend walking along a borrow pit, breaking the backs of moccasins with a heavy branch. Despite this frantic killing, the snakes swirled slowly through the shallows but did not flee to the middle of the pit. This puzzled Linda. Were they lethargic from the suffocating heat? Or was it the poisonous fertilizer chemicals that drained off the fields whenever it rained? Her brother shot snakes with a .22 rifle, but this was different. With their backs broken, the serpents writhed and curled back upon themselves in endless figure eights until they drowned and became meat for the nutrias. Later, when that boy was inside her, she'd remembered how the snakes had twisted and cracked like whips, and she wondered if they'd been screaming. Could snakes scream? Could they hear each other screaming?

Linda walked until the skin on the back of her neck felt like it would split from sunburn, dragging her throbbing leg behind her, but by then she'd climbed the levee again and figured out where she was—and where she was going. She was on Deer Park Road, and while there were only a couple of farmhouses for many miles, she knew about a church that stood alone at the edge of the cotton fields, and this confirmed God's participation in her survival. She got so thirsty she licked the sweat from her arms, and this made her smile. Yankees whined about the heat and the humidity, but it was the humidity that made the heat bearable. Louisiana wasn't like the barren hills outside Las Vegas, a place so dry you hardly saw the sweat leave your skin. Here there was almost as much water in the air as in your body, and the sweat beaded on your skin like water on a car that had just been waxed.

The last time she'd climbed the levee, she'd seen the church. In her mind it was white and clean and straight, rising from a green ocean of soybeans, but in truth it lay beside an empty cotton field like an oversize box thrown carelessly from a truck. The bright tin roof she remembered was a mosaic of rust and primer, and the steeple looked like a doghouse someone had squashed onto the apex of a roof. But even so, even with the crucifix atop it looking like a broken TV antenna, she'd seen deliverance. Pastor Simpson was alone behind the building, walking from the back shed to the main building with two boxes under his arms.

Linda had wept with joy.

She'd never been to services at that church, but she'd gone to Pastor Simpson's old church for years. Linda's father had been strict Assembly of God, but Linda had discovered Pastor Simpson when a friend had taken her to the Oneness Branch of the church. The Oneness people believed God couldn't be split into three, but the main thing was, they hated the hypocrisy of the mainliners. Pastors preaching against television while buying big sets for their lake houses, where they thought nobody would see them. But while Linda was in Las Vegas, Pastor Simpson had splintered off from the Oneness people too and had formed something called the Wholeness Church. It wasn't official, but he had a small congregation of forty or fifty hard-core believers, and they'd gotten together to renovate the old church by the river. She'd heard about it when she got back to town and went to work on the boat.

When Linda limped down off the levee, she hadn't known what Pastor Simpson's argument with the Oneness people was, nor had she cared. All she knew was that for years Simpson had been a good pastor and tried to help people, especially the poor. There'd been some talk about him and a couple of the young girls in the congregation, but she'd never had any trouble with him.

He'd recognized Linda almost immediately, and he'd taken her into the church and washed her wounds with water from the sink in the one bathroom they had. She hadn't told him the truth of course—not because she didn't trust him, but because she was afraid she might bring terrible harm down onto him or his followers. He'd sat there for half an hour with his silver hair and red skin and sympathetic eyes while she told him a lie about getting involved with a man she'd met on the gambling boat, a man who'd been in prison, who had almost killed her with a beating, and who would kill her if he found her. No, she couldn't go to the police, she said, because the man had friends in the police, on both sides of the river. Pastor Simpson had shaken his head and promised to do all he could to help, including getting her out of town. And he'd stood by his word, so far. When she'd written out the long note for Mayor Cage, Simpson had called one of the girls in his church to come out from town and pick it up, a girl named Darla, and Darla had promised to deliver it, and to make sure the mayor had no idea where any of them were, or even who she was.

Linda wished time would speed up. She's going to have to move soon because there's an evening service coming, and the pastor told her to be hiding in the shed well before the first car pulled up. She dreads that fifty-foot walk like nothing in a long time, but she'll do it somehow. Because after the service, the pastor's nephew is going to drive her to Shreveport, to stay with another group of Wholeness worshippers. There she will be safe from the "convict" who is hunting her. Linda lifts her shirt and wipes the sweat from her brow, which is burning like the skin around her torn leg. She needs a doctor, but she can hold out another few hours. They might even have a doctor in the church in Shreveport, she thinks. No matter how bad things look, God has taken her into his blessed hands. To know that's true, all Linda has to do is think about Ben Li.

CHAPTER

30

"You can talk in here," Kelly says, gunning the 4Runner and heading out of the parking lot. "No bugs, guaranteed."

"We're going to the cemetery."

"Okay. Why?"

"The disc is there. Not only that—Linda Church is alive."

Kelly looks at me. "How do you know that?"

I quickly relate what happened at the Ramada and describe the contents of the tape and the note. Caitlin supplements my account from the backseat.

"Wait a minute," says Kelly, turning

onto Homochitto Street. "Two different people approached you at this one event?"

"Yeah, I figured you saw them."

"I saw a girl watching you early on, but I was looking for males. I'm thinking of the coincidence."

"I know, but remember what you asked me early this morning? Everyone in town knew I would be at that event. It was published in the newspaper. Both Jewel and that girl knew they could talk to me without seeming to try to. It could look accidental. But what about you? You said we have a problem."

"One thing at a time. Do you know where Linda is?"

"No, but she's safely hidden, and her note says she's leaving town."

"You didn't recognize the girl who gave you the note?"

"You said she looked familiar," Caitlin reminds me.

"I could say that about almost everyone in this town. Do you know how many people I've spoken to since becoming mayor? And during the campaign? I think the part of my brain that connects names and faces has been short-circuited."

"I wouldn't mind having Linda Church in our back pocket," Kelly says. "I think you're going to need her as a witness before this mess is through."

"What the hell's going on? What's the problem you talked about?"

"Blackhawk got a bounceback on Jonathan Sands."

"A bounceback?"

"A return query. Rebound request. Someone in Washington wants to know who's asking about Sands."

Caitlin's eyes meet mine. "Washington?" she says. "*Who* in Washington?"

"They wouldn't tell me, and that's not a good sign. The company says they're covering for me, but I've got to be straight with you. Seventy-five percent of Blackhawk's revenues come from the Defense Department, and that number goes up every month. If Washington demands something, sooner or later the company's going to cave. They value my services, but in the end I'm just a grunt."

A wave of fear rolls through me. "Are you saying Blackhawk might give up Annie's location if the government pushed hard enough?"

"No, no. But they might give up my name, and maybe yours. Sands could find out I'm involved and figure you're trying to bust him, not help him."

"I see."

Kelly gives me a sidelong glance. "What *are* you going to do with that disc, if you find it?"

The truth is, I'm not sure, but I keep that to myself. "I hope you're about to find out."

"So how did you figure out the clues?" Kelly asks.

"He hasn't even told me that," Caitlin says with pique.

"When I searched the cemetery yesterday, I searched the graves of everyone Tim and I both knew. Classmates we've lost, people from St. Stephen's who died young. I even searched all the famous graves I knew. But I left out one grave. It never even *occurred* to me that Tim would use it."

"Whose was it?"

"A high school senior who was killed by a drunk driver in 1979."

Caitlin leans up between the seats. "Why didn't you think of him the other day?"

"Because Tim Jessup was the driver who killed him."

"My God. But how did the clue make you think of him?"

"The boy's name was Patrick McQueen."

Kelly smiles after a moment, but Caitlin shrugs. Sometimes a ten-year age gap causes issues.

"The Great Escape?" I prompt. "Steve McQueen . . . ? He ran from the Nazis on a motorcycle? Crashed into barbed wire at the end?"

"Oh . . . okay, I get it."

"I never considered Patrick's grave because I couldn't imagine Tim thinking about him in a desperate moment like that. Tim spent a year in jail because of that accident, and it ruined most of his life. I figured he'd done everything he could to get Patrick out of his mind. But I should have known better. He's probably thought about Patrick every day of his life since that night. Especially lately. I think he'd been trying to make up for what he did by living a good life."

Caitlin shakes her head sadly.

"But what does 'dog pack' mean?" Kelly asks. "What's that part of it?'

"Tim and I used to ride our bikes in the cemetery when we were kids. Once a pack of wild dogs chased us there. I'm not positive about the connection, but I think I know. We'll be sure in two minutes. When you get up to the flat part of this road, you'll see the river on your left. Turn at the main gate."

As Kelly does so, Caitlin touches my shoulder. "Are you sure you can't remember anything else about the girl who gave you the note? Something must have triggered that feeling of familiarity. What was it?"

I try to recall the girl's face, but the harder I concentrate on it, the less distinct it becomes. "I really can't place her. I have this vague feeling . . . she reminded me of a girl who used to wait on me across the river somewhere. A store or a restaurant in Vidalia, maybe. But the girl I'm thinking of was really heavy, and a lot plainer. I'm probably way off."

"Don't stop thinking about it. Maybe it will come to you later."

"I do better with remembering when I'm not trying to."

Despite this assertion, I plumb my

memory for some connection to the girl's face, but as we climb Maple Street toward the hill from which the Charity Hospital used to look down upon the cemetery, a very different memory rises. In the summer after sixth grade, a bunch of us were staying overnight with a friend who lived downtown. Most of us lived in subdivisions, but a few schoolmates still lived in ramshackle Victorians fronted with wrought-iron fences and backed by narrow alleys and deep gullies. We'd ride our jerry-built banana bikes downtown, pretending to be Evel Knievel, then spend the night tearing around the city streets, trying to do enough yelling to get the police to chase us.

We were just old enough that when Davy Cass suggested we should invade the cemetery, no one dared to say he was afraid to do it. I certainly didn't. Partly it was the idea of a deserted graveyard that scared me, but another part knew that the cemetery lay on the north side of town, uncomfortably close to the Negro sections of the city. During that era, no black male with his wits about him would have dared say a cross word to a white child, but we didn't know that. There was old Jim Clay, who lived in a shack on the Fenton property and who would fire rock salt from a shotgun if we got too near his place. Nook Wilson at the gas station had killed his wife with a butcher knife and sometimes looked at you like he'd just as soon kill you too. That was who I thought about when our bike routes took us close to the north side after dark, and not Ruby Flowers, our maid, who lived out that way and would have coldcocked anyone who tried to hurt me. But mostly—and wisely—we feared the unknown.

Our first thirty minutes in the cemetery were euphoric. We flashed down the narrow lanes between the mausoleums like the superheroes we worshipped, riding no-hands and seeing who could shut his eyes the longest without crashing. I rode from the main gate to Catholic Hill without once touching the handlebars, holding my arms out like wings (and only peeking a couple of times). But this hyperexcited state ended with the sound of a single growl. Barks wouldn't have frightened us, since most of us owned dogs. But when Davy suddenly skidded to a stop, the rest of us slammed into him from behind, and then we saw what had stopped him.

Crouching in the middle of the path was a black cur that had to weigh sixty pounds. Behind him a dozen more dogs stood alert, awaiting an attack signal. The cur had his teeth bared and his ears back, and when I saw his feverish eyes glint in the moonlight, I cringed with prehistoric fear. The lane cut between walls of earth twelve feet high, so our only escape route lay behind us. I felt my bladder turn to stone, then communal panic flashed through our little tribe. By the time we got our bikes turned, fifteen or twenty dogs were in pursuit. We'd had trouble with wild packs before, usually in the woods, and every summer our mothers reminded us that Billy Jenkins had been forced to take twenty-three rabies shots in his stomach because of a dog bite. This knowledge made us pedal like madmen for the gates, praying for deliverance as the frenzied animals snapped at our legs.

We didn't have a chance. Only the savant-level survival instincts of Trey Stacy saved us. When he jumped from his bike and dashed for the low-hanging branch of an oak tree, the herd instinct kicked in. Soon seven boys were treed like coons in the great gnarled branches of the oak. The furious dogs leaped and gnashed their teeth, barking and howling like demons among the gravestones, but that was their undoing. Their baying eventually drew the attention of a passing motorist, who called the police. The first cop shot one dog with his pistol, but the pack didn't retreat until his red-haired partner killed the alpha male with a shotgun. Several boys were crying as the police hauled us back to our sleepover, not for fear of their parents, but from the shock of seeing the dogs killed. I was shivering myself and glad when my father arrived to take me home rather than let me stay the night.

Caitlin touches my shoulder again and says, "Penn? We just went through the main gate. Where are we going?"

I point along a rank of oaks that line the nearby lane. When we reach the oak of my memory, I tell Kelly to stop. Its trunk is massive now, and its great branches hang so low that weather-treated four-by-fours have been propped beneath to keep them from sagging to the ground. Across the lane from the tree, beneath a twisted limb, lies the grave of Patrick McQueen.

With Caitlin trailing, I walk to his gravestone, a tall slab of granite with the text of Housman's "To an Athlete Dying Young" engraved on its face. One quick scan tells me that no disc is hidden beside the stone, but I'm certain now that Tim told me what I need to know. Leaving the stone, I walk out to where the crooked limb almost touches the grass. Then I set my foot in its crook, grip the rising branch with both hands, and begin climbing toward the trunk of the tree.

I don't have to go far. Fifteen feet from where I mounted the limb, wedged into a forked branch, is a hardcover copy of my third novel, *Nothing but the Truth.* The sight of its jacket moves me strangely, but the feeling passes as I look down and see Patrick McQueen's grave almost directly beneath me. For an infinite second, I feel as though I *am* Tim Jessup, clinging here in the dark, desperate to preserve the evidence I've stolen from the men I hate so deeply. Closing my eyes for a moment, I let this déjà vu bleed out of me. Then I fan the pages of my own book.

A flash of silver makes my heart thump. Lying between pages 342 and 343 is a DVD in a transparent plastic sleeve. There's no mark or label on the disc, and from the purplish color and look of the data side, it appears to be homemade.

"What did you find?" Caitlin calls from below. "It looks like a book."

"The disc is in it. We need a computer with a DVD drive."

"I can grab a notebook computer from the office."

Kelly steps up beside her, his blond hair bright beside her black mane. "I'd feel better with four walls around us. And we need to make some copies."

"We're two minutes from the office," Caitlin says. "We can lock the building. If Sands tried to storm the *Examiner,* that would make national headlines."

"That doesn't mean he won't," says Kelly. "We don't know what's on that disc. I'll cover the building while you two check it out. If there's anything you think I should see, call me on the Star Trek."

Closing the disc back into the book, I slide a little way down the limb, then drop six feet to the soft earth below.

"Tim died for this."

Caitlin nods slowly, then puts her arms around me and lays her head on my chest. "You can't bring him back. All you can do is finish what he started."

"Is that the plan?" Kelly asks.

My thoughts on Annie, I pull away from Caitlin and put the book into her hands. "What do you think?"

She looks back at me with the least feminine expression I've ever seen on her face. "I'm not your mother. I say nail the son of a bitch to the wall."

Caitlin and I are sitting in front of an Apple Cinema Display in the office of the *Examiner*'s publisher. Behind us Daniel Kelly stands alert, a Heckler and Koch MP5 submachine gun in his hands. Kelly thought he should stand guard outside, but I want him to see whatever's on the DVD. He certainly knows more about data encryption than Caitlin and me.

"It's coming up now," Caitlin says, pointing at a small, spinning beach ball on the blue screen. Then the screen goes black. "Do you think there's any risk of destroying the data by playing it on the wrong machine or anything?"

"I doubt it," says Kelly. "The disc may not boot without a code, though. Let's see. Look—"

From out of the blackness comes an image of weathered, old Corinthian columns against a summer sky. The camera pans along the leaves of the capitals, then pulls back to reveal a square of great columns with no building between them, fronted by a set of broad steps that lead into thin air.

"What the hell?" asks Kelly.

"I know that place," says Caitlin. "That's the Windsor Ruins, isn't it?"

"Yes," I say, a chill of foreboding in my chest.

"What's the Windsor Ruins?" Kelly asks.

Caitlin's shaking her head in confusion. "It's where Elizabeth Taylor and Montgomery Clift filmed *Raintree County*." She turns and looks at me with disbelieving eyes. "Penn, is this . . . ?"

"Maybe."

A couple of years after Caitlin moved to Natchez, she watched *Raintree County* with me on cable one night. When I told her that part of the movie had been filmed close to Natchez, she'd insisted on visiting the burned-out mansion. We took a video camera with us, and as we toured the columns, which stand like silent sentinels in the deep woods north of town, we thought it would be fun to film a romantic kiss on the steps where Taylor and Clift had shot their scene. As was common during that phase of our relationship, things quickly got heated, and we retired behind the huge base of one column to finish what we'd begun on the steps. We'd had some wine, and since we were alone at the site, Caitlin suggested we leave the camera running. I have a feeling that the results of that suggestion are about to flash up on the screen before us.

"Oh, God," Caitlin cries, as a shot of her moving ardently beneath me fills the screen. Feminine moans come from the computer's speakers.

"I'll close my eyes," Kelly offers, "but will somebody tell me what the hell is going on? Did you put in the wrong disc?"

They both turn to me as though I'm playing some childish joke on them.

"That's the DVD that was in the book," I say softly. "What the hell?"

There's a jerky cut, then Caitlin is sitting astride me, her bare breasts flushed, her neck mottled pink.

"You want me to leave?" asks Kelly, staring in confusion at the screen.

"I don't care if you see my tits," Caitlin snaps, "I want to know what's going on!"

I'm about to stop the player when the scene changes. This image is lower resolution than the first, because it was shot on an early eight-millimeter video camera, one my father bought around 1993. In this video, Annie is three years old, and she's pretending to make her way hand-over-hand across a horizontal ladder. Beneath her, trying to stay out of the frame, are her mother and me. Annie giggles with the unalloyed joy that no parent can hear without a tug at the heart, and Sarah laughs every time Annie giggles.

"You're almost there!" Sarah yells encouragingly. "You've almost done it!"

Explosive giggles fill the soundtrack as Annie reaches out and grips the last crossbar with her plump little hand. When I pull her free and set her on my shoulders,

Sarah hugs us both, then raises her hand in triumph. Too upset to speak, I reach out, turn the red trackball on the desk, and pause the video.

"Penn?" Caitlin says worriedly. "What is this? Are you okay?"

"It's not the videos that bother me," I say, lying just a little. "That first one? The one of us doing it?"

"Yes?"

"I didn't want Annie to see this tape by accident, so I put it in my safety-deposit box at the bank."

Caitlin blinks rapidly, trying to work out what's going on.

Kelly gets there first. "Sands made this disc. Or Quinn. Sometime before this afternoon, they found the real disc, then made this one and replaced the original with it. That's what you're saying, right?"

"It's the only explanation."

"And the tape of you and Caitlin—the one in your safe-deposit box was the only copy?"

"Absolutely. Does that mean someone at the bank helped them?"

"Not necessarily. Sands may have a box at the same bank. Depending on bank procedures, he or Quinn could have gone in to see their box, then broken into yours. They probably did it as soon as Sands perceived you as a threat. Same with your house. That's probably where he got the old home movies, right?"

"No. Those were in my dad's house."

"The fact that he got to this stuff is the message. Even though he got his stolen disc back, he's saying he can get to you anyplace, anytime."

"We'd better watch the rest of the tape, just to be sure."

Caitlin looks at me. "Are you sure you want to see it?"

"Me? What about you?"

"Kelly already saw me naked. Big whoop. It's you I'm worried about." Her voice goes quiet. "Stuff with Sarah? Things you might not want to see with me? Or me to see at all?"

I take her hand, and Kelly looks away. "It's okay. Whatever there is, you can watch."

Caitlin swallows hard, and her eyes soften. Then she sighs, composes herself, and clicks the button on the trackball.

On the screen, Sarah and Annie and I

fade to black. Then Annie appears again, alone this time. She can't be more than ten months old, and she's sitting on the steps of our house in Houston. She looks into the lens, then reaches for someone outside the frame. When no one takes her, her eyes fill with confusion and she begins to cry. Just as Sarah's hands enter the frame to take her, the sound of mad-dened dogs bursts from the speakers. The savage cacophony hurls me thirty years back in time, to the night Tim and I pedaled for our lives in the cemetery. From the sound, five or six dogs are fighting over something, but then the snarls and snap-ping teeth are punctuated by a sound that freezes my blood. It's a man screaming— first like a man, then like a little boy being torn apart by wolves. Male voices shout in the background, but I can't make out dis-tinct words. The screams become shrieks, rising in pitch and volume until they're suddenly cut off. What follows can only be the sound of animals fighting over meat. As we stare in stunned horror, the screen goes blue.

"That's the worst thing I've ever heard,"

Caitlin says. "Do you think the disc has fingerprints on it?"

"Yours," I say. "These guys don't make that kind of mistake."

"Who *are* these people? That wasn't dogfighting."

"That was a snuff tape," Kelly says, a strange awe in his voice. "I'll bet they have video too. They just couldn't risk showing it to us."

"You think it shows them?" I ask.

"Maybe. I'll bet we could ID the victim from it."

"Ben Li?" I suggest.

Kelly shrugs. He's already read Linda's note and listened to the tape of Tim's car chase. "Could have been. This guy sounded older to me when he first screamed, though. Late thirties, forties maybe."

"*Jesus,*" says Caitlin. "You can guess people's ages by their screaming?"

The Delta veteran shrugs again. "Occupational hazard."

She turns to me and starts to speak, then steps close. "Penn? I've never seen you look like that. Except maybe . . . after Ruby was in the fire."

"Sands got what he wanted, right?" I say too loudly. "He found his missing disc. So why go to all this trouble? Why keep *fucking* with me?"

"Because they're still vulnerable," Kelly says. "They don't have all the variables locked down. The USB drive copy may still be out there. And now we find out this Ben Li kid may have kept some kind of insurance. Sands means to keep you on the hook for that stuff too. That's what he's saying with this."

"Surely if they found the DVD, they found the other stuff long ago. They've known about Ben Li from the beginning."

"I doubt they hired the kid because he was stupid."

The screen saver has started on the Mac's display; pastoral scenes of the four seasons fade in and out, providing jarring visual counterpoint to what we just heard.

"What do we do now?" Caitlin asks.

"I'm tempted to call Sands," I say. "Tell him that as far as I'm concerned, everything is settled. He's got his DVD, and I'm going back to normal life."

Kelly shakes his head. "That won't accomplish anything. Not unless you're really backing off. Is that what you're doing?"

Caitlin looks at me expectantly.

"You mean tonight?" I ask. "The kayaks? The photo op?"

Kelly nods. "They probably feel more secure right now than they have since the night Jessup died."

I close my eyes, trying to see the larger picture.

"Look at it this way," Kelly says. "Do you feel good about bringing Annie back to town as things stand?"

"No."

"There you go."

"How did Sands find that DVD?" I ask. "Even if he somehow heard Tim's message—if Shad Johnson played it for him—he couldn't have understood Tim's clues."

"Who knows?" says Kelly. "Metal detector, maybe. He's probably had flunkies searching that cemetery ever since Jessup died. Don't worry about it."

An insistent buzzing starts in the room.

"Is that your cell phone?" Caitlin asks Kelly.

Kelly reaches into his pocket and

silences the phone. "There's only one way to get these guys out of your life. Send them to prison or kill them. We can put an end to this thing tonight. Three good photos and you've got them on felony charges. Then you can take back-bearings and fill in the missing pieces. Linda Church. The USB drive. Ben Li. The freaking 'bird' thing, whatever that is. What do you say, boss?"

"I'll get the boats. Are Danny and Carl on line for it?"

"What do you think?" Kelly smiles at Caitlin. "Why don't you make a few copies of Linda's note? It wouldn't hurt to dub Tim's voice memo either, and make some backups of the last part of that DVD."

She nods excitedly, glad for something to do.

Kelly looks at me. "Are you going to share any of this with Chief Logan?"

I don't answer immediately, but I know what my gut is telling me. "I don't think we can risk anyone finding out that Linda Church is alive."

Kelly nods in agreement. "Logan didn't tell you about the voice memo, did he? Even though it was meant for you."

This hadn't struck me until now. "I wonder if he knows about it. Maybe Shad Johnson took the phone the night of the murder, and Logan never saw anything but the texts. When I asked him at the station if he had the phone, he wouldn't tell me."

"So we're definitely not showing the DA anything?"

I actually laugh at the absurdity of this idea, then sit back on the chair, suddenly drained by the release of tension. When Kelly takes out his phone to check his message, it's instantly obvious that something is wrong. Before I can ask him what, he hands me the phone. There's a text message on the screen, short and to the point:

> **Cease all inquiry re Jonathan Sands immediately. Conflict of interest. The assets will be protected, but you're to stand down in Mississippi soonest. TOC Kabul 48 hours. Burton.**
> **PS Don't push this.**

"Daniel?" I say, handing the phone to Caitlin. "Are Annie and my mother the 'assets'?"

"Yeah."

"Oh, no," Caitlin says. "This is crazy."

"Are they truly safe, Kelly?"

"Absolutely. I've checked on them twice today."

"It looks like things are changing fast."

Kelly squats beside me, his eyes intense. "Personal protection is what Blackhawk was founded on. They've never lost a client, and they can't afford to now. Especially people related to someone who can make as much noise as you can."

"I don't feel reassured."

"Me either," says Caitlin.

Kelly squeezes my shoulder. "I know the guys guarding them, Penn. Both shifts. Even if someone at the company gave out information, these guys would take out anybody who made a move."

"What if Blackhawk people showed up at the door?"

Kelly licks his lips, then seems to take a silent decision. "Look, they're not even where the company thinks they are, okay? Not anymore. As soon as I got the call about that bounceback on the Sands query, I told the guys to move them."

My heart begins to race. "So you *are* worried."

"No. I just don't take chances. Annie's fine, man. I told you how to make her truly safe. Stick to the plan. When you get this deep in, only one thing can get you out. Leverage."

"You made that plan before you got the text message."

"The message changes nothing."

"*What?* You're ready to lose your job over this?"

Kelly's blue eyes are as steady as a man's can be. "I took that risk the minute I moved Annie and your mother. I don't know who's protecting Jonathan Sands, but I know this: They're on the wrong fucking side."

CHAPTER

31

The river is black glass tonight, and I'm thankful for it. It's been three months since I've been on water in anything but a ski boat, and then only on a lake. We put in our kayaks a half mile above the city, on the Louisiana side of the river. The western shore is dark except for the digital depth markers the push boat pilots use to find the main channel. The sky to the south glows from the ambient light of Natchez. The air over the water is chilly and calm, but high above us black clouds are scudding across the face of the moon.

Kelly paddles beside me with smooth assurance, like a wingman flying escort. He learned his moves when his Delta team did an exchange program with Britain's Special Boat Squadron; their commandos taught him the mysteries of handling small craft of all types. Our kayaks are Seda gliders, nineteen-foot touring boats with razor bows that move through the water like Kevlar arrows. With a seasoned paddler in the cockpit, they can do twelve miles an hour going downstream. The steamboats of the 1870s moved only slightly faster than this. I'm a recreational paddler, but I've mastered the art of powering the boat with my torso and hips, using the rudder pedals as braces for my long touring stroke. Kelly uses a power stroke, keeping his offset blades close to the kayak throughout his movement.

We can easily talk as we paddle, as long as he stays within ten or fifteen feet of me, which he has made a point of doing. Kayaks are inherently unstable, and push boats can throw up four-foot waves in their wake as they drive their barges up and down the river. I can almost feel Kelly tensing to perform a rescue every time our boats hit a boil in the otherwise smooth river.

We almost scrubbed tonight's mission five minutes before we put the kayaks in the river. That was when I confessed to Kelly that I'd contacted my closest friend in the FBI about Jonathan Sands. I probably wouldn't have risked it if it weren't a Sunday, but I knew Peter Lutjens would be home with his family, and not in the Puzzle Palace—FBI headquarters—where he works in the IT department of the National Security Division. The result wasn't what I'd hoped for. In less than two hours, Lutjens called back and told me that no information could be given out about Sands under any circumstances, and I should be very careful whom I questioned about him.

I was about to hang up when Lutjens asked about Annie. I answered briefly, and then we chatted for a while about his son, who was having trouble with a science project. Lutjens told a lengthy anecdote about a next-door neighbor who'd turned out to be a retired physicist, who'd helped the boy finish the project. "Some-times," Lutjens concluded, "help comes from the most unexpected places." I thanked him for his time, wondering what he could mean by that. Whatever he meant, it's unlikely to help us on the river tonight.

Our kayaks glide past the northern reaches of Vidalia and Natchez almost without sound, the lights of the houses on Clifton Avenue glittering above us. Three-quarters of a mile to our left, the casino boats line the foot of the bluff, spaced about evenly for almost a mile. First comes the *Magnolia Queen,* then the *Zephyr,* the *Evangeline,* and finally the *Lady Belle.* I think of Tim as I pass the *Queen* because the cemetery sits on the ground high above it, but guilt will not help me tonight. Kelly didn't even want me along, and I mean to prove that I won't slow him down.

Danny McDavitt and Carl Sims are somewhere in the sky to the south of us, shadowing the VIP boat. Danny must be flying very high or very low because I can't hear his helicopter. Our journey has been a milk run so far, but that will soon change, and knowing that Carl is riding shotgun in the chopper with his sniper rifle gives me a sense of confidence I might otherwise lack.

"Looking good," Kelly says, his voice coming clear over the water. "You feeling okay?"

"Yeah. Trying to get used to working the rudder again."

"The real work's below the waist."

"I feel it."

As the twin bridges slide past high above our heads, Kelly stops paddling and adjusts the ear bud connected to the Star Trek in his pocket.

"Any word from Danny and Carl?" I ask.

"The VIP boat's still cruising south, but not in any hurry."

He pulls back a piece of canvas and checks the GPS unit Velcroed to the coaming of his boat. "We've been doing six miles an hour. Not bad, but let's see if we can find some faster water."

His kayak shoots forward without apparent extra effort on his part, then turns toward the middle of the river. I grip my two-bladed paddle and pull as strongly as

I can, trying to stay up with him. On a river as broad as the Mississippi, the surface moves at different speeds in different places. Soon we're moving at a steady nine miles per hour, and the lights of the town fall quickly behind us.

The land beyond the levee to our right is all former plantation land, and most of it's still farmed today. From faintly silhouetted landmarks such as grain silos, I can tell we're passing the old Morville Plantation, the one my father mentioned as a den of white slavery and gambling in the 1960s. Remembering this gives me a feeling of futility, as though Tim's effort to stop what he saw as the rape of his hometown was nothing more than a vain quest to fight vices that will always be with us. The ironies are almost unbearable, if I think about them. Kelly and I are paddling this river to photograph men committing illegal cruelty upon animals, in order to "save" a city built upon the incalculable cruelty of slavery. The land on both sides of this river was watered with the sweat and blood of slaves, and their descendants still struggle to find their place in the life of

the community. I've dealt with the conse-
quences of that history every day of my
term as mayor, and it lies at the root of the
most intractable problem I've ever faced.

"Something weird's going on," Kelly
says. "The VIP boat's barely moving, but
they still haven't stopped anywhere."

"What do you think?"

He looks across the space between us.
"Could they be fighting dogs *on* the boat?
Down below or something?"

"I guess. Caitlin told me urban dogfighters hold fights in basements and places
like that. But that's an expensive cabin
cruiser. I can't imagine them fighting dogs
in there."

Kelly stops paddling and lets his boat
drift with the current. "In five minutes we'll
be at the place they docked last night. If
they haven't stopped anywhere by then, I
say we get out and wait. Scout the place
out. They could actually be coming back
to the same spot."

"You think?"

Kelly chuckles softly. "They might just
be cruising around drinking, getting
hyped up for the fight. Maybe the handlers haven't got the dogs here yet. Yeah,

this might be perfect. We can videotape everybody as they get off the cruiser."

"What if somebody heard Danny's chopper, and it spooked them?"

Kelly's smile vanishes. "Don't put the hex on us, man. Let's go."

He digs his paddle into the black water and heads for the Louisiana shore. Another mile of river slides beneath us, then Kelly holds up his hand. After I stop paddling, he checks his GPS, then says, "We're there. Let's take 'em in."

"I see a sandbar. Do you want to land there?"

"Let's go about forty yards farther down, where those weeds are."

To my surprise, Kelly lets me lead. I pull up my rudder with the lanyard, then drive the bow of my boat onto the gently sloping river bottom. When my motion stops, I lay the shaft of my paddle behind me, just aft of the cockpit, and brace the flat of the blade on the sand. Using this to stabilize the boat, I extricate my legs from the cockpit and step out into the water. Kelly does the same as I drag my kayak into the weeds, and soon we're standing under some small cottonwoods, surveying the land where Danny saw the VIP boat anchor last night.

Kelly takes a night scope from his pack and glasses the darkness in front of us. To me the landscape looks like a black-and-white photograph tinted slightly blue. The hum of insects is annoyingly loud, and the only light comes from the half-moon over our heads. Kelly's view is completely different, of course. To him this night is a montage of ghostly greens, one he can navigate with the sure-footedness of a deer feeding at dusk.

"What do you see?" I ask.

"Nothing much. Let's move inland."

All I can do is follow orders and walk in his tracks. The soil is sandy, the weeds and nettles thick. As we get farther from the river, the cottonwood trees tower above us.

"Any signs of people?"

"There's a shed about forty meters to the north," he says. "No lights. Looks like a swing set or something beside it."

As we pick our way through the tree trunks, Kelly adds, "I see a few benches and chairs."

Though the chill of fall was in the air on

the river, here the night is thick with the smell of green foliage, and I've begun to sweat. It's as though we've stumbled into some low-lying region where summer never ends.

Kelly curses as I collide with his back. He stands immobile, head cocked as though he's listening for something. When I start to speak, he flips up a hand and whispers, "Give it a second. You'll understand."

Then I do. The smell of death is in the air—thick and powerful enough to smother the green scent I savored only moments ago. The odor isn't alien; it's what you smell when you're forced to drive slowly past an armadillo that's been dead for two days.

"This place feels deserted," I whisper.

Kelly lowers the scope, then raises his neck and turns his head like a meerkat moving in slow motion. "No, there's something here. Something alive."

"Deer?"

"Let's find out."

I have no desire to walk any closer to whatever is producing that reek. But when

Kelly creeps forward, I realize I have even less desire to stand here by myself.

As I follow him, the stench of death grows overpowering. I can barely suppress my gag reflex. Beneath the putrid smell of decay is a pungent, ammoniac funk that almost burns the nostrils. Lifting the crook of my left arm to my face, I bury my nose in my jacket sleeve and survey what little I can see by moonlight.

There's the swing set Kelly mentioned. It's a standard A-frame set, like the one my parents bought at Western Auto in the 1960s, but no swings are attached to its crossbar—only some heavy-gauge springs and short links of chain. The chains end in hooks, while large carabiners dangle from the springs. Fifteen yards to my right is some sort of contraption that looks like a piece of antique playground equipment. It has two metal arms jutting from a central pillar that looks as though it's meant to rotate so the arms can turn in a circle. But I can't quite solve the puzzle of its function. One of the arms ends in a hook, and a short length of chain dangles from the second, a few feet behind that one.

"What is this place?" I whisper.

"It's for training," Kelly murmurs, clicking on a flashlight with a red filter on its lens. "They hang things the dogs want from the hooks and springs. Pit bulls will leap up and bite and hang there for hours. They do it to strengthen the dogs' jaws."

"What's that thing that looks like a homemade merry-go-round?"

"You don't want to know."

"I do."

Kelly points his red beam at the strange machine and walks over to it. "See this front arm?" He points to the one that ends in a hook. "They hang a pet caddy from this hook with a kitten or something else inside it. Then they chain the dog to this arm back here. The cat goes crazy from terror, of course, and the dog chases it, pushing against the resistance in the machine."

"Jesus."

"It's sort of like dog races—only with this deal, when the dog's through running, they let him kill the cat. Sometimes they don't even use a pet caddy. They just hang the bait animal from the hook. I've seen that in Kabul. I think they call this thing a jenny, or something like that."

Suddenly the red beam vanishes, and I feel Kelly's hand on my arm.

"What is it?" I ask, feeling my heart kick. "Did you hear something?"

"A cat, I think. Listen."

He's right. Beneath the whine of insects, I hear a tiny feline mewling, like the kind you hear behind Dumpsters at fast-food restaurants.

"I think it's coming from the shed," Kelly says. "Come on."

I follow reluctantly, still thinking about the jenny.

Kelly quickly covers the distance to the shed, but as I follow, my right foot bangs into a bucket on the ground, sending a hollow clang through the trees. Before the sound dies, a cat screams inside the shed. Then something scuffles against the wall boards.

"Very smooth," Kelly says, trying the door handle. "It's locked."

"I saw a silencer on your pistol. Just shoot it off."

"No." He runs his hand down the faces of the weathered boards. Slipping his fingertips into a crack between two boards at shoulder level, he yanks a board right off the shed, then jumps back as though he expects a wildcat to leap out of the dark opening. When nothing emerges but the stench of old urine, he switches on his flashlight and shines it into the shed.

"This is fucked-up," he says.

"I can smell it. I don't need to look."

"You said you needed to be able to testify about what we found, right? Well, here it is."

I peer through the hole long enough to see half a dozen malnourished, extremely dehydrated cats. Three or four others appear to be dead. Half-buried piles of excrement litter the dirt floor. My horror deepens when I realize that some of the cats are wearing collars. Mercifully, Kelly shines his light into the corner of the shed away from the animals, onto some short metal bars leaning in the corner.

"What are those?" I ask.

"Break sticks. Bars to pry a bulldog's jaws loose from something."

Kelly takes out his camera and begins videotaping the contents of the shed.

"We've got to let them go," I say.

Kelly makes a humming sound I can't interpret, but it sounds negative. "We don't want anybody to know we were here. I'm going to put that board back in place."

I look back at him for a few seconds, then kneel and yank one end of the bottom-most board away from the wall. While Kelly stares with a curious look on his face, two cats shoot through the opening and race away into the darkness.

"Put the other board back up," I tell him. "They don't know how many cats were in here."

"There go the rest," says Kelly, pointing at several dark shapes escaping cautiously through the opening. The last cat through seems barely able to keep its feet.

"Okay, Gandhi," says Kelly, hammering the top board back on with his hand. "Let's put it back like we found it."

As I wedge the bottom board back into place, a chilling sound reaches my ears. It's a low, haunting howl, coming from somewhere deeper in the trees. It sounds like the crying of a soul that's wandered lost for a thousand years.

"I *know* I don't want to see that," I whisper. "Whatever it is. Let's get the fuck out of here."

"Wait," says Kelly. "Danny's talking to me."

I'd forgotten that Kelly's still wearing his earpiece.

"The VIP boat's getting close to where we are," he says.

"What do we do?"

"Let's check out that noise, and by then we'll know if they're going to put in here or not."

With a silent groan I follow him toward the wavering howl.

"We're on a path," he says, shining the red beam along a sandy track worn through the grass. "I bet this ends where they fight the dogs."

Thirty yards farther on, the path terminates in a small clearing. In the middle of the clearing lies a shallow pit dug in the earth. It's about eight feet square, and eighteen inches deep.

"That's where they do it," says Kelly. "One place, anyway. In Afghanistan they fight them right in the street, but most places use a pit."

Staring into the hole, I try to imagine two heavy-muscled pit bulls exploding out of the corners and smashing into each other, dueling for a death grip. But even standing in this spot, it's difficult to believe that happens here. The howl comes again—lower in pitch, but much closer now.

"Over there," Kelly says, pointing the beam toward the trees.

He trots across the ground, and I reluctantly follow. The first thing I see when I reach the trees is some sort of block and tackle hanging from a branch, the kind deer hunters use to gut animals. But as I try to look closer, the red light vanishes. Kelly has knelt to examine something at the base of the tree.

"Easy now," he says, as though talking to a child. "Just take it easy. We're not going to hurt you."

Dread flows into me like an icy tide, but after a deep breath, I force myself to take a step to my right. Four feet in front of Kelly, at the base of a cottonwood tree, a pit bull terrier lies shivering on its belly. It's a brindle, I think, but so much of its coat is covered with dried blood that it's hard to be sure. The howling has stopped. Now all I hear is panting, accompanied by a strange whistling sound.

"What's wrong with it?" I ask, wondering why the dog hasn't bolted in terror. "Can't it move?"

"I don't think so," says Kelly. "I think her back is broken."

"How do you know it's a her?"

"No balls. Just checked."

"Can a dog break its back in a dogfight?"

"No way. Easy, girl, easy," Kelly murmurs, sweeping his beam around the tree. The light stops at the trunk of the next tree. "That's what did it."

Leaning against the next tree, a blue aluminum softball bat gleams dully in the red light. Like the dog, it's covered with dried blood. Beside the bat, three car batteries stand on a small square of plywood. Kelly shakes his head and aims the beam back at the wounded dog. The terrier's eyes look plaintive, almost human, but shock and exposure have obviously taken their toll. Both forelegs have deep, suppurating gashes at the shoulder.

Kelly edges forward, but I grab his arm. "That dog can still take your hand off."

"Don't worry, I know what I'm doing."

As he moves closer to the dog, I ask, "What's that whistling sound?"

He leans over the animal, training the beam on the top of its skull. Even with its back broken, the dog instinctively jerks its head away from Kelly's arm.

"Christ," Kelly says in a stunned voice. "They cracked her skull with the bat. When she breathes, the air goes through it. Kind of like a sucking chest wound, I guess. I can't believe she's still alive."

As I stare in horror, Kelly takes out his camera and videotapes the wounds, then painstakingly videotapes everything in the clearing. As sick as it makes me, I can't take my eyes off the suffering animal. Her plight is beyond understanding, like that of so many human victims I encountered in Houston. The sound of running footsteps makes me jump, then Kelly is at my side.

"What is it?" I ask. "Did the VIP boat land here?"

"No, it passed us. Goddamn it!"

"Maybe they *are* fighting dogs on the boat."

"No. That cruise was some kind of con—a diversion. It's like they knew we were coming. I think we'd better get out of here."

He stuffs his camera into his pack and starts walking away.

"Wait," I call. "What about her?"

He stops and looks back at me. "I told you. They can't know we were here. We got nothing tonight, unless Sands himself owns the land we're standing on. We're going to have to do this *again*."

"We can't leave her like this. Can't you . . ."

"What?"

"Shoot her?"

Kelly shakes his head. "I can't be sure the wound wouldn't show, and I can't get close enough to stick the gun in her mouth."

"We can't leave her like this," I insist.

He sighs like a soldier being forced to consider the feelings of civilians. "You want to put her out of her misery?" He shines his flashlight back on the softball bat. "There you go."

A wave of nausea rolls through me. "They already hit her with that," I stammer, recoiling at the thought.

"They weren't trying to help her. They were having a party. If you hit the cervical spine as hard as you can, death should be instantaneous."

I look down at the dog, then back at Kelly.

"You wanted to come," he says, shining the light in my eyes. "If you want to finish it, finish it."

This is not like Kelly at all. Whenever we've worked together, he's always been ready and willing to do whatever dirty work was required. I've never completely understood the dynamic between us, or what motivated him to go beyond what I consider the call of duty. He's always operated by a private code, one I thought I understood. It's as though together, we function as a complete man—a rational mind capable of enforcing its decisions with implacable force. But in the past, I realize now, Kelly's willingness to kill has always been demonstrated while he was protecting me or my family. This situation falls outside those parameters. In fact, letting the dog die in agony is probably the safer choice, from that perspective. But I can see that Kelly feels for the animal. Is he testing me? Is the iron fist performing a gut check on the mind that wields it? Or is he trying to find out whether I'll let my emotions override my reason? Knowing there's no sure answer to any of these questions, I walk to the tree and lift the bat, certain that the last person who did so was the one who battered the helpless dog into what huddles at my feet now.

"Wait," says Kelly.

I stand over the shivering dog, waiting to feel the bat taken from my hands.

"Danny thinks he's got something. Uh-huh . . . Right . . . How far?" He checks his watch, then says, "Shit, we can do that. We'll come in the boats. . . . No, no, if you drop us in close enough, they'll hear the chopper. Stay well clear. If they leave before we get there, try to get a license plate, but don't let them know you're there. I'll radio our coordinates en route. . . . Right. Out."

"What's going on?" I ask.

"Danny saw something suspicious earlier on the FLIR, down past where the VIP boat turned around. He went back and checked it out. It's a big metal building, and it's throwing off heat. There's a couple of SUVs out front with men sitting behind the wheel like drivers waiting for people."

"What do you think it is?"

"Tonight's dogfight. I think they tried to pull a fast one on us. They knew we might be following the boat, so they handled transport a different way."

"Where are they?"

"An island. About five miles downriver."

"Five miles?"

"Yeah. If we dig in, we can make it in twenty or twenty-five minutes."

"Won't the fight be over by then?"

"Not necessarily. A single dogfight can go two hours or more. But we don't have time to waste. Put the bat back, and let's move."

"Damn it, Kelly, just shoot the dog. We can throw her in the river. They'll never know."

"Bullshit. Dogs aren't like cats to these people. They were punishing this dog, probably for losing a fight. They know she can't move, and when they come back, they'll expect to find her here, dead. Come on."

Kelly takes two backward steps, but he

doesn't turn away. I feel the weight of his gaze upon me. There's a pregnant tension between us, but I won't kill a helpless creature because a man is testing me. Stepping over the dog's rump with my left foot, I brace my foot against a tree root, then grip the bat's taped handle with both hands and raise it over my right shoulder. The terrier lifts her head, trying to look back at me, but before her eyes find mine I swing the bat with all my strength, aiming for the neck, where the spine meets the skull. In the adrenaline-flushed second that the bat completes its arc, instinct tells me to shut my eyes, but I keep them open, knowing that to look away could result in more torture.

The bat doesn't ring on impact, but it jolts my arms and rattles my spine down to my pelvis as a wet crack like a boy stomping on a sodden limb echoes through the trees. The awful whistling has stopped. The dog lies motionless. I stumble back to the other tree, lean the bat against it, then march past Kelly toward the river.

As I wedge my knees through the cockpit of my kayak, he walks into the shallow water and looks down at me. "You did the right thing. But I think that's enough for tonight. I should take it from here."

Thrusting my legs forward, I set my feet against the pedals, jerk the lanyard that flips down my rudder, and push away from the sandbar. "I'll see you down there."

CHAPTER

32

Walt Garrity takes a sip of ice-cold Maker's Mark and gazes around the vast gaming floor of the Magnolia Queen. Most casino boats are floating barns filled with slot machines and few table games, but the Magnolia Queen is magnificent, harkening back to the days of the floating palaces that cruised the river after the Civil War. The Queen has a three-hundred-foot salon built in the style known as steamboat Gothic, with Gothic arches, stained-glass skylights, gilt pendants, and eight massive chandeliers. There are hundreds of slot machines, yes, but there are also table games of every type.

Walt spent the first part of the evening putting on the same kind of show he'd given on the Zephyr last night, making a spectacle of himself at the craps table and tipping everyone beyond all reason. He's stayed with Nancy because since their scene in the RV they've had a certain understanding about the sexual component of their relationship that he doesn't want to explain to a succession of prostitutes.

She stands a few feet away, losing wads of Penn Cage's money at the blackjack table. Nancy doesn't seem to mind Walt's frequent absences, so long as the flow of chips and alcohol continues uninterrupted. She probably assumes that a man of his age is making repeated trips to the restroom. In fact, Walt has conducted a casual but very thorough inspection of Golden Parachute's floating casino. This is the second time they've been aboard the Queen *today. They first visited it after lunch, then spent some time on both the Zephyr and the Evangeline. Walt was glad to learn that the opulence of the* Magnolia Queen *would justify J. B. Gilchrist's spending most of his time in Natchez aboard her, and not the lesser boats.*

During his first visit, Walt twice saw Jonathan Sands—the first time coming down the escalator from the upper deck where Walt now knows Sands's office is, and the second in the cashier's cage, talking to some employees. Despite his bespoke suit, Sands moved like an alert and graceful animal padding through a herd of less sentient creatures. Most of the gamblers on the boat blunder around like shoppers in a mall, their eyes on the slot machines, the tables, or the young women that seem so plentiful. Sands's eyes miss nothing. He actually made eye contact with Walt long enough to register that he was being watched as he descended the escalator. Even after seeing Sands only twice, Walt knows the Irishman will be a difficult man to outwit, much less capture.

Walt has paid some attention to the women as well. Several of the younger ones are Chinese, and from their behavior he guessed they were prostitutes. Nancy confirmed this when Walt asked about them and showed more than a little jealousy when she did. Apparently this perk of the Magnolia Queen is becoming well-known to out-of-town businessmen, who don't seem to mind that the girls speak little or no English. Walt understands the attraction. As a young soldier in 1953, he fell in love with a young Japanese girl during an extended R&R in Kobe, Japan. Most of the women he'd met in Korea were prostitutes, but Kaeko was a nurse he met by chance in a restaurant. Walt had married his high school sweetheart before shipping out, and he'd sworn to be faithful while he was overseas. Kaeko had tested his vow to the limit, not physically so much as by slowly and completely inhabiting his soul.

The Chinese girls on the Magnolia Queen look different from Kaeko, but their resemblance is enough to trigger a feeling in Walt that shames the twinge of lust he felt when Nancy bared her bottom in the van.

"Why do you keep running off?"

Nancy asks. "You're tired of me, aren't you?"

"No, I'm just taking it all in. I've been on a lot of boats, but I haven't seen one like this in many a year."

Thus reassured, Nancy begins chattering mindlessly, but Walt suddenly becomes aware that several people are looking up over his shoulder. When he turns, he sees one of the most beautiful women he has ever encountered descending the escalator. She looks like a princess being carried down steps in a royal litter. She wears a jade green dress that lies close against her petite body, and her hair is long and straight. What strikes Walt, though, as it must have the other watchers, is the sense of self-possession radiated by the girl. Reaching behind him, he takes hold of Nancy's cheap dress and turns her so that she can see the escalator.

"Daddy, I'm playing," she protests. *"Hit," she tells the dealer. "Stay."*

"Do you know who that is?" Walt asks.

"Who?"

"That girl on the escalator."

Nancy turns and stares for a few seconds. "No, I never seen that one before. She looks like she thinks her you-know-what don't stink, though."

Nancy's harsh voice intrudes on Walt's reverie like the squawk of a crow startling a man contemplating a pristine dawn. He cannot imagine that the girl on the escalator could be for sale. If she were, the price for a night with her would have to be ten times that for a night with the Nancys so common on the boats. But Walt knows one thing: If her time is for sale, he intends to buy as much as he can afford.

CHAPTER

33

As we near the island, I start to ease my kayak along the sandy shore, but Kelly pulls alongside and points. "Farther down. That brush'll keep the boats out of sight if a patrol comes down to the main bank."

I nod and wait for him to lead the way. I almost vomited during our sprint down-river from the first stop. Sweat is pouring off me, but not from the eighty-strokes-per-minute pace Kelly set. Not even from the shock of killing the dog, which was an act of mercy by any measure. What has shaken me to the core is that the glimpse of hell I saw under the trees was less than five miles from the place where I grew up. My meditation on the ironies of Tim's "heroic quest" as Kelly and I paddled down from Natchez has filled me with shame, and any doubt about our purpose tonight has vanished. Standing among the chains and hooks and infernal machines, I felt as though I'd stumbled into a death camp, one designed for animals rather than humans. The eerie whistling of the dog breathing through its skull will haunt me to my grave.

"Penn? You with me?"

"Right behind you."

Kelly turns his rudder and knifes silently toward the shore. He pulls parallel to an overgrown bank that looks a little steep for my taste—not to mention snaky—then braces his paddle and climbs out of his cockpit. As I pull in behind him and follow suit, Kelly drags his boat behind some kudzu, then unloads his pack and takes out his night-vision scope.

"Come on," he says, seizing the grab handle on my bow and dragging the Seda into the weeds.

I insert the earbud Kelly gave me for

my Star Trek—which I've discovered is on the blink—and follow Kelly up the bank. According to Danny McDavitt, no dogs or guards are on the river side of the towhead, only a couple of men by the building that he believes could be the site of tonight's dogfight.

When I get up to the sandy hump where Kelly stands, I see that we're in a line of trees beside a marshy field. Across the field, faint yellow light spills from a windowless metal building that looks like a small warehouse, and beyond this stands a black wall of trees.

"Turn off your Star Trek," Kelly says.

"Why?"

"You're going to be with me, and we don't need any noise-pollution accidents. Also, we want Danny to airlift us off the river later, and your radio is our spare batteries."

Before I obey his order, he lifts his Star Trek and says, "How we looking on sentries, Pave Low?"

Pave Low is McDavitt's code name for tonight; it's the model of helicopter he flew in the air force.

"You got a couple of dogs prowling on the far side of the building," he answers. "Pay attention."

"What about the field?"

"Nothing. Some deer bedded down in the tree line about seventy meters to the north of you."

Standing in near darkness, it's strange to know that Danny McDavitt is looking down on us with a God's-eye view that sees every warm-blooded creature around us.

"Hold up," McDavitt says in my ear. "Do you see that?"

Across the field, a horizontal bar of light appears, growing rapidly into a rectangle.

"That's an overhead door," says Kelly. "Shit!"

As the rattling whine of a chain drive reaches us, a black SUV roars out of the building, followed by two more just like it. Their headlights flash on when they leave the spill from the open door.

"We're too late?" Kelly says in disbelief. "What the . . . ?"

"What do you want me to do?" McDavitt asks. "Cover you or go with the vehicles?"

"Go with the SUVs!"

"Ten-four."

Kelly winces, then looks longingly across the field. "I'm tempted to go into that building and see what they left behind." He keys his Star Trek. "Did they take the dogs with them?"

"Negative."

"Okay, we're bugging out. We'll see you a couple miles downriver."

Through the trees I see three pairs of headlights cutting through the dark, moving north at gravel-road speed. Carl Sims's voice replaces McDavitt's.

"I can take out those dogs for you, no problem."

Kelly considers this. "No. We don't know that we'll get anything from the building. If you waste the dogs, they'll know we know about this place. Find out where the SUVs go—that's all."

With a last look across the field, Kelly shakes his head. Far to my right, the headlights turn away, and I see taillights that remind me of those I saw on Cemetery Road the night Tim died.

"All this work," I mutter, "and it's come to nothing."

"Maybe not nothing. We'll see what Danny turns up."

"Should we just call the Highway Patrol and have them stopped on some pretext?"

"No, they're clean now, away from the scene. Honestly, I'll be surprised if the plates on those SUVs are traceable. But we'll find out who owns this land and see if we can learn something that way."

As Kelly turns away from the field, a pale shadow flashes across my sight from right to left. I fall backward as Kelly goes down with a thud. Scrambling to my feet, I see a huge white dog mauling his left arm, trying to reach his throat. I yank out my Star Trek and yell, "Danny! Carl! We need help!"

Kelly's gun is still in his gear bag, and the bag is behind him. As I crab-walk toward it, my eyes on the attacking dog—a Bully Kutta, I see now—the dog whips its head from side to side, trying to rip off Kelly's blocking arm. Kelly's struggling to get his right hand under the dog's belly. Yanking the gear bag clear of the fight, I struggle with the zipper, but before I get it open, the Bully Kutta arches its back, its four paws galloping in midair as it tries to wrench away from Kelly, who is jerking a knife from the dog's scrotum to its rib cage. When I see a loop of intestine spill out in silence, I know that this dog too has had its vocal cords removed. As the animal rolls on the ground in its death throes, Kelly cinches his belt around his left biceps as a tourniquet.

"Are you okay?" I ask. "I couldn't get the bag open!"

"It's okay. Find me a rock."

"A rock?"

"A rock! Half an inch thick—flat, if possible."

Three feet away I find a flat pebble smoothed round by the river. Kelly takes it and wedges it under his tourniquet, against the artery, I guess. Both sides of his forearm show puncture wounds, and the flesh is ripped near his inner elbow.

"This isn't good," he says, staring at the wounds. "I don't even know—"

A sound like running hoofbeats makes us whirl. This time the flying shadow is black, not white. Before I can even backpedal, I hear a bullwhip crack, and the wolf-size dog slides harmlessly to my feet, a quivering pile of muscle and bone. I leap backward, but Kelly just shakes his head and holds up his wired earpiece.

"That dog knocked it out of my ear," he says.

"What just happened?" I ask, trying to get my breath. "Did you shoot that dog?"

"Hell no." Kelly pulls his pistol from the gear bag and shows it to me. "Carl shot it from the chopper."

Kelly inserts his earpiece and says, "Thanks, buddy. You cut that kind of close."

"You're lucky I even saw the damn thing," Carl replies. "I missed with my first shot. That was the second."

McDavitt's voice cuts through the chatter. "What's the situation down there, Delta? You want me to follow the vehicles or do you need a hospital? My partner says it looks like a dog got to one of you."

"We're fine," Kelly lies. "We need to ID those vehicles."

"I already got a license plate."

"I want to know where they're headed."

"Okay."

"Are there any more of these monster

dogs out there? That old Ranger sure was right. I didn't hear a damned thing till it hit me."

"The two dogs by the building are still there. I don't know where those came from."

Kelly chuckles darkly. "I think they're the 'deer' you thought you saw bedded down. They're big, man."

"Penn? Penn, are you there?"

Kelly looks sharply at me as the new voice breaks into the conversation, but I recognize the tone immediately. It's my father.

"I'm here," I tell him. "What's the matter?"

"Jenny was just run off the road in Bath. Her car flipped."

I swallow hard as an image of my sister lying dead beside an English motorway flashes through my mind. "Is she alive?"

"Yes. She called me from the hospital, and I spoke to her doctor. She's in mild shock, but she could easily have been killed."

"When did it happen?"

"About an hour ago. She'd dropped the kids with a friend and was on her way to the university."

A wave of heat rushes over my face as guilt suffuses me. "Where are you?"

"On my way to the safe house." Kelly insisted that we have an empty house within ten miles of the operation to review any evidence we collected without having to go to a place Sands could know about. "Caitlin's with me," adds my father.

"Doc?" Kelly cuts in. "I know you're upset, but go easy on the names, okay?"

"Fuck that," says my father. "I've had it with these sons of bitches."

"How soon will you reach the house?" Kelly asks, his eyes moving right and left like those of a man thinking fast.

"Twenty minutes. And I want you there. I want everybody there."

Kelly looks down at the corpse of the white dog. His left hand is balled into a fist, probably against pain, but I sense that he's weighing the possibility of progress against the immediate crises. His entire posture communicates frustration; he looks as though he's about to kick the dead dog.

"Pave Low?" he says into the Star Trek.

"Here."

"Come get us."

"Ten-four. You want me to set down right where you are?"

"No. We can't be sure that building's empty. We'll find a sandbar downstream. A mile, maybe."

"I'll be flying right over the water, coming upstream. Out."

I key my Star Trek again. "Dad, we're on the way."

"I heard. Don't waste any time."

As I shove the walkie-talkie into my pocket, the sound of my father angrily carving a Sunday roast makes me turn. But it's a trick of the mind. Kelly has the Bully Kutta's head wedged between his knees, and he's sawing through the lower part of its neck like a man being paid for piecework, not by the hour.

"What are you *doing*?"

"Rabies," he grunts without looking up. The spinal column slows him down for a few seconds, but Kelly's obviously field-dressed a lot of game in his time. "I don't know if this fucker's had his shots or not. You gotta get the brainstem and everything for that test." When the head tears free, Kelly lifts it by its wrinkled face and stuffs it into his gear bag. Then he straps on his pack, heaves the dog's carcass over his right shoulder, and stands with a groan. "What are you waiting for? Pick up the other one."

"Where are we going?"

"To throw them in the river."

With a strange buzzing in my head, I kneel beside the black dog, lever my right arm under it, then wrestle it over my shoulder in an awkward fireman's carry. The damn thing must weigh a hundred pounds, and it stinks. I'm winded before I cover twenty yards, but Kelly's already far ahead.

This is one time I should have let him do the job alone.

When I reach the river's edge, the white carcass is already spinning slowly downstream under the stars, and Kelly is stuffing the dog's head into the rear cargo hold of his kayak. With the last of my strength, I stagger downstream from the boats and heave my burden into the current. The Bully Kutta disappears with a splash, then bobs to the surface.

"They actually went after my sister," I say with breathless disbelief. "I haven't heard my dad sound that upset since Ruby died."

Kelly squats and rinses his wounded forearm with river water. "I'll tell you what I think," he says softly, scrubbing the half-clotted blood from his skin.

"What?"

He looks up, his mild blue eyes like those of a choirboy. "I think Jonathan Sands has become a one-bullet problem."

CHAPTER

34

"A one-bullet problem?" Caitlin asks, echoing Kelly's repeated phrase. "You mean you want to kill Sands? In cold blood?"

Kelly looks around the circle of faces in the room. Along with Kelly and Caitlin, Carl Sims, my father, and I are seated in chairs in the den of a lake house owned by Chris Shepard, my father's youngest partner. Because it's after Labor Day, most of the houses used as second homes by Natchezians are empty now. As I drew the curtains over the broad glass doors on the far wall, I saw the narrow black line of Lake Concordia, the oxbow lake that carries the name of the parish, behind the house. I also saw James Ervin, who's guarding us from the lake side, while his brother Elvin guards the road entrance. Danny McDavitt is sitting in the chopper across the lake road, in the cotton field where we landed.

"Actually," says Kelly, "my blood is still pretty hot at this point."

"Mine too," says my father. "Gutless bastards."

While my father dressed Kelly's wounded arm, we listened to his account of Jenny being attacked on the highway (not even the British police believe it was an accident), then brought Dad up to speed on the events on the river. While we talked, Carl tied the Bully Kutta's severed head in a trash bag, then stored it in the refrigerator, so that its brain can be examined by the path lab in the morning. Coming after the events beside the river tonight, this scene was so surreal that I could scarcely separate thought from emotion. Kelly's assertion that the time has come to kill Jonathan Sands seems perfectly natural to me, given the situation. I can tell by Caitlin's hard-set face that she doesn't agree. She doesn't want to antagonize my father, but she's not going to be silent when the matter at hand is assassination.

"Look, I want the guy to go down," she says. "He's scum, okay? No question. But you can't just kill him. I mean, if it's all right for you to decide who lives and dies, the same goes for everyone else. Who empowered you? If you're free to do that, where does it end? Back in the cave, that's where."

Kelly listens patiently until she stops. "Let me tell you a secret, Caitlin. We're still in the cave. It's just bigger, and we wear nicer clothes. We make alliances and try to be civil, we save the weak instead of leaving them out in the cold to die. But guys like Sands, Quinn, Po . . . they play by the ancient rules. To them, life is a zero-sum game. You win or lose, live or die. And the most important rule of all is, you take everything you can, when you can, until somebody draws a line and says, 'No more.'"

"Is that your view of life?"

"If it were, I wouldn't be offering to kill a man in front of witnesses. You probably studied existentialism in college, right? Survey of philosophy course? I'm not trying to patronize you, okay? But I *am* an existentialist. A soldier. Asleep or awake, in uniform or out. There's war in Afghanistan, but there's war here too. When Sands threatened to kill Penn's child, he opened hostilities and declared the rules of engagement. We know from Linda Church's note that Sands probably murdered Ben Li, or else ordered it done. It's a miracle Linda isn't dead too—*if* she's still alive, which we don't know for sure. I'm sure they're hunting for her as we speak."

Caitlin shivers at this thought.

Kelly nods with certainty. "Given where things stand now, we have only one practical solution. Remove Sands from the equation."

"You're willing to do that?" Dad asks. "If we say here and now that that's what we want . . . then Sands will die?"

Kelly nods soberly. "Quinn too, I think. Unavoidable."

Caitlin shakes her head in amazement. "And you'll go back to Afghanistan and never lose a night's sleep over it?"

"I'll sleep better."

What strikes me most about Kelly's cool assertion is that a couple of hours ago, he was unwilling to put a dying dog out of its misery. But that mystery will have to wait. I look at my father, who's rubbing his white beard with arthritically curled hands.

"It's tempting," Dad says. "When I think of Jenny rolling over in that car, I could do it myself."

"I'm sorry to be a drag here, guys," Caitlin says. "But this is *way* over the line. What does killing Sands even accomplish? If Edward Po is the problem, who's to say he won't carry on the vendetta and send men here to kill Penn and every member of his family?"

"She's got a point," Carl says. "You'd be crazy not to consider that."

"I've considered it," Kelly says. "Edward Po is a businessman. Whatever he's up to here, he ultimately views it in terms of profit and loss. You can't go around murdering government officials in small-town America. It draws the wrong kind of attention. That's bad business. Sands is Po's cat's-paw, his control mechanism for Golden Parachute. If Sands dies, Po will simply order Craig Weldon to put someone else in that job."

"Yet you're arguing that Sands *will* murder government officials," Caitlin points out. "Or their families."

"I think he's proved that he will. I don't think Sands is motivated primarily by money."

"You don't know that Po is either. You're ignoring the question of face. If Po is a criminal, can he afford to let other criminals know that his lieutenants can be killed without reprisals?"

"I considered face," Kelly says patiently. "Also *guanxi.* I think killing Sands is actually the most elegant solution to our problem—and not just for us. If Sands is killed, I suspect Po will claim credit for the murder—unofficially, of course. Competitors will assume that Po had Sands murdered for interfering with his niece, Jiao, whom Po vowed to protect from people like Sands."

Everyone is silent, not least because Kelly seems two steps ahead of us all.

"We either kill him or we back off," Kelly concludes. "Conventional methods are too slow. They're just going to get someone we care about killed."

"Carl?" Caitlin says pointedly. "Would *you* kill Sands?"

The sniper gives her a "Why me?" look, like a grade-school student being called on by his teacher. "Kelly's a free agent," he mumbles. "The man makes his own decisions."

"I'm asking about *you.*"

"Depends on the situation. If somebody was going to die because I didn't, I would, yeah."

"But would you shoot him sitting at his breakfast table?"

Carl turns up his palms. "I don't think so, but it's complicated. I *have* shot somebody who was eating dinner, because the Marine Corps told me he needed to die. Now, I don't know Jonathan Sands from Jonathan Livingston Seagull. But if I knew he was going to kill my sister or my mother . . . then I'd vaporize him."

Caitlin turns to me, as though I'm the court of last resort. "You're an attorney, sworn to uphold the law. You've sent people to death row for doing exactly what Kelly's offering to do now. Are you really going to send him out of this house to commit murder?"

The fact that I think Kelly is right surprises even me. I've been in similar situations before, with the power of life and death over someone almost as evil as Sands, and I chose to use the court system, even with the chance that they might escape punishment. But Sands is a special case. I wish Caitlin and I could have this discussion in private, because she tends to get more stirred up when she's in front of people. But there's no alternative now.

"I have sent people to death row," I concede in a level voice. "But not for doing something like this. This is a unique situation. Tim stumbled into something far bigger and more complicated than he knew. Blackhawk's position and Peter Lutjens's warning prove that. We still don't really know what we're dealing with. We only know that the government is involved in some way, and that Sands and Quinn are prepared to kill to prevent anyone from learning what they're doing. I also know that wherever they are, my mother and Annie are scared to death.

They're holding their chins up, but they're terrified that they'll get a phone call saying that Dad or me is dead. And I believe that's a real possibility."

"That sounded like a summation, not an answer," Caitlin says, her tone still challenging.

"Caitlin . . . this is like a stalking case. When I was a prosecutor, I saw a lot of women die needlessly because the police had no effective way to intervene until after they were dead. A lot of the men who killed those women went to prison afterward. But the women were still dead."

This time I get no ricochet response.

"In this case, there are four women who could die," I go on, "all of whom I love. And one of them is you."

"Don't do that," she says with startling intensity. "Don't use me to justify killing someone."

"Maybe we should take a vote," Kelly suggests.

"No!" snaps Caitlin. "We're not taking any goddamn vote. No one here has the right to vote on murder. If you kill Sands, you've done it on your own."

"What would you do if he went through

with it?" I ask. "Would you report Kelly to the police?"

She gets to her feet and turns to my father. "Tom, you're not seriously condoning this?"

Dad looks up at her with sad eyes. "I understand your feelings, Kate. I believe in the rule of law. And Sands hasn't killed a member of my family—yet. But that's only thanks to chance. My daughter could easily have died two hours ago."

"But she *didn't,* Tom. She's going to be all right. We have time to take another path."

"What path would that be?"

"We could go public. I can have this story on the front page of twenty-three papers tomorrow, and a lot more than that, if I bring my father into this. I'd hate to do that, but if we're to the point of assassinating someone, then I think it's time to break the story nationwide."

"If we go public," I point out, "Edward Po won't set foot on U.S. soil for ten years, at least. Whatever he's doing here, he won't be nailed for it."

Caitlin looks at me like I'm an idiot. "What do you think Po is going to do if you murder Sands? You lose Po that way too."

"What exactly would you print?" I ask. "Unsubstantiated allegations?"

Kelly leans forward and says, "I know going public seems like a magic solution, throwing light onto people who live in the shadows. But men like Po don't see the world the way you do. They're not politicians. While you're stirring up your media storm, they will be *acting.* To them, this is war. And if they take you out, or Annie or Peggy or Penn, none of us is going to feel comforted by the fact that you splashed Sands's and Po's names in the paper. Because that won't bring back the dead."

Dad seems to be weighing all the arguments in his mind. "You saw those two old black men outside?" he says to Caitlin. "The ones watching over us?"

She nods.

"Before they were cops, before there even *were* black cops in Natchez, they were members of something called the Deacons for Defense."

"What's that?"

"A group of men who got fed up with their friends and neighbors being terrorized, beaten, and killed. They patrolled their neighborhoods with pistols, lay out all night in ditches with shotguns, all to keep their people safe. They did that because they couldn't turn to the police. The law had failed to protect them, so they did it themselves."

"Has the law failed to protect us?" Caitlin asks, looking around our circle. "We haven't even *asked* for help yet."

"Kate," my father says gently. "Let me tell you a story a patient of mine once told me. Back in the sixties and seventies, they had gambling and prostitution not far from where we are now. A place called Morville Plantation. Very close to where Penn and Kelly got attacked. Some of the girls who worked at Morville were held there against their will. God only knows where they'd been taken from, or what hell they'd been through. But one day, one girl got away from there. Half naked, she walked all the way to the sheriff's department. She was crying with relief while she told her story. The sheriff listened, then put her in his car and drove her right back to the whorehouse."

Caitlin stares at my father in silence.

"Kate, you're sitting in a parish that didn't have jury trials for almost ten years—from 1956 to 1966."

"We're not living in that time anymore," Caitlin says quietly.

"That's true. But how far are we from the story of that poor girl? If we believe Tim Jessup, the same thing is going on today."

Dad's mention of Tim seems to move Caitlin to silence.

"This is what I know," I conclude. "Peter Lutjens warned me to stay away from Sands, said he could give me no information whatever. Peter would only do that if Sands was involved with the government in some way. Sands is either a target, an agent, or an informant. I'm almost afraid to find out which. But the fact is, he's been committing felonies since he arrived here, up to and including murder. Yet he's still roaming free."

"Maybe the government doesn't know he's doing that!" Caitlin argues.

"The same government you want to pillory for its handling of Katrina and Iraq?" I shake my head. "Either we've stumbled into something really rotten, or something so serious that we can't even grasp its significance. Either way, we have to assume that if Tim's death didn't matter to whoever's in charge of this mess, none of ours would either."

Caitlin looks as if she's winding up again, but before she speaks, Dad says, "I think Penn and I have to make this decision alone. Caitlin, you and Carl will have no part in it."

"But we *know* about it. We *are* a part of it, whether we want to be or not."

As passionate as she is about this, some part of me wonders about Caitlin's true motive.

"If we decide to go ahead," Dad says, "you do whatever you feel you must."

The room is so quiet that my cell phone vibrating in my pocket stops the conversation. It's late enough that I feel I need to check it. The screen shows one new text message. The area code is 202—Washington, D.C.—but I don't recognize the number. The message reads: GO OUT-SIDE AND TURN ON YOUR SATELLITE PHONE.

"What is it?" Kelly asks, seeing the color drain from my face.

I toss the phone to him. He reads the

screen, then jumps to his feet and grabs his gear bag.

"What is it?" Dad asks worriedly. "Is it Annie or Peggy?"

"I don't know what it is," Kelly says, "but it ain't good." He looks at me. "Who have you given the sat number to?"

"Nobody."

"Shit. Either it's someone from Blackhawk, or they gave the number to somebody in D.C."

"What do I do?" I ask. "How do they know I'm inside?"

"They tried to call the satphone and you didn't answer. Take it easy. They can't see us or anything. But you've got to take the call. I'll go out with you."

We brush aside the curtain and go out the patio doors. Caitlin follows. As soon as Kelly sets up the link to the satellite, the phone starts to buzz.

"This is Penn Cage."

"Hello, Mr. Cage," says a voice with a vestigial Southern accent. "My name is William Hull. I'm an attorney with the Justice Department."

"They're a pretty big employer. Could you be more specific?"

"I'm special counsel to the Department of Homeland Security."

"That sounds ominous."

"Very boring, I assure you. Being an assistant DA in Houston is twice as exciting."

"What are you calling about, Mr. Hull? And how did you get this number?"

"We have some mutual friends. They were kind enough to give me your private number. As for the purpose of my call, it's about Jonathan Sands."

"What about him?"

"Well, this is a delicate matter. We—"

"Mr. Hull, when you say *delicate,* I hear *dirty.*"

Hull pauses, his rhythm disturbed. "Jonathan Sands has an important relationship to the federal government at this time."

I look at Kelly and shake my head in disbelief. "You mean he's an informant."

"I didn't say that."

"Well, what did you say? Is Sands employed by the federal government?"

"Of course not."

"Is he a close personal friend of someone in the administration?"

"Don't be ridiculous."

"Then he's an informant."

Hull sighs like a man unaccustomed to frustration. "Mr. Cage, there's an investigation pending—a very large and complex investigation—that began almost three years ago. It involves both the Department of Homeland Security and the Justice Department, through the Special Task Force on Money Laundering. The target is a Chinese national named Edward Po."

"I know who Po is."

"Do you? In any case, Mr. Sands is important to the aforementioned investigation. That's all I am authorized to tell you, and given my position, it should be enough."

"Well, it's not. I've played this game before, Mr. Hull. I've dealt with some pretty unsavory characters in order to nail worse ones, so I know the rules. But I also know that at some point you have to draw a line. Being a confidential informant isn't a free pass to commit murder."

Hull takes his time with this. At length he says, "You were an assistant district attorney in Houston, Texas. You were dealing with state crimes. I'm talking about the national security of the United States."

"That rubric has been stretched to cover a lot of sins lately. The last time I checked, Mississippi was part of the United States. And her citizens count just as much as those in Georgetown or Chevy Chase. What happens to Sands after your investigation of Po is concluded? Does he walk?"

There's another hitch in Hull's rhythm. "That hasn't been determined yet."

"Then tell me this: What chance do you really have of nailing a Chinese billionaire in U.S. federal court?"

"There's a first time for everything."

"You're telling me somebody up in the Justice Department has finally grown some balls?"

"It happens. Mr. Cage, I need your personal assurance that you won't interfere any further, as of this moment."

"You're not going to get that. Not tonight, anyway."

"I'm sure I don't need to remind you that you have no law enforcement authority. You're no longer a prosecutor."

"The local DA reminds me of that all the time. I am, however, an American citizen."

"Meaning?"

"Hull, if you've forgotten what that means, we might as well hang up now."

"I sense a certain naïveté in your attitude, Mr. Cage. Maybe you've been out of the city too long."

At last my outrage boils over. "Do you have any idea what kind of criminal acts Jonathan Sands is committing down here?"

"Knowing the man's résumé, I can guess."

"My sister was nearly killed in England two hours ago by a hit-and-run driver."

"You can prove that was linked to Jonathan Sands?"

"It wasn't coincidence. But even that pales next to kidnapping and murder."

"Are you referring to the death of Timothy Jessup?"

"And possibly others."

"Mr. Cage, try to set aside your personal concerns and listen to me for one minute. A little over a month ago, more than two thousand people drowned in New Orleans. If the numbers I'm seeing are any indicator, we're likely to find another thousand corpses or so, and many will remain unaccounted for. So, as for a few dogs being fought in some backwater Louisiana parish, we don't have time for it. As for prostitution and gambling, the authorities in Babylon had the same problem. It's not going away."

"I'm not talking about dogfighting and prostitution."

"I heard you. Murder is serious business—if murder is in fact what you have down there. But Edward Po is smuggling illegal aliens into this country by the hundred, some of whom will work in industrial jobs, others as prostitutes or drug couriers. More importantly, through massive and complex money-laundering schemes, Po is meddling with the currency of the United States. The number of people who've been injured because of his criminal enterprises probably can't be overestimated. So while I'm sure Mr. Jessup was a close friend of yours, you need to take a step back and get some perspective. The target here is Po, not some Irish punk who likes to fight dogs and run whores in his spare time. I talked to your old boss Joe Cantor. He told me that you generally have a good sense of priorities, but that you're an idealist. In these times, idealism is a luxury we can't afford. Am I getting through to you?"

"You've made your position clear."

"That's not what I'm asking."

"That's the only answer you're going to get. I'll consider what you've said, but you should be aware of this. My family has been threatened by your informant. I've had to send my mother and daughter into hiding. Because of that, I've taken certain steps. If I or my father die or disappear for any length of time, every detail of these matters will be made public in the most sensational way I could contrive."

This silences Hull for some seconds. "Mr. Cage, there's no need for threats. We're on the same side."

"That's the one thing I'm not clear on after this conversation, Mr. Hull. Good night."

"Wait! Please don't do anything rash. For your own sake. You have my phone number now, on your satellite phone."

"I don't need your number. You can tell

your masters this. Besides being a citizen, I'm also a lawyer. And I don't cringe when I say that. I'm not a backroom, Washington Beltway, cuff-links-and-suspenders kind of lawyer—and by that I mean *your* kind of lawyer. I'm a trial lawyer. A former state prosecutor. And when somebody starts treating the laws of my state like their own personal toilet paper, I know how to tear them a new asshole. Am I getting through to you, sir?"

"In graphic detail. Mr. Cage, you remind me of what I loved and hated about the South."

"I take that as a compliment."

"Take care of yourself. And please inform Daniel Kelly that he's made himself subject to severe criminal penalties for misappropriating army property. He can be arrested at any time."

When I click END, I realize that my father has come outside as well. He and Caitlin are watching me with a mix of concern and awe.

"I love you," says Caitlin, hugging me tight. "You realize that, right?"

"Jesus."

"That was . . . freaking awesome."

"No, it was stupid. This isn't a Frank Capra movie."

"Who were you talking to?" Kelly asks.

"Claimed he was special counsel to the Department of Homeland Security. Name of Hull. Ever hear of him? William Hull."

"No. But it sounds like we'd better forget what we were talking about back in the house."

"Yeah. Killing federal informants is a bad idea."

"Sands is a government informant?" Dad asks.

"He's their leverage against Po. And they want Po for all sorts of major crimes. Human smuggling, prostitution, money laundering. All the stuff Walt talked about the other night. If my experience is any guide, Sands is probably part of a sting designed to lure Po onto U.S. soil. Then they can grab him, and Sands can testify against him."

Kelly sighs in disgust. "And then Sands walks? Is that the deal?"

"I honestly don't know. But with a target that big, and in this paranoid security climate, it's possible. They couldn't care less what crimes Sands is committing down here. For all we know, Sands could be doing that stuff specifically to lure Po here."

"That's just *nuts,*" Caitlin sputters. "It's fascism!"

My father lays a hand on her shoulder. "It burns me up to think they'd write off what we've been going through, but the government makes those kinds of decisions all the time. All governments do."

"But *ours* isn't supposed to."

Kelly laughs cynically. "Caitlin, you sound like a schoolgirl, not a journalist."

"So, we're just going to back off?" she says in disbelief. "That's what you're all saying?"

"You think we want to back off?" I ask incredulously. "We're the ones who wanted to shoot the son of a bitch!"

"There's got to be a middle path," she says doggedly.

"Don't go Buddhist on us," Kelly says wearily, probing his wounded arm. "We've got new information now. We've got to pull back a little to reassess. I've got four guys risking their careers to protect Annie and Peggy right now. That's asking a lot of men who don't even know them."

"Hull knows all about you," I tell Kelly. "The Star Treks, everything. Blackhawk sold you out. Hull threatened you with arrest."

Kelly shrugs as if this were only to be expected. "You could still try to nail Sands on murder charges after the feds get custody of Po, right?"

"Yes. They don't have the power to grant Sands immunity on state charges. Not unless they've suspended the Constitution."

Caitlin stares at me with narrowed eyes, then steps forward. "Don't do this, Penn. You can't cave in to bastards like Hull."

"I hate to say it, but I've been in the same position he's in. Not exactly the same, but similar ones. Justice is about compromise, Caitlin. Trade-offs."

"*Justice?* Don't shit on that word by using it to describe what's about to happen here."

I sigh heavily, then lift the satellite phone and call the lawyer back.

Dad takes Caitlin's arm. "Let's just be thankful Jenny wasn't killed, and that none of us was either. We've been lucky, considering what we're mixed up in."

In her present mood, Caitlin would jerk her arm away from anyone else. But not my father. Instead, she leans into him and rests her head on his shoulder.

"Hello, Mr. Cage," Hull says in a smug voice. "Have you thought things over?"

"Yes."

"I know emotions are probably running high down there. But with your legal background, I felt certain you'd see the logic of things."

"I have a precondition for backing off, Mr. Hull."

"What's that?"

"You call off the dogs, as of this moment. That means Sands, Quinn, and any goons who are watching us. Also any agency that's eavesdropping, trying to find my kid, whatever. All that stops as of this moment. Is that understood?"

There's a brief silence. "I can't speak to those specific concerns, but I feel sure you can stop worrying about your loved ones from this point forward. No one knows better than I that Sands can be difficult to deal with. Things probably got a little out of hand down there. I may be coming down myself soon, to help manage things."

"If you want your prosecution to succeed, please don't make me call you again."

"More threats?"

"That's no threat. How would you like this story to go page one across the country? We can make that happen, if you push us."

This silences Hull longer than anything else.

"Do we have an understanding?" I ask.

"D'accord," he says. "You go back to your lives, we'll go back to making America safe. Good-bye."

I kill the connection. "God, what an arrogant bastard."

"Let's go," Caitlin says in a flat voice. "How are we getting back?"

"You two ride in the helicopter with Danny and Carl," Dad says. "Kelly and I will follow in the car. If that's okay with you, Kelly. I'd like to keep an eye on that arm."

"Sure."

The subtext is clear: No one wants to be around Caitlin for the thirty minutes it will take to drive back to town. I'd just as soon ride in the car with Kelly and Dad, but that wouldn't go over well with the offended lady.

"Let me get that dog's head and lock the house," Dad says, "and we'll run you over to the chopper."

"It's only a couple of hundred yards," Caitlin says. "We'll walk it. There's no danger anymore, right?'

Dad's face darkens. "I'm not so sure—"

"We'll walk it," I tell him, looking over at the running lights of the chopper on the far side of the lake road.

Kelly squeezes my arm and says, "I'll see you back at the house."

"You sticking around town awhile?"

He somehow manages a grin as my father walks back to the door. "I can't afford to lose this gig. You're my only employer now."

"Good, because I need you to bring Annie back from Texas. You're definitely still on the payroll."

"Sounds like a pretty cushy job." Kelly stops smiling and points past me. "You better look after her."

Caitlin has already started walking toward the helicopter. I don't hurry to catch up, but my longer stride brings us even soon enough. At first she says nothing. But when I don't speak, she says, "You know what's funny about the way that just went down?"

"What?"

"Two minutes before that lawyer called, you were ready to wipe Jonathan Sands off the planet without even a warning. But the second some Beltway lawyer told you that Sands should go scot-free for God and country, you bent over and said, 'Thank you, sir, may I have another.'"

"Caitlin . . . nothing I say is going to make you feel better."

"No, I want to hear your rationale. Is there something more than the 'good German' defense here?"

"Yes, unpalatable though it may be. Edward Po represents a greater threat to a larger number of people than Sands. If the only way to nail Po is to let Sands walk, then that's what the government will do. They're choosing to stop the greater of two evils. If that sounds lame, let me tell you something. When I was an ADA, I once had to go down to the port and walk into a ship container that held twenty-seven bodies. They were Mexicans who'd died of dehydration. Five extended families, all dead. Men, women, children. Put Chinese faces on those bodies, and you get an idea of the kind of thing Edward Po is into for profit."

Caitlin is shaking her head in frustration. "But you're just taking their word about Po. What do you really know about him?"

"We got Po's history from Blackhawk before they sold Kelly out. The bottom line is that however crazy Sands may be, he's protected right now. That's a fact of life. And if he feels threatened, he won't hesitate to kill my father, my mother, my daughter, or even you. It would be insane to risk that."

"I told you not to use me to justify murder. Don't use me to justify chickening out either. Aren't you putting an awful lot of trust in a bureaucrat you've never met, to keep Sands in line?"

She's right about that much, I think, as we cross the black strip of asphalt in the night. Carl's probably watching us through his night scope from the helicopter and wondering why we're risking this walk across open ground without Kelly.

As we draw close enough to hear the slowly turning rotors whoosh through the air, she says, "I really feel down. I can't explain it. It's more than just what happened tonight."

"No, it's not. After I told off Hull, you were flying high. Now, facing reality, you're depressed. I know I've disappointed you. But I have too much at stake to fight Hull and Sands. You want me to leave you out of my calculations? Okay. The bottom line is this. I have a child, you don't. That was a big part of my reasoning about executing Sands, as well. Until you have a child of your own, you can't understand the absolute imperative you feel to protect that innocent life."

Caitlin stops short of the helicopter and looks up at me, her eyes bright and wet. "I *want* a child. I wanted one with you. I always have. That's why I've been treading water for a year and half, even though I'm almost thirty-five. You think *I* can't deal with reality? What about you and your fantasy of saving Natchez?"

I reach out to take her hand, but she slaps mine away. "You told me you ran for mayor to save your hometown. That's what you told yourself, your parents, Annie, and everyone else. Well, I wasn't sure it could be saved from the things you wanted to take on. Not by one person. But I know this: It damn sure needs saving now. And what are you doing? Folding your tent. Pissing on the fire and calling in the dogs, as they say down here." She shakes her head and starts to turn away. "Honestly . . . I don't think I've ever been more shocked in my life. Or more wrong about someone."

At this point, a wise man would offer an apology and get into the helicopter. But something's been nagging at me ever since the argument about killing Sands.

"As long as we're being honest," I say to her back, "let me ask you one question. When you argued so passionately against killing Sands, was that really because you believe it would be morally wrong to do it?"

"Of course!" she snaps, whirling on me. "What did you think?"

"I wondered whether you might be arguing that way because, if we'd gone that route, you'd never have been able to write the story. Not as it really happened, anyway."

Caitlin has pale skin, but what little color she has drains from her face. "You son of a bitch." She looks as if she'd like to gouge my eyes out, but instead she simply turns and climbs into the cabin of the helicopter.

I look back at the road, where my father's nine-year-old BMW is swinging onto the asphalt to head back toward Mississippi. No matter what I told Caitlin, there's no escaping one unalterable reality: Despite my deal with the devil, Tim Jessup's blood still cries out from the ground. And I am not deaf. Only one thought brings me solace now.

My daughter is coming home.

CHAPTER

35

Linda is sitting in the front pew of the church, near the wooden rail. Pastor Simpson sits facing her, his hands hanging between his knees. He looks like a laborer forced to put on a suit for a funeral, but when you feel his hands, you know he hasn't done real labor in years. He's a talker, soft-spoken and sincere. He's been talking to Linda about the totality of God, but she can't keep her mind on the words. She's burning up, her leg is throbbing, and her ride is late, hours late, picking her up.

"I'm sorry it's taken so long, honey,"

Simpson says for the twentieth time. "That dern nephew of mine can't hardly get no work, and now he gets called out to rig like this . . . and after what you said, I didn't think we should tell nobody else but Darla about you being here."

"I understand," Linda says, trying to keep her mind clear through the fever. "But the Bargain Barn closed a long time ago."

"I told you, hon, Darla sits with sick folks sometimes after she gets off, and tonight she had to check on a patient. Somebody probably ran off and stuck her with their mama or something. Happens all the time. Darla don't charge half of what professional sitters charge, so people are all the time taking advantage."

"Where exactly are we going?"

"Oh, you're gonna love it. My brother's got a place way out in the country. Ain't nothing there but trees and ponds. Nobody to hurt you, or even see you. Just an old cabin. You can stay out there however long you need, till the coast is clear."

"All by myself?"

"Well, Darla can stay awhile to get you fixed with food and sundries. But after that—" Simpson falls silent at the sound of an engine. "See there? All that worry for nothing."

Linda feels a dizzying rush of relief. The pastor reaches out and steadies her. "She's gonna knock three times, so we'll know it's her. Okay?"

"Okay. You said Mayor Cage got my note, right?"

"That's what Darla said. Now, let's get on down the aisle."

As Simpson helps Linda to her feet, three loud knocks reverberate through the cold church, like someone banging on a castle door.

"Come in," the pastor calls. "We're coming."

The door opens, and Linda sees a tall silhouette in the door. Darla, for sure. But as the silhouette moves forward, Linda perceives its narrow waist and broad shoulders. Then a shaft of light falls on the handsome face of Seamus Quinn.

Linda's stomach heaves in terror,

and she whirls toward Pastor Simpson, who's looking at her with terrible shame on his face.

Quinn strides up the aisle with two big men flanking him. Linda recoils and tries to run toward the altar, but her torn knee gives way and she collapses in the aisle. The two men rush forward and lift her to her feet.

"How can you do this?" she asks, her eyes on Pastor Simpson. "You're a man of God!"

"Just a man, Linda. I'm weak, like everybody else. I sin like everyone else. It's the curse of my life."

Simpson turns to Quinn and says, "We're square now, right? That's what you said? All debts canceled?"

Quinn gives him a broad grin and slaps his back. "No worries, Padre. For now. I'm sure you'll be back at the tables soon enough."

"No!" Simpson cries. "Never. This finishes all that!"

Quinn's laughter reverberates through the church as they drag Linda toward the door.

"They're going to kill me!" she screams, looking back at Simpson with pleading eyes. "You know they are!"

"The Lord will keep you, child! Have no fear. You're a child of God, perfect in his eyes. But I must to render unto Caesar what is Caesar's. My family needs me, Linda. My congregation needs me. You'll be saving all of that with your sacrifice, just as our Lord did at Calvary!"

"Fuckin' hell!" Quinn shouts, laughing. "Shut your fucking gob already! You're worse than the bloody Taigs!"

As Simpson falls to his knees at the altar and begins to pray, Linda's knee gives way at the door. The men lift her bodily and carry her toward a black SUV.

"Who's going first?" asks one of the men holding her.

"High card wins," says the second.

"Get your arses up front," snaps Quinn. "Age before beauty, that's the rule."

He lifts the rear gate on the SUV and

the men slide Linda into the cargo area on her back. "Get on with you," Quinn says. "This is no peep show."

One man slams the rear door down, and they get into the front seat. After the motor starts, Quinn leans down beside Linda's ear. "You led me a merry chase, darlin'. But I like a game bitch. I've been waiting a long time for this. I've already seen pictures, now let's see the real thing."

Linda struggles as his hand slides down her stomach, but when a razor-edged knife grazes her throat, she freezes. Seconds later, her pants have been cut from her body as smoothly as if by a nurse in an ER.

Quinn's eyes glint in the dark. "So that's what kept the boss in such a state," he whispers. "Not bad . . . not bad."

"What do you want?"

"Everything you gave him," *Quinn whispers. "Then more."*

Linda's shock and fever have held her at some chemical remove from the situation, but now reality is settling into her bones. God has not delivered her anywhere but into the hands of Tim's murderers.

"Please don't hurt me any more," she whispers. "I'll do anything you say."

"Course you will." Quinn laughs harshly, then hits the front seat twice to signal the driver to go. "Everybody does, in the end."

CHAPTER

36

Kelly and I are standing at the foot of the broad gangplank of the *Magnolia Queen,* having a last talk before we go aboard. Kelly believes Sands needs to hear directly from us that we're disengaging from our covert war, and we need his assurance that he's doing the same. I've agreed because I want no misunderstanding on that score, especially since Kelly and Danny McDavitt are flying to Houston this afternoon to bring back Annie and my mother.

"We're just going to talk, right?" I ask a little anxiously.

"Clear the air," Kelly says. "Everybody can get whatever they have to say off their chests, and we can all relax a little."

"That's kind of hard for me to visualize, given the past few days."

"Nah. Come on."

As I follow him up the broad gangplank, I say, "Did that SAS sergeant ever get back to you? About Sands's life pre-1989? The Northern Ireland stuff?"

Kelly's face darkens. "He did, but he didn't have anything for me. He thinks Sands probably isn't a real name. I faxed him a photo, but that could take longer. My guy's not on active duty anymore."

"I just wish we knew more about this asshole."

"We're about to. You're not carrying a weapon or a wire, are you?"

"No. Why?"

"They're bound to search us. Wand us, everything."

"I'm clean. You?"

Kelly rolls his eyes. "I asked you first."

At the end of the gangway we pass through the main entrance, where a guard in a burgundy uniform stands greeting gamblers. Seeing us, he speaks into a collar radio. Seconds later, two men appear at our sides and lead us to an elevator hidden behind a wall partition. As we rise to the upper floor known as the hurricane deck, our escorts pat us down thoroughly, then run wands along the lengths of our bodies.

"Rub a little harder down there," Kelly quips. "You're giving me a chubby."

The guy pulls back, muttering something about queers and ponytails. He'd probably be shocked to learn that this ponytailed hippie could take him apart without raising his pulse rate.

The other guy finishes Kelly's patdown, stopping at his left forearm. Kelly pulls up the sleeve of his sweatshirt, exposing a white bandage. "Dog bite," he says with a smile. The guy fingers the entire length of the bandage while Kelly grits his teeth. Then the man presses a remote in his pocket.

The doors open onto a carpeted corridor where the jangling sound of slots does not intrude. The men motion for us to walk past simulated gasoliers to a set of stainless-steel doors at the end of the hall.

As we reach them, the doors part as

though by magic, and I catch my breath. The steamboat-Gothic motif that dominates the *Magnolia Queen* ends at the door of Jonathan Sands's office. Behind his sleek black desk stands a solid glass wall that offers a breathtaking vista of the upstream bend of the Mississippi River, the great reddish tide flowing down out of verdant green bluffs on the east, and flat delta earth to the west. Sands sits behind his desk wearing an olive green commando sweater with patches on the elbows. He's furnished the room with Barcelona chairs, an Eames lounger, and several other iconic pieces. The office feels as though it was ordered in a single shipment from Ultra Modern or Design Within Reach.

"Well, Mr. Kelly," he says. "We meet at last."

Kelly nods but says nothing.

"Where did you come from, if you don't mind my asking?"

"I flew in from a place called Qalat. You know where that is?"

Sands gives a surprised smile. "Actually, I do. I passed a few years there one afternoon, back in the nineties."

"I figured maybe you had. Or some-where like it."

"So. Brothers-in-arms."

"I wouldn't go that far."

"Well, get on with it. Why are you here?"

"Diplomacy. To make sure something's understood."

"I'm listening."

"At the request of the government, we're going to cease and desist trying to nail your hide to the barn door."

As Sands laughs, the doors hiss open behind us. When I glance back, I see Seamus Quinn, his face clouded with suspicion. After Quinn comes the white Bully Kutta I last saw at Sands's house. The dog walks around us and sits calmly to the right of Sands's desk, the piercing eyes staring out of its wrinkled face.

"That's already been communicated to me," Sands says.

"From Hull, no doubt," I say.

"We're here to add the personal touch," Kelly says. "I have a message of my own for you."

Sands raises one eyebrow.

"I want you to understand that the only thing keeping you alive is this man standing here."

Sands looks back and forth from me to Kelly.

"Penn is your old-school type guy. A gentleman and a scholar. Officer material, you might say. I'm more the direct type. A grunt. A grunt's grunt might be more accurate. I have certain skills that your average grunt doesn't. When the brass sees a problem they can't solve with a TV-guided bomb or an Abrams tank, they point guys like me at it. The paper pushers call it discretionary warfare. Doesn't sound very bloody, does it?" Kelly smiles. "But you know the real definition, don't you? Mate?"

Sands's good humor seems to be wearing thin. I doubt he's accustomed to being challenged in his own office.

"I know what you did to his sister," Kelly says mildly. "And he told me what you said you'd do to his little girl. I'm a big fan of that little girl. I like the way she smells—like clothes that just came out of a dryer. So when Mayor Cage asked my opinion of your recent activities, I told him you were a one-bullet problem. Do you require a translation, Mr. Sands?"

Sands chuckles in appreciation. "You're all balls, aren't you, Danny boy? Where was your grandfather from? Derry?"

"South Boston. You can play it as cool as you want, but you see me. You hear me. And I don't want any misunderstanding after I leave this room. We're not your problem anymore, and you're not ours. You guys can rob this town blind for all we care. Neither I nor the mayor is going to lift a finger to stop you. Am I right, Penn?"

"Right."

"But," Kelly adds, "if anything happens to my friend or his family—if his father should suffer a minor heart attack while walking through the produce section of the local Wal-Mart, say . . . then you, Jonathan Sands, will cease to exist. Your pal standing behind me too—but purely as an afterthought. I'd take him out just to get rid of the bog stink."

I hear Quinn shifting his weight, but Sands stops him with a glance.

"Are we clear?" Kelly asks.

"Danny, Danny," says Sands. "Who do you think you're dealing with?"

"Rats," Kelly says. "Informers. But that's an old IRA tradition, isn't it? That's why you have the kneecapping with the power drills and all that, to try to keep your mates from selling you out for a bottle of Bushmills."

Sands's eyes harden remarkably fast.

"You're ratting Po to the government," Kelly goes on, despite my trying to shut him up with a glance, "which sounds like a risky proposition to me, even if they get him. But if I were you, I'd be worried about what your lapdog behind me's going to do if Po *doesn't* take the bait. Hull is going to want something to show for his years of investigation. Quinn might decide to flip on you and turn state's evidence to keep his own ass out of jail. Yeah, I'd be thinking hard about that."

I hear a quick sliding sound, and then Quinn is flying over Kelly, a gun in his hand. At first I think he's pistol-whipping Kelly, but when the motion stops, Kelly is wrapped around the Irishman like a boa constrictor, his bulging calf locked across Quinn's thighs, his forearm wrapped around Quinn's neck. The Irishman's spine is bowed to the point of breaking around

Kelly's other knee. Sometime during this commotion Sands whistled and the white Bully Kutta went alert, but something makes Sands call him off. The dog stands with his forelegs braced three feet from Kelly and Quinn, his clipped ears back, his bunched muscles quivering, tongue panting in frustrated energy.

Then I see why.

Kelly's free hand is holding something small and black against Quinn's bulging neck. Thin and irregularly shaped, it looks like the ancient flint knives I used to see in my father's anthropology books. Where the point should be, I see only skin; then a trail of blood begins to make its way down the flesh of Quinn's neck. Sands is on his feet behind his desk, as ready as his dog to burst into action, but he can do nothing, short of ordering his dog to attack me.

"Pick up the gun, Penn," Kelly says in a steady voice.

I look down. Quinn's automatic is lying on the floor, two feet in front of me. It would be nothing to pick it up—if Sands's dog weren't here.

"You give that animal an attack order," says Kelly, "Quinn will be spurting blood like the *Texas Chainsaw Massacre,* and I'll gut the dog before he's dead. Pick up the gun, Penn. *Now.*"

I feel like I'm reaching into a cobra's basket, but I bend at the waist and pick up the gun. There's no question about who's in charge in this room.

"Don't point it at the dog," Kelly says calmly. "Point it at his master."

I turn to Sands, which brings the barrel of the pistol in line with his stomach.

"That's right," says Kelly, like a man giving instructions to toddlers. "That dog could take three or four rounds from a nine mil, but Mr. Sands will have a hard time surviving one."

Quinn suddenly jerks hard in Kelly's grip, but Kelly tightens his arm and leg, and I hear a sound like rope being stretched taut. Quinn groans, then screams in agony.

"How do you like being on the receiving end?" Kelly asks mildly. He drags the black blade farther along Quinn's neck, and blood begins to stream from the cut.

"You're a dead man," Sands says quietly.

Kelly laughs. "It takes one to know one.

Open the door, Penn. Nice and slow. Just put your foot in front of it. Anyone but Penn moves, I'll sever Quinn's carotid. Fair warning."

"He's bluffing," gasps Quinn, still struggling against the hold.

With a strained smile, Kelly tightens his calf muscle, and Quinn screams like a heretic on the rack.

"I never bluff," Kelly says. "You came after me with a gun. I kill you, it's self-defense all the way. Right, Mr. Prosecutor?"

"Absolutely. Any reasonable person would have been in fear for his life."

"Yeah, I almost shit myself from fear. Now, open the door."

I obey, but slowly, the dog watching me all the way.

"Okay," says Kelly, his voice strained from the effort of holding Quinn immobile, "just so we're all clear. First, I'm going to let this piece of shit go. Then Penn and I are going to walk off this tub. And you two, after licking your wounds, are going to realize that business is business. You crossed the line when you brought Penn's family into this, and I've pointed out your mistake. Now we're all going to go our separate ways."

"Are we?" says Sands. "I think we have some unfinished business. You killed two of my dogs last night. I had an investment in those animals."

"Consider it overhead. Now, I know what you're thinking. As soon as the door closes, Quinn will say, 'We've got to kill that bastard. I'm not spending the rest of my life looking over my shoulder for him.' But you don't have to do that, you see? For two reasons. First, because I'm a man of my word. We're backing off. And second, because it would be a waste of time. You'd never see me coming anyway."

Sands is smiling again, but the effect is more frightening than a scowl on a normal person. "Before you go, Mr. Kelly, let me tell you something about myself. I don't often do that, but you've earned it, so I'll make an exception. You ever hear of the Shankill Butchers?"

Kelly thinks for a few seconds. "Northern Ireland. They were a Prod bunch, right? Mass murderers. More gangsters than political."

"One of the bloodiest gangs as ever

stalked the streets of Belfast. Scum,
really. Grabbed Catholics at random off
the streets and tortured them. Cut them to
ribbons, beat them to death. When they
couldn't get Catholics, they took whatever
they found. I know, because I worked with
them now and again, on legitimate UDF
missions. For a while they were protected
by the Brits because they occasionally
topped an IRA man or two. But eventually, everyone on both sides knew something had to be done."

"My arm's getting tired," Kelly says.
"Can you cut to the chase?"

Sands smiles, then rubs the Bully
Kutta's head and speaks in a barely audible voice. "I killed their headman, Mr. Kelly.
When two armies of killers who couldn't
agree on a fucking thing for thirty years
decided one of their own needed killing,
they came to me. And I wasn't even
twenty. Oh, it's a famous murder. Never
solved."

"What's your point?"

"Let's don't be making threats that it's
in neither of our interests to back up.
We're both tough boys, but there's room

in the jungle for both of us. At least until
Mr. Hull and I conclude our business. We
have a cease-fire until then."

"That's exactly what we came to get."

"After that, we can renegotiate new
terms, if you like. I hear you may be looking for work soon." Sands gives me a
pointed look. "*You* go back to worrying
about city ordinances and garden clubs.
However, if you should come across that
data that Jessup copied, make sure it gets
to me. If you find out somebody else has
it, you do the same. No copies. No games.
Are we clear?"

"No problem," I say. "It's your property
anyway."

"Right." Sands doesn't move, but the
sense of dismissal is unmistakable. "I think
we're done here, gentlemen."

In a burst of motion almost as fast as
the one with which he restrained Quinn,
Kelly disengages from the Irishman and
bounds to his feet. Then he takes the gun
from me, and we back out of the office,
the dog watching us like a wolf cheated of
a kill.

"I'll leave the gun with your doorman,"

Kelly says. "Have a grand day altogether, gentlemen."

The doors hiss closed.

Outside, stepping off the far end of the gangplank, I finally take my first easy breath.

"I know that was tense," Kelly says, "but it was necessary. Especially if I'm leaving town for a few hours to get Annie back."

"Why did you provoke them like that?"

"Guys like that only understand one thing. Force. I wanted them to know who they're dealing with, and I wanted more information about Sands than we had before. I accomplished both things."

"You did that, all right. Sands shocked me when he asked about the USB drive. I've assumed they had that for a while now."

"I think Quinn has it," Kelly says. "But he's keeping it for himself. It's his ace in the hole if the Po sting goes bad. A chip in the game with Hull. That's one reason Quinn flipped out and attacked me. I was dead right about him getting positioned to stab his boss in the back."

"Do you think it's really safe to bring Annie back?"

"As long as we stick to the agreement. They have nothing to gain by antagonizing you further, and now they understand they have a lot to lose."

"What do you mean?"

"They know we'll bypass the law as easily as they will. That's something they needed to know."

I look into Kelly's eyes for a while but say nothing. When I start to shake his hand, he turns and starts walking toward the parking lot.

"What's the matter?"

"Quinn's bound to be watching us. We don't want anything that looks like a good-bye scene. We want them thinking I'm right around the corner, day and night."

"Sorry."

Kelly laughs softly as I catch up to him. "That felt good, didn't it?"

The last knot of tension is starting to uncoil in me. "I've got to say, seeing Quinn on the floor with the knife to his throat beat any courtroom moment I ever had. How did you get the knife in there?"

"Flint doesn't show up on the wands. No metal."

"Where was it hidden?"

"Lower back, in the little valley over my spine. I guess it's my version of Walt Garrity's derringer necklace. People miss it all the time."

"A flint knife," I marvel. "A caveman's weapon."

Kelly turns back and gives me a serious look. "Remember what I told Caitlin last night. We're still in the cave. It's just bigger now." He pats my shoulder. "Tonight you're going to eat dinner with your little girl. Let's get to the airport."

CHAPTER

37

Linda Church crouches naked and shivering in the corner of the kennel stall, praying for deliverance to a God she has almost given up on. There's a dog collar around her neck, and a heavy chain runs from the collar to a steel post anchored in cement. The kennel is a long, low building with a tin roof, hidden entirely beneath a tall shed so that it can't be seen from the air. The two rows of gated stalls are made of Cyclone fencing, with an office and a storeroom made of plywood at one end. There's a barred window in her room, but she doesn't dare try to break out of it. The kennel is surrounded by a high fence, and a half dozen ravenous pit bulls roam free between the outer wall and the fence.

That's why Quinn feels confident leaving her alone here. Even if she could somehow get the chain off, Linda couldn't leave the kennel. But the truth is, she hasn't the strength for any of that.

When someone is hurting you and you beg them to stop—and they don't stop—something breaks inside you. Linda learned that very young, and she's lived most of her life trying to escape that feeling, to heal what was broken inside her. Tim was the first man who ever really helped her with that, and Quinn killed him. He's already admitted that. The first time Quinn raped her in the kennel, he described Tim's last minutes on earth, the desperate attempt to make them think he had wrecked his car, his flight into the woods near the Devil's Punchbowl. But Tim hadn't counted on Sands's dog. The Bully Kutta had run him down in minutes and savaged him before the men could pull him off.

Linda shuts her eyes and tries not to think about last night, but it's impossible. On top of her infected leg and torn knee, she's getting a urinary-tract infection. The pain is almost unbearable when she pees, like a razor blade in her urethra, and she shivers for two or three minutes after she's finished. She stopped drinking water to keep from having to endure any more pain, but that seemed to make it worse. She can't understand why a man would want to have sex with a woman in the shape she's in, but Quinn does. Maybe the pain arouses him; maybe that's the whole point.

She's cried until she has no tears left. She believed with all her being that her escape from the boat had been divine providence, that she was really going to get clear as a reward for her bravery on the boat—which had in reality been a willingness to accept death, if necessary. To take that step and then be betrayed by the very servant of God, or one who put himself up as that . . . this had broken her. She feels valueless. Doomed. Like the altar boy must feel when he realizes that the priest who is using him doesn't love him, doesn't care for him at all, but sees him only as a means to an end.

Linda has never truly wished for death, despite enduring very hard times. She's known girls who committed suicide, but she could never believe that they hadn't had some better choice, if only they had looked hard enough. But here, in this place, she sees no hope of deliverance. Only more rape, more pain, and a terrible death in the end. Quinn has told her he means to feed her to the dogs when he tires of her, and she knows he will do it. He has hated her for being Sands's favorite, and thus unavailable to him. Quinn would sometimes come sniffing around the Devil's Punchbowl, but he couldn't risk it often because the cameras were always on, and Sands might see him from the security suite or the interrogation room. Still, she always felt Quinn's eyes creeping over her body whenever he was near. She'd turned to find him staring at her so many times that she'd come to think of his hungry gaze as she did the hairy black caterpillars she'd feared as a child, the ones that injected an anesthetic as they stung you. By the time you looked down and saw one of the revolting things on your leg, you knew it had been there for a long time, injecting its poison. And half an hour later the burning would begin.

Now Quinn is free to do with her what he will. Linda has never seen so much hatred and anger knotted up inside a man, but she knows she will bear the brunt of it until she can bear no more. So she prays hopelessly for she knows not what, while the wind rattles the fences and the dogs prowl the dirt beyond the plywood wall.

"Please, Lord, help me," she whimpers in the dead air of the kennel. "Please send me an angel. I'm too sick to help myself. I can't do no more."

CHAPTER

38

Caitlin has not come to Tim's funeral. This morning she called and told me that the way to honor Tim's life was not to grieve in a church, but to carry on his work. If we couldn't do that, she said, she couldn't bear to sit in the cathedral and dishonor his memory. When I asked what she intended to do instead, she said she was going down to the newspaper office to think about all that had happened and to try to make some decisions about her future. Her tone made it plain I was not to be a part of this process.

Skipping the funeral wasn't an option for me; I'm a pallbearer. Eight of us are sitting behind the Jessup family in the center pews of St. Mary's, a beautiful Gothic Revival cathedral built in 1843. Most pallbearers in Natchez are old men grown too frail to carry their dead friends, but today I'm seated among seven strapping boys I went to high school with—men now, of course—who have flown in from every corner of the country. Los Angeles, Chicago, Wisconsin, Oregon, Atlanta, D.C., other places. To my surprise and relief, not one man that Tim's father asked to perform this duty made an excuse not to show. More surprising, at least twenty-five people from our senior class are present, and most have traveled far to be here. Since we had only thirty-two students in our graduating class, this is a significant percentage. Earlier, we held a sort of unofficial reunion outside the cathedral, trading updates on kids, careers, class gossip. After we pallbearers received our instructions inside, a couple of my old friends asked some pointed questions about what had brought us all together. I told them only that Tim had lost his life while trying to help the city, and that he'd transformed that life before he died.

After the processional was complete, I was amazed to find St. Mary's filled nearly to capacity. I had worried that, like his wake, Tim's funeral would draw few mourners, but it seems that a decision has been taken by the congregation to support Tim and his family despite the poison being spread by Charlotte McQueen. These people understand that one of their children could easily have killed someone during a drunken drive to the county line during college, as Tim did, and only the grace of God spared them such a tragedy. The Catholics in Natchez have always seemed to me a great extended family, and they're proving it today.

Father Mullen made the right choice in the end: Tim is getting the full Catholic funeral mass. This, along with the presence of my friends and the large turnout, warmed my heart initially. But as the ritual proceeds, that warmth slowly dissipates in the vaulted vastness of the cathedral. Father Mullen, dressed in white vestments, begins a reading through coughs and throat clearings and the stifled cries of infants. He's chosen a passage from 2 Timothy, one that has more relevance than the name of the book.

"Remember the gospel that I carry, 'Jesus Christ risen from the dead, sprung from the race of David': it is on account of this that I have to put up with suffering, even to being chained like a criminal. But God's message cannot be chained up. So I persevere for the sake of those who are chosen, so that they, too, may obtain the salvation that is in Christ Jesus with eternal glory. Here is a saying that you can rely on: If we have died with him, then we shall live with him. If we persevere, then we shall reign with him. If we disown him, then he will disown us."

Perhaps my private testimonial to Tim's heroism moved Father Mullen to be brave. As the priest continues, my gaze drops from his face to the heads and shoulders of the family in front of me. Dr. and Mrs. Jessup are as shattered as any parents whose child precedes them in death. Julia sits beside them with the baby on her lap, bereft and bewildered. She has not made eye contact with me today, though we've stood only a few feet apart more than once. But now her son peeks over her shoulder and finds my eyes, his own filled with bemused innocence. I search for the father in the boy's face, but where I find Tim is twenty feet closer to the altar, in the gleaming bronze casket I will soon help carry to the cemetery where we met on the night before he was murdered.

That night, Tim told me not to blame myself if anything happened to him. But today the very silence of his closed coffin seems a screaming indictment of all my recent failures. Am I the only one who hears it? I probably look normal, even detached, to those assembled here. But inside, a storm of emotion is slowly gathering force. Here in this mystical atmosphere of candles and incense and holy water, other things Tim said that night come back with the accusatory weight of deathbed charges. I had promised the people so much, he reminded me. How could I consider walking away from a battle I'd scarcely even joined? The silent echo of his words makes me bow my head in shame, and with shame comes anger and resentment.

Stealing a covert glance at the disinterested faces behind me, I wonder how these people would react if I resigned as mayor. They know nothing of the actions of Jonathan Sands, or of the threat posed by the *Magnolia Queen.* My stepping down would send a short-lived wave of gossip through the city, and then someone else would take over the job. Life would go on as before. Many in these pews would be happy to see me go. Several among them fiercely resisted my early efforts to change the educational system in Natchez, as one would expect from a group that supports a strong Catholic school. And all pointed out the contradiction of my preaching a move to the public schools while supporting my alma mater, which is private.

Despite his bold reading, Father Mullen's homily is vague and aimed squarely at the faithful in the pews. He might have written it specifically not to offend Charlotte McQueen. As he speaks, I sense melancholy regret in the crowd, but not the dazed sorrow people usually feel at the funeral of a man in his forties. Most here today—certainly my peers— always expected Tim Jessup to die young, probably long before now. Except for the lingering questions about how he died, there's a sense of anticlimax about this ceremony. As people kneel and sit and stand as though controlled by a central computer, I feel a wild urge to stand, take the pulpit, and do what Dr. Jessup has probably given up hope that I will do—tell the truth about Tim's life and death.

But what would it accomplish? Would these people rise as one, march down Silver Street, and drag Sands and Quinn off the boat to face a rough justice? Would they burn the *Magnolia Queen* where she lies? Such things have happened in Natchez before. Games of chance and horse racing were always popular here, among both the aristocracy on the bluff and the riff-raff below. But in 1835, when the organized gamblers of Vicksburg fled to Natchez Under-the-Hill after several of their number were hanged, prominent Natchez attorney John Quitman led a group of citizens down Silver Street, rounded up the offenders, flogged them savagely, and drove them out of town. Such "clean outs" occurred regularly in the old days, and sometimes involved more than horsewhips. But no similar uprising would happen today. Such things are left to the police now. If the authorities don't pursue a case, people assume there's no real wrongdoing, at least none they need concern themselves about.

My frustration feels alien after the buoyant exaltation I experienced outside the cathedral, where my old classmates expressed endless admiration for my work as mayor. Seeing so many boyhood friends gathered together was a shock to my system—a different kind of shock than those I've endured for the past few days, but a shock nonetheless. For two years, I've received a steady stream of calls and e-mails expressing thanks and respect for my commitment to the town. All have written or spoken of how much they miss Natchez, and how badly they would like to return. I never doubted their sincerity, at least during their nostalgic moments. But the fact is, almost none *have* returned. Most can't, of course. They're successful, ambitious professionals who cannot earn

a living in a town without a thriving economy. They've established families elsewhere, most in the suburbs of large cities.
During holiday visits over the past two decades, they've noted that Natchez has
declined from the idyllic years they remember, and they've expressed a desire to
help save it. Yet this urge passes, and
few bother to send annual checks to St.
Stephen's Prep, much less to inquire what
they can do for the town. I can't condemn
them for that. Prior to moving back home,
I experienced the same sentimental feelings during my own rare visits, yet I didn't
move back to Natchez with the intention of
staying, but rather to give Annie and me a
safe haven to grieve over Sarah. I certainly
didn't come back to save the town.

And I have not saved it.

In fact, I have conspicuously failed to do
so. Since I was twelve years old, I've
known that the key to renewing this city is
leading the white population back to the
public schools, yet I have proved unequal
to the task. The reasons are complex and
deeply rooted in the history of the state,
but also of the nation as a whole. Sitting
with my old classmates, I see that more

clearly now. For despite living in suburbs in the north or west, most of their children do not attend public schools. Before the funeral I heard one mother complain (brag) about how long she'd had to camp out to get her youngest child admitted to kindergarten at the most exclusive private school in Portland, Oregon. The petrified truth is that throughout history the affluent have always sent their children to exclusive schools. What makes Natchez's problem seem special is that the poor and lower-middle-class populations are predominantly black. This results in a system that appears to be racist but which is actually segregated by economics—as are the schools in most other states. Racism may contribute to this economic reality, but that's a national problem. To imagine that I could solve in four years a problem that the best minds in government have been unable to solve in five decades was pure hubris—as Caitlin pointed out before I ran for office.

Father Mullen is preparing to conduct Communion. As ushers begin escorting the Catholics down the outer aisles, I ponder what my old schoolmates said outside the cathedral. The pipe organ fills the foot-shuffling silence, but when the cantor's voice joins in, I block out both and focus on my memory of the voices I heard on the cathedral steps. At last I recognize the unfamiliar timbre I heard there. It was the tone one uses when speaking to a martyr, or to a fool. Though they don't verbalize this feeling, the men and women I grew up with are amazed that I've been willing to pay the costs of returning home to try to change things. First among those is the education of my child—not because we have a racist school system, but because the first-class education I received at St. Stephen's is no longer to be had here at any price—*not even at St. Stephen's.* This realization steals my breath for a few moments, and to fully accept it is almost more than I can bear.

The only thing that could have prevented the present crisis was foresight during the boom years of my childhood. If community leaders had worked *then* to diversify the local economy away from oil production, and if white citizens had supported the public schools, Natchez would be a different city today. Political and economic opportunities were squandered that may never present themselves again. But short of a time machine, what I need to save this town is the people who have flown in for this funeral. Natchez needs the bright young citizens who benefited during her prime to return the favor. She needs their intelligence and energy, their desire to remake the city into the image of their dreams, a place where their children can experience the kind of childhood they enjoyed, but where those kids can also return and raise their own families if they choose to. But that is a pipe dream. The conversations I had a half hour ago told me that. Tomorrow, my old classmates will say good-bye to their aging parents and fly back to their own families. Other towns and cities will be the beneficiaries of their energy and intelligence; other schools will receive the fruits of their labor. They will always speak wistfully of Natchez, and many may retire here after their children leave for college, but with a few exceptions, that's it. The same is true of most young black people who leave Natchez after high school.

So, I wonder, with a wretched emptiness

that borders on despair, *what the hell am I doing here?*

What does it mean to "save" a town anyway? American towns have been growing and withering since the 1600s. The idea that a city that has survived for almost three hundred years needs me to save it is more than a little egotistical. Natchez will always be here in one form or another. It stands on high ground, well watered and fertile, with a mild climate hospitable to crops. Even in 1927, when the Mississippi swelled to a terrifying seventy miles *wide* at Natchez, the city stood high and dry above the closest thing to Armageddon the Mississippi valley has ever known. In my messianic zeal to resurrect what I saw as the best part of the city's past, I simply lost sight of the fact that no matter what I do, Penn Cage will be but a footnote in the long history of this once great river town.

As the Communion service proceeds, and Father Mullen drones about the body and blood of Christ, my thoughts turn to my own family. For the past two years, I've tried not to think about what my political crusade has cost, but the price has been high. I lost Caitlin at the outset, because she didn't share my vision. I deprived Annie of the culturally rich experience she might have had in a larger city. I put my writing career on hold, giving up an absurdly large amount of money in exchange for a public servant's salary. And for this I got the privilege of beating my head against a wall of stubborn provincialism and hidebound tradition for two dispiriting years. Ironically, my actions have actually exacerbated some problems. The magic I worked on Mrs. Pierce opened the gates to the *Magnolia Queen* and all its depredations. Tim Jessup lies dead twenty feet away from me, and despite my national reputation as a prosecutor, I've been unable to bring his killer to justice.

Pathetic. That's my verdict on the Penn Cage administration.

While I waited for Tim in the cemetery that first night, I reflected that I'd rarely failed at anything, and that I'd never quit. True Southerners, I was always taught, surrender only when the means to fight no longer exist. But the Southern mythos of noble defeat gives me no comfort today.

Am I to sacrifice the education of my child in a vain quest to "save" something that is merely changing, as all things do?

"Penn?" whispers Sam Jacobs, nudging me in the side. "It's time to do our thing."

The Communion service has ended. Father Mullen is walking around Tim's casket, sprinkling holy water. Rising like a sleepwalker, I take my place beside the casket and help roll it down the long aisle to the cathedral doors.

I recognize almost every face in the pews. As I pass, dozens of eyes seek mine with a beseeching look. What are they asking? How did Tim die? Why did he die? Or do they have deeper questions? In their puzzled faces, I sense a longing to know why the feeling of unity they experience on occasions like this cannot be sustained throughout the year, as it once was in this town. But the answer is sitting among them. A town that cannot sustain its children through adulthood cannot survive, except as a shadow of itself.

When the ushers open the cathedral

doors, the sunlight blinds me for several seconds. Luckily, my pupils adapt by the time we reach the head of the broad steps, where we lift the heavy casket from the gurney and carry Tim down the ten steps that have brought older pallbearers to grief. Without quite admitting it to myself, I had hoped to find Caitlin waiting outside, but one scan of the intersecting streets tells me she's not here. As we slide the casket along the rollers inside the waiting hearse, Sam Jacobs, a Jew, pats the side of the coffin and says, "See you at the cemetery, Timmy." In that moment I recall two thoughts I had the last time I saw Tim alive, which was at the cemetery, on Jewish Hill.

One is the lesson my father learned in Korea: *Heroism is sacrifice.* The second is that most of the heroes I know are dead. Tim was one of those heroes. He chose a martyr's death as surely as some deluded saint from the Middle Ages. Looking down Union Street, lined with the rental cars of everyone but Caitlin Masters, the selfish voice that I usually suppress speaks loud and clear in my mind:

Are you going to live a martyr's life? Will you sacrifice your daughter's education and the second love of your life to fight a battle you no longer believe is winnable?

"Penn?" says a man's voice. "Are you okay?"

Turning away from the hearse, I find Paul Labry standing beside me. Paul is Catholic, but he did not attend St. Stephen's with Tim and me, and so was not asked to be a pallbearer. Despite this, he's stayed close to me today, knowing that I'm working under great strain, even if he doesn't fully understand the reasons for it.

"I'm fine, Paul. Thanks for asking."

"Are you riding with Drew and the other guys?"

Looking past Labry, I see Drew Elliott beckoning me to a black BMW a few cars behind the hearse. "I guess so. You're going to the burial, right?"

"Of course. Unless you need me to do something else."

"No, I want you to come. I want to speak to you afterward."

Paul's face takes on a worried cast, but he knows this isn't the place to ask for details. The congregation is spilling down the steps now, and car engines are starting all along Union and Main. "Is anything wrong?" he asks softly.

"No, no. I just want to ask you something. Something I should have asked you two years ago."

Intrigued, Labry takes my elbow and starts leading me away from the crowd, but I pull free and quietly assure him that nothing is wrong. "I'm just upset by Tim's death," I tell him. "We'll talk after the burial, okay?"

"Sure. I'll see you at the cemetery."

While Paul heads up Main Street, presumably to get his car, I tread slowly toward Drew Elliot's BMW like a man crossing the last mile of a desert. The flicker of an impulse to search for Caitlin's face among those on the sidewalk goes through my mind, but I don't raise my head. She's not here. She made that decision this morning. Squinting against the glare coming off the concrete, I suddenly realize that I know the answer to my silent questions. Some people have chosen to see me as a hero in the past. I traded on that reputation to gain the mayor's office.

But I'm no hero, not by my father's measure. I'm certainly no martyr. My work here is not finished, not by a long shot. But I am. This time, when my old friends leave Natchez to return to their families, I will follow them with mine. This time I choose the future, not the past.

My crusade is over.

CHAPTER

39

Caitlin crosses the Mississippi River Bridge with her heart pounding. She is sure she has found the girl who passed Linda Church's note to Penn at the Ramada, and she did it with two phone calls. The trick was figuring out whom to call. Caitlin had only caught a glimpse of the girl at the hotel, and mostly walking away, at that. But she'd seen enough. The giveaway was the hair. At first glance the girl's hair had looked short, but as she walked away, Caitlin had seen the telltale mane hanging out from the tail of the jacket. Caitlin hardly ever saw waist-length hair anymore, and when she did, it usually meant one thing—in the Deep South, anyway. The other thing was the girl's eye makeup. Not only had she worn twice as much as she needed, but it looked as though it had been applied by an eight-year-old trying to imitate her teenage sister. These two things together told Caitlin that the girl was wearing her idea of a disguise. And what she was disguising was her religion.

Caitlin had been fascinated when Penn told her that Mississippi had the highest per capita number of churches and also the lowest literacy rate. Three years ago, she had used these statistics as the launching point of a story on charismatic religions. People speaking in tongues, faith healing. For her, the most disturbing thing about doing the story had been her contact with the younger girls in the churches. She could see that they aspired to be like other teenage girls, but they had been raised in families with nineteenth-century values, or certainly pre-Eisenhower-era twentieth-century values. Her portrayal of these churches as patriarchal and sexist had upset a lot of their members and got some girls in trouble with their pastors, but it had also opened a lot of eyes to a closed society.

A couple of the women she'd spoken to had remained kind to her, and so the moment Caitlin suspected that the girl who delivered the note might be Pentecostal, she had checked her files at the Examiner *and made some phone calls. Using what she'd gleaned from Penn's description, she said she was looking for a tall girl who had probably lost a lot of weight in the past year or two, and who might have a job in Vidalia. That was all it had taken to get the two pieces of information she needed: a name and a location. Darla McRaney, the Bargain Barn on Highway 15.*

At first Caitlin had been tempted to tell Penn what she'd discovered. But then she'd realized it would only prove to him that his jab about her penchant for following a story was on target. If this trip led any closer to Linda Church, Caitlin had promised herself, she'd tell Penn immediately.

The Bargain Barn is a long, low-slung building just off the highway, that looks as if it might once have been a brand-name store. During all the time Caitlin lived in Natchez, she'd only been inside it once, but her memory is clear. The store sells everything from clothing to housewares, medicine to ant poison, all of it cheap both in quality and price.

Only a few cars are in the lot. Caitlin parks between two of them, then locks her car and walks through the glass door. An elderly man wearing an orange vest greets her with a puzzled smile, and she walks past him into the clothing section.

"Can I help you?" asks a middle-aged woman sorting dresses on a circular rack.

"I'm looking for Darla McRaney."

"Darla mostly stays over in housewares."

Caitlin quickly navigates the empty aisles until she reaches an area filled with thin metal pots and imitation Tupperware. In the next aisle, above a rack of blenders, she sees Darla McRaney's head. She knows it's Darla because a girl would have to be almost six feet tall to be seen above the blenders.

Making a U around the end of the aisle, Caitlin approaches Darla cautiously, like a naturalist trying not to spook a timid animal. In spite of this, Darla looks up sharply and takes a step back, blushing scarlet.

"I didn't see you," she says. "Can I help you?"

"Darla, my name is Caitlin. I'm a very good friend of Penn Cage."

The girl stares back for several moments, neither breathing nor blinking. Then she starts to back away.

"Wait," Caitlin says. "Please, wait. I know you gave Penn that note at the Ramada Inn. I know you tried to disguise yourself, but he recognized you. He thought you worked at a restaurant, but I found you anyway."

"I used to work at a restaurant," the girl says in a dazed voice. "Franky's Pizza. I liked it there, but I kept putting on weight. I had to quit."

Caitlin nods with empathy.

"But I don't know nothing about no

note," Darla says, twice as loudly as she'd spoken before.

Caitlin can't help but smile at this obvious lie.

"But you knew exactly what I was referring to when I mentioned the Ramada and Penn Cage."

Darla licks her lips, then looks around as though suspicious someone is watching her.

"I was at the Ramada," she says. "So were a lot of people. And I did see the mayor there. But I don't know nothin' 'bout no note. I haven't passed notes to men since grade school."

Caitlin takes a step forward and speaks with sisterly intimacy. "I'm trying to help Linda Church. She's in terrible danger, more even than she knows. I know you've been trying to help her, you and your friends. But she needs more help than that."

Fear glitters in Darla's eyes. "I told you, I don't know nothin' 'bout any a that. I gotta get back to work. I got customers."

"I don't see any customers," Caitlin says gently. "But I'll be glad to buy something if you'll tell me just a little bit of the truth."

"I did," Darla insists.

"Have you seen Linda yourself? The reason I'm asking you is because of your eye makeup. I saw you didn't know how to put it on, and I figured that if Linda was with you, she would have fixed it for you."

Darla looks on the verge of tears. Her neck is splotchy, and her breath is going shallow. "I can't talk anymore. Please, go away. Leave me alone."

Caitlin reaches into her purse and hands Darla a card with her cell number on it. "I want the same thing you do, Darla. I want Linda to be safe. Please call me later. Think about all this. You'll know it's the right thing to do."

Darla accepts the card with a shaking hand, then turns and hurries down the aisle toward a collection of Chinese lawn mowers.

Caitlin knows the girl is lying, but sometimes you have to stop pushing and let the source make her own decision. With a girl as skittish as Darla McRaney, it shouldn't take long.

CHAPTER

40

Car doors close with a disturbing finality in cemeteries. Tim lies under the earth now, a few flowers on top of his coffin, dropped in by family and friends. He wasn't buried on Catholic Hill, but he does lie within sight of it. This wasn't a punishment, but a matter of limited space. Green Astroturf carpet conceals the mound of dirt that the backhoe will use to fill in the grave. The familiar green canopy of McDonough's funeral home keeps the sun off the few people who remain: Dr. Jessup and his wife, some relations from California, Julia and the baby.

A second knot of people stands several yards away, mostly pallbearers, myself among them. These men I knew as boys flew so far to do their somber duty, and though most of us haven't seen each other much in the past twenty-five years, we're as comfortable as brothers who live on separate coasts. Paul Labry stands with us, waiting, as I asked him to do at the cathedral.

After a couple of quiet jokes, well-concealed smiles, and well-meant but empty promises to stay in touch, the guys head for their rented cars. After the short line of vehicles disappears up the lane, I turn to Paul, but find myself facing Julia Jessup. She's left Tim junior with his grandmother. Her eyes are bloodshot, the skin around them raw and swollen.

Labry takes a step back out of courtesy, but one hard glance from Julia sends him back another twenty feet.

"I know I look bad," she says in a cracked voice. "I'm not getting much sleep. Tim used to help me with the baby. A lot more than most men do, I think. And Tim junior's not sleeping well at all now."

"I'm sorry, Julia."

"Are you?" Her hollow eyes probe mine. "I came over here because I want you to know something. I didn't want Tim doing what he did. The thing that got him killed. But he did it anyway. I think you should know that he did it for his father, and for you."

A wave of heat goes through my face. "Me?"

She nods with conviction. "Tim really had you up on a pedestal. A lot of people do, I think. He never forgot how close you were when you were young, and when you stopped being friends, he blamed himself. He thought he'd let you down somehow. You went on to be a big success, and he wound up dealing cards on a casino boat. I told him that was honest work and nothing to be ashamed of, but it didn't help. He was ashamed. And after he found out whatever was really going on with that boat, it just ate at him until he had to do something."

"I'm truly sorry, Julia. Tim was a good man, and I wish he hadn't gotten involved with any of that. I wish I hadn't let him."

"I just want to know if it did any good," she says. "Because my son is going to have to live the rest of his life without a father. Was it worth it, Penn? Did Tim accomplish one goddamned thing by dying?"

While I try to find a suitable answer, Julia says, "What about *you*? Have you done what you promised you would do?"

As I try to recall exactly what I promised Tim that night, his widow turns and walks back to his grave without waiting for an answer.

"What was that about?" Labry asks, coming up behind me.

"Did you hear any of it?"

He shakes his head. "She made it pretty clear that was a private conversation."

I take deep breath and blow out a long rush of air, trying to flush the guilt from my system. "Let's go over there, away from the family."

We walk a little way up the lane, then climb some steps to a hill shaded by cedar trees. Like most of the names in this cemetery, the one engraved on the stones in this plot is familiar to me. A cool but gentle breeze blows over the hill, and the sun shines bright enough to warm the bricks of the wall around the plot. Leaning back against the wall, I regard Paul Labry.

Where most of the Catholics in Natchez are Irish or Italian, Paul is of French descent. By marriage, he's related to the Acadians forced by the Spanish to live near what would become the infamous Morville Plantation. Labry has dark eyes and skin and he's still handsome despite losing some hair and putting on weight. He looks more like an aging poet than the manager of an office-supply business, but I never cease to be amazed by how poorly some people fit the stereotype of their occupation.

"Paul, I want to tell you something that I haven't told anyone else."

"I thought you wanted to ask me something."

"That too. I've decided to step down as mayor."

"*What?*" He looks me from head to toe. "You're not sick, are you?"

Tim asked me the same thing the night we met here. "No, it's not that. My reasons are personal, mostly to do with Annie and Caitlin."

Paul's watching me like a man who still

can't believe what he's hearing. "Are you guys getting back together? You and Caitlin?"

"If she'll have me."

"Are you kidding? You know she loves you."

"Not enough to live here with me."

He purses his lips while he mulls this over. "Is that it, then? You want to stay in Natchez, but you feel you can't?"

"No. It's time for me to go. The reason I'm talking to you is that I want you to stand for mayor in the special election after I'm gone."

Labry draws back, his face pale. "Are you serious?"

"It should have been you two years ago. I should never have run."

"Oh, that's bullshit."

"No, it's not. You're the man for the job, Paul. I think you should announce on the same day I resign, and I'll throw you my full support."

Labry turns away, looking thoughtfully toward the tent over Tim's grave. "I used to think I might try it," he says. "But I'm forty-four now, and I'm starting to think I don't understand the world anymore. My father's business is going down, Penn. Wal-Mart and the rest have about killed it. I've tried to save it, but the hole just keeps getting deeper." His cheeks redden in embarrassment. "All the old retail places are going down. Hell, we don't have more than a handful of Jewish families left in town, and they were the backbone of the retail economy when we were growing up."

I hoped I wouldn't have to play the next card, but Paul's not giving me any choice. "I'm sorry to hear that. Because if you don't run, you know who's going to get the job."

Paul blanches again. "Shad Johnson?"

"Yep."

"Christ."

"Who knows? Maybe that wouldn't be such a bad thing."

"Bullshit." Paul lowers his voice. "I was talking to Father Nightingale, from out at Mandamus Baptist? He speaks for a lot of the black community. He doesn't even like Shad being district attorney. Said you can't trust him as far as you'd throw him. I'm not sure the blacks would even turn out for him."

"They will if you're not in the race. But if

you're in it, they'll vote for you. They know where your heart is."

Labry looks away for a while, then turns back to me. "Penn, if you can't accomplish the things we dreamed about, what chance do I have?"

"That's the wrong way to look at it. I aimed too high. I wanted to solve the education problem because that's where salvation lies, but I couldn't do it. I used to blame the whites for that, but there's blame on both sides."

He nods dejectedly. "You know what I think the real obstacle is?"

"Does it even matter? The existing public facilities couldn't absorb the kids from the private schools even if their parents decided to send them."

"Oh, hell, that's just a matter of money. If we really brought all those kids into one system, what you'd have is a bunch of white kids who couldn't make the athletic teams and a bunch of black kids who couldn't make their grades. You talk about something nobody wants? *That's* it."

There's truth in what Labry says, but he knows the reasons run deeper. "Paul, if I was going to live up to my principles, I would have moved Annie to the public school on the day I was elected. But I didn't. I was unwilling to risk my child's education, and maybe her safety, unless there were a dozen other white kids in there with her. It's time for someone with more conviction and a different list of priorities to give it a shot. And that's you."

Labry's blushing now. "You know, I think when we lost the Toyota plant, we lost the mandate you had after the election. We'll eventually get there on education. But people's first concern is high-paying jobs."

"You'll never get the latter without the former. But there are lots of other things to be done. Annexation of county land. Pushing through the eco-preserve on the creek. Keeping the selectmen from covering the bluff with RV parks. Schmoozing people like Hans Necker. You're twice as good as I am at that stuff. Be honest, Paul. Don't you want the job?"

Labry looks down and twists the toe of his shoe into the grass. "From what I've seen these past years, being mayor's about dealing with a bunch of people who all think they're something special."

"Well, aren't they? If anyone still believes that, I figured it was you."

"Sure they are. But no more special than anybody else. We get in trouble when we start thinking we're better than our neighbor. Or that somebody else is better than the rest of us. But that's what people always do."

"Is that how you see me? As a guy who thinks he's better than other people?"

Paul laughs softly. "That's the funny thing. You *are* better, in a lot of ways. Oh, I'm sure you've got your secrets; everybody does. But knowing you like I do, knowing all you've accomplished in your past, and then seeing you fail in your own eyes . . ."

"I'm not a politician, Paul. That's why I never ran for DA in Houston. I was a lawyer at heart. Now I'm a novelist, and I think that spoiled me. When you write a book, you have total control of the universe and everyone in it. When you're mayor of a town, you're lucky if you can control yourself, much less anyone else."

Labry steps onto a low concrete wall and sweeps his hand to take in the whole of the cemetery. "Look out there. Jewish Hill, Catholic Hill, Protestants between. Colored Ground. Babyland, where the unwed mothers' babies went if they died. We try so hard to stay separate from each other that we even do it in death. It's tribal, man, and it's not just the South." Paul turns and points toward the rear of the cemetery. "But the truth is over there behind Catholic Hill, in those thick woods. Paupers' Field. There's three thousand bodies back there, just dropped in holes in the ground. In the dark under those trees, there's no separation. The roots are growing down through all of them, just alike."

"I'm not sure I see where you're going. But it doesn't sound like you're too interested in being mayor."

"We're all equal before God," Labry says. "That's what I'm saying. But nobody walking this planet seems to get that. Everybody sins, Penn. *Everybody.* That's the great leveler. Not death. *Sin.*"

"I was hoping for a more definitive answer."

Labry gazes into the forest for a while. Then without warning he springs off the wall and looks up at me with a grin. "Hell, yes, I'll do it. I'll be the damnedest mayor this town ever had!"

I look back in amazement for a few moments, then we both burst out laughing.

CHAPTER

41

Caitlin hunches low behind the wheel of her car and takes a sip from a can of diet Dr Pepper. She's parked between two trucks in the lot of the Bargain Barn on Highway 15. She knows Darla was lying. The girl was so flustered that she's bound to panic and leave the store at her first opportunity. Forty minutes have passed since Caitlin left the store, but her cell phone has not rung. Despite Caitlin's promises of confidentiality, Darla was too rattled for that. But Caitlin has dealt with enough sources to recognize the signs of panic. This is a lot like fishing, or what she remembers her father trying to teach her of it during the summers she stayed with him. Only out here there's nowhere to pee.

Using her cell phone, she's trying to Google some more recent information on local Pentecostals when Darla McRaney hurries through the door of the Bargain Barn, looks right and left, then runs to an ancient Pacer hatchback parked in the corner of the lot. Once she's inside, Caitlin starts her own car but stays low behind the wheel until the Pacer reaches the highway turn.

Darla crosses the westbound lanes, then turns east toward Vidalia and Natchez. Caitlin follows, but since there aren't many traffic lights on this road, she leaves ten or twelve car lengths between them.

Less than a mile down the highway, the Pacer turns into a used-car dealership. It's a small operation with older-model cars and pickup trucks parked on a vacant lot with the grass worn down to mud in many places. Garish signs scream EASY TERMS! and NO MONEY DOWN! while the banner over the gate reads NO CREDIT, NO PROBLEM!

Caitlin pulls onto the shoulder fifty yards from the entrance, then gets out and walks into the parking lot of the adjacent business, a small engine-repair shop. Its parking lot is crowded, making a covert approach to the car lot easy.

Ten yards from the border between the lots, she sees Darla gesturing vehemently at a silver-haired, red-faced man. They're standing between a van and a large SUV, apparently to shield their conversation from anyone in the trailer that serves as the dealership's office, but Caitlin has a good view of them both. She creeps along the side of a trailer until she hears Darla call the man Pastor Simpson. That's got to be right, *Caitlin thinks, because now she remembers Simpson from the story she did on charismatic religions.*

Having heard enough to be sure of what she's seeing, Caitlin steps out of cover and walks right up to the pair. "Pastor Simpson?" she says. "I'd like to speak to you for a minute."

Simpson looks up sharply, as though prepared to respond angrily, but then he mistakes Caitlin for a customer.

"Ma'am, I'm busy just now, but if you'll wait a minute, I'll be right with you."

"I'm not here about a car."

"That's her," Darla says anxiously. *"The newspaper lady."*

"Aw, hell," Simpson says. "What do you want with me?"

"I'm here about Linda Church."

"I don't know who you're talking about. I never heard a nobody by that name."

Caitlin sighs wearily. "I find that hard to believe, since the first person Darla ran to after I questioned her about Linda was you."

"Well, you flustered this poor girl. I'm her pastor. She's afraid you're going to put her in the newspaper or somethin'."

Caitlin holds up both hands in a placating gesture. "I'm not here to put anybody in the newspaper."

"That's a bald-faced lie," says Simpson with conviction. "That's what you live for, to see your name in the paper. I remember the story you did on our church, don't think I don't. You twisted the truth ever which way to make us look like fools. I got nothin' to say to you."

Caitlin steps closer and speaks with all the sincerity she can muster. "Sir, my only concern is the safety of Linda Church. She's a material witness to a major crime, and I believe her life is in danger."

"Well, what's that got to do with us?"

"I believe you helped Linda. I think you got Darla to carry a note from Linda to Penn Cage."

"What makes you think that?"

"The mayor and I are very close friends."

Simpson snorts. "Livin' in sin is what you mean, ain't it?"

"Mr. Simpson, I believe you acted as a Good Samaritan to Linda, just as your faith teaches, but I'm not sure you understand how dangerous the people who are looking for her are. If you really want to help Linda, you'll tell me how to find her. I'll make sure she receives around-the-clock protection."

Simpson stares at Caitlin for a long time, as though about to come clean. Then he says, "It's hard to stay protected when you're on the front page of a newspaper. I tell you what, missy. If Linda Church had asked me for help—and I'm not saying she did—I woulda got her straight outta town where no slimy sons-of-bitches could hurt her. Okay? Now, that's all you're gonna get from me without the sheriff."

Caitlin turns to Darla, but before she can speak, Simpson interposes himself between them. "You leave this girl here alone too, or I'll have some law on you. We don't take kindly to harassment on this side of the river, especially by the likes of you. Now, get off my lot."

Caitlin tries to step around Simpson to address Darla directly, but he steps in front of her and shoves her backward.

"That's assault," Caitlin says quietly.

"You don't get your ass off my property," Simpson snarls, his eyes blazing, "I'll show you some battery too. Git!"

Caitlin holds her ground for a face-saving moment, then turns and walks back to her car.

Walt Garrity blinks in surprise as he's ushered into Jonathan Sands's office. He expected the antebellum decor to be uniform throughout the boat, but this room could be the office of a European investment banker. The play that brought him here is simple: He's told the pit boss that he needs to speak to the manager about a special group event, one the standard event planner won't be able to okay without the manager's approval, and since that's the case, he'd rather talk directly to the man with the power to answer his questions.

Sands looks bigger than he did walking the casino floor. He has an imposing density that Walt has seen in natural fighters, and he has a fighter's eyes as well, always probing for vulnerability. Yet when he rises from his desk, the watchfulness recedes, and he offers his hand with a smile. Walt takes it, gauging the power in it. It's the hand of a laborer or an infantry soldier.

"Hello, Mr. Gilchrist," Sands says in a cultured English accent. "It's good to have a real gambler aboard."

"Aw, you must see my type all the time."

"You'd be surprised. The average player on a Mississippi boat loses about fifty dollars. Our average is higher, because we have a higher percentage of table games, and we draw the affluent clientele that does exist. But still. It's good to have a real player aboard."

"Winning, losing, hell, it's all the same after a while. It's the risk that keeps you going. Just like the oil business. I hate a duster, but, goddamn, it just makes it all the sweeter when you hit that pay sand on the next one. You know?"

"A man after my own heart," Sands says. "A man who can live out Kipling's famous advice about victory and defeat—to treat those two impostors as the same."

Walt laughs. "You Brits sure have a way with words. I'll bet the ladies just fall over and beg for it when they hear that accent, don't they?"

Sands smiles and takes his seat. "What business are you in?"

"Oil."

"Not too much of it left around here, is there?"

"More than you'd think. And with the price through the roof, the numbers on old wells look a lot better than they used to. Course, you're right. In the fifties and sixties, they found some fifty-million-barrel fields over here. Most of them are still producing. But I'm rambling. Times have changed, that's for sure."

"You mentioned a group event in the future."

"Right. But it's not your standard-type junket."

Sands smiles expansively. "I always have time for a man with an interesting proposition."

"I'm the same way myself. You never know what'll come your way if you keep your ears open."

"What sort of event do you have in mind?"

Walt hesitates as he once did when asking a pharmacist for a condom, but inside he's feeling a too-long-absent thrill. He loves nothing more than facing his mark and winging it, which is what he's always done best. If you look a criminal in the eye and come right at him—tempt him toward a crime as though it's your idea—he frequently forgets to doubt you. Of course that can get into entrapment issues, these days. But in the heyday of the Rangers, there'd been a lot of latitude when it came to that kind of thing, and not much concern about procedure. Case notes tended to be spare, running a line or two every couple of days. "Drove from Austin to Dallas. Located suspect in barn. Killed him at dawn. Returned to Austin" was one Walt remembered fondly. Times have changed of course, but this meeting has some of the flavor of the old days.

"Mr. Sands," he says, "when you get to my age, like me and my friends, there's not much you haven't seen. It tends to take a lot to get the old ticker racing."

A sympathetic smile from Sands. "All pleasures grow stale, don't they?"

"Indeed. But in about a month, I'm bringing over a bunch of boys for a visit. We've been looking for a place to blow off some steam without the wives, and we got to talking about Natchez. We used to come over here for a golf tournament they had every year, the local oilmen. Man, after that thing was over, we'd go back to the hotel, and they'd have the girls waiting. There were lines out the doors of some rooms, and local guys charging admission just to watch."

"That's the kind of action you're looking for?"

"Some of that would be appreciated. With enough to go around, of course."

"Oh, that's never a problem here."

"Not just girls, though. I'm talking about the gambling too."

"Well, you've seen the boat."

"And a fine one she is too, as far as she goes."

Sands cocks one eyebrow. "Meaning?"

"Legal gambling's all right, in its place. But it's kind of . . . restrictive, if you get my meaning. It's like sex in a medical clinic with all the lights on. Takes the zing out of it. Half the fun's the sneaking around, the mystery of it. That's what gets the blood pumping—the forbidden. You with me?"

"Oh, yes."

When I was a boy, before I went into the army, I used to work in a gambling joint down in Galveston. Illegal, of course, like all the best places. Man, there was nothing *they didn't have. I'm talking sport, now. Bare-knuckles boxing, strictly for interested parties. Cockfighting. Shooting contests. That's the kind of action I'm talking about."*

Sands mulls this over, watching Walt with unblinking eyes. "I see. You ever put money on dogs?"

"Dog racing?"

"Dog fighting," says Sands, his eyes as insinuating as those of a pimp offering a young boy to a tourist.

"Oh, I get you. Twenty, twenty-five years ago we had a good bit of that in my neck of the woods, but the governor got a bug up his ass and the state troopers started cracking down. The Rangers too. I saw old Red fight in Taos. She was bred out of Arkansas Blackie. Hell of a leg dog. Went for the foreleg every time, but she could really break 'em down. A real champion. That was years ago, though. I've heard they do a lot of hogs-and-dogs-type stuff out at the hunting camps, and I've seen a little of that. But straight fighting? Pit fighting? Not in a while."

"Well, we have a variety of activities available to players accustomed to more intense games. I'll give it a think and see what I come up with. As for ladies, do you have any preference?"

"I gotta tell you, I like those oriental girls. You seem to have a surplus too."

Sands's eyes flicker with light.

"When I first got to town, I was thinking about a colored girl, but these young ladies you got remind me of some I spent time with in Korea."

"Recently?"

"Hell, no. I'm talking 1952–53."

For the first time, Sands looks truly interested. "You fought there?"

"All along that godforsaken thirty-eighth parallel, with those hookers' granddaddies launching human-wave attacks every night. Only one out of two of those bastards even had a rifle in his hands when they started, but soon as one man would fall, the unarmed fella would pick up his gun and keep a'comin'."

"A very effective tactic," Sands says, "if you can find personnel fanatical enough to carry it out."

Walt laughs. "That's your basic Chink soldier right there. Fanatical. I'll bet you couldn't find a hundred Americans on the East Coast who would do that."

"Quite right. If one American dies in Iraq, it's national news."

"You look like a man who's spent some time in uniform."

Sands shrugs. "When I was young and stupid, I confess. But the real fighting isn't always done in uniform."

"I imagine you're right, there. Anyway, it goes without saying that anybody who can help us out with extracurricular activities would be handsomely compensated."

Sands dismisses this with a flick of his hand. "I have no worries on that score, Mr. Gilchrist."

"J.B., please."

"You know, of course, that the type of action we're discussing is illegal, both in Mississippi and Louisiana."

"Ain't just about everything worth doing illegal? That's the way this country works. Pure hypocrisy, from Plymouth Rock on down."

Sands sniffs and leans forward,

subtly signaling that the meeting is over. "Which hotel are you staying at?"

"The Eola."

"If you'll call ahead on your next trip, we'll comp you a suite at our hotel."

"I appreciate it, but I've got a soft spot for those grand old dames. The downtowns may be dying, but the great hotels soldier on, in the good towns anyway. Course, I don't mind putting the boys up in your hotel. We'll make that part of the deal if it makes things easier."

"It does simplify issues like transport."

"It's a deal, then."

Walt gets up, not wanting to press, but Sands comes around his desk and says, "Are you interested in any special action during this visit? A test-drive, say?"

"A girl, you mean? Or the blood sport?"

"You seem quite able to manage the ladies on your own. I was thinking of sport."

"Well, I wouldn't be against it. I got three, four more days here. I was planning on getting to know one of those little China girls better. But I'm open to anything. You get something good going, I'm in."

Sands shakes Walt's hand and leads him to the door with a smile. "I'm sure we can accommodate you."

Walt has shaken a lot of hands in his life, and he knows the feel of great strength under restraint. The manager of the Magnolia Queen *could tear a deck of cards in half.*

CHAPTER

43

Kelly and Major McDavitt flew Annie and my mother back from Houston this afternoon, arriving at my house just after seven. My mother insisted on cooking for us. We tried to make Kelly eat, but he privately told me that he wanted to go down to the *Magnolia Queen* and make sure that Sands appeared to be keeping his part of the deal. "I like to know where my enemies are" was how he put it. Kelly expressed visible relief when Dad informed him that Sands's guard dog had tested negative for rabies, and laughed that he might have to celebrate.

Living in the Texas safe house for a few days had been surprisingly comfortable, my mother claimed. The simple fact of separation had proved to be the ordeal. Though Mom sensed that the crisis that had necessitated their fleeing was not fully resolved, we assured Annie that the bad guys were all taken care of. When she asked why James Ervin and his brother were standing guard on the front porch and in the backyard, I told her that we just needed to play it safe for a couple of days.

"In case the bad guys' friends are mad, right?" she said.

"Sort of," I admitted.

My parents left a half hour ago, with James Ervin driving. His brother Elvin stayed behind to await Kelly's return. Annie took a quick bath, then climbed into bed and called for me to tuck her in.

It's obvious that being home has given her a great sense of relief, no matter how hard she pretends that living on the run was no big deal.

"The second house was scarier," she says, looking up at me from the covers as I sit on the edge of the bed.

"Why?"

"The first one was a condo, really. Like a vacation. But then Mr. Kelly called, and Mr. Jim said we had to move. The place he took us to then wasn't near as nice. I think it belonged to a lady he knew. The house was okay, but I could tell that Mr. Jim and his friends were worried. At the first house I never saw their guns, but at the second one, they had them out all the time."

"I'm sorry you had to go through that, baby. But it's over now."

"How was Mr. Tim's funeral? Was it sad?"

"It was. All funerals are sad, but when the dead person is young, it's harder."

Confusion clouds Annie's eyes. "Mr. Tim wasn't young."

I smile. "I guess I'm not either, then. He was the same age I am."

"Well, you're not *old*," she says, obviously a little embarrassed. "But you're not young either. I guess what I mean is, Mr. Tim seemed a lot older than you."

"That's because he didn't take care of himself when he was young. He had some bad luck, and he"—I hesitate—"he turned to drugs to try to deal with it."

"You don't have to tell me not to do drugs. I already know."

"I know you do. But life looks different to people as they grow older. Fate always throws something you don't expect in your path, and sometimes it's really tough."

"Like Mom getting sick."

The rush of emotion that hits me is almost dizzying. "Yes. Like that." I look away for a moment and gather myself. "We're okay, though. Right?"

Annie nods with reasonable certainty.

"I want to ask you a question, squirt. A big one, okay?"

"Okay."

"What would you think if I wasn't the mayor anymore?"

Her eyes widen, but I can't tell what she's feeling. "What do you mean? Are you going to get voted out or something?"

"No, no. But for a while now I've been thinking that I haven't been able to accomplish the things I wanted to. The things I wanted to change for you and the kids your age. I think only time is going to fix those things, and you and I only have a certain amount of time together. Time to get you the education you deserve, to—"

"What?"

"To *live,* I guess. It's hard to explain, really."

Annie works her mouth like someone trying to solve a difficult problem. "I liked it better when you just wrote books. You were home a lot more."

"I sure was."

"But to have things back like they were before, you'd have to quit, right?"

"Yes."

"You always tell me never to quit, no matter what."

"I know. I've been struggling with that. But this job is about serving the people of the city. And if I'm not giving my full self to that job, then I'm betraying those people."

Annie looks at the ceiling, considering.

"It's been done before," I tell her. "The last mayor resigned, remember? That's how I was elected, during a special election. That's what would happen this time."

"But Mr. Doug had cancer. Who would be mayor if you stopped?"

I give her a smile. "I know someone who's wanted to be mayor for a long time."

"Not Mr. Johnson!"

Laughing at her sound political instincts,

I say, "No, no. Shad's always wanted it, but I was thinking of Paul Labry."

Annie's eyes brighten. "Yeah! Mr. Labry would be a great mayor. He's so nice, and he likes being out talking to people on the streets. You don't like that part of the job so much. That's not good."

"You see a lot, don't you?" I rub her head affectionately. "Annie, I think what I'm really feeling is this. Natchez was the right place for me to grow up, but I don't think it is for you. The town was different when I was a boy. I ran for mayor because I thought I could bring back some of the good ways life used to be, and at the same time fix the things that were wrong back then. But that job's too big for one person. I want us to be somewhere there are more kids like you—as smart as you—and also more who are different from you. I want you to be exposed to everything that's out there. You deserve all that."

She knots the blanket in her right hand and speaks in a voice that is subtly changed. "When you say 'us,' do you just mean you and me?"

This is the unspoken heart of our conversation.

"Well . . . you know my decision to run for mayor was probably the main reason that Caitlin and I broke up."

"Uh-huh." *That's why I'm asking this now, dummy,* her eyes seem to say. "But I don't think she really wanted to leave us."

"I don't either."

"She kept her house here."

"Yes. And I think that house was sort of a symbol. A reminder that she was still out there, hoping I would come to her. But this town is too small for Caitlin. If we were all going to be together, I think it would have to be somewhere else. And I'm not sure that's what you want, since you'd have to leave behind the friends you've made here."

Annie's face can be difficult to read, but in this moment her mother's eyes shine out at me with certainty. "I don't care where we live, Daddy. As long as we're together."

"By 'we,' do you mean you and me?"

Annie shakes her head. "I mean the three of us. I want Caitlin to be my mom. I think that's how it's supposed to be."

When the tears swell in the corners of my eyes, I turn and look toward the door.

Annie rises up and puts her arms

around my neck. "It's okay, Dad. I think even Mom would want that. She'd want us to be happy. She'd want you to have someone to take care of you."

"And you," I choke out.

"You've taken good care of me. But I think you're right. I think it's time to let Mr. Paul take care of the town, and us take care of each other."

I lean down and hug her as tight as I dare. When I rise back up, she says, "I think Caitlin needs us too."

This brings a wave of warmth into my chest. "I think you're right. Now, you need to get some sleep."

"I will. I'm glad to be in my own bed again."

I smile, kiss her once more, then turn out the light and leave the room.

As I reach the bottom of the stairs, I see Kelly walking through the front door. He's moving more slowly than usual, and his eyes look bleary. Then I see the Styrofoam cup in his hand. The smell of alcohol hits me with his first words.

"Hey, Penn, how's everybody doing?"

"It's all good. We're glad to be back together. How about you? You okay?"

"I'm good."

I reach out and squeeze his shoulder. "You look pretty out of it."

"Well . . . I haven't done much sleeping since I got here. I don't need much, but I need some."

"Well tonight you can finally get some."

He gives an exaggerated nod. "Yep. I finally took me a drink too. I didn't want to buy one on the *Queen*. That fucking Quinn would love to get me that way. I'll bet he was watching me on the CCTVs the whole time."

"Where'd you go?"

"Stopped at a little bar on the way back here, down on the corner of Canal Street. It's called the Corner Bar, fittingly enough." Kelly almost giggles, which makes me laugh.

"Dude, you need some serious sleep."

"Yeah. I'm going to sit on the couch in the den for a while. Zone out and watch a movie. Will that bother Annie?"

"Nah. I do it all the time."

"Hey," Kelly says, as though just remembering something important. "I just saw Caitlin pull into her driveway."

Something stirs in my chest. "Really?"

"Yeah. She didn't look too happy. I think you ought to go talk to her."

"I don't think she wants that right now."

"Bullshit. When you think they don't want to talk to you . . . that's *exactly* when they want you to talk to them. Take it from me."

The truth is, I very much want to talk to Caitlin. Before doubt can stop me, I dial her cell and am surprised when she doesn't let it go to voice mail.

"Penn?" she says.

"Yes."

"Is anything wrong?"

"No. I was wondering if I could come over and talk to you."

"I'm pretty wiped out, actually. Is it important?"

Kelly motions for me to push it. "I think it is. It won't take long."

There's a long silence. Then she says, "All right, I'll be on the porch."

"Thanks. I'm on my way."

"Way to go!" Kelly says, slapping my back. "I told you."

As I smile back at him, I see that he must have had quite a few drinks at the Corner Bar. His eyes are bloodshot slits.

But if anybody's earned a few drinks, Kelly has.

"I'll see you, bro," I say.

"I hope not. You need to stay over there tonight."

"Is Carl there?"

"Yeah. But I'll text him to put some Kleenex in his ears. Go on, man. She's waiting for you."

I wave him off and hurry out.

CHAPTER

44

Caitlin waits on her porch with her arms folded, her hair down around her neck. She's wearing a blue cashmere sweater and jeans, and from her expression I get the feeling she's not planning on being out here long. I walk up the steps and stop a few feet short of her.

"Long day?" I ask.

She shrugs. "Yes and no. Lots to think about. No big epiphanies. What about you?"

"I did a lot of thinking during Tim's funeral. About Annie, about the town. But about us, mostly."

Caitlin doesn't prompt me to continue, but there's no point backing away from it now. "I realized today that I lost you the first time because I was too idealistic, which you told me at the time. I wanted to do something that you thought was impossible, and I didn't really listen to your objections. I thought you didn't see the situation as deeply as I did, so I went on and did it anyway. And you left."

She's watching me with interest now. She doesn't often get abject admissions of fault from me.

"I really thought you were never coming back," I go on. "But you did. And I think you were open to us when you came back. And the irony is, now I'm losing you again, only this time it's because you want me to do something *I* think is impossible, at least for the time being. Now it's your idealism that's separating us."

Her mouth opens in amazement. "So it's *my* fault? That's what you're saying?"

"No. I'm saying that you were right the first time. I was wrong to think I could save this town by myself. It was hubris. And though my parents raised me never to quit anything, I think that for a lot of reasons, the time has come for me to step down and focus on what the people I care about really need."

She looks steadily back at me, but I can't read her expression. Whatever she feels, it's clearly not what I'd hoped for.

"I spoke to Paul Labry today about running for mayor after I resign."

"Resign?" She draws back as though she can't quite believe this. "And what do you plan to do after that?"

"Move somewhere that you can be happy working in your job, and where Annie can go to a top-flight school."

Caitlin blinks several times, then looks curiously at me. "And you?"

"I can write anywhere."

She turns toward the street and leans on her porch rail. "I don't know what to say."

"I thought you'd be happy to hear that. More than happy, actually."

A sad smile touches her mouth. "I would have thought so too. I've waited a long time to hear it. A very long time. But now that I have, what it sounds like is . . . you're running away."

"Running away? From what? The job?"

"I don't know." She turns to me with anger in her eyes. "From Tim's death, from Sands, this whole dirty mess. And, yes, the job too. What about the noble work that meant so much to you two years ago? I don't get it. It's like for the first time in your life, you're trying to take the easy road. And I don't—that's not the man I fell in love with."

I'm so stunned I can hardly get my thoughts together. "You want me to *stay* here? Finish out my term? Is that it? You want Annie to stay in St. Stephen's?"

"That's not what I want, no. But I don't want you to slink away from this place either. Or from what's caused this problem between us."

A surge of resentment rises in me, but I press it down. "Look, it's not like I'm Achilles sulking in his tent, okay? I've made some decisions about the case too. I'm a lawyer, Caitlin. And I'm going to attack the Sands problem like a lawyer. After Po is in custody and Sands is in the system, I'm going to use every resource in my power to have him indicted on state murder charges. And if I can't prove them, I'll get him on the others. Kidnapping, dogfighting, money laundering, whatever it takes to put him behind bars."

She nods distantly, as though this is the minimum I should do. "What if they don't get Po?"

"Then Sands won't be of any use to the government anymore. He'll lose his protection from Hull. Hull will probably nail Sands himself."

"No, he won't. Don't you see? *That's* my fear. You're so naïve sometimes. It will just go on and on, this teasing game, where Hull thinks he's running Sands, but it's really the other way around."

"So what do you want to do? Take it all public?"

Her jaw tightens abruptly. "Maybe. I'm thinking about it. If the Po sting doesn't work, it's certainly an option. And please don't remind me of our deal. As far as I'm concerned, you've stepped away from this case, and I'm free to make my own decisions."

This statement starts an alarm ringing in my head. "What have you been doing today?"

"Trying very hard not to think about all this."

I know she doesn't want me to pry, but I can't help myself. "What are your plans tomorrow?"

"I've been talking to those people I was in touch with on the Katrina stories. The Danziger Bridge incident, mainly, but also trying to sort out what really happened in the convention center down there. And the Superdome."

The bridge incident means her "friend's" documentary.

"Yes, I've spoken to Jan today, if that's what you're wondering. He's shooting some footage tomorrow with some Danziger witnesses. I'm thinking of going down to help out. He doesn't have much crew down there."

This prospect bothers me far more than I would have expected it to. I mean, I practically just asked this woman to marry me, and she's telling me she's going to New Orleans to shoot a film with another guy. "When were you thinking of leaving?"

"Tomorrow."

I should conceal my feelings better, but I realize I'm shaking my head angrily. "I don't know what to say. This isn't the reaction I expected. The opposite, in fact. I guess . . . I'd better think about what you've said. What you're doing."

She nods and gives me the sad smile again. "I want to think about what you said, as well. Resigning would be a very big step for you. I didn't mean to belittle it. Like I said, I've waited a long time to hear you say what you did."

"Too long, maybe?"

"I don't know. I'm not sure why this Sands thing has affected me so deeply."

Without thinking, I reach out and take her hand. "Will you have lunch with me tomorrow? At the Castle, like we used to? Maybe we'll have some perspective on this by then."

She looks at me a long time, leaving her hand in mine. "If I'm still in town, I will." Her fingers slide out of my grasp. "If I don't show up, that means I had to take more time with it. Do you understand?"

I nod slowly. "I wish I didn't."

She hugs herself against the chill. "I'd better go in."

"Thanks for letting Carl stay with you."

"I know there's danger. I'm not going to

compromise my safety just to make some kind of point."

I'm glad she's thinking clearly on this issue, at least. Last night she seemed perfectly willing to do just that.

"I'm sorry I didn't come see Annie," she says. "I just don't want to confuse her right now."

"No, you're right. If this is how you feel, it's better that way."

"I know she's glad to be home."

"She is. Good night."

Caitlin waves, then slips inside her door.

I find Kelly splayed out on the couch in my den, the Styrofoam cup in his lap, his eyes nearly closed. The television's playing an old Sydney Pollack film, *Three Days of the Condor,* very low.

"Hey?" I say. "You okay?"

Kelly's head slides forward in what might be a nod. I'm about to turn and go upstairs when he says, "That didn't take long. I guess it didn't go so good, huh?"

"Understatement of the millennium."

"Don't worry about it. She's just young. Still got a few illusions left. Give her time."

I know he's right, but I hate to think I'm

waiting for Caitlin to become as jaded as Kelly and I about human nature and the legal process. "Maybe she's right. Maybe we should just go public with the whole stinking mess."

"No way. Then Po skates for sure. I just wish we'd wasted Sands before we knew the bigger picture. Then we could say. 'Uh-oh,' and go about our business." Kelly laughs softly, but for once his dark sense of humor strikes a dissonant note.

I walk deeper into the den and look down at him. "You say that so easily. Like killing Sands would be no big deal. But last night you wouldn't even kill that dying dog."

Kelly's red eyes open momentarily, but he doesn't look up. "I told you . . . we had to leave that place like we found it."

"There was more to it than that. Were you testing me or something?"

His chest rises as he takes a long breath. Then he sighs heavily, the sound almost like a snore. "You got it done, man. Just let it go."

"I want to know."

He scowls, then sips from his cup, swallows audibly. "When I went into Delta

training, I was ready. Ninety-seven percent of the volunteers wash out, and they
come from elite units to begin with. Then
there's the mental shit they put you
through. I got through that just fine. But
later on, after I was in, they put me in a
rotation called dog lab."

One eye opens and seeks me out, trying to see if I've heard of this. I shrug.

"The idea," he says, "is to prepare you
to handle the kinds of wounds you might
encounter in the field. I mean, we didn't
have medics along on our ops. We were
our own medics."

"So what was dog lab?"

"Well . . . it's pretty simple. The army
takes some stray dogs and shoots them—
or 'inflicts missile wound trauma'—usually
with the kinds of rounds you're likely to be
hit by in the field. AK-47s, shit like that.
Then they give you the wounded dogs.
You have your medical kit. You're supposed to stabilize the dog, then nurse it
back to health. Every guy gets his own
dog. They're in shock when you get them,
of course, like that dog last night. Bleeding out fast, panicked eyes, howling in

pain. You start an IV, do everything you'd do for a human being. And that's when you realize that textbook training doesn't mean shit. In the field, it's different. So all you do for a week, ten days, is try to save your dog. You live with it, and with the other guys and their dogs. The guys bond with the animals in weird ways. They name them, and they get territorial about their dog's space, or other people touching their dog. Some die, of course. But most of them make it—the ones that survive the initial shootings."

Kelly takes another noisy sip from his cup.

"My dog got septicemia," he says. "I had him on antibiotics, but not the right kind, I guess. He was dying steadily, and the other guys were riding me about it. I wanted to load him into a jeep and drive off-base to a fucking veterinarian. But you couldn't do that. So when it got really bad, I took a syrette of morphine and put him down. The officer in charge of us went batshit, of course. I flunked dog lab. But I'd done so well on the hard-core stuff, they weren't about to wash me out for that."

"So last night—"

"Last night, when I leaned over that pit bull, I was back in dog lab. Canine PTSD. Isn't that a riot? I've killed human beings without batting an eye, but I go to pieces over a fucking mutt."

"I'd say that's a good sign."

Kelly shakes his head with sudden vehemence. "It ain't that simple, boss. Loving dogs doesn't make you a humanitarian. *Hitler* loved dogs. He had a dog named Blondi. He loved Blondi, but he still murdered millions of people. He offed the retards and the handicapped people too. *Homo sapiens* is one fucked-up species, Penn. Sometimes I wish I was still like Caitlin."

I lean over and squeeze his knee. "Don't think about it. Just go get in the bed."

"I'm good right here."

"You sure?"

"I'm good."

As I climb the stairs, my cell phone buzzes to announce a text message. When I check it, I'm surprised to see it's from Caitlin. It reads: I THINK YOU'RE MAKING THE RIGHT DECISION FOR ANNIE, WHETHER IT'S RIGHT FOR YOU AND ME OR NOT. I LOVE YOU.

Halfway up the stairs, I stop and key in my reply: I LOVE YOU, TOO. I HOPE I SEE YOU TOMORROW.

Then I walk up the steps and collapse onto my bed.

CHAPTER

45

Caitlin stands in her kitchen, reading Penn's text message and blinking back tears. In all her time with him, she's never lied like that, not even by omission. But the deepest hurt is from shock at her own lack of feeling. She's waited a year and a half for him to make the decision he made today, but tonight, hearing the words, she felt . . . betrayed. It made no sense, but that was what she felt.

Wiping the corners of her eyes, she reaches back and switches off the gas burner. She'd started making tea, but the last thing she wants is to lie in bed for an hour thinking about what just happened. She walks down the hall to the stairs and stops suddenly, startled by the sight of a man sitting on the floor of her living room. Carl Sims looks up from a copy of Shotgun News *with a friendly smile. There's a pistol on the floor by his knee, and his sniper rifle leans against the wall beside his shoulder.*

"**Everything okay?**" **he asks.** "**Didn't mean to scare you.**"

"**It's all right. I just forgot. Where were you when I came in?**"

"**Well, I was out there when you were talking to Mayor Cage. I mean, I wasn't close enough to listen or anything. I was just covering you guys. You know.**"

"**Thank you, Carl. I'm sorry I don't have a TV down here for you.**"

"*That's okay. I'm fine for the night. I've got this magazine, and I got one of Mr. Cage's novels to read if I get tired of the* News. *Major McDavitt keeps telling me I ought to read one, so I'll probably give it a try tonight. They any good?*"

Caitlin walks to the foot of the stairs

and stops. "I think so. The first three, especially."

"The major told me you might be in one or two of them. Kind of disguised, like."

"Oh, I don't know. Maybe parts of me."

Carl smiles knowingly.

"You like Penn, don't you, Carl?"

Sims sticks out his lower lip as though pondering the question. "I do, yeah."

"Why, do you think?"

"Same as the major, I guess. He's somebody who does the right thing, if there's any way to do it."

"Isn't that what you do?"

"Well . . . I try to. But seeing what's right, and doin' it—that's two different things."

"What about what we've been going through this past week?"

The sniper shrugs. "Life gets complicated. That's a fact. But I know this. Taking an enemy from the front ain't always the best way. I figure Mr. Cage knows what he's doing—even if he don't know he knows it himself yet. You know what I'm saying?"

Caitlin is surprised to hear herself laugh. "Actually, I think I do. I'm not sure I agree with you in this case. But I understand."

Carl watches her for a few moments, then suddenly looks down, like a boy caught staring. "I didn't mean to keep you down here."

"No, it's all right. I appreciate hearing what you have to say."

He looks back up at her. "You know what I think? I think you two gonna be all right. Sometimes it just takes a while."

"How old are you, Carl?"

"Twenty-six."

"You look thirty. And you sound like you're sixty."

He laughs warmly. "I'm just quoting what my daddy's said to me."

"Well . . . let's hope he's right."

"Oh, he usually is. Good night, Mrs. Cage—oops, my bad."

Caitlin smiles and shakes her finger at him. "I know that was on purpose."

The deputy laughs and looks back at his newspaper.

"Call me if you need anything, Carl."

"Same to you. I'm the one guarding you, remember?"

She smiles.

Caitlin ascends the long staircase, wondering why Penn's words didn't resonate in her as they would have only a week ago. She walks into her bedroom and opens the dresser, wishing she'd packed more clothes for the trip. As she takes off her sweater and bra and slips on a T-shirt, her thoughts go back to her conversation with Pastor Simpson in the afternoon. Tying back her hair with an elastic band, she hears a noise from downstairs. Thinking it might be Carl knocking on the wall for attention, she goes to the door and sticks her head out.

A rush of movement from the right makes her jerk left, then a black hood descends over her head. As she shouts for Carl, someone yanks a drawstring tight, cutting off her air. Lashing out with both hands, she tries to break free, but a needle-sharp sting like a wasp's pierces her neck below the jaw. Within seconds her limbs stop obeying her brain. She tries to yell Carl's name, then screams for Penn, but all that emerges from her mouth is the blubbering of someone being shoved underwater.

CHAPTER

46

Walt Garrity stands between the Devil's Punchbowl and a row of blinking slot machines, sipping a Maker's Mark and trying to avoid Nancy. Since making his play with Sands earlier, he's felt a nice buzz, and the whiskey only makes it better. He's also realized that the case isn't the only thing on his mind. The image of the Chinese beauty descending the escalator will not leave him. He's been half-consciously searching for her all night. The search hasn't been easy, because Nancy seems to be noticing his absences more now. In fact, she ought to be running out of chips about now, and he's going to have to put in a little time with her at the craps table.

Setting his empty glass on a table outside the bar, he heads for the main escalator that leads to the grand salon. Just as he reaches for the moving handrail, a hidden door used by the staff opens in the wall to his left, and the Chinese beauty steps out, wearing what looks like a silk kimono. She's not looking at Walt, but she's less than ten yards away and doesn't seem to be in a hurry.

He moves to his left, gently intercepting her, and says, "Excuse me, ma'am. Could I talk to you for a minute?"

"You want talk?" she asks in musical voice. "My English not good."

Her ingenuousness melts something in Walt. "That's all right. I'll keep it simple. I really just want to sit with you for a couple of minutes."

"Sit?"

"In the bar maybe? The Devil's Punchbowl?"

She crinkles her nose. "Food not so good there. I no like."

"We don't have to eat anything."

She looks mildly anxious, as if she has somewhere else to be.

"Am I holding you up?"

"With someone else tonight. You understand?"

"You're with someone else? You have a date?"

"Date, yes." The girl smiles and nods, and Walt's heart sinks.

She nods considerately, then moves to go. But after walking a few feet, she turns and glides back to him. "No date tomorrow," she says softly, her eyes shining. "You come back tomorrow, I be your date."

Something kicks in Walt's chest, and it can only be his heart. He'd hardly dared hope that this woman could be had by a simple business transaction. But here she stands, waiting for his answer.

"You come tomorrow?" she asks. "Or I make another date?"

Walt swallows, trying to get his mind around the reality of what's being offered.

"You no be sorry," the girl whispers. "Me number one girl. Make you come many time. You feel twenty again. You like?"

Walt gulps as he did as an eighteen-year-old in Tokyo when the first streetwalker climbed onto his leg and offered him something he'd never heard of. Prostitution had been legal in Japan then, but it certainly wasn't in Texas, and he'd almost popped the moment her warm flesh settled against the leg of his uniform.

"Tomorrow," he says finally. "I'll be your date tomorrow."

The girl extends her graceful hand and traces one fingernail along his chest. "I like you. What I call you?"

"J.B."

"Zhaybee?"

"Good enough."

"Okay. I go now. Date waiting."

She turns away again, but this time, emboldened by her frankness, Walt reaches out and lays a fingertip on her scalloped collarbone. When she turns this time, he thinks he sees a flash of annoyance, but then the submissive smile of the Orient he remembers from so long ago returns. "Yes, Zhaybee?"

"What do I call you?"

Her smile broadens. "So sorry. I forgot. I am Ming."

"Ming?"

"Ming. Like the vase, yes?"

"I won't forget."

"Bye for now."

Walt watches her lithe form glide across the carpet until she slips into the mass of fat American bodies crowding the slot machines.

"I guess you're dumping me now, huh?" Nancy says petulantly from behind him.

Walt turns, takes in the genuine hurt in her face, and tries to let her down easy. "We've had a good run, Nancy. Haven't we?"

"What's so great about her?"

What's not? *Walt wonders.*

"She's too damn skinny," Nancy says, "too skinny by half. Nothing to hold on to when you get in the saddle."

Walt gives her a patient smile.

"Course I guess that doesn't matter, since you can't saddle up anymore."

Despite the venom in her voice, Walt

takes out his wallet and peels off $500 of Penn's money.

"We had a good run, honey. Will you take some advice from an old man?"

"That's the only kind of vice I don't like," Nancy says, her face hard again. "Advice."

Walt holds her eye, forcing her to see him straight.

"Okay, okay, let's hear it."

"It's nothing you haven't heard before. But I want you to listen this time. Find another line of work."

"Great. Thanks, granddad. You know how hard it is in this town to find a job that pays what I make on my back?"

"Find a new town. Girls don't live long in this racket."

For a few brief seconds Nancy looks back at him without affect, completely vulnerable, almost hopeful, but then a dealer calls a win, and she blinks, and the walls go back up, her eyes as opaque as plaster marbles.

"Take care, Nancy. And thanks. You brought me luck."

CHAPTER

47

Caitlin has no idea how long she's been locked in the car trunk when the vehicle finally stops. As soon as she woke up, she found a taillight with her foot and kicked it out, but though she stuck her hand through the hole and waved it wildly, no one stopped the car.

Two doors open and close, then the trunk pops open. Someone lifts the lid. She hears gruff commands—the accents Irish. Powerful hands seize her and lift her out of the trunk, letting her feet dangle to the ground. Fear is loose in her like a wild thing, but she keeps telling herself that if they meant to kill her, they could have done it before now. She's glad they're holding her up. With the hood over her head, it's difficult to maintain balance.

"I'm holding a Taser," says a voice. "Try to run, I'll juice you. You won't like it. I can tell you from experience."

They march her forward at a rapid clip, then stop. There's a jangle of keys. Suddenly she hears panting. A barrage of barking erupts close to her, and she hears heavy bodies slamming into a Cyclone fence. All at once she remembers Linda's note, about Quinn feeding Ben Li to dogs.

"Get 'em back!" shouts an Irishman. "Goddamn it, go! Use bait if you have to."

One man lets go of Caitlin, but the yammering dogs keep hitting the fence. Caitlin wants to speak, but duct tape holds her jaw immobile. After about a minute, the dogs race away and slam into what must be a different fence. There's a metallic rattle, then the sound of an opening gate.

The man drags her through, then

opens a door and leads her into a closed space that stinks of urine, old food, and dirty animals. She smells alcohol too, rubbing alcohol, plus other medical odors she can't identify. The floor feels like bare cement. They march her twenty steps, then stop and open another door with a key. This sounds like a real door, not a gate. Someone shoves her between the shoulder blades, driving her into the room. She almost stumbles, but keeps her feet long enough to collide with a wall opposite the door.

"We're going to take the hood off. Be still, or you get the juice. Nod if you understand."

Caitlin nods once.

The black hood is whipped off her head, and blinding fluorescent light stabs her eyes. After a few seconds, she realizes it's just a cheap bulb, and her vision clears. One man stands in front of her, wearing a balaclava mask. His lips show through the mask; they look bright red, filled with blood. His eyes are gray and hungry.

"Take off your clothes," he says.

"What?"

"Get 'em off!"

"No."

He jabs the Taser at her. "You do it or I do. It'll hurt less if you do it."

"Why do you want my clothes?"

"Fuckin' hell, you mouthy cunt. Do what I tell ya!"

Caitlin pulls her T-shirt over her head, then slides her jeans down and steps out of them.

"Panties too. Everything."

With a hiss of anger, she pulls down the panties and tosses them at his feet.

"Not bad," he says, his voice muffled by the hood. "A little skinny for my taste, but, damn, you're a thoroughbred, aren't you?"

"What do you think this is going to accomplish?"

"Ah . . . well, that's up to your boyfriend, I reckon. You too. Lucky for you, he's got something we need. But let's see how cooperative you can be, eh? You shave it a little close down there, don't ya? I like it natural."

It takes a supreme act of will, but

Caitlin turns and faces the wall. A barred window is set in it, but the bars don't look strong enough to hold a determined prisoner. She expects to feel the bite of the Taser at any moment, but all she hears is a closing door.

She starts to turn, but then the door opens again, just wide enough for a head. "Hey, I like that side too. Better than the front, I think. I'll be seein' ya, princess. Oh, yeah. Lots to look forward to."

This time when the door closes, a key turns in the lock, a heavy bolt shoots home, and muted steps go down the corridor.

Caitlin turns slowly in place, taking in every detail of the room. It's a simple square with plywood walls, a concrete floor, and a low ceiling that looks like the underside of a tin roof. A plastic dog bowl sits on the floor, filled with water. A pail stands beside it, empty, and she realizes that this is to be her toilet. A door slams somewhere, and the walls of her cell vibrate.

"Well, this is what you get," she says aloud, walking forward and testing the

bars with a steady pull. The bars aren't set in the window, but screwed over it. She could have them off in a couple of hours. It can't be that easy, she thinks. Then she remembers the dogs.

"Fuck," she whispers, realizing her situation at last. The bars weren't put here to hold a human in this room, but a dog. I can use my wonderful opposable thumb to get the bars off, but the dogs are outside, hoping I'll drop through that window like food through a chute.

The sound of an engine reaches her, and after a grinding of gears, it slowly recedes into silence. Thinking they've left her alone, Caitlin nearly jumps out of her skin when something bumps the wall to her left. At first she thinks it's a dog, but then the sound comes again, a steady tapping against the plywood, low down on the wall. She drops into a crouch and puts her cheek against the wood.

"Is someone there?"

Three slow taps respond.

"Who are you?" Caitlin asks.

"Who are you?"

"Caitlin Masters."

There's silence for a few moments. Then a muffled female voice says, "Penn Cage's old girlfriend?"

"Yes! Tell me your name."

There's a long pause. Then the voice says, "Are you for real?"

"What do you mean?"

"You could be with them. Helping them. Quinn."

"My God, no! They just kidnapped me. I've been looking for Linda Church. Is that you, Linda?"

"You tell me the rest first. Why would they kidnap you?"

"Penn got your note—from that Pentecostal girl. He thought you'd got away safe, but I wasn't sure. I wanted to find you. I never stopped looking for you, Linda. I traced that girl from the Oneness church. And then the preacher, Simpson."

Caitlin hears soft whimpering. "I want to believe you."

"Linda, is it really you? Please tell me. What can it hurt? They already know you're here. They put you here."

"I guess. I can't think right anymore. I'm sick. My leg's infected."

Caitlin remembers this from the note. She'd forgotten it, assuming that Linda had got medical care by now. "Do you have fever?"

"I'm burning up. But that's not the worst part."

"What's the matter?"

"He's been doing it to me. Quinn."

"Doing it?"

"Raping me. He started last night. He's done it so much that I'm getting a UTI. It hurts so bad when I have to pee, and I shiver all over afterward."

"Did you tell Quinn that?"

"He gave me some pills he said would help. Antibiotics. They're for dogs, I think, but he said it's all the same. But they're not helping. If it gets any worse, I don't know what I'll do. I stopped drinking water so I won't have to pee."

"You can't do that, Linda. You have to drink. You'll die if you don't."

"I'm going to die anyway. They'll never let me out of here alive. He's going to use me till he's tired of me, then feed me to the dogs. He told me."

Fear and outrage rush through

Caitlin in a flood. "That's not going to happen. Listen to me, Linda. We're getting out of here!"

"How? Does anybody know where you are?"

Caitlin doesn't want to admit the truth, but she can't bring herself to lie. "No."

"Then how are we going to get out? There's dogs outside this kennel. Bull-dogs and something else too. Big dogs. They don't even leave men to guard me most of the time. They don't have to. It's twenty feet to the fence. Even if you could get out of here, they'd tear you to pieces before you got to it."

"Is that what this building is? A ken-nel?"

"Uh-huh. You're in a regular room like an office. But the rest of it's just two lines of fenced stalls with an aisle between. There's cats in one stall down by the door. That's it."

"That helps. The more I know, the bet-ter chance we have. I'll think of some-thing. You just drink your water and try to stay strong. Maybe the antibiotics will start to work. I know the bladder infection

*hurts. I've had those myself. But you lis-
ten to me, girl. We are getting out of here.
Do you hear me?"*

"Yes."

"Say it, Linda."

"We're getting out."

"Say it like you believe it."

"I'm sorry. My throat hurts. Did they put a collar on you?"

"What?"

"A dog collar."

"No."

"They've got a dog collar on me, and it's chained to a post. He only takes it off when he does it to me."

Jesus Christ.

"If you're going to do something, please do it quick."

Caitlin thinks frantically. "Are we by ourselves now? Did they really leave?"

"I think so."

"I'm sure I can get these bars off the window."

"No! Don't do that! You'll draw the dogs. They could jump through that window if they tried."

"Okay, okay, I won't." Caitlin looks around her cell again, then lifts her gaze to the cheap tin roof. "What about the roof? Do you care if I try to get part of that open? Then I could get up on top and see what's out there."

After a brief silence, Linda says, "I guess that's okay. Just don't fall off."

Caitlin flexes her hands, then takes hold of the window bars at shoulder height. With a mighty effort, she leans back and starts walking her feet up the wall, first to chest level, then past the window. Skinning the cat, they called it when she was a kid. *Surprised she can still manage the maneuver, she keeps stretching and extending until her bare feet reach the edge of the low-lying ceiling, then begins kicking. By the fourth kick she's put a dent in the tin, but soon she has to unwind and drop back to the floor, panting and rubbing her hands. She's not sure how long she can keep it up, but she's pretty sure a roofing nail has started to lift out of the two-by-four at the top of the wall.*

CHAPTER

48

Today will be Annie's first day back at St. Stephen's, and she seems a little uncertain as we coast down the long drive of the school. I'm not exactly at peace myself. Despite my cease-fire agreement with Jonathan Sands, I've warned the headmaster and security guard to be on the lookout for strangers on the campus, and not to be shy about calling 911 if they see any. Chief Logan has prepped the dispatcher to send two squad cars to St. Stephen's with sirens blaring if there's even a hint of trouble.

"Are you all right?" I ask, glancing over to the passenger seat. "You seem quiet."

"I had another dream."

"What about?" I ask, easing the car right, toward the middle school.

"Caitlin again."

I glance at Annie, but she keeps her eyes focused forward. "Was it bad or good?"

"Bad."

"Will you tell me what it was?"

Her face tightens with indecision, but then she says, "I dreamed Mom was alive again."

This surprises me, since Annie was only four when Sarah died and has few clear memories of her. "What happened in it?"

"I don't want to say. It was creepy."

"Everybody has creepy dreams sometimes."

"Well, we went to visit Mom's grave, like we've done before, but Mom was *with* us. And the thing is . . . the creepy thing . . ."

"It's all right, baby."

"*Caitlin* was the one who was gone. In

Mom's grave. And Mom was with us, looking down at the stone."

Sensing that Annie is really disturbed, I pull onto the grassy shoulder of the driveway and put the Saab in park. Cars loaded with children glide past, then slow and empty their charges at the door of the middle school.

"Maybe you dreamed that because of the talk we had last night. What do you think?"

"I don't know. It's just that the last time I dreamed about Caitlin, me and Gram ended up having to hide out of town."

I pat her knee, then squeeze it reassuringly. "That didn't have anything to do with your dream. That was something to do with my work."

She looks skeptically at me for a while. "Did you talk to her about what we said last night?"

"A little bit. We're going to talk some more today, I think."

"You think? Or you know?"

"We're not sure yet. Sometimes big things like this take a little time to work out."

She looks down at the glove box and nods with quick assertiveness, as though she knows her voice will crack if she speaks while looking at me. "Did you tell her I wanted her to be my mom?"

"Did you want me to?"

"Did you?"

I sigh in resignation, knowing she can outlast me at this game. "No. I didn't."

"Good. I'm worried it might scare her."

"No, no. Why would you think that?"

"Well, she's going to want her own babies and stuff. She may not want to think of herself as my mom."

Annie's fear of rejection brings tears to my eyes. I squeeze her hand. "I'll tell you a secret. I think Caitlin's always wanted to be your mom."

Annie looks up at me and blinks three times, her eyes wide and vulnerable. "Really?"

"She's tried to do all the things Mom would have done, if she'd lived. I think Caitlin worries that you'll think she's trying to take Mom's place."

Annie's mouth falls open. "But I don't think that!"

As perceptive as she is sometimes, it surprises me that Annie doesn't see the relationship of her dream to what's happening in our lives. "Well, that's the hard part about these kinds of situations. People are scared to say what they really feel, and sometimes they wait too long to do it."

"Have you done that? Waited too long?"

"I don't know. I don't think so. I think we're going to get everything worked out."

Looking up, I see no more cars at the door. One of the teachers looks up the hill at us and gives a friendly wave.

"You're going to be late, baby."

She takes my hand and squeezes it. "It doesn't matter, Dad."

"No. I guess it doesn't."

"Let's go," she says brightly, as though everything has been resolved. "Like Gram says, 'One way or another, everything's going to be fine.'"

I laugh and drive down to the door of the school. Annie leans over and kisses my cheek, then lifts her backpack from the floor. When I start to speak, she presses her finger to my lips.

"You don't have to tell me not to worry, or not to talk about any of this. I know how things work."

With that, she smiles, gets out, and disappears through the door of the school I loved as a child, the school that made me what I am, the school that my daughter will soon be leaving forever.

CHAPTER

49

Caitlin hunches naked on the balls of her bloody feet, listening to Linda's chain rattle. She can tell by the sound that the chain is heavy, the kind with big, bright links that farmers use to tie tractors to flatbed trailers. Some people, Caitlin knows now, use them to strengthen fighting dogs, by making them drag the chains around every minute of their lives, as Linda must do now. Linda sleeps fitfully in her fever, moving frequently, shifting the dog collar that holds her to the chain.

Caitlin has not slept. She feels as

though she's awakened in some night-mare version of The Count of Monte Cristo, *but instead of solitude as her curse, she must endure the cries of a woman who has suffered thirty hours of rape and abuse, while being powerless to help her. Caitlin doesn't intend to stay that way. She knows a lot more about her situation than she did when she arrived last night, and she doesn't believe their plight hopeless, as Linda so clearly does.*

Being betrayed by her former pastor seems to have cracked the foundation of Linda's religious faith. Caitlin senses that her will to live is fragile, her injuries and infections no doubt aggravating the situation.

From long and careful questioning of Linda during the night, Caitlin believes they're not far from Natchez. Yesterday, Seamus Quinn visited the kennel building that is their prison three separate times, with only a few hours between each visit. Caitlin is sure he must be driving back and forth to Natchez between the bouts of rape.

What interests her more is that Quinn has told Jonathan Sands that Linda is already dead. Quinn was apparently supposed to kill her on the night Ben Li died, but by a brave leap from the boat, Linda saved herself. Quinn found her again by quietly putting out the word among hard-luck gamblers that all debts would be forgiven if someone could deliver Linda Church to him. Quinn's ploy paid off, and he's apparently kept her alive because he always coveted his master's favorite mistress.

That Quinn would lie to his boss about something so important might offer a chance to drive a wedge between the two men, but the more frightening aspect of this lie is that Quinn must mean to kill Linda soon, so that Sands will never know he failed in his first effort—or risked letting Caitlin hear what she's already heard. This, Caitlin knows, is the worst indicator of her own likely future. For if they mean to let her live, why would they allow her to see or hear what they've done to Linda Church? Her best hope is that some disconnect between Sands and Quinn has resulted in this scenario. Otherwise, she has only one chance: escape.

During the night, Caitlin kicked at the kennel's tin roof for two hours, off and on, taking breaks before repeating the skin-the-cat move required to get her feet up to where the tin meets the wall. Her feet were bruised and bleeding after ten minutes, and the pit bulls outside went crazy while she did it, but no humans appeared. Quinn apparently believes that the dogs alone are sufficient to prevent an escape.

After she got a section of tin pried up, she learned why. The kennel building is surrounded by a heavy Cyclone fence eight feet high, set back twenty feet on all sides, and hidden from the air by a huge shed, like those that house machine shops. The metal struts that support its roof are twenty feet above her head. If she had a rope, she might be able to reach one of the rafters, but she doesn't know if there's rope in the kennel. Even if there is, and she could climb hand over hand to the struts, Linda would not be able to follow.

According to Linda, the kennel building is forty paces long and hardly more than a glorified doghouse. They placed Caitlin in the structure's only room with four walls, other than a locked storeroom that occupies one end of the building. The remainder of the kennel's interior consists of two rows of empty dog stalls partitioned by heavy Cyclone fencing, with a central aisle running between them. The first stall on the right, past the entry door, holds several live cats to be used as training bait. Despite Linda's fevered state of mind, all this conforms to what Caitlin remembers from her hooded journey down the central aisle.

Using this knowledge, she reconnoitered the entire roof, looking for a weak spot where she might drop down into another part of the kennel. Everywhere she went, the dogs followed, looking up with the obsessive fascination that only real hunger can bring. The pit bulls have narrow waists and massive chests, like those of steroid-addicted bodybuilders. The musculature of a couple of them actually looks human in the chest and forelegs area. Still, she thinks, based on the Internet reading she's done on dogfighting, these are probably not true fighting dogs. If they were, they wouldn't be left to run loose in the same yard; they'd be chained far enough away from each other not to do any damage. Instead they're probably guard or "protection" dogs, which can be controlled by commands, at least by the proper person. What puzzles Caitlin is what happened when she was brought through the yard to the kennel last night. The dogs weren't ordered away by command. She remembers Quinn telling a man to "use bait if you have to" to get them away from the gate. This makes her think the pit bulls might just be a pack of dogs they use for training purposes, kept hungry to intimidate Linda—and now her—into staying put.

The comment about using bait stayed with her, though, and before much time passed, the rudiments of a plan had formed in her mind. If she could somehow get to the stall that holds the cats, she could pry off the bars of a window on one side of the kennel, toss a couple of cats out as bait, then jump through a window on the opposite side and sprint for the fence. If the dogs are hungry enough, she feels sure she can cover the twenty feet required before they figure out her trick. Of course, getting to the cats proved impossible last night. Prying up a sheet of tin from the top side of the roof had proved much harder than kicking up a section from below. If she didn't have to worry about sliding off into the jaws of ravenous pit bulls, it might be easier, but there's no point thinking like that. She's made decent progress on the tin sheet over the spot where, by the sound of mewling, she judges the cats to be, but she stopped with first light, worried that Quinn would show up. It will take another hour's work to get the sheet pried up enough to drop down and get at the cats.

The real problem with her escape plan is Linda. Even if Caitlin can somehow free Linda from her collar and chain, her leg injuries might keep her from running quickly enough to the fence—never mind climbing it.

The only other option Caitlin can think of is the storeroom. Quinn has taken Linda into the storeroom to rape her, and Linda recalls seeing a drug cabinet and stacks of bagged puppy chow inside it. She does not, however, recall seeing any tools. If the cabinet contains tranquilizers like the one they used on Caitlin, there might be some chance of drugging the dogs. But unless she can get down through the roof of the storeroom, that option is off the table. And according to Linda, the men who feed and train the dogs are likely to show up soon—they come once in the morning and once in the evening—and Quinn could appear at any time.

The chain next door rattles louder than before, and Caitlin stops bobbing in her crouch. She hears Linda groan through the plywood, then a parched sobbing sound.

"Linda? It's Caitlin. I'm here."

The chain rattles loudly, and Caitlin hears plastic slide.

"Oh my God," Linda whines. "I have to pee. What am I going to do?"

"Just grit your teeth and do it. That's all you can do."

"I can't! I can't take it!"

"You have to. I'm with you."

The plastic pail slides again, and there's momentary silence. Then Caitlin hears urine hitting the plastic pail, and Linda begins to scream. Caitlin hugs herself and tries to block it out. Once, when she was hiking in Belize with a boyfriend, she developed a urinary tract infection from too frequent sex. The pain was almost unbearable, and by the time they got back to civilization, it had spread to her kidneys. She'd spent three days in a hospital on IV antibiotics, wondering what women had done before the discovery of penicillin. Surely millions must have died, and in the same agony that Linda Church is suffering now.

There's a heavy bump against the plywood wall, and the chain rattles loudly. Linda is gasping. Caitlin is about to try to comfort her when she hears the sound of an engine. The pit bulls begin barking wildly.

"Oh, no," Linda says. "Nooo . . ."

The engine dies, and a door slams.

Linda's sobs grow louder. "I can't

do this!" she wails. "Oh, God, don't let them do this."

Caitlin speaks a few words of reassurance, but her heart is skipping from fear. She's never been at the mercy of a man the way Linda has these past hours, much less a sadistic psychopath. As she struggles to gain control of herself, she hears Linda reciting a Bible verse. Caitlin doesn't recognize it, but the sound of the terrified woman steels something within her. Long ago Caitlin determined that she would not go through life as a victim, and she has no intention of becoming one now.

By the time the door of the kennel building slams open, she's standing naked but erect in her cell, right over the bloody footprints that could alert her captors to her nocturnal efforts. She's used some of her precious drinking water to try to lighten the bloody marks, but the only real result was to make them larger. If anyone notices, she plans to tell them she's started her period.

She hears booted feet come up the

aisle between the stalls, then stop just short of her room. Though she can't see Quinn, she remembers his photograph from the Golden Parachute file Penn showed her. He was handsome in what some call the black-Irish way, with curly black hair, dark eyes, and good bone structure. But even in the photograph the whole effect was spoiled by what appeared to be gray, badly-cared-for teeth.

"Top of the mornin' to you, ladies," Quinn calls. Then his voice moves closer to Caitlin's door. "How you doin' in there, princess?"

"She needs medicine!" Caitlin shouts. "She's really sick."

"I gave her some antibiotics."

"They're not working!"

"I'll give her something else then. We definitely don't want anything interfering with our party."

"Just let her alone! She's in agony!"

"You want to take her place, princess?"

The question seems so genuine that something jumps in Caitlin's chest.

"I wouldn't mind a piece of you, dar-lin'. Cleanest I've ever had, by the look of you."

For one primal moment Caitlin won-ders if Linda wishes he would turn his attention to Caitlin today. Of course she does. And I can't blame her . . .

A key rattles in the lock on Linda's cage, and Linda begins to shriek.

"LET HER ALONE!" Caitlin shouts.

"Ah, it'll pass, now she's done her business. She'll be ready for another workout in no time."

Caitlin crushes her palms over her ears as she hasn't done since she was a child.

CHAPTER

50

I'm sitting at a private table in a side room of the Castle, the restaurant Caitlin and I frequented most often when she lived here. It's a Gothic outbuilding of Dunleith, the most magnificent antebellum mansion in the city. I often make sure that people who are flying in to look at industrial sites stay here, and to prime them for the experience, I tell them that the main house makes Tara in *Gone With the Wind* look like a utility shed. No one has ever argued the point.

Caitlin and I have had good meals and bad ones at the Castle, not because of the quality of the food, but because we've worked through so many phases of our relationship over the tables here. When times were good, we ate at the small table in back, beside the window overlooking the verdant grounds. When times weren't so great, we ate in the private dining room where I'm waiting now. If Caitlin does show up, she won't be surprised to find me at this table.

It's 12:25 now, and though I hate to admit it to myself, she's probably not coming. Caitlin tends to be late now and then, but she wouldn't be on a day such as this. I can't quite believe she'd leave me sitting here without even a phone call, or at least a text message. But I guess she feels strongly enough about where things are to view standing me up as her statement on the subject. I should probably just order lunch and try to parse out her feelings, but given my conversations with Annie, I don't think I can put this event—or nonevent— behind me without being sure Caitlin hasn't been delayed by something unforeseen.

I speed-dial her cell, but it kicks me immediately to voice mail. Either she switched off her phone, anticipating upsetting calls from me, or else she's driving south and chatting happily to Jan about the documentary she'll soon be working on.

Searching my contact list, I call the *Examiner* office and ask for Kim Hunter, the reporter who is Caitlin's best remaining friend on the staff. It takes some time for Kim to come to the phone.

"Hello?" says a young male voice free of any Southern accent.

"Kim, it's Penn Cage."

"Hey."

"Look, I'm down at the Castle, and I thought Caitlin was going to be joining me for lunch. Do you know anything about that?"

"No. She didn't say anything to me."

"You saw her this morning?"

"No. I haven't seen her since yesterday afternoon. She came in and pulled some old stories she worked on."

"Do you know what stories?"

"Something she did on charismatic religions. You know, foot washers and faith healers, that kind of stuff."

Maybe the stories have something to do with her interviews in New Orleans, I think, though it seems unlikely. "Did she say anything to you about going to New Orleans today?"

This time the silence is longer, and Hunter sounds uncertain about telling me more. "She said she might be going down to do some interviews for a documentary being shot there."

"I know about all that, Kim. About Jan, everything. Please tell me anything you know."

"Hang on. Mike would know more about that. He's been taking messages from the guy."

"From the filmmaker?"

"Right. He's called here two or three times this morning. Hang on."

I hear the phone clatter onto something hard.

An alarm is buzzing in my head. . . . If Caitlin had made plans to be in New Orleans today, she would have made them directly with Jan—of that I'm sure.

"Penn?"

"I'm here."

"Mike said the guy called just a few minutes ago. He's been trying to get Caitlin all morning. Apparently Mike figured Caitlin was with you, working on whatever you guys have been doing this past couple of days."

"Thanks, Kim, I appreciate it. If you hear from her, please have her call me immediately, okay?"

"I will. Is something wrong? Should we be worried?"

"I don't know. Just try to find her if you can."

My next call is to the landline at Caitlin's house, but by the fifth ring I'm already out of the restaurant and running to my car.

My tires screech as I skid into the curb in front of Caitlin's house. Her door is standing open. It was closed this morning when Annie and I left for school. For a moment I think everything might be okay, but then I realize Caitlin's rental car isn't in the driveway.

Bounding up the steps, I go through the door and find Kelly crouched over Carl Sims, trying to unwrap duct tape from his wrists. Carl is lying on the floor, his eyes closed, his usually mahogany skin almost gray.

"What happened?" I ask. "Where's Caitlin?"

"Not here, that's all I know. I just got here. Carl's fucked up. They darted him with something." Kelly points to an orange feather lying on the floor, then looks up at me. "I think they've taken her."

"*Taken* her?"

"Kidnapped her."

"Sands?"

"Who else? But why, I have no idea."

My vision begins to blur as panic rushes through me. "I tried to call you on my way here. Why didn't you answer?"

"I can't find my cell phone."

"Is Carl alive?"

"His heart's beating. They must have hit him with some kind of big-game tranquilizer. I just called 911."

"You didn't check in with him last night?"

"Dude, I didn't wake up until two minutes ago. I think they drugged me too. Somebody must have slipped something into my drink at the Corner Bar."

"Why the hell would they take Caitlin now? We had an agreement!"

Kelly gently slaps Carl's face. "Either

they want something from you, or they want to keep you from doing something."

"I already told them I was backing off!"

"I just thought of a third possibility."

"What?"

"Caitlin wasn't too happy about our deal to back off. What if she *didn't*? What if she kept working the case?"

Immediately, I know Kelly's right. Still, I say, "She wouldn't do that."

He gives me a look. "Come on, man. This is Caitlin we're talking about."

She told me last night that she considered our agreement terminated—

"Do you know where she was yesterday?" Kelly asks. "What she did all day? Because Carl wasn't with her a lot of the time. She told him she needed some time alone, and she meant it. I was surprised she let him stay here last night."

"That's *why* she let him stay," I think aloud. "She knew there was risk, because she was still working this thing. Damn it!"

Kelly puts his ear to Carl's chest, then feels his pulse.

"What should I do? Call the FBI? Caitlin's father?"

"No way. Hell no."

"That's what anybody else would do. That's why this was such a stupid move on their part!"

"Sands expects you to know the rules. Calling in the FBI automatically risks the life of the hostage. You go public, like her father might, you'd be signing her death sentence. Think about it: If Caitlin kept pushing the case, Sands would assume you were too. So he thinks *you* broke the agreement. They don't want to kill her. But they could. That's the whole point of taking her. You've got to stay cool. You'll hear from them soon. You should go across the street and check your message machine."

"They know my damned cell number!"

As Kelly and I stare at each other, Carl begins to cough in his arms. Then he vomits onto Kelly's leg and the hardwood floor.

"Thank God he didn't do that last night," Kelly says. "He had duct tape over his mouth. He would have done a Jimi Hendrix right here."

"We can't just wait around for Sands to make the next move."

Kelly wipes vomit off his pants. "I should've just thrown him in the car instead of waiting on an ambulance. Jeez." Kelly looks up at me with weary disgust. "What do you want to do?"

"Grab Sands or Quinn off the street and squeeze them until they tell us where she is. You told Sands yesterday that you'd kill him if he fucked with my family. Well, Caitlin is family."

"She is, absolutely. But we won't be able to get to them now. They've gone to the mattresses."

Carl seems to be breathing better, but he's not yet coherent.

"But *why*?" I ask. "Sands isn't stupid. Why take the risk of me calling the FBI and blowing up the whole Po sting?"

"I told you, either Caitlin gave them no choice, or you have something they want."

"But I don't!"

"Maybe they think you do. Sands thinks there're still variables floating around out there. The USB drive, for instance. And whatever that computer kid had on him. The bird lover. And don't forget Linda Church."

Kelly's right, especially about Linda. "I could see Caitlin trying to find her."

"The worst scenario," he says, "is that Caitlin was planning to go public, and they found out about it. They probably have somebody on their payroll down at the paper. Only makes sense."

"Jesus. Do you think they took her just to kill her? Kill her and lose her body?"

"No. They'd have taken Carl too. This is like when kings used to exchange hostages to prevent wars from happening. Gangs still do that kind of thing."

"How is this like that? They have Caitlin, and we have nothing."

"Sands must *think* you have something. Probably Ben Li's insurance."

As soon as these words leave Kelly's mouth, I know what to do. I take out my cell phone, but before I punch a key, Kelly says, "Whoa, what are you doing?"

"Watch and learn." I speed-dial Seamus Quinn, and the Irishman answers with his usual smug sarcasm.

"Top of the morning to ya, Mr. Mayor."

"It's after lunch, Quinn."

"Is it? I'll bet some people are just wakin' up, though."

I nod meaningfully to Kelly. "We both know what happened last night, so let's skip the games. I know you won't talk about it. I just want you to know one thing."

"You're not gonna threaten me again, are you? I'm getting a bit tired of that."

"Do you remember our conversation on the *Queen* on Monday?"

"I remember your bodyguard assaulted me. With a deadly weapon. I'm thinking of pressing charges."

"Listen to me, you stupid bastard—"

Calm down, Kelly mouths, shaking his head.

"Your boss discussed some missing data. Do you remember that?"

Quinn's answer is silence.

When we left the *Magnolia Queen* yesterday morning, Kelly assumed that Quinn had possession of the missing USB drive, and was holding it to use in a possible deal with Hull. I agreed. But if Sands and Quinn are desperate enough to kidnap Caitlin, something tells me that they have neither Ben Li's stash nor the USB drive. And if Quinn doesn't have it, logic leaves only one other likely candidate—someone who heard the voice memo Tim made on his cell phone before he died. Knowing Shad Johnson as I do—as a political creature above all else—I judge that it's worth the risk of bluffing Quinn on this point.

"I've got it, Quinn."

"You're lying," says the Irishman, and for a moment my confidence wavers. But something in his voice tells me to push on, and with the dizzying rush that a cliff diver must feel, I say, "I've got your boss by the short hairs, you bastard, and there's only one way he's getting it back. A trade."

"Even if you have it, you can't use it," Quinn says with more certainty. "Your own government would bury you. You still don't know what you're dealing with."

Hope and excitement have filled my chest. "I'll tell you what I know. Your government buddy Hull's like a vampire—he can't stand the light. If I go public, he'll vanish into a puff of smoke. Keep your focus, Quinn. The thumb drive is the thing. And if you put one scratch on Caitlin, you and Sands will spend the rest of your lives on Parchman Farm. You think Irish prisons are tough? You'd be better off dead, *mate.* You'll be hearing from me soon."

"Wait—"

When the connection goes dead, I pump my fist. "They don't have it."

"That's great," says Kelly, cradling Carl's head. "The problem is, you don't either."

"No. But I know who does."

The wail of a siren echoes up Washington Street at last.

"Just in the nick of time," mutters Kelly. "Christ."

"Stay with him until they get here," I say, backing through the door.

"Where are you going?"

"The DA's office. You can find me there or City Hall."

CHAPTER

51

It's only three blocks from Caitlin's house to the DA's office. I use the brief drive to call Chief Logan at police headquarters.

"Haven't heard from you in a while, Mr. Mayor," Logan says with subtle sarcasm.

"I could say the same. I've been pretty busy. What about you?"

"You could say that."

"I'm calling to give you a head's up on something. There was a kid named Ben Li who worked on the *Magnolia Queen*. Computer specialist. I think he's in trouble—maybe even dead."

"What makes you think that?"

"Just trust me, Chief. You ought to look into it. I'd pay special attention to things like safe deposit boxes or storage rooms the kid might have rented. You could search his house too, but I don't think you're going to find anything there."

Logan doesn't speak for a few seconds. Then he says, "I sure wish you'd decided to tell me this a little earlier. Like yesterday."

"Why's that?'

"Did this Li kid live on Park Place?"

"I don't know. Why?"

"Because a house owned by someone of that name burned to the ground before dawn this morning."

A cold blade of premonition slices through me, but Logan pushes on too quickly for me to read its significance.

"I'd like to ask you a couple of questions, Penn. Face to face, if possible."

I've reached City Hall, and just in time. "I'd like that too, Don, but I'll have to get back to you. I'm about to go into a meeting with the district attorney."

"That right? Be sure and give him my warmest regards." The sarcasm drips from Logan's voice. "Not that he gives a shit. He thinks the only thing we're here for is to fix speeding tickets for his buddies—who are few and far between."

"I hear you. I'll get back to you when I can."

"I'll see what I can find out about this Li kid."

I tell Logan I appreciate it, then park in my private spot and start toward the building that houses the DA's office. The lunch crowd is returning to the city offices, but I hardly respond to their greetings, my mind on a fire that was surely no accident, and that must have meaning for those with the wits to read it.

It's a measure of what Sands has done to this town that as I pass long-familiar faces, I wonder whether I can trust any of them.

Rose, my secretary, is walking up the sidewalk from the parking lot.

"Paul Labry's waiting for you in your office," she calls. "Apparently he showed up halfway through lunch, and he's been there ever since. Dora says he's very upset."

"Why didn't you call me?"

"I just found out myself. He didn't want you disturbed. Said you had to talk face-to-face and nobody should mention him to you on the phone."

Veering right, I trot across the grass to the door of City Hall.

Two women in the foyer dart out of my path with a cry as I take the steps two at a time. All I can think of is that it was Labry who first gave me the name of Edward Po, from his Golden Parachute files. Asking him had been a selfish thing to do; it put both him and his family at risk. But now I sense that this act is going to come back to haunt me—or has already cost Labry dearly. If he looked deeper into the Golden Parachute investors on his own . . .

"Where is he, Dora?" asks a loud and insistent male voice. "Damn it, he never gets back this late from lunch!"

"Paul?" I call, opening the door. "I'm here, man. What's going on?"

The man who stumbles toward me looks like a caricature of the dignified civil servant who accepted the citizenship award from me at the Ramada two days ago. He looked tired at Tim's burial yesterday, but now his eyes are bloodshot, his cheeks flushed, and his clothes in disarray, the front left tail of his poly-cotton-blend button-down hanging askew.

Dora gives me a look bordering on desperation.

"Let's go in my office, Paul. Come on back."

Labry stares at me like he's about to burst into tears, then throws his hand twice in the direction of my office, walks into it, and collapses in the chair opposite my desk.

I give Dora a placating gesture just as Rose comes in behind me. "Is everything okay?" she asks.

"We're fine," I tell her. "Will you check and see whether Shad Johnson's in his office?"

"You want me to buzz you or wait till you're done?"

"Buzz me when you know."

Shutting the door softly behind me, I lay my hand on Paul's shoulder and squeeze it. "What's happened, Paul? I've never seen you look like this."

"I've never felt like this," he says, staring over my desk as if I'm sitting on the other side of it, and not looking down at the top of his head.

When he remains silent, I go around my desk and take my seat.

"I wanted to come talk to you this morning," he says, "but . . . I couldn't get up the nerve."

"What is it, Paul? Is it what I talked to you about yesterday? Running for mayor?"

Labry laughs so hard at this that mucus drips from his nose. He wipes it with his sleeve, but when he lowers his arm, the smile is gone. "I can't ever be mayor now. Never."

"Why not?"

"I wouldn't get fifty votes. I don't deserve fifty votes."

"Why not? What's the matter?"

"I'll be bankrupt in a month. My father too, only he doesn't know it. We're going to lose everything. The business . . . our houses. All of it."

"What?"

"I told you yesterday that retail's gone down the toilet. Well, I did some things to try to compete with the big guys. Expand, you know? But I just made things worse.

The debts just grew and grew. Then I did some gambling, hoping to make up the shortfall."

This takes me completely off guard. "I didn't know you gambled."

"I don't, really. Just enough to get to know some of the people who run the casinos. Which is crazy, when you think about it, because I didn't even want the damned casinos here. But it was Sands who bailed me out, man. He got me out of—"

"Sands?" I ask sharply. "Jonathan Sands?"

"Right. One night I got a little drunk and started bitching about the banks hounding me, and Sands offered to help out. He did too. But now . . ." Paul looks helplessly at me, then grabs his own shirtfront and jerks it upward. "They own me, man. They *own* me. I owe them so much money, I could never pay it back. There's no way I can be mayor with them pulling my strings like a puppet. It'd be a travesty of everything you and I ever talked about doing."

"Jesus, Paul . . . I had no idea. Why didn't you come to me? I would have tried to help."

"Come to you? Do you have *any* idea how hard that would have been? Come to you and tell you I'm a total fuckup? My old man already thinks I drove the business into the ground. He doesn't get it, how the world has changed."

"Paul—look, I know you're in trouble, but I've got something really big going on right now. I've got to make some calls."

He's shaking his head again. "No, no, I told you, I was supposed to come see you this morning. I just couldn't do it. That's why I started drinking. I couldn't face you, man."

"What are you talking about?"

At last all his frenetic twitching stops, and he looks me dead in the eye. "They sent me to talk to you. To give you a message."

"Who did?"

"Sands's security guy. Quinn. It's about Caitlin."

For a moment I'm not sure I've heard right, but then my face goes cold.

"Whatever it is you're doing," Labry says, "you've got to stop it for thirty-six hours. That's the message. They don't have any intention of hurting her. They've got her in a hotel somewhere."

I'm pushing myself slowly away from my desk, trying to process what I'm hearing as panic and rage rise in me. "How long have you known this, Paul?'

"Quinn came to the store this morning. Look, I know it sounds bad. But they have some big deal about to go down, and they said you guys were going to screw it up somehow, by going public with something. I don't even know if you know about it. Maybe it was mostly Caitlin, but . . . Penn, don't look at me like that. You look like I took her or something. I love Caitlin. She's got more—"

"Get out of my sight, Paul."

Labry stares as though I've slapped his face, then begins sobbing. I stand and walk past him, heading for the stairs.

"Where are you going?" he cries, running after me as Rose gapes.

"To see Shad Johnson."

"Shad? Why?" He catches up with me on the staircase and pulls me to a stop. "Penn, if you report this, they'll kill her."

"You just said they wouldn't!"

Labry is fidgeting again, trying to think of anything he can to stop me. "I don't *know*! I have no idea what's really going on. But you must, right? Just do whatever it is they need, and she'll be fine!"

"Get out of my way, or I'll throw you down these stairs. I'm not going to Shad about the kidnapping."

He backs away, looking stricken. "Why, then?"

"He has something I need."

"What?"

"You're still trying to get something for Sands, aren't you?"

"No! I had to do this, Penn. He was going to tell my father everything! Pop would die of shame, man."

I leap down the stairs and race out of the building, headed down the block to the DA's office. Labry chases after me, yelling where anyone can hear. A deputy going into the sheriff's office looks up and stares after us.

"Let me make it up to you, man!" Labry screams. "I'll do anything."

"Get her back for me!" I shout over my shoulder. "Can you do that? That's the only way to make this up."

As I enter the building that houses the district attorney's office, a sudden epiphany hits me. I run up the stairs, knowing that Labry will follow. When I reach the top, Paul calls out from the landing, trying to keep from being heard by the people on the upper floor.

"Penn, don't! Don't say anything you can't take back! Let's go talk to Sands. I'm sure we can work something out. You've got money—"

"They don't care about *money!* Not the kind we have. They could buy this town a thousand times over!"

"There's got to be something we can do!"

"There is. Come up here, and I'll tell you."

Labry climbs warily toward me, then stops one step below the top as I make room for him at the head of the staircase.

I reach out and pull him up to the top step, then speak quietly. "You're going to come into Shad's office with me and tell him just what you told me. The message you gave me, and who told you to give it."

Labry jerks back, his eyes wide, then tries to turn to go back downstairs. I reach out and grab his shirt, half to hold him here, half to keep him from breaking his neck. But panic has seized him. He windmills his arms to get his balance, then strikes out at me hard enough to disengage us. As we separate, he falls backward, but the wall catches him, and he practically rides it to the bottom of the steps.

"How could you do it?" I shout. "Our children *play* together!"

Labry is sobbing again, staring up in despair. "I had no choice," he says in a dead voice. "No choice."

He looks as if he's about to say something else, but then his eyes go wide, and he backs out of the building.

"What the hell was that about?" asks a clipped baritone voice behind me.

I turn and look into the face of Shadrach Johnson. He regards me with cool detachment, waiting for me to explain my presence on his territory.

"You and I need to talk," I tell him. "But first get rid of your secretary. You don't want any witnesses to this conversation."

CHAPTER

52

Caitlin is staring out the window of her plywood cell, into the sharklike eyes of a giant white dog. After Quinn took Linda to the storeroom, her screams stopped, but soon men arrived in a pickup hauling a long trailer behind it. What caught Caitlin's attention was a man wearing a heavily padded suit that made him look like the Michelin tire man. She assumed this was for working with dangerous dogs, and her assumption soon proved correct.

The trailer unloaded four white dogs that dwarfed the pit bulls outside. Their heads reached the men's waists, and they had wrinkled faces with cropped ears that gave them the look of some hybrid fighting creature she had never before seen. The pit bulls went wild when the white dogs appeared; several cowered near the kennel. A few minutes later, a second trailer appeared with more men. They opened the gate of the kennel yard, gathered up the pit bulls, loaded them into their trailer, and drove away in a cloud of dust. Then the white dogs were released into the kennel yard.

After studying them for a while, Caitlin felt sure these new dogs must be Bully Kuttas, like the dog Penn described on his porch the night Sands revealed himself. Penn had thought the dogs that attacked him and Kelly on the river island were also Bully Kuttas, but he couldn't be sure. In any case, these white dogs frighten Caitlin more than the pit bulls, something that hadn't seemed possible an hour ago.

The sound of a closing door pulls her away from the window. Linda's door rattles the wall of Caitlin's room, then she hears Linda's gate close. Quinn says something too soft for Caitlin to make out, and Linda doesn't reply. Then the booted feet stump off down the kennel.

After the door closes, Caitlin says, "Linda? Are you all right?"

"My stomach hurts."

"Did he hurt you again?"

"No. He gave me some different pills. I think that's why my stomach hurts."

"Well, try to hold them down. Drink some water if you can. That will dilute your urine, and it won't hurt as bad when you pee."

A sound like a scoff comes through the wood.

"Linda, I've got an idea about how to get out of here. I want you to listen to me. Will you do that?"

After a brief silence, Linda says, "I'm listening."

Quickly, Caitlin describes her plan to use a cat as bait to distract the dogs to one side of the kennel, while she and Linda make a break for the fence on the other side. She makes it sound as plausible as she can, but Linda's lack of questions worries her. "Well?" she asks at last. "What do you think?"

"It won't work."

Caitlin tries to suppress her frustration. "Why not?"

"Because first you have to get the cats. And just getting the roof off won't get you through the Cyclone fence. It's over my head too, not just walls."

Caitlin starts to argue, but Linda's still talking.

"And even if you get the bars off the windows, you'll never get this chain off my neck."

"I will. After everyone leaves, I'm going to get into that storeroom and find a way. There has to be a key in there. Or some kind of tool. Didn't you say he takes the collar off when he abuses you?"

"Sometimes. Other times he hooks it to a bolt on a table with a shorter chain."

"Where does he get the key when he takes it off you?"

"From the same ring as his car keys."

Damn.

"You have to leave me out of it,"

Linda says, almost too low to hear. "You know that."

"No, I don't."

"You do. Because even if you get the collar off, I'll never make it to that fence. Not before the dogs get me. And I can't die like that. I can't."

"You're not going to die, Linda. You're going to get out of here with me."

Silence.

"What if I drugged the dogs?"

"With what?"

"There might be tranquilizers in the storeroom."

"They took all that stuff out. I looked when I was in there a minute ago, like you told me to. When he was getting me the pills. All I saw was junk that looked like steroids and supplements. I used to date a bodybuilder in Oklahoma City, and he took the same kind of stuff."

"Linda, you have to stop thinking it's impossible. If you think that way, you make it so. I'm going to get us out of here."

To her amazement, Caitlin hears what sounds like sad laughter. "You think that because you're different from me. Stuff works out for girls like you. That's just the way life is. But for me . . . it's different. No matter what I do, something always goes wrong."

"I want you to stop saying that kind of thing! There's no difference between you and me."

"You're wrong," Linda says wearily. "I got away once. I risked everything and jumped off that boat. I put myself in God's hands. And here I am. You can't get me out. Go without me. Maybe you can bring help back in time."

Caitlin considers this. The odds of Quinn leaving Linda alive once he knew Caitlin had escaped would be zero. And how long might it take her to find help?

"I'm not going without you," she says.

"Caitlin?" Linda says in a tighter voice.

"Yes?"

"I haven't told you everything."

The hair rises on Caitlin's neck. There is no terror like the terror of the unknown. "What is it? Tell me."

"I know what those white dogs are for."

"What?"

"They're going to fight them against a man."

Caitlin looks at the wall, as if she could read Linda's face through it. "What? You mean like feed a man to them?"

"No. A man's gonna fight them. Try to kill them in a pit."

"How do you know that?"

"I heard them talking, and I've seen them getting ready for it."

"What did you see?"

"Yesterday morning, they brought a man into the kennel and put him in a stall. They were waiting for those white dogs to get here. The guy looked like a homeless man they pulled off the street. A drunk. Later Quinn told me he was."

"What did they do with him?"

"First they put some kind of vest on him."

"Like that protective suit? The padded thing?"

"No. More like a bulletproof vest. I saw a lot of those in Las Vegas. And they put some kind of plates on his arms. When they were done, he looked like a gladiator or something."

Caitlin can scarcely form her next question. "What did they do then?"

"They took him out there and let one of those dogs loose on him."

She closes her eyes. "What happened?"

"It took that dog about twenty seconds to kill him. Ripped his throat out. Then they let the rest of the dogs tear him up."

"Why did they do that? To give them a taste of human blood?"

"No. They were testing the suit. The armor. I heard them talking outside. They just wanted to see how it would stand up to the dogs' teeth and jaws. The suit is special-made. They killed that man just to find out how good it worked."

Caitlin tries to shut out her horror and think logically. "Have they ever had

a fight like that before? Dogs against a man?"

"Once. They have a videotape of it. He had it."

"Who? Quinn?"

"No. Him."

"Sands?"

"Mm-hm."

"Why did you wait till now to tell me this?"

"I didn't want to scare you. I know you're brave . . . but I'm telling you, those dogs out there are devils. They're war dogs. They're like the one he has. He knows everything about them. Jonny's dad raised dogs back in Ireland. When he was a boy, his daddy gave him a puppy to raise . . . and then he made him kill it. To teach him how the world was, he said. Sands knows dogs like no one I ever met. And the dogs he trains . . . you don't want to be close to them. You may fool them for a second or two with those cats, but what they live for is killing. I don't want to see you torn to pieces out there."

"Linda, when is this fight supposed to take place?"

"Soon. That's all I know."

"Will it just be another victim, some drunk or something?"

"No. A man's coming in to fight them special. He'll have a weapon. A knife, maybe two."

"I wonder who he is."

"I think he's a convict, from what they were saying. One of those UFC-type fighters. Some walleyed redneck, I'm sure. But they're all getting ready for it."

Caitlin takes this in, analyzing their situation in light of these new developments.

"Linda, have you ever heard of a man named Edward Po?"

"No."

"What about a girl named Jiao?"

Linda hisses. "Oh, I know who she is all right. The Queen of Sheba. She don't know nothing about who Sands really is. How he screws all the girls on the boat. That Jiao . . . she lives down there in New Orleans, away from all this. At least she did until Katrina, anyway. Now . . . I don't know. Maybe that's one reason he wants me dead. I've seen her look at me like she knows I mean something to him. Or meant something."

"Have you heard Jiao has a cousin? From China?"

"I did hear that. He flew in for one of the fights a while back. He brought his own dog with him."

Caitlin is starting to see the outline of a larger picture. "Linda, listen to me. I want you to tell me everything you know about Jiao and her cousin. And Sands. Everything, no matter how trivial it may seem. Will you do that?"

"I think that medicine may be working," Linda says softly. "My God. The pain isn't as bad."

"You're going to make it, I promise. Penn and his friends are looking for us with everything in their power right now. I know they are. A friend of his actually killed one of those white dogs the other night, with nothing but a knife."

"I don't believe it."

"It's true. He cut the dog's head off to make sure it didn't have rabies. You have to hang on, Linda. You have to believe. They're coming to get us."

"If that's true, then why risk your life to try to get past those devil dogs?"

Caitlin thinks about this. "Because you can't wait around to be saved. This isn't Cinderella, *honey. It's* Beauty and the Beast, *but there's no prince hidden inside the beast. After the feeders come this evening, I'm breaking through the roof and getting two of those cats. And then I'm getting that collar off your neck, if I have to chew through the leather to do it. Okay?"*

"If you say so."

"I do. Now—tell me about Jiao."

53

Shad speaks over his shoulder as he ushers me in. "Why was one of our most distinguished selectmen drunk in the middle of the day?"

I glance briefly around the district attorney's office. He has a huge, antique desk pilfered from one of the historic buildings owned by the city—three-quarters the size of a billiards table. The wall behind him is covered with diplomas and plaques, while the one to my right almost bulges from the weight of framed photographs: Shadrach Johnson's Wall of Respect. In most of the pictures, Shad stands beside the nationally famous black politicians and celebrities who visited Natchez during his 1996 mayoral campaign against Wiley Warren. Fewer than half of those figures returned to the city two years ago when Shad ran against me during the special election. Apparently, during the interim, they'd learned that Shad was primarily interested in advancing the cause of Shad Johnson, and no one else, no matter what color they might be. Many politicians share this illness, of course, but Shad has a particularly virulent strain of it.

"Did you come in to look at the pictures?" Shad asks.

I turn and look deep into his eyes. "Caitlin Masters was kidnapped last night. She was taken by Jonathan Sands and Seamus Quinn. Paul Labry just informed me that if I do nothing against Sands for thirty-six hours, they'll return her to me unharmed."

Shad's eyes go wide, then narrow slowly. "Labry works for Sands?"

"You thought you were the only one?"

The district attorney jabs his forefinger at me. "That's slander."

"Sue me. Why aren't you advising me to call the FBI, Shad?"

He looks toward his window, then back at me. "If that's what you wanted to do, you'd already have done it. What are you really doing here, Cage? What do you want from me?"

"That's a long list, buddy. I want to know why you soft-pedaled the murder of Tim Jessup. Why you misappropriated evidence and withheld facts critical to the investigation from the police chief. Why you're not pushing to find out what happened to a computer programmer named Ben Li, who was also probably murdered. But I already know the answer, don't I?"

"I don't know anything about that. Any of it. Those are police matters."

"The night Tim died, you made a point of telling me you were the chief law enforcement officer of the city. So why does your police chief think the last thing you want him to do is make progress on any of these investigations?"

Shad folds his hands together and leans back in his chair. "Chief Logan and I don't always see eye to eye. That's no secret."

I stand and put my hands on his desk, then lean over him. "I'll tell you why I'm here. Right now, Jonathan Sands thinks I have a certain item that Tim Jessup stole from the *Magnolia Queen.* A USB thumb drive. But *you* know I don't have it. Don't you?"

The district attorney's face remains impassive. Shad is good in a courtroom, and he'd be a hell of a poker player, though I hear he prefers bridge. While he ponders my statement, I glance over at his Wall of Respect. One photograph draws my attention. It shows a huge boar hog, probably five or six hundred pounds, hanging by its hind legs from a hoist. Shad stands on one side of the hog, while on the other, wearing a bright orange jersey with the number 88 on it, stands a tall black man with a hunting rifle lying across his muscular forearms.

"I didn't know you were a hunter, Shad. I thought bridge was your game. Or the odd set of tennis."

Johnson regards me with silent hatred.

"Is that Darius Jones?" I ask. "The wide receiver for San Antonio?"

"You know it is."

"Was that photo taken around here?"

Shad shifts in his seat. "On DeSalle Island. Hunting camp."

DeSalle Island lies farther downriver than we paddled last night, almost to Angola Prison, but it's exactly the kind of remote spot in which Sands has been holding his dogfights.

"I think I've got the picture," I say quietly. "Darius win any money on the dogs?"

"On the what?"

I give Shad a knowing look. "I guess it doesn't matter. Darius has got it to lose, right? Long as he doesn't get caught."

"You're wearing out your welcome, Cage. I don't know anything about any computer drive."

I lean farther over the desk, into Shad's personal space. "I know you have it. You're the only person who could. You had Tim's cell phone. You heard the voice memo he made before he died. And somehow you got into the morgue—or got someone to go in there for you—and you got that drive. You want to dig into dead men's asses for fun and profit, that's your business. But I need that drive. If I don't have something to trade for Caitlin, they're going to kill her. Do you read me, Shad?"

The district attorney remains stone-faced.

"I think I know where you are on this," I say, trying to help him along. "You think that drive is your ace in the hole, if everything goes to hell. I don't know how badly compromised you are, or what Sands has on you. But you need to figure out which side you're on. Because if you give me that drive now, I'll make sure you stay out of trouble when the wheels come off of this deal."

"I have no idea what you're talking about," Shad says evenly. "But even if I did, you don't have the power to offer anybody any kind of deal—certainly not immunity from prosecution. I'm the DA, Cage, and I could jail you for assault right now, based on what I saw five minutes ago."

I want to snatch Shad up from his chair and bang his head against the desk, but that's not going to get me the drive. I'd find myself in the county jail in short order, and it's right across the street.

"Shad, there's a federal investigation

going on in this county, and my guess is you don't know a thing about it. Or if you do, you only know enough to make your asshole pucker. When the feds don't tell you they're on your turf, it's bad news for you. So, I repeat, you need to decide which side you're on. And the best way to prove you're on the right one is to give me that drive."

Shad gives me a tired smile. "I think we're done here."

I make no move to leave or even straighten up. "After I leave, you might be tempted to destroy that drive. I could see the logic of it, from your point of view. But that would be a mistake. You're going to need a friend when this blows up. And if Caitlin dies because you didn't give it to me, I'll hound you right into Parchman, I swear to God. You'll have a cell right next to Sands."

There's a sudden rush of heavy footsteps outside, and then someone pounds on Shad's door. I jump to my feet and open the door, expecting to see Paul Labry making another plea for forgiveness. But it's Mitch Catton, a deputy from the sheriff's department, and he's breathing hard.

"What is it, Deputy?" Shad asks calmly.

"Paul Labry was just killed in a car accident!"

"What?"

"He hit a bridge abutment. Must have been doing seventy, at least."

"Was anyone else hurt?" I ask.

"Nope. One-car accident. There was an empty bottle of vodka in the car too. Sally, over to the clerk's office, told me Mr. Labry'd been hanging around here all during lunch. Said he smelled like a liquor cabinet."

I look down at Shad, my eyes filled with foreboding.

"Thank you, Mitch," Shad says. "Mayor Cage and I need to finish our conversation."

"Okay, sorry. I just figured you'd want to know. I mean, is there anything special we should do because it's a selectman?"

"No, just follow your normal procedures."

Catton stares at us in puzzlement for a few seconds, then shuts the door and bangs down the stairs.

"This town is under siege," I say softly. "And the biggest threat always comes from within. Don't kid yourself that you can come out of this clean. Not without me. I don't know if Paul committed suicide or if they killed him, but when this is all over, there's going to be a reckoning. Pick your side, Shad. Fast. That thumb drive is your only get-out-of-jail-free card. You know how to reach me."

"Get out of my office."

I hold up my forefinger and point at him, my eyes burning, then turn and go.

CHAPTER

54

Caitlin stands naked in the storeroom of the kennel, a leather dog collar tight around her neck, its thick chain binding her to the wooden support post of some shelves behind her. She's bound so tightly that she can't turn her head, which forces her to watch the scene taking place before her. She's shut her eyes as long and as often as she could, but Quinn has sworn to Taser her if she does it again.

Linda Church lies bent forward over a crude table, her collar chained to a ringbolt set in its top. Naked from the waist down, Seamus Quinn plunges relentlessly into her from behind, his eyes on Caitlin to be sure she's watching. Linda screamed so much when he began that Quinn wrapped four long pieces of duct tape around her face. Caitlin is afraid Linda will vomit and aspirate it before Quinn can get the tape off—if he'd even try.

"Don't pretend you don't want to look," Quinn says, panting from exertion. "Everything that walks on two legs would watch this . . . if they knew nobody was looking. Why do you think Romans paid their last coin to see this kind of thing? This is what we are, princess. The emperors gave the people what they wanted—sex and death. Everything else is just window dressing."

Caitlin keeps her eyes on Quinn but speaks to Linda. "Think about something else," she says in what she hopes is a maternal voice. "Anything but this. This will pass, like every other thing in life. You don't believe me right now, but it will—"

"Shut your gob!" Quinn shouts, seizing Linda's haunches and driving harder. "You know what they really loved in the arena? Women and animals. They'd take the urine of female animals and spread it on virgins, sometimes twenty at a time. Then they'd let the trained males at them. Baboons and mandrills, bulls and boars, dogs and leopards, even giraffes. That's history—real, every bit of it." Quinn shows Caitlin his gray teeth. "People don't change, and you're no different."

Caitlin can't bear to look at Linda's face. All she can think to do is deflect some of Quinn's bottomless rage onto herself. "I'd like to see you get it this rough," she says. "See how you like being on the receiving end."

Quinn huffs and laughs. "A man does the givin', princess. The woman does the takin'. I'm not particular, so long as it's warm and tight."

"Your day is coming," Caitlin says in a barely audible voice. "There are places not far from here where men twice your size will be happy to give you what you're giving her. Twice as much, from what I saw when you dropped your pants."

Quinn pulls out and starts toward Caitlin, but before he can reach her, the door to her right bursts open and two men enter the room. One wears a black balaclava hood, the other a green one. The man in the black mask looks from Quinn to Caitlin, then back at Quinn. It's as though Linda isn't in the room.

"What are you doing here?" Quinn asks in a dazed voice.

"Liam called me." The black-masked man's voice seems hardly distinguishable from Quinn's. "About a day late, by the look of it."

"You told me I could do what I wanted with her."

"You bloody sod. For one night, I said." The man looks at Caitlin, eyes glinting through the slanted eyeholes cut in the balaclava. "Has he touched you?"

Caitlin is certain that the man in the black balaclava is Jonathan Sands, but given the circumstances, letting him know that could be fatal. "Only to put this collar on me," she says. "He's raped her for two days straight, though. She has some serious infections, her leg and her urinary tract. She needs an emergency room right away."

Quinn laughs, then cuts off the sound with a cough.

The man in the black balaclava takes two steps toward Quinn and leans forward as though to speak, but then his right hand lashes out and cracks the bridge of Quinn's nose. Blood erupts from the Irishman's face, and he topples backward, holding his nose with both hands.

The third man watches without reaction.

Quinn gets to his knees but remains doubled over, blood pouring through his hands. Sands extends his arm to help him up, but when Quinn takes the hand, Sands snaps his boot into Quinn's rib cage with a crunch. The force of the blow lifts Quinn bodily from the cement. He drops flat on his belly, gasping for air.

"Get up, you piece of shite."

Quinn gets slowly to his knees, covering his belly like a beaten dog preparing for another kick, then slides up the wall behind him until he's erect.

Sands jerks his head toward Caitlin. "Where's her clothes?"

"Over there. In the cabinet."

"Get 'em. And take that fuckin' collar off her."

"Why? Are you trading her?"

"Get her bloody clothes. And keep your mouth shut while you're about it. Jaysus."

Quinn goes to the cabinet and retrieves Caitlin's jeans and T-shirt. "You broke my ribs," he grunts, as he hands them to her.

"I ought to give you a proper digging," Sands mutters. "You ignore another order and I'll have Liam kneecap you. I've half a mind to do it here and now. Got a drill in the lorry."

Quinn holds up both hands, silently pleading for mercy.

"What about it, ladies?" Sands asks. "You want to hear this bastard scream?"

"We just want to go home," Caitlin

says. "We don't care about you or him or whatever you're doing."

A toothy smile flashes through the mouth of the balaclava. "That's what you say now. But you'll feel different later."

"What are you going to do with us?"

Sands sniffs and keeps looking at her, but says nothing. Slowly, his eyes travel from her breasts to her ankles, then back to her eyes. As this happens, she realizes that there is no "us" for Sands or Quinn. In their minds, Linda is already dead.

"You'll be home in twenty-four hours, good as new," Sands says. "That's a promise."

"I don't believe you."

"You don't have to. It's the truth."

"What about Linda?"

Sands glances to his right, where Linda remains bent over the table, sobbing through her nose, covering the duct tape with glistening mucus.

"She'll be looked after. She can't go back home, though. Not right away. She'll have to start over somewhere else. We'll either give her a job on one of our other boats or see she has the money to start somewhere else. Money's no problem."

Caitlin knows he's lying, but there's nothing to be done. She wishes Linda believed what he was saying, but who knows better than Linda Church how worthless Sands's promises are?

Quinn takes a key from atop the cabinet, then comes over and unlocks the thick leather collar from Caitlin's neck. He's still naked from the waist down, but his erection's gone, his penis shrunk to a nub.

"Go ahead," Sands says to Caitlin.

"What?"

"Kick him. Right in the bollocks. He deserves it for being so bloody stupid."

As Quinn darts out of reach of her feet, Caitlin recalls what he asked Sands: Are *you trading her? Penn must be trying to negotiate her release by trading something for her. What? Could he be onto Ben Li's private insurance policy? During the night, Linda told her that Quinn had several times asked her what "The birds know" might mean. Apparently*

Ben Li had screamed this phrase several times as he was being interrogated belowdecks on the Magnolia Queen. *Maybe Penn has cracked this mysterious code—*

"Put her back in the office," Sands says to Quinn, who's pulling on his pants.

"What about the other one?"

"Wherever you had her before. And get her some fucking medicine. Human medicine. You know where to get it."

Quinn looks puzzled by this order, but he signals his willingness to obey with a nod.

"I'll take Masters," Sands says, motioning Caitlin toward the storeroom door.

Her door is the first outside the storeroom, the only other room with four walls. Now she can see the rest of the kennel, and it's just as Linda described it, two rows of Cyclone-fence stalls, the cats housed in the one nearest the main door.

Sands pauses outside her room, waiting for her to enter first. Caitlin looks through the eyeholes of the balaclava. "Will you give Linda her clothes back? Please?"

Sands stares into her eyes for a long time. Then he shouts, "Give Linda her clothes!" and prods Caitlin into her cell.

Caitlin goes to the corner and squats over her bloody footprints, but not in time. Sands grabs her wrist and pulls her across the floor. Staring down at the prints, he looks around the walls, then up at the roof. An appreciative smile shows through the mouth hole.

"Seamus?" he calls.

"Yeah?"

"Get those fucking cats out of here."

"Why?"

"Just do it!"

"What am I supposed to do with them?"

"What do I care? Just get 'em outside the fence, yeah?"

"Okay."

Sands takes a strand of Caitlin's hair between his fingers, rubs it softly. "Very fine," he says in the tone of a man judging an animal pelt.

She pulls away but makes a point of

not jerking back, so as not to appear afraid.

Sands smiles again, then looks back at the bent tin of the roof.

"Smart girl," he says. "Cage is a lucky man."

CHAPTER

55

When I come out of the district attorney's office, I find Kelly sitting on the concrete wall by the courthouse, beneath the shade of a gnarled oak. His rented 4Runner is parked in front of him, but when he points at it, I shake my head and sit beside him on the wall.

"What's the deal?" he asks.

"Shad has the thumb drive, but he's not giving it up unless I get more leverage."

"He admitted having it?"

"No. But he's got it. I'd like to take you back in there and sweat it out of him, but he is the DA. Two minutes after we left him, we'd be in there."

Kelly looks to where I'm pointing, a tall pile of red brick with slit windows above the sheriff's department across the street. He nods. "Okay, what's plan B?"

"While Shad's at work, I want you to search his house. If you don't find it there, come back to his office after work and search that. Can you get his safe open?"

"No problem."

"Okay. We need to check Ben Li's place too. They burned it down, but we should check the yard, anything. I've got Chief Logan looking into any other property he might have had. Storage units, safe-deposit boxes, like that. Maybe we'll get lucky."

"You trust Logan?" Kelly asks, as two women come down the courthouse steps and turn our way.

"As much as anyone in this town." One of the women waves. I do the same, acting as if I recognize her.

"What about you? What are you going to do?"

"Run the bluff of my life."

"What's your play?"

"The only way to increase the odds of Caitlin living through the night is to make Hull think I'm willing to blow his case wide-open if they hurt her. That they've pushed me so far I no longer give a shit about Po or anything else."

"That shouldn't be a tough sell. If the time limit Labry gave you is right—thirty-six hours—and he was supposed to tell you that this morning, the Po sting must be set up for tomorrow. Tomorrow night at the latest. Hull will be sweating bullets until then."

"Exactly. But I have to be careful. I can't demand that they trade Caitlin for something I don't have, and I don't want Sands to panic. He could kill her and split."

"He'll figure the moment Caitlin's loose, she'll go public anyway."

"Right. What I want is to know Caitlin's alive."

Kelly scratches his chin. "Proof of life. It's like you're keeping your cool, but you know better than to trust Sands and Quinn. Do you think Hull knew they were going to take her?"

I shake my head. "He would have tried

to stop that. I think they panicked and did it, then presented him a fait accompli—if they've told him at all."

"So what will you ask for? A phone call from her?"

"They won't do that. We could back-track with the cell company and figure out where she called from."

"A photo with today's newspaper is standard. They could text it to you."

"I'm thinking of something even faster and simpler."

"What?"

"A question only she would know the answer to."

Kelly gives me a thumbs-up. "Do it."

I speed-dial Hull, but he doesn't answer. There's a click that I think is his voice mail, but suddenly his voice comes from the phone.

"Yes? Who is this?"

"Penn Cage."

"I'm in a meeting. What is it?"

"You'd better take a bathroom break if you want Edward Po's scalp on your wall."

"Don't use that name on an open line."

"Buddy, I'm sixty seconds from calling

the FBI and telling it to their kidnap squad."

"Kidnap squad?" Hull sounds genuinely shocked.

"Is that news to you?"

"I don't know what you're talking about," he says under his breath. "But I told you, the FBI is part of my task force."

"*Part* of the FBI is part of your task force. The National Security Branch, I'm guessing. And the Money Laundering Task Force. But I know how the FBI works kidnappings, Hull. Five minutes after I call the New Orleans and Jackson field offices, they'll call the Puzzle Palace, and you'll have a world-class clusterfuck on your hands."

"Give me just a minute," Hull says softly. "I'll be right back."

I hear shuffling, then a closing door. "Cage, I don't know what the hell you're up to, but we're into endgame on this. You're begging for an obstruction-of-justice charge."

I laugh out loud. "Last night Caitlin Masters was kidnapped from her home. A sworn officer of the law was almost killed protecting her. I don't know how much you know about this, and I don't give a shit. I want proof that she's alive."

"How can I—"

"Do you have any idea who that girl's father is? Clinton Masters owns twentysome newspapers across the Southeast. He's got Rupert Murdoch on speed dial. If I pick up the phone and tell him what's happened, you can kiss Edward Po smack on the ass as he flutters out of your net. *Capisce?*"

Kelly's smiling and nodding encouragement.

"Let's just calm down," Hull temporizes. "If there has been a kidnapping, you should know this: Going public sometimes results in the death of the hostage. The Bureau can tell you that."

"You're not hearing me, William. Your pet psychopaths crossed the line down here. I no longer give a shit about your investigation, and I have enough evidence to arrest Sands for money laundering on my own hook right now. I want proof of life, and I want it in fifteen minutes. If I don't get it, your investigation goes straight down the toilet. Make it happen."

"What kind of proof do you have in mind?"

"I want an answer from Caitlin Masters to a question that only she would know."

"What is it?"

"Who did you lose your virginity to?"

Kelly gives me a strange look.

"You got that, Hull?"

"Yes, but—"

"Make it happen. Once I know she's alive, we'll go from there. If I don't have the answer in fifteen minutes, I pull the trigger."

Hull is still trying to talk when I hang up.

Kelly stands and stretches. "Are we waiting here for their answer?"

"Might as well. I want to ask you something. I think it's bothering me down so deep that I couldn't quite voice it. But there's no use hiding from it."

"You're wondering if they're planning to kill her no matter what. Right?"

"Yeah. Kidnapping alone carries the death penalty in Mississippi. How could they hope to let her go and get away clean? No matter what kind of immunity deal they have with Hull."

"I think it depends on what that plea

deal is—what Sands's plans are after Po is busted. If he's planning to go back to China and take over Po's operations, I guess he could let Caitlin go."

"But what about Po's son? He'll want the China operations, right?"

Kelly begins a set of what look like isometric exercises with his hands. "No doubt. More likely, they've cut a private deal for Sands to keep the U.S. casinos, while the son takes over the China stuff."

"And in that case?"

"I don't think Sands will want Caitlin running around screaming about kidnapping. Much easier to kill her, lose the body, and never worry about it again."

The detachment in Kelly's voice nudges my nestled fear back toward panic. "But even if that's his plan, he has to keep her alive until the sting. Right?"

"Absolutely."

"So we've got what, thirty hours to find her?"

"Or to find something to trade for her." Kelly sits on the wall again and hits my knee with his fist. "And we will, man. We will."

The buzz of my cell phone makes both

of us jump, but the caller isn't Hull or Sands. It's my father. "Dad?"

"Penn, I need you to come by the house, if you can."

"What's the matter? You're not at work?"

"Take it easy. Peggy called me. Annie called her from school, saying she had a stomachache, and Peggy called me to come home and look at her. I think she's having a delayed reaction to the separation in Houston. All she really needs is to see you. To see all of us together."

Remembering our conversation in the car this morning, this doesn't surprise me. But Annie has almost never asked to be checked out of school. I wonder if Dad could be getting me home for some other reason.

"I'm on my way."

"Good."

Kelly is on his feet again. "Everything okay?"

"We need to get to my dad's house."

We move quickly to Kelly's 4Runner. "Can we talk in here?" I ask, climbing into the passenger seat.

"Swept it right before I drove down here. We're okay."

Kelly is turning left on Wall Street when my cell phone chirps, signaling a text message. Closing my eyes briefly, I take my cell out of my pocket and check the message. It reads: PHILIP RIVERS.

"What is it?" Kelly asks. "Caitlin's answer?"

I nod, thinking.

"Is it the right answer?"

"It's *an* answer. But not the right one. Not quite."

"What does that mean?"

"It's part right and part wrong. The message says Philip Rivers. The guy's name was Philip, but Philip McKey."

"Okay, then. That's Caitlin doing that. She's handing you information. A clue about something. Philip means she's alive. What does *rivers* mean?"

"The river!" I cry.

"She's by a goddamn river," Kelly agrees. "But which river?"

"The Mississippi. Has to be, right? That's where all the action has been. All the dogfights and training stuff. They probably have her at one of those camps, or on an island."

"But she said 'ri-*vers*,' plural."

"The singular would be too obvious. Wouldn't sound like a name."

"Maybe. But she could also be on a tributary, something that flows into the Mississippi."

"Who cares? Either way, we know she's alive, and she's somewhere close to a river. Odds are, it's the Mississippi."

"So, what are you thinking?" Kelly asks.

"I'm thinking Danny McDavitt and his FLIR pod."

"Classic. We can fly the river as soon as it gets dark. I'll be his TFO."

"His what?"

"Tactical flight officer. You need two guys to run FLIR from a chopper. The pilot to fly the ship and hold position, and a TFO to control the pod and read the monitor. That's why they missed those dogs that hit us the other night. Carl doesn't have any hours on a FLIR screen. Just rifle scopes. But I've done time in an AH-64 in Afghanistan. I've spotted IEDs from six miles out in pitch-darkness. And we know how these guys roll. Wherever she is, there'll be guard dogs, shit like that." Kelly jams his elbow into my side. "If she's on the river, we'll find her."

Excitement flashes through me . . . hope, even. "Let's get over to my dad's place. Quick."

"Can you get us out of a speeding ticket?"

"That's *one* thing I still have the power to do."

Kelly laughs and floors it.

James Ervin is standing outside the door of my father's house. The familiar beagle eyes of the old cop always make me smile.

"How you doing, Penn?" he asks.

"Better than I was this morning. What about you?"

"I'm all right. Got a little surprise waiting in there."

My pulse quickens. "Good or bad?"

"Same as last time."

"What?"

"You'll see."

I move quickly through the door and into my parents' den. Dad is sitting in the La-Z-Boy from which he dictates his medical charts, facing a stranger wearing a three-piece suit and heavy-rimmed glasses.

"Who's this?" I ask sharply, wondering if it could be William Hull.

The stranger takes off his glasses, and the unfamiliar face coalesces into that of Walt Garrity, Texas Ranger. "I figured it was time to check in," Walt says. "Hated to risk it, but I have some news, and I had a feeling things might be popping on your end."

"In that getup, you're a man transformed. What's your news?"

Walt's lips crack into a thin smile. "J. B. Gilchrist just got invited to a dogfight. I'm in, boys."

"When's the fight?" Kelly asks.

"I won't know till the last minute, but I'm guessing tonight."

"How'd you wangle that?"

"Just played my part and stuck to it. Lost enough of Penn's money to attract attention, then let Sands know I was interested in some real action."

"You're sure nobody followed you here?"

"Give me some credit, soldier. If somebody was following me, they think I'm still in the Natchez Mall, where my Roadtrek is parked. My clothes are hidden in a storage cabinet in a department store. I picked these up on my way out."

Dad says, "What do you think, Penn?"

"We need to tell you guys something. Caitlin was kidnapped last night."

While they listen with growing anxiety, I relate the morning's events. Dad hasn't even heard the news about Paul Labry, probably because he left work early.

"Where's Annie?" I ask. "Is she really here?"

"She and Peggy are in the back watching TV. She really did call with a stomachache, but she's fine."

Walt says, "This puts a new spin on everything. I'll keep my eyes and ears open tonight, especially if we're on the river. Maybe I'll pick up a clue to where Caitlin could be."

"I doubt it," says Kelly. "More likely they're just testing you. We think the Po sting is set for tomorrow night. I don't think they'd let somebody they don't know close to anything important with that cooking."

"I've been thinkin' about that," says Walt.

"What?" I ask.

"Po. You gotta figure this mandarin motherfucker can see just about any- thing he gets an itch to see over there in China. If not, then in Russia or Thailand. What the hell could Sands offer that would make the old man risk setting foot on U.S. soil?"

"God only knows," I say. "It could be an orgy with fifty blond twelve-year-olds, or dinner and a show with Barbra Streisand."

"I'd say the former's more likely," says Kelly.

"You never know with moneyed folk," drawls Walt. "Especially your oriental types. They got all kinds of strange fixa- tions about America. Course, it could be a simple business meeting. Straighten- ing a few things out, or replacing some people."

"It doesn't matter," says Kelly. "All that matters to us is the time limit. The sting is our ticking clock. According to Labry, we had thirty-six hours to find Caitlin. By now, I say we figure on twenty-four."

"Well," says Walt, standing, "I guess it's back to business. What are you boys gonna be doing today?"

"This and that," says Kelly. "But we're

going to fly the river tonight with a FLIR chopper, hoping to pick up something."

Walt looks suitably impressed. "Well, if you get in a bind trying to save the girl, or if you're outgunned somewhere and you need backup, call the Louisiana Highway Patrol. Ask for the man in charge and give him my name. I was saving this for later in the game, but it sounds like it's time to call in all the heat we've got."

"You trust him?"

"Yessir. And there seems to be a shortage of cops we can trust around here."

"What makes you trust him?" Kelly asks bluntly.

Walt smiles. "He started out as a Texas Ranger."

"Good enough," Kelly says, and shakes Garrity's hand. "Thanks for the tip, and good luck."

"Good luck to you boys. We don't want to lose that girl."

"Penn," Dad says, getting up much slower than Walt, his knees creaking. "I got a package today, FedEx. I think it's for you."

"Who's it from?"

"It said Dwight Stone."

This piques my interest. Dwight Stone is a retired FBI agent who helped me nail the former director of the Bureau.

"Here you go," says Dad, having retrieved a thick envelope from the kitchen.

"While I'm thinking about it," I tell him, "I'd like you to do me a favor this afternoon, if you can."

"What is it?"

"Find Jewel Washington and speak to her face-to-face. I think Shad Johnson has the USB drive that matches the cap the pathologist in Jackson took out of Tim's rectum. I want Jewel to use her contacts at the hospital to find out if anyone saw Shad there the night Tim died. Or if Shad has any particular connection with anybody who has access to the morgue. One more thing. If she can, have her find out the exact model of the drive that mates with that cap. No phone calls, though. This has to be face-to-face."

"That shouldn't be a problem."

"Thanks. I also think we should all stay in my house tonight. You, Mom, Annie, everybody."

Dad's face darkens. "Why's that?"

"Things are moving fast now, and we

don't know what might happen. We're safer all together. And my house has the old shutters that really work. We can shut those things and lock the place down."

"Sounds like a plan," Kelly says.

"Sounds like a pain in the ass," Dad grumbles. "But okay."

Holding up the FedEx package, I glance at Kelly, and he nods. Inside it I find a thick sheaf of typed, single-spaced pages. Taped to the top sheet is a typed note that reads, *Sometimes help comes from the most unexpected places.*

"It's from Lutjens!" I say. "Peter Lutjens."

"What is it?" asks Kelly.

I crumple the note and read the top of the first page. It begins, "Case Black. Distribution List Restricted. Subject: Edward Po, Macau."

"It could be gold."

My cell phone is buzzing again. I look down. "That's William Hull."

Kelly motions me out of the room.

Walking into the kitchen, I hit SEND and say, "Penn Cage."

"Are you feeling reassured about your lady friend?"

"Why would I?"

"I have no idea. I'm just calling to reiter-ate that I have no knowledge of what we discussed in your earlier call."

"Well, now that we both know what we're not talking about, are we done?"

"Just about," says Hull. "I have one question."

"I'm listening."

"You said you had enough evidence to convict Jonathan Sands of money laun-dering on your own."

"That's correct."

"I'd like to see that evidence."

"I'd like a chocolate chip cookie with-out the chips."

"Mr. Cage—"

"Unless your informant wants to trade my lady friend for said evidence, you won't be seeing anything. And don't bother look-ing for it, or sending people to look for it. They won't find it."

"I wonder if that's because you have no such evidence."

"You'll be wondering that all night. Look, Hull, I've been where you are, okay? How long did you say you've been trying to bust Po? A couple of years? More?"

"Almost three actually."

"And everything you've done in that time comes down to tomorrow. You're living on caffeine and adrenaline and doughnuts. You've probably got the AG bitching about all the money you've spent, and now— right here at the end—you finally realize that everything you've done hangs on the actions of one psychopathic informant. You thought you were running him, but right now, the tail's wagging the dog. I know you wouldn't have okayed them snatching Caitlin, but for whatever reason, they did it. And the truth is, you're probably relieved that they took her off the board. Just until your sting goes down. Because right now, you're the living embodiment of the end justifies the means. Nailing Po is all you live for. I get that, William. But you're not so far gone that you've forgotten this. If Caitlin Masters dies in the custody of your informant, it won't matter what kind of evidence you have on Po. Your case is blown, and you'll end up sitting in a cell right next to Sands when it's all over. That's not a threat. That's lawyer to lawyer. So you've got one job, my friend. Make sure that not one hair on Caitlin's head is harmed. Not *one*."

There's a long silence. Then Hull says, "All I can do is give you my word that I'll look into the situation. But my instinct is that—no, let me rephrase that—as regards anyone involved in my investigation, you should have no concerns whatever regarding the safety of Ms. Masters."

"I have your word on that?"

"As regards anyone involved in my investigation, yes. Now, if she's simply run off somewhere—"

"Her bodyguard was shot with a tranquilizer dart."

"Well . . . she *is* an investigative journalist. We can't know what sort of stories she might be pursuing."

"I don't like what you're suggesting, William. I'm getting a very uneasy feeling. And I think the best way for you to alleviate that feeling is to get on a Learjet, switch on the afterburners, and get your ass down here. *Tonight.* You need to get a handle on your informant, before I decide to have him jailed myself."

"I can't possibly do that."

"Why not?"

"I can't tell you. But I will be coming south tomorrow. Meanwhile, I can't imagine that jailing Mr. Sands would be anything but counterproductive—for all of us. I think that if you can be patient for a little longer, your patience will be rewarded."

"I'm not a patient man," I say, and cut the connection.

"Learjets don't have afterburners," Kelly says. "But it sounded good. Is he coming?"

"He says he can't be here until tomorrow. He's got to be bullshitting me."

"Maybe not. He's probably trying to get a leash on Sands from where he is, but he's got too many balls in the air to control them all. He's doing just what you said— praying everything will hold together until tomorrow night."

"I hope so."

"There is one other option." Kelly smiles. "You said Homeland Security was part of this task force, right?"

"Yeah."

"The threat of Mr. Masters going public could have pushed Hull over the edge. He might just be stalling long enough to get a rendition team down here to make us all disappear."

"You're kidding, right?"

Kelly laughs. "Hell, yeah. They're not that crazy. And it's not going to matter anyway. We're going to find her ourselves tonight."

CHAPTER

56

"I told you it wouldn't work," Linda says through the plywood wall. "He doesn't miss anything. He took one look in there and knew what you were thinking. That's why he took the cats."

Caitlin balls her bloody fists in frustration and tries to keep her voice level. "It doesn't matter. I can get into the storeroom now."

"So what? You can't get away without the cats to distract them."

"I'm going to use the puppy chow."

Linda laughs without mirth. "You think those dogs want puppy chow?

They eat meat, and nothing but. You're crazy if you try it."

"Have you got the bars off your window yet?"

Linda says nothing.

"Linda?"

"I got two of them loose. What does it matter? You can't get this chain off, and even if you do, I can't run. How many times do I have to tell you that?"

"You can tell me a thousand times and I won't listen."

There's another long silence, during which Caitlin hears the trainers outside working the Bully Kuttas. From what she's seen through her window, any man who would climb into a pit with one of them with only a knife would have to be certifiably insane, no matter how much armor he wore. Still, Daniel Kelly managed to kill one on the river-bank, so it's not impossible. But Kelly is an elite commando; she can't have any illusions about what would happen if one of the dogs caught hold of an ankle as she climbed the fence. They would literally eat her alive.

"I'm not leaving without you," Caitlin

says again. "But we have to go as soon as those trainers leave. Quinn's going to be furious after what Sands did to him today. He's going to want to take it out on you. As soon as the trainers leave, you get those other bars off."

"I know what they're going to do," she says. "They're going to take you away, and then they'll put that armor suit on me and throw me to the dogs."

"No!" Caitlin shouts, but she suspects Linda is right.

"You saw how they acted. They can't afford to kill you. That's why they came and asked who popped your cherry. The mayor's working some kind of deal for you. But I won't get that. I've seen too much."

"If they are letting me go, then they can't kill you. I've seen you. I could tell people you were alive. You see?"

A shout with a ring of finality echoes across the yard beneath the great shed, and Caitlin hears the lid of a pickup's toolbox clang down.

"They're getting ready to leave," she says, feeling her heart pound with anticipation. "Get ready to get those bars down. The second they're gone, I'm getting up on the roof."

"Caitlin?"

"Yes?"

"You shouldn't try it. They're going to let you go, if you'll just wait for the trade. But if you go out there with those dogs, you're going to die. Puppy chow won't hold them for five seconds. They'll smell you coming, and they'll rip you to pieces."

"I'm not waiting."

"I'll pray for you, then."

"I don't want a prayer. I want you with me."

"I can't run no more!"

Caitlin can't sustain the deception any longer. "Linda, if you don't run, you're going to die. You're right. Quinn means to kill you. It's only twenty feet to that fence. I'll help you across the space, and I'll boost you up."

There's a long silence. "I can't let you do that," Linda says finally. "It wasn't meant to be. This is my time, that's all. If you're really going to do it, just go."

"I won't. Not without you."

"Yes, you will. Don't feel bad about it either. You're a good person, Caitlin. Not stuck-up like I would have thought. I wish we could've been friends. I haven't had a good girlfriend since grade school."

"We can be friends. We are friends. You're a good person too, and you deserve a long, happy life!"

This time the silence drags. "I done some bad things in my life," Linda says. "Stuff I wouldn't want my mama to know about."

"We all have, Linda. Trust me on that."

"Maybe. I don't imagine you've seen the world from some of the places I have. But at least I can say this. I never took money for it."

Outside, the truck engine rumbles to life, and two doors slam.

"That's it," Caitlin says, jumping to her feet. "Get those bars off your windows. I'm going to the storeroom. When Quinn gets back, he's not going to find anything but empty stalls!"

She grabs her window bars and

starts her skin-the-cat inversion, but stops before pushing up the tin sheet above her. "Linda?" she says. "Linda?"

She hears nothing but the receding truck at first, then the rattle of the chain next door.

"Are you working on them?" she calls, as the blood pools in her head.

"Uh-huh. It hurts."

"No pain, no gain. Get them off!"

"Caitlin?"

"What?"

"Thanks for getting my clothes back."

"You're welcome. I'll see you in a few minutes, okay?"

"Okay."

"No more Quinn, right?"

"Right. No more."

Caitlin almost rejoices in the pain as she kicks the tin sheet upward, then drops to the floor and climbs onto the windowsill, bent nearly double. In one smooth motion she straightens her legs and catches hold of the outside roof, then raises herself through the hole by main strength. When the cool breeze hits her face, it feels like freedom, and when the four Bully Kuttas gather below her, their upturned faces watching her with unmistakable malice, she leans out just a little and speaks softly.

"Let's see who's smarter, eh? Dogs or women?"

CHAPTER

57

Despite our enthusiasm when we climbed aboard Danny McDavitt's helicopter, it didn't take long to figure out that even with the first-class equipment aboard the Athens Point JetRanger—and Kelly's proficiency at reading a FLIR screen—the mathematics of our mission are going to kill us. Even assuming that Caitlin's "rivers" clue meant the Mississippi River, and confining our search to the sixty miles of river between Natchez and DeSalle Island (the site of the hunting camp where Shad Johnson had his picture taken with Darius Jones), we're conducting the equivalent of a single-aircraft search for a lifeboat over a small sea. Actually, our situation is worse, because at least on the ocean, it's a matter of sighting a boat on empty water. Moreover, my sixty-mile figure was calculated as the crow flies. Flying the tortuous bends of the river easily doubles that distance, while covering both banks doubles that again. If we try to search more than a half mile deep into Mississippi or Louisiana, the square-miles numbers go stratospheric.

Compounding this, we're flying at night, using infrared radar to see through the darkness. Because FLIR sees everything with a temperature warmer than the earth, Kelly is having to sort through the thousands of living creatures moving or sleeping on the ground below the chopper, hoping to find something that looks suspicious. We've landed seven times already, checking out groups of dogs that seemed to be kenneled in out-of-the-way places. In almost every case we found ourselves in hunting camps, and in one case were almost shot at by an irate landowner. McDavitt feels sure that complaint calls have already been made, and if anyone wrote down our registration number, the

pilot could be in deep trouble. Nevertheless, he hasn't asked to return the ship to
the airport. Like the rest of us, he knows
that we may be Caitlin's only chance.

We're flying at fifteen hundred feet, our
speed sixty knots, which Major McDavitt
and Kelly agree is ideal for FLIR work.
It keeps the chopper out of the "dead
man's curve" (high enough to perform an
emergency autorotation in case of engine
failure), but low enough for good FLIR
imaging. Kelly also told us that fifteen
hundred feet is high enough to present a
difficult target for small arms at night. The
former Delta operator is sitting in the left
cockpit seat, his eyes glued to the screen
before him. McDavitt's in the right seat,
flying the ship and holding position whenever Kelly says he wants to take a closer
look at something. I'm sitting in the cabin
with Carl Sims, listening to Kelly and
McDavitt work the land below, and thinking about the afternoon's events.

Per my instructions, Kelly searched
Shad Johnson's house while Shad was at
work, and his office immediately afterward, but Kelly didn't find the thumb drive.
He also searched Ben Li's yard for signs

that anything had been buried or unburied recently, and found nothing. Finally, Kelly spent a couple of hours trying to track down Sands or Quinn, hoping that one or the other might lead him to Caitlin. While he'd seen plenty of Jiao, her daily routine as regular as clockwork, he hadn't found a trace of either Irishman.

While Kelly was busy with this, I had Chief Logan trace the license plate that Carl picked up in his rifle scope on Sunday night. It had been stolen off a similar make of vehicle from a parking lot in Baton Rouge. The SUV's owner hadn't missed it. I personally checked out the owners of the land where Kelly and I had made our kayak landings, but both were absentee landlords who leased to hunting clubs and had little idea what might be happening on their property.

The one positive development of the afternoon was that Jewel Washington had located a hospital aide that she believed had removed the thumb drive from Tim Jessup's rectum prior to his body being transported to Jackson for the autopsy. The aide didn't admit this outright, but Jewel thinks he will for the right price, and that he might crack under aggressive police questioning. I wasn't prepared to tell Logan to arrest the man yet, but I did call Shad and tell him I was now positive he had the thumb drive, and that if he destroyed it, I would make good on my threat to send him to prison, one way or another.

I've brought along the file on Edward Po that Peter Lutjens sent to my father's house, but despite my having taken Dramamine before we took off, efforts to read the dense type by the cabin lights have twice brought me to the point of vomiting. All I know at this point is that the file summarizes a shocking maze of criminal activities and associations spanning the globe, with personal and psychological profiles of Po and his associates that trivialize the Blackhawk bio Kelly gave us when he arrived. The one thing my limited study of the file has made clear is why William Hull and his task force are so aggressively pursuing the crime lord.

We've been airborne for hours, and the combined vibrations of the engine, the main rotor, the tail rotor, and the buffeting air have pushed me past my limit. If our goal were anything but rescuing Caitlin, I would have begged to be taken back to the airport long ago. During the first half hour of the flight, I leaned forward and tried to read the screen myself, but I soon got a headache. The FLIR unit is set to "white-hot," which means the images detected by the sensor mounted beneath the chopper's nose are displayed in a gradient from black to white, black being coldest, white hottest. A deer running along the ground appears bright white against black, but the scenes Kelly has to sort through are much more complex. Vehicles appear white on their hoods (where the engines are) and also beneath (where heat is radiating), but dark near the trunk. Most of the roads appear lighter than the land they cross, and build-ings register differently, depending on how well heated and insulated they are. In sev-eral cases Kelly spotted dogs beneath sheds by seeing them from the side, but none of these sightings led to anything. Worst of all, vegetation degrades the sys-tem, so whenever we get into heavy cover, Kelly's job becomes that much tougher.

Carl has tried to keep me upbeat, but like me he knows that in spite of our best efforts, if Caitlin is being held one mile north of Natchez, our initial assumption that she's being held to the south doomed our mission before we lifted off. That assumption was based on the sites where we encountered evidence of dogfighting, as well as the island where Shad Johnson probably attended a dogfight himself. In addition, most of the better deer camps are to the south, though there are certainly some famous ones to the north.

"Penn?" says Kelly. "We're about three miles east of the Red River now. It doesn't flow into the Mississippi for a good ways yet, but I wondered if you might want to head over and take a quick look."

"If we try to fly every river and bayou that drains into the Mississippi along here, we'll run out of fuel in no time."

"We're using it fast, as it is," says McDavitt.

"Let's stick to the Mississippi," I decide. "Louisiana bank, is my guess, based on what we know."

"Okay."

"If we're that far south, we're about to leave Concordia Parish. Now that I see how tough this is, I think the practical thing is to stay within twenty miles of town. Let's start flying a grid search of the Louisiana bank, starting close to the river and moving slowly westward."

"You figuring they want to stay close to town?" Kelly asks.

"I think they have to. They don't know what we might do, and they need to be able to react fast. I think we have to play the percentages."

"We still looking for dogs?"

"I think so. Don't you?"

"Yeah," Kelly says wearily. "I'm just starting to think there's more damned dogs in Louisiana than people."

"You're doing good. The next pack you find could be guarding her."

"Oh, I'm staying with it. I'm gonna find that girl. When I think about her tied up somewhere with those sons of bitches—"

"Kelly . . ."

"Sorry, man. Let's do it, Major. Take her back north."

McDavitt banks wide, and my stomach rolls again.

CHAPTER

58

Walt Garrity stands at the periphery of a crowd that looks like a New York film director's idea of a Southern lynch mob. Under the roof of a dilapidated barn, two dozen people have gathered to watch dogs try to kill each other in a shallow pit. Boys of eight or ten tussle around the edges, worming their way through the adults when they hear a shout indicating a change in the status of the dogs locked together at the center of the circle. The men are dressed in camo or overalls, the women in

T-shirts and halter tops made tolerable by hissing propane heaters behind them. Two dowdy women have babies slung on their hips, and one white-whiskered man who must be ninety sits in a wheelchair at the edge of the pit, apparently a place of honor.

The expressions on their faces look exactly like those Walt has seen in photographs taken at lynchings. The women are bug-eyed with rapture, fascinated, even aroused by the primal spectacle. The men look grim yet ecstatic, riding an intoxicating flood of testosterone sparked by the sight of blood and combat. They watch the canine battle with total absorption, occasionally making comments, then screaming in frustration or jubilation when the fight takes a turn, and changing their bets according to the fortunes of their chosen dog.

The two pit bulls—a brindle called Genghis and a black named Mike—have been in the pit for nearly an hour, their handlers goading them from the corners, but no real damage was done until a few minutes ago, when Genghis sunk his jaws into Mike's brisket and began trying to rip his foreleg off.

At Walt's side, Ming stands motionless, her eyes forward as though watching the fight, but she must only be catching glimpses through the heaving mass of bodies in front of her. When she and Walt arrived—they were driven here in a limo by a casino bouncer—the crowd gaped at Ming in her silk kimono as though she were an alien being set down among them. The women reacted like territorial cats, practically baring their teeth at the incomprehensibly foreign beauty. Ming looked back at them the way a cloistered princess might look down upon her subjects while she waited for Walt to lead her where he would. It was their age disparity that broke the tension. After the crowd realized that Ming was "with" Walt, serving as his hired escort for the evening, she was slotted into place as a whore, and the world made sense again. Walt chose a spot that was close enough to the pit to make it seem as if he actually wanted to see the fight, but far enough that blood wouldn't spatter their clothes.

He hasn't seen a dogfight in fifteen years, and he'd hoped never to do so again. The practice had waxed and waned in popularity in Texas during his tenure as a Ranger, but there had always been a core group of fanatical breeders who kept at it year after year. Rangers always had more important cases to work, but occasionally they would run afoul of dogfighters during an anti-gambling crusade. Such crusades were always politically motivated—they tended to come just before state elections—and thus very unpopular among the Rangers. Busting gaming operations was a no-win proposition. People loved to gamble, and they were going to find a way to do it, no matter what the law said. Fighting that reality meant risking life and limb to generate headlines for some politician, while the best you could accomplish was a brief interruption of the illegal activity. This dogfight was a prime example of the lure of the forbidden. Gambling was legal right across the river at Natchez, yet here stood this pack of fools, betting hard-earned money on something that could send them to the penitentiary for ten years.

Twice in his career, Walt had actually stopped dogfights in progress. It was hard to imagine a more chaotic scene of flight. While the panicked spectators raced for their trucks or four-wheelers—and sometimes even horses—the handlers would snatch up their dogs and hightail it into the woods, leaving their vehicles behind. The aftermath of those cases was always the same. After tracking a handler or owner to his home, Walt would find dogs chained in such pitiful conditions that he wanted to manacle the owner to one of the poles and let the dogs into the house to live. In one case he'd actually done that, but only for half an hour, while he waited for the state troopers and animal control officers to show up. He'd hoped the experience might give the owner some empathy for his dogs, but it hadn't. A year later, the man had been stabbed to death beside a pit during a dispute over whether his dog's coat had been laced with poison.

"You like fight?" Ming asks, standing on tiptoe to speak in Walt's ear above the howling crowd.

"Not much." Walt realizes that he's hardly paid attention to the dogs since they first exploded out of their corners like projectiles shot from a gun. "This is bush league," he says, truthfully.

"Bush?" Ming asks, clearly confused.

"Amateur hour. Low-rent. I can't believe they sent us to this dump."

Ming's remarkable eyes narrow in concern. "You no like?"

"No. These dogs are mismatched. The brindle outweighs the black by two and a half pounds."

"You want go closer? I take you front row."

"I'm fine right here, hon." It strikes Walt that Ming may not be as disgusted by the scene as he is. "Do you like the fight?"

The young woman shrugs, then whispers, "No like people."

Her warm breath in the shell of his ear starts his heart pounding.

"They no like me either," she adds. "To hell with them, yes?"

Walt chuckles at her frankness. "More than likely, is my guess. You want to leave?"

Ming shrugs, then smiles and runs her finger along his forearm. "Whatever you want, Zhaybee."

Walt considers the matter. He knows he's not thinking as clearly as he should. He ought to have been working the crowd for clues to Caitlin Masters's whereabouts, but he's just stood beside Ming, like the lazy old fart he's pretending to be. It's not the dogfight that's messing him up. It's the girl. But it's not like it matters tonight. In his gut he knows he will find no clues here.

Sands is testing me, *he thinks.* He has to be. This is how they screen prospective spectators. A thrown-together dogfight like this wouldn't attract the kinds of gamblers Jessup had told Penn about. Not even the ones who wanted to go slumming. *No rap star, NFL player, Arab prince, or Chinese billionaire was going to spend five minutes with this pathetic collection of pasty-*

faced, Skoal-dipping rednecks. They're still talking about the "kickass" hog vs. dog exhibition that preceded the pit fight.

Who's watching me? *Walt wonders. Someone in this room was studying him right now, evaluating every reaction. One of the men on the far side of the crowd probably. But the spy could be Ming herself. Sands or Quinn might be planning to question her later and draw out every detail of how he'd behaved during the fight. He'd have to make sure that nothing she said would arouse suspicion.*

"**You want me call driver?**" **Ming asks.**

Walt stands on tiptoe, pretending to base his decision on what's happening in the pit. Genghis, the brindle, still has a lock on the foreleg of the black, and Mike has lost a lot of blood. The floor of the pit is viscous with it. Mike's handler looks worried, and Walt senses that Genghis is about to try for his throat.

"*I guess,*" *Walt says in a bored voice.* "*Hell, I'd rather be back on the* Queen *than in this dump.*"

Ming takes his callused hand in her

soft fingers and looks up at him with liquid eyes. "Or in hotel room, maybe?"

Walt swallows hard, trying to conceal how desperately he wants to be alone with her. Ming removes a cell phone from her tiny handbag, presses a key, and puts a finger into her opposite ear. Their driver had told them he couldn't wait outside, since a random bust was always possible. If that happened, they were to run into the nearby woods and wait until the police left, then call him on Ming's cell phone. Because they're far out in the woods, Walt figures the limo is at least twenty minutes away.

Ming stands on tiptoe again, and he leans down. "Driver come back fifteen minutes," she says. "Okay, Zhaybee?"

"That'll do. This fight will be over by then, anyway. The black's about had it."

Ming peeks between some people in front of her. "Yes."

Now all Walt has to do is pretend to be excited about cruelty and slaughter for fifteen minutes.

The black's handler is shouting at

Genghis to break off the fight. The other handler looks angry about this, but the fight's being conducted under "Cajun Rules," a code that strictly governs all aspects of a fight from the washing, weighing, and handling of the dogs to what constitutes a turn and a scratch—even the duties of the referee and timekeeper. Any dog handler with experience ought to know that Cajun Rules allow the handlers to yell at both dogs.

To Walt's surprise, a sharp cry from Mike's handler finally distracts Genghis, and Mike tears himself free, twisting away in a move that warrants a cessation of the fight. As Mike limps back to his corner on three legs, the referee calls a turn, signaling that the black has tried to break off the battle. Mike's handler straddles his gasping dog, rubbing him vigorously after only a cursory check of the injured leg, which is almost surely broken.

"Get ready, Mike!" he yells, tossing a bloody towel aside. "You ain't out of it yet. You got your second wind now. Get ready to scratch, boy!"

To scratch, Mike will have to limp across a line in the dirt four feet in front of him—within two seconds of the referee's signal—then voluntarily engage Genghis, whose handler is struggling to hold him in his corner. Walt tries to imagine a boxing trainer encouraging a human fighter to continue with a broken, mangled shoulder. They don't even do that in UFC fighting.

"Let go!" shouts the referee, and the timekeeper begins counting. Before the second syllable dies in his throat, Mike limps out of his handler's grasp and hobbles across the scratch line. Half the crowd whoops with approval. Across the pit, Genghis strains in his handler's arms, almost mad to finish the battle. Mike hesitates at the center of the pit, then tucks his tail between his legs and starts to turn away.

"Goddamn it, don't you turn!" screams his handler. "Hit him! Hit! Hit!"

Mike looks back across the pit, then lowers his square head, charges across the bloody dirt and lunges at Genghis, seizing the brindle's nose in his jaws.

When Genghis's handler releases him, Mike tries to roll him over, but the broken leg prevents his getting enough leverage to do it. As the churning dogs wheel to one side, Genghis rips his nose free and darts out of Mike's reach, then hurls himself bodily into the smaller dog, knocking him onto his back. Genghis leaps for Mike's exposed throat, but Mike twists his trunk at the last instant, and the massive jaws bite deep into his chest instead. The crowd roars and stomps the floor in approval.

Genghis thrashes his head from side to side, grinding his jaws, widening the wound. A rush of blood soaks Mike's ribs, glistening on the black coat, and for a moment both dogs stop moving. Genghis seems content to rest in this dominant position, his jaws locked in Mike's chest, his tail held high. Mike gazes back at his handler with cloudy eyes, like a boy who has disappointed his father.

"Get up!" the handler screams. "You goddamn worthless sack of meat!"

At this furious cursing, Mike jerks weakly, his back legs paddling the air as he tries to wrestle free from the terrible jaws, but his effort only spurs Genghis to drive deeper into the wound. The brindle whips his head back and forth with monstrous power, flinging Mike bodily across the pit, and the crowd shouts in manic anticipation of the kill.

"Finish him!" yells a woman from the throng.

"Kill him, G! Gut that black cur!"

Walt's stomach heaves, unable to tolerate the mixture of anger and disgust flooding through him. This is like standing in a room where prisoners are forced to fight or copulate for the pleasure of their guards. The Nazis did that, and the Japanese, and probably the jailers of all nations in all epochs of history. Walt knows men who have done it; he witnessed such a fight once at an army stockade. The specter of Abu Ghraib rises in his mind. The terrible truth is that brutality is part of human nature, and all the laws in the world can't neuter it. That's the accursed nub of the thing. Some people in this barn probably think he's obscene—a geezer on the wrong side of seventy with a delicate

*beauty hardly past twenty. Of course,
they don't know that being with Ming is
simply part of his job, just as being with
Nancy had been. Although . . . the two
aren't quite the same. Being with Nancy
felt like work. Being with Ming feels like
the first rush after a good shot of whiskey,
dilated into a constant state of euphoria.
Ming is one of those rare women who
draws every eye wherever she goes.
Every man wants her, and every woman
hates her because they can't be her.
Her very existence is an affront to other
women's efforts to attract the opposite
sex.*

**But Walt doesn't want Ming for the
reason these rednecks thinks he does.
She's beautiful, yes, and she radiates
sensuality like a magnetic field. But for
him the girl is a living door to the past:
a time when he felt more alive to love
than at any other time in his life. He
can't bear to think about Kaeko in this
obscene place, but the pain of being
forced to leave her in Japan returns
with even the faintest memory. Walt
had been so despondent that he'd gone
half out of his head. He'd stopped**

thinking right, stopped paying attention, and that got men killed in Korea. If it hadn't been for Tom Cage, Walt would have died during the retreat from Chosin Reservoir.

Ming touches his arm, stands on tiptoe, and says, "We must go, Zhaybee. Now."

"Is the driver here?"

She hands him her cell phone and points to a text message on its LCD screen. It reads GET OUT NOW. HELICOPTER SEARCHING FIVE MILES AWAY. HIDE IN WOODS. WILL CALL SOON.

As Walt reads these words, the referee calls a turn, which silences the puzzled crowd. There's been no turn. Genghis is standing over Mike with his head still buried in the black's chest.

"Folks," cries the ref, "we may be about to get a visit from the sheriff. I designate location number four as the site to finish this battle, if Mike's still game."

The crowd begins to swirl around the pit like water around a drain, as people pick up coats, gather children, and toss beer bottles at the overflowing trash cans.

The ref looks at Mike's handler. "Is your dog still game?"

"Hell, no," the man mutters. "Sumbitch is good as dead. You call it. Collins can have the purse."

At this concession, the crowd explodes into motion. Walt feels like he's in an ant pile some kid stomped on. Wads of cash change hands as people make for the doors, and nearly everyone has a cell phone jammed against his ear.

"We go now!" Ming says, real fear in her eyes.

"No, we don't," says Walt.

Engines roar to life outside, shaking the barn. Dirt and gravel hammer the walls as the vehicles flee.

"Yes, yes. Must go now!"

"Take it easy. After these yahoos clear out with their dogs, we've got nothing to worry about."

"Helicopter coming!"

The barn is empty now, save for Walt and Ming and a pile of black fur in the pit. Mike's handler has left him behind. Walt steps down into the pit, kneels beside the valiant bulldog. Thankfully, Mike is dead. Walt closes his eyes for a moment, thinking of soldiers he'd known who died just as uselessly as Mike did.

"You want go to jail?" Ming cries.

Walt isn't worried about jail. He's almost certain that the helicopter is being flown by Danny McDavitt. Still, if some gung-ho sheriff's deputy were to show up on a random raid, Walt would either have to blow his cover to get out of it or spend the night in some parish shithole. With a heavy sigh he stands and climbs out of the pit, then takes Ming by the hand and leads her to the barn door.

"You crazy man?" Ming asks gravely.

Walt thinks of the howling crowd and the bleeding dogs and wonders how he wound up in the middle of nowhere while the real action went down somewhere else.

"Maybe so," he says wearily.

The limousine waits outside like a long black hearse, its engine purring in the dark. When the driver jumps out and opens the rear door, Walt helps Ming in, then settles back into the leather seat beside her.

"Any sign of that chopper?" he asks.

"It moved off toward the river," says the driver.

"Good."

"Are we going back to the boat?"

Ming clenches his hand and puts her lips against his ear. "Hotel now. Make you forget dogs. Yes?"

Walt draws back and looks into her bottomless eyes. Back on the Queen, *outside the Devil's Punchbowl, they had seemed opaque, but now he feels he could lose himself in their depths.*

He looks up and sees the driver watching them in his rearview mirror, smug judgment in his eyes.

"Eola Hotel," Walt says. "And if you look back here again, I'll cut your right ear off. Comprende?"

"Yes, sir."

"Then move out."

CHAPTER

59

Caitlin stands alert on the tin roof of the kennel, her ears attuned to the slightest sound. For a few moments she thought she'd heard the distant drumbeat of a helicopter, but it faded so quickly that she decided it had been some resonant vibration of her feet on the tin. Even if a chopper was searching for her, it would be unable to spot her beneath the shed that shields the kennel from the sky.

It had taken half an hour, but she'd finally got two sacks of puppy chow onto the roof. The Bully Kuttas made no noise other than a sort of strangled cough, and she'd realized that this was what it sounded like when they tried to bark. But they'd followed her as remorselessly as sharks, and she wondered if Linda was right—that they were too smart to be distracted by a pile of puppy chow. Caitlin had searched the storeroom for other possible distractions but had found none. Nor drugs that might sedate the dogs. Quinn had removed everything that might help them to escape.

Very carefully, she carries a heavy sack of puppy chow to the hole above her prison room. She's studied the Cyclone fence from the roof and decided that barefoot is the way to go at it. The Bully Kuttas are tall, and instinct tells her that a full-out sprint followed by a leap for the highest point she can reach—a leap with all four limbs grasping for holds—will offer the best chance of escape. Bare toes will surely fit into the openings in the fence better than the toes of her shoes. It will probably hurt like hell, but compared to the jaws that will be pursuing her, such pain is meaningless.

Of course, this reasoning goes to hell when she considers Linda. The reality is, she will be dragging Linda across the open space at a snail's pace, probably gagged to keep her from crying out in pain. As soon as she tries to boost Linda up, the fence wire will ring against the poles, and at least one dog will come to investigate the noise—if they've been distracted at all.

Caitlin wonders if she'll have the courage to stay on the ground if the dogs come running and Linda is slow to climb. Will she risk being eaten alive to help someone who has little chance of making it over the top without her? Can she live with the memory of standing safe on the far side of the fence while four dogs tear a helpless woman to pieces?

Stop, *she tells herself, humping the second bag across the roof on her shoulder.* Cross that bridge when you come to it.

More than once she's wondered

whether, if she went over alone and ran nonstop from the time she cleared the fence, she might be able to bring back help before Quinn returned to do whatever Sands has ordered him to do. Linda could probably get onto the roof and hide there, and Caitlin could pull the tin back down into place before she made her break. Surely such a ruse would have some chance of working— not on Sands, of course, but maybe on Seamus Quinn.

Pausing beside the hole over her room, Caitlin considers bringing this up to Linda. Linda would agree, of course. She doesn't want to risk the dogs anyway. Offering her the choice is the same as copping out on trying to save her.

"You don't even know if you can get the chain off her," Caitlin mutters. "Quit borrowing trouble."

Being careful of the tin's sharp edges, Caitlin drops the first sack down the hole in the roof. It hits with a solid thud. She looks at it a moment, then lifts the second bag and drops it onto the first. From the ground below, the four white dogs watch with ardent curiosity.

"Bye-bye, suckers," she says with a wave.

Then she flattens her palms on both sides of the hole, lets herself down, and drops to the floor.

"Linda?" she says, tearing open one of the bags. "You got those bars off yet?"

No answer.

"Linda? Talk to me."

Caitlin leans close against the plywood wall. She hears nothing. This time she shouts Linda's name, but there's no reply, and suddenly she realizes she didn't really expect one. Screaming irrationally, Caitlin climbs to the windowsill and lifts herself onto the roof again. The dogs are making barking motions, and she hears their hacking coughs, but she ignores them and runs to the hole over the storeroom.

Dropping through it, she cries out when her bruised feet hit the cement, but she doesn't slow down. She runs to the door and tests it by pulling on the handle. She's done this already and thought it too strong, but now adrenaline has electrified her muscles.

Taking two steps back, she throws her shoulder against the door. It moves in the frame, but the impact tells her it will take many more such blows to make headway.

Looking around desperately, her eyes fall on the medicine cabinet. She hadn't noticed before, but the cabinet is resting on casters. Without even thinking, she heaves the heavy cabinet away from the wall and places it perpendicular to the door, about eight feet away. Then she braces her shoulder against the cabinet and drives it against the door with all the power in her legs.

This time the door rattles hard, and she hears wood splinter. Moving around the cabinet, she braces her back against the door and reorients the cabinet for another rush. This time she drives it even faster into the wood, and when the impact comes, she feels the frame give way. Dragging the cabinet back just far enough to squeeze by, she darts into the hall and stops in front of Linda's stall.

What she sees steals her breath

entirely. Linda appears to be standing by the left side of her stall, but in truth she's hanging by her dog collar, its shortened chain bound to the Cyclone fence with what looks like one of the bars from the window, twisted into a hook. She's wearing a waitress's uniform, with an emblem of a steamboat embroidered on the blouse. Her wrists are bound tightly with a pair of cotton panties, and her face is blue.

Caitlin stands frozen for a moment, then looks down and jerks open the latch that keeps Linda's stall closed. With the collar and chain holding her, Quinn never felt the need to lock her in, saving himself the trouble of finding another key whenever he had the urge to rape her.

Caitlin bends her knees and tries to lift Linda high enough to ease the pressure on her neck, but it's no use. Cursing in panic, she searches for a pulse. She waits, counting slowly, but feels nothing.

"Damn it!" she screams. "Goddamn it, Linda! You gave up!"

But inside she knows this isn't true.

Linda was afraid that Caitlin would risk death by forcing her to try to escape, or by remaining with her if Linda refused to try. Linda had hanged herself to release Caitlin from this burden.

Caitlin stares at the woman whose face she has never seen in life before this moment and thinks of the nude pictures she was shown, those supposedly taken from the house of Tim Jessup. She'd condemned the girl in those photos out of hand, and now . . . now she owes that woman her life. Caitlin has met so many women like Linda during her years in Mississippi, girls with plenty of native sense, but who married right out of high school, and, if they were lucky, did two years of junior college before the first baby came. What could Linda Church have accomplished had she been born with Caitlin's advantages? So many women from Caitlin's world pretended to ask these questions, but down deep they felt a sense of entitlement that assured them that their rarefied places in the nation's elite schools and corporations were based on merit alone. Caitlin reaches out and lays a hand on Linda's arm—then freezes.

She's heard the sound of a motor. Not a helicopter, but a car or truck. Maybe even a jeep.

Her body jerks as though she's grabbed hold of a 220-volt cable. A fraction of a second later she's racing to the storeroom, certain of what she must do. High on both side walls of the storeroom are windows without bars. Caitlin slides open the one on the side opposite Linda's stall. Then she runs back to Linda's stall and listens.

The engine is louder now, intermittent but getting closer.

Wedging both hands behind Linda's distended neck, she pulls on the twisted bar that Linda somehow managed to bend into a hook. It takes more strength than Caitlin expected to open the loop. Almost . . .

Linda pitches forward onto her face, the chain rattling behind her.

Caitlin feels once more for a pulse. Nothing. Now the engine is a smooth rumble. How far is that sound traveling over the flat ground? A half mile? A mile?

With a silent prayer, she looks down at Linda's body, then gets to her knees and hauls Linda onto her shoulder. It takes most of her strength to bear the dead weight, but this is not enough. She has to get to a standing position. Breathing hard, she redoubles her effort and drives herself to her feet.

Holding the body in a fireman's carry, she turns until Linda's feet are pointing toward the unbarred window and drives one of Linda's heels through the brittle plastic pane. A chorus of coughs enters the stall. Then something heavy slams against the wall. The Bully Kuttas are leaping for the window.

Filled with shame and horror, Caitlin presses Linda's lower legs together and shoves them through the window. Any worry about how she would push more of the body through the small space vanishes, for the moment the legs clear the frame, Linda's weight is yanked from Caitlin's arms and shoulders as though by a threshing machine.

The sounds that follow send a bolt of primal terror through her. After one paralyzed second, she breaks for the storeroom. The whole building is rattling from the force of the dogs trying to drag Linda's corpse through the window. Caitlin feels her stomach trying to come up, but she forces down the bile and runs to the storeroom window.

No sound, *she thinks, like a child playing hide-and-seek.* I can't make a single sound. . . .

Standing on tiptoe, she pokes her head far enough through the window to make sure no dog waits below. The engine is much louder than before. The far wall of the building sounds as if a construction crew is demolishing it.

First, she tries to put her feet through the window frame, but she can't manage it. She'll have to go through headfirst, then roll and sprint for the fence. She checks the dark yard again, then wriggles through the window and falls facefirst onto the ground.

Bounding to her feet, she runs for the fence without looking to either side. If I look back, I'm dead, *she thinks. Halfway to the fence, she hears a cough, then a sound like galloping hooves. Even as her brain calculates how far the dog must run, she's leaping for the top of the eight-foot fence.*

Her fingers lock into the heavy wire, and she whips her thighs and ankles up beneath her, spread-eagling them like an Olympic gymnast as a Bully Kutta slams into the fence below her rump. She's already climbing as the dog falls, and by the time he leaps again, her hands are on the top bar and she's flinging her legs over.

Another dog has joined the first. They leap for her again and again, their frenzied hacking like the rage of mute wolves. Panting hard, Caitlin feels a dizzy moment of triumph, then drops to the far side of the fence and sprints into the trees. She hears no engine, no dogs—nothing but the dull thump of her feet on the sandy soil. If the engine was Quinn's, she knows, those dogs will be set loose on her trail in moments. And if they are . . .

CHAPTER

60

"Penn?" Major McDavitt says in my head-set.

"Yeah?" I jerk out of the nauseated doze into which four hours in a free-floating roller coaster have submerged me. Leaning forward and looking at the FLIR screen, I see that we're flying along what looks like a one-lane road.

"We're getting into a fuel situation. We're into the reserve. My GPS is set to the airport, and we're already going to be cutting it close. We need to get back and refuel."

"Kelly?" I say. "You seen anything?"

"SOS, man. Sorry. We need the air cav for this job. A fleet of these bitches."

"I'm willing to keep going," says McDavitt, "but we've got to be honest with ourselves. Without more specific intel, these are really long odds."

I rub my eyes hard and try to see the larger picture, but exhaustion and airsickness are taking their toll. The only thing I can hold clearly in my mind is an image of Caitlin standing on her porch with her arms folded, the night we had our last talk. Remembering this, I try to imagine telling Annie that Caitlin was kidnapped and won't ever be coming back.

"Let's refuel and keep going," I say. "I know it's a lot to ask, but we all know what's at stake."

Nobody says anything.

"Am I being stupid? Is there no chance at all?"

"Outside," says McDavitt. "But if it were my wife, I'd keep looking."

"Carl?" I say.

"Keep going. All night if we gotta. If I'd kept my damned eyes open, she wouldn't ever have got took."

"Forget that. You don't know that. Let's

head back to the airport and fill her up, Major."

McDavitt starts to bank the chopper, but Kelly says, "Hold up. I've got something on the road."

"What is it?"

"Two legs, foot-mobile. Can you circle, Major?"

McDavitt takes us into a slow revolution of the bright white human form on Kelly's screen.

"Looks female to me," Kelly says. "We're in Bumfuck, Egypt, too. Let's set down and check it out."

McDavitt descends rapidly, then touches the cyclic and flares at the last moment. As we settle gently onto the road, he puts the throttle into flight idle to conserve fuel.

"Where'd she go?" asks Carl. "Did she run?"

"There," says McDavitt, pointing left of the cockpit. "She's running!"

"I'll get her," says Kelly, opening the side door and leaping down to the pavement. I'm still trying to get my harness off when Kelly climbs back into the cockpit, shaking his head.

"Who was it?" I ask.

"A drunk. Black woman, about sixty-five. I offered her a ride, but she told me to get the hell off her driveway. She thought we were a UFO until I caught up to her."

Carl settles back in his seat, obviously demoralized.

"Let's take this bird back to the barn and gas up," Kelly says. "Caitlin's still out there somewhere."

I'm expecting the chopper to rise and tilt forward, but we don't move. Then I see McDavitt holding his headset tight against his ear. "Ten-four," he says in an angry voice. "On my way."

"Who was that?" Kelly asks.

"The sheriff of Lusahatcha County. We just lost our helicopter."

"How come?" Carl asks, leaning forward again. "What does Billy Ray need with the chopper this time of night?"

"It's not that. The guy from that hunting camp saw the insignia on our fuselage and called the sheriff's department, screaming bloody murder."

"Goddamn it," Carl mutters.

McDavitt turns in his seat and looks back at me with genuine regret. "I'm sorry, Penn. We can probably get another chopper, but this is the only FLIR unit between Baton Rouge and Jackson."

"It's okay. It was a long shot anyway."

The JetRanger rises on a cushion of air, then reaches translational lift. The nose tilts forward and we head into the darkness. As I look to the horizon, battling airsickness once more, something Kelly said pings back into my mind. *Let's take this bird back to the barn. . . .* For the life of me, I don't know why, but I keep hearing the phrase, even in my semicoma of nausea and depression.

And suddenly I know why: The term *bird* doesn't remind me of helicopters, but of a young man I never met in life. Ben Li. A computer genius who told Tim Jessup to "ask the birds" about his insurance policy. What I don't understand is why, if Li had a cache of sensitive data, he didn't use it to save his life when Sands and Quinn began to torture him. If I can answer that question, maybe I can find what no one else has been able to: something valuable enough—or dangerous enough—to purchase Caitlin's freedom.

CHAPTER

61

Caitlin has been walking so long that her feet are numb. If she hadn't had to kick so hard to get the roof open, she would still be running, running along the road until she reached a town. She could do ten miles if she had to. But the bruises in her heels are to the bone—she can hardly take the pressure of her own weight on the asphalt.

Six times she's seen the lambent glow of headlights in the sky, then raced into fields beside the road before the lights appeared. As the

sound of the engines grew, a frantic compulsion to leap out of the field and flag down the driver would grow in her chest, but each time she fought the urge into submission. Over and over she hears the voice of Tom Cage telling the story of the poor girl who escaped from Morville Plantation and reached the sheriff's office, only to be driven back into forced sexual slavery by squad car.

Before her feet became numb, Caitlin had found herself sobbing every few minutes. Nothing she did could block the memories rising out of the dark. The rape wasn't the worst of it. The worst was Linda hanging from the Cyclone fence, her dress tucked as modestly around her legs as she could make it, a last attempt at dignity from a girl who'd had all dignity stripped away from her. Caitlin's memory of heaving Linda's legs out through the window is growing vague. The sight of a Bully Kutta hanging suspended from a dead knee seems beyond comprehension, something Caitlin dreamed in a fever. But it happened, *she tells herself.* I did that. It's like those soccer players who survived that plane crash in the Andes. You do what you have to do. . . .

Sooner or later, I'll come to a place that has a phone. If not, I'll just keep on until I drop or the sun comes up.

CHAPTER

62

Kelly, my father, and I are seated around my kitchen table with half-drunk cups of coffee in front of us, three pistols centered between them. Danny and Carl have taken the JetRanger back to Athens Point. Because of the guilt he feels about Caitlin's kidnapping, Carl tried to remain behind, but the sheriff ordered him back, and that was that. The Ervin brothers are still outside, guarding us as they have almost from the beginning. Mom and Annie are sleeping in Annie's bed upstairs. We're on our third pot of coffee, and though everyone is exhausted, no one has made a move to a bedroom. I've been trying to wade through the Po file Lutjens sent me, but there's so much raw data that I can't really digest it. Ever since we were forced to abandon the helicopter search, a feeling of desperation has been growing in me. I want to do something—anything—to get Caitlin back.

"You want me to give you a shot so you can sleep?" Dad asks. "Just put you out for a while?"

"No. We don't know how things might break tonight. I have to be ready for whatever happens."

"Okay."

"This is the toughest kind of situation to take," Kelly says. "You have no control over events, and that's hard to handle when you're used to having it."

"I'm about ready to say to hell with Po, call Caitlin's father, and break this story nationwide."

"Worst thing you could do. That's the one thing that might force them to kill her. Po would be gone, and Hull would vanish like a puff of smoke."

"He's right," Dad says softly.

"I know."

Kelly leans forward and forces me to look him in the eye. "Sands isn't going to kill her, Penn."

"How can you be sure?"

"Put yourself in his shoes. Sands took her because he felt he had no choice. I don't know what Caitlin did, but somehow she made herself a threat to the Po sting. As for why I'm sure they won't kill her— apart from everything we've discussed—it comes down to this: Sands was looking into my eyes when I made that promise Monday morning. He knows that if Caitlin dies, he dies. Maybe not today, but one day soon. He doesn't want to look over his shoulder for the rest of his life."

"I think he's lived that way since he was a kid. It's a way of life for him."

"He won't kill her."

Dad looks less certain. "Remember, Son, our greatest hopes and our worst fears are seldom realized."

"That's a fine sentiment. But in this case my greatest hope and my worst fear are opposite sides of the same coin. It's either/or. Caitlin's alive or dead. She's coming back or she's not. And as things

stand, we have no control over the out-
come."

"She's alive," Dad says with conviction.
"I know she is. I can feel it."

My father has never been the mystical
type. "Feel it? Aren't you the one who told
me that when you die, you're dead?"

"I am. But sometimes I have a feeling
about things. Things as they're supposed
to be."

"What's your feeling now?" Kelly asks.

Dad takes my hand and squeezes
as hard as he can with his diminished
strength. "Caitlin's going to be part of this
family for a long time. I *know* that. I refuse
to accept any other possibility."

For a few seconds I actually believe
him. Then Kelly sits erect, grabs his pistol, and jumps to his feet. "There's somebody outside."

He's right. Someone's knocking softly
on the front door. With Kelly in the lead, all
three of us walk to the foyer. He motions
us back, then, holding his pistol along his
leg, leans against the wall beside the door
and says, "Who's there?"

"Walt," says a male voice. "Walt Garrity."

We all look at each other in surprise. Kelly reaches out and opens the door, aiming his gun through the crack. After a moment, he pulls Walt through the door and shuts it behind him.

"What happened?" I asked. "You have any word on Caitlin?"

Walt shakes his head dejectedly. "Nothing. I'm sorry, boys. I'm blown."

"What do you mean?"

"My end of this operation's over."

"Let's get back in the kitchen," says Kelly. "You want some coffee, Walt?"

"I wouldn't turn it down. I got a long drive ahead of me."

In the kitchen Walt sits to my father's right, and I sit opposite him while Kelly pours the coffee. Walt waves his hand over the cup to indicate he wants it black.

"So what happened?" I ask.

"They had the dogfight tonight, like I said. I went. Took a hooker with me for cover. I've had one with me every night. Started out with a white girl, local. Tipped her heavy and sent her home at the end of each night. But tonight I had a different one. Anyhow, when I got to the fight, it looked like Kelly was right. They were testing me. It was just a bunch of country boys fighting a couple of pit bulls. Had some hog dogs there too. Strictly low-rent. Still, everything was going all right. Then the fight broke up. Guess they got word somebody was flying the river in a chopper."

"That was us."

"I figured. After that, I told the hooker I wanted to go back to the hotel. I figured I had more chance learning something about Caitlin from her than from anyone else."

"And?"

"You said the first hooker was white," Kelly says. "Was this girl black?"

"No. Chinese. They got quite a few Chinese girls on Sands's boat, and I thought she might have some inside poop, because of the Po connection. Her English was pretty bad, but there was something different about this girl. She reminded me of a girl I knew in Japan, during the war." Walt looks at my father. "Kaeko, remember? That girl in Kobe I told you about?"

Dad nods.

"This girl's name was Ming. . . ." Walt trails off.

"So what happened in the room?" Kelly prompts.

"I don't know, exactly. I just wanted to talk to her, which was stupid, because of the language problem, but when we got in there, she took off her dress and started to get in the bed. I told her I just wanted to talk. And then . . . then *I* started to talk. I told her about Kaeko, about my R and R in Japan, that stuff. She was listening, but she was taking off my jacket and shirt too. She got real quiet when she saw my derringer hanging around my neck, but then she smiled and took that off like it was no big deal. She pushed me down on the bed and started to get on top of me . . . and that's when it happened."

"What?" Dad asks.

"She stood up straight and started talking in a different voice. She went from sounding like a Hong Kong streetwalker to Greer Garson in about half a second. Told me to go back home to Texas if I wanted to stay alive."

With a chill of foreboding, I get up and go to the counter, then shuffle through the pages in the FedEx package Lutjens sent.

"She took my derringer," Walt says. "She held it on me as she backed out of the room."

"What exactly did she say?" Kelly asks.

"She said, 'You're a long way from home, old man. Go back to Texas, if you want to live.'"

"Ming the Merciless," Dad says softly.

"Ming the Merci*ful*," Kelly corrects him.

Walt watches curiously as I cross the room and hand him a five-by-seven photo of Jiao Po. Then he looks down, stares for a couple of seconds, and says, "That's her. Son of a bitch. Who is she?"

"Jonathan Sands's girlfriend. The niece of Edward Po."

Walt's head snaps up, his weathered cheeks flushed.

"She was supposed to kill you," Kelly says. "Or to set you up for it, anyway. But something made her stop at the last minute."

Walt blinks at Kelly.

"I bet the hotel maid would have found you dead tomorrow morning, probably from an apparent heart attack. A little Viagra by the bed . . . end of story."

"Why didn't she do it?" I muse.

Walt snorts and shakes his head. "Because she saw I was a broke-dick old bastard in way over his head. *Damn,* that's hard to bear."

"Would you rather be dead?" Kelly asks.

"Maybe," Walt mutters. "What a way to finish up." He looks over at my father, then me. "I haven't helped you boys one damn bit. All I did was lose a bunch of your money. And I still don't know how they copped to me."

"They could have followed you here yesterday," I point out.

"No. I'm sure about that."

"Were you doing anything with the white hooker?" Kelly asks. "Sexual stuff, I mean?"

"Naw. Told her I was too old to get it up anymore, and she was fine with that. Less work for the same money."

Kelly rubs his thumb and forefinger together with a sandpaper sound. "Still, if she told any of the other girls that, it might have drawn some interest. I doubt many johns pay good money without wanting something at the end of the night. At least a little strip show, if not a blow job."

"Maybe," allows Walt. "But I don't think she would have told. She wanted me to herself. Why share an easy mark?"

"It doesn't matter now," I tell him. "You did what you could. Sands is a smart son of a bitch. You probably just pushed too far too fast."

"I am getting impatient in my old age."

Kelly gives Walt a "buck-up" smile. "No, you're getting too decent for the work. If you'd screwed that first whore silly, they'd never have caught onto you."

Walt's face remains wrinkled with concentration. "It was the girl. Ming, or Jiao, whatever. Sands sent her to try and read me, and she did. Just like a book. To tell you the truth, I feel a little shaky now. Kelly's right. I came close to buying it tonight, without even knowing it."

Dad gets up slowly and gives his old friend a consoling pat on the shoulder. "That means your luck's holding, Walt. That's something to celebrate."

The old Ranger shakes his head, his sense of failure palpable in the room. "No. I'd say that's about as clear a message as a man gets that it's time to hang up his spurs."

"You're not serious about driving back tonight, are you?"

"Yep. I never want to see that hotel room again, and I couldn't sleep now anyway. Too much to think about. And Carmelita's been patient with me. I need to get on back to Texas."

Dad doesn't waste time trying to persuade his friend to stay. He knows Walt's mind is made up. "What can we do for you?"

"Walk me to the door, partner. That's it."

We all rise and follow him into the foyer. "A pretty poor showing for me," Walt says, shaking hands all around. "But don't lose heart. Kelly, you quoted that old 'One riot, one Ranger' saw to me on the night we first met. I'll leave you with the real one we used to live by."

The foyer falls silent, and Walt Garrity speaks with quiet conviction.

" 'No man in the wrong can stand up against a fellow that's in the right and keeps on a'comin'.' Cap'n Bill McDonald said that. Don't you boys forget it, either, just 'cause things look black." The old Ranger nods once for emphasis. "I'll catch you on the turnaround."

Kelly opens the door, checks the street, then leads Walt out to his Roadtrek. Dad and I follow, my hand on the pistol in my pocket. As Walt reaches his door, I hear the whine of a small engine being driven hard, then headlights flash over us. A Volkswagen runs the stop sign at Union Street, races up to where we stand, and skids to a stop.

Kelly has his pistol out a full second before I do, the weapon light mounted beneath its barrel illuminating the face of Kim Hunter, the reporter for the *Examiner.* The guy holds up both hands and shouts, "Penn, it's me! Kim!"

"He's okay!" I tell Kelly. "What are you doing here?"

"Are we safe out here?"

"Safe as anywhere."

"I'm getting out." Hunter climbs out of the Volkswagen, then walks to the rear of the vehicle and pops open his trunk. "Come here." He bends out of our sight. "Hurry."

Kelly lifts his gun again, but as we get to the back of the car, I'm stunned to find Caitlin staring up out of the small trunk. Her face is gaunt and her feet are a bloody mess, but her eyes are filled with tears of relief.

"She wouldn't let me call the police," Hunter says. "Or take her to the hospital. I've been driving around the block trying to see if it was safe to stop. When I saw you come out, I decided to go for it. She's scared to death, and she can barely walk. What the hell's going on?"

"We've got her," I say, lifting Caitlin bodily from the trunk and holding her shivering body. "Thanks, Kim. Go home, before somebody sees you. Don't talk about this to anybody, and don't let anybody at the paper print one word."

"Okay. Are you sure she's going to be all right?"

"We've got her," Kelly says. "We owe you, buddy."

"No, you don't. I love that lady, man."

Kelly grins and pushes Hunter toward the open driver's door. "Get going."

As the Volkswagen pulls away, Kelly ushers Caitlin and me back toward my porch, his back to us as he turns left and right, covering the street behind us with his pistol. As we move through the door, I see Dad wave at Walt in the driver's seat of the Roadtrek. Then the long, silver RV rolls up the street after the Volkswagen.

"Linda Church is dead," Caitlin says, her bruised hands wrapped around a mug of coffee. "She hanged herself. I saw it. I mean, I found her right afterward. She was being held next to me. In a dog kennel."

Caitlin's sitting on my knee at the kitchen table, her bandaged feet resting on a pillow, my arms wrapped around the blanket my father put over her shoulders.

"How did you get away?"

She shakes her head as if there's too much to explain.

"Do you know where the kennel was? We flew the river for hours looking for you."

"I don't. I walked so far, and everything looked the same. They took my cell phone, and I knew I couldn't call you even if I had it, because they might hear. I saw a few cars, but I didn't dare risk flagging anyone down. I kept thinking about that story your father told us, about the girl who got away from the brothel. I was afraid to talk to anyone."

"How did you find Kim?"

"I finally came to a building in the middle of nowhere. A farm equipment place. I broke in and used their telephone. I figured Kim was my safest bet. But I was afraid to wait there for him. I thought the police might come."

I lay my cheek against her back and hold her tight. "It's going to be all right. You're home now."

"You don't have any idea where Linda's body might be?" Kelly asks, ever practical.

Caitlin closes her eyes and shakes her head. "I don't . . . the dogs—"

"I'm going to put her in bed," I say, seeing that she's about to break down. "Dad, I want you to call every cop you ever treated and put a ring of steel around this house. I'll talk to Logan in a few minutes. Kelly—"

"I'm there, bro. Going to the mattresses. About fucking time."

Dad's already picking up the phone.

To my surprise, Caitlin allows me to carry her to the ground-floor guest room. When I pull back the covers, she raises her arms for me to remove her sweat-soaked top, then pulls her pants off and climbs under the sheet.

"Did they hurt you?" I ask, surprised by how afraid I am to hear the answer.

She lies on her side, staring blankly toward my hip. "Not really. But the things I saw . . . what they did to Linda. I wish I'd let Kelly kill them. Quinn . . ." Caitlin lifts a shaking hand to her eyes, as though to hide them from some awful sight. "He made me watch him rape Linda, and she was *sick.* I don't understand it."

Almost afraid to touch her, I stroke her hair gently. "Beyond a certain point, there isn't any understanding it. Sometimes the only way to deal with people like that is on their own terms."

She lets her hand fall and blinks back tears, as though still witnessing some immutable horror. "I never really under-stood that. I'll *never* be the person I was before. I'll never talk to another victim of a crime the same way again."

"Don't think about it now. Just try to rest."

She closes her eyes, then opens them again.

"What about what Kelly asked?" I say. "You don't have any idea where Linda might be?"

"I'm sorry, I don't. Kim can probably tell you more than I can."

"But you're positive she's dead?"

Caitlin blinks twice, then her chin begins to quiver, and tears stream down across her nose. "Penn . . . I had to use her body to get away."

I don't quite understand this statement, but something tells me not to ask for details.

"To distract the dogs," she whispers. "I don't . . . I don't think there'll be anything left to find."

I lay my hand on her forehead and say, "Shhh," just the way I do with Annie.

Caitlin wipes her nose and looks up at me, her eyes pleading for absolution. "I tried to get her to go with me. I tried so hard. But they'd broken her. You understand? She was alive, but there was nothing really left of her."

"I'm sorry. Whatever you did, I'm sure it was the right thing."

She squeezes her eyes tight, then

nods once. "She couldn't have made it. She knew that. She was so brave. . . . I see now. She gave her life for me."

"I want you to stop thinking about it, if you can. You're never going to forget what happened, but right now you need to let it go, just for a while. You're alive, and you deserve to be. Sometimes survivors don't get that. I'm going to go out there and make some decisions. But I want you to call me if you can't sleep."

She tries to smile but fails. "I will."

I stand slowly, shattered by the sight of this woman I know to be so strong reduced to near helplessness.

"Will you do me one favor?" she asks softly.

"Anything."

"I want Seamus Quinn dead." Caitlin locks her fingers around my wrist and squeezes until her arm shakes. "Not just dead. I want him to *suffer*."

I nod but don't reply.

"Will you promise?" she asks, her eyes bright in the shadows.

"Let's see how you feel after some sleep. We can talk about it then."

Her eyes hold mine for several seconds, then she releases my wrist and turns over. "Nothing's going to change my mind," she says quietly.

"I'll see you when you wake up."

"Nothing."

CHAPTER

63

Burned houses remind me of dead bodies. There's the same feeling of senseless waste, of life extinguished. Family homes are the worst. Stumbling over a charred doll or a half-burned photo album always brings a sharp pang of sadness, the knowledge that apart from life itself, talismans of the past are our true treasures.

Ben Li's house is not like that. A modest wood-frame structure on Park Place, near Duncan Park, it burned nearly to the ground before the fire department arrived. According to Chief Logan, the fire chief has no doubt that it was arson. The house must have been filled with accelerants to have gone up so fast.

In the hazy blue light of dawn, smoke still rises from the charred wood beneath the brick piers that once supported the house. It's 6:15 a.m., but the older people in the neighborhood are already up and moving, getting their papers or walking their dogs. A few have strolled up to the house to stare at the ruin, as people do. One guy even picked through the wreckage as though hunting for souvenirs, until I chased him away.

I'm here because sometime during the night, in that semicomatose state between sleep and wakefulness, the one true epiphany of this case came to me. I don't know why I didn't think of it sooner— probably because I was so focused on the stolen USB drive—but perhaps also because the tension generated by Caitlin's kidnapping was blocking me. But after her return last night, some tightly wrapped coil of stress must have let go, for a chain of logical thought rose out of my subconscious as effortlessly as a string of bubbles seeking the surface of a lake.

Jonathan Sands hired Ben Li because

he was a computer expert. Tim Jessup believed that Li had maintained some sort of "insurance" to protect himself from his employers, probably sensitive data. When I first heard Tim say this—in the voice memo he made before he died—I assumed that Li would have hidden whatever data he had on some remote digital server, accessible only by himself or someone with the password. I also assumed that Li's instruction to "ask the birds" about this somehow related to such a password, and that if Ben Li kept cockatoos, maybe they could speak the required phrase or numbers. Sands and Quinn almost certainly made the same assumption. But if the birds could speak the password, they did not do so for Sands. If they had, he would not have felt the need to burn down Ben Li's house.

More to the point, last night, during Caitlin's periods of fitful sleep, she told me something of her captivity with Linda Church. Through the rapes and abuse Linda suffered, Quinn had kept after her about one subject: Ben Li's birds. While torturing Li in the interrogation room in the bowels of the *Magnolia Queen,* Sands and Quinn had asked him about anything incriminating he might have stored off the boat. Li had still been under the influence of whatever drugs Tim had given him, and was half-delirious, but in that state he had babbled something to the effect of "The birds know! Ask the birds!"

I haven't come to Ben Li's house because I've figured out his password. I've come because I believe there *is* no password. There never was. A computer wizard like Li would know that every movement through cyberspace leaves digital footprints as surely as a man walking through snow. And Li couldn't be sure that he was the only computer wizard working for Sands. If Ben Li wanted to keep sensitive data to protect himself from his criminal employers, he would have wanted it close to hand, where he could reassure himself it was safe any time he felt nervous, and probably to add to it as more incriminating data fell within his grasp. As a prosecutor, I saw this kind of behavior all the time. Hoarding secrets is a primal human instinct.

Jonathan Sands obviously came to the same conclusion sometime yesterday and, being unable to locate the data, decided on a scorched-earth policy. But why did he assume that Li's insurance would be inside the house? Li might have buried it, not knowing that water finds its way into even the most tightly sealed containers left underground. I can't even recall all the ruined caches of contraband I saw as an ADA: documents, photographs, cash, drugs, bloody clothing, body parts—literally everything imaginable.

And so . . . as the sun rose, I stood here in the smoking ruins, trying to open myself to inspiration. I've searched the yard and found no sign of recent digging, as Kelly predicted, having already done the same himself. The only trees in the backyard have high limbs, and Ben Li seems to have had no ladder.

I'm about ready to surrender and walk back to my car when a vaguely familiar man in his early fifties approaches me from the adjoining yard. He smiles as he walks toward me, holding up a hand to show he doesn't mean to bother me.

"Mayor Cage?" he says. "Bobby DeWitt."

I hesitate for a moment, trying to place the name, but the man does look familiar.

"I played ball at the public school," he says, "about eight years ahead of you. I saw some of your games out at St. Stephen's. Y'all had a good team."

Now I remember him . . . a tight end.

"So did you guys," I tell him, shaking his hand firmly. "State championship, right?"

"Yeah, we won the Shrimp Bowl, but that was a long time ago."

DeWitt looks over at the ruined house. "Terrible, ain't it? For a while we thought it might spread to our place, but we were lucky. I wet our roof down with my pressure washer, and that saved us, I reckon."

"That's good. Did you know the kid who lived here at all?"

"Ben? Naw. He kept to hisself most of the time. Hardly ever left the house. For a long time, I didn't even know what he did for a living. Wasn't hardly no furniture in that place. Just some glass tables with computers on 'em. A big old beanbag chair, and one of them futon things in the back. And the birdcages, of course. He had them two parrots."

"You'd been inside the house, then?"

"Oh, yeah, I fixed a busted pipe for him

one time. He was a nice kid. Real quiet. Might've been into drugs a little. I thought I smelled some pot a couple of times. But, hey, that's his business. He wasn't hurtin' nobody."

I look back at the pipes sticking out of the soggy ground, wondering if broken pipes could somehow be a clue to Ben Li's hiding place.

"Did you ever hear the parrots talk?"

DeWitt laughs. "Shit, they talked all the time."

"What did they say?"

"Lines from old movies, mostly. Humphrey Bogart–type stuff. One of 'em always said, 'I'll be back,' like in *The Terminator*."

"Really," I say, trying to guess if this might have some meaning.

"Yeah," DeWitt says in a reflective tone. "Ben was shy all right. About the only person he ever talked to was old Mrs. Bassett, who lives in that house yonder. Widow woman."

"Which one?" I ask.

"Back behind that fence there." DeWitt points to a weathered board fence shrouded by overhanging limbs.

"What did those two have in common, I wonder?"

DeWitt laughs. "Don't know. I think they just got to talkin' by the fence one day and took a shine to each other. Mrs. Bassett's about half-blind, and she has arthritis so bad, she can't hardly do for herself no more. I think Ben felt sorry for her. He used to go over there and help take care of her bird feeders and stuff."

Two seconds after the word *bird* leaves DeWitt's lips, my mouth goes dry. "What bird feeders? Like hummingbird feeders?"

"Well, yeah. She's got all kinds of bird-baths and feeders and stuff over there. Ben even climbed up in that tree back there and fixed her birdhouse for her. A martin house, you know? He brought it down to his place, fixed it, hand-painted it—the whole works. Then he remounted it on the pole for her."

I'm trying to remain calm, but even DeWitt can see my excitement. "How did he get up there? I don't see a ladder."

"He borrowed my extension ladder."

"Would you mind if I borrowed it for a minute?"

"Hell, no. I'll get it for you. You want to

look at that birdhouse?" He looks puzzled, but not particularly bothered, by my request.

"I do. Can you tell me where it is?"

"It's back there in those limbs that hang over the fence, about twenty-five feet up. In the winter you can see it plain as day, but with the leaves still on the trees, you can't hardly find it. The pole's set in the ground right behind the fence.

Two minutes later, I'm climbing the aluminum extension ladder that Bobby DeWitt has leaned against a high oak limb. Ten feet above me is the simple white birdhouse that you see in half the yards in Mississippi. Only this one looks as if it were hand-painted by an Asian artist. The three circular holes in the wall of the house have a tracery of exotic leaves painted around them, and several ladybugs that look almost real have been painted under the eaves of the roof.

"You okay?" DeWitt calls from below, where he's holding the ladder steady.

"Yeah."

Suppressing my excitement, I slip two fingers into the first hole and feel in the dark space, hoping I won't find a brown recluse spider. There's nothing inside but bare wood. The center hole holds a few small twigs and something that feels like crusted bird crap. But as my fingers probe the leftmost hole, my fingertips touch plastic.

Moving them back and forth, I know immediately that I'm touching a Ziploc bag. It's taped to the inside wall of the birdhouse. Tugging gently, I remove the baggie from the hole, taking care not to let DeWitt see it. As I look down, my heart begins to race.

Inside the sandwich-size Ziploc is a stack of SD memory cards, the kind used in some digital cameras. I count five of them, and the topmost card is labeled 2G HIGH SPEED. Keeping my hand close to my body, I slide the baggie into my front pants pocket. I can barely keep my balance as I descend the ladder, and when I release the aluminum rails, my hands are shaking.

"Find anything up there?" DeWitt asks.

"No. I'm not even sure what I was looking for."

"Huh, I wondered. You ain't the only one's been around here looking. Some guys searched his house a couple nights ago, before the fire. I figured they were cops, but I had a funny feeling about them."

"Why's that?"

"Well, I was standing outside when they come out. And they looked at me like I was just dogshit. On my own property too."

"Did they ask you any questions?"

"Hell, no. I wouldn't of told them nothing if they had."

Intoxicated with hope, I slap DeWitt on the back and say, "Good man, Bobby. I'll see you around, okay?"

"Anytime. Hey, you reckon you could get something done about these potholes on our street?"

I laugh and turn my head as I'm running to my car. "Bobby, by next week, this street will be smooth as a baby's butt!"

"I'll believe that when I see it!"

"Count on it!"

CHAPTER

64

As I feared, the data on Ben Li's SD cards were encrypted. Normally, this would have stopped me for at least a couple of days while I located an expert, but Kelly is accustomed to such challenges. Three and a half hours ago, he transmitted the data to a retired buddy from the Army Signal Corps.

Caitlin has spent that time reading the file Peter Lutjens FedEx'd to my father yesterday. Dad had dressed her hands and feet with bandages after treating the lacerations, but she insisted on keeping her fingers free to turn pages. Apparently the detailed history of Edward Po, his extended family, and his worldwide criminal operations is the only thing capable of taking Caitlin's mind off the horrors she endured while being held prisoner. She's still sitting cross-legged on the sofa in the den when Kelly comes running in from my study.

"Decryption's coming through. And from the sound of Joey's e-mail, it's hot stuff."

Caitlin sets the file aside and hobbles toward the study. Soon the three of us are gathered around my computer to review the result of Joey's efforts.

Caitlin presses a button on my trackball, and over a hundred tiny thumbnail images appear on my display. Some of them represent data files, but others are clearly JPEG images.

"Do I see frontal nudity?" asks Kelly, leaning closer and squinting.

"You do," says Caitlin, double-clicking on one image. "Oh my God . . . look."

On the screen, Linda Church leans over a bathroom counter, bracing herself on her forearms while Jonathan Sands thrusts into her from behind. Sands's left hand seems to be yanking her head back by the hair, while his right holds a digital camera high to capture the scene. The camera's flash is a bright star in the mirror of what looks like a hotel bathroom.

Caitlin turns away. "I'm sorry. It's not the sex, I just can't look at her, knowing what I know."

"There's one question answered," I say. "Sands shot the nude pictures of Linda that were planted in Tim's house."

"Can I change the picture?" Caitlin asks in a distressed voice.

"Sorry, yeah, go."

She clicks the trackball again, and a photo of Sands having sex with a different woman fills the screen.

"Ben Li couldn't have taken these, could he?" asks Kelly.

"No. He must have hacked into Sands's private computer and copied whatever he found. Keep going. Skip down a ways."

"There's a *lot* more folders," Caitlin says, scrolling through the contents of the disc. "They're mostly pictures too."

I'm beginning to understand. "Ben Li shot the cell phone pictures that Tim showed me in the cemetery that first night. I'll bet those pictures are in here too. Stuff from the dogfights. I think Ben Li liked pictures."

"I don't get this," Caitlin says in a puzzled voice.

"What?"

"If Ben Li had all these pictures of Sands, why didn't he use them to save his life? Why sit there and be tortured and yell elliptical clues? It doesn't make sense."

"Think about it," I tell her, having solved this riddle during my drive back from Li's burned house. "He has these pictures stashed. When he wakes up and figures out Tim has been using him, he calls Sands or Quinn and reports what happened, probably thinking he has no choice. Next thing he knows, they've got him strapped in a chair with an electrode up his behind. Aside from the obvious stupidity of calling Quinn, this kid was a genius. Simply telling Sands and Quinn that he had these pictures—or anything else that might be on these discs—wasn't going to save him. They'd just retrieve the discs from the birdhouse and kill him anyway. He needed to figure out a way to barter the discs for his life. He probably passed out while he was trying to do that. And he was high as a kite, remember, from whatever Tim had given him. He probably didn't wake up until he was in Quinn's boat."

Caitlin is nodding slowly. "And when he tried to stop Quinn from getting Linda, Quinn shot him."

"Right. So the discs stayed hidden."

Caitlin lowers her head for a few moments, then raises it and clicks on another thumbnail image. Now we're looking at a well-known local attorney—a very married attorney—having sex with a Chinese girl who looks barely sixteen.

"Is that who I think it is?" asks Caitlin.

"It is."

"Jesus."

"Keep going. This is important, but it's not what we need."

She clicks through several more images of people having sex, mostly Sands with a variety of women. But several familiar local faces pop up, as well, most of them of people with political or financial influence.

"What are we looking for here?" Kelly asks.

"How about this?" asks Caitlin, pulling

up an image of a group of men gathered around two bloody dogs savaging each other in a pit.

She clicks through this sequence, which depicts what appears to be three or four different dogfights. The dogs and the people change in the pictures, but here too I recognize quite a few locals. When one image pops up, I seize Caitlin's shoulder. It's the photo I saw on Shad Johnson's wall yesterday: Shad and Darius Jones standing beside a dead boar hog hanging from a hoist.

"I see him," Caitlin says. "Son of a bitch."

"Keep going," I tell her, my hand flexing with hopeful tension.

Three more shots of Shad and the wide receiver follow. Two show the hog, while in the third the two men stand arm in arm with drunk grins on their faces. But Caitlin gasps when the next photo fills the screen. In it, a blood-soaked pit bull hangs from its neck from a tree branch while three men look on. The dog's spine is bowed from the animal jerking its hindquarters away from something in one of the men's hands. A cattle prod. The man holding it is Darius

Jones. But to Jones's right, staring with what appears to be primal fascination, is District Attorney Shadrach Johnson.

"Holy God," Caitlin breathes.

I squeeze her shoulder again. "That's it. *That's* what we needed."

"Do you know what that is?" she says in a stunned voice.

"What?" asks Kelly.

"That's two black men at a lynching. Only they're not the ones being lynched."

I'm shaking my head in disbelief, but after so many days of feeling helpless, a bracing surge of power is rising in me.

"You *own* Shad Johnson," Caitlin says. "The question is . . . what are you going to buy with that picture?"

"Anybody want to guess?"

"Thumb drive," says Kelly.

I smile and nod with satisfaction. "For a start."

CHAPTER

65

I'm staring at Shad Johnson across the compulsively neat surface of his antique desk. The district attorney looks as though he hasn't slept since our meeting yesterday, and having seen the contents of Ben Li's secret files, I'm not surprised.

"You look a little green around the gills, Shad."

"Skip the bullshit, okay?"

I glance to my right, to his Wall of Respect. The picture of Shad and Darius Jones with the dead hog is conspicuously absent. In its place hangs a framed photo of Shad sitting beside a state senator at a political banquet.

"Looks like you're missing a photograph."

"I said cut the bullshit," snaps Johnson. "Why are you here?"

I give him my most cordial smile. "You know what they say about a career in Mississippi politics, don't you?"

"What's that?"

"The same thing they say about Louisiana politics. The only way to truly end your career is to get caught with a dead woman or a live boy."

Shad licks his lips as his gaze flicks to the window. His political instincts are well-honed; he knows something's coming, only he doesn't know what. Taking a manila envelope from inside my windbreaker, I remove an eight-by-ten printout of the dog-lynching photo and slide it faceup across his desk.

"I think that picture is the exception to the rule."

Shad hesitates before looking down, knowing that after he does, his life will never be the same. At last his chair creaks and he leans forward, lowering his eyes to the image on the paper. Shad is a light-skinned black man, but he perceptibly lightens another shade.

"Looks a little bit like you and Darius with the hog, doesn't it? Only it's a little different. Especially when considered from a legal perspective."

Shad seems to have lost his voice altogether.

"You're a smart man, Shad. So I know there's no misunderstanding about where we stand now."

"What do you want?" he asks hoarsely.

"You already know. The USB drive. I know you've got it, and I know how you got it. But if you hand it over now and come up with a plausible story, I'm willing to run with that. You're not who I'm after."

The district attorney clears his throat, then speaks in his professional voice. "I was about to call you about that drive, Mr. Mayor. As a matter of fact, someone slid a sealed envelope underneath my door last night."

"Is that so?" I smile to let him see that I'm willing to play along.

"Sure did. Even in this day and age,

you'll find a Good Samaritan doing whatever he can to help the cause of law and
order."

"I'd like to see that envelope."

Shad reaches into his pocket, takes out
a key, then unlocks his bottom desk
drawer. He looks down into it for a long
time, and for a couple of seconds I have a
crazy feeling that he's about to pull a pistol. I'm sure he'd like nothing better, if he
could get away with it, but when he
straightens up, he's holding a sealed,
bone-white envelope. He tosses it across
the desk.

Ripping the envelope open, I tilt the
torn side to my palm. A small, gray Sony
thumb drive falls into it, no heavier than a
child's LEGO block.

"Do you know what's on it?" I ask.

"How could I? I never even opened the
envelope."

I give him a hard look. "What's on it,
Shad?"

He shrugs, then sighs. "No idea. It's
encrypted. I couldn't get into it."

I slip the thumb drive into my pants
pocket and stand.

"What are you going to do with that?" Shad asks.

"I'm going to run those Irish bastards out of town. Do you know why you're still sitting here, and not in a jail cell?"

He swallows audibly. "Why?"

"Because you could have turned that drive over to them, and you didn't. I know you didn't do that from a noble motive— probably just self-preservation. But whatever the reason, you didn't do the worst thing you could have done."

"So, what now? Is this the end of it?"

"Oh, no. Today's a big day, my friend. A red-letter day. I'll be in touch about what I need from you."

Shad rises behind his desk as I move toward the door.

"Whatever you want, Penn. You can count on me one hundred percent."

"Oh, I know that."

He clears his throat. "What about the original of that photo? The negative, or the disc or whatever?"

"Let's see how things go. I'll make my decision later."

I turn and walk through the doorway,

then stop and poke my head back through it. Shad is studying the photograph like a man being forced to peer into the darkest corner of his soul.

"One more thing," I say quietly.

"What?" he says without looking up.

"Soren Jensen. You just pled him down to probation and a drug treatment program. He doesn't spend one more day in jail."

"He's out on bail now."

"Say it," I tell him.

"Done. Probation."

"Stay by your phone. I'll be in touch."

CHAPTER

66

Caitlin is sitting at the kitchen table, poring over the Po file like a novel she can't put down. One hour ago, Kelly sent a copy of the data on the USB thumb drive to his Signal Corps friend, who warned us that it could take longer to crack than the SD cards. In the meantime, Kelly and I have been discussing how best to use the results, should they prove to be as incriminating as we believe they will be.

"Let's just assume," Caitlin says, abruptly dropping the file and joining our conversation, "that the thumb drive is what you think it is. Conclusive proof of systematic money laundering by Golden Parachute Gaming Corporation, and that it incriminates both Sands and Po."

"Okay."

She smiles like a woman with a secret. "Proof is no longer our problem. Chief Logan could arrest Sands at that moment for money laundering. He could arrest him right now for dogfighting based on Ben Li's pictures, and the district attorney to boot."

"Keep going."

"The problem is Edward Po."

"How so?"

"What is your worst fear at this point?"

I think about this for a few seconds. "Legally, I guess the worst scenario would be for Po to actually show up for the sting, and for Hull to grant Sands immunity in exchange for his testimony. Hull might grab Sands and keep him out of our reach for a long time using national security as a justification."

"Hull has made that deal already, right? I mean, would Sands lure Po here without a signed plea agreement? Something Hull can't renege on?"

"No. You're right."

"On the other hand, if Po doesn't show up for this Roman-spectacle freak show they have planned, Hull will likely take down Sands as a consolation prize, right?"

"If he can. Hull has tolerated enough of Sands's crimes that Sands may have significant leverage over him."

"Can Hull stop the State of Mississippi from pursuing murder charges against Sands?"

"Hard to imagine," I say thoughtfully.

"Not for me," says Kelly. "Post-9/11? Hull's task force is part FBI, part Homeland Security, remember?"

"Yes."

"What if they designate Sands as some kind of special informant to the task force? Hell, they could put him on the payroll of the CIA. They could say he's been working for them all along. You've got to think about how the world has changed, Penn. I mean, Sands could disappear, and you'd never even know where he was. They could do it."

"*That's* my worst fear. Sands walks away from both murders and never suffers a day for all the hell he brought down on this town."

Caitlin threads her fingers together, then twists her arms inside out to stretch. Through a grimace of pain, I see the gleam of satisfaction in her eyes. "So the person you really need to be able to control is—"

"William Hull," I finish. "The real architect of this clusterfuck."

"How do you get that?"

I sigh heavily. "Hull has definitely pushed the envelope, but given the nature of his target, the government may sweep a lot of that under the rug. You have to get guys like Hull to hang themselves."

"By?"

"Wearing a wire. You get them somewhere they feel safe, lead them into saying things, and let them convict themselves. But he won't do that with me."

"So, what's your plan?"

"Hull is probably in town already, prepping for tonight's sting. I'm going to demand a meeting with him and find out the details of his plea agreement with Sands."

"Using the thumb drive for leverage?"

"If it's what I think it is. I can threaten to arrest Sands based on that evidence and blow Hull's Po operation, unless he modifies the plea agreement."

"But if he calls your bluff, and you blow the operation, Po walks away. Right?"

"Right."

"And you told me yourself he's the bigger target. The greater of two evils."

"Yes. I just want Sands more."

Caitlin's smile vanishes. "So do I."

"I'm also going to demand that two Natchez plainclothes detectives remain in Sands's presence right up until the moment of the sting. That way, if Po doesn't show, we can bust Sands before he has a chance to flee."

"But if Po does show—and the plea agreement remains unchanged—you have your original problem. Sands vanishes into the federal system, and we might never see him again."

"Right."

Caitlin sets aside the file in her lap and lets the blanket fall away from her shoulders. She's wearing one of my dress shirts and nothing else, but at this moment, even Kelly is looking only at her eyes, which gleam with intensity.

"What if I could tell you a way to get both Sands and Hull on tape, discussing all the shit that Sands has pulled this past week?"

"Is this a trick question?" Kelly asks.

Caitlin shakes her head, then picks up the stack of pages she's been reading the past few hours. "There's a direct pipeline into the heart of Sands's operation. One that's never even crossed his paranoid mind."

"Quinn?" says Kelly. "We've thought of that. Hull certainly has too. If Po doesn't show, he'll flip Quinn against Sands."

"Not Quinn," she says, smiling with supreme confidence. "Jiao."

"Jiao?" Kelly echoes. "The girl?"

"Yes."

"The one who let Walt live?"

"Exactly. Jiao Po."

"You think she'd turn against Sands?" I ask.

Caitlin leans over and holds up a print-out of Sands giving Linda Church oral sex. "Don't you?"

Kelly sucks his bottom lip, thinking hard. "Okay, I get it. But still . . ."

"Jiao has been living in New Orleans the

whole time Sands has been in Natchez. Even before that, when he was opening other casinos along the river. She only moved up here after Hurricane Katrina forced her out of her house down there. I don't think she has any idea what Sands's been up to all that time. Not as far as the women, anyway. The dogfighting she may not mind, since her uncle's always done it." Caitlin looks at me. "You talked to her the morning your balloon was shot down, right? You saw them together. How did they seem?"

I think back to that morning in Sands's drug-lord-style mansion. "She walked in on her own. He wasn't expecting her. He let her do some of the talking, but he seemed annoyed that she'd come in."

Caitlin nods knowingly.

"She threatened me too, though. Subtly, but she left no doubt about what she meant."

"That doesn't surprise me. Women will go to amazing lengths to protect their family unit, or what they perceive as that. When women kill, it's usually to protect. Right, Mr. Prosecutor?"

"You're right."

"I've seen that in war zones," Kelly says. "Okay, I'm buying it. If Jiao got angry enough at Sands, that same instinct might make her try to take him down."

"I think this girl is very confused," Caitlin says. "She's only twenty-seven. And she's about to stand by while her lover delivers the uncle who practically raised her to the American government. If I can shake her faith in Sands, I think we might be surprised at what she might do."

"Whoa," I say, seeing where this is going at last. "What do you think you're about to try?"

"I'm just going to talk to her. Face-to-face. A little girl talk."

"Caitlin—"

"I like it," says Kelly. "Shit, where's the harm?"

"Are you serious? Caitlin would be risking her life. The sting's tonight. What can we really hope to get this girl to do, even if you turn her?"

Caitlin smiles. "Wear a wire, of course."

Now Kelly shakes his head. "That, I can't see. Jiao's been around these guys a long time. She knows what would happen if they caught her wearing a wire."

"But they won't! They won't even *check* her. That's the beauty of this."

I hold up both hands, trying to calm Caitlin down. "You've got a good idea, but it won't work that way. Jiao won't know how to steer the conversation. She doesn't know what we need in a legal sense."

"A discussion of murder? What's hard about that?"

"Between Hull and Sands? How does she engineer that? I think I've got a better idea. Thanks to your inspiration."

Caitlin looks skeptical. "What is it?"

"I knew this cop in Houston. He told me about a sting they pulled on a mob guy once. Superparanoid. Nobody could get close to him with a wire, swept his houses all the time. But they took their time and got an informant close to him, and he got a feel for the guy's habits. Based on that, they prewired several outdoor spots he liked to visit when he needed to talk to somebody. And the night before they knew a big discussion was going down, they wired them all. They used two dozen recorders, all told, but they got him."

"How does that relate to Jiao?" Caitlin asks.

"We don't need two dozen recorders. We only need two."

Caitlin is shaking her head, but Kelly is nodding, his tactical sense kicking in.

"I'm going to demand the meeting I told you about a few minutes ago. But not just with Hull. I'm going to demand that Sands be there too. He won't want to come, but if the thumb drive is what we think it is, I can make it happen. I pressure Hull, Hull pressures Sands."

Caitlin's listening now.

"There's only one place Sands is going to feel safe in a meeting like that," Kelly says.

She blinks in silence. "The *Magnolia Queen*?"

"You got it," I say. "And so far as I know, there are only two places on that casino boat not being recorded by surveillance equipment twenty-four hours a day. The first is Sands's office, where Kelly and I talked to him. And the second is—"

"The torture room," Caitlin says. "The Devil's Punchbowl. Jesus."

"If Jiao will hide voice-activated recorders in those two rooms, I can do the rest. Fifteen minutes alone with Hull and

Sands, and I'll have them both by the balls."

"And you know what happens then," Kelly says, watching Caitlin like a hopeful teacher.

She smiles. "Their hearts and minds will follow."

Kelly laughs and looks at his watch. "Right now, Jiao Po is taking a PiYo class at Mainstream Fitness."

"Are you kidding?" I ask.

Kelly shakes his head. "Hell, no. She's like a Mafia wife. People are dying left and right, and she's worried about her cellulite."

"She doesn't have any," Caitlin says. "I've seen the pictures. Is that where I approach her?"

Kelly shakes his head. "She likes to go down to the coffee bar on Franklin Street after her workout, for green tea and a bran muffin."

"That's it," I say, squeezing my right hand into a fist.

"I have a feeling," says Caitlin, "that her muffin won't be going down so well today."

CHAPTER

67

Caitlin is sitting at a small, round table in the Natchez Coffee Bar, a long, narrow space downtown, not far from the club where Jiao Po takes her PiYo class. Jiao sits across the table, not an arm's length away, her eyes deep and remote. People have often told Caitlin that her skin resembles porcelain, but Jiao's skin is perfect, without blemish. She radiates a self-possession that Caitlin finds intimidating, and her light eyes seem startlingly alive in the Chinese face. The coffee bar is almost empty, but when Caitlin asked to sit with Jiao, the woman did not object. Only when Caitlin identified herself did Jiao's eyes rise to take her in.

"Is anyone watching you?" Caitlin asks. "Any of Sands's men, I mean?"

Kelly has already assured Caitlin that Jiao isn't being tailed, but Caitlin wants to make sure.

"What do you want?" Jiao asks, regarding her coolly. "A human interest story for your newspaper?"

"No. I want to show you something. A photograph."

Jiao rises from the table.

"You stayed in New Orleans too long," Caitlin says quickly. "I know you must suspect about the women."

The girl slows almost imperceptibly.

"I know you went to Cambridge, Ms. Po. I know you don't miss much. But sometimes we blind ourselves intentionally to things we don't want to see."

Jiao stops and looks back, her body utterly motionless. "What does this photograph show?"

Caitlin shakes her head. "You have to see it. Either you have something to fear or you don't. I'm not here to hurt you. Only people you trust can do that."

Jiao steps back to the table with regal poise and gives Caitlin an impatient look. "Well?"

"Will you sit down?"

Jiao sighs lightly, then takes her seat again. "Show me."

Caitlin takes a five-by-seven manila envelope from her bag and removes the bathroom-mirror photograph of Sands screwing Linda Church. With an eerie sense of detachment, she slides the photo across the table, just as Penn told her he did with Shad Johnson.

Jiao doesn't flinch or even blink. After a few seconds, Caitlin can't tell if the woman's breathing.

"Is this the only one?" Jiao asks at last.

"No."

"Show me."

Caitlin removes five more photographs, each showing Sands having sex with a different woman, every one an employee on the Magnolia Queen. Jiao must have seen many of these women over the past few weeks. The final photo shows only a male organ entering a woman's anus, but Caitlin is sure that Jiao knows whose penis she's looking at. Her doll-like lips purse for a few seconds, then without lifting her eyes from the top image, she says, "Do you have money?"

"Do you need money?" Caitlin asks, confused. Perhaps Jiao has been cut off by her uncle and fears she can't survive without Sands's support.

A fleeting smile crosses Jiao's face, and the aquamarine eyes rise to Caitlin's. "No, I mean, were you raised with money?"

"Yes."

"My father made little, but my uncle saw that we never went without. Father wouldn't touch that money for himself, but we children got the necessities. After he died, I lacked for nothing. But I found that whether women have money or not, we look for men who are strong enough to be providers. Strong enough to protect us, yes? But with that strength comes things we do not want so much. A wandering eye, aggressiveness, even cruelty. Yet the men who would always be faithful, the ones who worship us, we ignore or kick away. Do you find this to be true?"

"I've made mistakes like that. But some men are both strong and kind."

Jiao's eyes move over Caitlin's face. "I think my father was like your lover. He was a professor. He taught law in Communist China. What could be more absurd? When I was young, I thought he was a fool. After he died, I attended school in England, as you said. But during breaks I went to Macao, to live under my uncle's protection. He didn't want me there, but I insisted. I was seduced by his power, his money, the unimaginable wealth. And I fell in love with Jonathan Sands. He seemed a glamorous figure to me, an Irishman who could carve out a place for himself among my uncle's henchmen. He was white, yet my uncle respected him. And of course, my mother was a Scot."

The coffee bar's single waitress walks toward them. Caitlin lays the manila envelope over the explicit photos as the woman passes and goes to the restroom. "You must have been very young when you fell for Sands."

Jiao shrugs. "Older than my mother when she married. But, yes, I was young. Too young to see what I was to him. A way to rise in the hierarchy, to reach the inner circle. He was playing a role from the beginning, I think."

Caitlin is impressed by the girl's sangfroid, but it makes her doubt the soundness of her plan. Without an angry Jiao, nothing of value will be accomplished here.

"I'm curious about something. Did they let you see the violent part of what they did?"

Jiao takes a quick breath, then expels it. "They tried to insulate me from that, my uncle especially. But everyone has a primal fascination with violence. At that point in my life I was curious. But my curiosity was quickly satisfied. Death holds no mystery for me. I think women are interested in life, men in death. What do you think?"

Jiao's genuine interest in her opinions takes Caitlin off guard. This meeting reminds her of conversations during college. "I think there's some truth in that."

Jiao toys with what's left of the muffin on her plate. "At first I thought violent sport was something that came along with male strength. They admired in others what they aspired to in themselves."

She slides the envelope off the picture and stares clinically at her lover fucking another woman. "I saw much dogfighting in Macao. My uncle lives for it. He and his friends. Breeding the dogs, training them—most of all fighting them. But what I learned watching those men was this: They prized the dogs that would fight to the death, beyond all hope of survival. The ones too weak to do that, they killed. In the end, though, all the dogs died." Jiao looks earnestly into Caitlin's eyes. "They prized some dogs, you see, but they loved none of them."

This insight silences Caitlin for a while. "Is Sands like that?"

Jiao ignores the question, her gaze still on the photograph. "They see us the same way," she whispers.

"How do you mean?"

The girl's eyes rise to Caitlin's. "You're a beautiful woman, Ms. Mas-

ters. Don't protest, please, you know you are. It's a fact, like strength or height. All your life you've benefited from this attribute, as I have."

Caitlin can feel herself blushing. "Yes. I have."

"Men prize beautiful women, they pursue us with all their power, shower us with wealth. They settle for those of medium attractiveness, and the ugly ones they treat as slaves."

Caitlin isn't sure what to say. "That might be a little extreme."

"Do you think so? I do not."

"Well—"

Jiao silences her with an upraised finger. "We all lose our beauty one day, Ms. Masters. All of us. Never forget that."

"That day is a long way off for you."

Jiao smiles. "In the eyes of the man I thought I wanted, it has already come and gone. I sensed it long ago. I've tried to deny it. I have been a fool."

Caitlin says nothing.

"What do you want me to do?"

CHAPTER

68

It's 6:00 p.m. as Kelly and I drive down Pierce's Mill Road toward the *Magnolia Queen,* the flaming sun beginning to set above the bridges behind us. I wanted the meeting earlier, but I was lucky to get it at all. Had the thumb drive not turned out to contain the legal dynamite I'd hoped it would, Hull would have told me to go to hell. As it was, he tried to sidestep my intent by offering a quick meeting between the two of us, but I demanded that Sands be present, and despite Sands's resistance, Hull forced him to accede to my wishes. What gave me the boost of confidence I feel now was Sands's insistence that the meeting take place aboard the *Queen.* I'd worried that I might have to insist on this venue myself, but as I'd anticipated, Sands considered it a victory to force his home territory on us.

"What are you thinking?" Kelly asks, braking his 4Runner as we descend the long hill.

"I'm not."

"Bullshit."

To my left, the Mississippi River blazes orange under the falling sun, and five hundred hundred yards below us, the fake smokestacks of the *Magnolia Queen* suggest the opening shot of a Technicolor version of *Huckleberry Finn.* "Seriously. Whenever I had to go into court for a summation, or even a critical cross-examination, I winged it. I figured if I didn't already know everything I needed to, I was lost anyway."

"I don't know if that makes me feel better or worse about this."

"Everything depends on Hull. I envisioned a bow-tied Beltway tight-ass, but the more I've talked to him, the more I've realized he's a pro. He's just been working this case too long. I can't imagine what trying to run a guy like Sands as a CI would be like. They're probably like two scorpions in a bottle by now."

Kelly laughs wickedly. "That I don't doubt."

"Hull and I will be a little like that. More like boxers, maybe. The wire idea was genius. That's what's going to make him let his guard down."

"Nothing increases the odds of victory more than letting the enemy think he's already taken your secret weapon."

Hidden in my belt is a digital transmitter Kelly brought along in his Blackhawk gear bag. Given Kelly's flint-knife surprise in Sands's office, we feel sure that Quinn will search every nook and cranny of our bodies before allowing us near Sands. When his search turns up the wire, that should convince our marks that we have no other way to record the conversation. After that everything depends on Sands's steering us to his office or to the interrogation room below deck.

"You know what I'm wondering?" Kelly says.

"What?"

"Did Jiao really hide those recorders in there?"

"You mean where she was supposed to?"

He gives me a sidelong glance. "I mean at all."

"She did. Don't even think about it."

"Why are you so sure?"

I turn to him, a slight smile showing. "Hell hath no fury, brother. It's a law of the universe. Like gravity."

The grade levels out at last, and Kelly pulls the 4Runner alongside the massive barge with the faux steamboat built atop it. The structure dwarfs everything around it, and only the steel cables running above our heads that moor the casino to the shore betray that it's a vessel and not a building. A red-coated valet approaches the 4Runner, but Kelly rolls down his window and waves him off, then raises the window with a whir.

"Listen," he says, all levity gone from his voice. "No matter how you look at this, we're about to walk into hostile territory. Indian country. I don't know if Po is coming to this party later or not, but you can bet that Sands, Hull, and Quinn have contingency plans in case things don't go their way. At a certain point, every situation becomes every man for himself. Understand?"

"You're saying if it goes to shit, I'm on my own?"

"No. I'm saying those guys won't hesitate to fuck each other or anyone else who gets in their way. Trust does not exist among these people. Not even Quinn and Sands, who probably grew up together. But Sands's biggest fear is *you.* You're the loose cannon on his deck. While he had Caitlin, he felt he had you under control, but now . . . I don't think he'd hesitate to kill you if he thought you were going to have him arrested."

"I get you."

"After you, his fear is Hull. If Po doesn't show, Hull's going after Sands's scalp. So Sands has to have an exit strategy in that event too. Just keep all that in mind while you're 'winging it.'"

"I will."

Kelly grins at last. "We've been here before, bro. If the wheels come off, hit the deck and listen for me. I'll be right with you."

"I know you will."

Kelly looks to his left, over the long gangplank that leads to the main deck of the *Queen.* "There's our buddy," he says, lifting a hand to wave at Seamus Quinn. "I'm gonna give you one for Linda Church before we're done, you mick bastard."

"Aren't you Irish too?"

"Sure. What?"

"Nothing. Just take it easy. We didn't come to fight."

"I'm easy, baby. Let's do it."

As we walk across the broad gangplank, I lean toward Kelly. "You think it'll be Sands's office or belowdecks?"

"Interrogation room," he whispers. "The Devil's Punchbowl."

"Why there?"

He laughs loudly, as though I've just told a joke. "In case they decide to shoot us. Easier to dump the bodies."

I can't tell if he's kidding or not, and before I have time to think about it, we're through the main door of the casino, where a doorman with gold-braid epaulets and a captain's cap greets us in an "Ol' Man River" bass.

"This way, gents," Quinn says from behind him in a surprisingly professional voice. We're within earshot of fifty customers playing the slot machines, so some rudimentary courtesy is called for. Quinn leads us down the length of the three-hundred-foot-long saloon. The sunset has lit the skylights a brilliant orange with purple shading, and for a moment this sight behind the glittering chandeliers makes me dizzy. A second later, though, I see Chief Don Logan standing at the head of the escalator that leads to the *Queen*'s upper or "hurricane" deck.

Logan and a handpicked team of plainclothes police detectives are here to take charge of the recorders planted by Jiao as soon as we vacate the room where the meeting is held. Logan will kill time playing slots on the hurricane deck, and when I appear afterward—either from Sands's office or from the interrogation room in the bowels of the barge—I'll signal the chief by touching the top of my head, and he and his men will move to retrieve the appropriate recorder.

"What did I tell you?" Kelly says softly.

Quinn has walked us behind a partition

three-quarters of the way down the saloon, where a brass-plated elevator waits discreetly for staff with business belowdecks.

Quinn punches a nine-digit code into a keypad beside the doors, and they open with a soft whir. The elevator is surprisingly spacious, and Kelly stands unnecessarily close to Quinn during the brief descent.

"Stand back, queer boy," Quinn says, now that we're away from the paying customers.

Kelly laughs but doesn't move.

When the doors open, three security men in black coats stand waiting for us, wands in hand.

"Assume the position," Quinn says, gesturing at the wall to our left.

Kelly and I flatten our hands on the wall and spread our legs, though Kelly mutters under his breath for effect. As per the terms set for this meeting, neither of us is carrying a weapon, but as strong hands pat and probe me, Quinn says, "I've half a mind to poke a light up Ponytail's arse, to make sure he hasn't got one o' them knives stuck up it."

Kelly mocks a girlish squeal. "That's

just the excuse you need to check out what you been craving since you saw me, isn't it?"

Quinn is cursing when one of the wands stops and hovers at my belly button, beeping softly.

"What is it?" asks Quinn.

"Probably my belt buckle," I say, straightening up.

"Not so fast," says Quinn, gripping my upper arm. "Take your belt off."

"What for?"

"Jaysus, just do it."

With obvious reluctance I remove my belt. The guard wands my belly while Quinn feels his way along the belt. His hand stops, then with a chiding smirk he draws a knife from his boot and slices the leather on the inside of the belt. One flick of the knifepoint exposes a thin wire antenna, and he rips out the transmitter with a laugh.

"Sneaky bastard. Wouldn't have thought it of you, Your Honor."

Quinn uses this find as an excuse to have the men go over Kelly again, but they discover nothing. Telling the guards to stay where they are, Quinn leads us down a narrow corridor. The barge really feels like a ship down here, with hatches dividing the compartments instead of doors. Suddenly Quinn stops, then twists the wheel on a hatch, pushes it open, and motions for us to follow him.

Kelly enters first, and I follow him into a long, dim room. The walls are black, but two large TV screens in a far corner to my right glow with changing images of the casino decks above. Three chairs have been placed in a rough triangle near the hatch, facing inward. Two are occupied, the nearest by Jonathan Sands, who's wearing a business suit, and the other by a man who must be William Hull, who looks nothing like I imagined. He has a lean, well-muscled frame, and his face is long and angular. The bureaucrat I imagined vanishes, replaced by this figure who looks more like a Cold War–era military officer.

Deeper into the room stands a single, more substantial chair. With a roll of my stomach I realize this is the chair where Ben Li and Linda Church were tortured. Beside it stands the cart that held the electrical generator. Inside this cart, Jiao is supposed to have planted one of the microrecorders.

"You a furniture aficionado?" Hull asks with his faint trace of Southern accent. South Carolina, maybe.

Beyond the torture chair, against what must be the hull of the barge, a metal staircase leads up to a hatch near the ceiling of the room. *An escape hatch?* At some level I register that we must be below the level of the river. "I was just thinking about something that happened in that chair."

"Nothing's ever happened in that chair," Sands says, looking up at me with unnerving intensity. The skin of his balding head seems stretched even tighter over his skull, if that's possible, and his cheeks look hollow. Apparently not even Jonathan Sands is immune to the effects of stress.

"Why are we down here?" I ask.

"Privacy," says Hull.

"We never shut off the security cameras on the boat," says Sands. "If we were anywhere but in here or my office, you could subpoena our hard drives."

"Look what I found on Hizzoner," says Quinn, handing the small transmitter to

Sands. "Bastard was planning to tape the whole meeting."

Hull gives a theatrical frown, then looks up at me. "Is there any further point to this meeting, Cage? If this was just an excuse for you to entrap us, you should let us get on with our business."

"The tape wasn't the point," I say. "I've just never seen a government attorney act with such cavalier disregard for the law, and I wanted some kind of record."

"Sorry to disappoint. Sit down and speak your piece."

As I take my chair, I realize there's a man standing in the shadows behind Hull. He looks more like a Green Beret than an FBI agent. Quinn closes the door behind us, leaving six of us in the room. With an almost antiquated feeling of symmetry, Kelly stands behind me, Quinn behind Sands, and the Green Beret behind Hull.

"Well?" says Hull.

"I want to know the terms of your plea agreement with Sands. What happens to him after tonight, if the Po sting is successful?"

"He testifies against Po in federal court."

"In exchange for?"

Hull shakes his head. "I'm not at liberty to disclose that."

"Mr. Hull . . . that's why we're here. I think you'd do just about anything to get Po's scalp, at this point. For instance, you might promise to let Sands keep his interest in Golden Parachute. You might even try to use some Homeland Security, national-interest bullshit to keep the State of Mississippi from prosecuting him on other charges. I'm here to make sure that doesn't happen."

Sands looks expectantly at Hull, but Hull doesn't deliver the withering broadside Sands apparently expects.

"That's what I figured," I say. "Well, it's not going to happen."

Hull sighs. "What exactly do you want?"

"I want to know that Sands isn't going to vanish into federal custody the second Po is in your hands."

"And how do I prove that to you? You want a letter of agreement?"

I chuckle at this. "I want plainclothes Natchez police detectives beside Sands from now until five minutes before Po's expected touchdown, and within sight of him until the moment you take Po into custody."

"He's out of his fucking mind," says Sands, not even deigning to look at me.

Hull gestures for the Irishman to be silent.

"That could create practical difficulties," the lawyer says calmly. "If Po has anyone watching Sands—and he well may—then seeing men like that might spook him. Small-town police detectives don't have the training to blend into the scene I foresee tonight."

"I'm not negotiating, Hull. I'm telling you what I need in order to give you the time you need to bust Po. Otherwise, we take Sands now. I've got police standing by to arrest him, and I've got the district attorney ready to take him before a grand jury in the morning."

Sands shifts in his seat like a man preparing to spring to his feet. Quinn looks even more tense.

"Shad Johnson's no longer playing for your team," I tell Sands. "I've got the evidence to bury you right now, and Shad knows it."

Hull holds up his hands to calm his informant, and in this moment I sense the frightening tension between them. "Penn, you've got to be reasonable here. You've got to try to see the larger picture."

"I've tried to do that, William. I honestly have. As a former prosecutor, I have a lot of empathy for your position. But the crimes your informant has committed in the past week alone—"

"Were part of the very operation that's about to take place. The dogfighting—"

"Dogfighting doesn't even register on the scale he's established in the past few days."

Hull looks at his steel watch and winces. "Edward Po's a well-known breeder of fighting dogs. Sands had to use whatever bait he could to lure Po onto U.S. soil."

"That doesn't change the fact that every instance of it is a felony."

"Christ, Cage, you can't be *that* much of a Boy Scout. You worked in Houston for twelve years. You dealt with major crimes."

"Mostly murder. Not this pseudo-spook stuff. That's why this case sticks in my craw. Jonathan Sands murdered or ordered the murders of Tim Jessup, Ben Li, and Linda Church, all employees of the *Magnolia Queen,* all of whom were in a position to supply enough evidence to put him in state prison for the rest of his life. He also ordered the kidnapping of Caitlin Masters. All those crimes are capital offenses in Mississippi. Tim Jessup was a friend of mine, but even if he weren't, this man would not go unpunished. I don't give a damn what federal authority you try to invoke, once you have Po, this son of a bitch is going to jail. Either he does hard time as part of your plea with him, or Shad Johnson sends him to Parchman for murder and kidnapping."

Sands leans in from my left and laughs in my face. "You don't get it, mate. If I don't cooperate, Hull doesn't get Po. And I don't cooperate unless I'm guaranteed immunity from prosecution. *Full* immunity. End of story."

"Not quite," I say. "If Edward Po doesn't show up for your little Roman spectacle tonight—and I'd lay ten-to-one odds that he won't—do you really believe that Hull's going back to Washington empty-handed? After all the time and money he's spent on this? No. In that case Quinn's going to get the free pass, and *you'll* wake up as the most vicious criminal in America. I can see the headlines now: 'Irish mob man kills defenseless dogs, launders money for the Chinese triads. Possible links to terrorism.'"

As Quinn glares at me from behind Sands's head, I see that Sands has obviously considered this possibility.

"After all," I go on, "all we're sure Seamus did is rape Linda Church and kill a few dogs. Maybe he killed Tim Jessup, maybe he didn't. But he can tell us everything *you* did. And without Po in hand, you're the big fish everyone's going to want to fry."

"Why the fuck are we even listening to this?" Sands snaps, getting to his feet so fast that Quinn jumps back to get clear.

"Because I have evidence, Mr. Sands" I say evenly. "Hard evidence. I can bust you for money laundering right now. Chief Logan is standing by on the shore, and all the FBI agents in the world can't stop him." I lean back and look up at Sands with all the hatred in my heart flowing through my eyes. "This is still the United *States* of America, asshole. *That's* why you're listening."

Hull looks worried. "You don't have cops where somebody could see them, do you?"

"Take it easy, William. I want Po busted almost as badly as you do. I understand the priorities here. But I don't think he's coming. And I'm making sure that in the heat of the moment, this psycho doesn't slip away to a fairy-tale ending."

While Sands flexes his fists like a man preparing to beat down a door, Hull stands, turns his chair around, then straddles it and looks at me like a sergeant about to dress down his troops. I probably already have enough audio evidence to ruin Hull's career, but I have a feeling we're headed into serious criminal territory.

"Let me give you the facts of life," the lawyer says in a stern voice. "Sands may be a psychopath, but who really gives a fuck? Do you think I'd be wasting my time with him if he couldn't deliver? The NSA confirmed that Po's Dassault Falcon lifted off from Madrid Barajas Airport in Spain five hours ago. He was directly observed loading three Tosa Tokens aboard, and—"

"Tosa Tokens?"

"Fighting dogs, Cage! Po thinks he's bringing them here to fight a man."

The reality that Edward Po might actually be falling for Hull's trap hits me for the first time, and the force of the realization shocks me. "How long till he gets here?"

"Barring unforeseen delay—like this absurd bullshit—three to four hours."

Sands looks down at Hull. "You'd better straighten this bastard out, Will."

"He's seeing the light. Cage, do you know who you are in all this? I've read your file from cover to cover. You think you're Atticus Finch and Thomas Jefferson rolled into one, but I'll tell you who you are. Barney Fife. Barney fucking Fife, with one bullet in your gun, aimed straight at your own foot. I'm fighting for the national security of this nation, and you're busting my balls over collateral damage that doesn't add up to one day's casualties in Iraq or Afghanistan. Do you read me?"

"Loud and clear. But we're not in Iraq. And the laws of this country apply to you as well as to Sands. When you gave me the proof of life I asked for yesterday, you proved yourself an accessory to kidnapping."

Hull laughs outright. "You're joking, right? Do you seriously think you'll be able to trace that text message back to me? There are so many cutouts between those communications . . . shit, you won't even be permitted to access the records." He gets to his feet and kicks over the chair he was straddling. "This meeting's over."

I stand also, knowing I've got more evidence than I'd hoped for.

"All right," I say with seeming resignation. "If Po is really coming, take your best shot at getting him. I want you to get him. But I want Natchez cops standing by within a half mile of the sting."

Hull shakes his head. "We can't risk it. I give you my word, Sands will still be on U.S. soil tomorrow. That's the best I can do."

"You gave me your word that Caitlin Masters would be safe last night, but she was nearly killed by your informant's attack dogs, and the woman she was being held with died as Sands's prisoner.

Your word means nothing to me. I'm calling in my cops."

"We can't let you do that."

"How are you going to stop me? If I don't walk off this boat under my own power, Logan's men come aboard. If we have a shoot-out, or even a standoff, Po's jet is heading back to Spain."

Hull looks at Sands, then back at me. "One man," he says finally. "You can put one detective with us tonight."

"No," says Sands, feeling the tide turn against him.

"It makes no difference," Hull says, looking hard at the Irishman.

"It does to me."

"Well, that's the way it is. Who do you want, Cage? Whoever it is, make sure he has a nice suit."

"Kelly," I say without hesitation.

"No fucking way," blurts Quinn.

Sands, too, is shaking his head.

"Anybody else is like no guard at all," I say. "Sands could put down a city cop without breaking stride. I want someone who can control him."

"Kelly it is," says Hull. "Does he own a suit?"

"He'll have one in fifteen minutes."

"Then we're done here." Hull nods at the door, and the Green Beret steps forward and opens it. Quinn and Sands look like they're on the ragged edge of making a move, but Hull's bodyguard projects the feeling that he wasn't party to the firearms prohibition governing this meeting.

Kelly's hand is in the small of my back, pushing me through the hatch. He clearly doesn't want the two of us left in the room with Sands and Quinn. As I pass into the corridor, I'm acutely conscious that I'm leaving behind the taped evidence that will give me control of William Hull, but there's nothing to be done about this, short of fighting the two Irishmen for it. I'll have to trust that Logan and his men can get down here and retrieve the recorder without trouble.

What fills my mind as we move up the passageway behind Hull is the real possibility of nailing Edward Po. I never quite believed that the billionaire would risk stepping onto U.S. soil, but maybe Hull knew his prey well, and did what was required to draw him into the net.

At the elevator we all bunch up again

as we wait for Quinn to arrive and punch in the security code. The other three guards have gone, but when the elevator arrives and the doors open, it's all we can do to fit the six of us inside the car.

Seldom have I felt more free-floating testosterone than I do in this elevator. Sands and Kelly, predictably, have gained the back wall, but I have to stand with Quinn's chest pressing into my back. I half expect the knife he used to slice open my belt to slide between my kidneys.

"Fifteen minutes," Hull says, as the car stops on the main deck. "You don't have Kelly a suit by then, we're leaving without him."

"He'll have it," I say, my mind on the recorder downstairs as the doors open.

Hull and his man are first out. When they step around the partition, Hull beckons Kelly forward. As Kelly moves past me, I feel a hand grab my shirt and pull me backward, then a man's breath in my ear. "Remember that night on your porch?" Sands whispers. "You make all the agreements you want with Hull, mate. Just remember this. Nothing in my world gets resolved on paper. *Nothing*."

As I pull away, he twists a piece of flesh on my side hard enough to pop blood vessels, but nothing matters at this point. Nothing but signaling Chief Logan to get the recorder from below. Kelly fades back to me with a curious look, as though sensing that something has transpired, but I shake my head and push him forward.

Rounding the partition, I look up to the head of the escalator, but Logan isn't there. A large crowd is upstairs, and I try to pick the chief from the moving mass of bodies as Kelly takes my wrist and tugs me forward.

The ring of a cell phone behind me makes me turn. When I do, I see Seamus Quinn holding his phone close to his ear, trying to hear above the jangling noise of the casino. I'm about to turn forward again when Quinn's eyes go wide, and he grabs the arm of Jonathan Sands, who's two feet to his right. Sands looks annoyed, but Quinn jerks him sideways and speaks urgently into his ear.

Every instinct tells me something has gone horribly wrong. Without even sighting Logan, I raise my hand to the top of my head and pat it three times. Sands's eyes lock onto mine from a distance of ten feet, the malice in them absolute. For a brief time we are joined by mutual hatred, then his hand darts into his pocket, my eyes scarcely able to follow the swift movement.

A burst of white lights the night outside the casino, then a staccato blast like fireworks rattles the windows. The crowd falls into a shocked hush, and then the whole casino lurches away from the shore, sending hundreds of people reeling. As a collective scream of panic fills the saloon, Sands gives me a savage grin, then turns and races toward the stern of the barge, Quinn close behind him.

"Get off the boat!" Kelly shouts, knocking me aside as he flies past in pursuit. *"Go, go, go! I'll get the tape!"*

CHAPTER

69

Water cascades from the sprinkler system, and alarms ring shrilly while a recorded voice directs people to the exits with absurd calm. The bow of the barge seems to be drifting away from the riverbank, slowly but with increasing speed, like a log being pulled into a flooding river. The sensation is eerie, as though a huge hotel ballroom had begun to spin on its axis.

A scream of terror draws my gaze to the escalator. Chief Logan stands at its head, shouting for calm. Below him, a surging mass of gamblers has clogged the motorized staircase. Many have fallen, and people higher up are trampling them in their headlong flight to reach the main deck. Logan tries to stop the stampede, but the crowd swells over him like a tide, everyone with a single thought in mind—reaching the main exit.

Whirling from the mob scene, I look for Kelly, but I can't find him in the seething mass of bodies. Then, to my right, I see his blond ponytail disappearing through a service door disguised as a section of wall. Maybe the elevator has stopped working.

I charge through the door where Kelly disappeared and immediately hear footsteps on the staircase below. Leaning over the rail, I see the top of his head as he crashes through a fire door. Taking the stairs two at a time, I follow. Are Sands and Quinn somewhere ahead? Or is Kelly only after the tape? All I know is that whatever happened to this vessel was triggered by Jonathan Sands. Someone phoned Quinn with information, he relayed it to Sands, and Sands triggered the explosions.

Beyond the fire door, I see Kelly sprinting down a narrow passage that seems to run the length of the lower deck. It's the same corridor we were in only a minute ago. Ten yards past Kelly, Seamus Quinn veers right and disappears, and I realize he's back in the room we just left—the torture room nicknamed the Devil's Punchbowl.

Could Quinn know about the tape? Did someone betray the presence of the recorder?

Kelly darts though the hatch where Quinn disappeared. Before I can follow, the boat abruptly stops drifting, and I crash to the floor. Either the barge has hit something or it's reached the limit of any mooring cables that remain intact. Scrambling to my feet, I move through the hatch after Kelly.

The interrogation room is lit only by red emergency lights. Kelly stands thirty feet from me on the landing of the metal stairs by the far wall, his back braced against a steel hatch. One arm is locked around Quinn's neck, the other pins one of the security chief's arms. Jonathan Sands crouches two steps down from the landing, both hands raised, his fingers curled inward. There's blood on the side of his face. He seems to want to get to the hatch, but when he lunges toward it, Kelly flicks out a lightning kick, driving him back.

"Where's the recorder?" I shout. "Did they get it?"

"I don't know!" Kelly answers, wrenching his arm tighter around Quinn's neck.

The cart at the center of the room looks undisturbed. Before I can reach it, the boat shifts again, and a thunderous rumble rolls through the barge. Then a vibration like thousands of running feet rattles the hull. On the monitor screens to my right, I see screaming passengers trying frantically to escape the upper deck.

As Sands rushes the hatch once more and Kelly drives him back, I snatch open the lower door of the cart and probe with my hand, unwilling to take my eyes off Kelly. Feeling several hard objects, I rake everything onto the floor. The recording device is there, amid rolls of wire and duct tape, but I have to blink before I can take in what also lies beside the recorder: a tiny, antique-looking pistol with a leather string attached to its curved butt.

Walt Garrity's derringer.

Jiao . . .

Sands's lover obviously feared that he'd

never be taken as easily as we'd thought. Scooping up the recorder, I stand without reaching for the gun. There's no need for it.

"Kelly, let them go! I've got it! Don't risk your life! *They can't get away!*"

Sands looks back at me and laughs, then makes another try for the hatch. Kelly drives him off with a kick, but as he does Quinn shifts in his grasp, and Kelly almost loses him.

"Danny and Carl are out there!" I shout. "It's time to get off the boat! Carl can blow them away if they go through that hatch!"

"Sands still has the detonator!" Kelly screams. "Call Logan! We need cops down here!"

As the significance of *detonator* hits me, Quinn smashes an elbow into Kelly's chin, stunning him long enough for Sands to kick him away from the hatch. While Quinn engages Kelly, Sands spins the hatch wheel, then seizes the heavy metal door and throws it to the foot of the stairs with a clang. I drop to my knees, grabbing for the derringer, but too late. Kelly twists like a cat, flinging Quinn bodily over his shoulder in a judo throw. The Irishman's legs slam the rim of the open hatch, and I hear the crack of bone. I'm running forward with the gun when Quinn snatches Kelly's shirt from behind and yanks him backward with all his strength. Sands kicks out at the same moment, and Kelly tumbles through the open hatch, snatching Quinn after him as he falls out of the barge.

Sands and I are alone.

I stop at the foot of the stairs, aiming the derringer up at the Irishman's back. He's standing in the hatch, staring down at what must be Kelly and Quinn fighting in the water. Certain that Kelly can handle himself against Quinn, I'm tempted to run for the main deck, but I can't leave Sands with a detonator in his hand—not if any unexploded charges remain aboard.

"Back away!" I yell. "Get back! We're going up to the main deck!"

Sands looks over his shoulder and laughs again. "Look at those screens! Do you want to be trampled to death? Do you want to drown under a thousand people?"

The monitor screens are blinking erratically, but I can still see that the grand

saloon is teeming with panicked gamblers
who have nowhere to run. Sands is right.
Trying for the main exit at this point would
be crazy. And the likelihood that Logan
and his squad can impose any kind of
order on that mob is minuscule. Climbing
the first two steps, I steady the tiny derringer in my right hand and aim between
Sands's shoulder blades.

"Look at me, damn it! Give me the detonator!"

Sands turns from the hatch and raises
his right hand, turning a small metal box
in the red light. "What are you going to do
with that peashooter? You need to press
that against a man's belly to be sure of
hitting him."

I take another step upward, and Sands's
grin disappears. He looks out the hatch,
curses, then turns back to me.

"That first charge was nothing. Primacord on the mooring cables. I can blow the
bottom out of this tub anytime. You might
hit me if you shoot, but that pimp gun won't
kill me. Not before I push the button."

Come on, Kelly, I think, wishing the
commando would catapult back through

the hatch like a ninja assassin. The river can't be more than three feet below the hatch, if that.

"They're gone," Sands says, reading my mind. "You got what you wanted, Cage. You threw a wrench into the works. You queered my deal with Hull and cost me my fucking casino. Jiao helped you, didn't she? She planted the recorder."

"If you step through that hatch, a sniper's going to blow your head off."

Holding the detonator tight, Sands crouches and looks out over the darkening river. "I don't think so."

"He's got a night-vision scope."

"Oh, I'm sure. But where is he?"

"Helicopter."

"Well, then. You're going to call him off."

"Why would I do that?" I move one step higher.

Sands wields the detonator like a Taser. "Because if you don't, I'll send this bitch to the bottom. I've got seven or eight hundred hostages in my hand."

"You can't destroy this boat while you're still on it."

Sands gives me a defiant sneer and presses the remote.

The *Magnolia Queen* shudders like a bell being pounded with a sledgehammer. When the reverberations subside, the sound of screams reaches my ringing ears. Whether they're coming from the speakers or from other parts of the casino I don't know, but I'm certain Sands has mortally wounded the barge.

"If they don't seal the forward hold in sixty seconds," he says, "this tub is going to the bottom. Call off your sniper, Cage. I have two more charges left."

The barge shifts beneath my feet, wallowing in the river.

"Okay! I'll do it." I take out my cell phone and pretend to make a call, but there's no way I can let Sands leave this hold. If he gets twenty feet from the hull, he'll blow every charge he has left just for spite.

"Call him off," Sands says, scanning the river from the hatch. "I'm leaving. You can stay and die with the white trash and niggers you love so dearly."

Walt's derringer spits flame as I pull the trigger.

Sands's eyes register an instant of terror, but his fear fades into a smirk when the ricochet pings off against the steel wall.

"What did I tell you?" he cries, laughing. "One shot left."

"No. I've got four left, thanks to a good friend. And your old lover."

Sands's arrogance twists into rage before my eyes. He whistles shrilly, then spins toward the hatch as I fire again. A bloom like a red paintball round blossoms on his right shoulder blade, then he drops through the hatch.

No splash, I'm thinking when I hear metal scrape behind me. Whirling, I see only a blur of white against the red wash of emergency lights.

I twist away, but too late.

The jaws of Sands's Bully Kutta clamp down on my left upper arm, then hurl me bodily off the steps and slam me to the deck. Releasing my arm to go for my throat, the dog opens its maw and lunges downward, digging into my shoulder and neck. With the speed of blind reflex I whip my gun hand under its jaw and pull the derringer's trigger. There's a muffled pop, then the Bully Kutta lurches and topples onto its side, paws paddling the air as it voids its bladder and bowels on the deck.

The sound of a revving outboard motor echoes through the room. Scrambling up to the hatch, I look down and see Sands seated three feet below me in a gray Zodiac raft. Bright red blood covers his back and right side, but his right hand still holds the detonator, which has several buttons on its face. With his left hand, he's struggling to unmoor the raft from a cleat mounted on the barge's side. Bracing myself in the hatch, I point the derringer down at him.

"Turn off the motor!"

The Irishman looks up in exhausted surprise, then holds up the detonator like a cross against a vampire. "Do you really want to die here, Cage?"

"No more than you! That sniper's an ex-marine. The same one who shot your dog on the island. He can put a round through your brainstem before you push your buttons."

Sands looks over the darkening river, then winces in pain. "I'll take my chances. I've still got a few lives left."

As he struggles to free the line with his good hand, I swing Walt's derringer to the left and fire a round through the Zodiac's side.

Sands screams in rage at the hiss of escaping air, but the Zodiac's line is almost free of the cleat. Though part of the raft is deflating, it still looks seaworthy. And while Carl is out there somewhere, he has no idea what's happening in this small recess in the barge's side. He and McDavitt are probably trying to rescue people from the deck of the sinking casino—or from the river itself.

I'm on the verge of firing at Sands's head when I see riverbank twenty yards behind him. What I should see is three-quarters of a mile of water and the Louisiana shore. The *Queen*'s stern must have broken away from the bank and now must be pointing downstream. The three huge ramps providing egress from the boat must be hanging in the main channel of the river. Escape for the passengers is truly impossible. If Sands gets clear of the barge and blows the remaining charges, hundreds will drown in the fast-moving water of the cut bank.

Sands shouts in triumph as the line comes free.

Afraid of missing with a headshot, I aim at the center of his chest and fire. The shock of the impact jolts him. He looks down at his chest, then up at me in amazement. While his eyes bulge with incomprehension, I leap for the bloody hand holding the detonator.

My momentum topples us both into the river. The cold water shocks me, but I scrabble for his hand, my only thought to submerge the detonator long enough to short it out. The metal box goes under, but Sands drives his arm upward and gets it clear again, just out of reach. To keep it there, he clings to a length of cable on the barge's side with his good arm, while I cling to him. He's wheezing with every breath, but hatred still burns like molten glass in his eyes.

I must have hit a lung, not his heart. . . .

Unable to reach the detonator, I climb Sands's bloodied body like a drowning man, and my weight begins to push him down. Using the cable for leverage, he snaps up both knees and almost jars me loose. The powerful current tugs at my body, and I wonder briefly where Kelly is.

Sands brings up his knees again, but this time I'm ahead of him, clawing at his chest, searching for the bullet hole. When my forefinger finds the opening, I drive it deep into the hole and tear at the muscle, hoping to find his heart. *It's all he can do to stay afloat,* I think, but as I turn to look for the detonator, Sands slams his forehead into my right ear. There's a flash of white, and my hands go limp, but as the river begins to pull me away, I feel his shirtsleeve tangled in my fingers, and I yank it down with all my strength.

This time the detonator goes under and stays there. Sands bellows and tries to fight, but his strength is failing. His lung must be filling with blood. I'm riding his arm now, leverage on my side, the detonator wedged against my groin.

With his last reserve of strength, Sands releases the cable and smashes his good hand into my face. So powerful is this blow that I nearly lose consciousness, but one thought glows in my fading mind: *Hang on to the detonator.* He pounds the side of my head again and again, but each blow carries less force than the last, until the beating ceases and the arm in my hands goes limp. Then I'm clinging not to Sands, but to the crumpling Zodiac, and Sands is spinning out into the river.

CHAPTER

70

Caitlin and I are walking toward the pier at Drew Elliott's house on Lake St. John. It's one thirty in the morning. The moon is high, the air is cold, and the lake looks as deserted as it must have when the Mississippi River cut off this wayward bend long ago.

We're here because Daniel Kelly called me at City Hall three hours ago and asked me to bring Caitlin out here—alone. I was stunned to learn that Kelly had survived— Chief Logan and the Coast Guard had written him off as drowned—but Kelly would give me no details over the phone.

When I asked about Quinn, he told me the Irishman was dead. He would explain the rest in person, he said, at Lake St. John, but Caitlin and I must come alone and be absolutely sure we weren't followed.

It seemed a strange request given all that had happened on the river, and it was difficult to get away from town, even at this late hour. The insanity of the early evening had devolved into a night of phone calls to the state capital and to Washington, meetings with Shad Johnson and the police, visits to the hospital, and a few stolen moments with my family. Annie is staying at my parents' house, under the watchful eyes of James Ervin, his brother, and my father, who refuses to believe that all danger has passed. We found the lake house locked when we arrived, with no lights on, no cars parked in the driveway, and no sign of Kelly. Unsure what to do, we decided to walk down to the pier and sit by the lake.

"Look," says Caitlin, pointing to a wooden swing hanging from an oak limb in the backyard. "Let's just sit here."

I sit slowly, taking care not to bang my

wounded arm on the swing or chain. Dad prescribed pain pills and antibiotics for my injuries, but my head still throbs from Sands's blows, and my arm burns where his Bully Kutta ripped the skin.

"What do you think Kelly is up to?" she asks, pulling her fleece jacket close around her. "Why bring us all the way out here?"

"It could be anything. The Justice Department might be trying to arrest him. He might need help getting out of the country. We'll just have to wait and see."

"He wouldn't tell you what happened to Quinn?"

"Are we off the record?"

Caitlin nods, her gaze on the mirrorlike surface of the lake beyond the cypress trees.

"Quinn's dead."

She sighs deeply, but asks nothing more.

Caitlin has been strangely quiet tonight, especially during the forty-five minute ride from town. The chaos that followed the explosions on the *Magnolia Queen* meant one of the biggest news stories in the town's history, but she has acted as if covering it hardly interests her. I think her greatest fear was that I would not survive the near-disaster, which she'd watched from the bluff near the *Examiner* offices. When I called her cell phone and told her that the Coast Guard had rescued me from the river, something in her gave way, and a sort of delayed shock set in—probably caused by whatever she'd endured while being held prisoner with Linda Church. As we drove through the dark farmland between Natchez and Ferriday, we simply held hands and dwelled in our own thoughts.

There was a lot I didn't know when I was dragged aboard the Coast Guard river tender that responded to the distress call from the *Magnolia Queen*. I didn't know what had happened to the barge itself, or to the passengers, and it took some time for Logan, the Coast Guard, and the fire chief to determine those things.

Jonathan Sands had rigged all the mooring cables with Primacord—a rope-like explosive with a wide range of uses—in case the meeting I had demanded proved to be a trap. The foundering casino would provide the diversion he needed to escape, should it prove necessary. By sheer luck, one of the wireless detonators failed, leaving a single cable intact. This proved strong enough to keep the casino from careening downriver toward the twin bridges a mile downstream. There were 753 people aboard the *Queen* when the cables snapped, and no lifeboats are required on such a barge. Had the casino collided with the bridge pilings, many lives could have been lost. But that possibility paled compared with what might have happened.

As Sands had claimed in the hold, two unexploded charges remained in the bowels of the barge when he went through the hatch—not Primacord, but C-4. If he had blasted out the bottom of the *Magnolia Queen* while she was in the main channel of the river, everyone aboard would almost certainly have perished. Despite having a brave crew, the Coast Guard vessel at Natchez doesn't have the resources to rescue large numbers of people from a fast-sinking ship.

As for why Sands blew the cables when

he did, Chief Logan sussed this out in short order, much to his chagrin. A member of Logan's handpicked team had called Seamus Quinn's cell phone just as Quinn and Sands emerged from the elevator after our meeting. This was the call I'd seen Quinn take before the cables blew. Alerted by the traitor, Quinn simply leaned into Sands's ear and repeated the news he'd just heard: that we'd planted recording devices on the boat, and Logan's team was about to retrieve them. Sands had known then that, no matter what happened to Edward Po, I intended to make sure the casino manager spent the rest of his life in a Mississippi prison.

Chief Logan blamed himself for the leak. He'd kept our plan to himself until the penultimate moment, but as he waited at the head of the escalator for me to appear, his nerves got the better of him, and he confided their true mission to his men. There were twelve cops on that detail, and eleven proved loyal. The biblical symbolism of the numbers escaped no one. After reporting this betrayal to me by phone, Chief Logan drove to City Hall and handed me his letter of resignation. I tore it up while he watched, then told him to get back to work.

The status of Edward Po remains unknown. Just before Logan arrested William Hull on the riverbank, the lawyer took a call from the NSA, informing him that Po's jet had turned back for Spain six minutes after Sands blew the cables. Improbable as it seems, Po was apparently bound for Louisiana in the belief that the planned gladiatorial spectacle would take place. Had Logan's traitor not caused Sands to panic, Hull's plan to capture the Chinese crime lord might actually have worked.

I've wondered privately whether Jiao—who also watched the explosions from the bluff—might have warned her uncle that he hadn't chosen the best day for a visit to the United States. But I suspect it was one of the young Chinese prostitutes aboard the *Queen.* Jiao has not fled the city, as I feared she might, and she has reaffirmed her intent to sign a plea agreement and provide a full description of the stunning variety of criminal activities overseen by Jonathan Sands.

Sands himself was plucked unconscious

from the river by Carl Sims, who was hanging from a skid on Danny McDavitt's helicopter. By then the sheriff's department rescue boat and chopper had arrived, so McDavitt airlifted Sands to St. Catherine's Hospital. There he was stabilized, then sent north to the University Medical Center in Jackson, where he lies chained to a bed under round-the-clock guard by the Mississippi State Police. The legal wrangling over his case has scarcely begun, but like me, Shad Johnson intends to make sure that Sands spends the rest of his life at Parchman Farm.

The only real mystery of the night was the disappearance of Kelly and Quinn. The sheriff's department and the Coast Guard combed both sides of the river for hours but turned up nothing. By ten p.m., a consensus was building that the river had taken both men, as it had so many before them. Knowing Kelly as I do, I wasn't as quick to write him off, but even I was relieved to hear his voice on the phone when he called my office three hours ago.

"Look," says Caitlin, pointing out toward the lake. "Did you see that?"

"What?"

"A light. There."

Out over the water, probably at the end of Drew's pier, a yellow flashlight beam flashes twice in quick succession.

"That's got to be him," I say, getting to my feet. "Come on."

"What if it's not?" Caitlin asks. "What if it's Quinn?"

I start to say this is ridiculous, but something stops me. "Quinn's dead. Kelly told me himself."

"Still. I don't like this. Did you bring a gun?"

"In the car. Should I go back and get it?"

The light flashes again, then stays lit, shining upward. In the haze of its beam I see the glint of long blond hair. Then I hear a high, keening whistle that I've only ever heard from the lips of Daniel Kelly.

"That's him! Come on."

As we trot down to the pier, the light vanishes. Our feet make hollow bangs on the sun-warped boards, but as we reach the end of the dock, the rumble of an engine rolls over the water.

"Down here!" Kelly calls. "In the boat. Get in."

Peering down from the platform, I see

Kelly sitting behind the wheel of Drew Elliot's newest toy. Drew's old boat was the Bayrider parked in the metal building where we met Walt and Carl and Danny. This is a thirty-foot Four Winns, with an enclosed cuddy cabin below the forward deck. It's really too much boat for this lake, but Drew sometimes takes it out on the Mississippi, or even down to the Gulf to fish with his wife and son.

I help Caitlin down the ladder, then follow her into the boat. After giving Kelly a long hug, she sits in the padded passenger seat behind the windshield. I sit behind her. Kelly gives me a little salute, then pushes the throttle forward. The boat glides away from the pier with a softly churning wake behind it.

St. John is much larger than Lake Concordia, where Chris Shepard has his summer house. When we're fifty yards from the pier, Kelly pushes the throttle again, and the big Volvo engine propels the bow up out of the water. In seconds we're racing over the glassy surface, headed to the western end of the oxbow lake. Kelly looks pretty good, considering what he's been through. His blond hair flying in the wind gives him a deceptively youthful cast.

"Where are we going?" Caitlin asks, leaning back to me. "Seriously."

"I don't know. With Kelly, you just have to be patient."

Thirty seconds of silence is all she can manage. "Danny McDavitt's going to drop out of the sky and pick him up, isn't he? We're here to take the boat back."

"I truly have no idea." Reaching out with my foot, I touch Kelly's hip. "What are we doing?" I call over the whipping wind.

"Getting closure," he replies.

Caitlin looks curiously at me, but Kelly offers nothing further.

He's steering toward the far end of the lake—the shallow end, as Tim referred to it on the night we first met in the cemetery. The boat is really moving now, hydroplaning with perfect trim, the sensation as close to flight as you can get without lifting completely off the water. We're making more noise than I'd like, and Kelly is running without navigation lights, but he seems unconcerned. The houses thin out on this end of the lake, and there's zero chance of a patrol boat this late.

Caitlin turns her captain's chair sideways and takes my hand in hers. Normally, I'd expect her to be chattering about what happened to the *Magnolia Queen,* or badgering Kelly about our destination, but she seems withdrawn, even depressed. For the first time it strikes me that she might not be thinking about the recent past, but the future. About leaving Natchez again.

Leaving me.

As I ponder this reality, Kelly pulls back on the throttle, and the bow settles into the water. Except for our collapsing wake, the lake is perfectly still, with thin fog hovering low over the surface. As we glide forward at a fraction of our former speed, thick cypress trunks close around us. The bellow of bullfrogs is startlingly loud, and a chorus of chirping insects joins in. The smell of decay is claustrophobic, like the floor of a swamp, thick with rotting vegetation and dead fish, burping methane. As the trunks come within a few feet of the boat on both sides, the cypress limbs arch into a ceiling above us, blocking out the moon in some places.

"You're going too fast," I say. "There

are fallen trees under the water here. You don't want to hole out down on this end."

"No?" he says, staring into the darkness ahead of him.

"Take my word for it."

Now and then there's a wet sound as of something heavy sliding into the water. Caitlin squeezes my hand tighter. I wouldn't want to be driving this boat with only moonlight to steer by, and I don't feel particularly safe even with Kelly at the wheel.

"Dude," I say, "there's nothing down here but an old fishing camp. What's the mission?"

He pulls back on the throttle until we're barely moving, but he's too late. A second later the boat shudders as though we've struck a granite boulder. I feel nausea as it rebounds and floats backward.

"What are we *doing*?" Caitlin asks, looking up at the overhanging limbs. "Didn't you tell me water moccasins hang off of those limbs and drop into fishing boats?"

"Sometimes," I admit. "If it happens, don't jump out of the boat. We'll be all right."

Kelly carefully reverses direction, eases

forward, then puts the engine in neutral. The cypresses surround us like ranks of giant soldiers in the night, stretching back to muddy banks thick with undergrowth. Switching on his flashlight, Kelly shines it onto the deck, reflecting enough light upward to see our faces.

"Everybody good?"

"No," says Caitlin. "Enough with the mystery. Let's do whatever we came to do."

"We're about to. But before we do, I want to show you something."

Kelly sweeps the yellow beam along the waterline at the base of the cypress trunks. There, among the smooth wooden knees, dozens of red eyes reflect the light back to us with chilling effect.

Caitlin leaps from her seat and seizes my arm. "What the hell is *that*? Penn? What are they?"

Another thud comes from below, but this time the boat doesn't shudder.

"Did we hit something else?" Caitlin asks anxiously.

In answer, Kelly sweeps the light along the waterline on both sides of the boat, then aims it into the cypresses again. The red eyes glow in pairs, some only a couple of inches apart, others more widely spaced.

"What *are* those things?"

"Alligators," I say. "Locals call this place Alligator Alley."

As she shakes her head in disbelief, a loud slapping sound reverberates over the lake.

"They're headslapping," Kelly says. "Warning us to get out."

"I want to go back," Caitlin says anxiously. "This is crazy."

"This is karma," Kelly says enigmatically. "We've all been through a lot this past week, but nobody more than you. Nobody who lived, anyway."

She looks back at him in confusion. "And?"

"You remember that talk we had at that other lake house? About Sands being a one-bullet problem?"

Now he has her attention. "Yes."

"Tom told you it wasn't up to you, only to him and Penn."

"I remember."

"Well, this time you get a vote."

"A vote?" She glances at me, then looks back at Kelly. "On what?"

He passes the flashlight to me, then steps down and opens the door to the forward cabin.

"What's he doing?" Caitlin asks.

Kelly disappears into the cabin and pulls the door shut behind him.

"I'm not sure." Even as I say this, I know it's a lie. I've known Kelly too long to be surprised. Now I know what he means by *closure.*

I hear muted ripping sounds, some scuffling, and then the cabin door opens and Kelly drags a human form up onto the deck. When I shine the light down onto it, Caitlin gasps.

Seamus Quinn lies on the deck carpet, bound and gagged with duct tape, both eyes blackened and burning with virulent hatred. He's wearing dark pants, a blood-stained white T-shirt, and one shoe. His other ankle and foot are too grossly swollen to fit inside the other.

Why has he done this? I wonder. Kelly and I have come to this fork in the road before, and I chose the rule of law. Why would he think I'd decide any different now? My decision to assassinate Sands was defensive; killing Quinn would be revenge. Also, stupid. We need Quinn as a witness against Sands. *Although, I reflect, if Jiao continues to cooperate with Shad, Quinn's testimony would be superfluous.*

There's something going on here that I don't understand. Could Kelly simply be flirting with an idea that he knows I'll never agree to, but one I might push far enough to teach a murderer a lesson he'll never forget? *No.* He wouldn't waste his time hazing somebody. He's hard-core, all the way. But whatever he's up to, one thing is sure: He won't kill Quinn unless Caitlin and I tell him to do it.

"I thought this guy was dead," I say.

Kelly shrugs. "As far as anybody knows, he is."

After a few seconds of dazed comprehension, Caitlin breaks away from me and kicks the Irishman savagely in the ribs. He grunts but doesn't attempt to defend himself. Caitlin draws back her foot and kicks him again, harder this time. When Quinn shows no sign of terror, she throws the flashlight at his head, then hammers her foot into his arm, his neck, and his head. Quinn rolls away from the blows, but the bulkhead stops him. After that, he absorbs the kicks with resignation, like a man accustomed to beatings. Caitlin, by contrast, is crying and whining as she struggles to make Quinn feel some fraction of the pain he inflicted on Linda Church.

Caitlin stops after half a minute, probably because she's winded. I too am breathing hard, as though I participated in the assault. But my distress is emotional. Never have I seen Caitlin lose complete control, much less become violent. Even now she seems poised to begin kicking Quinn again. Her chin is quivering, and her eyes are wild. What I thought might be a reflexive discharge of pent-up fury seems to be only the first flicker of an unquenchable anger. What, I wonder, would it take to drive her into such a state?

And that's when I realize that Kelly's decision to bring us here has nothing to do with me. He's done this for Caitlin's sake. *Because he knows something you don't,* says a childlike voice within me.

Something awful. My throat tightens as I perceive something huge and dark beyond the surface of things, like a misshapen form behind a curtain I've been unwilling to pull back. Did Quinn's bruises and blackened eyes result from his fight on the *Magnolia Queen*? Or when Kelly uprooted every detail of his crimes from the toxic soil of his memory? *Kelly knows what happened in the dog kennel,* says the voice. *And whatever it was, he thinks she needs to witness this kind of punishment to exorcise it.*

Kelly has laid his hands on Caitlin's shoulders, as though to hold her back. Without knowing why, I kneel and rip the tape from Quinn's mouth.

"You going to drown me, Your Honor?" the Irishman asks, working his lower jaw up and down as though to relieve a cramp. "That the plan?"

"That's up to the lady," Kelly says softly. "What do you figure your odds are?"

"Drownin's not so bad," Quinn says philosophically. "I've drowned many a runt for the good of the litter. There's worse ways to go."

Kelly smiles appreciatively. "You're right about that, ace."

Caitlin looks warily from me to Kelly, then back to me again. "Is he serious?"

"Oh, he's serious, all right."

The Caitlin I thought I knew would be yelling for us to take Quinn back to Natchez and hand him over to the police. But the woman before me is not doing that. Instead, she takes the flashlight from me and shines it around the boat in a slow circle, watching the reptilian eyes watch her.

I try to catch Kelly's eye, but he's gazing at Caitlin like a knight awaiting a decision from his queen. Christ. When I first saw Quinn lying on the deck, I thought Kelly had chosen a cruel path by exposing Caitlin to such a situation. But now I understand that she's already far down a road I wouldn't have expected her to set foot on before tonight. She's no longer the woman I knew before she was taken prisoner. She is sister to a thousand women I knew and tried to serve as an assistant DA in Houston. She's a victim: violated, bereft, forever changed. A rush of emotions too powerful to understand swells in my chest, making it difficult to breathe.

Kelly was clever to choose this place. It's difficult to step outside the law when you're surrounded by all its tangible expressions. But here, in this prehistoric darkness under the cypress trees, it's easy to ask why we should bother taking Seamus Quinn back to the world of cops and lawyers and plea bargains. Intellectually, I know the answer to that, of course. But the shape behind the curtain is becoming clearer to me, even as I try to hold the curtain shut.

"What the fuck's she gawkin' at?" Quinn asks.

Caitlin swings the beam away from the red eyes and aims it down at Quinn. Then she switches off the flashlight and covers her face with a shaking hand. Five minutes ago I thought of Caitlin's period of captivity as a transient nightmare she had miraculously managed to escape. Now I know she might never escape it. Thinking this is like cracking the gate to hell.

"Stand him up," she says. "Let him see."

Kelly grabs Quinn under the arms and

heaves him up onto one of the seats. The Irishman looks out, but all is darkness around the boat. Then Caitlin shines the light toward the cypress knees, and the red eyes gleam like rubies in its beam.

"Bloody hell," says Quinn, his voice in a higher register. "What's that?"

The satisfaction I feel at the sound of fear in his voice cannot be denied. "American alligator," I inform him. "*Alligator mississippiensis.* I'm sure you've seen them on TV."

As Quinn slowly draws back his head, a throaty bellow blasts out of the dark at unbelievable volume. His bound feet scrape against the deck, but he has nowhere to run.

"You're a big fan of people fighting animals," Caitlin says. "You told me all about the Romans and their games, how they made animals rape girls."

Reaching out my right hand, I touch her shoulder softly. "Caitlin . . . ? What did he do?"

She looks back at me, her eyes wet with tears. "It's what he didn't do."

"What didn't he do?"

"He didn't *stop*. It was . . . unforgivable."

Anger like corrosive acid burns the lining of my heart.

"Where's your Christian mercy, darlin'?" Quinn asks mockingly, but his eyes are those of a cornered animal—desperate and calculating. He looks at Kelly. "It's always the women. The most bloodyminded creatures ever the Lord made."

"That's why you treat them with respect, Seamus."

Another hard slap rebounds over the water, and Caitlin whips the beam over to the cypress trees. Quinn can't tear his gaze away from the glowing eyes. When Kelly claps him on the back, the Irishman jumps in terror.

"Ready, tough guy? Here's your chance to prove what a badass you are. Ultimate Fighting Challenge times fifty."

"Ah, you're bluffin'," Quinn says, turning back from the water and smiling like a man who can appreciate being the butt of a good joke. "Cage is a lawyer. He won't have any part of this. He can't."

"Do you remember what I told you outside Sands's house?" I ask.

Quinn nods. "Sure. This isn't Northern Ireland. You were right about that."

"'Stay away from my family.' That's what I told you. Well, Caitlin is family. And this is Mississippi. You remember what I told you about that?"

"Cage, listen—"

"I said, 'We know how to play rough too.' But you didn't believe me. And now here we are, with you telling me about the law."

Recognizing the steel in my voice, Kelly eases the throttle forward, and we begin creeping through the narrow chute. Caitlin shines the light over the bow to assist him, and Quinn stares along the beam as though hypnotized by the unblinking eyes that surround us. After a couple of minutes, the chute opens into a wide pool. The old fishing camp stands somewhere in the trees to our left, but I can't see it. The place is deserted now, and there's nothing else down this way. The water's too shallow and dangerous for people to build here. With seemingly infinite patience, Kelly turns the boat and heads back up the chute.

Quinn's naturally pale skin looks as white as a movie vampire's in the moonlight. Fear has drained the blood from his face. This man has fed human beings to dogs. He may even have imagined what it might be like to suffer such a death. But he has never contemplated the fate Daniel Kelly has set before him. Kelly has appointed himself the instrument of the karma he believes in, and for him the terror Quinn suffers now is as important as his dying.

"I've heard a lot of guys brag about the biting strength of pit bulls," Kelly says in an offhand tone. "But I'll tell you something. A gator could bite a chunk out of a *car fender.*"

"Alligators don't usually attack people," I recall aloud. "It's usually by mistake, or if one feels threatened."

"This is a unique situation," Kelly says with relish. "*Lots* of gators out there tonight. Protective females, territorial males." He glances back at Quinn. "They don't need to see you, man. They *smell* you. Which reminds me . . ."

Motioning for me to take the wheel, Kelly lifts a seat cushion and opens the lid of an ice chest. A rotten smell instantly permeates the boat.

"That's awful!" cries Caitlin, holding her nose. "What is it?"

"I'm not sure. Got it out of the Dumpster behind the Mexican restaurant."

Kelly reaches across me and shifts the engine into neutral, then pulls on a gardening glove and reaches into the ice chest. I pinch my nostrils shut as he tosses something heavy into the trees. The splash silences the frogs, but they soon resume their dissonant chorus.

No one speaks. Something primitive holds us spellbound. Then I hear a single, powerful swish, like a sound effect from a horror movie: a heavy, armored tail moving water. A primitive grunt comes from the dark, then a choked bellow. More swishes follow. Too many to count.

"Feeding time," says Kelly. He pulls a knife from a sheath on his ankle. Quinn jerks in his seat when Kelly leans down and slices the duct tape binding his ankles. After a few seconds, Quinn stands erect on his good foot and holds out his wrists, but Kelly shakes his head.

"Come on!" says Quinn. "Jaysus, give a

man a chance. Give me something to work with."

I point at Quinn's feet. "He just did."

Caitlin turns the flashlight on Quinn. "More of a chance than you gave Linda Church."

"The water's only four feet deep here," I offer. "Kind of tough to run in that, but I know you'll give it all you've got."

"I wouldn't do that," Kelly advises. "I'd swim for it. *Real* slow. Alligators have some kind of organ that picks up vibrations in the water."

Quinn's dark eyes are bulging. "You're wired, right?" he says in a hyperexcited voice. "You want a confession? Fine. Let's start with Jessup."

"Save your breath," mutters Kelly.

"Wait a second," I say. "What about Ben Li?"

Quinn shakes his head angrily. "That kid attacked me on the boat! That crazy Linda jumped into the river, and when I turned around to find her, the chink went crazy. He was kicking me and screaming nonsense. I had to shoot him to try to save Linda."

Caitlin looks incredulous. "You killed

Ben Li to save Linda? So that you could rape her later?"

Panic arcs from Quinn's eyes.

"Do you have any idea what she went through?" Caitlin asks. "She *hanged* herself because of what you did."

"There you go!" he cries. "She killed her*self.* That's not murder!"

"Enough of this," says Kelly. "Let's get it done."

He turns to Caitlin as though for final permission, but her eyes are locked on Quinn.

"Linda *begged* you to stop," she says. "She begged you, but you kept on. She was *sick.* She was in pain. But you wouldn't stop."

"I was only doing what Sands ordered me to do!"

"*Liar!* He beat you for it."

"What do you think that was but *show*?" Quinn barks a hysterical laugh. "He did that in case he had to let you go later. So you could tell everyone what a merciful bastard he is."

Caitlin turns to me, her eyes luminous in the half dark. "How long would Quinn spend in prison?"

I lower my voice. "I can't answer that without knowing what happened. Everything that happened."

She closes her eyes. "Beyond a reasonable doubt," she says instantly. "That's the standard for murder, right?"

"Yes."

"He's guilty, Penn."

"I know."

"Come on then, ya fuckin' cunt!" Quinn roars, dropping his mask of submission. "Stop asking for absolution. Kill me if you've got the guts!"

She turns and takes a step toward him. "You think I won't?"

"No. You'll have your hard boy there do it." Quinn leers at Caitlin like an uncle with a dirty secret. "But why don't you tell them the real reason? Eh? You don't want your man to know what *really* happened in the kennel."

Caitlin raises the flashlight as though to strike him.

"Go on," Quinn says, grinning. "Tell him. Nothing to be ashamed of, lass. Tell him what you did for me, yeah?"

When she doesn't speak, Quinn looks over her shoulder at me. "She sucked me like a ten-dollar whore, Cage. Didn't think twice about it. They'll do anything for a little extra food and toilet paper. Swallowed it all too—"

Caitlin throws the flashlight, but Quinn deflects it with his bound forearms.

"That's it!" he says, laughing. "That's my little wildcat. Katie likes it rough, gents." He winks at me. "But then you know that already, don't you?"

I want to smash my fist into his windpipe, but something keeps me rooted where I stand.

"Or do you?" Quinn looks back at Caitlin and raises an eyebrow. "You play the lady for him, eh? That's the way of it?" He laughs crudely, then begins describing Caitlin's naked body—accurately— and how she serviced him in the kennel in exchange for certain privileges.

Kelly watches Caitlin and me with animal alertness, waiting for a signal that we've had enough. One word from either of us would send Quinn into the lake. This knowledge feels like a loaded gun in my hand.

Caitlin stands like a sapling against the torrent of sewage coming from Quinn's mouth, but her hands are quivering at her sides. If she had a gun, she might shoot him. With no more than six feet of deck separating her from Quinn, she could probably hit him. Kelly's probably thinking the same thing. But no matter how Caitlin feels right now, she would never be able to live with herself if she did that. The three of us stand like judges being taunted by a madman we have the power to silence at any moment, but who lack the last measure of will to do so.

Quinn rants on, like a man driving a car a hundred miles an hour along a cliff edge. "She took it in every hole, mate! She was scared at first, but I went deeper than you ever have. And she *loved* it. She told me that. She'll never forget it, and you won't either. No matter what you do to me tonight, you'll lie awake thinking how I filled her up—"

Caitlin snaps first, lunging for him with outstretched hands, and only then do I realize what he's wanted throughout his tirade.

A hostage.

My thought is far ahead of my muscles. Even as I fling out my arms to pull Caitlin back, Quinn's eyes flash with triumph, and he grabs her left arm with his bound hands, twisting her into him. They're almost one form when a blast of flame lights them like a flashbulb, and a deafening report echoes across the water.

Caitlin cries out, backpedaling away from Quinn and falling against me. Quinn staggers like a boxer who's taken a blow to the solar plexus, then looks down at the black hole between his shoulder and his heart. Clawing at the T-shirt, he grunts in disbelief, then looks up openmouthed at Kelly, his eyelids pinned back over bulging eyes. Kelly reaches out with his free hand and pushes Quinn backward, flipping him over the gunwale into the lake.

The splash barely registers in my ringing ears, but I feel Caitlin panting against me. She's hyperventilating.

"Are you hit?" I ask, lifting her to her feet and pulling off her fleece jacket.

"She's not hit," Kelly says, sliding his pistol into a storage slot in the boat's dash panel.

"Is he dead?" Caitlin asks, leaning on the gunwale and looking out into the dark.

"If he is, he got off easy. A bullet's a lot better than what's waiting out there."

"People had to hear that shot. Oh, my God."

"It's all right," I assure her, even as my heart bangs against my chest wall. "People shoot snakes and armadillos all the time up here."

"It's almost deer season," Kelly says. "Already bow season. Folks will figure it's poachers trying to get a jump on a big buck. There might be a game warden out this way, but twenty minutes from now, there won't be anything left to find."

Caitlin shivers in the wind. As I pick up her jacket and help her into it, Kelly eases the boat thirty yards up the chute. When he puts the engine in neutral again, the rumble of the engine quiets, and a heavy swish of water reaches us. Kelly removes a monocular night-vision scope from his pocket and pans across the water.

"Do you see him?" I ask.

"No."

Caitlin turns from the gunwale, walks to me, and splays her palm on my chest. "He was lying," she says, looking into my eyes with steady intensity. "About raping me. He was just trying to hurt you. He thought . . . we were really going to kill him."

"Weren't we?" Kelly asks.

She glances back at him, but Kelly keeps the scope trained on the surface of the water. Caitlin pushes her palm deeper into my chest.

"You believe me, don't you?"

"Of course." *What else can I say?*

"If you ever worry about what he was saying, then Quinn got what he wanted."

"I know."

Her anxious eyes remain on mine for several seconds; then she hugs her cheek against my chest. As I stroke her hair, three quick splashes come out of the dark.

Caitlin stiffens. "What's happening?"

"It's starting," says Kelly. "Jesus."

"He's dead, isn't he?"

A shriek of terror pierces the night.

"Guess not."

"Have they got him?" she asks, squeezing my wrist tight enough to cut off my circulation.

The next scream is defiant, like that of a hiker shouting at a grizzly bear to forestall an attack. Sound can carry for miles over water, and from this distance it's as though the nightmare is playing out only a few feet from us. Wild splashing echoes over the lake, as though a dozen kids are leaping into it from tree limbs. Then a high wail rolls out of the dark, rising in pitch until a glottal squawk cuts it off, and I know without looking that Quinn's head was just dragged beneath the surface. The sound of thrashing water makes my skin crawl.

"I can't listen," Caitlin says, shuddering against me. "Do something, Kelly. Make it stop."

Keeping the night-vision scope trained on its target, Kelly reaches back blindly toward the dashboard. I step around Caitlin and give him his pistol from the storage slot. He raises it quickly with his right hand, aiming along a path parallel to the scope held against his eye.

"I need light."

I scoop the flashlight from the aft deck and point it along the path of his aim, but I see neither man nor beast in its beam, only a churning maelstrom of water like a sand boil behind a saturated levee.

"My God," breathes Caitlin.

"He's gone," Kelly says with finality.

"We should go too."

Kelly lowers his pistol, but he doesn't take his eyes from the slowly subsiding frenzy.

"Let's *go*," Caitlin pleads. "I want to forget this."

I nod, thinking, *You never will.*

EPILOGUE

FIVE DAYS LATER

The season has turned at last. Before we even got off Lake St. John, a wall of rain rolled out of the west and covered the land for twelve hours before moving on. Behind the rain came a cold wind that took the last illusions of summer with it. The leaves on most trees are still green, some so dark they're almost black, but now the bluff is splashed with orange and yellow sprays of autumnal color.

Caitlin and I are on the river again, this time in Drew Elliott's old Bayrider, which I borrowed from his storage building. We've come to spread Linda Church's ashes.

We chose the river because it was the place where Tim and Linda found each other. On shore, Tim belonged to his wife and son. But on the *Magnolia Queen,* where he went to work as a sort of penance for his squandered birthright, he found another lost soul who might have become much more, had she been born with Tim's advantages.

Caitlin and I haven't spoken much since the night Quinn died on Lake St. John. I've spent most of my private time with Annie and my parents, mulling over the past and wondering about our future, but the aftermath of what happened on the *Magnolia Queen* has kept Caitlin busy day and night. In addition to writing stories and fending off requests from other media, she has funded and overseen the effort to rescue the fighting dogs Sands kept on both sides of the river, and also to return the many stolen pets to their owners. Some of the fighting dogs had to be put down, but others will be adopted. So far, twenty-three dogs and cats have been returned to homes as far away as Little Rock, Arkansas. I suspect that this whirlwind of activity has helped distract Caitlin from the aftermath of what we did on the lake that night.

Kelly left town the morning after Quinn died. We walked down to the bluff together and watched the big diesel boats push barges up and down the river for a while. The *Magnolia Queen* had already been towed to a refitting yard for repairs, so once again Pierce's Landing Road led only to an empty stretch of water. Leaning on the fence near the gazebo, Kelly told me that he'd spent the previous night reading a copy of Mark Twain's *Life on the Mississippi* that my father had lent him. It seemed an odd choice after what we'd done at the lake, but I supposed Kelly needed a way to come down from all that had happened that final day.

"You know," he said, "if you count the Missouri as the main channel of this river, the Mississippi was the longest river in the world until army engineers shortened it by three hundred miles. Longer than both the Nile and the Amazon."

"I didn't know that."

"Me either. In 1811, there was an earthquake so big that part of the river flowed backward for hours."

"I have heard that story. New Madrid, right?"

Kelly nodded. "Created a hole so big that the lower Mississippi flowed backward until the hole filled up. There's a lake there now. It's in Tennessee."

Kelly rarely chatters to hear his own voice, so his musings prompted a question. "Why do I get the feeling there's a message here? Are you going Zen on me?"

"Maybe so, grasshopper. *Change.* That's the message. Man wants to control this river, but the river wants to go where it will. And in the end, it will."

"I still don't get it. Beyond the obvious, I mean."

"Look out there," he said, gesturing with his arm to take in the great sweep of the river. "River pilots like Sam Clemens had to learn everything about the Mississippi. Every bend, cut, crossing, chute, island, hill, sandbar, and snag along thirteen hundred miles. Then they had to learn it all over again on each passage, because the river changed that fast. Not many men had the brains to do that, and even fewer had the guts to risk the lives of a boat full of people at every turn. Steamboats wrecked all the time."

"Uh-huh. And?"

"Well . . . I could see how a river pilot might start feeling like his job was futile— even absurd. There certainly were easier ways to make money."

I suddenly saw where he was going. "Like writing, for instance?"

"Well, Twain did a little writing, yeah. But he did his share of piloting too. And he was proud of it."

"How much piloting did he do?"

"I'm not sure." Kelly turned to me, his blue eyes as mild as ever. "But I know one thing. He never walked off a boat halfway down the river, leaving his passengers stranded in a storm."

I nodded to show that I'd taken Kelly's point, but my thoughts weren't on local politics. Despite my promise to Caitlin, Seamus Quinn's final raving words had been preying on my mind since the last night on the lake.

"What's wrong?" Kelly asked. "Something's eating you, man. Cough it up."

"Do you think Caitlin was telling the truth? About Quinn?"

His face darkened. "You think she'd lie about being raped?"

"Maybe. To protect me. So I'd never have to think about it. I want to believe her, but . . . she was ready to have you throw Quinn out of the boat. She wouldn't have done that unless he'd done something terrible to *her*—personally."

Kelly shook his head. "I disagree. For some people, seeing somebody suffer an atrocity can be as bad as it happening to them. Worse, sometimes. They feel impotent, you know? Guilty because they stood by and did nothing."

Uncertainty must have shown on my face, because Kelly put his hand on my shoulder and said, "I'm telling you, that's what happened with Caitlin and Linda. Quinn didn't rape Caitlin."

"He described her naked body."

Kelly sighs heavily. "Bro. I was alone with him for a long time before you guys showed up. There's *nothing* I don't know about that cocksucker. He saw her naked, yeah, but Sands showed up and made him give her clothes back. Quinn never raped her, Penn. He wanted to. But if he had,

Sands would have killed him. You can let go of that."

I felt shamed by the rush of relief that coursed through me after this assurance, but the idea that Caitlin might have chosen to suffer something so terrible alone rather than let me try to help her had been more than I could bear. "Thanks," was all I could manage.

An hour after this conversation, Danny McDavitt picked Kelly up at the Natchez airport and flew him to Baton Rouge. By now he's back in the mountains of Afghanistan, working for an outfit I never heard of, but almost certainly some version of Blackhawk Risk Management. The last thing Kelly said to me was "Spartacus." Then he handed me a scrap of paper with a phone number on it. I embraced him, shook hands with McDavitt, and drove back to my house on Washington Street to try to sort out my feelings.

Each day since then has brought more developments, some surprising, others predictable. Jiao has cooperated with Shad Johnson's office, but not yet with the FBI. Most of her testimony up to this point has implicated Jonathan Sands, but not her uncle in Macao. I can't fault the woman for her survival instincts. Edward Po is not someone you want angry at you.

No one knows this better than Jonathan Sands. The former general manager of the *Magnolia Queen* seems quite content to be tried in Mississippi for murder rather than in federal court on money-laundering charges. Without William Hull to protect him—and with Po at large in the world, rather than in custody—Sands would be a fool to implicate the crime lord in even a misdemeanor. Sands may hope to escape Po's legendary vengeance by remaining silent, or he may simply be posturing to lure the Justice Department into offering him protective custody in exchange for his testimony. Either way, I don't think he has much chance of living out the year. The State of Mississippi has no intention of turning Sands over to federal authorities without a fight, and Edward Po's arm is very long.

As a powerful Chinese national, Po will not be extradited to the U.S. even if Sands survives to testify against him. But under the broad powers of the Patriot Act, he will be declared a terrorist and stripped of his U.S. assets. Since Po legally owns less than five percent of the Golden Parachute Gaming Corporation, Craig Weldon, the California entertainment lawyer, will finally gain control of the company he naïvely thought was his in the first place. The Golden Parachute casino boats will run as legitimate businesses now, and continue to pump much needed money into Mississippi's struggling economy.

William Hull's days as a rogue lawyer are over, but I doubt he'll spend a day in prison. Like the men he pursued, Hull was the type to maintain detailed records of all he did in the service of his masters. Such is the currency of politics, and Hull was, if anything, a political creature. This was verified when Shad Johnson received a call from the Director of Homeland Security, asking that Hull be released into federal custody. To Shad's credit, he called to ask my opinion before he agreed. After some thought, I decided that I had no moral authority to judge Hull. Last week, I almost ordered Kelly to assassinate Jonathan Sands without even the semblance of due process. As for what happened on Lake

St. John . . . though I'm loath to admit it, the difference between Hull and myself is one of degree rather than kind.

No one has learned the fate of Seamus Quinn. Perhaps those who rolled over in their beds during the wee hours of that night on Lake St. John have an inkling that something happened, but gunshots are common there, and it would take a small skirmish to warrant a call to the sheriff's department. The ignorance of the public doesn't mean Quinn is forgotten. Kelly will remember him as one more face in the shadow gallery of those who saw him last upon the earth. For Kelly, the existentialist, there is no moral issue: The deed is done, today is a new day. For Caitlin and me, however, the thing is more complex. Here in this place where the past is never dead, or even past, Quinn rises between us at odd moments, most often when we moralize or make the easy generalizations that we as "liberals" tend to make. Caitlin now knows that all the fine words spoken down the centuries mean nothing when you have watched someone remorselessly brutalize a member of your tribe— even if that tribe includes all the women of the world. When offered a choice between certain death for the transgressor or a fair trial with the prospect of acquittal, she came close to choosing death. I did also. Moreover, she did not shy from delivering blows herself. The temptation we felt that night haunts us both and makes us question all we'd stood for until last week.

The awful philosophical musings that Quinn shared with Caitlin and Linda in the kennel are partly true, and they echo what Kelly told Caitlin in Chris Shepard's lake house: *We're still in the cave.* As with the dogs that Sands twisted into killers, there are urges in the blood that that no amount of socialization will ever remove. Lies and cruelty and murder are in us all.

All.

"Is that it?" Caitlin asks, pointing to a deep seam in the overgrown riverbank.

"Maybe," I say, throttling back and getting to my feet in the gently rocking boat. "I just don't know."

The "it" she's referring to is the Devil's Punchbowl. The real one. We figured that since the great defile lies north of town, it would be a good landmark to use for spreading Linda's ashes on the water. From there they would drift down past the remaining casinos, then under the bridges and past the old plantations where Sands imprisoned dogs and women alike, as other men had done before him. Three or four days later, what's left of Linda Church would flow through New Orleans and out into the Gulf of Mexico.

"I don't think we're going to find it without a GPS," I confess. "The bank's still too overgrown."

Caitlin shrugs. "It doesn't matter. We're far enough north. Let's do it out in the main channel."

I turn the boat to port and push the throttle forward. When we're midway between Mississippi and Louisiana, I kill the engine. I don't like doing that in the middle of the river, but given the occasion, it seems necessary. Caitlin removes a simple bronze urn from beneath one of the seats and rests it on the gunwale.

"Should we say something?" I ask.

"Anything we say now is too late."

Squinting into the sun, she looks back at Natchez high on the bluff, then across at the levee on the Louisiana side. I don't know what she's thinking, but I don't intend to disturb her. The extremity of what she endured with Linda in the kennel remains unknown to me. And while I take Kelly at his word that Quinn never raped Caitlin, the few details she has revealed were enough to convince me that Seamus Quinn deserved an express ticket to hell. Whatever really happened, it inspired Caitlin to pay for Linda's cremation and memorial service, which was attended by a handful of cocktail waitresses and no one else.

"I'll never forget her," Caitlin says, still looking westward toward the place of their captivity.

"She'd be glad to know that."

"She would. She had a high opinion of me, for some reason. She taught me how lucky I was to have the childhood I had. I'm not a poor little rich girl anymore. Linda gets the credit for that."

I smile at this rare display of self-deprecation.

"You want to know a secret?" she says, removing the lid from the urn. The breeze catches some dust from the opening and sends it dancing over the water like a swarm of gnats.

"Sure."

Caitlin raises her eyes until we're looking directly at each other. "I sprinkled some of this over Tim's grave this morning."

"Did you really?"

"I couldn't see the harm. Julia will never know, and it would have meant the world to Linda."

"To Tim too." I can't help but smile. "Just when I start believing you're a real cynic, you show your romantic streak."

Caitlin turns back to the water. "I've always been a romantic. You know that. Here goes nothing."

Lifting the urn by its base, she flings the ashes far over the orange-red water. A hiss like falling rain reaches the boat, and then only a small cloud of dust hangs over the river, dissipating slowly in the wind.

"How long till she gets to New Orleans?" Caitlin asks.

"That depends on a lot of things. No more than a week. Maybe sooner."

She watches the ashes drift away from

the boat. "The other day, you asked me if I'd learned anything about Tim's last minutes while I was with Linda. I did, actually. Quinn told her about it between the rapes. To torment her."

"Christ."

"I'm going to tell you, but I don't ever want to talk about it again. Nothing about Quinn."

"All right."

Caitlin sits on one of the padded seats and crosses her legs. She tugs at the end of her ponytail as she speaks, her gaze on the fiberglass deck. "When Tim stole the DVD from the *Magnolia Queen,* there was already a homing device on his car. Quinn tracked him sometimes to see if he was at Linda's apartment. Ben Li woke up and called Quinn to warn him just after Tim left the casino. Quinn and a couple of goons tracked Tim up to the cemetery in a security van. Then they switched on a cell phone jammer and started hunting. They found Tim's car right away. They left one guy guarding it, then fanned out through the graveyard. Tim must have been hiding the DVD in the tree about then."

"Because he couldn't find me."

Caitlin pauses, then nods in sober agreement. "After he hid the disc, Tim somehow got back to his car and over-powered the guard, then took off for town. But Quinn had already called for help. The second vehicle blocked the road, so Tim turned and headed out Cemetery Road as fast as he could."

"That's when he made the voice memo in his phone."

"Right. The plan he mentioned in his memo was simple. He ran his car off the cliff into the Devil's Punchbowl and dived out at the last second. He was trying to make them think he'd spun out and killed himself."

"Why didn't it work?"

"Think about it."

This takes only a moment. "Dogs."

"*Dog,* singular. The backup team had brought Sands's Bully Kutta in the second vehicle. Tim hid in the woods across the road from the Punchbowl, but he didn't have a chance with that monster hunting him."

"My God," I whisper, remembering the massive white dog pinning me to the wall of my house.

Caitlin closes her eyes. Recounting this is obviously a struggle for her. "The dog mauled Tim pretty badly, as you saw. But the real torture happened in the backseat of the SUV. They were taking him back to the *Queen* to question him with electricity, but naturally Quinn couldn't wait. He beat Tim with a club to subdue him, then started on him with a cigarette." She wrings her hands as though unsure what to do with them. "Quinn told Linda a lot of horrible things, but I think he was just trying to make her suffer. Tim was only in the SUV for a couple of minutes. At least I hope he was."

"A couple of minutes of fire is more pain than most people can imagine."

Caitlin pulls her jacket tighter around her. "Tim had passed out by the time they reached the bluff—or so they thought. But just as they passed Bowie's Tavern, he exploded off the seat and started hitting everyone in sight. Then he grabbed his cell phone and jumped out of the SUV."

"Where the witnesses first saw him."

"I doubt Tim even knew where he was when he started running."

My throat constricts when I think of Tim

giving his last reserves of strength to escape his torturers. By then he must have been thinking only of Julia and his son. But now I remember Logan telling me that Tim tried to call me just before he went over the bluff. This memory brings blood to my face and tears to my eyes.

"It was Quinn who chased him?" I whisper.

"Yes. I think Quinn panicked. They switched on the jammer to stop Tim from calling anybody, but Quinn wasn't sure he could get Tim back into the vehicle before a crowd gathered. That's why he shot him."

"They would have killed him in the end anyway."

"Yes." Caitlin reaches out and touches my hand. "Penn, there's a reason I told you this story. I wouldn't want you to have that stuff in your head unless I thought it was necessary."

"What do you mean?"

"You blame yourself for Tim's death. I know it. I don't think you could have done what we did at the lake unless you did."

My throat is so tight that breath can hardly pass through it. She's right. When

Kelly shoved Quinn off the boat, I didn't protest because I had focused all my guilt and self-disgust on him. But Quinn's death has not lightened *my* guilt—or eased my suffering.

"Look at me," Caitlin says. "Sit down and look at me."

I do.

"You think Tim died because you were late for that meeting."

"Didn't he?"

"No. He died because he put himself into a situation he didn't understand, with some very bad people. Only one thing would be different today if you had showed up at the cemetery on time. You'd be dead too."

"You don't know that. I had a gun with me."

Caitlin shakes her head. "Don't kid yourself. You and Tim were no match for Quinn, his gang, and that dog. You were lucky to get off the *Queen* alive the other day, and you were only fighting Sands."

She's right again. "I know that. My real mistake was letting Tim go forward at all. I knew what could happen when—"

"Stop," she says sharply. "You have to

stop. You'll drive yourself crazy. Do you want me to spend the rest of my life torturing myself for not saving Linda?"

"You couldn't have—"

"*Stop.* You have to let go, Penn. Now, out here, today. And I mean all of it. Tim, Quinn, everything. When you start this boat again, we're going to leave it behind us, in the river."

She stands and comes to my seat, then pulls my head against her abdomen and runs her fingers through my hair. I haven't been this way with her in so long that a dizzying feeling comes over me.

"Are you still planning to resign?" she asks softly.

When I don't answer, she says, "Paul Labry must have mentioned your talk with him to someone before he died, because the rumor's already spreading."

"I know. Drew asked me about it when I called to borrow this boat."

Caitlin steps backward and looks down expectantly. "Well?"

She's waiting for me to say yes. Hoping for it. I can see that as plainly as the sun over the river. But from the moment Kelly gave me his Mark Twain speech on the bluff, I've been questioning my decision. Surprisingly, my father gave me his blessing only a day after Kelly left. The two had evidently discussed my dilemma, and Dad was aware that my reluctance to disappoint him had already kept me in office longer than I might have stayed otherwise. He told me that, considering all that had happened, he wouldn't think less of me if I felt I had to step down. I don't know if he meant that, but he said it, and he said it knowing that if I resigned, I would probably move Annie to a new town far away. But yesterday, as I watched two black men in overalls lower Paul Labry's casket into the earth not far from Tim's grave, I knew with utter certainty that if I resigned, I would think less of myself for the rest of my life.

"It would be wrong to quit now," I say in a shaky voice. "I wish that weren't the case. But I made a commitment to the town. I made promises, and people believed me. If Paul were still alive, I might feel differently. But now . . . as badly as I want to go away with you, I don't feel I should leave the job in the hands of those most likely to get it."

Caitlin's eyes narrow for a few seconds, then she turns to her right, looking out over the water. She's hiding tears.

"Was that a no?"

Despite my best intentions, the truth emerges when I speak. "No. No matter what it costs me, I can't lose you again. I can't do it."

She raises a hand to her face and wipes her eyes. "Then I'll stay."

The words don't quite register at first. "You don't mean that."

She turns to face me, her green eyes wide and filled with resolve. "I do. I'll stay until the end of your term. For two years, I'll use all my power to make this town worthy of Tim's death, and of what you've worked for. I'll fight to make it a place where I can feel good about Annie living and going to school."

Blinking in disbelief, I feel the first rush of euphoria that comes with the knowledge that life is granting you the grace of a dream realized. "Caitlin, you don't—"

"Wait a second. I have one condition."

"What? We leave town after my term is up?"

Her face tightens with irritation. "Would you let me talk?"

"Sorry."

Holding up two fingers, she gestures at me like the beautiful schoolteacher of some little boy's dreams. "After two years, we look hard at what we've accomplished, then reassess where we are."

"Of course. Absolutely."

"That wasn't my condition. That's a given."

"Oh."

She lowers her hand and squares her shoulders like a woman about to walk to the end of a very high diving platform. "My condition is that you marry me."

At first I think she's joking, but I've never seen her look more serious.

"Don't fall down with joy," she says.

"I'm shocked, that's all. The way you've been acting for the past few days—"

"Penn, you're the dumbest smart man I've ever met. Annie needs a mother, not a girlfriend hanging around year after year."

The depth of her commitment hits me like a sudden pitch of the boat. "I agree," I say softly.

"She needs a sister too. Or a brother, if that's the best we can do. I'm thirty-five, and I'm not getting any younger."

The laughter I hear is mine. "You're moving pretty fast, aren't you?"

"Have you ever known me to move any other way?"

"No."

"Well, then," she says, her face still severe. "You should probably kiss me now."

Reaching out, I take her hand and pull her toward me. For the first time in a year and a half, this intimacy is not a dream or a memory, but real. She hesitates, then spreads her palm flat on my chest and smiles with such intensity that her eyes shine.

"I've missed you," she says. "I've missed you so much."

"Why didn't you let me know?"

"Because it was everything or nothing. It had to be."

Before I can speak again, she leans forward and brushes her lips against mine. This close, her scent is overwhelming. Taking her in my arms, I kiss her as I longed to the first time we were ever alone, and she melts against me. When she finally pulls back, her cheeks are flushed, her eyes bright and wet.

"Do you remember our first time?" she asks.

"The party at that surgeon's house. In the garden. Before the Del Payton case broke."

"Does it feel the same to you?"

"Yes. No. As good as that was, this is better."

She closes her eyes as though saying a silent prayer. "Was that your first kiss after your wife died?"

"Yes."

"I've always wondered that."

"You must have known."

She opens her eyes and touches my right cheek with her finger. "I thought it was. I wanted to think it. That's why I never asked."

Over Caitlin's shoulder, I see a long string of barges pushing around the north bend of the river. "When can we tell Annie?" I ask, moving behind the wheel and starting the engine.

"Today. It's long overdue."

"What about asking your father's permission, all that?"

"We're pretty old for that, aren't we? He'd love it, of course."

"It's the right thing. In this case, anyway."

Spying the barges, Caitlin stows the empty urn, then sits in the passenger seat. "Do whatever you want about that. But I'm about to surprise you."

"Oh, God. Are you pregnant? With a little filmmaker?"

She smacks me on the shoulder hard enough to bruise. "It's about the wedding."

"Let me guess. No fuss, no church, just a quick trip to Fiji or somewhere."

"Boy, you *are* dumb. I want the church, the dress, engraved invitations, a string quartet, the whole thing. I know it's all bullshit, but I want it anyway."

"I literally can't believe that."

She smiles broadly, elated at having surprised me. "If I'm going to stay in Mississippi, I'm taking the good with the bad. Come on, let's go before that barge runs us over."

Putting the boat into gear, I push the throttle forward, make a wide turn, and head downstream.

"The day we get married," she says above the roar of the wind, "I'm going to pour a glass of champagne into this river. Don't let me forget."

"I won't."

"I mean it." She takes my hand, then pulls out her ponytail holder and lets the wind fling her dark veil of hair behind her. "Do you know how lucky we are?"

"Yes."

She intertwines her fingers in mine.

The ski boat skims the surface of the river, bouncing gently as we make for the distant landing at Silver Street. High above us, the city stretches along the rim of the bluff from the homes of Clifton Avenue to the gazebo where a kissing couple watched Tim die. Past the highway cut and the bridges stands the Ramada and the Briars, where Jefferson Davis was married, and then the land descends to the lumber mill and the sandbar near the old Triton Battery site, where Hans Necker will someday build his recycling plant.

We're less than a mile from the landing

when my cell phone vibrates in my pocket. Expecting Annie, I'm surprised to see my mother's cell number on the LCD screen. She only uses the thing in emergencies, so my pulse quickens at the sight.

"Hello?"

"Penn, it's Mom."

The way she said my name reveals the stress she's under. "What is it? What's happened?"

"Are you driving?"

"Mom, what's the matter?"

"Your father had a heart attack."

I close my eyes, preparing for the worst. "Is he alive?"

Caitlin clenches my hand, and I tell her what's happened.

"He's at St. Catherine's Hospital," Mom goes on. "I'm on my way there now. Drew used the office defibrillator on him. Tom probably would have died without it."

"Is he conscious?"

"Yes."

"Is Annie still with the babysitter?"

"Yes. I didn't want to scare either one of them."

"Caitlin and I are on the river, but we'll

pick up Annie and get to the hospital as fast as we can. Thirty minutes, max."

"Hurry, Penn. I talked to him for a few seconds. Tom said he has something important to tell you. He was very emphatic."

"What's that about?"

"I have no idea. He wasn't completely coherent, but he sounded like he doesn't think he's going to make it."

My father always hides pain, and my mother doesn't exaggerate. This is not good news.

"Just hurry so he won't be anxious about whatever it is."

"I'm on my way, Mom. You pay attention to the road. We'll be there before you know it."

"Be careful." When she clicks off, I press END and shove the throttle to the wall. The Bayrider leaps forward, then planes out and begins to bounce on the river, jumping and smacking down like some great porpoise. "Damn it!" I curse.

Caitlin points toward Natchez Under-the-Hill. "We're almost there. We'll just tie up and run straight for the car."

I nod, but I'd already made that decision, though it means risk for Drew's boat.
There's no real dock at Silver Street, only
a steep ramp. I'll tie the thing to the Evangeline casino if I have to. Boiling with frustration, I slam my hand against the wheel.
"It's always something, you know?"

"What do you mean?" Caitlin asks.

"Whenever life gets too good, whenever fate hands you something wonderful, something else gets taken away."

She squeezes my shoulder and shakes
her head. "Stop thinking like that. For one
thing, life hasn't been that great lately. And
for another, your dad's not going to die."

It's a nice sentiment, but she has no
idea what shape my father is in right now.
He could be dead already. "You don't
think this could have something to do with
what we just went through, do you? With
Sands or Po?"

"No. Absolutely not. This is just life,
okay? But it's going to be all right this time.
I know it, Penn. We're together again, and
Tom's not going to die on us."

"He seems to think he is. He told Mom
that he has something important to tell
me."

Caitlin absorbs this in silence. "Well, we have something important to tell him too. We'll tell him before we tell Annie. You know how that news will make him feel."

"You're right," I admit, picturing the scene. My father wanted me to marry Caitlin a week after he met her. "He'll be the happiest, apart from Annie."

"He will. Now, keep thinking that." Caitlin hugs me tightly from the side. "Okay?"

"Okay." With shaking hands, I turn the wheel and point the boat toward the Silver Street landing.

Toward home.

ACKNOWLEDGMENTS

None of my novels could be written without the generous help of many friends and acquaintances. Mimi Miller of the Natchez Historic Foundation and Stanley Nelson of *The Concordia Sentinel* were especially helpful this time around. Stanley is a fine local historian, and some of his articles are available online. Natchezians are always happy to help with my research, even though the fictional city that sometimes results seems a less than desirable place to live. We who live here know the truth, and wouldn't live anywhere else. This time around, I want to thank: Judge

George Ward; Sally Durkin; Mayor Jake Middleton; former mayor Tony Byrne; Chief Mike Mullins; Major Jody Waldrop; Keith Benoist; Kevin Colbert; Billy Ray Farmer; Jim Easterling; Don Estes; Mike Wheelis, M.D.; and helicopter pilot John Goodrich.

Thanks to the usual suspects on the personal support side: Jerry Iles, M.D.; Betty Iles; Geoff Iles; Jane Hargrove; and Courtney Aldridge.

Thank you, Ed Stackler, for midwifing most of this one into being during a long and stressful October. Thanks to novelist Charlie Newton for his Las Vegas expertise. My warm gratitude also goes out to a few good people who shall remain nameless.

For being patient with this book, my heartfelt thanks to the crew at Simon & Schuster: Carolyn Reidy, Susan Moldow, Louise Burke, Colin Harrison, Dan Cuddy, and my buddy Gene Wilson out in Texas. Thanks also to Wayne Brookes at HarperCollins UK, and to the gang at S&S Canada, for a good time at Niagara Falls and great support year round.

Finally, thanks to Aaron Priest, Lucy Childs, and Lisa Erbach-Vance for holding down the left-brain stuff for right-brain guys like me.

To those readers who took the trouble to read this page: Penn Cage will be back next year. That wasn't my intent, but what was originally meant to be half of this book grew into something far too important to be only part of a novel. So, enjoy!

For those considering a trip to Natchez, please be aware that at this time the city has only one riverboat casino in operation. During the writing of this novel, two more casinos were in the works, but the changing economy has affected those plans. I know that many of my readers travel to Natchez to see some of the sights depicted in my books, and I urge you to search the Web for accurate tourism information, which can vary quite a bit from the fictional world I've created for Penn Cage. That said, Natchez is a beautiful and mysterious place, and well worth the trip. The annual hot-air balloon festival is one of the highlights of the year, and while I have taken dramatic license with the scheduling of certain events, the three-day festival is truly spectacular.

Finally, all mistakes in this novel are mine.